CHARLES DICKENS

was born in a little house in Landport, Portsea, England, on February 7, 1812. The second of eight children, he grew up in a family frequently beset by financial insecurity. At the age of eleven, Dickens was taken out of school and sent to work in a London blacking warehouse, where his job was to paste labels on bottles for six shillings a week. His father, John Dickens, was a warmhearted but improvident man. When he was condemned to Marshalsea Prison for unpaid debts, he unwisely agreed that Charles should stay in lodgings and continue working while the rest of the family joined him in the jail. This three-month separation caused Charles much pain; his experiences as a child alone in a huge city—cold, isolated, with barely enough to eat—haunted him for the rest of his life.

When the family fortunes improved, Charles went back to school, after which he became an office boy, a freelance reporter and finally an author. With *Pickwick Papers* (1836–7) he achieved immediate fame; in a few years he was easily the most popular and respected writer of his time. It has been estimated that one out of every ten persons in Victorian England was a Dickens reader. *Oliver Twist* (1837), *Nicholas Nickleby* (1838–9) and *The Old Curiosity Shop* (1840–1) were huge successes. *Martin Chuzzlewit* (1843–4) was less so, but Dickens followed it with his unforgettable *A Christmas Carol* (1843). *Bleak House* (1852–3), *Hard Times* (1854), and *Little Dorrit* (1855–7) reveal his deepening concern for the injustices of British society. *A Tale of Two Cities* (1859), *Great Expectations* (1860–1), and *Our Mutual Friend* (1864–5) complete his major works.

Dickens's marriage to Catherine Hogarth produced ten children but ended in separation in 1858. In that year he began a series of exhausting public readings; his health gradually declined. After putting in a full day's work at his home at Gads Hill, Kent, on June 8, 1870, Dickens suffered a stroke, and he died on the following day.

Our
Mutual
Friend

by Charles Dickens

BANTAM BOOKS

NEW YORK · TORONTO · LONDON · SYDNEY · AUCKLAND

OUR MUTUAL FRIEND

A Bantam Classic Book / August 1990

PRINTING HISTORY
Our Mutual Friend *was first published 1865*

ISBN 0-553-21386-5

Published simultaneously in the United States and Canada

Bantam Books are published by Bantam Books, a division of
Bantam Doubleday Dell Publishing Group, Inc. Its trademark,
consisting of the words "Bantam Books" and the portrayal of a
rooster, is Registered in U.S. Patent and Trademark Office and
in other countries. Marca Registrada. Bantam Books, 666 Fifth
Avenue, New York, New York 10103.

PRINTED IN THE UNITED STATES OF AMERICA

OPM 0 9 8 7 6 5 4 3 2 1

THIS BOOK IS
INSCRIBED BY ITS AUTHOR TO

SIR JAMES EMERSON TENNENT

AS A MEMORIAL OF FRIENDSHIP

CONTENTS

BOOK THE FIRST

THE CUP AND THE LIP

BOOK THE SECOND

BIRDS OF A FEATHER

BOOK THE THIRD

A LONG LANE

BOOK THE FOURTH

A TURNING

BOOK THE FIRST
THE CUP AND THE LIP

Chapter 1
On the Look Out

In these times of ours, though concerning the exact year there is no need to be precise, a boat of dirty and disreputable appearance, with two figures in it, floated on the Thames, between Southwark Bridge which is of iron, and London Bridge which is of stone, as an autumn evening was closing in.

The figures in this boat were those of a strong man with ragged grizzled hair and a sun-browned face, and a dark girl of nineteen or twenty, sufficiently like him to be recognizable as his daughter. The girl rowed, pulling a pair of sculls very easily; the man, with the rudder-lines slack in his hands, and his hands loose in his waistband, kept an eager look out. He had no net, hook, or line, and he could not be a fisherman; his boat had no cushion for a sitter, no paint, no inscription, no appliance beyond a rusty boathook and a coil of rope, and he could not be a waterman; his boat was too crazy and too small to take in cargo for delivery, and he could not be a lighterman or river-carrier; there was no clue to what he looked for, but he looked for something, with a most intent and searching gaze. The tide, which had turned an hour before, was running down, and his eyes watched every little race and eddy in its broad sweep, as the boat made slight head-way against it, or drove stern foremost before it, according as he directed his daughter by a movement of his head. She watched his face as earnestly as he watched the river. But, in the intensity of her look there was a touch of dread or horror.

Allied to the bottom of the river rather than the surface, by reason of the slime and ooze with which it was covered, and its sodden state, this boat and the two figures in it obviously were doing something that they often did, and were seeking what they often sought. Half savage as the man showed, with no covering on his matted head, with his brown arms bare to between the elbow and the shoulder, with the loose knot of a looser kerchief lying low on his bare breast in a wilderness of beard and whisker, with such dress as he wore seeming to be made out of the mud that begrimed his boat, still there was business-like usage in his steady gaze. So with every lithe action of the girl, with every turn of her wrist, perhaps most of all with her look of dread or horror; they were things of usage.

'Keep her out, Lizzie. Tide runs strong here. Keep her well afore the sweep of it.'

Trusting to the girl's skill and making no use of the rudder, he eyed the coming tide with an absorbed attention. So the girl eyed him. But, it happened now, that a slant of light from the setting sun glanced into the bottom of the boat, and, touching a rotten stain there which bore some resemblance to the outline of a muffled human form, coloured it as though with diluted blood. This caught the girl's eye, and she shivered.

'What ails you?' said the man, immediately aware of it, though so intent on the advancing waters; 'I see nothing afloat.'

The red light was gone, the shudder was gone, and his gaze, which had come back to the boat for a moment, travelled away again. Wheresoever the strong tide met with an impediment, his gaze paused for an instant. At every mooring-chain and rope, at every stationary boat or barge that split the current into a broad-arrowhead, at the offsets from the piers of Southwark Bridge, at the paddles of the river steamboats as they beat the filthy water, at the floating logs of timber lashed together lying off certain wharves, his shining eyes darted a hungry look. After a darkening hour or so, suddenly the rudder-lines tightened in his hold, and he steered hard towards the Surrey shore.

Always watching his face, the girl instantly answered to the action in her sculling; presently the boat swung round, quivered as from a sudden jerk, and the upper half of the man was stretched out over the stern.

The girl pulled the hood of a cloak she wore, over her head and over her face, and, looking backward so that the front folds of this hood were turned down the river, kept the boat in that direction going before the tide. Until now, the boat had barely held her own, and had hovered about one spot; but now, the banks changed swiftly, and the deepening shadows and the kindling lights of London Bridge were passed, and the tiers of shipping lay on either hand.

It was not until now that the upper half of the man came back into the boat. His arms were wet and dirty, and he washed them

over the side. In his right hand he held something, and he
washed that in the river too. It was money. He chinked it once,
and he blew upon it once, and he spat upon it once,—'for luck,'
he hoarsely said—before he put it in his pocket.

'Lizzie!'

The girl turned her face towards him with a start, and rowed
in silence. Her face was very pale. He was a hook-nosed man,
and with that and his bright eyes and his ruffled head, bore a
certain likeness to a roused bird of prey.

'Take that thing off your face.'

She put it back.

'Here! and give me hold of the sculls. I'll take the rest of
the spell.'

'No, no, father! No! I can't indeed. Father!—I cannot sit so
near it!'

He was moving towards her to change places, but her
terrified expostulation stopped him and he resumed his seat.

'What hurt can it do you?'

'None, none. But I cannot bear it.'

'It's my belief you hate the sight of the very river.'

'I—I do not like it, father.'

'As if it wasn't your living! As if it wasn't meat and drink
to you!'

At these latter words the girl shivered again, and for a
moment paused in her rowing, seeming to turn deadly faint. It
escaped his attention, for he was glancing over the stern at
something the boat had in tow.

'How can you be so thankless to your best friend, Lizzie?
The very fire that warmed you when you were a baby, was
picked out of the river alongside the coal barges. The very basket
that you slept in, the tide washed ashore. The very rockers that I
put it upon to make a cradle of it, I cut out of a piece of wood
that drifted from some ship or another.'

Lizzie took her right hand from the scull it held, and
touched her lips with it, and for a moment held it out lovingly
towards him: then, without speaking, she resumed her rowing, as
another boat of similar appearance, though in rather better trim,
came out from a dark place and dropped softly alongside.

'In luck again, Gaffer?' said a man with a squinting leer,
who sculled her and who was alone, 'I know'd you was in luck
again, by your wake as you come down.'

'Ah!' replied the other, drily. 'So you're out, are you?'

'Yes, pardner.'

There was now a tender yellow moonlight on the river, and the new comer, keeping half his boat's length astern of the other boat looked hard at its track.

'I says to myself,' he went on, 'directly you hove in view, Yonder's Gaffer, and in luck again, by George if he ain't! Scull it is, pardner—don't fret yourself—I didn't touch him.' This was in answer to a quick impatient movement on the part of Gaffer: the speaker at the same time unshipping his scull on that side, and laying his hand on the gunwale of Gaffer's boat and holding to it.

'He's had touches enough not to want no more, as well as I make him out, Gaffer! Been a knocking about with a pretty many tides, ain't he pardner? Such is my out-of-luck ways, you see! He must have passed me when he went up last time, for I was on the lookout below bridge here. I a'most think you're like the wulturs, pardner, and scent 'em out.'

He spoke in a dropped voice, and with more than one glance at Lizzie who had pulled on her hood again. Both men then looked with a weird unholy interest at the wake of Gaffer's boat.

'Easy does it, betwixt us. Shall I take him aboard, pardner?'

'No,' said the other. In so surly a tone that the man, after a blank stare, acknowledged it with the retort:

'—Arn't been eating nothing as has disagreed with you, have you, pardner?'

'Why, yes, I have,' said Gaffer. 'I have been swallowing too much of that word, Pardner. I am no pardner of yours.'

'Since when was you no pardner of mine, Gaffer Hexam Esquire?'

'Since you was accused of robbing a man. Accused of robbing a live man!' said Gaffer, with great indignation.

'And what if I had been accused of robbing a dead man, Gaffer?'

'You COULDN'T do it.'

'Couldn't you, Gaffer?'

'No. Has a dead man any use for money? Is it possible for a dead man to have money? What world does a dead man belong to? 'Tother world. What world does money belong to? This world. How can money be a corpse's? Can a corpse own it, want it, spend it, claim it, miss it? Don't try to go confounding the rights and wrongs of things in that way. But it's worthy of the sneaking spirit that robs a live man.'

'I'll tell you what it is—.'

'No you won't. *I*'ll tell you what it is. You've got off with a short time of it for putting your hand in the pocket of a sailor, a live sailor. Make the most of it and think yourself lucky, but don't think after that to come over *me* with your pardners. We have worked together in time past, but we work together no more in time present nor yet future. Let go. Cast off!'

'Gaffer! If you think to get rid of me this way—.'

'If I don't get rid of you this way, I'll try another, and chop you over the fingers with the stretcher, or take a pick at your head with the boat-hook. Cast off! Pull you, Lizzie. Pull home, since you won't let your father pull.'

Lizzie shot ahead, and the other boat fell astern. Lizzie's father, composing himself into the easy attitude of one who had asserted the high moralities and taken an unassailable position, slowly lighted a pipe, and smoked, and took a survey of what he had in tow. What he had in tow, lunged itself at him sometimes in an awful manner when the boat was checked, and sometimes seemed to try to wrench itself away, though for the most part it followed submissively. A neophyte might have fancied that the ripples passing over it were dreadfully like faint changes of expression on a sightless face; but Gaffer was no neophyte and had no fancies.

Chapter 2
The Man from Somewhere

MR AND MRS VENEERING were bran-new people in a bran-new house in a bran-new quarter of London. Everything about the Veneerings was spick and span new. All their furniture was new, all their friends were new, all their servants were new, their plate was new, their carriage was new, their harness was new, their horses were new, their pictures were new, they themselves were new, they were as newly married as was lawfully compatible with their having a bran-new baby, and if they had set up a great-grandfather, he would have come home in matting from the

Pantechnicon, without a scratch upon him, French polished to the crown of his head.

For, in the Veneering establishment, from the hall-chairs with the new coat of arms, to the grand pianoforte with the new action, and upstairs again to the new fire-escape, all things were in a state of high varnish and polish. And what was observable in the furniture, was observable in the Veneerings—the surface smelt a little too much of the workshop and was a trifle stickey.

There was an innocent piece of dinner-furniture that went upon easy castors and was kept over a livery stable-yard in Duke Street, Saint James's, when not in use, to whom the Veneerings were a source of blind confusion. The name of this article was Twemlow. Being first cousin to Lord Snigsworth, he was in frequent requisition, and at many houses might be said to represent the dining-table in its normal state. Mr and Mrs Veneering, for example, arranging a dinner, habitually started with Twemlow, and then put leaves in him, or added guests to him. Sometimes, the table consisted of Twemlow and half a dozen leaves; sometimes, of Twemlow and a dozen leaves; sometimes, Twemlow was pulled out to his utmost extent of twenty leaves. Mr and Mrs Veneering on occasions of ceremony faced each other in the centre of the board, and thus the parallel still held; for, it always happened that the more Twemlow was pulled out, the further he found himself from the centre, and the nearer to the sideboard at one end of the room, or the window-curtains at the other.

But, it was not this which steeped the feeble soul of Twemlow in confusion. This he was used to, and could take soundings of. The abyss to which he could find no bottom, and from which started forth the engrossing and ever-swelling difficulty of his life, was the insoluble question whether he was Veneering's oldest friend, or newest friend. To the excogitation of this problem, the harmless gentleman had devoted many anxious hours, both in his lodgings over the livery stable-yard, and in the cold gloom, favourable to meditation, of Saint James's Square. Thus, Twemlow had first known Veneering at his club, where Veneering then knew nobody but the man who made them known to one another, who seemed to be the most intimate friend he had in the world, and whom he had known two days—the bond of union between their souls, the nefarious conduct of the committee respecting the cookery of a fillet of veal, having been accidently cemented at that date. Immediately upon this, Twemlow received an invitation to dine with Veneering, and dined: the man being of the party. Immediately upon that, Twemlow received an

invitation to dine with the man, and dined: Veneering being of
the party. At the man's were a Member, an Engineer, a Payer-
off of the National Debt, a Poem on Shakespeare, a Grievance,
and a Public Office, who all seemed to be utter strangers to
Veneering. And yet immediately after that, Twemlow received
an invitation to dine at Veneerings, expressly to meet the Member, the Engineer, the Payer-off of the National Debt, the Poem
on Shakespeare, the Grievance, and the Public Office, and,
dining, discovered that all of them were the most intimate friends
Veneering had in the world, and that the wives of all of them
(who were all there) were the objects of Mrs Veneering's most
devoted affection and tender confidence.

Thus it had come about, that Mr Twemlow had said to
himself in his lodgings, with his hand to his forehead: 'I must
not think of this. This is enough to soften any man's brain,'
—and yet was always thinking of it, and could never form a
conclusion.

This evening the Veneerings give a banquet. Eleven leaves
in the Twemlow; fourteen in company all told. Four pigeon-
breasted retainers in plain clothes stand in line in the hall. A fifth
retainer, proceeding up the staircase with a mournful air—as
who should say, 'Here is another wretched creature come to
dinner; such is life!'—announces, 'Mis-ter Twemlow!'

Mrs Veneering welcomes her sweet Mr Twemlow. Mr Veneering welcomes his dear Twemlow. Mrs Veneering does not
expect that Mr Twemlow can in nature care much for such
insipid things as babies, but so old a friend must please to look at
baby. 'Ah! You will know the friend of your family better,
Tootleums,' says Mr Veneering, nodding emotionally at that
new article, 'when you begin to take notice.' He then begs to
make his dear Twemlow known to his two friends, Mr Boots and
Mr Brewer—and clearly has no distinct idea which is which.

But now a fearful circumstance occurs.

'Mis-ter and Mis-sis Podsnap!'

'My dear,' says Mr Veneering to Mrs Veneering, with an air
of much friendly interest, while the door stands open, 'the
Podsnaps.'

A too, too smiling large man, with a fatal freshness on him,
appearing with his wife, instantly deserts his wife and darts at
Twemlow with:

'How do you do? So glad to know you. Charming house
you have here. I hope we are not late. So glad of this opportunity, I am sure!'

When the first shock fell upon him, Twemlow twice skipped back in his neat little shoes and his neat little silk stockings of a bygone fashion, as if impelled to leap over a sofa behind him; but the large man closed with him and proved too strong.

'Let me,' says the large man, trying to attract the attention of his wife in the distance, 'have the pleasure of presenting Mrs Podsnap to her host. She will be,' in his fatal freshness he seems to find perpetual verdure and eternal youth in the phrase, 'she will be so glad of the opportunity, I am sure!'

In the meantime, Mrs Podsnap, unable to originate a mistake on her own account, because Mrs Veneering is the only other lady there, does her best in the way of handsomely supporting her husband's, by looking towards Mr Twemlow with a plaintive countenance and remarking to Mrs Veneering in a feeling manner, firstly, that she fears he has been rather bilious of late, and, secondly, that the baby is already very like him.

It is questionable whether any man quite relishes being mistaken for any other man; but, Mr Veneering having this very evening set up the shirt-front of the young Antinous in new worked cambric just come home, is not at all complimented by being supposed to be Twemlow, who is dry and weazen and some thirty years older. Mrs Veneering equally resents the imputation of being the wife of Twemlow. As to Twemlow, he is so sensible of being a much better bred man than Veneering, that he considers the large man an offensive ass.

In this complicated dilemma, Mr Veneering approaches the large man with extended hand and, smilingly assures that incorrigible personage that he is delighted to see him: who in his fatal freshness instantly replies:

'Thank you. I am ashamed to say that I cannot at this moment recall where we met, but I am so glad of this opportunity, I am sure!'

Then pouncing upon Twemlow, who holds back with all his feeble might, he is haling him off to present him, as Veneering, to Mrs Podsnap, when the arrival of more guests unravels the mistake. Whereupon, having re-shaken hands with Veneering as Veneering, he re-shakes hands with Twemlow as Twemlow, and winds it all up to his own perfect satisfaction by saying to the last-named, 'Ridiculous opportunity—but so glad of it, I am sure!'

Now, Twemlow having undergone this terrific experience, having likewise noted the fusion of Boots in Brewer and Brewer in Boots, and having further observed that of the remaining seven guests four discreet characters enter with wandering eyes and wholly decline to commit themselves as to which is Veneering, until Veneering has them in his grasp;—Twemlow having profited by these studies, finds his brain wholesomely hardening as he approaches the conclusion that he really is Veneering's oldest friend, when his brain softens again and all is lost, through his eyes encountering Veneering and the large man linked together as twin brothers in the back drawing-room near the conservatory door, and through his ears informing him in the tones of Mrs Veneering that the same large man is to be baby's godfather.

'Dinner is on the table!'

Thus the melancholy retainer, as who should say, 'Come down and be poisoned, ye unhappy children of men!'

Twemlow, having no lady assigned him, goes down in the rear, with his hand to his forehead. Boots and Brewer, thinking him indisposed, whisper, 'Man faint. Had no lunch.' But he is only stunned by the unvanquishable difficulty of his existence.

Revived by soup, Twemlow discourses mildly of the Court Circular with Boots and Brewer. Is appealed to, at the fish stage of the banquet, by Veneering, on the disputed question whether his cousin Lord Snigsworth is in or out of town? Gives it that his cousin is out of town. 'At Snigsworthy Park?' Veneering inquires. 'At Snigsworthy,' Twemlow rejoins. Boots and Brewer regard this as a man to be cultivated; and Veneering is clear that he is a remunerative article. Meantime the retainer goes round, like a gloomy Analytical Chemist: always seeming to say, after 'Chablis, sir?'—'You wouldn't if you knew what it's made of.'

The great looking-glass above the sideboard, reflects the table and the company. Reflects the new Veneering crest, in gold and eke in silver, frosted and also thawed, a camel of all work. The Heralds' College found out a Crusading ancestor for Veneering who bore a camel on his shield (or might have done it if he had thought of it), and a caravan of camels take charge of the fruits and flowers and candles, and kneel down to be loaded with the salt. Reflects Veneering; forty, wavy-haired, dark, tending to corpulence, sly, mysterious, filmy—a kind of sufficiently well-looking veiled-prophet, not prophesying. Reflects Mrs Veneering; fair, aquiline-nosed and fingered, not so much light hair as she might have, gorgeous in raiment and jewels, enthusiastic, propitiatory, conscious that a corner of her husband's veil is over herself. Reflects Podsnap; prosperously feeding, two little light-coloured wiry wings, one on either side of his else bald head, looking as like his hairbrushes as his hair, dissolving view of red beads on his forehead, large allowance of crumpled shirt-collar up behind. Reflects Mrs Podsnap; fine woman for Professor Owen, quantity of bone, neck and nostrils like a rocking-horse, hard features, majestic head-dress in which Podsnap has hung golden offerings. Reflects Twemlow; grey, dry, polite, susceptible to east wind, First-Gentleman-in-Europe collar and cravat, cheeks drawn in as if he had made a great effort to retire into himself some years ago, and had got so far and had never got any farther. Reflects mature young lady; raven locks, and complexion that lights up well when well powdered—as it is—carrying on considerably in the captivation of mature young gentleman; with too much nose in his face, too much ginger in his whiskers, too much torso in his waistcoat, too much sparkle in his studs, his eyes, his buttons, his talk, and his teeth. Reflects charming old Lady Tippins on Veneering's right; with an immense obtuse drab oblong face, like a face in a tablespoon, and a dyed Long Walk up the top of her head, as a convenient public approach to the bunch of false hair behind, pleased to patronize Mrs Veneering opposite, who is pleased to be patronized. Reflects a certain 'Mortimer', another of Veneering's oldest friends; who never was in the house before, and appears not to want to come again, who sits disconsolate on Mrs Veneering's left, and who was inveigled by Lady Tippins (a friend of his boyhood) to come to these people's and talk, and who won't talk. Reflects Eugene, friend of Mortimer; buried alive in the back of his chair, behind a shoulder—with a powder-epaulette on it—of the mature young lady, and gloomily resorting to the champagne chalice whenever proffered by the Analytical Chemist. Lastly, the looking-glass reflects Boots and Brewer, and two other stuffed Buffers interposed between the rest of the company and possible accidents.

The Veneering dinners are excellent dinners—or new people wouldn't come—and all goes well. Notably, Lady Tippins has made a series of experiments on her digestive functions, so extremely complicated and daring, that if they could be published with their results it might benefit the human race. Having taken in provisions from all parts of the world, this hardy old cruiser has last touched at the North Pole, when, as the ice-plates are being removed, the following words fall from her:

'I assure you, my dear Veneering—'

(Poor Twemlow's hand approaches his forehead, for it would seem now, that Lady Tippins is going to be the oldest friend.)

'I assure you, my dear Veneering, that it is the oddest

affair! Like the advertising people, I don't ask you to trust me, without offering a respectable reference. Mortimer there, is my reference, and knows all about it.'

Mortimer raises his drooping eyelids, and slightly opens his mouth. But a faint smile, expressive of 'What's the use!' passes over his face, and he drops his eyelids and shuts his mouth.

'Now, Mortimer,' says Lady Tippins, rapping the sticks of her closed green fan upon the knuckles of her left hand—which is particularly rich in knuckles, 'I insist upon your telling all that is to be told about the man from Jamaica.'

'Give you my honour I never heard of any man from Jamaica, except the man who was a brother,' replies Mortimer.

'Tobago, then.'

'Nor yet from Tobago.'

'Except,' Eugene strikes in: so unexpectedly that the mature young lady, who has forgotten all about him, with a start takes the epaulette out of his way: 'except our friend who long lived on rice-pudding and isinglass, till at length to his something or other, his physician said something else, and a leg of mutton somehow ended in daygo.'

A reviving impression goes round the table that Eugene is coming out. An unfulfilled impression, for he goes in again.

'Now, my dear Mrs Veneering,' quoth Lady Tippins, 'I appeal to you whether this is not the basest conduct ever known in this world? I carry my lovers about, two or three at a time, on condition that they are very obedient and devoted; and here is my old lover-in-chief, the head of all my slaves, throwing off his allegiance before company! And here is another of my lovers, a rough Cymon at present certainly, but of whom I had most hopeful expectations as to his turning out well in course of time, pretending that he can't remember his nursery rhymes! On purpose to annoy me, for he knows how I doat upon them!'

A grisly little fiction concerning her lovers is Lady Tippins's point. She is always attended by a lover or two, and she keeps a little list of her lovers, and she is always booking a new lover, or striking out an old lover, or putting a lover in her black list, or promoting a lover to her blue list, or adding up her lovers, or otherwise posting her book. Mrs Veneering is charmed by the humour, and so is Veneering. Perhaps it is enhanced by a certain yellow play in Lady Tippins's throat, like the legs of scratching poultry.

'I banish the false wretch from this moment, and I strike him out of my Cupidon (my name for my Ledger, my dear,) this very night. But I am resolved to have the account of the man from Somewhere, and I beg you to elicit it for me, my love,' to Mrs Veneering, 'as I have lost my own influence. Oh, you perjured man!' This to Mortimer, with a rattle of her fan.

'We are all very much interested in the man from Somewhere,' Veneering observes.

Then the four Buffers, taking heart of grace all four at once, say:

> 'Deeply interested!'
> 'Quite excited!'
> 'Dramatic!'
> 'Man from Nowhere, perhaps!'

And then Mrs Veneering—for Lady Tippins's winning wiles are contagious—folds her hands in the manner of a supplicating child, turns to her left neighbour, and says, 'Tease! Pay! Man from Tumwhere!' At which the four Buffers, again mysteriously moved all four at once, exclaim, 'You can't resist!'

'Upon my life,' says Mortimer languidly, 'I find it immensely embarrassing to have the eyes of Europe upon me to this extent, and my only consolation is that you will all of you execrate Lady Tippins in your secret hearts when you find, as you inevitably will, the man from Somewhere a bore. Sorry to destroy romance by fixing him with a local habitation, but he comes from the place, the name of which escapes me, but will suggest itself to everybody else here, where they make the wine.'

Eugene suggests, 'Day and Martin's.'

'No, not that place,' returns the unmoved Mortimer, 'that's where they make the Port. My man comes from the country where they make the Cape Wine. But look here, old fellow; it's not at all statistical and it's rather odd.'

It is always noticeable at the table of the Veneerings, that no man troubles himself much about the Veneerings themselves, and that any one who has anything to tell, generally tells it to anybody else in preference.

'The man,' Mortimer goes on, addressing Eugene, 'whose name is Harmon, was only son of a tremendous old rascal who made his money by Dust.'

'Red velveteens and a bell?' the gloomy Eugene inquires.

'And a ladder and basket if you like. By which means, or by others, he grew rich as a Dust Contractor, and lived in a hollow in a hilly country entirely composed of Dust. On his own small estate the growling old vagabond threw up his own mountain range, like an old volcano, and its geological formation was Dust. Coal-dust, vegetable-dust, bone-dust, crockery dust, rough dust and sifted dust,—all manner of Dust.'

A passing remembrance of Mrs Veneering, here induces Mortimer to address his next half-dozen words to her; after which he wanders away again, tries Twemlow and finds he doesn't answer, ultimately takes up with the Buffers who receive him enthusiastically.

'The moral being—I believe that's the right expression—of this exemplary person, derived its highest gratification from anathematizing his nearest relations and turning them out of doors. Having begun (as was natural) by rendering these attentions to the wife of his bosom, he next found himself at leisure to bestow a similar recognition on the claims of his daughter. He chose a husband for her, entirely to his own satisfaction and not in the least to hers, and proceeded to settle upon her, as her marriage portion, I don't know how much Dust, but something immense. At this stage of the affair the poor girl respectfully intimated that she was secretly engaged to that popular character whom the novelists and versifiers call Another, and that such a marriage would make Dust of her heart and Dust of her life—in short, would set her up, on a very extensive scale, in her father's business. Immediately, the venerable parent—on a cold winter's night, it is said—anathematized and turned her out.'

Here, the Analytical Chemist (who has evidently formed a very low opinion of Mortimer's story) concedes a little claret to the Buffers; who, again mysteriously moved all four at once, screw it slowly into themselves with a peculiar twist of enjoyment, as they cry in chorus, 'Pray go on.'

'The pecuniary resources of Another were, as they usually are, of a very limited nature. I believe I am not using too strong an expression when I say that Another was hard up. However, he married the young lady, and they lived in a humble dwelling, probably possessing a porch ornamented with honeysuckle and woodbine twining, until she died. I must refer you to the Registrar of the District in which the humble dwelling was situated, for the certified cause of death; but early sorrow and anxiety may have had to do with it, though they may not appear in the ruled pages and printed forms. Indisputably this was the case with Another, for he was so cut up by the loss of his young wife that if he outlived her a year it was as much as he did.'

There is that in the indolent Mortimer, which seems to hint that if good society might on any account allow itself to be

impressible, he, one of good society, might have the weakness to
be impressed by what he here relates. It is hidden with great
pains, but it is in him. The gloomy Eugene too, is not without
some kindred touch; for, when that appalling Lady Tippins
declares that if Another had survived, he should have gone down
at the head of her list of lovers—and also when the mature young
lady shrugs her epaulettes, and laughs at some private and
confidential comment from the mature young gentleman—his
gloom deepens to that degree that he trifles quite ferociously
with his dessert-knife.

Mortimer proceeds.

'We must now return, as the novelists say, and as we all
wish they wouldn't, to the man from Somewhere. Being a boy of
fourteen, cheaply educating at Brussels when his sister's expulsion befell, it was some little time before he heard of it—
probably from herself, for the mother was dead; but that I don't
know. Instantly, he absconded, and came over here. He must
have been a boy of spirit and resource, to get here on a stopped
allowance of five sous a week; but he did it somehow, and he
burst in on his father, and pleaded his sister's cause. Venerable
parent promptly resorts to anathematization, and turns him out.
Shocked and terrified boy takes flight, seeks his fortune, gets
aboard ship, ultimately turns up on dry land among the Cape
wine: small proprietor, farmer, grower—whatever you like to
call it.'

At this juncture, shuffling is heard in the hall, and tapping
is heard at the dining-room door. Analytical Chemist goes to the
door, confers angrily with unseen tapper, appears to become
mollified by descrying reason in the tapping, and goes out.

'So he was discovered, only the other day, after having
been expatriated about fourteen years.'

A Buffer, suddenly astounding the other three, by detaching
himself, and asserting individuality, inquires: 'How discovered,
and why?'

'Ah! To be sure. Thank you for reminding me. Venerable
parent dies.'

Same Buffer, emboldened by success, says: 'When?'

'The other day. Ten or twelve months ago.'

Same Buffer inquires with smartness, 'What of?' But herein
perishes a melancholy example; being regarded by the three
other Buffers with a stony stare, and attracting no further attention from any mortal.

'Venerable parent,' Mortimer repeats with a passing remembrance that there is a Veneering at table, and for the first time addressing him—'dies.'

The gratified Veneering repeats, gravely, 'dies'; and folds his arms, and composes his brow to hear it out in a judicial manner, when he finds himself again deserted in the bleak world.

'His will is found,' said Mortimer, catching Mrs Podsnap's rocking-horse's eye. 'It is dated very soon after the son's flight. It leaves the lowest of the range of dust-mountains, with some sort of a dwelling-house at its foot, to an old servant who is sole executor, and all the rest of the property—which is very considerable—to the son. He directs himself to be buried with certain eccentric ceremonies and precautions against his coming to life, with which I need not bore you, and that's all—except—' and this ends the story.

The Analytical Chemist returning, everybody looks at him. Not because anybody wants to see him, but because of that subtle influence in nature which impels humanity to embrace the slightest opportunity of looking at anything, rather than the person who addresses it.

'—Except that the son's inheriting is made conditional on his marrying a girl, who at the date of the will, was a child of four or five years old, and who is now a marriageable young woman. Advertisement and inquiry discovered the son in the man from Somewhere, and at the present moment, he is on his way home from there—no doubt, in a state of great astonishment —to succeed to a very large fortune, and to take a wife.'

Mrs Podsnap inquires whether the young person is a young person of personal charms? Mortimer is unable to report.

Mr Podsnap inquires what would become of the very large fortune, in the event of the marriage condition not being fulfilled? Mortimer replies, that by special testamentary clause it would then go to the old servant above mentioned, passing over and excluding the son; also, that if the son had not been living, the same old servant would have been sole residuary legatee.

Mrs Veneering has just succeeded in waking Lady Tippins from a snore, by dexterously shunting a train of plates and dishes at her knuckles across the table; when everybody but Mortimer himself becomes aware that the Analytical Chemist is, in a ghostly manner, offering him a folded paper. Curiosity detains Mrs Veneering a few moments.

Mortimer, in spite of all the arts of the chemist, placidly refreshes himself with a glass of Madeira, and remains unconscious of the document which engrosses the general attention, until Lady Tippins (who has a habit of waking totally insensible), having remembered where she is, and recovered a perception of surrounding objects, says: 'Falser man than Don Juan; why don't you take the note from the Commendatore?' Upon which, the chemist advances it under the nose of Mortimer, who looks round at him, and says:

'What's this?'

Analytical Chemist bends and whispers.

'*Who?*' says Mortimer.

Analytical Chemist again bends and whispers.

Mortimer stares at him, and unfolds the paper. Reads it, reads it twice, turns it over to look at the blank outside, reads it a third time.

'This arrives in an extraordinarily opportune manner,' says Mortimer then, looking with an altered face round the table: 'this is the conclusion of the story of the identical man.'

'Already married?' one guesses.

'Declines to marry?' another guesses.

'Codicil among the dust?' another guesses.

'Why, no,' says Mortimer; 'remarkable thing, you are all wrong. The story is completer and rather more exciting than I supposed. Man's drowned!'

Chapter 3
Another Man

As THE disappearing skirts of the ladies ascended the Veneering staircase, Mortimer, following them forth from the dining-room, turned into a library of bran-new books, in bran-new bindings liberally gilded, and requested to see the messenger who had brought the paper. He was a boy of about fifteen. Mortimer looked at the boy, and the boy looked at the bran-new pilgrims on the wall, going to Canterbury in more gold frame than procession, and more carving than country.

'Whose writing is this?'

'Mine, sir.'

'Who told you to write it?'

'My father, Jesse Hexam.'

'Is it he who found the body?'

'Yes, sir.'

'What is your father?'

The boy hesitated, looked reproachfully at the pilgrims as if they had involved him in a little difficulty, then said, folding a plait in the right leg of his trousers, 'He gets his living along-shore.'

'Is it far?'

'Is which far?' asked the boy, upon his guard, and again upon the road to Canterbury.

'To your father's?'

'It's a goodish stretch, sir. I come up in a cab, and the cab's waiting to be paid. We could go back in it before you paid it, if you liked. I went first to your office, according to the direction of the papers found in the pockets, and there I see nobody but a chap of about my age who sent me on here.'

There was a curious mixture in the boy, of uncompleted savagery, and uncompleted civilization. His voice was hoarse and coarse, and his face was coarse, and his stunted figure was coarse; but he was cleaner than other boys of his type; and his writing, though large and round, was good; and he glanced at the backs of the books, with an awakened curiosity that went below the binding. No one who can read, ever looks at a book, even unopened on a shelf, like one who cannot.

'Were any means taken, do you know, boy, to ascertain if it was possible to restore life?' Mortimer inquired, as he sought for his hat.

'You wouldn't ask, sir, if you knew his state. Pharaoh's multitude that were drowned in the Red Sea, ain't more beyond restoring to life. If Lazarus was only half as far gone, that was the greatest of all the miracles.'

'Halloa!' cried Mortimer, turning round with his hat upon his head, 'you seem to be at home in the Red Sea, my young friend?'

'Read of it with teacher at the school,' said the boy.

'And Lazarus?'

'Yes, and him too. But don't you tell my father! We should have no peace in our place, if that got touched upon. It's my sister's contriving.'

'You seem to have a good sister.'

'She ain't half bad,' said the boy; 'but if she knows her letters it's the most she does—and them I learned her.'

The gloomy Eugene, with his hands in his pockets, had strolled in and assisted at the latter part of the dialogue; when the boy spoke these words slightingly of his sister, he took him roughly enough by the chin, and turned up his face to look at it.

'Well, I'm sure, sir!' said the boy, resisting; 'I hope you'll know me again.'

Eugene vouchsafed no answer; but made the proposal to Mortimer, 'I'll go with you, if you like?' So, they all three went away together in the vehicle that had brought the boy; the two friends (once boys together at a public school) inside, smoking cigars; the messenger on the box beside the driver.

'Let me see,' said Mortimer, as they went along; 'I have been, Eugene, upon the honourable roll of solicitors of the High Court of Chancery, and attorneys at Common Law, five years; and—except gratuitously taking instructions, on an average once a fortnight, for the will of Lady Tippins who has nothing to leave—I have had no scrap of business but this romantic business.'

'And I,' said Eugene, 'have been "called" seven years, and have had no business at all, and never shall have any. And if I had, I shouldn't know how to do it.'

'I am far from being clear as to the last particular,' returned Mortimer, with great composure, 'that I have much advantage over you.'

'I hate,' said Eugene, putting his legs up on the opposite seat, 'I hate my profession.'

'Shall I incommode you, if I put mine up too?' returned Mortimer. 'Thank you. I hate mine.'

'It was forced upon me,' said the gloomy Eugene, 'because it was understood that we wanted a barrister in the family. We have got a precious one.'

'It was forced upon me,' said Mortimer, 'because it was understood that we wanted a solicitor in the family. And we have got a precious one.'

'There are four of us, with our names painted on a door-post in right of one black hole called a set of chambers,' said Eugene; 'and each of us has the fourth of a clerk—Cassim Baba, in the robber's cave—and Cassim is the only respectable member of the party.'

'I am one by myself, one,' said Mortimer, 'high up an awful staircase commanding a burial-ground, and I have a whole clerk to myself, and he has nothing to do but look at the burial-ground, and what he will turn out when arrived at maturity, I cannot conceive. Whether, in that shabby rook's nest, he is always plotting wisdom, or plotting murder; whether he will grow up, after so much solitary brooding, to enlighten his fellow-creatures, or to poison them; is the only speck of interest that presents itself to my professional view. Will you give me a light? Thank you.'

'Then idiots talk,' said Eugene, leaning back, folding his arms, smoking with his eyes shut, and speaking slightly through his nose, 'of Energy. If there is a word in the dictionary under any letter from A to Z that I abominate, it is energy. It is such a conventional superstition, such parrot gabble! What the deuce! Am I to rush out into the street, collar the first man of a wealthy appearance that I meet, shake him, and say, "Go to law upon the spot, you dog, and retain me, or I'll be the death of you"? Yet that would be energy.'

'Precisely my view of the case, Eugene. But show me a good opportunity, show me something really worth being energetic about, and *I'll* show you energy.'

'And so will I,' said Eugene.

And it is likely enough that ten thousand other young men, within the limits of the London Post-office town delivery, made the same hopeful remark in the course of the same evening.

The wheels rolled on, and rolled down by the Monument and by the Tower, and by the Docks; down by Ratcliffe, and by Rotherhithe; down by where accumulated scum of humanity seemed to be washed from higher grounds, like so much moral sewage, and to be pausing until its own weight forced it over the bank and sunk it in the river. In and out among vessels that seemed to have got ashore, and houses that seemed to have got afloat—among bow-sprits staring into windows, and windows staring into ships—the wheels rolled on, until they stopped at a dark corner, river-washed and otherwise not washed at all, where the boy alighted and opened the door.

'You must walk the rest, sir; it's not many yards.' He spoke in the singular number, to the express exclusion of Eugene.

'This is a confoundedly out-of-the-way place,' said Mortimer, slipping over the stones and refuse on the shore, as the boy turned the corner sharp.

'Here's my father's, sir; where the light is.'

The low building had the look of having once been a mill. There was a rotten wart of wood upon its forehead that seemed

to indicate where the sails had been, but the whole was very
indistinctly seen in the obscurity of the night. The boy lifted the
latch of the door, and they passed at once into a low circular
room, where a man stood before a red fire, looking down into it,
and a girl sat engaged in needlework. The fire was in a rusty
brazier, not fitted to the hearth; and a common lamp, shaped like
a hyacinth-root, smoked and flared in the neck of a stone bottle
on the table. There was a wooden bunk or berth in a corner, and
in another corner a wooden stair leading above—so clumsy and
steep that it was little better than a ladder. Two or three old
sculls and oars stood against the wall, and against another part of
the wall was a small dresser, making a spare show of the
commonest articles of crockery and cooking-vessels. The roof of
the room was not plastered, but was formed of the flooring of the
room above. This, being very old, knotted, seamed, and beamed,
gave a lowering aspect to the chamber; and roof, and walls, and
floor, alike abounding in old smears of flour, red-lead (or some
such stain which it had probably acquired in warehousing), and
damp, alike had a look of decomposition.

'The gentleman, father.'

The figure at the red fire turned, raised its ruffled head, and
looked like a bird of prey.

'You're Mortimer Lightwood Esquire; are you, sir?'

'Mortimer Lightwood is my name. What you found,' said
Mortimer, glancing rather shrinkingly towards the bunk; ''is it
here?'

' 'Tain't not to say here, but it's close by. I do everything
reg'lar. I've giv' notice of the circumstarnce to the police, and
the police have took possession of it. No time ain't been lost, on
any hand. The police have put into print already, and here's what
the print says of it.'

Taking up the bottle with the lamp in it, he held it near a
paper on the wall, with the police heading, BODY FOUND. The
two friends read the handbill as it stuck against the wall, and
Gaffer read them as he held the light.

'Only papers on the unfortunate man, I see,' said Lightwood, glancing from the description of what was found, to the
finder.

'Only papers.'

Here the girl arose with her work in her hand, and went out
at the door.

'No money,' pursued Mortimer; 'but threepence in one of
the skirt-pockets.'

'Three. Penny. Pieces,' said Gaffer Hexam, in as many sentences.

'The trousers pockets empty, and turned inside out.'

Gaffer Hexam nodded. 'But that's common. Whether it's the wash of the tide or no, I can't say. Now, here,' moving the light to another similar placard, '*his* pockets was found empty, and turned inside out. And here,' moving the light to another, '*her* pocket was found empty, and turned inside out. And so was this one's. And so was that one's. I can't read, nor I don't want to it, for I know 'em by their places on the wall. This one was a sailor, with two anchors and a flag and G.F.T. on his arm. Look and see if he warn't.'

'Quite right.'

'This one was the young woman in grey boots, and her linen marked with a cross. Look and see if she warn't.'

'Quite right.'

'This is him as had a nasty cut over the eye. This is them two young sisters what tied themselves together with a handkecher. This the drunken old chap, in a pair of list slippers and a nightcap, wot had offered—it afterwards come out—to make a hole in the water for a quartern of rum stood aforehand, and kept to his word for the first and last time in his life. They pretty well papers the room, you see; but I know 'em all. I'm scholar enough!'

He waved the light over the whole, as if to typify the light of his scholarly intelligence, and then put it down on the table and stood behind it looking intently at his visitors. He had the special peculiarity of some birds of prey, that when he knitted his brow, his ruffled crest stood highest.

'You did not find all these yourself; did you?' asked Eugene.

To which the bird of prey slowly rejoined, 'And what might *your* name be, now?'

'This is my friend,' Mortimer Lightwood interposed; 'Mr Eugene Wrayburn.'

'Mr Eugene Wrayburn, is it? And what might Mr Eugene Wrayburn have asked of me?'

'I asked you, simply, if you found all these yourself?'

'I answer you, simply, most on 'em.'

'Do you suppose there has been much violence and robbery, beforehand, among these cases?'

'I don't suppose at all about it,' returned Gaffer. 'I ain't one of the supposing sort. If you'd got your living to haul out of the

river every day of your life, you mightn't be much given to
supposing. Am I to show the way?'

As he opened the door, in pursuance of a nod from Lightwood, an extremely pale and disturbed face appeared in the
doorway—the face of a man much agitated.

'A body missing?' asked Gaffer Hexam, stopping short; 'or
a body found? Which?'

'I am lost!' replied the man, in a hurried and an eager
manner.

'Lost?'

'I—I—am a stranger, and don't know the way. I—I—want
to find the place where I can see what is described here. It is
possible I may know it.' He was panting, and could hardly
speak; but, he showed a copy of the newly-printed bill that was
still wet upon the wall. Perhaps its newness, or perhaps the
accuracy of his observation of its general look, guided Gaffer to
a ready conclusion.

'This gentleman, Mr Lightwood, is on that business.'

'Mr Lightwood?'

During a pause, Mortimer and the stranger confronted each
other. Neither knew the other.

'I think, sir,' said Mortimer, breaking the awkward silence
with his airy self-possession, 'that you did me the honour to
mention my name?'

'I repeated it, after this man.'

'You said you were a stranger in London?'

'An utter stranger.'

'Are you seeking a Mr Harmon?'

'No.'

'Then I believe I can assure you that you are on a fruitless
errand, and will not find what you fear to find. Will you come
with us?'

A little winding through some muddy alleys that might have
been deposited by the last ill-savoured tide, brought them to the
wicket-gate and bright lamp of a Police Station; where they
found the Night-Inspector, with a pen and ink, and ruler, posting
up his books in a whitewashed office, as studiously as if he were
in a monastery on top of a mountain, and no howling fury of a
drunken woman were banging herself against a cell-door in the
back-yard at his elbow. With the same air of a recluse much
given to study, he desisted from his books to bestow a distrustful
nod of recognition upon Gaffer, plainly importing, 'Ah! we
know all about *you*, and you'll overdo it some day;' and to

inform Mr Mortimer Lightwood and friends, that he would attend them immediately. Then, he finished ruling the work he had in hand (it might have been illuminating a missal, he was so calm), in a very neat and methodical manner, showing not the slightest consciousness of the woman who was banging herself with increased violence, and shrieking most terrifically for some other woman's liver.

'A bull's-eye,' said the Night-Inspector, taking up his keys. Which a deferential satellite produced. 'Now, gentlemen.'

With one of his keys, he opened a cool grot at the end of the yard, and they all went in. They quickly came out again, no one speaking but Eugene: who remarked to Mortimer, in a whisper, 'Not *much* worse than Lady Tippins.'

So, back to the whitewashed library of the monastery—with that liver still in shrieking requisition, as it had been loudly, while they looked at the silent sight they came to see—and there through the merits of the case as summed up by the Abbot. No clue to how body came into river. Very often was no clue. Too late to know for certain, whether injuries received before or after death; one excellent surgical opinion said, before; other excellent surgical opinion said, after. Steward of ship in which gentleman came home passenger, had been round to view, and could swear to identity. Likewise could swear to clothes. And then, you see, you had the papers, too. How was it he had totally disappeared on leaving ship, 'till found in river? Well! Probably had been upon some little game. Probably thought it a harmless game, wasn't up to things, and it turned out a fatal game. Inquest to-morrow, and no doubt open verdict.

'It appears to have knocked your friend over—knocked him completely off his legs,' Mr Inspector remarked, when he had finished his summing up. 'It has given him a bad turn to be sure!' This was said in a very low voice, and with a searching look (not the first he had cast) at the stranger.

Mr Lightwood explained that it was no friend of his.

'Indeed?' said Mr Inspector, with an attentive ear; 'where did you pick him up?'

Mr Lightwood explained further.

Mr Inspector had delivered his summing up, and had added these words, with his elbows leaning on his desk, and the fingers and thumb of his right hand, fitting themselves to the fingers and thumb of his left. Mr Inspector moved nothing but his eyes, as he now added, raising his voice:

'Turned you faint, sir! Seems you're not accustomed to this kind of work?'

The stranger, who was leaning against the chimneypiece with drooping head, looked round and answered, 'No. It's a horrible sight!'

'You expected to identify, I am told, sir?'

'Yes.'

'*Have* you identified?'

'No. It's a horrible sight. O! a horrible, horrible sight!'

'Who did you think it might have been?' asked Mr Inspector. 'Give us a description, sir. Perhaps we can help you.'

'No, no,' said the stranger; 'it would be quite useless. Good-night.'

Mr Inspector had not moved, and had given no order; but, the satellite slipped his back against the wicket, and laid his left arm along the top of it, and with his right hand turned the bull's-eye he had taken from his chief—in quite a casual manner—towards the stranger.

'You missed a friend, you know; or you missed a foe, you know; or you wouldn't have come here, you know. Well, then; ain't it reasonable to ask, who was it?' Thus, Mr Inspector.

'You must excuse my telling you. No class of man can understand better than you, that families may not choose to publish their disagreements and misfortunes, except on the last necessity. I do not dispute that you discharge your duty in asking me the question; you will not dispute my right to withhold the answer. Good-night.'

Again he turned towards the wicket, where the satellite, with his eye upon his chief, remained a dumb statue.

'At least,' said Mr Inspector, 'you will not object to leave me your card, sir?'

'I should not object, if I had one; but I have not.' He reddened and was much confused as he gave the answer.

'At least,' said Mr Inspector, with no change of voice or manner, 'you will not object to write down your name and address?'

'Not at all.'

Mr Inspector dipped a pen in his inkstand, and deftly laid it on a piece of paper close beside him; then resumed his former attitude. The stranger stepped up to the desk, and wrote in a rather tremulous hand—Mr Inspector taking sidelong note of every hair of his head when it was bent down for the purpose—'Mr Julius Handford, Exchequer Coffee House, Palace Yard, Westminster.'

'Staying there, I presume, sir?'

'Staying there.'

'Consequently, from the country?'

'Eh? Yes—from the country.'

'Good-night, sir.'

The satellite removed his arm and opened the wicket, and Mr Julius Handford went out.

'Reserve!' said Mr Inspector. 'Take care of this piece of paper, keep him in view without giving offence, ascertain that he *is* staying there, and find out anything you can about him.'

The satellite was gone; and Mr Inspector, becoming once again the quiet Abbot of that Monastery, dipped his pen in his ink and resumed his books. The two friends who had watched him, more amused by the professional manner than suspicious of Mr Julius Handford, inquired before taking their departure too whether he believed there was anything that really looked bad here?

The Abbot replied with reticence, couldn't say. If a murder, anybody might have done it. Burglary or pocket-picking wanted 'prenticeship. Not so, murder. We were all of us up to that. Had seen scores of people come to identify, and never saw one person struck in that particular way. Might, however, have been Stomach and not Mind. If so, rum stomach. But to be sure there were rum everythings. Pity there was not a word of truth in that superstition about bodies bleeding when touched by the hand of the right person; you never got a sign out of bodies. You got row enough out of such as her—she was good for all night now (referring here to the banging demands for the liver), 'but you got nothing out of bodies if it was ever so.'

There being nothing more to be done until the Inquest was held next day, the friends went away together, and Gaffer Hexam and his son went their separate way. But, arriving at the last corner, Gaffer bade his boy go home while he turned into a red-curtained tavern, that stood dropsically bulging over the causeway, 'for a half-a-pint.'

The boy lifted the latch he had lifted before, and found his sister again seated before the fire at her work. Who raised her head upon his coming in and asking:

'Where did you go, Liz?'

'I went out in the dark.'

'There was no necessity for that. It was all right enough.'

'One of the gentlemen, the one who didn't speak while I was there, looked hard at me. And I was afraid he might know what my face meant. But there! Don't mind me, Charley! I was all in a tremble of another sort when you owned to father you could write a little.'

'Ah! But I made believe I wrote so badly, as that it was odds if any one could read it. And when I wrote slowest and smeared out with my finger most, father was best pleased, as he stood looking over me.'

The girl put aside her work, and drawing her seat close to his seat by the fire, laid her arm gently on his shoulder.

'You'll make the most of your time, Charley; won't you?'

'Won't I? Come! I like that. Don't I?'

'Yes, Charley, yes. You work hard at your learning, I know. And I work a little, Charley, and plan and contrive a little (wake out of my sleep contriving sometimes), how to get together a shilling now, and a shilling then, that shall make father believe you are beginning to earn a stray living along shore.'

'You are father's favourite, and can make him believe anything.'

'I wish I could, Charley! For if I could make him believe that learning was a good thing, and that we might lead better lives, I should be a'most content to die.'

'Don't talk stuff about dying, Liz.'

She placed her hands in one another on his shoulder, and laying her rich brown cheek against them as she looked down at the fire, went on thoughtfully:

'Of an evening, Charley, when you are at the school, and father's—'

'At the Six Jolly Fellowship Porters,' the boy struck in, with a backward nod of his head towards the public-house.

'Yes. Then as I sit a-looking at the fire, I seem to see in the burning coal—like where that glow is now—'

'That's gas, that is,' said the boy, 'coming out of a bit of a forest that's been under the mud that was under the water in the days of Noah's Ark. Look here! When I take the poker—so—and give it a dig—'

'Don't disturb it, Charley, or it'll be all in a blaze. It's that dull glow near it, coming and going, that I mean. When I look at it of an evening, it comes like pictures to me, Charley.'

'Show us a picture,' said the boy. 'Tell us where to look.'

'Ah! It wants my eyes, Charley.'

'Cut away then, and tell us what your eyes make of it.'

'Why, there are you and me, Charley, when you were quite a baby that never knew a mother—'

'Don't go saying I never knew a mother,' interposed the boy, 'for I knew a little sister that was sister and mother both.'

The girl laughed delightedly, and her eyes filled with pleasant tears, as he put both his arms round her waist and so held her.

'There are you and me, Charley, when father was away at work and locked us out, for fear we should set ourselves afire or fall out of window, sitting on the door-sill, sitting on other door-steps, sitting on the bank of the river, wandering about to get through the time. You are rather heavy to carry, Charley, and I am often obliged to rest. Sometimes we are sleepy and fall asleep together in a corner, sometimes we are very hungry, sometimes we are a little frightened, but what is oftenest hard upon us is the cold. You remember, Charley?'

'I remember,' said the boy, pressing her to him twice or thrice, 'that I snuggled under a little shawl, and it was warm there.'

'Sometimes it rains, and we creep under a boat or the like of that: sometimes it's dark, and we get among the gaslights, sitting watching the people as they go along the streets. At last, up comes father and takes us home. And home seems such a shelter after out of doors! And father pulls my shoes off, and dries my feet at the fire, and has me to sit by him while he smokes his pipe long after you are abed, and I notice that father's is a large hand but never a heavy one when it touches me, and that father's is a rough voice but never an angry one when it speaks to me. So, I grow up, and little by little father trusts me, and makes me his companion, and, let him be put out as he may, never once strikes me.'

The listening boy gave a grunt here, as much as to say 'But he strikes *me* though!'

'Those are some of the pictures of what is past, Charley.'

'Cut away again,' said the boy, 'and give us a fortune-telling one; a future one.'

'Well! There am I, continuing with father and holding to father, because father loves me and I love father. I can't so much as read a book, because, if I had learned, father would have thought I was deserting him, and I should have lost my influence. I have not the influence I want to have, I cannot stop some dreadful things I try to stop, but I go on in the hope and trust that the time will come. In the meanwhile I know that I am in some things a stay to father, and that if I was not faithful to him he would—in revenge-like, or in disappointment, or both—go wild and bad.'

'Give us a touch of the fortune-telling pictures about me.'

'I was passing on to them, Charley,' said the girl, who had not changed her attitude since she began, and who now mournfully shook her head; 'the others were all leading up. There are you—'

'Where am I, Liz?'

'Still in the hollow down by the flare.'

'There seems to be the deuce-and-all in the hollow down by the flare,' said the boy, glancing from her eyes to the brazier, which had a grisly skeleton look on its long thin legs.

'There are you, Charley, working your way, in secret from father, at the school; and you get prizes; and you go on better and better; and you come to be a—what was it you called it when you told me about that?'

'Ha, ha! Fortune-telling not know the name!' cried the boy, seeming to be rather relieved by this default on the part of the hollow down by the flare. 'Pupil teacher.'

'You come to be a pupil-teacher, and you still go on better and better, and you rise to be a master full of learning and respect. But the secret has come to father's knowledge long before, and it has divided you from father, and from me.'

'No it hasn't!'

'Yes it has, Charley. I see, as plain as plain can be, that your way is not ours, and that even if father could be got to forgive your taking it (which he never could be), that way of yours would be darkened by our way. But I see too, Charley—'

'Still as plain as plain can be, Liz?' asked the boy playfully.

'Ah! Still. That it is a great work to have cut you away from father's life, and to have made a new and good beginning. So there am I, Charley, left alone with father, keeping him as straight as I can, watching for more influence than I have, and hoping that through some fortunate chance, or when he is ill, or when—I don't know what—I may turn him to wish to do better things.'

'You said you couldn't read a book, Lizzie. Your library of books is the hollow down by the flare, I think.'

'I should be very glad to be able to read real books. I feel my want of learning very much, Charley. But I should feel it much more, if I didn't know it to be a tie between me and father.— Hark! Father's tread!'

It being now past midnight, the bird of prey went straight to roost. At mid-day following he reappeared at the Six Jolly Fellowship Porters, in the character, not new to him, of a witness before a Coroner's Jury.

Mr Mortimer Lightwood, besides sustaining the character of one of the witnesses, doubled the part with that of the eminent solicitor who watched the proceedings on behalf of the representatives of the deceased, as was duly recorded in the newspapers. Mr Inspector watched the proceedings too, and kept his watching closely to himself. Mr Julius Handford having given his right address, and being reported in solvent circumstances as to his bill, though nothing more was known of him at his hotel except that his way of life was very retired, had no summons to appear, and was merely present in the shades of Mr Inspector's mind.

The case was made interesting to the public, by Mr Mortimer Lightwood's evidence touching the circumstances under which the deceased, Mr John Harmon, had returned to England; exclusive private prosprietorship in which circumstances was set up at dinner-tables for several days, by Veneering, Twemlow, Podsnap, and all the Buffers: who all related them irreconcilably with one another, and contradicted themselves. It was also made interesting by the testimony of Job Potterson, the ship's steward, and one Mr Jacob Kibble, a fellow-passenger, that the deceased Mr John Harmon did bring over, in a hand-valise with which he did disembark, the sum realized by the forced sale of his little landed property, and that the sum exceeded, in ready money, seven hundred pounds. It was further made interesting, by the remarkable experiences of Jesse Hexam in having rescued from the Thames so many dead bodies, and for whose behoof a rapturous admirer subscribing himself 'A friend to Burial' (perhaps an undertaker), sent eighteen postage stamps, and five 'Now Sir's to the editor of the Times.

Upon the evidence adduced before them, the Jury found, That the body of Mr John Harmon had been discovered floating in the Thames, in an advanced state of decay, and much injured; and that the said Mr John Harmon had come by his death under highly suspicious circumstances, though by whose act or in what precise manner there was no evidence before this Jury to show. And they appended to their verdict, a recommendation to the Home Office (which Mr Inspector appeared to think highly sensible), to offer a reward for the solution of the mystery. Within eight-and-forty hours, a reward of One Hundred Pounds was proclaimed, together with a free pardon to any person or persons not the actual perpetrator or perpetrators, and so forth in due form.

This Proclamation rendered Mr Inspector additionally studious, and caused him to stand meditating on river-stairs and causeways, and to go lurking about in boats, putting this and that together. But, according to the success with which you put this and that together, you get a woman and a fish apart, or a Mermaid in combination. And Mr Inspector could turn out nothing better than a Mermaid, which no Judge and Jury would believe in.

Thus, like the tides on which it had been borne to the knowledge of men, the Harmon Murder—as it came to be popularly called—went up and down, and ebbed and flowed, now in the town, now in the country, now among palaces, now among hovels, now among lords and ladies and gentlefolks, now among labourers and hammerers and ballast-heavers, until at last, after a long interval of slack water it got out to sea and drifted away.

Chapter 4
The R. Wilfer Family

REGINALD WILFER is a name with rather a grand sound, suggesting on first acquaintance brasses in country churches, scrolls in stained-glass windows, and generally the De Wilfers who came over with the Conqueror. For, it is a remarkable fact in genealogy that no De Any ones ever came over with Anybody else.

But, the Reginald Wilfer family were of such commonplace extraction and pursuits that their forefathers had for generations modestly subsisted on the Docks, the Excise Office, and the Custom House, and the existing R. Wilfer was a poor clerk. So poor a clerk, though having a limited salary and an unlimited family, that he had never yet attained the modest object of his ambition: which was, to wear a complete new suit of clothes, hat and boots included, at one time. His black hat was brown before he could afford a coat, his pantaloons were white at the seams and knees before he could buy a pair of boots, his boots had worn out before he could treat himself to new pantaloons, and, by the time he worked round to the hat again, that shining modern article roofed-in an ancient ruin of various periods.

If the conventional Cherub could ever grow up and be clothed, he might be photographed as a portrait of Wilfer. His chubby, smooth, innocent appearance was a reason for his being always treated with condescension when he was not put down. A stranger entering his own poor house at about ten o'clock P.M. might have been surprised to find him sitting up to supper. So boyish was he in his curves and proportions, that his old schoolmaster meeting him in Cheapside, might have been unable to withstand the temptation of caning him on the spot. In short, he was the conventional cherub, after the supposititious shoot just mentioned, rather grey, with signs of care on his expression, and in decidedly insolvent circumstances.

He was shy, and unwilling to own to the name of Reginald, as being too aspiring and self-assertive a name. In his signature he used only the initial R., and imparted what it really stood for, to none but chosen friends, under the seal of confidence. Out of this, the facetious habit had arisen in the neighbourhood surrounding Mincing Lane of making christian names for him of adjectives and participles beginning with R. Some of these were more or less appropriate: as Rusty, Retiring, Ruddy, Round, Ripe, Ridiculous, Ruminative; others, derived their point from their want of application: as Raging, Rattling, Roaring, Raffish. But, his popular name was Rumty, which in a moment of inspiration had been bestowed upon him by a gentleman of convivial habits connected with the drug-markets, as the beginning of a social chorus, his leading part in the execution of which had led this gentleman to the Temple of Fame, and of which the whole expressive burden ran:

> 'Rumty iddity, row dow dow,
>   Sing toodlely, teedlely, bow wow wow.'

Thus he was constantly addressed, even in minor notes on business, as 'Dear Rumty'; in answer to which, he sedately signed himself, 'Yours truly, R. Wilfer.'

He was clerk in the drug-house of Chicksey, Veneering, and Stobbles. Chicksey and Stobbles, his former masters, had both become absorbed in Veneering, once their traveller or commission agent: who had signalized his accession to supreme power by bringing into the business a quantity of plate-glass window and French-polished mahogany partition, and a gleaming and enormous door-plate.

R. Wilfer locked up his desk one evening, and, putting his

bunch of keys in his pocket much as if it were his peg-top, made for home. His home was in the Holloway region north of London, and then divided from it by fields and trees. Between Battle Bridge and that part of the Holloway district in which he dwelt, was a tract of suburban Sahara, where tiles and bricks were burnt, bones were boiled, carpets were beat, rubbish was shot, dogs were fought, and dust was heaped by contractors. Skirting the border of this desert, by the way he took, when the light of its kiln-fires made lurid smears on the fog, R. Wilfer sighed and shook his head.

'Ah me!' said he, 'what might have been is not what is!'

With which commentary on human life, indicating an experience of it not exclusively his own, he made the best of his way to the end of his journey.

Mrs Wilfer was, of course, a tall woman and an angular. Her lord being cherubic, she was necessarily majestic, according to the principle which matrimonially unites contrasts. She was much given to tying up her head in a pocket-handkerchief, knotted under the chin. This head-gear, in conjunction with a pair of gloves worn within doors, she seemed to consider as at once a kind of armour against misfortune (invariably assuming it when in low spirits or difficulties), and as a species of full dress. It was therefore with some sinking of the spirit that her husband beheld her thus heroically attired, putting down her candle in the little hall, and coming down the doorsteps through the little front court to open the gate for him.

Something had gone wrong with the house-door, for R. Wilfer stopped on the steps, staring at it, and cried:

'Hal—loa?'

'Yes,' said Mrs Wilfer, 'the man came himself with a pair of pincers, and took it off, and took it away. He said that as he had no expectation of ever being paid for it, and as he had an order for another LADIES' SCHOOL door-plate, it was better (burnished up) for the interests of all parties.'

'Perhaps it was, my dear; what do you think?'

'You are master here, R. W.,' returned his wife. 'It is as you think; not as I do. Perhaps it might have been better if the man had taken the door too?'

'My dear, we couldn't have done without the door.'

'Couldn't we?'

'Why, my dear! Could we?'

'It is as you think, R. W.; not as I do.' With those submissive words, the dutiful wife preceded him down a few stairs to a little basement front room, half kitchen, half parlour, where a girl of about nineteen, with an exceedingly pretty figure and face, but with an impatient and petulant expression both in her face and in her shoulders (which in her sex and at her age are very expressive of discontent), sat playing draughts with a younger girl, who was the youngest of the House of Wilfer. Not to encumber this page by telling off the Wilfers in detail and casting them up in the gross, it is enough for the present that the rest were what is called 'out in the world,' in various ways, and that they were Many. So many, that when one of his dutiful children called in to see him, R. Wilfer generally seemed to say to himself, after a little mental arithmetic, 'Oh! here's another of 'em!' before adding aloud, 'How de do, John,' or Susan, as the case might be.

'Well Piggywiggies,' said R. W., 'how de do to-night? What I was thinking of, my dear,' to Mrs Wilfer already seated in a corner with folded gloves, 'was, that as we have let our first floor so well, and as we have now no place in which you could teach pupils even if pupils—'

'The milkman said he knew of two young ladies of the highest respectability who were in search of a suitable establishment, and he took a card,' interposed Mrs Wilfer, with severe monotony, as if she were reading an Act of Parliament aloud. 'Tell your father whether it was last Monday, Bella.'

'But we never heard any more of it, ma,' said Bella, the elder girl.

'In addition to which, my dear,' her husband urged, 'if you have no place to put two young persons into—'

'Pardon me,' Mrs Wilfer again interposed; 'they were not young persons. Two young ladies of the highest respectability. Tell your father, Bella, whether the milkman said so.'

'My dear, it is the same thing.'

'No it is not,' said Mrs Wilfer, with the same impressive monotony. 'Pardon me!'

'I mean, my dear, it is the same thing as to space. As to space. If you have no space in which to put two youthful fellow-creatures, however eminently respectable, which I do not doubt, where are those youthful fellow-creatures to be accommodated? I carry it no further than that. And solely looking at it,' said her husband, making the stipulation at once in a conciliatory, complimentary, and argumentative tone—'as I am sure you will agree, my love—from a fellow-creature point of view, my dear.'

'I have nothing more to say,' returned Mrs Wilfer, with a meek renunciatory action of her gloves. 'It is as you think, R. W.; not as I do.'

Here, the huffing of Miss Bella and the loss of three of her men at a swoop, aggravated by the coronation of an opponent, led to that young lady's jerking the draught-board and pieces off the table: which her sister went down on her knees to pick up.

'Poor Bella!' said Mrs Wilfer.

'And poor Lavinia, perhaps, my dear?' suggested R. W.

'Pardon me,' said Mrs Wilfer, 'no!'

It was one of the worthy woman's specialities that she had an amazing power of gratifying her splenetic or wordly-minded humours by extolling her own family: which she thus proceeded, in the present case, to do.

'No, R. W. Lavinia has not known the trial that Bella has known. The trial that your daughter Bella has undergone, is, perhaps, without a parallel, and has been borne, I will say, Nobly. When you see your daughter Bella in her black dress, which she alone of all the family wears, and when you remember the circumstances which have led to her wearing it, and when you know how those circumstances have been sustained, then, R. W., lay your head upon your pillow and say, "Poor Lavinia!" '

Here, Miss Lavinia, from her kneeling situation under the table, put it that she didn't want to be 'poored by pa', or anybody else.

'I am sure you do not, my dear,' returned her mother, 'for you have a fine brave spirit. And your sister Cecilia has a fine brave spirit of another kind, a spirit of pure devotion, a beau-ti-ful spirit! The self-sacrifice of Cecilia reveals a pure and womanly character, very seldom equalled, never surpassed. I have now in my pocket a letter from your sister Cecilia, received this morning—received three months after her marriage, poor child!—in which she tells me that her husband must unexpectedly shelter under their roof his reduced aunt. "But I will be true to him, mamma," she touchingly writes, "I will not leave him, I must not forget that he is my husband. Let his aunt come!" If this is not pathetic, if this is not woman's devotion——!' The good lady waved her gloves in a sense of the impossibility of saying more, and tied the pocket-handkerchief over her head in a tighter knot under her chin.

Bella, who was now seated on the rug to warm herself, with her brown eyes on the fire and a handful of her brown curls in her mouth, laughed at this, and then pouted and half cried.

'I am sure,' said she, 'though you have no feeling for me, pa, I am one of the most unfortunate girls that ever lived. You know how poor we are' (it is probable he did, having some reason to know it!), 'and what a glimpse of wealth I had, and how it melted away, and how I am here in this ridiculous mourning—which I hate!—a kind of a widow who never was married. And yet you don't feel for me.—Yes you do, yes you do.'

This abrupt change was occasioned by her father's face. She stopped to pull him down from his chair in an attitude highly favourable to strangulation, and to give him a kiss and a pat or two on the cheek.

'But you ought to feel for me, you know, pa.'

'My dear, I do.'

'Yes, and I say you ought to. If they had only left me alone and told me nothing about it, it would have mattered much less. But that nasty Mr Lightwood feels it is his duty, as he says, to write and tell me what is in reserve for me, and then I am obliged to get rid of George Sampson.'

Here, Lavinia, rising to the surface with the last draughtman rescued, interposed, 'You never cared for George Sampson, Bella.'

'And did I say I did, miss?' Then, pouting again, with the curls in her mouth; 'George Sampson was very fond of me, and admired me very much, and put up with everything I did to him.'

'You were rude enough to him,' Lavinia again interposed.

'And did I say I wasn't, miss? I am not setting up to be sentimental about George Sampson. I only say George Sampson was better than nothing.'

'You didn't show him that you thought even that,' Lavinia again interposed.

'You are a chit and a little idiot,' returned Bella, 'or you wouldn't make such a dolly speech. What did you expect me to do? Wait till you are a woman, and don't talk about what you don't understand. You only show your ignorance!' Then, whimpering again, and at intervals biting the curls, and stopping to look how much was bitten off, 'It's a shame! There never was such a hard case! I shouldn't care so much if it wasn't so ridiculous. It was ridiculous enough to have a stranger coming over to marry me, whether he liked it or not. It was ridiculous enough to know what an embarrassing meeting it would be, and how we never could pretend to have an inclination of our own, either of us. It was ridiculous enough to know I shouldn't like him—how *could* I like him, left to him in a will, like a dozen of spoons, with everything cut and dried beforehand, like orange chips. Talk of orange flowers indeed! I declare again it's a shame! Those ridiculous points would have been smoothed away by the money, for I love money, and want money—want it dreadfully. I hate to be poor, and we are degradingly poor, offensively poor, miserably poor, beastly poor. But here I am, left with all the ridiculous parts of the situation remaining, and, added to them all, this ridiculous dress! And if the truth was known, when the Harmon murder was all over the town, and people were speculating on its being suicide, I dare say those impudent wretches at the clubs and places made jokes about the miserable creature's having preferred a watery grave to me. It's likely enough they took such liberties; I shouldn't wonder! I declare it's a very hard case indeed, and I am a most unfortunate girl. The idea of being a kind of a widow, and never having been married! And the idea of being as poor as ever after all, and going into black, besides, for a man I never saw, and should have hated—as far as *he* was concerned—if I had seen!'

The young lady's lamentations were checked at this point by a knuckle, knocking at the half-open door of the room. The knuckle had knocked two or three times already, but had not been heard.

'Who is it?' said Mrs Wilfer, in her Act-of-Parliament manner. 'Enter!'

A gentleman coming in, Miss Bella, with a short and sharp exclamation, scrambled off the hearth-rug and massed the bitten curls together in their right place on her neck.

'The servant girl had her key in the door as I came up, and directed me to this room, telling me I was expected. I am afraid I should have asked her to announce me.'

'Pardon me,' returned Mrs Wilfer. 'Not at all. Two of my daughters. R. W., this is the gentleman who has taken your first-floor. He was so good as to make an appointment for to-night, when you would be at home.'

A dark gentleman. Thirty at the utmost. An expressive, one might say handsome, face. A very bad manner. In the last degree constrained, reserved, diffident, troubled. His eyes were on Miss Bella for an instant, and then looked at the ground as he addressed the master of the house.

'Seeing that I am quite satisfied, Mr Wilfer, with the rooms, and with their situation, and with their price, I suppose a memorandum between us of two or three lines, and a payment down, will bind the bargain? I wish to send in furniture without delay.'

Two or three times during this short address, the cherub addressed had made chubby motions towards a chair. The gentleman now took it, laying a hesitating hand on a corner of the table, and with another hesitating hand lifting the crown of his hat to his lips, and drawing it before his mouth.

'The gentleman, R. W.,' said Mrs Wilfer, 'proposes to take your apartments by the quarter. A quarter's notice on either side.'

'Shall I mention, sir,' insinuated the landlord, expecting it to be received as a matter of course, 'the form of a reference?'

'I think,' returned the gentleman, after a pause, 'that a reference is not necessary; neither, to say the truth, is it convenient, for I am a stranger in London. I require no reference from you, and perhaps, therefore, you will require none from me. That will be fair on both sides. Indeed, I show the greater confidence of the two, for I will pay in advance whatever you please, and I am going to trust my furniture here. Whereas, if you were in embarrassed circumstances—this is merely supposititious—'

Conscience causing R. Wilfer to colour, Mrs Wilfer, from a corner (she always got into stately corners) came to the rescue with a deep-toned 'Per-fectly.'

'—Why then I—might lose it.'

'Well!' observed R. Wilfer, cheerfully, 'money and goods are certainly the best of references.'

'Do you think they *are* the best, pa?' asked Miss Bella, in a low voice, and without looking over her shoulder as she warmed her foot on the fender.

'Among the best, my dear.'

'I should have thought, myself, it was so easy to add the usual kind of one,' said Bella, with a toss of her curls.

The gentleman listened to her, with a face of marked attention, though he neither looked up nor changed his attitude. He sat, still and silent, until his future landlord accepted his proposals, and brought writing materials to complete the business. He sat, still and silent, while the landlord wrote.

When the agreement was ready in duplicate (the landlord having worked at it like some cherubic scribe, in what is conventionally called a doubtful, which means a not at all doubtful, Old Master), it was signed by the contracting parties, Bella looking on as scornful witness. The contracting parties were R. Wilfer, and John Rokesmith Esquire.

When it came to Bella's turn to sign her name, Mr Rokesmith, who was standing, as he had sat, with a hesitating hand upon the table, looked at her stealthily, but narrowly. He looked at the pretty figure bending down over the paper and saying, 'Where am I to go, pa? Here, in this corner?' He looked at the beautiful brown hair, shading the coquettish face; he looked at the free dash of the signature, which was a bold one for a woman's; and then they looked at one another.

'Much obliged to you, Miss Wilfer.'

'Obliged?'

'I have given you so much trouble.'

'Signing my name? Yes, certainly. But I am your landlord's daughter, sir.'

As there was nothing more to do but pay eight sovereigns in earnest of the bargain, pocket the agreement, appoint a time for the arrival of his furniture and himself, and go, Mr Rokesmith did that as awkwardly as it might be done, and was escorted by his landlord to the outer air. When R. Wilfer returned, candlestick in hand, to the bosom of his family, he found the bosom agitated.

'Pa,' said Bella, 'we have got a Murderer for a tenant.'

'Pa,' said Lavinia, 'we have got a Robber.'

'To see him unable for his life to look anybody in the face!' said Bella. 'There never was such an exhibition.'

'My dears,' said their father, 'he is a diffident gentleman, and I should say particularly so in the society of girls of your age.'

'Nonsense, our age!' cried Bella, impatiently. 'What's that got to do with him?'

'Besides, we are not of the same age:—which age?' demanded Lavinia.

'Never *you* mind, Lavvy,' retorted Bella; 'you wait till you are of an age to ask such questions. Pa, mark my words! Between Mr Rokesmith and me, there is a natural antipathy and a deep distrust; and something will come of it!'

'My dear, and girls,' said the cherub-patriarch, 'between Mr Rokesmith and me, there is a matter of eight sovereigns, and something for supper shall come of it, if you'll agree upon the article.'

This was a neat and happy turn to give the subject, treats being rare in the Wilfer household, where a monotonous appearance of Dutch-cheese at ten o'clock in the evening had been rather frequently commented on by the dimpled shoulders of

Miss Bella. Indeed, the modest Dutchman himself seemed conscious of his want of variety, and generally came before the family in a state of apologetic perspiration. After some discussion on the relative merits of veal-cutlet, sweetbread, and lobster, a decision was pronounced in favour of veal-cutlet. Mrs Wilfer then solemnly divested herself of her handkerchief and gloves, as a preliminary sacrifice to preparing the frying-pan, and R. W. himself went out to purchase the viand. He soon returned, bearing the same in a fresh cabbage-leaf, where it coyly embraced a rasher of ham. Melodious sounds were not long in rising from the frying-pan on the fire, or in seeming, as the firelight danced in the mellow halls of a couple of full bottles on the table, to play appropriate dance-music.

The cloth was laid by Lavvy. Bella, as the acknowledged ornament of the family, employed both her hands in giving her hair an additional wave while sitting in the easiest chair, and occasionally threw in a direction touching the supper: as, 'Very brown, ma;' or, to her sister, 'Put the saltcellar straight, miss, and don't be a dowdy little puss.'

Meantime her father, chinking Mr Rokesmith's gold as he sat expectant between his knife and fork, remarked that six of those sovereigns came just in time for their landlord, and stood them in a little pile on the white tablecloth to look at.

'I hate our landlord!' said Bella.

But, observing a fall in her father's face, she went and sat down by him at the table, and began touching up his hair with the handle of a fork. It was one of the girl's spoilt ways to be always arranging the family's hair—perhaps because her own was so pretty, and occupied so much of her attention.

'You deserve to have a house of your own; don't you, poor pa?'

'I don't deserve it better than another, my dear.'

'At any rate I, for one, want it more than another,' said Bella, holding him by the chin, as she stuck his flaxen hair on end, 'and I grudge this money going to the Monster that swallows up so much, when we all want—Everything. And if you say (as you want to say; I know you want to say so, pa) "that's neither reasonable nor honest, Bella," then I answer, "Maybe not, pa—very likely—but it's one of the consequences of being poor, and of thoroughly hating and detesting to be poor, and that's my case." Now, you look lovely, pa; why don't you always wear your hair like that? And here's the cutlet! If it isn't very brown, ma, I can't eat it, and must have a bit put back to be done expressly.'

However, as it was brown, even to Bella's taste, the young lady graciously partook of it without reconsignment to the frying-pan, and also, in due course, of the contents of the two bottles: whereof one held Scotch ale and the other rum. The latter perfume, with the fostering aid of boiling water and lemon-peel, diffused itself throughout the room, and became so highly concentrated around the warm fireside, that the wind passing over the house roof must have rushed off charged with a delicious whiff of it, after buzzing like a great bee at that particular chimneypot.

'Pa,' said Bella, sipping the fragrant mixture and warming her favourite ankle; 'when old Mr Harmon made such a fool of me (not to mention himself, as he is dead), what do you suppose he did it for?'

'Impossible to say, my dear. As I have told you time out of number since his will was brought to light, I doubt if I ever exchanged a hundred words with the old gentleman. If it was his whim to surprise us, his whim succeeded. For he certainly did it.'

'And I was stamping my foot and screaming, when he first took notice of me; was I?' said Bella, contemplating the ankle before mentioned.

'You were stamping your little foot, my dear, and screaming with your little voice, and laying into me with your little bonnet, which you had snatched off for the purpose,' returned her father, as if the remembrance gave a relish to the rum; 'you were doing this one Sunday morning when I took you out, because I didn't go the exact way you wanted, when the old gentleman, sitting on a seat near, said, "That's a nice girl; that's a *very* nice girl; a promising girl!" And so you were, my dear.'

'And then he asked my name, did he, pa?'

'Then he asked your name, my dear, and mine; and on other Sunday mornings, when we walked his way, we saw him again, and—and really that's all.'

As that was all the rum and water too, or, in other words, as R. W. delicately signified that his glass was empty, by throwing back his head and standing the glass upside down on his nose and upper lip, it might have been charitable in Mrs Wilfer to suggest replenishment. But that heroine briefly suggesting 'Bed-time' instead, the bottles were put away, and the family retired; she cherubically escorted, like some severe saint in a painting, or merely human matron allegorically treated.

'And by this time to-morrow,' said Lavinia when the two

girls were alone in their room, 'we shall have Mr Rokesmith here, and shall be expecting to have our throats cut.'

'You needn't stand between me and the candle for all that,' retorted Bella. 'This is another of the consequences of being poor! The idea of a girl with a really fine head of hair, having to do it by one flat candle and a few inches of looking-glass!'

'You caught George Sampson with it, Bella, bad as your means of dressing it are.'

'You low little thing. Caught George Sampson with it! Don't talk about catching people, miss, till your own time for catching—as you call it—comes.'

'Perhaps it has come,' muttered Lavvy, with a toss of her head.

'What did you say?' asked Bella, very sharply. 'What did you say, miss?'

Lavvy declining equally to repeat or to explain, Bella gradually lapsed over her hair-dressing into a soliloquy on the miseries of being poor, as exemplified in having nothing to put on, nothing to go out in, nothing to dress by, only a nasty box to dress at instead of a comodious dressing-table, and being obliged to take in suspicious lodgers. On the last grievance as her climax, she laid great stress—and might have laid greater, had she known that if Mr Julius Handford had a twin brother upon earth, Mr John Rokesmith was the man.

Chapter 5
Boffin's Bower

OVER against a London house, a corner house not far from Cavendish Square, a man with a wooden leg had sat for some years, with his remaining foot in a basket in cold weather, picking up a living on this wise:—Every morning at eight o'clock, he stumped to the corner, carrying a chair, a clothes-horse, a pair of trestles, a board, a basket, and an umbrella, all strapped together. Separating these, the board and trestles became a counter, the basket supplied the few small lots of fruit and sweets that he offered for sale upon it and became a foot-warmer, the unfolded clothes-horse displayed a choice collection of halfpenny ballads and became a screen, and the stool planted within it became his post for the rest of the day. All weathers saw the man at the post. This is to be accepted in a double sense, for he contrived a back to his wooden stool, by placing it against the lamp-post. When the weather was wet, he put up his umbrella over his stock in trade, not over himself; when the weather was dry, he furled that faded article, tied it round with a piece of yarn, and laid it cross-wise under the trestles: where it looked like an unwholesomely-forced lettuce that had lost in colour and crispness what it had gained in size.

He had established his right to the corner, by imperceptible prescription. He had never varied his ground an inch, but had in the beginning diffidently taken the corner upon which the side of the house gave. A howling corner in the winter time, a dusty corner in the summer time, an undesirable corner at the best of times. Shelterless fragments of straw and paper got up revolving storms there, when the main street was at peace; and the water-cart, as if it were drunk or short-sighted, came blundering and jolting round it, making it muddy when all else was clean.

On the front of his sale-board hung a little placard, like a kettle-holder, bearing the inscription in his own small text:

> *Errands gone*
> *On with fi*
> *Delity By*
> *Ladies and Gentlemen*
> *I remain*
> *Your humble Servt:*
> *Silas Wegg*

He had not only settled it with himself in course of time, that he was errand-goer by appointment to the house at the corner (though he received such commissions not half a dozen times in a year, and then only as some servant's deputy), but also that he was one of the house's retainers and owed vassalage to it and was bound to leal and loyal interest in it. For this reason, he always spoke of it as 'Our House,' and, though his knowledge of its affairs was mostly speculative and all wrong, claimed to be in its confidence. On similar grounds he never beheld an inmate at any one of its windows but he touched his hat. Yet, he knew so little about the inmates that he gave them names of his own invention: as 'Miss Elizabeth', 'Master George', 'Aunt Jane', 'Uncle Parker'—having no authority whatever for any such designations, but particularly the last—to which, as a natural consequence, he stuck with great obstinacy.

Over the house itself, he exercised the same imaginary power as over its inhabitants and their affairs. He had never been in it, the length of a piece of fat black water-pipe which trailed itself over the area-door into a damp stone passage, and had rather the air of a leech on the house that had 'taken' wonderfully; but this was no impediment to his arranging it according to a plan of his own. It was a great dingy house with a quantity of dim side window and blank back premises, and it cost his mind a world of trouble so to lay it out as to account for everything in its external appearance. But, this once done, was quite satisfactory, and he rested persuaded, that he knew his way about the house blindfold: from the barred garrets in the high roof, to the two iron extinguishers before the main door—which seemed to request all lively visitors to have the kindness to put themselves out, before entering.

Assuredly, this stall of Silas Wegg's was the hardest little stall of all the sterile little stalls in London. It gave you the face-ache to look at his apples, the stomach-ache to look at his oranges, the tooth-ache to look at his nuts. Of the latter commodity he had always a grim little heap, on which lay a little wooden measure which had no discernible inside, and was considered to represent the penn'orth appointed by Magna Charta. Whether from too much east wind or no—it was an easterly corner—the stall, the stock, and the keeper, were all as dry as the Desert. Wegg was a knotty man, and a close-grained, with a face carved out of very hard material, that had just as much play of expression as a watch-man's rattle. When he laughed, certain jerks occurred in it, and the rattle sprung. Sooth to say, he was so wooden a man that he seemed to have taken his wooden leg naturally, and rather suggested to the fanciful observer, that he might be expected—if his development received no untimely check—to be completely set up with a pair of wooden legs in about six months.

Mr Wegg was an observant person, or, as he himself said, 'took a powerful sight of notice'. He saluted all his regular passers-by every day, as he sat on his stool backed up by the lamp-post; and on the adaptable character of these salutes he greatly plumed himself. Thus, to the rector, he addressed a bow, compounded of lay deference, and a slight touch of the shady preliminary meditation at church; to the doctor, a confidential bow, as to a gentleman whose acquaintance with his inside he begged respectfully to acknowledge; before the Quality he delighted to abase himself; and for Uncle Parker, who was in the army (at least, so he had settled it), he put his open hand to the side of his hat, in a military manner which that angry-eyed buttoned-up inflammatory-faced old gentleman appeared but imperfectly to appreciate.

The only article in which Silas dealt, that was not hard, was gingerbread. On a certain day, some wretched infant having purchased the damp gingerbread-horse (fearfully out of condition), and the adhesive bird-cage, which had been exposed for the day's sale, he had taken a tin box from under his stool to produce a relay of those dreadful specimens, and was going to look in at the lid, when he said to himself, pausing: 'Oh! here you are again!'

The words referred to a broad, round-shouldered, one-sided old fellow in mourning, coming comically ambling towards the corner, dressed in a pea over-coat, and carrying a large stick. He wore thick shoes, and thick leather gaiters, and thick gloves like a hedger's. Both as to his dress and to himself, he was of an overlapping rhinoceros build, with folds in his cheeks, and his forehead, and his eyelids, and his lips, and his ears; but with bright, eager, childishly-inquiring, grey eyes, under his ragged eyebrows, and broad-brimmed hat. A very odd-looking old fellow altogether.

'Here you are again,' repeated Mr Wegg, musing. 'And what are you now? Are you in the Funns, or where are you? Have you lately come to settle in this neighbourhood, or do you own to another neighbourhood? Are you in independent circumstances, or is it wasting the motions of a bow on you? Come! I'll speculate! I'll invest a bow in you.'

Which Mr Wegg, having replaced his tin box, accordingly did, as he rose to bait his gingerbread-trap for some other devoted infant. The salute was acknowledged with:

'Morning, sir! Morning! Morning!'

('Calls me Sir!' said Mr Wegg, to himself. '*He* won't answer. A bow gone!')

'Morning, morning, morning!'

'Appears to be rather a 'arty old cock, too,' said Mr Wegg, as before. 'Good morning to *you*, sir.'

'Do you remember me, then?' asked his new acquaintance, stopping in his amble, one-sided, before the stall, and speaking in a pounding way, though with great good-humour.

'I have noticed you go past our house, sir, several times in the course of the last week or so.'

'Our house,' repeated the other. 'Meaning—?'

'Yes,' said Mr Wegg, nodding, as the other pointed the clumsy forefinger of his right glove at the corner house.

'Oh! Now, what,' pursued the old fellow, in an inquisitive manner, carrying his knotted stick in his left arm as if it were a baby, 'what do they allow you now?'

'It's job work that I do for our house,' returned Silas, drily, and with reticence; 'it's not yet brought to an exact allowance.'

'Oh! It's not yet brought to an exact allowance? No! It's not yet brought to an exact allowance. Oh!—Morning, morning, morning!'

'Appears to be rather a cracked old cock,' thought Silas, qualifying his former good opinion, as the other ambled off. But, in a moment he was back again with the question:

'How did you get your wooden leg?'

Mr Wegg replied, (tartly to this personal inquiry), 'In an accident.'

'Do you like it?'

'Well! I haven't got to keep it warm,' Mr Wegg made answer, in a sort of desperation occasioned by the singularity of the question.

'He hasn't,' repeated the other to his knotted stick, as he gave it a hug; 'he hasn't got—ha!—ha!—to keep it warm! Did you ever hear of the name of Boffin?'

'No,' said Mr Wegg, who was growing restive under this examination. 'I never did hear of the name of Boffin.'

'Do you like it?'

'Why, no,' retorted Mr Wegg, again approaching desperation; 'I can't say I do.'

'Why don't you like it?'

'I don't know why I don't,' retorted Mr Wegg, approaching frenzy, 'but I don't at all.'

'Now, I'll tell you something that'll make you sorry for that,' said the stranger, smiling. 'My name's Boffin.'

'I can't help it!' returned Mr Wegg. Implying in his manner the offensive addition, 'and if I could, I wouldn't.'

'But there's another chance for you,' said Mr. Boffin, smiling still, 'Do you like the name of Nicodemus? Think it over. Nick, or Noddy.'

'It is not, sir,' Mr Wegg rejoined, as he sat down on his stool, with an air of gentle resignation, combined with melancholy candour; 'it is not a name as I could wish any one that I had a respect for, to call *me* by; but there may be persons that would not view it with the same objections.—I don't know why,' Mr Wegg added, anticipating another question.

'Noddy Boffin,' said that gentleman. 'Noddy. That's my name. Noddy—or Nick—Boffin. What's your name?'

'Silas Wegg.—I don't,' said Mr Wegg, bestirring himself to take the same precaution as before, 'I don't know why Silas, and I don't know why Wegg.'

'Now, Wegg,' said Mr Boffin, hugging his stick closer, 'I want to make a sort of offer to you. Do you remember when you first see me?'

The wooden Wegg looked at him with a meditative eye, and also with a softened air as descrying possibility of profit. 'Let me think. I ain't quite sure, and yet I generally take a powerful sight of notice, too. Was it on a Monday morning, when the butcher-boy had been to our house for orders, and bought a ballad of me, which, being unacquainted with the tune, I run it over to him?'

'Right, Wegg, right! But he bought more than one.'

'Yes, to be sure, sir; he bought several; and wishing to lay out his money to the best, he took my opinion to guide his choice, and we went over the collection together. To be sure we did. Here was him as it might be, and here was myself as it might be, and there was you, Mr Boffin, as you identically are, with your self-same stick under your very same arm, and your very same back towards us. To—be—sure!' added Mr Wegg, looking a little round Mr Boffin, to take him in the rear, and identify this last extraordinary coincidence, 'your wery self-same back!'

'What do you think I was doing, Wegg?'

'I should judge, sir, that you might be glancing your eye down the street.'

'No, Wegg. I was a listening.'

'Was you, indeed?' said Mr Wegg, dubiously.

'Not in a dishonourable way, Wegg, because you was singing to the butcher; and you wouldn't sing secrets to a butcher in the street, you know.'

'It never happened that I did so yet, to the best of my

remembrance,' said Mr Wegg, cautiously. 'But I might do it. A man can't say what he might wish to do some day or another.' (This, not to release any little advantage he might derive from Mr Boffin's avowal.)

'Well,' repeated Boffin, 'I was a listening to you and to him. And what do you—you haven't got another stool, have you? I'm rather thick in my breath.'

'I haven't got another, but you're welcome to this,' said Wegg, resigning it. 'It's a treat to me to stand.'

'Lard!' exclaimed Mr Boffin, in a tone of great enjoyment, as he settled himself down, still nursing his stick like a baby, 'it's a pleasant place, this! And then to be shut in on each side, with these ballads, like so many book-leaf blinkers! Why, it's delightful!'

'If I am not mistaken, sir,' Mr Wegg delicately hinted, resting a hand on his stall, and bending over the discursive Boffin, 'you alluded to some offer or another that was in your mind?'

'I'm coming to it! All right. I'm coming to it! I was going to say that when I listened that morning, I listened with hadmiration amounting to haw. I thought to myself, "Here's a man with a wooden leg—a literary man with—" '

'N–not exactly so, sir,' said Mr Wegg.

'Why, you know every one of these songs by name and by tune, and if you want to read or to sing any one on 'em off straight, you've only to whip on your spectacles and do it!' cried Mr Boffin. 'I see you at it!'

'Well, sir,' returned Mr Wegg, with a conscious inclination of the head; 'we'll say literary, then.'

' "A literary man—*with* a wooden leg—and all Print is open to him!" That's what I thought to myself, that morning,' pursued Mr Boffin, leaning forward to describe, uncramped by the clothes-horse, as large an arc as his right arm could make; ' "all Print is open to him!" And it is, ain't it?'

'Why, truly, sir,' Mr Wegg admitted, with modesty; 'I believe you couldn't show me the piece of English print, that I wouldn't be equal to collaring and throwing.'

'On the spot?' said Mr Boffin.

'On the spot.'

'I know'd it! Then consider this. Here am I, a man without a wooden leg, and yet all print is shut to me.'

'Indeed, sir?' Mr Wegg returned with increasing self-complacency. 'Education neglected?'

'Neg—lected!' repeated Boffin, with emphasis. 'That ain't no word for it. I don't mean to say but what if you showed me a B, I could so far give you change for it, as to answer Boffin.'

'Come, come, sir,' said Mr Wegg, throwing in a little encouragement, 'that's something, too.'

'It's something,' answered Mr Boffin, 'but I'll take my oath it ain't much.'

'Perhaps it's not as much as could be wished by an inquiring mind, sir,' Mr Wegg admitted.

'Now, look here. I'm retired from business. Me and Mrs Boffin—Henerietty Boffin—which her father's name was Henery, and her mother's name was Hetty, and so you get it—we live on a compittance, under the will of a diseased governor.'

'Gentleman dead, sir?'

'Man alive, don't I tell you? A diseased governor? Now, it's too late for me to begin shovelling and sifting at alphabeds and grammar-books. I'm getting to be a old bird, and I want to take it easy. But I want some reading—some fine bold reading, some splendid book in a gorging Lord-Mayor's-Show of wollumes' (probably meaning gorgeous, but misled by association of ideas); 'as'll reach right down your pint of view, and take time to go by you. How can I get that reading, Wegg? By,' tapping him on the breast with the head of his thick stick, 'paying a man truly qualified to do it, so much an hour (say twopence) to come and do it.'

'Hem! Flattered, sir, I am sure,' said Wegg, beginning to regard himself in quite a new light. 'Hew! This is the offer you mentioned, sir?'

'Yes. Do you like it?'

'I am considering of it, Mr Boffin.'

'I don't,' said Boffin, in a free-handed manner, 'want to tie a literary man—*with* a wooden leg—down too tight. A halfpenny an hour shan't part us. The hours are your own to choose, after you've done for the day with your house here. I live over Maiden-Lane way—out Holloway direction—and you've only got to go East-and-by-North when you've finished here, and you're there. Twopence halfpenny an hour,' said Boffin, taking a piece of chalk from his pocket and getting off the stool to work the sum on the top of it in his own way; 'two long'uns and a short'un—twopence halfpenny; two short'uns is a long'un and two two long'uns is four long'uns—making five long'uns; six nights a week at five long 'uns a night,' scoring them all down separately, 'and you mount up to thirty long'uns. A round'un! Half a crown!'

Pointing to this result as a large and satisfactory one, Mr Boffin smeared it out with his moistened glove, and sat down on the remains.

'Half a crown,' said Wegg, meditating. 'Yes. (It ain't much, sir.) Half a crown.'

'Per week, you know.'

'Per week. Yes. As to the amount of strain upon the intellect now. Was you thinking at all of poetry?' Mr Wegg inquired, musing.

'Would it come dearer?' Mr Boffin asked.

'It would come dearer,' Mr Wegg returned. 'For when a person comes to grind off poetry night after night, it is but right he should expect to be paid for its weakening effect on his mind.'

'To tell you the truth Wegg,' said Boffin, 'I wasn't thinking of poetry, except in so fur as this:—If you was to happen now and then to feel yourself in the mind to tip me and Mrs Boffin one of your ballads, why then we should drop into poetry.'

'I follow you, sir,' said Wegg. 'But not being a regular musical professional, I should be loath to engage myself for that; and therefore when I dropped into poetry, I should ask to be considered so fur, in the light of a friend.'

At this, Mr Boffin's eyes sparkled, and he shook Silas earnestly by the hand: protesting that it was more than he could have asked, and that he took it very kindly indeed.

'What do you think of the terms, Wegg?' Mr Boffin then demanded, with unconcealed anxiety.

Silas, who had stimulated this anxiety by his hard reserve of manner, and who had begun to understand his man very well, replied with an air; as if he were saying something extraordinarily generous and great:

'Mr Boffin, I never bargain.'

'So I should have thought of you!' said Mr Boffin, admiringly.

'No, sir. I never did 'aggle and I never will 'aggle. Consequently I meet you at once, free and fair, with—Done, for double the money!'

Mr Boffin seemed a little unprepared for this conclusion, but assented, with the remark, 'You know better what it ought to be than I do, Wegg,' and again shook hands with him upon it.

'Could you begin to-night, Wegg?' he then demanded.

'Yes, sir,' said Mr Wegg, careful to leave all the eagerness to him. 'I see no difficulty if you wish it. You are provided with the needful implement—a book, sir?'

'Bought him at a sale,' said Mr Boffin. 'Eight wollumes. Red and gold. Purple ribbon in every wollume, to keep the place where you leave off. Do you know him?'

'The book's name, sir?' inquired Silas.

'I thought you might have know'd him without it,' said Mr Boffin slightly disappointed. 'His name is Decline-And-Fall-Off-The-Rooshan-Empire.' (Mr Boffin went over these stones slowly and with much caution.)

'Ay indeed!' said Mr Wegg, nodding his head with an air of friendly recognition.

'You know him, Wegg?'

'I haven't been not to say right slap through him, very lately,' Mr Wegg made answer, 'having been otherways employed, Mr Boffin. But know him? Old familiar declining and falling off the Rooshan? Rather, sir! Ever since I was not so high as your stick. Ever since my eldest brother left our cottage to enlist into the army. On which occasion, as the ballad that was made about it describes:

'Beside that cottage door, Mr Boffin,
    A girl was on her knees;
She held aloft a snowy scarf, Sir,
    Which (my eldest brother noticed) fluttered in the breeze.
She breathed a prayer for him, Mr Boffin;
    A prayer he could not hear.
And my eldest brother lean'd upon his sword, Mr Boffin,
    And wiped away a tear.'

Much impressed by this family circumstance, and also by the friendly disposition of Mr Wegg, as exemplified in his so soon dropping into poetry, Mr Boffin again shook hands with that ligneous sharper, and besought him to name his hour. Mr Wegg named eight.

'Where I live,' said Mr Boffin, 'is called The Bower. Boffin's Bower is the name Mrs Boffin christened it when we come into it as a property. If you should meet with anybody that don't know it by that name (which hardly anybody does), when you've got nigh upon about a odd mile, or say and a quarter if you like, up Maiden Lane, Battle Bridge, ask for Harmony Jail, and you'll be put right. I shall expect you, Wegg,' said Mr Boffin, clapping him on the shoulder with the greatest enthusiasm, 'most joyfully. I shall have no peace or patience till you come. Print is now opening ahead of me. This night, a literary man—*with* a wooden leg—' he bestowed an admiring look upon that decoration, as if it greatly enhanced the relish of Mr Wegg's attainments—'will begin to lead me a new life! My fist again, Wegg. Morning, morning, morning!'

Left alone at his stall as the other ambled off, Mr Wegg subsided into his screen, produced a small pocket-handkerchief of a penitentially-scrubbing character, and took himself by the nose with a thoughtful aspect. Also, while he still grasped that feature, he directed several thoughtful looks down the street, after the retiring figure of Mr Boffin. But, profound gravity sat enthroned on Wegg's countenance. For, while he considered within himself that this was an old fellow of rare simplicity, that this was an opportunity to be improved, and that here might be money to be got beyond present calculation, still he compromised himself by no admission that his new engagement was at all out of his way, or involved the least element of the ridiculous. Mr Wegg would even have picked a handsome quarrel with any one who should have challenged his deep acquaintance with those aforesaid eight volumes of Decline and Fall. His gravity was unusual, portentous, and immeasurable, not because he admitted any doubt of himself, but because he perceived it necessary to forestall any doubt of himself in others. And herein he ranged with that very numerous class of impostors, who are quite as determined to keep up appearances to themselves, as to their neighbours.

A certain loftiness, likewise, took possession of Mr Wegg; a condescending sense of being in request as an official expounder of mysteries. It did not move him to commercial greatness, but rather to littleness, insomuch that if it had been within the possibilities of things for the wooden measure to hold fewer nuts than usual, it would have done so that day. But, when night came, and with her veiled eyes beheld him stumping towards Boffin's Bower, he was elated too.

The Bower was as difficult to find, as Fair Rosamond's without the clue. Mr Wegg, having reached the quarter indicated, inquired for the Bower half a dozen times without the least success, until he remembered to ask for Harmony Jail. This occasioned a quick change in the spirits of a hoarse gentleman and a donkey, whom he had much perplexed.

'Why, yer mean Old Harmon's, do yer?' said the hoarse

gentleman, who was driving his donkey in a truck, with a carrot for a whip. 'Why didn't yer niver say so? Eddard and me is a goin' by *him*! Jump in.'

Mr Wegg complied, and the hoarse gentleman invited his attention to the third person in company, thus;

'Now, you look at Eddard's ears. What was it as you named, agin? Whisper.'

Mr Wegg whispered, 'Boffin's Bower.'

'Eddard! (keep yer hi on his ears) cut away to Boffin's Bower!'

Edward, with his ears lying back, remained immoveable.

'Eddard! (keep yer hi on his ears) cut away to Old Harmon's.'

Edward instantly pricked up his ears to their utmost, and rattled off at such a pace that Mr Wegg's conversation was jolted out of him in a most dislocated state.

'Was-it-Ev-verajail?' asked Mr Wegg, holding on.

'Not a proper jail, wot you and me would get committed to,' returned his escort; 'they giv' it the name, on accounts of Old Harmon living solitary there.'

'And-why-did-they-callitharm-Ony?' asked Wegg.

'On accounts of his never agreeing with nobody. Like a speeches of chaff. Harmon's Jail; Harmony Jail. Working it round like.'

'Doyouknow-Mist-Erboff-in?' asked Wegg.

'I should think so! Everybody do about here. Eddard knows him. (Keep yer hi on his ears.) Noddy Boffin, Eddard!'

The effect of the name was so very alarming, in respect of causing a temporary disappearance of Edward's head, casting his hind hoofs in the air, greatly accelerating the pace and increasing the jolting, that Mr Wegg was fain to devote his attention exclusively to holding on, and to relinquish his desire of ascertaining whether this homage to Boffin was to be considered complimentary or the reverse.

Presently, Edward stopped at a gateway, and Wegg discreetly lost no time in slipping out at the back of the truck. The moment he was landed, his late driver with a wave of the carrot, said 'Supper, Eddard!' and he, the hind hoofs, the truck, and Edward, all seemed to fly into the air together, in a kind of apotheosis.

Pushing the gate, which stood ajar, Wegg looked into an enclosed space where certain tall dark mounds rose high against the sky, and where the pathway to the Bower was indicated, as the moonlight showed, between two lines of broken crockery set in ashes. A white figure advancing along this path, proved to be nothing more ghostly than Mr Boffin, easily attired for the pursuit of knowledge, in an undress garment of short white smock-frock. Having received his literary friend with great cordiality, he conducted him to the interior of the Bower and there presented him to Mrs Boffin:—a stout lady of a rubicund and cheerful aspect, dressed (to Mr Wegg's consternation) in a low evening-dress of sable satin, and a large black velvet hat and feathers.

'Mrs Boffin, Wegg,' said Boffin, 'is a highflyer at Fashion. And her make is such, that she does it credit. As to myself, I ain't yet as Fash'nable as I may come to be. Henerietty, old lady, this is the gentleman that's a going to decline and fall off the Rooshan Empire.'

'And I am sure I hope it'll do you both good,' said Mrs Boffin.

It was the queerest of rooms, fitted and furnished more like a luxurious amateur tap-room than anything else within the ken of Silas Wegg. There were two wooden settles by the fire, one on either side of it, with a corresponding table before each. On one of these tables, the eight volumes were ranged flat, in a row, like a galvanic battery; on the other, certain squat case-bottles of inviting appearance seemed to stand on tiptoe to exchange glances with Mr Wegg over a front row of tumblers and a basin of white sugar. On the hob, a kettle steamed; on the hearth, a cat reposed. Facing the fire between the settles, a sofa, a footstool, and a little table, formed a centrepiece devoted to Mrs Boffin. They were garish in taste and colour, but were expensive articles of drawing-room furniture that had a very odd look beside the settles and the flaring gaslight pendent from the ceiling. There was a flowery carpet on the floor; but, instead of reaching to the fireside, its glowing vegetation stopped short at Mrs Boffin's footstool, and gave place to a region of sand and sawdust. Mr Wegg also noticed, with admiring eyes, that, while the flowery land displayed such hollow ornamentation as stuffed birds and waxen fruits under glass-shades, there were, in the territory where vegetation ceased, compensatory shelves on which the best part of a large pie and likewise of a cold joint were plainly discernible among other solids. The room itself was large, though low; and the heavy frames of its old-fashioned windows, and the heavy beams in its crooked ceiling, seemed to indicate that it had once been a house of some mark standing alone in the country.

'Do you like it, Wegg?' asked Mr Boffin, in his pouncing manner.

'I admire it greatly, sir,' said Wegg. 'Peculiar comfort at this fireside, sir.'

'Do you understand it, Wegg?'

'Why, in a general way, sir,' Mr Wegg was beginning slowly and knowingly, with his head stuck on one side, as evasive people do begin, when the other cut him short:

'You *don't* understand it, Wegg, and I'll explain it. These arrangements is made by mutual consent between Mrs Boffin and me. Mrs Boffin, as I've mentioned, is a highflyer at Fashion; at present I'm not. I don't go higher than comfort, and comfort of the sort that I'm equal to the enjoyment of. Well then. Where would be the good of Mrs Boffin and me quarrelling over it? We never did quarrel, before we come into Boffin's Bower as a property; why quarrel when we *have* come into Boffin's Bower as a property? So Mrs Boffin, she keeps up her part of the room, in her way; I keep up my part of the room in mine. In consequence of which we have at once, Sociability (I should go melancholy mad without Mrs Boffin), Fashion, and Comfort. If I get by degrees to be a higher-flyer at Fashion, then Mrs Boffin will by degrees come for'arder. If Mrs Boffin should ever be less of a dab at Fashion than she is at the present time, then Mrs Boffin's carpet would go back'arder. If we should both continny as we are, why then *here* we are, and give us a kiss, old lady.'

Mrs Boffin who, perpetually smiling, had approached and drawn her plump arm through her lord's, most willingly complied. Fashion, in the form of her black velvet hat and feathers, tried to prevent it; but got deservedly crushed in the endeavour.

'So now, Wegg,' said Mr Boffin, wiping his mouth with an air of much refreshment, 'you begin to know us as we are. This is a charming spot, is the Bower, but you must get to appreciate it by degrees. It's a spot to find out the merits of, little by little, and a new'un every day. There's a serpentining walk up each of the mounds, that gives you the yard and neighbourhood changing every moment. When you get to the top, there's a view of the neighbouring premises, not to be surpassed. The premises of Mrs Boffin's late father (Canine Provision Trade), you look down into, as if they was your own. And the top of the High Mound is crowned with a lattice-work Arbour, in which, if you don't read out loud many a book in the summer, ay, and as a friend, drop many a time into poetry too, it shan't be my fault. Now, what'll you read on?'

'Thank you, sir,' returned Wegg, as if there were nothing new in his reading at all. 'I generally do it on gin and water.'

'Keeps the organ moist, does it, Wegg?' asked Mr Boffin, with innocent eagerness.

'N-no, sir,' replied Wegg, coolly, 'I should hardly describe it so, sir. I should say, mellers it. Mellers it, is the word I should employ, Mr Boffin.'

His wooden conceit and craft kept exact pace with the delighted expectation of his victim. The visions rising before his mercenary mind, of the many ways in which this connexion was to be turned to account, never obscured the foremost idea natural to a dull over-reaching man, that he must not make himself too cheap.

Mrs Boffin's Fashion, as a less inexorable deity than the idol usually worshipped under that name, did not forbid her mixing for her literary guest, or asking if he found the result to his liking. On his returning a gracious answer and taking his place at the literary settle, Mr Boffin began to compose himself as a listener, at the opposite settle, with exultant eyes.

'Sorry to deprive you of a pipe, Wegg,' he said, filling his own, 'but you can't do both together. Oh! and another thing I forgot to name! When you come in here of an evening, and look round you, and notice anything on a shelf that happens to catch your fancy, mention it.'

Wegg, who had been going to put on his spectacles, immediately laid them down, with the sprightly observation:

'You read my thoughts, sir. *Do* my eyes deceive me, or is that object up there a—a pie? It can't be a pie.'

'Yes, it's a pie, Wegg,' replied Mr Boffin, with a glance of some little discomfiture at the Decline and Fall.

'*Have* I lost my smell for fruits, or is it a apple pie, sir?' asked Wegg.

'It's a veal and ham pie,' said Mr Boffin.

'Is it indeed, sir? And it would be hard, sir, to name the pie that is a better pie than a weal and hammer,' said Mr Wegg, nodding his head emotionally.

'Have some, Wegg?'

'Thank you, Mr Boffin, I think I will, at your invitation. I wouldn't at any other party's, at the present juncture; but at yours, sir!—And meaty jelly too, especially when a little salt, which is the case where there's ham, is mellering to the organ, is very mellering to the organ.' Mr Wegg did not say what organ, but spoke with a cheerful generality.

So, the pie was brought down, and the worthy Mr Boffin exercised his patience until Wegg, in the exercise of his knife and fork, had finished the dish: only profiting by the opportunity to inform Wegg that although it was not strictly Fashionable to keep the contents of a larder thus exposed to view, he (Mr Boffin) considered it hospitable; for the reason, that instead of saying, in a comparatively unmeaning manner, to a visitor, 'There are such and such edibles down stairs; will you have anything up?' you took the bold practical course of saying, 'Cast your eye along the shelves, and, if you see anything you like there, have it down.'

And now, Mr Wegg at length pushed away his plate and put on his spectacles, and Mr Boffin lighted his pipe and looked with beaming eyes into the opening world before him, and Mrs Boffin reclined in a fashionable manner on her sofa: as one who would be part of the audience if she found she could, and would go to sleep if she found she couldn't.

'Hem!' began Wegg, 'This, Mr Boffin and Lady, is the first chapter of the first wollume of the Decline and Fall off——' here he looked hard at the book, and stopped.

'What's the matter, Wegg?'

'Why, it comes into my mind, do you know, sir,' said Wegg with an air of insinuating frankness (having first again looked hard at the book), 'that you made a little mistake this morning, which I had meant to set you right in, only something put it out of my head. I think you said Rooshan Empire, sir?'

'It is Rooshan; ain't it, Wegg?'

'No, sir. Roman. Roman.'

'What's the difference, Wegg?'

'The difference, sir?' Mr Wegg was faltering and in danger of breaking down, when a bright thought flashed upon him. 'The difference, sir? There you place me in a difficulty, Mr Boffin. Suffice it to observe, that the difference is best postponed to some other occasion when Mrs Boffin does not honour us with her company. In Mrs Boffin's presence, sir, we had better drop it.'

Mr Wegg thus came out of his disadvantage with quite a chivalrous air, and not only that, but by dint of repeating with a manly delicacy, 'In Mrs Boffin's presence, sir, we had better drop it!' turned the disadvantage on Boffin, who felt that he had committed himself in a very painful manner.

Then, Mr Wegg, in a dry unflinching way, entered on his task; going straight across country at everything that came before him; taking all the hard words, biographical and geographical; getting rather shaken by Hadrian, Trajan, and the Antonines; stumbling at Polybius (pronounced Polly Beeious, and supposed by Mr Boffin to be a Roman virgin, and by Mrs Boffin to be responsible for that necessity of dropping it); heavily unseated by Titus Antoninus Pius; up again and galloping smoothly with Augustus; finally, getting over the ground well with Commodus: who, under the appellation of Commodious, was held by Mr Boffin to have been quite unworthy of his English origin, and 'not to have acted up to his name' in his government of the Roman people. With the death of this personage, Mr Wegg terminated his first reading; long before which consummation several total eclipses of Mrs Boffin's candle behind her black velvet disc, would have been very alarming, but for being regularly accompanied by a potent smell of burnt pens when her feathers took fire, which acted as a restorative and woke her. Mr Wegg, having read on by rote and attached as few ideas as possible to the text, came out of the encounter fresh; but, Mr Boffin, who had soon laid down his unfinished pipe, and had ever since sat intently staring with his eyes and mind at the confounding enormities of the Romans, was so severely punished that he could hardly wish his literary friend Good-night, and articulate 'To-morrow.'

'Commodious,' gasped Mr Boffin, staring at the moon, after letting Wegg out at the gate and fastening it: 'Commodious fights in that wild-beast-show, seven hundred and thirty-five times, in one character only! As if that wasn't stunning enough, a hundred lions is turned into the same wild-beast-show all at once! As if that wasn't stunning enough, Commodious, in another character, kills 'em all off in a hundred goes! As if that wasn't stunning enough, Vittle-us (and well named too) eats six millions' worth, English money, in seven months! Wegg takes it easy, but upon-my-soul to a old bird like myself these are scarers. And even now that Commodious is strangled, I don't see a way to our bettering ourselves.' Mr Boffin added as he turned his pensive steps towards the Bower and shook his head, 'I didn't think this morning there was half so many Scarers in Print. But I'm in for it now!'

Chapter 6
Cut Adrift

THE Six Jolly Fellowship Porters, already mentioned as a tavern of a dropsical appearance, had long settled down into a state of hale infirmity. In its whole constitution it had not a straight floor, and hardly a straight line; but it had outlasted, and clearly would yet outlast, many a better-trimmed building, many a sprucer public-house. Externally, it was a narrow lopsided wooden jumble of corpulent windows heaped one upon another as you might heap as many toppling oranges, with a crazy wooden verandah impending over the water; indeed the whole house, inclusive of the complaining flag-staff on the roof, impended over the water, but seemed to have got into the condition of a faint-hearted diver who has paused so long on the brink that he will never go in at all.

This description applies to the river-frontage of the Six Jolly Fellowship Porters. The back of the establishment, though the chief entrance was there, so contracted that it merely represented in its connexion with the front, the handle of a flat iron set upright on its broadest end. This handle stood at the bottom of a wilderness of court and alley: which wilderness pressed so hard and close upon the Six Jolly Fellowship Porters as to leave the hostelry not an inch of ground beyond its door. For this reason, in combination with the fact that the house was all but afloat at high water, when the Porters had a family wash the linen subjected to that operation might usually be seen drying on lines stretched across the reception-rooms and bed-chambers.

The wood forming the chimney-pieces, beams, partitions, floors and doors, of the Six Jolly Fellowship Porters, seemed in its old age fraught with confused memories of its youth. In many places it had become gnarled and riven, according to the manner of old trees; knots started out of it; and here and there it seemed to twist itself into some likeness of boughs. In this state of second childhood, it had an air of being in its own way garrulous about its early life. Not without reason was it often asserted by the regular frequenters of the Porters, that when the light shone full upon the grain of certain panels, and particularly upon an old corner cupboard of walnut-wood in the bar, you might trace little forests there, and tiny trees like the parent tree, in full umbrageous leaf.

The bar of the Six Jolly Fellowship Porters was a bar to soften the human breast. The available space in it was not much larger than a hackney-coach; but no one could have wished the bar bigger, that space was so girt in by corpulent little casks, and by cordial-bottles radiant with fictitious grapes in bunches, and by lemons in nets, and by biscuits in baskets, and by the polite beer-pulls that made low bows when customers were served with beer, and by the cheese in a snug corner, and by the landlady's own small table in a snugger corner near the fire, with the cloth everlastingly laid. This haven was divided from the rough world by a glass partition and a half-door, with a leaden sill upon it for the convenience of resting your liquor; but, over this half-door the bar's snugness so gushed forth, that, albeit customers drank there standing, in a dark and draughty passage where they were shouldered by other customers passing in and out, they always appeared to drink under an enchanting delusion that they were in the bar itself.

For the rest, both the tap and parlour of the Six Jolly Fellowship Porters gave upon the river, and had red curtains matching the noses of the regular customers, and were provided with comfortable fireside tin utensils, like models of sugar-loaf hats, made in that shape that they might, with their pointed ends, seek out for themselves glowing nooks in the depths of the red coals, when they mulled your ale, or heated for you those delectable drinks, Purl, Flip, and Dog's Nose. The first of these humming compounds was a speciality of the Porters, which, through an inscription on its door-posts, gently appealed to your feelings as, 'The Early Purl House'. For, it would seem that Purl must always be taken early; though whether for any more distinctly stomachic reason than that, as the early bird catches the worm, so the early purl catches the customer, cannot here be resolved. It only remains to add that in the handle of the flat iron, and opposite the bar, was a very little room like a three-cornered hat, into which no direct ray of sun, moon, or star, ever penetrated, but which was superstitiously regarded as a sanctuary

replete with comfort and retirement by gaslight, and on the door
of which was therefore painted its alluring name: Cosy.

Miss Potterson, sole proprietor and manager of the Fellowship Porters, reigned supreme on her throne, the Bar, and a man
must have drunk himself mad drunk indeed if he thought he
could contest a point with her. Being known on her own authority as Miss Abbey Potterson, some water-side heads, which (like
the water) were none of the clearest, harboured muddled notions
that, because of her dignity and firmness, she was named after,
or in some sort related to, the Abbey at Westminster. But,
Abbey was only short for Abigail, by which name Miss Potterson
had been christened at Limehouse Church, some sixty and odd
years before.

'Now, you mind, you Riderhood,' said Miss Abbey Potterson,
with emphatic forefinger over the half-door, 'the Fellowship
don't want you at all, and would rather by far have your room
than your company; but if you were as welcome here as you are
not, you shouldn't even then have another drop of drink here this
night, after this present pint of beer. So make the most of it.'

'But you know, Miss Potterson,' this was suggested very
meekly though, 'if I behave myself, you can't help serving me,
miss.'

'*Can't* I!' said Abbey, with infinite expression.

'No, Miss Potterson; because, you see, the law—'

'*I* am the law here, my man,' returned Miss Abbey, 'and
I'll soon convince you of that, if you doubt it at all.'

'I never said I did doubt it at all, Miss Abbey.'

'So much the better for you.'

Abbey the supreme threw the customer's halfpence into the
till, and, seating herself in her fireside-chair, resumed the
newspaper she had been reading. She was a tall, upright, well-
favoured woman, though severe of countenance, and had more
of the air of a schoolmistress than mistress of the Six Jolly
Fellowship Porters. The man on the other side of the half-door,
was a waterside-man with a squinting leer, and he eyed her as if
he were one of her pupils in disgrace.

'You're cruel hard upon me, Miss Potterson.'

Miss Potterson read her newspaper with contracted brows,
and took no notice until he whispered:

'Miss Potterson! Ma'am! Might I have half a word with you?'

Deigning then to turn her eyes sideways towards the suppli-
ant, Miss Potterson beheld him knuckling his low forehead, and
ducking at her with his head, as if he were asking leave to fling

himself head foremost over the half-door and alight on his feet in the bar.

'Well?' said Miss Potterson, with a manner as short as she herself was long, 'say your half word. Bring it out.'

'Miss Potterson! Ma'am! Would you 'sxcuse me taking the liberty of asking, is it my character that you take objections to?'

'Certainly,' said Miss Potterson.

'Is it that you're afraid of—'

'I am not afraid of *you*,' interposed Miss Potterson, 'if you mean that.'

'But I humbly don't mean that, Miss Abbey.'

'Then what do you mean?'

'You really are so cruel hard upon me! What I was going to make inquiries was no more than, might you have any apprehensions—leastways beliefs or suppositions—that the company's property mightn't be altogether to be considered safe, if I used the house too regular?'

'What do you want to know for?'

'Well, Miss- Abbey, respectfully meaning no offence to you, it would be some satisfaction to a man's mind, to understand why the Fellowship Porters is not to be free to such as me, and is to be free to such as Gaffer.'

The face of the hostess darkened with some shadow of perplexity, as she replied: 'Gaffer has never been where you have been.'

'Signifying in Quod, Miss? Perhaps not. But he may have merited it. He may be suspected of far worse than ever I was.'

'Who suspects him?'

'Many, perhaps. One, beyond all doubts. I do.'

'*You* are not much,' said Miss Abbey Potterson, knitting her brows again with disdain.

'But I was his pardner. Mind you, Miss Abbey, I was his pardner. As such I know more of the ins and outs of him than any person living does. Notice this! I am the man that was his pardner, and I am the man that suspects him.'

'Then,' suggested Miss Abbey, though with a deeper shade of perplexity than before, 'you criminate yourself.'

'No, I don't, Miss Abbey. For how does it stand? It stands this way. When I was his pardner, I couldn't never give him satisfaction. Why couldn't I never give him satisfaction? Because my luck was bad; because I couldn't find many enough of 'em. How was his luck? Always good. Notice this! Always good! Ah! There's a many games, Miss Abbey, in which there's chance, but there's a many others in which there's skill too, mixed along with it.'

'That Gaffer has a skill in finding what he finds, who doubts, man?' asked Miss Abbey.

'A skill in purwiding what he finds, perhaps,' said Riderhood, shaking his evil head.

Miss Abbey knitted her brow at him, as he darkly leered at her.

'If you're out upon the river pretty nigh every tide, and if you want to find a man or woman in the river, you'll greatly help your luck, Miss Abbey, by knocking a man or woman on the head aforehand and pitching 'em in.'

'Gracious Lud!' was the involuntary exclamation of Miss Potterson.

'Mind you!' returned the other, stretching forward over the half door to throw his words into the bar; for his voice was as if the head of his boat's mop were down his throat; 'I say so, Miss Abbey! And mind you! I'll follow him up, Miss Abbey! And mind you! I'll bring him to book at last, if it's twenty year hence, I will! Who's he, to be favoured along of his daughter? Ain't I got a daughter of my own!'

With that flourish, and seeming to have talked himself rather more drunk and much more ferocious than he had begun by being, Mr Riderhood took up his pint pot and swaggered off to the tap-room.

Gaffer was not there, but a pretty strong muster of Miss Abbey's pupils were, who exhibited, when occasion required, the greatest docility. On the clock's striking ten, and Miss Abbey's appearing at the door, and addressing a certain person in a faded scarlet jacket, with 'George Jones, your time's up! I told your wife you should be punctual,' Jones submissively rose, gave the company good-night, and retired. At half-past ten, on Miss Abbey's looking in again, and saying, 'William Williams, Bob Glamour, and Jonathan, you are all due,' William, Bob, and Jonathan with similar meekness took their leave and evaporated. Greater wonder than these, when a bottle-nosed person in a glazed hat had after some considerable hesitation ordered another glass of gin and water of the attendant potboy, and when Miss Abbey, instead of sending it, appeared in person, saying, 'Captain Joey, you have had as much as will do you good,' not only did the captain feebly rub his knees and contemplate the fire without offering a word of protest, but the rest of the company murmured, 'Ay, ay, Captain! Miss Abbey's right; you be guided by Miss Abbey, Captain.' Nor, was Miss Abbey's vigilance in anywise abated by this submission, but rather sharpened; for, looking round on the deferential faces of her school, and descrying two other young persons in need of admonition, she thus bestowed it: 'Tom Tootle, it's time for a young fellow who's going to be married next month, to be at home and asleep. And you needn't nudge him, Mr Jack Mullins, for I know your work begins early tomorrow, and I say the same to you. So come! Good-night, like good lads!' Upon which, the blushing Tootle looked to Mullins, and the blushing Mullins looked to Tootle, on the question who should rise first, and finally both rose together and went out on the broad grin, followed by Miss Abbey; in whose presence the company did not take the liberty of grinning likewise.

In such an establishment, the white-aproned pot-boy with his shirt-sleeves arranged in a tight roll on each bare shoulder, was a mere hint of the possibility of physical force, thrown out as a matter of state and form. Exactly at the closing hour, all the guests who were left, filed out in the best order: Miss Abbey standing at the half door of the bar, to hold a ceremony of review and dismissal. All wished Miss Abbey good-night and Miss Abbey wished good-night to all, except Riderhood. The sapient pot-boy, looking on officially, then had the conviction borne in upon his soul, that the man was evermore outcast and excommunicate from the Six Jolly Fellowship Porters.

'You Bob Gliddery,' said Miss Abbey to this pot-boy, 'run round to Hexam's and tell his daughter Lizzie that I want to speak to her.'

With exemplary swiftness Bob Gliddery departed, and returned. Lizzie, following him, arrived as one of the two female domestics of the Fellowship Porters arranged on the snug little table by the bar fire, Miss Potterson's supper of hot sausages and mashed potatoes.

'Come in and sit ye down, girl,' said Miss Abbey. 'Can you eat a bit?'

'No thank you, Miss. I have had my supper.'

'I have had mine too, I think,' said Miss Abbey, pushing away the untasted dish, 'and more than enough of it. I am put out, Lizzie.'

'I am very sorry for it, Miss.'

'Then why, in the name of Goodness,' quoth Miss Abbey, sharply, 'do you do it?'

'*I* do it, Miss!'

'There, there. Don't look astonished. I ought to have begun with a word of explanation, but it's my way to make short cuts at things. I always was a pepperer. You Bob Gliddery there, put the chain upon the door and get ye down to your supper.'

With an alacrity that seemed no less referable to the pepperer fact than to the supper fact, Bob obeyed, and his boots were heard descending towards the bed of the river.

'Lizzie Hexam, Lizzie Hexam,' then began Miss Potterson, 'how often have I held out to you the opportunity of getting clear of your father, and doing well?'

'Very often, Miss.'

'Very often? Yes! And I might as well have spoken to the iron funnel of the strongest sea-going steamer that passes the Fellowship Porters.'

'No, Miss,' Lizzie pleaded; 'because that would not be thankful, and I am.'

'I vow and declare I am half ashamed of myself for taking such an interest in you,' said Miss Abbey, pettishly, 'for I don't believe I should do it if you were not good-looking. Why ain't you ugly?'

Lizzie merely answered this difficult question with an apologetic glance.

'However, you ain't,' resumed Miss Potterson, 'so it's no use going into that. I must take you as I find you. Which indeed is what I've done. And you mean to say you are still obstinate?'

'Not obstinate, Miss, I hope.'

'Firm (I suppose you call it) then?'

'Yes, Miss. Fixed like.'

'Never was an obstinate person yet, who would own to the word!' remarked Miss Potterson, rubbing her vexed nose; 'I'm sure I would, if I was obstinate; but I am a pepperer, which is different. Lizzie Hexam, Lizzie Hexam, think again. Do you know the worst of your father?'

'Do I know the worst of father!' she repeated, opening her eyes.

'Do you know the suspicions to which your father makes himself liable? Do you know the suspicions that are actually about, against him?'

The consciousness of what he habitually did, oppressed the girl heavily, and she slowly cast down her eyes.

'Say, Lizzie. Do you know?' urged Miss Abbey.

'Please to tell me what the suspicions are, Miss,' she asked after a silence, with her eyes upon the ground.

'It's not an easy thing to tell a daughter, but it must be told. It is thought by some, then, that your father helps to their death a few of those that he finds dead.'

The relief of hearing what she felt sure was a false suspicion, in place of the expected real and true one, so lightened Lizzie's breast for the moment, that Miss Abbey was amazed at her demeanour. She raised her eyes quickly, shook her head, and, in a kind of triumph, almost laughed.

'They little know father who talk like that!'

('She takes it,' thought Miss Abbey, 'very quietly. She takes it with extraordinary quietness!')

'And perhaps,' said Lizzie, as a recollection flashed upon her, 'it is some one who has a grudge against father; some one who has threatened father! Is it Riderhood, Miss?'

'Well; yes it is.'

'Yes! He was father's partner, and father broke with him, and now he revenges himself. Father broke with him when I was by, and he was very angry at it. And besides, Miss Abbey! —Will you never, without strong reason, let pass your lips what I am going to say?'

She bent forward to say it in a whisper.

'I promise,' said Miss Abbey.

'It was on the night when the Harmon murder was found out, through father, just above bridge. And just below bridge, as we were sculling home, Riderhood crept out of the dark in his boat. And many and many times afterwards, when such great pains were taken to come to the bottom of the crime, and it never could be come near, I thought in my own thoughts, could Riderhood himself have done the murder, and did he purposely let father find the body? It seemed a'most wicked and cruel to so much as think such a thing; but now that he tries to throw it upon father, I go back to it as if it was a truth. Can it be a truth? That was put into my mind by the dead?'

She asked this question, rather of the fire than of the hostess of the Fellowship Porters, and looked round the little bar with troubled eyes.

But, Miss Potterson, as a ready schoolmistress accustomed to bring her pupils to book, set the matter in a light that was essentially of this world.

'You poor deluded girl,' she said, 'don't you see that you can't open your mind to particular suspicions of one of the two, without opening your mind to general suspicions of the other? They had worked together. Their goings-on had been going on for some time. Even granting that it was as you have had in your thoughts, what the two had done together would come familiar to the mind of one.'

'You don't know father, Miss, when you talk like that. Indeed, indeed, you don't know father.'

'Lizzie, Lizzie,' said Miss Potterson. 'Leave him. You needn't break with him altogether, but leave him. Do well away from him; not because of what I have told you to-night—we'll pass no judgment upon that, and we'll hope it may not be—but because of what I have urged on you before. No matter whether it's owing to your good looks or not, I like you and I want to serve you. Lizzie, come under my direction. Don't fling yourself away, my girl, but be persuaded into being respectable and happy.'

In the sound good feeling and good sense of her entreaty, Miss Abbey had softened into a soothing tone, and had even drawn her arm round the girl's waist. But, she only replied, 'Thank you, thank you! I can't. I won't. I must not think of it. The harder father is borne upon, the more he needs me to lean on.'

And then Miss Abbey, who, like all hard people when they do soften, felt that there was considerable compensation owing to her, underwent reaction and became frigid.

'I have done what I can,' she said, 'and you must go your way. You make your bed, and you must lie on it. But tell your father one thing: he must not come here any more.'

'Oh, Miss, will you forbid him the house where I know he's safe?'

'The Fellowships,' returned Miss Abbey, 'has itself to look to, as well as others. It has been hard work to establish order here, and make the Fellowships what it is, and it is daily and nightly hard work to keep it so. The Fellowships must not have a taint upon it that may give it a bad name. I forbid the house to Riderhood, and I forbid the house to Gaffer. I forbid both, equally. I find from Riderhood and you together, that there are suspicions against both men, and I'm not going to take upon myself to decide betwixt them. They are both tarred with a dirty brush, and I can't have the Fellowships tarred with the same brush. That's all *I* know.'

'Good-night, Miss!' said Lizzie Hexam, sorrowfully.

'Hah!—Good-night!' returned Miss Abbey with a shake of her head.

'Believe me, Miss Abbey, I am truly grateful all the same.'

'I can believe a good deal,' returned the stately Abbey, 'so I'll try to believe that too, Lizzie.'

No supper did Miss Potterson take that night, and only half her usual tumbler of hot Port Negus. And the female domestics—two robust sisters, with staring black eyes, shining flat red faces, blunt noses, and strong black curls, like dolls—interchanged the sentiment that Missis had had her hair combed the wrong way by somebody. And the pot-boy afterwards remarked, that he hadn't been 'so rattled to bed', since his late mother had systematically accelerated his retirement to rest with a poker.

The chaining of the door behind her, as she went forth, disenchanted Lizzie Hexam of that first relief she had felt. The night was black and shrill, the river-side wilderness was melancholy, and there was a sound of casting-out, in the rattling of the iron-links, and the grating of the bolts and staples under Miss Abbey's hand. As she came beneath the lowering sky, a sense of being involved in a murky shade of Murder dropped upon her; and, as the tidal swell of the river broke at her feet without her seeing how it gathered, so, her thoughts startled her by rushing out of an unseen void and striking at her heart.

Of her father's being groundlessly suspected, she felt sure. Sure. Sure. And yet, repeat the word inwardly as often as she would, the attempt to reason out and prove that she was sure, always came after it and failed. Riderhood had done the deed, and entrapped her father. Riderhood had not done the deed, but had resolved in his malice to turn against her father, the appearances that were ready to his hand to distort. Equally and swiftly upon either putting of the case, followed the frightful possibility that her father, being innocent, yet might come to be believed guilty. She had heard of people suffering Death for bloodshed of which they were afterwards proved pure, and those ill-fated persons were not, first, in that dangerous wrong in which her father stood. Then at the best, the beginning of his being set apart, whispered against, and avoided, was a certain fact. It dated from that very night. And as the great black river with its dreary shores was soon lost to her view in the gloom, so, she stood on the river's brink unable to see into the vast blank misery of a life suspected, and fallen away from by good and bad, but knowing that it lay there dim before her, stretching away to the great ocean, Death.

One thing only, was clear to the girl's mind. Accustomed from her very babyhood promptly to do the thing that could be done—whether to keep out weather, to ward off cold, to postpone hunger, or what not—she started out of her meditation, and ran home.

The room was quiet, and the lamp burnt on the table. In the bunk in the corner, her brother lay asleep. She bent over him softly, kissed him, and came to the table.

'By the time of Miss Abbey's closing, and by the run of the tide, it must be one. Tide's running up. Father at Chiswick, wouldn't think of coming down, till after the turn, and that's at half after four. I'll call Charley at six. I shall hear the church-clocks strike, as I sit here.'

Very quietly, she placed a chair before the scanty fire, and sat down in it, drawing her shawl about her.

'Charley's hollow down by the flare is not there now. Poor Charley!'

The clock struck two, and the clock struck three, and the clock struck four, and she remained there, with a woman's patience and her own purpose. When the morning was well on between four and five, she slipped off her shoes (that her going about, might not wake Charley), trimmed the fire sparingly, put water on to boil, and set the table for breakfast. Then she went up the ladder, lamp in hand, and came down again, and glided about and about, making a little bundle. Lastly, from her pocket, and from the chimney-piece, and from an inverted basin on the highest shelf, she brought halfpence, a few sixpences, fewer shillings, and fell to laboriously and noiselessly counting them, and setting aside one little heap. She was still so engaged, when she was startled by:

'Hal-loa!' From her brother, sitting up in bed.

'You made me jump, Charley.'

'Jump! Didn't you make *me* jump, when I opened my eyes a moment ago, and saw you sitting there, like the ghost of a girl miser, in the dead of the night.'

'It's not the dead of the night, Charley. It's nigh six in the morning.'

'Is it though? But what are you up to, Liz?'

'Still telling your fortune, Charley.'

'It seems to be a precious small one, if that's it,' said the boy. 'What are you putting that little pile of money by itself for?'

'For you, Charley.'

'What do you mean?'

'Get out of bed, Charley, and get washed and dressed, and then I'll tell you.'

Her composed manner, and her low distinct voice, always had an influence over him. His head was soon in a basin of water, and out of it again, and staring at her through a storm of towelling.

'I never,' towelling at himself as if he were his bitterest enemy, 'saw such a girl as you are. What *is* the move, Liz?'

'Are you almost ready for breakfast, Charley?'

'You can pour it out. Hal-loa! I say? And a bundle?'

'And a bundle, Charley.'

'You don't mean it's for me, too?'

'Yes, Charley; I do, indeed.'

More serious of face, and more slow of action, than he had been, the boy completed his dressing, and came and sat down at the little breakfast-table, with his eyes amazedly directed to her face.

'You see, Charley dear, I have made up my mind that this is the right time for your going away from us. Over and above all the blessed change of by-and-bye, you'll be much happier, and do much better, even so soon as next month. Even so soon as next week.'

'How do you know I shall?'

'I don't quite know how, Charley, but I do.' In spite of her unchanged manner of speaking, and her unchanged appearance of composure, she scarcely trusted herself to look at him, but kept her eyes employed on the cutting and buttering of his bread, and on the mixing of his tea, and other such little preparations. 'You must leave father to me, Charley—I will do what I can with him—but you must go.'

'You don't stand upon ceremony, I think,' grumbled the boy, throwing his bread and butter about, in an ill-humour.

She made him no answer.

'I tell you what,' said the boy, then, bursting out into an angry whimpering, 'you're a selfish jade, and you think there's not enough for three of us, and you want to get rid of me.'

'If you believe so, Charley,—yes, then I believe too, that I am a selfish jade, and that I think there's not enough for three of us, and that I want to get rid of you.'

It was only when the boy rushed at her, and threw his arms round her neck, that she lost her self-restraint. But she lost it then, and wept over him.

'Don't cry, don't cry! I am satisfied to go, Liz; I am satisfied to go. I know you send me away for my good.'

'O, Charley, Charley, Heaven above us knows I do!'

'Yes, yes. Don't mind what I said. Don't remember it. Kiss me.'

After a silence, she loosed him, to dry her eyes and regain her strong quiet influence.

'Now listen, Charley dear. We both know it must be done, and I alone know there is good reason for its being done at once. Go straight to the school, and say that you and I agreed upon it—that we can't overcome father's opposition—that father will never trouble them, but will never take you back. You are a credit to the school, and you will be a greater credit to it yet, and they will help you to get a living. Show what clothes you have brought, and what money, and say that I will send some more money. If I can get some in no other way, I will ask a little help of those two gentlemen who came here that night.'

'I say!' cried her brother, quickly. 'Don't you have it of that chap that took hold of me by the chin! Don't you have it of that Wrayburn one!'

Perhaps a slight additional tinge of red flushed up into her face and brow, as with a nod she laid a hand upon his lips to keep him silently attentive.

'And above all things mind this, Charley! Be sure you always speak well of father. Be sure you always give father his full due. You can't deny that because father has no learning himself he is set against it in you; but favour nothing else against him, and be sure you say—as you know—that your sister is devoted to him. And if you should ever happen to hear anything said against father that is new to you, it will not be true. Remember, Charley! It will not be true.'

The boy looked at her with some doubt and surprise, but she went on again without heeding it.

'Above all things remember! It will not be true. I have nothing more to say, Charley dear, except, be good, and get learning, and only think of some things in the old life here, as if you had dreamed them in a dream last night. Good-bye, my Darling!'

Though so young, she infused in these parting words a love that was far more like a mother's than a sister's, and before which the boy was quite bowed down. After holding her to his breast with a passionate cry, he took up his bundle and darted out at the door, with an arm across his eyes.

The white face of the winter day came sluggishly on, veiled in a frosty mist; and the shadowy ships in the river slowly changed to black substances; and the sun, blood-red on the eastern marshes behind dark masts and yards, seemed filled with the ruins of a forest it had set on fire. Lizzie, looking for her father, saw him coming, and stood upon the causeway that he might see her.

He had nothing with him but his boat, and came on apace. A knot of those amphibious human-creatures who appear to have some mysterious power of extracting a subsistence out of tidal water by looking at it, were gathered together about the causeway. As her father's boat grounded, they became contemplative of the mud, and dispersed themselves. She saw that the mute avoidance had begun.

Gaffer saw it, too, in so far as that he was moved when he set foot on shore, to stare around him. But, he promptly set to work to haul up his boat, and make her fast, and take the sculls and rudder and rope out of her. Carrying these with Lizzie's aid, he passed up to his dwelling.

'Sit close to the fire, father, dear, while I cook your breakfast. It's all ready for cooking, and only been waiting for you. You must be frozen.'

'Well, Lizzie, I ain't of a glow; that's certain. And my hands seem nailed through to the sculls. See how dead they are!' Something suggestive in their colour, and perhaps in her face, struck him as he held them up; he turned his shoulder and held them down to the fire.

'You were not out in the perishing night, I hope, father?'

'No, my dear. Lay aboard a barge, by a blazing coal-fire.— Where's that boy?'

'There's a drop of brandy for your tea, father, if you'll put it in while I turn this bit of meat. If the river was to get frozen, there would be a deal of distress; wouldn't there, father?'

'Ah! there's always enough of that,' said Gaffer, dropping the liquor into his cup from a squat black bottle, and dropping it slowly that it might seem more; 'distress is for ever a going about, like sut in the air—Ain't that boy up yet?'

'The meat's ready now, father. Eat it while it's hot and comfortable. After you have finished, we'll turn round to the fire and talk.'

But, he perceived that he was evaded, and, having thrown a hasty angry glance towards the bunk, plucked at a corner of her apron and asked:

'What's gone with that boy?'

'Father, if you'll begin your breakfast, I'll sit and tell you.'

He looked at her, stirred his tea and took two or three gulps, then cut at his piece of hot steak with his case-knife, and said, eating:

'Now then. What's gone with that boy?'

'Don't be angry, dear. It seems, father, that he has quite a gift of learning.'

'Unnat'ral young beggar!' said the parent, shaking his knife in the air.

'—And that having this gift, and not being equally good at other things, he has made shift to get some schooling.'

'Unnat'ral young beggar!' said the parent again, with his former action.

'—And that knowing you have nothing to spare, father, and not wishing to be a burden on you, he gradually made up his mind to go seek his fortune out of learning. He went away this morning, father, and he cried very much at going, and he hoped you would forgive him.'

'Let him never come a nigh me to ask me my forgiveness,' said the father, again emphasizing his words with the knife. 'Let him never come within sight of my eyes, nor yet within reach of my arm. His own father ain't good enough for him. He's disowned his own father. His own father therefore, disowns him for ever and ever, as a unnat'ral young beggar.'

He had pushed away his plate. With the natural need of a strong rough man in anger, to do something forcible, he now clutched his knife overhand, and struck downward with it at the end of every succeeding sentence. As he would have struck with his own clenched fist if there had chanced to be nothing in it.

'He's welcome to go. He's more welcome to go than to stay. But let him never come back. Let him never put his head inside that door. And let you never speak a word more in his favour, or you'll disown your own father, likewise, and what your father says of him he'll have to come to say of you. Now I see why them men yonder held aloof from me. They says to one another, "Here comes the man as ain't good enough for his own son!" Lizzie— !'

But, she stopped him with a cry. Looking at her he saw her, with a face quite strange to him, shrinking back against the wall, with her hands before her eyes.

'Father, don't! I can't bear to see you striking with it. Put it down!'

He looked at the knife; but in his astonishment still held it.

'Father, it's too horrible. O put it down, put it down!'

Confounded by her appearance and exclamation, he tossed it away, and stood up with his open hands held out before him.

'What's come to you, Liz? Can you think I would strike at you with a knife?'

'No, father, no; you would never hurt me.'

'What should I hurt?'

'Nothing, dear father. On my knees, I am certain, in my heart and soul I am certain, nothing! But it was too dreadful to bear; for it looked—' her hands covering her face again, 'O it looked—'

'What did it look like?'

The recollection of his murderous figure, combining with her trial of last night, and her trial of the morning, caused her to drop at his feet, without having answered.

He had never seen her so before. He raised her with the utmost tenderness, calling her the best of daughters, and 'my poor pretty creetur', and laid her head upon his knee, and tried to restore her. But failing, he laid her head gently down again, got a pillow and placed it under her dark hair, and sought on the table for a spoonful of brandy. There being none left, he hurriedly caught up the empty bottle, and ran out at the door.

He returned as hurriedly as he had gone, with the bottle still empty. He kneeled down by her, took her head on his arm, and moistened her lips with a little water into which he dipped his fingers: saying, fiercely, as he looked around, now over this shoulder, now over that:

'Have we got a pest in the house? Is there summ'at deadly sticking to my clothes? What's let loose upon us? Who loosed it?'

Chapter 7
Mr Wegg Looks After Himself

SILAS WEGG, being on his road to the Roman Empire, approaches it by way of Clerkenwell. The time is early in the evening; the weather moist and raw. Mr Wegg finds leisure to make a little circuit, by reason that he folds his screen early, now that he combines another source of income with it, and also that he feels it due to himself to be anxiously expected at the Bower. 'Boffin will get all the eagerer for waiting a bit,' says Silas, screwing up, as he stumps along, first his right eye, and then his left. Which is something superfluous in him, for Nature has already screwed both pretty tight.

'If I get on with him as I expect to get on,' Silas pursues, stumping and meditating, 'it wouldn't become me to leave it here. It wouldn't be respectable.' Animated by this reflection, he stumps faster, and looks a long way before him, as a man with an ambitious project in abeyance often will do.

Aware of a working-jeweller population taking sanctuary about the church in Clerkenwell, Mr Wegg is conscious of an interest in, and a respect for, the neighbourhood. But, his sensations in this regard halt as to their strict morality, as he halts in his gait; for, they suggest the delights of a coat of invisibility in which to walk off safely with the precious stones and watch-cases, but stop short of any compunction for the people who would lose the same.

Not, however, towards the 'shops' where cunning artificers work in pearls and diamonds and gold and silver, making their hands so rich, that the enriched water in which they wash them is bought for the refiners;—not towards these does Mr Wegg stump, but towards the poorer shops of small retail traders in commodities to eat and drink and keep folks warm, and of Italian frame-makers, and of barbers, and of brokers, and of dealers in dogs and singing-birds. From these, in a narrow and a dirty street devoted to such callings, Mr Wegg selects one dark shop-window with a tallow candle dimly burning in it, surrounded by a muddle of objects vaguely resembling pieces of leather and dry stick, but among which nothing is resolvable into anything distinct, save the candle itself in its old tin candlestick, and two preserved frogs fighting a small-sword duel. Stumping with fresh vigour, he goes in at the dark greasy entry, pushes a little greasy dark reluctant side-door, and follows the door into the little dark greasy shop. It is so dark that nothing can be made out in it, over a little counter, but another tallow candle in another old tin candlestick, close to the face of a man stooping low in a chair.

Mr Wegg nods to the face, 'Good evening.'

The face looking up is a sallow face with weak eyes, surmounted by a tangle of reddish-dusty hair. The owner of the face has no cravat on, and has opened his tumbled shirt-collar to work with the more ease. For the same reason he has no coat on:

only a loose waistcoat over his yellow linen. His eyes are like
the over-tried eyes of an engraver, but he is not that; his expression and stoop are like those of a shoemaker, but he is not that.

'Good evening, Mr Venus. Don't you remember?'

With slowly dawning remembrance, Mr Venus rises, and
holds his candle over the little counter, and holds it down
towards the legs, natural and artificial, of Mr Wegg.

'To be *sure!*' he says, then. 'How do you do?'

'Wegg, you know,' that gentleman explains.

'Yes, yes,' says the other. 'Hospital amputation?'

'Just so,' says Mr Wegg.

'Yes, yes' quoth Venus. 'How do you do? Sit down by the
fire, and warm your—your other one.'

The little counter being so short a counter that it leaves the
fireplace, which would have been behind it if it had been longer,
accessible, Mr Wegg sits down on a box in front of the fire, and
inhales a warm and comfortable smell which is not the smell of
the shop. 'For that,' Mr Wegg inwardly decides, as he takes a
corrective sniff or two, 'is musty, leathery, feathery, cellary,
gluey, gummy, and,' with another sniff, 'as it might be, strong
of old pairs of bellows.'

'My tea is drawing, and my muffin is on the hob, Mr
Wegg; will you partake?'

It being one of Mr Wegg's guiding rules in life always to
partake, he says he will. But, the little shop is so excessively
dark, is stuck so full of black shelves and brackets and nooks and
corners, that he sees Mr Venus's cup and saucer only because it
is close under the candle, and does not see from what mysterious
recess Mr Venus produces another for himself, until it is under
his nose. Concurrently, Wegg perceives a pretty little dead bird
lying on the counter, with its head drooping on one side against
the rim of Mr Venus's saucer, and a long stiff wire piercing its
breast. As if it were Cock Robin, the hero of the ballad, and Mr
Venus were the sparrow with his bow and arrow, and Mr Wegg
were the fly with his little eye.

Mr Venus dives, and produces another muffin, yet untoasted;
taking the arrow out of the breast of Cock Robin, he proceeds to
toast it on the end of that cruel instrument. When it is brown, he
dives again and produces butter, with which he completes his
work.

Mr Wegg, as an artful man who is sure of his supper
by-and-bye, presses muffin on his host to soothe him into a
compliant state of mind, or, as one might say, to grease his

works. As the muffins disappear, little by little, the black shelves and nooks and corners begin to appear, and Mr Wegg gradually acquires an imperfect notion that over against him on the chimney-piece is a Hindoo baby in a bottle, curved up with his big head tucked under him, as he would instantly throw a summersault if the bottle were large enough.

When he deems Mr Venus's wheels sufficiently lubricated, Mr Wegg approaches his object by asking, as he lightly taps his hands together, to express an undesigning frame of mind:

'And how have I been going on, this long time, Mr Venus?'

'Very bad,' says Mr Venus, uncompromisingly.

'What? Am I still at home?' asks Wegg, with an air of surprise.

'Always at home.'

This would seem to be secretly agreeable to Wegg, but he veils his feelings, and observes, 'Strange. To what do you attribute it?'

'I don't know,' replies Venus, who is a haggard melancholy man, speaking in a weak voice of querulous complaint, 'to what to attribute it, Mr Wegg. I can't work you into a miscellaneous one, no how. Do what I will, you can't be got to fit. Anybody with a passable knowledge would pick you out at a look, and say,—"No go! Don't match!"'

'Well, but hang it, Mr Venus,' Wegg expostulates with some little irritation, 'that can't be personal and peculiar in *me*. It must often happen with miscellaneous ones.'

'With ribs (I grant you) always. But not else. When I prepare a miscellaneous one, I know beforehand that I can't keep to nature, and be miscellaneous with ribs, because every man has his own ribs, and no other man's will go with them; but elseways I can be miscellaneous. I have just sent home a Beauty—a perfect Beauty—to a school of art. One leg Belgian, one leg English, and the pickings of eight other people in it. Talk of not being qualified to be miscellaneous! By rights you *ought* to be, Mr Wegg.'

Silas looks as hard at his one leg as he can in the dim light, and after a pause sulkily opines 'that it must be the fault of the other people. Or how do you mean to say it comes about?' he demands impatiently.

'I don't know how it comes about. Stand up a minute. Hold the light.' Mr Venus takes from a corner by his chair, the bones of a leg and foot, beautifully pure, and put together with exquisite neatness. These he compares with Mr Wegg's leg; that gentleman looking on, as if he were being measured for a riding-boot. 'No, I don't know how it is, but so it is. You have got a twist in that bone, to the best of my belief. *I* never saw the likes of you.'

Mr Wegg having looked distrustfully at his own limb, and suspiciously at the pattern with which it has been compared, makes the point:

'I'll bet a pound that ain't an English one!'

'An easy wager, when we run so much into foreign! No, it belongs to that French gentleman.'

As he nods towards a point of darkness behind Mr Wegg, the latter, with a slight start, looks round for 'that French gentleman,' whom he at length descries to be represented (in a very workman-like manner) by his ribs only, standing on a shelf in another corner, like a piece of armour or a pair of stays.

'Oh!' says Mr Wegg, with a sort of sense of being introduced; 'I dare say you were all right enough in your own country, but I hope no objections will be taken to my saying that the Frenchman was never yet born as I should wish to match.'

At this moment the greasy door is violently pushed inward, and a boy follows it, who says, after having let it slam:

'Come for the stuffed canary.'

'It's three and ninepence,' returns Venus; 'have you got the money?'

The boy produces four shillings. Mr Venus, always in exceedingly low spirits and making whimpering sounds, peers about for the stuffed canary. On his taking the candle to assist his search, Mr Wegg observes that he has a convenient little shelf near his knees, exclusively appropriated to skeleton hands, which have very much the appearance of wanting to lay hold of him. From these Mr Venus rescues the canary in a glass case, and shows it to the boy.

'There!' he whimpers. 'There's animation! On a twig, making up his mind to hop! Take care of him; he's a lovely specimen. —And three is four.'

The boy gathers up his change and has pulled the door open by a leather strap nailed to it for the purpose, when Venus cries out:

'Stop him! Come back, you young villain! You've got a tooth among them halfpence.'

'How was I to know I'd got it? You giv it me. I don't want none of your teeth; I've got enough of my own.' So the boy pipes, as he selects it from his change, and throws it on the counter.

'Don't sauce *me,* in the wicious pride of your youth,' Mr Venus retorts pathetically. 'Don't hit *me* because you see I'm down. I'm low enough without that. It dropped into the till, I suppose. They drop into everything. There was two in the coffee-pot at breakfast time. Molars.'

'Very well, then,' argues the boy, 'what do you call names for?'

To which Mr Venus only replies, shaking his shock of dusty hair, and winking his weak eyes, 'Don't sauce *me,* in the wicious pride of your youth; don't hit *me,* because you see I'm down. You've no idea how small you'd come out, if I had the articulating of you.'

This consideration seems to have its effect on the boy, for he goes out grumbling.

'Oh dear me, dear me!' sighs Mr Venus, heavily, snuffing the candle, 'the world that appeared so flowery has ceased to blow! You're casting your eye round the shop, Mr Wegg. Let me show you a light. My working bench. My young man's bench. A Wice. Tools. Bones, warious. Skulls, warious. Preserved Indian baby. African ditto. Bottled preparations, warious. Everything within reach of your hand, in good preservation. The mouldy ones a-top. What's in those hampers over them again, I don't quite remember. Say, human warious. Cats. Articulated English baby. Dogs. Ducks. Glass eyes, warious. Mummied bird. Dried cuticle, warious. Oh, dear me! That's the general panoramic view.'

Having so held and waved the candle as that all these hetero-geneous objects seemed to come forward obediently when they were named, and then retire again, Mr Venus despondently repeats, 'Oh dear me, dear me!' resumes his seat, and with drooping despondency upon him, falls to pouring himself out more tea.

'Where am I?' asks Mr Wegg.

'You're somewhere in the back shop across the yard, sir; and speaking quite candidly, I wish I'd never bought you of the Hospital Porter.'

'Now, look here, what did you give for me?'

'Well,' replies Venus, blowing his tea: his head and face peering out of the darkness, over the smoke of it, as if he were modernizing the old original rise in his family: 'you were one of a warious lot, and I don't know.'

Silas puts his point in the improved form of 'What will you take for me?'

'Well,' replies Venus, still blowing his tea, "I'm not prepared, at a moment's notice, to tell you, Mr Wegg.'

'Come! According to your own account I'm not worth much,' Wegg reasons persuasively.

'Not for miscellaneous working in, I grant you, Mr Wegg; but you might turn out valuable yet, as a—' here Mr Venus takes a gulp of tea, so hot that it makes him choke, and sets his weak eyes watering; 'as a Monstrosity, if you'll excuse me.'

Repressing an indignant look, indicative of anything but a disposition to excuse him, Silas pursues his point.

'I think you know me, Mr Venus, and I think you know I never bargain.'

Mr Venus takes gulps of hot tea, shutting his eyes at every gulp, and opening them again in a spasmodic manner; but does not commit himself to assent.

'I have a prospect of getting on in life and elevating myself by my own independent exertions,' says Wegg, feelingly, 'and I shouldn't like—I tell you openly I should *not* like—under such circumstances, to be what I may call dispersed, a part of me here, and a part of me there, but should wish to collect myself like a genteel person.'

'It's a prospect at present, is it, Mr Wegg? Then you haven't got the money for a deal about you? Then I'll tell you what I'll do with you; I'll hold you over. I am a man of my word, and you needn't be afraid of my disposing of you. I'll hold you over. That's a promise. Oh dear me, dear me!'

Fain to accept his promise, and wishing to propitiate him, Mr Wegg looks on as he sighs and pours himself out more tea, and then says, trying to get a sympathetic tone into his voice:

'You seem very low, Mr Venus. Is business bad?'

'Never was so good.'

'Is your hand out at all?'

'Never was so well in. Mr Wegg, I'm not only first in the trade, but I'm *the* trade. You may go and buy a skeleton at the West End if you like, and pay the West End price, but it'll be my putting together. I've as much to do as I can possibly do, with the assistance of my young man, and I take a pride and a pleasure in it.'

Mr Venus thus delivers himself, his right hand extended, his smoking saucer in his left hand, protesting as though he were going to burst into a flood of tears.

'That ain't a state of things to make you low, Mr Venus.'

'Mr Wegg, I know it ain't. Mr Wegg, not to name myself as a workman without an equal, I've gone on improving myself in my knowledge of Anatomy, till both by sight and by name I'm perfect. Mr Wegg, if you was brought here loose in a bag to be articulated, I'd name your smallest bones blindfold equally with your largest, as fast as I could pick 'em out, and I'd sort 'em all, and sort your wertebræ, in a manner that would equally surprise and charm you.'

'Well,' remarks Silas (though not quite so readily as last time), '*that* ain't a state of things to be low about.—Not for *you* to be low about, leastways.'

'Mr Wegg, I know it ain't; Mr Wegg, I know it ain't. But it's the heart that lowers me, it is the heart! Be so good as take and read that card out loud.'

Silas receives one from his hand, which Venus takes from a wonderful litter in a drawer, and putting on his spectacles, reads:

' "Mr Venus," '

'Yes. Go on.'

' "Preserver of Animals and Birds," '

'Yes. Go on.'

' "Articulator of human bones." '

'That's it,' with a groan. 'That's it! Mr Wegg, I'm thirty-two, and a bachelor. Mr Wegg, I love her. Mr Wegg, she is worthy of being loved by a Potentate!' Here Silas is rather alarmed by Mr Venus's springing to his feet in the hurry of his spirits, and haggardly confronting him with his hand on his coat collar; but Mr Venus, begging pardon, sits down again, saying, with the calmness of despair, 'She objects to the business.'

'Does she know the profits of it?'

'She knows the profits of it, but she don't appreciate the art of it, and she objects to it. "I do not wish," she writes in her own handwriting, "to regard myself, nor yet to be regarded, in that boney light".'

Mr Venus pours himself out more tea, with a look and in an attitude of the deepest desolation.

'And so a man climbs to the top of the tree, Mr Wegg, only to see that there's no look-out when he's up there! I sit here of a night surrounded by the lovely trophies of my art, and what have they done for me? Ruined me. Brought me to the pass of being informed that "she does not wish to regard herself, nor yet to be regarded, in that boney light"!' Having repeated the fatal expressions, Mr Venus drinks more tea by gulps, and offers an explanation of his doing so.

'It lowers me. When I'm equally lowered all over, lethargy sets in. By sticking to it till one or two in the morning, I get oblivion. Don't let me detain you, Mr Wegg. I'm not company for any one.'

'It is not on that account,' says Silas, rising, 'but because I've got an appointment. It's time I was at Harmon's.'

'Eh?' said Mr Venus. 'Harmon's, up Battle Bridge way?'

Mr Wegg admits that he is bound for that port.

'You ought to be in a good thing, if you've worked yourself in there. There's lots of money going, there.'

'To think,' says Silas, 'that you should catch it up so quick, and know about it. Wonderful!'

'Not at all, Mr Wegg. The old gentleman wanted to know the nature and worth of everything that was found in the dust; and many's the bone, and feather, and what not, that he's brought to me.'

'Really, now!'

'Yes. (Oh dear me, dear me!) And he's buried quite in this neighbourhood, you know. Over yonder.'

Mr Wegg does not know, but he makes as if he did, by responsively nodding his head. He also follows with his eyes, the toss of Venus's head: as if to seek a direction to over yonder.

'I took an interest in that discovery in the river,' says Venus. '(She hadn't written her cutting refusal at that time.) I've got up there—never mind, though.'

He had raised the candle at arm's length towards one of the dark shelves, and Mr Wegg had turned to look, when he broke off.

'The old gentleman was well known all round here. There used to be stories about his having hidden all kinds of property in those dust mounds. I suppose there was nothing in 'em. Probably you know, Mr Wegg?'

'Nothing in 'em,' says Wegg, who has never heard a word of this before.

'Don't let me detain you. Good night!'

The unfortunate Mr Venus gives him a shake of the hand with a shake of his own head, and drooping down in his chair, proceeds to pour himself out more tea. Mr Wegg, looking back over his shoulder as he pulls the door open by the strap, notices that the movement so shakes the crazy shop, and so shakes a momentary flare out of the candle, as that the babies—Hindoo,

African, and British—the 'human warious', the French gentleman, the green glass-eyed cats, the dogs, the ducks, and all the
rest of the collection, show for an instant as if paralytically animated; while even poor little Cock Robin at Mr Venus's elbow
turns over on his innocent side. Next moment, Mr Wegg is
stumping under the gaslights and through the mud.

Chapter 8
Mr Boffin in Consultation

WHOSOEVER had gone out of Fleet Street into the Temple at the
date of this history, and had wandered disconsolate about the
Temple until he stumbled on a dismal churchyard, and had
looked up at the dismal windows commanding that churchyard
until at the most dismal window of them all he saw a dismal boy,
would in him have beheld, at one grand comprehensive swoop of
the eye, the managing clerk, junior clerk, common-law clerk,
conveyancing clerk, chancery clerk, every refinement and department of clerk, of Mr Mortimer Lightwood, erewhile called in
the newspapers eminent solicitor.

Mr Boffin having been several times in communication with
this clerkly essence, both on its own ground and at the Bower,
had no difficulty in identifying it when he saw it up in its dusty
eyrie. To the second floor on which the window was situated, he
ascended, much pre-occupied in mind by the uncertainties besetting the Roman Empire, and much regretting the death of the
amiable Pertinax: who only last night had left the Imperial affairs
in a state of great confusion, by falling a victim to the fury of the
prætorian guards.

'Morning, morning, morning!' said Mr Boffin, with a wave
of his hand, as the office door was opened by the dismal boy,
whose appropriate name was Blight. 'Governor in?'

'Mr Lightwood gave you an appointment, sir, I think?'

'I don't want him to give it, you know,' returned Mr
Boffin; 'I'll pay my way, my boy.'

'No doubt, sir. Would you walk in? Mr Lightwood ain't in at the present moment, but I expect him back very shortly. Would you take a seat in Mr Lightwood's room, sir, while I look over our Appointment Book?' Young Blight made a great show of fetching from his desk a long thin manuscript volume with a brown paper cover, and running his finger down the day's appointments, murmuring, 'Mr Aggs, Mr Baggs, Mr Caggs, Mr Daggs, Mr Faggs, Mr Gaggs, Mr Boffin. Yes, sir; quite right. You are a little before your time, sir. Mr Lightwood will be in directly.'

'I'm not in a hurry,' said Mr Boffin.

'Thank you, sir. I'll take the opportunity, if you please, of entering your name in our Callers' Book for the day.' Young Blight made another great show of changing the volume, taking up a pen, sucking it, dipping it, and running over previous entries before he wrote. As, 'Mr Alley, Mr Balley, Mr Calley, Mr Dalley, Mr Falley, Mr Galley, Mr Halley, Mr Lalley, Mr Malley. And Mr Boffin.'

'Strict system here; eh, my lad?' said Mr Boffin, as he was booked.

'Yes, sir,' returned the boy. 'I couldn't get on without it.'

By which he probably meant that his mind would have been shattered to pieces without this fiction of an occupation. Wearing in his solitary confinement no fetters that he could polish, and being provided with no drinking-cup that he could carve, he had fallen on the device of ringing alphabetical changes into the two volumes in question, or of entering vast numbers of persons out of the Directory as transacting business with Mr Lightwood. It was the more necessary for his spirits, because, being of a sensitive temperament, he was apt to consider it personally disgraceful to himself that his master had no clients.

'How long have you been in the law, now?' asked Mr Boffin, with a pounce, in his usual inquisitive way.

'I've been in the law, now, sir, about three years.'

'Must have been as good as born in it!' said Mr Boffin, with admiration. 'Do you like it?'

'I don't mind it much,' returned Young Blight, heaving a sigh, as if its bitterness were past.

'What wages do you get?''

'Half what I could wish,' replied young Blight.

'What's the whole that you could wish?'

'Fifteen shillings a week,' said the boy.

'About how long might it take you now, at a average rate of

going, to be a Judge?' asked Mr Boffin, after surveying his small stature in silence.

The boy answered that he had not yet quite worked out that little calculation.

'I suppose there's nothing to prevent your going in for it?' said Mr Boffin.

The boy virtually replied that as he had the honour to be a Briton who never never never, there was nothing to prevent his going in for it. Yet he seemed inclined to suspect that there might be something to prevent his coming out with it.

'Would a couple of pound help you up at all?' asked Mr Boffin.

On this head, young Blight had no doubt whatever, so Mr Boffin made him a present of that sum of money, and thanked him for his attention to his (Mr Boffin's) affairs; which, he added, were now, he believed, as good as settled.

Then Mr Boffin, with his stick at his ear, like a Familiar Spirit explaining the office to him, sat staring at a little bookcase of Law Practice and Law Reports, and at a window, and at an empty blue bag, and at a stick of sealing-wax, and a pen, and a box of wafers, and an apple, and a writing-pad—all very dusty— and at a number of inky smears and blots, and at an imperfectly-disguised gun-case pretending to be something legal, and at an iron box labelled HARMON ESTATE, until Mr Lightwood appeared.

Mr Lightwood explained that he came from the proctor's, with whom he had been engaged in transacting Mr Boffin's affairs.

'And they seem to have taken a deal out of you!' said Mr Boffin, with commiseration.

Mr Lightwood, without explaining that his weariness was chronic, proceeded with his exposition that, all forms of law having been at length complied with, will of Harmon deceased having been proved, death of Harmon next inheriting having been proved, &c., and so forth, Court of Chancery having been moved, &c. and so forth, he, Mr Lightwood, had now the gratification, honour, and happiness, again &c. and so forth, of congratulating Mr Boffin on coming into possession as residuary legatee, of upwards of one hundred thousand pounds, standing in the books of the Governor and Company of the Bank of England, again &c. and so forth.

'And what is particularly eligible in the property Mr Boffin, is, that it involves no trouble. There are no estates to manage, no rents to return so much per cent. upon in bad times (which is an extremely dear way of getting your name into the newspapers), no voters to become parboiled in hot water with, no agents to take the cream off the milk before it comes to table. You could put the whole in a cash-box to-morrow morning, and take it with you to—say, to the Rocky Mountains. Inasmuch as every man,' concluded Mr Lightwood, with an indolent smile, 'appears to be under a fatal spell which obliges him, sooner or later, to mention the Rocky Mountains in a tone of extreme familiarity to some other man, I hope you'll excuse my pressing you into the service of that gigantic range of geographical bores.'

Without following this last remark very closely, Mr Boffin cast his perplexed gaze first at the ceiling, and then at the carpet.

'Well,' he remarked, 'I don't know what to say about it, I am sure. I was a'most as well as I was. It's a great lot to take care of.'

'My dear Mr Boffin, then *don't* take care of it!'

'Eh?' said that gentleman.

'Speaking now,' returned Mortimer, 'with the irresponsible imbecility of a private individual, and not with the profundity of a professional adviser, I should say that if the circumstance of its being too much, weighs upon your mind, you have the haven of consolation open to you that you can easily make it less. And if you should be apprehensive of the trouble of doing so, there is the further haven of consolation that any number of people will take the trouble off your hands.'

'Well! I don't quite see it,' retorted Mr Boffin, still perplexed. 'That's not satisfactory, you know, what you're a-saying.'

'Is Anything satisfactory, Mr Boffin?' asked Mortimer, raising his eyebrows.

'I used to find it so,' answered Mr Boffin, with a wistful look. 'While I was foreman at the Bower—afore it *was* the Bower—I considered the business very satisfactory. The old man was a awful Tartar (saying it, I'm sure, without disrepect to his memory) but the business was a pleasant one to look after, from before daylight to past dark. It's a'most a pity,' said Mr Boffin, rubbing his ear, 'that he ever went and made so much money. It would have been better for him if he hadn't so given himself up to it. You may depend upon it,' making the discovery all of a sudden, 'that *he* found it a great lot to take care of!'

Mr Lightwood coughed, not convinced.

'And speaking of satisfactory,' pursued Mr Boffin, 'why, Lord save us! when we come to take it to pieces, bit by bit, where's the satisfactoriness of the money as yet? When the old man does right the poor boy after all, the poor boy gets no good of it. He gets made away with, at the moment when he's lifting (as one may say) the cup and sarser to his lips. Mr Lightwood, I will now name to you, that on behalf of the poor dear boy, me and Mrs Boffin have stood out against the old man times out of number, till he has called us every name he could lay his tongue to. I have seen him, after Mrs Boffin has given him her mind respecting the claims of the nat'ral affections, catch off Mrs Boffin's bonnet (she wore, in general, a black straw, perched as a matter of convenience on the top of her head), and send it spinning across the yard. I have indeed. And once, when he did this in a manner that amounted to personal, I should have given him a rattler for himself, if Mrs Boffin hadn't thrown herself betwixt us, and received flush on the temple. Which dropped her, Mr Lightwood. Dropped her.'

Mr Lightwood murmured 'Equal honour—Mrs Boffin's head and heart.'

'You understand; I name this,' pursued Mr Boffin, 'to show you, now the affairs are wound up, that me and Mrs Boffin have ever stood, as we were in Christian honour bound, the children's friend. Me and Mrs Boffin stood the poor girl's friend; me and Mrs Boffin stood the poor boy's friend; me and Mrs Boffin up and faced the old man when we momently expected to be turned out for our pains. As to Mrs Boffin,' said Mr Boffin, lowering his voice, 'she mightn't wish it mentioned now she's Fashionable, but she went so far as to tell him, in my presence, he was a flinty-hearted rascal.'

Mr Lightwood murmured 'Vigorous Saxon spirit—Mrs Boffin's ancestors—bowmen—Agincourt and Cressy.'

'The last time me and Mrs Boffin saw the poor boy,' said Mr Boffin, warming (as fat usually does) with a tendency to melt, 'he was a child of seven years old. For when he came back to make intercession for his sister, me and Mrs Boffin were away overlooking a country contract which was to be sifted before carted, and he was come and gone in a single hour. I say he was a child of seven year old. He was going away, all alone and forlorn, to that foreign school, and he come into our place, situate up the yard of the present Bower, to have a warm at our fire. There was his little scanty travelling clothes upon him. There was his little scanty box outside in the shivering wind, which I was going to carry for him down to the steamboat, as the old man wouldn't hear of allowing a sixpence coach-money. Mrs Boffin, then quite a young woman and pictur of a full-blown rose, stands him by her, kneels down at the fire, warms her two open hands, and falls to rubbing his cheeks; but seeing the tears come into the child's eyes, the tears come fast into her own, and she holds him round the neck, like as if she was protecting him, and cries to me, "I'd give the wide wide world, I would, to run away with him!" I don't say but what it cut me, and but what it at the same time heightened my feelings of admiration for Mrs Boffin. The poor child clings to her for awhile, as she clings to him, and then, when the old man calls, he says "I must go! God bless you!" and for a moment rests his heart against her bosom, and looks up at both of us, as if it was in pain—in agony. Such a look! I went aboard with him (I gave him first what little treat I thought he'd like), and I left him when he had fallen asleep in his berth, and I came back to Mrs Boffin. But tell her what I would of how I had left him, it all went for nothing, for, according to her thoughts, he never changed that look that he had looked up at us two. But it did one piece of good. Mrs Boffin and me had no child of our own, and had sometimes wished that how we had one. But not now. "We might both of us die," says Mrs Boffin, "and other eyes might see that lonely look in our child." So of a night, when it was very cold, or when the wind roared, or the rain dripped heavy, she would wake sobbing, and call out in a fluster, "Don't you see the poor child's face? O shelter the poor child!"—till in course of years it gently wore out, as many things do.'

'My dear Mr Boffin, everything wears to rags,' said Mortimer, with a light laugh.

'I won't go so far as to say everything,' returned Mr Boffin, on whom his manner seemed to grate, 'because there's some things that I never found among the dust. Well, sir. So Mrs Boffin and me grow older and older in the old man's service, living and working pretty hard in it, till the old man is discovered dead in his bed. Then Mrs Boffin and me seal up his box, always standing on the table at the side of his bed, and having frequently heerd tell of the Temple as a spot where lawyer's dust is contracted for, I come down here in search of a lawyer to advise, and I see your young man up at this present elevation, chopping at the flies on the window-sill with his penknife, and I give him a Hoy! not then having the pleasure of your acquaintance, and by that means come to gain the honour. Then you, and the gentleman in the uncomfortable neck-cloth under the little archway in Saint Paul's Churchyard—'

'Doctors' Commons,' observed Lightwood.

'I understood it was another name,' said Mr Boffin, pausing, 'but you know best. Then you and Doctor Scommons, you go to work, and you do the thing that's proper, and you and Doctor S. take steps for finding out the poor boy, and at last you do find out the poor boy, and me and Mrs Boffin often exchange the observation, "We shall see him again, under happy circumstances." But it was never to be; and the want of satisfactoriness is, that after all the money never gets to him.'

'But it gets,' remarked Lightwood, with a languid inclination of the head, 'into excellent hands.'

'It gets into the hands of me and Mrs Boffin only this very day and hour, and that's what I am working round to, having waited for this day and hour a' purpose. Mr Lightwood, here has been a wicked cruel murder. By that murder me and Mrs Boffin mysteriously profit. For the apprehension and conviction of the murderer, we offer a reward of one tithe of the property—a reward of Ten Thousand Pound.'

'Mr Boffin, it's too much.'

'Mr Lightwood, me and Mrs Boffin have fixed the sum together, and we stand to it.'

'But let me represent to you,' returned Lightwood, 'speaking now with professional profundity, and not with individual imbecility, that the offer of such an immense reward is a temptation to forced suspicion, forced construction of circumstances, strained accusation, a whole tool-box of edged tools.'

'Well,' said Mr Boffin, a little staggered, 'that's the sum we put o' one side for the purpose. Whether it shall be openly declared in the new notices that must now be put about in our names—'

'In your name, Mr Boffin; in your name.'

'Very well; in my name, which is the same as Mrs Boffin's, and means both of us, is to be considered in drawing 'em up. But this is the first instruction that I, as the owner of the property, give to my lawyer on coming into it.'

'Your lawyer, Mr Boffin,' returned Lightwood, making a very short note of it with a very rusty pen, 'has the gratification of taking the instruction. There is another?'

'There is just one other, and no more. Make me as compact a little will as can be reconciled with tightness, leaving the whole of the property to "my beloved wife, Henerietty Boffin, sole executrix". Make it as short as you can, using those words; but make it tight.'

At some loss to fathom Mr Boffin's notions of a tight will, Lightwood felt his way.

'I beg your pardon, but professional profundity must be exact. When you say tight—'

'I mean tight,' Mr Boffin explained.

'Exactly so. And nothing can be more laudable. But is the tightness to bind Mrs Boffin to any and what conditions?'

"Bind Mrs Boffin?" interposed her husband. 'No! What are you thinking of! What I want is, to make it all hers so tight as that her hold of it can't be loosed.'

'Hers freely, to do what she likes with? Hers absolutely?'

'Absolutely?' repeated Mr Boffin, with a short sturdy laugh. 'Hah! I should think so! It would be handsome in me to begin to bind Mrs Boffin at this time of day!'

So that instruction, too, was taken by Mr Lightwood; and Mr Lightwood, having taken it, was in the act of showing Mr Boffin out, when Mr Eugene Wrayburn almost jostled him in the doorway. Consequently Mr Lightwood said, in his cool manner, 'Let me make you two known to one another,' and further signified that Mr Wrayburn was counsel learned in the law, and that, partly in the way of business and partly in the way of pleasure, he had imparted to Mr Wrayburn some of the interesting facts of Mr Boffin's biography.

'Delighted,' said Eugene—though he didn't look so—'to know Mr Boffin.'

'Thankee, sir, thankee,' returned that gentleman. 'And how do *you* like the law?'

'A—not particularly,' returned Eugene.

'Too dry for you, eh? Well, I suppose it wants some years of sticking to, before you master it. But there's nothing like work. Look at the bees.'

'I beg your pardon,' returned Eugene, with a reluctant smile, 'but will you excuse my mentioning that I always protest against being referred to the bees?'

'Do you!' said Mr Boffin.

'I object on principle,' said Eugene, 'as a biped—'

'As a what?' asked Mr Boffin.

'As a two-footed creature;—I object on principle, as a two-footed creature, to being constantly referred to insects and four-footed creatures. I object to being required to model my proceedings according to the proceedings of the bee, or the dog, or the spider, or the camel. I fully admit that the camel, for instance, is an excessively temperate person; but he has several stomachs to entertain himself with, and I have only one. Besides, I am not fitted up with a convenient cool cellar to keep my drink in.'

'But I said, you know,' urged Mr Boffin, rather at a loss for an answer, 'the bee.'

'Exactly. And may I represent to you that it's injudicious to say the bee? For the whole case is assumed. Conceding for a moment that there is any analogy between a bee, and a man in a shirt and pantaloons (which I deny), and that it is settled that the man is to learn from the bee (which I also deny), the question still remains, what is he to learn? To imitate? Or to avoid? When your friends the bees worry themselves to that highly fluttered extent about their sovereign, and become perfectly distracted touching the slightest monarchical movement, are we men to learn the greatness of Tuft-hunting, or the littleness of the Court Circular? I am not clear, Mr Boffin, but that the hive may be satirical.'

'At all events, they work,' said Mr Boffin.

'Ye-es,' returned Eugene, disparagingly, 'they work; but don't you think they overdo it? They work so much more than they need—they make so much more than they can eat—they are so incessantly boring and buzzing at their one idea till Death comes upon them—that don't you think they overdo it? And are human labourers to have no holidays, because of the bees? And am I never to have change of air, because the bees don't? Mr Boffin, I think honey excellent at breakfast; but, regarded in the light of my conventional schoolmaster and moralist, I protest against the tyrannical humbug of your friend the bee. With the highest respect for you.'

'Thankee,' said Mr Boffin. 'Morning, morning!'

But, the worthy Mr Boffin jogged away with a comfortless impression he could have dispensed with, that there was a deal of unsatisfactoriness in the world, besides what he had recalled as appertaining to the Harmon property. And he was still jogging along Fleet Street in this condition of mind, when he became aware that he was closely tracked and observed by a man of genteel appearance.

'Now then?' said Mr Boffin, stopping short, with his meditations brought to an abrupt check, 'what's the next article?'

'I beg your pardon, Mr Boffin.'

'My name too, eh? How did you come by it? I don't know you.'

'No, sir, you don't know me.'

Mr Boffin looked full at the man, and the man looked full at him.

'No,' said Mr Boffin, after a glance at the pavement, as if it were made of faces and he were trying to match the man's, 'I *don't* know you.'

'I am nobody,' said the stranger, 'and not likely to be known; but Mr Boffin's wealth—'

'Oh! that's got about already, has it?' muttered Mr Boffin.

'—And his romantic manner of acquiring it, make him conspicuous. You were pointed out to me the other day.'

'Well,' said Mr Boffin, 'I should say I was a disappointment to you when I *was* pinted out, if your politeness would allow you to confess it, for I am well aware I am not much to look at. What might you want with me? Not in the law, are you?'

'No, sir.'

'No information to give, for a reward?'

'No, sir.'

There may have been a momentary mantling in the face of the man as he made the last answer, but it passed directly.

'If I don't mistake, you have followed me from my lawyer's and tried to fix my attention. Say out! Have you? Or haven't you?' demanded Mr Boffin, rather angry.

'Yes.'

'Why have you?'

"If you will allow me to walk beside you, Mr Boffin, I will tell you. Would you object to turn aside into this place—I think it is called Clifford's Inn—where we can hear one another better than in the roaring street?'

('Now,' thought Mr Boffin, 'if he proposes a game at skittles, or meets a country gentleman just come into property, or produces any article of jewellery he has found, I'll knock him down!' With this discreet reflection, and carrying his stick in his arms much as Punch carries his, Mr Boffin turned into Clifford's Inn aforesaid.)

'Mr Boffin, I happened to be in Chancery Lane this morning, when I saw you going along before me. I took the liberty of following you, trying to make up my mind to speak to you, till you went into your lawyer's. Then I waited outside till you came out.'

('Don't quite sound like skittles, nor yet country gentleman, nor yet jewellery,' thought Mr Boffin, 'but there's no knowing.')

'I am afraid my object is a bold one, I am afraid it has little of the usual practical world about it, but I venture it. If you ask me, or if you ask yourself—which is more likely—what emboldens me, I answer, I have been strongly assured, that you are a man of rectitude and plain dealing, with the soundest of sound hearts, and that you are blessed in a wife distinguished by the same qualities.'

'Your information is true of Mrs Boffin, anyhow,' was Mr Boffin's answer, as he surveyed his new friend again. There was something repressed in the strange man's manner, and he walked with his eyes on the ground—though conscious, for all that, of Mr Boffin's observation—and he spoke in a subdued voice. But his words came easily, and his voice was agreeable in tone, albeit constrained.

'When I add, I can discern for myself what the general tongue says of you—that you are quite unspoiled by Fortune, and not uplifted—I trust you will not, as a man of an open nature, suspect that I mean to flatter you, but will believe that all I mean is to excuse myself, these being my only excuses for my present intrusion.'

('How much?' thought Mr Boffin. 'It must be coming to money. How much?')

'You will probably change your manner of living, Mr Boffin, in your changed circumstances. You will probably keep a larger house, have many matters to arrange, and be beset by numbers of correspondents. If you would try me as your Secretary—'

'As *what*?' cried Mr Boffin, with his eyes wide open.

'Your Secretary.'

'Well,' said Mr Boffin, under his breath, 'that's a queer thing!'

'Or,' pursued the stranger, wondering at Mr Boffin's wonder, 'if you would try me as your man of business under any name, I know you would find me faithful and grateful, and I hope you would find me useful. You may naturally think that my immediate object is money. Not so, for I would willingly serve you a year—two years—any term you might appoint—before that should begin to be a consideration between us.'

'Where do you come from?' asked Mr Boffin.

'I come,' returned the other, meeting his eye, 'from many countries.'

Mr Boffin's acquaintance with the names and situations of foreign lands being limited in extent and somewhat confused in quality, he shaped his next question on an elastic model.

'From—any particular place?'

'I have been in many places.'

'What have you been?' asked Mr Boffin.

Here again he made no great advance, for the reply was, 'I have been a student and a traveller.'

'But if it ain't a liberty to plump it out,' said Mr Boffin, 'what do you do for your living?'

'I have mentioned,' returned the other, with another look at him, and a smile, 'what I aspire to do. I have been superseded as to some slight intentions I had, and I may say that I have now to begin life.'

Not very well knowing how to get rid of this applicant, and feeling the more embarrassed because his manner and appearance claimed a delicacy in which the worthy Mr Boffin feared he himself might be deficient, that gentleman glanced into the mouldy little plantation or cat-preserve, of Clifford's Inn, as it was that day, in search of a suggestion. Sparrows were there, cats were there, dry-rot and wet-rot were there, but it was not otherwise a suggestive spot.

'All this time,' said the stranger, producing a little pocket-book and taking out a card, 'I have not mentioned my name. My name is Rokesmith. I lodge at one Mr Wilfer's, at Holloway.'

Mr Boffin stared again.

'Father of Miss Bella Wilfer?' said he.

'My landlord has a daughter named Bella. Yes; no doubt.'

Now, this name had been more or less in Mr Boffin's thoughts all the morning, and for days before; therefore he said:

'That's singular, too!' unconsciously staring again, past all bounds of good manners, with the card in his hand. 'Though, by-the-bye, I suppose it was one of that family that pinted me out!'

'No. I have never been in the streets with one of them.'

'Heard me talked of among 'em, though?'

'No. I occupy my own rooms, and have held scarcely any communication with them.'

'Odder and odder!' said Mr Boffin. 'Well, sir, to tell you the truth, I don't know what to say to you.'

'Say nothing,' returned Mr Rokesmith; 'allow me to call on you in a few days. I am not so unconscionable as to think it likely that you would accept me on trust at first sight, and take me out of the very street. Let me come to you for your further opinion, at your leisure.'

'That's fair, and I don't object,' said Mr Boffin; 'but it must be on condition that it's fully understood that I no more know that I shall ever be in want of any gentleman as Secretary—it *was* Secretary you said; wasn't it?'

'Yes.'

Again Mr Boffin's eyes opened wide, and he stared at the applicant from head to foot, repeating 'Queer!—You're sure it was Secretary? Are you?'

'I am sure I said so.'

—'As Secretary,' repeated Mr Boffin, meditating upon the word; 'I no more know that I may ever want a Secretary, or what not, than I do that I shall ever be in want of the man in the moon. Me and Mrs Boffin have not even settled that we shall make any change in our way of life. Mrs Boffin's inclinations certainly do tend towards Fashion; but, being already set up in a fashionable way at the Bower, she may not make further alterations. However, sir, as you don't press yourself, I wish to meet you so far as saying, by all means call at the Bower if you like. Call in the course of a week or two. At the same time, I consider that I ought to name, in addition to what I have already named, that I have in my employment a literary man—*with* a wooden leg—as I have no thoughts of parting from.'

'I regret to hear I am in some sort anticipated,' Mr Rokesmith answered, evidently having heard it with surprise; 'but perhaps other duties might arise?'

'You see,' returned Mr Boffin, with a confidential sense of dignity, 'as to my literary man's duties, they're clear. Professionally he declines and he falls, and as a friend he drops into poetry.'

Without observing that these duties seemed by no means clear to Mr Rokesmith's astonished comprehension, Mr Boffin went on:

'And now, sir, I'll wish you good-day. You can call at the Bower any time in a week or two. It's not above a mile or so from you, and your landlord can direct you to it. But as he may not know it by it's new name of Boffin's Bower, say, when you inquire of him, it's Harmon's; will you?'

'Harmoon's,' repeated Mr Rokesmith, seeming to have caught the sound imperfectly, 'Harmarn's. How do you spell it?'

'Why, as to the spelling of it,' returned Mr Boffin, with great presence of mind, 'that's *your* look out. Harmon's is all you've got to say to *him*. Morning, morning, morning!' And so departed, without looking back.

Chapter 9

Mr and Mrs Boffin in Consultation

BETAKING himself straight homeward, Mr Boffin, without further let or hindrance, arrived at the Bower, and gave Mrs Boffin (in a walking dress of black velvet and feathers, like a mourning coach-horse) an account of all he had said and done since breakfast.

'This brings us round, my dear,' he then pursued, 'to the question we left unfinished: namely, whether there's to be any new go-in for Fashion.'

'Now, I'll tell you what I want, Noddy,' said Mrs Boffin, smoothing her dress with an air of immense enjoyment, 'I want Society.'

'Fashionable Society, my dear?'

'Yes!' cried Mrs Boffin, laughing with the glee of a child. 'Yes! It's no good my being kept here like Wax-Work; is it now?'

'People have to pay to see Wax-Work, my dear,' returned her husband, 'whereas (though you'd be cheap at the same money) the neighbours is welcome to see *you* for nothing.'

'But it don't answer,' said the cheerful Mrs Boffin. 'When we worked like the neighbours, we suited one another. Now we have left work off, we have left off suiting one another.'

'What, do you think of beginning work again?' Mr Boffin hinted.

''Out of the question! We have come into a great fortune, and we must do what's right by our fortune; we must act up to it.'

Mr Boffin, who had a deep respect for his wife's intuitive wisdom, replied, though rather pensively: 'I suppose we must.'

'It's never been acted up to yet, and, consequently, no good has come of it,' said Mrs Boffin.

'True, to the present time,' Mr Boffin assented, with his former pensiveness, as he took his seat upon his settle. 'I hope good may be coming of it in the future time. Towards which, what's your views, old lady?'

Mrs Boffin, a smiling creature, broad of figure and simple of nature, with her hands folded in her lap, and with buxom creases in her throat, proceeded to expound her views.

'*I* say, a good house in a good neighbourhood, good things about us, good living, and good society. *I* say, live like our means, without extravagance, and be happy.'

'Yes. *I* say be happy, too,' assented the still pensive Mr Boffin.

'Lor-a-mussy!' exclaimed Mrs Boffin, laughing and clapping her hands, and gaily rocking herself to and fro, 'when I think of me in a light yellow chariot and pair, with silver boxes to the wheels—'

'Oh! you was thinking of that, was you, my dear?'

'Yes!' cried the delighted creature. 'And with a footman up behind, with a bar across, to keep his legs from being poled! And with a coachman up in front, sinking down into a seat big enough for three of him, all covered with upholstery in green and white! And with two bay horses tossing their heads and stepping higher than they trot long-ways! And with you and me leaning back inside, as grand as ninepence! Oh-h-h-h My! Ha ha ha ha ha!'

Mrs Boffin clapped her hands again, rocked herself again, beat her feet upon the floor, and wiped the tears of laughter from her eyes.

'And what, my old lady,' inquired Mr Boffin, when he also had sympathetically laughed: 'what's your views on the subject of the Bower?'

'Shut it up. Don't part with it, but put somebody in it, to keep it.'

'Any other views?'

'Noddy,' said Mrs Boffin, coming from her fashionable sofa to his side on the plain settle, and hooking her comfortable arm through his, 'Next I think—and I really have been thinking early and late—of the disappointed girl; her that was so cruelly disappointed, you know, both of her husband and his riches. Don't you think we might do something for her? Have her to live with us? Or something of that sort?'

'Ne-ver once thought of the way of doing it!' cried Mr Boffin, smiting the table in his admiration. 'What a thinking steam-ingein this old lady is. And she don't know how she does it. Neither does the ingein!'

Mrs Boffin pulled his nearest ear, in acknowledgment of this piece of philosophy, and then said, gradually toning down to a motherly strain: 'Last, and not least, I have taken a fancy. You remember dear little John Harmon, before he went to school? Over yonder across the yard, at our fire? Now that he is past all benefit of the money, and it's come to us, I should like to find some orphan child, and take the boy and adopt him and give him John's name, and provide for him. Somehow, it would make me easier, I fancy. Say it's only a whim—'

'But I don't say so,' interposed her husband.

'No, but deary, if you did—'

'I should be a Beast if I did,' her husband interposed again.

'That's as much as to say you agree? Good and kind of you, and like you, deary! And don't you begin to find it pleasant now,' said Mrs Boffin, once more radiant in her comely way from head to foot, and once more smoothing her dress with immense enjoyment, 'don't you begin to find it pleasant already, to think that a child will be made brighter, and better, and happier, because of that poor sad child that day? And isn't it pleasant to know that the good will be done with the poor sad child's own money?'

'Yes; and it's pleasant to know that you are Mrs Boffin,' said her husband, 'and it's been a pleasant thing to know this many and many a year!' It was ruin to Mrs Boffin's aspirations, but, having so spoken, they sat side by side, a hopelessly Unfashionable pair.

These two ignorant and unpolished people had guided themselves so far on in their journey of life, by a religious sense of duty and desire to do right. Ten thousand weaknesses and absurdities might have been detected in the breasts of both; ten thousand vanities additional, possibly, in the breast of the woman. But the hard wrathful and sordid nature that had wrung as much work out of them as could be got in their best days, for as little money as could be paid to hurry on their worst, had never been so warped but that it knew their moral straightness and respected it. In its own despite, in a constant conflict with itself and them, it had done so. And this is the eternal law. For, Evil often stops short at itself and dies with the doer of it; but Good, never.

Through his most inveterate purposes, the dead Jailer of Harmony Jail had known these two faithful servants to be honest and true. While he raged at them and reviled them for opposing him with the speech of the honest and true, it had scratched his stony heart, and he had perceived the powerlessness of all his wealth to buy them if he had addressed himself to the attempt. So, even while he was their griping taskmaster and never gave

them a good word, he had written their names down in his will.
So, even while it was his daily declaration that he mistrusted all
mankind—and sorely indeed he did mistrust all who bore any
resemblance to himself—he was as certain that these two people,
surviving him, would be trustworthy in all things from the
greatest to the least, as he was that he must surely die.

Mr and Mrs Boffin, sitting side by side, with Fashion
withdrawn to an immeasurable distance, fell to discussing how
they could best find their orphan. Mrs Boffin suggested advertisement in the newspapers, requesting orphans answering an-
nexed description to apply at the Bower on a certain day; but Mr
Boffin wisely apprehending obstruction of the neighbouring thoroughfares by orphan swarms, this course was negatived. Mrs
Boffin next suggested application to their clergyman for a likely
orphan. Mr Boffin thinking better of this scheme, they resolved
to call upon the reverend gentleman at once, and to take the
same opportunity of making acquaintance with Miss Bella Wilfer.
In order that these visits might be visits of state, Mrs Boffin's
equipage was ordered out.

This consisted of a long hammer-headed old horse, formerly
used in the business, attached to a four-wheeled chaise of the
same period, which had long been exclusively used by the
Harmony Jail poultry as the favourite laying-place of several
discreet hens. An unwonted application of corn to the horse, and
of paint and varnish to the carriage, when both fell in as a part of
the Boffin legacy, had made what Mr Boffin considered a neat
turn-out of the whole; and a driver being added, in the person of
a long hammer-headed young man who was a very good match
for the horse, left nothing to be desired. He, too, had been
formerly used in the business, but was now entombed by an
honest jobbing tailor of the district in a perfect Sepulchre of coat
and gaiters, sealed with ponderous buttons.

Behind this domestic, Mr and Mrs Boffin took their seats in
the back compartment of the vehicle: which was sufficiently
commodious, but had an undignified and alarming tendency, in
getting over a rough crossing, to hiccup itself away from the
front compartment. On their being descried emerging from the
gates of the Bower, the neighbourhood turned out at door and
window to salute the Boffins. Among those who were ever and
again left behind, staring after the equipage, were many youthful
spirits, who hailed it in stentorian tones with such congratula-
tions as 'Nod-dy Bof-fin!' 'Bof-fin's mon-ey!' 'Down with the
dust, Bof-fin!' and other similar compliments. These, the hammer-

headed young man took in such ill part that he often impaired the
majesty of the progress by pulling up short, and making as
though he would alight to exterminate the offenders; a purpose
from which he only allowed himself to be dissuaded after long
and lively arguments with his employers.

At length the Bower district was left behind, and the peaceful dwelling of the Reverend Frank Milvey was gained. The
Reverend Frank Milvey's abode was a very modest abode, because his income was a very modest income. He was officially
accessible to every blundering old woman who had incoherence
to bestow upon him, and readily received the Boffins. He was
quite a young man, expensively educated and wretchedly paid,
with quite a young wife and half a dozen quite young children.
He was under the necessity of teaching and translating from the
classics, to eke out his scanty means, yet was generally expected
to have more time to spare than the idlest person in the parish,
and more money than the richest. He accepted the needless
inequalities and inconsistencies of his life, with a kind of conventional submission that was almost slavish; and any daring
layman who would have adjusted such burdens as his, more
decently and graciously, would have had small help from him.

With a ready patient face and manner, and yet with a latent
smile that showed a quick enough observation of Mrs Boffin's
dress, Mr Milvey, in his little book-room—charged with sounds
and cries as though the six children above were coming down
through the ceiling, and the roasting leg of mutton below were
coming up through the floor—listened to Mrs Boffin's statement
of her want of an orphan.

'I think,' said Mr Milvey, 'that you have never had a child
of your own, Mr and Mrs Boffin?'

Never.

'But, like the Kings and Queens in the Fairy Tales, I
suppose you have wished for one?'

In a general way, yes.

Mr Milvey smiled again, as he remarked to himself, 'Those
kings and queens were always wishing for children.' It occurring
to him, perhaps, that if they had been Curates, their wishes
might have tended in the opposite direction.

'I think,' he pursued, 'we had better take Mrs Milvey into
our Council. She is indispensable to me. If you please, I'll call
her.'

So, Mr Milvey called, 'Margaretta, my dear!' and Mrs
Milvey came down. A pretty, bright little woman, something

worn by anxiety, who had repressed many pretty tastes and
bright fancies, and substituted in their stead, schools, soup,
flannel, coals, and all the week-day cares and Sunday coughs of a
large population, young and old. As gallantly had Mr Milvey
repressed much in himself that naturally belonged to his old
studies and old fellow-students, and taken up among the poor
and their children with the hard crumbs of life.

'Mr and Mrs Boffin, my dear, whose good fortune you have
heard of.'

Mrs Milvey, with the most unaffected grace in the world,
congratulated them, and was glad to see them. Yet her engaging
face, being an open as well as a perceptive one, was not without
her husband's latent smile.

'Mrs Boffin wishes to adopt a little boy, my dear.'

Mrs Milvey, looking rather alarmed, her husband added:

'An orphan, my dear.'

'Oh!' said Mrs Milvey, reassured for her own little boys.

'And I was thinking, Margaretta, that perhaps old Mrs
Goody's grandchild might answer the purpose.'

'Oh my *dear* Frank! I *don't* think that would do!'

'No?'

'Oh *no*!'

The smiling Mrs Boffin, feeling it incumbent on her to take
part in the conversation, and being charmed with the emphatic
little wife and her ready interest, here offered her acknowledgments and inquired what there was against him?

'I *don't* think,' said Mrs Milvey, glancing at the Reverend
Frank '—and I believe my husband will agree with me when he
considers it again—that you could possibly keep that orphan
clean from snuff. Because his grandmother takes so *many* ounces,
and drops it over him.'

'But he would not be living with his grandmother then,
Margaretta,' said Mr Milvey.

'No, Frank, but it would be impossible to keep her from
Mrs Boffin's house; and the *more* there was to eat and drink
there, the oftener she would go. And she *is* an inconvenient
woman. I *hope* it's not uncharitable to remember that last Christmas Eve she drank eleven cups of tea, and grumbled all the time.
And she is *not* a grateful woman, Frank. You recollect her
addressing a crowd outside this house, about her wrongs, when,
one night after we had gone to bed, she brought back the
petticoat of new flannel that had been given her, because it was
too short.'

'That's true,' said Mr Milvey. 'I don't think that would do. Would little Harrison—'

'Oh, *Frank*!' remonstrated his emphatic wife.

'He has no grandmother, my dear.'

'No, but I *don't* think Mrs Boffin would like an orphan who squints so *much*.'

'That's true again,' said Mr Milvey, becoming haggard with perplexity. 'If a little girl would do—'

'But, my *dear* Frank, Mrs Boffin wants a boy.'

'That's true again,' said Mr Milvey. 'Tom Bocker is a nice boy' (thoughtfully).

'But I *doubt*, Frank,' Mrs Milvey hinted, after a little hesitation, 'if Mrs Boffin wants an orphan *quite* nineteen, who drives a cart and waters the roads.'

Mr Milvey referred the point to Mrs Boffin in a look; on that smiling lady's shaking her black velvet bonnet and bows, he remarked, in lower spirits, 'that's true again.'

'I am sure,' said Mrs Boffin, concerned at giving so much trouble, 'that if I had known you would have taken so much pains, sir—and you too, ma'am—I don't think I would have come.'

'*Pray* don't say that!' urged Mrs Milvey.

'No, don't say that,' assented Mr Milvey, 'because we are so much obliged to you for giving us the preference.' Which Mrs Milvey confirmed; and really the kind, conscientious couple spoke, as if they kept some profitable orphan warehouse and were personally patronized. 'But it is a responsible trust,' added Mr Milvey, 'and difficult to discharge. At the same time, we are naturally very unwilling to lose the chance you so kindly give us, and if you could afford us a day or two to look about us,—you know, Margaretta, we might carefully examine the workhouse, and the Infant School, and your District.'

'To be *sure*!' said the emphatic little wife.

'We have orphans, I know,' pursued Mr Milvey, quite with the air as if he might have added, 'in stock,' and quite as anxiously as if there were great competition in the business and he were afraid of losing an order, 'over at the clay-pits; but they are employed by relations or friends, and I am afraid it would come at last to a transaction in the way of barter. And even if you exchanged blankets for the child—or books and firing—it would be impossible to prevent their being turned into liquor.'

Accordingly, it was resolved that Mr and Mrs Milvey should search for an orphan likely to suit, and as free as possible from the foregoing objections, and should communicate again with Mrs Boffin. Then, Mr Boffin took the liberty of mentioning to Mr Milvey that if Mr Milvey would do him the kindness to be perpetually his banker to the extent of 'a twenty-pound note or so,' to be expended without any reference to him, he would be heartily obliged. At this, both Mr Milvey and Mrs Milvey were quite as much pleased as if they had no wants of their own, but only knew what poverty was, in the persons of other people; and so the interview terminated with satisfaction and good opinion on all sides.

'Now, old lady,' said Mr Boffin, as they resumed their seats behind the hammer-headed horse and man: 'having made a very agreeable visit there, we'll try Wilfer's.'

It appeared, on their drawing up at the family gate, that to try Wilfer's was a thing more easily projected than done, on account of the extreme difficulty of getting into that establishment; three pulls at the bell producing no external result, though each was attended by audible sounds of scampering and rushing within. At the fourth tug—vindictively administered by the hammer-headed young man—Miss Lavinia appeared, emerging from the house in an accidental manner, with a bonnet and parasol, as designing to take a contemplative walk. The young lady was astonished to find visitors at the gate, and expressed her feelings in appropriate action.

'Here's Mr and Mrs Boffin!' growled the hammer-headed young man through the bars of the gate, and at the same time shaking it, as if he were on view in a Menagerie; 'they've been here half an hour.'

'Who did you say?' asked Miss Lavinia.

'Mr and Mrs BOFFIN!' returned the young man, rising into a roar.

Miss Lavinia tripped up the steps to the house-door, tripped down the steps with the key, tripped across the little garden, and opened the gate. 'Please to walk in,' said Miss Lavinia, haughtily. 'Our servant is out.'

Mr and Mrs Boffin complying, and pausing in the little hall until Miss Lavinia came up to show them where to go next, perceived three pairs of listening legs upon the stairs above. Mrs Wilfer's legs, Miss Bella's legs, Mr George Sampson's legs.

'Mr and Mrs Boffin, I think?' said Lavinia, in a warning voice.

Strained attention on the part of Mrs Wilfer's legs, of Miss Bella's legs, of Mr George Sampson's legs.

'Yes, Miss.'

'If you'll step this way—down these stairs—I'll let Ma know.'

Excited flight of Mrs Wilfer's legs, of Miss Bella's legs, of Mr George Sampson's legs.

After waiting some quarter of an hour alone in the family sitting-room, which presented traces of having been so hastily arranged after a meal, that one might have doubted whether it was made tidy for visitors, or cleared for blindman's buff, Mr and Mrs Boffin became aware of the entrance of Mrs Wilfer, majestically faint, and with a condescending stitch in her side: which was her company manner.

'Pardon me,' said Mrs Wilfer, after the first salutations, and as soon as she had adjusted the handkerchief under her chin, and waved her gloved hands, 'to what am I indebted for this honour?'

'To make short of it, ma'am,' returned Mr Boffin, 'perhaps you may be acquainted with the names of me and Mrs Boffin, as having come into a certain property.'

'I have heard, sir,' returned Mrs Wilfer, with a dignified bend of her head, 'of such being the case.'

'And I dare say, ma'am,' pursued Mr Boffin, while Mrs Boffin added confirmatory nods and smiles, 'you are not very much inclined to take kindly to us?'

'Pardon me,' said Mrs Wilfer. ' 'Twere unjust to visit upon Mr and Mrs Boffin, a calamity which was doubtless a dispensation.' These words were rendered the more effective by a serenely heroic expression of suffering.

'That's fairly meant, I am sure,' remarked the honest Mr Boffin; 'Mrs Boffin and me, ma'am, are plain people, and we don't want to pretend to anything, nor yet to go round and round at anything because there's always a straight way to everything. Consequently, we make this call to say, that we shall be glad to have the honour and pleasure of your daughter's acquaintance, and that we shall be rejoiced if your daughter will come to consider our house in the light of her home equally with this. In short, we want to cheer your daughter, and to give her the opportunity of sharing such pleasures as we are a going to take ourselves. We want to brisk her up, and brisk her about, and give her a change.'

'That's it!' said the open-hearted Mrs Boffin. 'Lor! Let's be comfortable.'

Mrs Wilfer bent her head in a distant manner to her lady visitor, and with majestic monotony replied to the gentleman:

'Pardon me. I have several daughters. Which of my daughters am I to understand is thus favoured by the kind intentions of Mr Boffin and his lady?'

'Don't you see?' the ever-smiling Mrs Boffin put in. 'Naturally, Miss Bella, you know.'

'Oh-h!' said Mrs Wilfer, with a severely unconvinced look. 'My daughter Bella is accessible and shall speak for herself.' Then opening the door a little way, simultaneously with a sound of scuttling outside it, the good lady made the proclamation, 'Send Miss Bella to me!' Which proclamation, though grandly formal, and one might almost say heraldic, to hear, was in fact enunciated with her maternal eyes reproachfully glaring on that young lady in the flesh—and in so much of it that she was retiring with difficulty into the small closet under the stairs, apprehensive of the emergence of Mr and Mrs Boffin.

'The avocations of R.W., my husband,' Mrs Wilfer explained, on resuming her seat, 'keep him fully engaged in the City at this time of the day, or he would have had the honour of participating in your reception beneath our humble roof.'

'Very pleasant premises!' said Mr Boffin, cheerfully.

'Pardon me, sir,' returned Mrs Wilfer, correcting him, 'it is the abode of conscious though independent Poverty.'

Finding it rather difficult to pursue the conversation down this road, Mr and Mrs Boffin sat staring at mid-air, and Mrs Wilfer sat silently giving them to understand that every breath she drew required to be drawn with a self-denial rarely paralleled in history, until Miss Bella appeared: whom Mrs Wilfer presented, and to whom she explained the purpose of the visitors.

'I am much obliged to you, I am sure,' said Miss Bella, coldly shaking her curls, 'but I doubt if I have the inclination to go out at all.'

'Bella!' Mrs Wilfer admonished her; 'Bella, you must conquer this.'

'Yes, do what your Ma says, and conquer it, my dear,' urged Mrs Boffin, 'because we shall be so glad to have you, and because you are much too pretty to keep yourself shut up.' With that, the pleasant creature gave her a kiss, and patted her on her dimpled shoulders; Mrs Wilfer sitting stiffly by, like a functionary presiding over an interview previous to an execution.

'We are going to move into a nice house,' said Mrs Boffin, who was woman enough to compromise Mr Boffin on that point, when he couldn't very well contest it; 'and we are going to set up a nice carriage, and we'll go everywhere and see everything.

And you mustn't,' seating Bella beside her, and patting her hand, 'you mustn't feel a dislike to us to begin with, because we couldn't help it, you know, my dear.'

With the natural tendency of youth to yield to candour and sweet temper, Miss Bella was so touched by the simplicity of this address that she frankly returned Mrs Boffin's kiss. Not at all to the satisfaction of that good woman of the world, her mother, who sought to hold the advantageous ground of obliging the Boffins instead of being obliged.

'My youngest daughter, Lavinia,' said Mrs Wilfer, glad to make a diversion, as that young lady reappeared. 'Mr George Sampson, a friend of the family.'

The friend of the family was in that stage of tender passion which bound him to regard everybody else as the foe of the family. He put the round head of his cane in his mouth, like a stopper, when he sat down. As if he felt himself full to the throat with affronting sentiments. And he eyed the Boffins with implacable eyes.

'If you like to bring your sister with you when you come to stay with us,' said Mrs Boffin, 'of course we shall be glad. The better you please yourself, Miss Bella, the better you'll please us.'

'Oh, my consent is of no consequence at all, I suppose?' cried Miss Lavinia.

'Lavvy,' said her sister, in a low voice, 'have the goodness to be seen and not heard.'

'No, I won't,' replied the sharp Lavinia. 'I'm not a child, to be taken notice of by strangers.'

'You *are* a child.'

'I'm not a child, and I won't be taken notice of. "Bring your sister," indeed!'

'Lavinia!' said Mrs Wilfer. 'Hold! I will not allow you to utter in my presence the absurd suspicion that any strangers—I care not what their names—can patronize my child. Do you dare to suppose, you ridiculous girl, that Mr and Mrs Boffin would enter these doors upon a patronizing errand; or, if they did, would remain within them, only for one single instant, while your mother had the strength yet remaining in her vital frame to request them to depart? You little know your mother if you presume to think so.'

'It's all very fine,' Lavinia began to grumble, when Mrs Wilfer repeated:

'Hold! I will not allow this. Do you not know what is due to guests? Do you not comprehend that in presuming to hint that this lady and gentleman could have any idea of patronizing any member of your family—I care not which—you accuse them of an impertinence little less than insane?'

'Never mind me and Mrs Boffin, ma'am,' said Mr Boffin, smilingly: 'we don't care.'

'Pardon me, but *I* do,' returned Mrs Wilfer.

Miss Lavinia laughed a short laugh as she muttered, 'Yes, to be sure.'

'And I require my audacious child,' proceeded Mrs Wilfer, with a withering look at her youngest, on whom it had not the slightest effect, 'to please to be just to her sister Bella; to remember that her sister Bella is much sought after; and that when her sister Bella accepts an attention, she considers herself to be conferring qui-i-ite as much honour,'—this with an indignant shiver,—'as she receives.'

But, here Miss Bella repudiated, and said quietly, 'I can speak for myself, you know, ma. You needn't bring *me* in, please.'

'And it's all very well aiming at others through convenient me,' said the irrepressible Lavinia, spitefully; 'but I should like to ask George Sampson what *he* says to it.'

'Mr Sampson,' proclaimed Mrs Wilfer, seeing that young gentleman take his stopper out, and so darkly fixing him with her eyes as that he put it in again: 'Mr Sampson, as a friend of this family and a frequenter of this house, is, I am persuaded, far too well-bred to interpose on such an invitation.'

This exaltation of the young gentleman moved the conscientious Mrs Boffin to repentance for having done him an injustice in her mind, and consequently to saying that she and Mr Boffin would at any time be glad to see him; an attention which he handsomely acknowledged by replying, with his stopper unremoved, 'Much obliged to you, but I'm always engaged, day and night.'

However, Bella compensating for all drawbacks by responding to the advances of the Boffins in an engaging way, that easy pair were on the whole well satisfied, and proposed to the said Bella that as soon as they should be in a condition to receive her in a manner suitable to their desires, Mrs Boffin should return with notice of the fact. This arrangement Mrs Wilfer sanctioned with a stately inclination of her head and wave of her gloves, as who should say, 'Your demerits shall be overlooked, and you shall be mercifully gratified, poor people.'

'By-the-bye, ma'am,' said Mr Boffin, turning back as he was going, 'you have a lodger?'

'A gentleman,' Mrs Wilfer answered, qualifying the low expression, 'undoubtedly occupies our first floor.'

'I may call him Our Mutual Friend,' said Mr Boffin. 'What sort of a fellow *is* Our Mutual Friend, now? Do you like him?'

'Mr Rokesmith is very punctual, very quiet, a very eligible inmate.'

'Because,' Mr Boffin explained, 'you must know that I'm not particularly well acquainted with Our Mutual Friend, for I have only seen him once. You give a good account of him. Is he at home?'

'Mr Rokesmith is at home,' said Mrs Wilfer; 'indeed,' pointing through the window, 'there he stands at the garden gate. Waiting for you, perhaps?'

'Perhaps so,' replied Mr Boffin. 'Saw me come in, maybe.'

Bella had closely attended to this short dialogue. Accompanying Mrs Boffin to the gate, she as closely watched what followed.

'How are you, sir, how are you?' said Mr Boffin. 'This is Mrs Boffin. Mr Rokesmith, that I told you of, my dear.'

She gave him good day, and he bestirred himself and helped her to her seat, and the like, with a ready hand.

'Good-bye for the present, Miss Bella,' said Mrs Boffin, calling out a hearty parting. 'We shall meet again soon! And then I hope I shall have my little John Harmon to show you.'

Mr Rokesmith, who was at the wheel adjusting the skirts of her dress, suddenly looked behind him, and around him, and then looked up at her, with a face so pale that Mrs Boffin cried:

'Gracious!' And after a moment, 'What's the matter, sir?'

'How can you show her the Dead?' returned Mr Rokesmith.

'It's only an adopted child. One I have told her of. One I'm going to give the name to!'

'You took me by surprise,' said Mr Rokesmith, 'and it sounded like an omen, that you should speak of showing the Dead to one so young and blooming.'

Now, Bella suspected by this time that Mr Rokesmith admired her. Whether the knowledge (for it was rather that than suspicion) caused her to incline to him a little more, or a little less, than she had done at first; whether it rendered her eager to find out more about him, because she sought to establish reason for her distrust, or because she sought to free him from it; was as yet dark to her own heart. But at most times he occupied a great amount of her attention, and she had set her attention closely on this incident.

That he knew it as well as she, she knew as well as he, when they were left together standing on the path by the garden gate.

'Those are worthy people, Miss Wilfer.'

'Do you know them well?' asked Bella.

He smiled, reproaching her, and she coloured, reproaching herself—both, with the knowledge that she had meant to entrap him into an answer not true—when he said 'I know *of* them.'

'Truly, he told us he had seen you but once.'

'Truly, I supposed he did.'

Bella was nervous now, and would have been glad to recall her question.

'You thought it strange that, feeling much interested in you, I should start at what sounded like a proposal to bring you into contact with the murdered man who lies in his grave. I might have known—of course in a moment should have known—that it could not have that meaning. But my interest remains.'

Re-entering the family-room in a meditative state, Miss Bella was received by the irrepressible Lavinia with:

'There, Bella! At last I hope you have got your wishes realized—by your Boffins. You'll be rich enough now—with your Boffins. You can have as much flirting as you like—at your Boffins. But you won't take *me* to your Boffins, I can tell you—you and your Boffins too!'

'If,' quoth Mr George Sampson, moodily pulling his stopper out, 'Miss Bella's Mr Boffin comes any more of his nonsense to *me*, I only wish him to understand, as betwixt man and man, that he does it at his per—' and was going to say peril; but Miss Lavinia, having no confidence in his mental powers, and feeling his oration to have no definite application to any circumstances, jerked his stopper in again, with a sharpness that made his eyes water.

And now the worthy Mrs Wilfer, having used her youngest daughter as a lay-figure for the edification of these Boffins, became bland to her, and proceeded to develop her last instance of force of character, which was still in reserve. This was, to illuminate the family with her remarkable powers as a physiognomist; powers that terrified R. W. when ever let loose, as being always fraught with gloom and evil which no inferior prescience was aware of. And this Mrs Wilfer now did, be it observed, in jealousy of these Boffins, in the very same moments when she was already reflecting how she would flourish these very same Boffins and the state they kept, over the heads of her Boffinless friends.

'Of their manners,' said Mrs Wilfer, 'I say nothing. Of their appearance, I say nothing. Of the disinterestedness of their intentions towards Bella, I say nothing. But the craft, the secrecy, the dark deep underhanded plotting, written in Mrs Boffin's countenance, make me shudder.'

As an incontrovertible proof that those baleful attributes were all there, Mrs Wilfer shuddered on the spot.

Chapter 10
A Marriage Contract

THERE is excitement in the Veneering mansion. The mature young lady is going to be married (powder and all) to the mature young gentleman, and she is to be married from the Veneering house, and the Veneerings are to give the breakfast. The Analytical, who objects as a matter of principle to everything that occurs on the premises, necessarily objects to the match; but his consent has been dispensed with, and a spring-van is delivering its load of greenhouse plants at the door, in order that to-morrow's feast may be crowned with flowers.

The mature young lady is a lady of property. The mature young gentleman is a gentleman of property. He invests his property. He goes, in a condescending amateurish way, into the City, attends meetings of Directors, and has to do with traffic in Shares. As is well known to the wise in their generation, traffic in Shares is the one thing to have to do with in this world. Have no antecedents, no established character, no cultivation, no ideas, no manners; have Shares. Have Shares enough to be on Boards of Direction in capital letters, oscillate on mysterious business between London and Paris, and be great. Where does he come from? Shares. Where is he going to? Shares. What are his tastes? Shares. Has he any principles? Shares. What squeezes him into

Parliament? Shares. Perhaps he never of himself achieved success in anything, never originated anything, never produced anything? Sufficient answer to all; Shares. O mighty Shares! To set those blaring images so high, and to cause us smaller vermin, as under the influence of henbane or opium, to cry out, night and day, 'Relieve us of our money, scatter it for us, buy us and sell us, ruin us, only we beseech ye take rank among the powers of the earth, and fatten on us'!

While the Loves and Graces have been preparing this torch for Hymen, which is to be kindled to-morrow, Mr Twemlow has suffered much in his mind. It would seem that both the mature young lady and the mature young gentleman must indubitably be Veneering's oldest friends. Wards of his, perhaps? Yet that can scarcely be, for they are older than himself. Veneering has been in their confidence throughout, and has done much to lure them to the altar. He has mentioned to Twemlow how he said to Mrs Veneering, 'Anastatia, this must be a match.' He has mentioned to Twemlow how he regards Sophronia Akershem (the mature young lady) in the light of a sister, and Alfred Lammle (the mature young gentleman) in the light of a brother. Twemlow has asked him whether he went to school as a junior with Alfred? He has answered, 'Not exactly.' Whether Sophronia was adopted by his mother? He has answered, 'Not precisely so.' Twemlow's hand has gone to his forehead with a lost air.

But, two or three weeks ago, Twemlow, sitting over his newspaper, and over his dry-toast and weak tea, and over the stable-yard in Duke Street, St James's, received a highly-perfumed cocked-hat and monogram from Mrs Veneering, entreating her dearest Mr T., if not particularly engaged that day, to come like a charming soul and make a fourth at dinner with dear Mr Podsnap, for the discussion of an interesting family topic; the last three words doubly underlined and pointed with a note of admiration. And Twemlow replying, 'Not engaged, and more than delighted,' goes, and this takes place:

'My dear Twemlow,' says Veneering, 'your ready response to Anastatia's unceremonious invitation is truly kind, and like an old, old friend. You know our dear friend Podsnap?'

Twemlow ought to know the dear friend Podsnap who covered him with so much confusion, and he says he does know him, and Podsnap reciprocates. Apparently, Podsnap has been so wrought upon in a short time, as to believe that he has been intimate in the house many, many, many years. In the friendliest manner he is making himself quite at home with his back to the fire, executing a statuette of the Colossus at Rhodes. Twemlow has before noticed in his feeble way how soon the Veneering guests become infected with the Veneering fiction. Not, however, that he has the least notion of its being his own case.

'Our friends, Alfred and Sophronia,' pursues Veneering the veiled prophet: 'our friends Alfred and Sophronia, you will be glad to hear, my dear fellows, are going to be married. As my wife and I make it a family affair the entire direction of which we take upon ourselves, of course our first step is to communicate the fact to our family friends.'

('Oh!' thinks Twemlow, with his eyes on Podsnap, 'then there are only two of us, and he's the other.')

'I did hope,' Veneering goes on, 'to have had Lady Tippins to meet you; but she is always in request, and is unfortunately engaged.'

('Oh!' thinks Twemlow, with his eyes wandering, 'then there are three of us, and *she's* the other.')

'Mortimer Lightwood,' resumes Veneering, 'whom you both know, is out of town; but he writes, in his whimsical manner, that as we ask him to be bridegroom's best man when the ceremony takes place, he will not refuse, though he doesn't see what he has to do with it.'

('Oh!' thinks Twemlow, with his eyes rolling, 'then there are four of us, and *he's* the other.')

'Boots and Brewer,' observes Veneering, 'whom you also know, I have not asked to-day; but I reserve them for the occasion.'

('Then,' thinks Twemlow, with his eyes shut, 'there are si—' But here collapses and does not completely recover until dinner is over and the Analytical has been requested to withdraw.)

'We now come,' says Veneering, 'to the point, the real point, of our little family consultation. Sophronia, having lost both father and mother, has no one to give her away.'

'Give her away yourself,' says Podsnap.

'My dear Podsnap, no. For three reasons. Firstly, because I couldn't take so much upon myself when I have respected family friends to remember. Secondly, because I am not so vain as to think that I look the part. Thirdly, because Anastatia is a little superstitious on the subject and feels averse to my giving away anybody until baby is old enough to be married.'

'What would happen if he did?' Podsnap inquires of Mrs Veneering.

'My dear Mr Podsnap, it's very foolish I know, but I have

an instinctive presentiment that if Hamilton gave away anybody else first, he would never give away baby.' Thus Mrs Veneering; with her open hands pressed together, and each of her eight aquiline fingers looking so very like her one aquiline nose that the bran-new jewels on them seem necessary for distinction's sake.

'But, my dear Podsnap,' quoth Veneering, 'there *is* a tried friend of our family who, I think and hope you will agree with me, Podsnap, is the friend on whom this agreeable duty almost naturally devolves. That friend,' saying the words as if the company were about a hundred and fifty in number, 'is now among us. That friend is Twemlow.'

'Certainly!' From Podsnap.

'That friend,' Veneering repeats with greater firmness, 'is our dear good Twemlow. And I cannot sufficiently express to you, my dear Podsnap, the pleasure I feel in having this opinion of mine and Anastatia's so readily confirmed by you, that other equally familiar and tried friend who stands in the proud position—I mean who proudly stands in the position—or I ought rather to say, who places Anastatia and myself in the proud position of himself standing in the simple position—of baby's godfather.' And, indeed, Veneering is much relieved in mind to find that Podsnap betrays no jealousy of Twemlow's elevation.

So, it has come to pass that the spring-van is strewing flowers on the rosy hours and on the staircase, and that Twemlow is surveying the ground on which he is to play his distinguished part to-morrow. He has already been to the church, and taken note of the various impediments in the aisle, under the auspices of an extremely dreary widow who opens the pews, and whose left hand appears to be in a state of acute rheumatism, but is in fact voluntarily doubled up to act as a money-box.

And now Veneering shoots out of the Study wherein he is accustomed, when contemplative, to give his mind to the carving and gilding of the Pilgrims going to Canterbury, in order to show Twemlow the little flourish he has prepared for the trumpets of fashion, describing how that on the seventeenth instant, at St James's Church, the Reverend Blank Blank, assisted by the Reverend Dash Dash, united in the bonds of matrimony, Alfred Lammle Esquire, of Sackville Street, Piccadilly, to Sophronia, only daughter of the late Horatio Akershem, Esquire, of York-shire. Also how the fair bride was married from the house of Hamilton Veneering, Esquire, of Stucconia, and was given away by Melvin Twemlow, Esquire, of Duke Street, St James's,

second cousin to Lord Snigsworth, of Snigsworthy Park. While
perusing which composition, Twemlow makes some opaque approach to perceiving that if the Reverend Blank Blank and the
Reverend Dash Dash fail, after this introduction, to become
enrolled in the list of Veneering's dearest and oldest friends, they
will have none but themselves to thank for it.

After which, appears Sophronia (whom Twemlow has seen
twice in his lifetime), to thank Twemlow for counterfeiting the
late Horatio Akershem Esquire, broadly of Yorkshire. And after
her, appears Alfred (whom Twemlow has seen once in his
lifetime), to do the same and to make a pasty sort of glitter, as if
he were constructed for candle-light only, and had been let out
into daylight by some grand mistake. And after that, comes Mrs
Veneering, in a pervadingly aquiline state of figure, and with
transparent little knobs on her temper, like the little transparent
knob on the bridge of her nose, 'Worn out by worry and excitement,' as she tells her dear Mr Twemlow, and reluctantly revived with curaçoa by the Analytical. And after that, the
bridesmaids begin to come by rail-road from various parts of the
country, and to come like adorable recruits enlisted by a sergeant
not present; for, on arriving at the Veneering depôt, they are in a
barrack of strangers.

So, Twemlow goes home to Duke Street, St James's, to
take a plate of mutton broth with a chop in it, and a look at the
marriage-service, in order that he may cut in at the right place
to-morrow; and he is low, and feels it dull over the livery
stable-yard, and is distinctly aware of a dint in his heart, made
by the most adorable of the adorable bridesmaids. For, the poor
little harmless gentleman once had his fancy, like the rest of us,
and she didn't answer (as she often does not), and he thinks the
adorable bridesmaid is like the fancy as she was then (which she
is not at all), and that if the fancy had not married some one else
for money, but had married him for love, he and she would have
been happy (which they wouldn't have been), and that she has a
tenderness for him still (whereas her toughness is a proverb).
Brooding over the fire, with his dried little head in his dried little
hands, and his dried little elbows on his dried little knees,
Twemlow is melancholy. 'No Adorable to bear me company
here!' thinks he. 'No Adorable at the club! A waste, a waste, a
waste, my Twemlow!' And so drops asleep, and has galvanic
starts all over him.

Betimes next morning, that horrible old Lady Tippins
(relict of the late Sir Thomas Tippins, knighted in mistake for

somebody else by His Majesty King George the Third, who, while performing the ceremony, was graciously pleased to observe, 'What, what, what? Who, who, who? Why, why, why?') begins to be dyed and varnished for the interesting occasion. She has a reputation for giving smart accounts of things, and she must be at these people's early, my dear, to lose nothing of the fun. Whereabout in the bonnet and drapery announced by her name, any fragment of the real woman may be concealed, is perhaps known to her maid; but you could easily buy all you see of her, in Bond Street; or you might scalp her, and peel her, and scrape her, and make two Lady Tippinses out of her, and yet not penetrate to the genuine article. She has a large gold eye-glass, has Lady Tippins, to survey the proceedings with. If she had one in each eye, it might keep that other drooping lid up, and look more uniform. But perennial youth is in her artificial flowers, and her list of lovers is full.

'Mortimer, you wretch,' says Lady Tippins, turning the eye-glass about and about, 'where is your charge, the bridegroom?'

'Give you my honour,' returns Mortimer, 'I don't know, and I don't care.'

'Miserable! Is that the way you do your duty?'

'Beyond an impression that he is to sit upon my knee and be seconded at some point of the solemnities, like a principal at a prize-fight, I assure you I have no notion what my duty is,' returns Mortimer.

Eugene is also in attendance, with a pervading air upon him of having presupposed the ceremony to be a funeral, and of being disappointed. The scene is the Vestry-room of St James's Church, with a number of leathery old registers on shelves, that might be bound in Lady Tippinses.

But, hark! A carriage at the gate, and Mortimer's man arrives, looking rather like a spurious Mephistophiles and an unacknowledged member of that gentleman's family. Whom Lady Tippins, surveying through her eye-glass, considers a fine man, and quite a catch; and of whom Mortimer remarks, in the lowest spirits, as he approaches, 'I believe this is my fellow, confound him!' More carriages at the gate, and lo the rest of the characters. Whom Lady Tippins, standing on a cushion, surveying through the eye-glass, thus checks off: 'Bride; five-and-forty if a day, thirty shillings a yard, veil fifteen pound, pocket-handkerchief a present. Bridesmaids; kept down for fear of outshining bride, consequently not girls, twelve and sixpence a yard, Veneering's flowers, snub-nosed one rather pretty but too conscious of her stockings, bonnets three pound ten. Twemlow; blessed release for the dear man if she really was his daughter, nervous even under the pretence that she is, well he may be. Mrs Veneering; never saw such velvet, say two thousand pounds as she stands, absolute jeweller's window, father must have been a pawnbroker, or how could these people do it? Attendant unknowns; pokey.'

Ceremony performed, register signed, Lady Tippins escorted out of sacred edifice by Veneering, carriages rolling back to Stucconia, servants with favours and flowers, Veneering's house reached, drawing-rooms most magnificent. Here, the Podsnaps await the happy party; Mr Podsnap, with his hairbrushes made the most of; that imperial rocking-horse, Mrs Podsnap, majestically skittish. Here, too, are Boots and Brewer, and the two other Buffers; each Buffer with a flower in his button-hole, his hair curled, and his gloves buttoned on tight, apparently come prepared, if anything had happened to the bridegroom, to be married instantly. Here, too, the bride's aunt and next relation; a widowed female of a Medusa sort, in a stoney cap, glaring petrifaction at her fellow-creatures. Here, too, the bride's trustee; an oilcake-fed style of business-gentleman with mooney spectacles, and an object of much interest. Veneering launching himself upon this trustee as his oldest friend (which makes seven, Twemlow thought), and confidentially retiring with him into the conservatory, it is understood that Veneering is his co-trustee, and that they are arranging about the fortune. Buffers are even overheard to whisper Thir-ty Thou-sand Pou-nds! with a smack and a relish suggestive of the very finest oysters. Pokey unknowns, amazed to find how intimately they know Veneering, pluck up spirit, fold their arms, and begin to contradict him before breakfast. What time Mrs Veneering, carrying baby dressed as a bridesmaid, flits about among the company, emitting flashes of many-coloured lightning from diamonds, emeralds, and rubies.

The Analytical, in course of time achieving what he feels to be due to himself in bringing to a dignified conclusion several quarrels he has on hand with the pastrycook's men, announces breakfast. Dining-room no less magnificent than drawing-room; tables superb; all the camels out, and all laden. Splendid cake, covered with Cupids, silver, and true-lovers' knots. Splendid bracelet, produced by Veneering before going down, and clasped upon the arm of bride. Yet nobody seems to think much more of the Veneerings than if they were a tolerable landlord and landlady doing the thing in the way of business at so much a head.

The bride and bridegroom talk and laugh apart, as has always been their manner; and the Buffers work their way through the dishes with systematic perseverance, as has always been *their* manner; and the pokey unknowns are exceedingly benevolent to one another in invitations to take glasses of champagne; but Mrs Podsnap, arching her mane and rocking her grandest, has a far more deferential audience than Mrs Veneering; and Podsnap all but does the honours.

Another dismal circumstance is, that Veneering, having the captivating Tippins on one side of him and the bride's aunt on the other, finds it immensely difficult to keep the peace. For, Medusa, besides unmistakingly glaring petrifaction at the fascinating Tippins, follows every lively remark made by that dear creature, with an audible snort: which may be referable to a chronic cold in the head, but may also be referable to indignation and contempt. And this snort being regular in its reproduction, at length comes to be expected by the company, who make embarrassing pauses when it is falling due, and by waiting for it, render it more emphatic when it comes. The stoney aunt has likewise an injurious way of rejecting all dishes whereof Lady Tippins partakes: saying aloud when they are proffered to her, 'No, no, no, not for me. Take it away!' As with a set purpose of implying a misgiving that if nourished upon similar meats, she might come to be like that charmer, which would be a fatal consummation. Aware of her enemy, Lady Tippins tries a youthful sally or two, and tries the eye-glass; but, from the impenetrable cap and snorting armour of the stoney aunt all weapons rebound powerless.

Another objectionable circumstance is, that the pokey unknowns support each other in being unimpressible. They persist in not being frightened by the gold and silver camels, and they are banded together to defy the elaborately chased ice-pails. They even seem to unite in some vague utterance of the sentiment that the landlord and landlady will make a pretty good profit out of this, and they almost carry themselves like customers. Nor is there compensating influence in the adorable bridesmaids; for, having very little interest in the bride, and none at all in one another, those lovely beings become, each one of her own account, depreciatingly contemplative of the millinery present; while the bridegroom's man, exhausted, in the back of his chair, appears to be improving the occasion by penitentially contemplating all the wrong he has ever done; the difference between him and his friend Eugene, being, that the latter, in the back of *his* chair, appears to be contemplating all the wrong he would like to do—particularly to the present company.

In which state of affairs, the usual ceremonies rather droop and flag, and the splendid cake when cut by the fair hand of the bride has but an indigestible appearance. However, all the things indispensable to be said are said, and all the things indispensable to be done are done (including Lady Tippins's yawning, falling asleep, and waking insensible), and there is hurried preparation for the nuptial journey to the Isle of Wight, and the outer air teems with brass bands and spectators. In full sight of whom, the malignant star of the Analytical has pre-ordained that pain and ridicule shall befall him. For he, standing on the doorsteps to grace the departure, is suddenly caught a most prodigious thump on the side of his head with a heavy shoe, which a Buffer in the hall, champagne-flushed and wild of aim, has borrowed on the spur of the moment from the pastrycook's porter, to cast after the departing pair as an auspicious omen.

So they all go up again into the gorgeous drawing-rooms—all of them flushed with breakfast, as having taken scarlatina sociably—and there the combined unknowns do malignant things with their legs to ottomans, and take as much as possible out of the splendid furniture. And so, Lady Tippins, quite undetermined whether today is the day before yesterday, or the day after to-morrow, or the week after next, fades away; and Mortimer Lightwood and Eugene fade away, and Twemlow fades away, and the stoney aunt goes away—she declines to fade, proving rock to the last—and even the unknowns are slowly strained off, and it is all over.

All over, that is to say, for the time being. But, there is another time to come, and it comes in about a fortnight, and it comes to Mr and Mrs Lammle on the sands at Shanklin, in the Isle of Wight.

Mr and Mrs Lammle have walked for some time on the Shanklin sands, and one may see by their footprints that they have not walked arm in arm, and that they have not walked in a straight track, and that they have walked in a moody humour; for, the lady has prodded little spirting holes in the damp sand before her with her parasol, and the gentleman has trailed his stick after him. As if he were of the Mephistopheles family indeed, and had walked with a drooping tail.

'Do you mean to tell me, then, Sophronia—'

Thus he begins after a long silence, when Sophronia flashes fiercely, and turns upon him.

'Don't put it upon *me*, sir. I ask you, do *you* mean to tell me?'

Mr Lammle falls silent again, and they walk as before. Mrs Lammle opens her nostrils and bites her under-lip; Mr Lammle takes his gingerous whiskers in his left hand, and, bringing them together, frowns furtively at his beloved, out of a thick gingerous bush.

'Do *I* mean to say!' Mrs Lammle after a time repeats, with indignation. 'Putting it on me! The unmanly disingenuousness!'

Mr Lammle stops, releases his whiskers, and looks at her. 'The what?'

Mrs Lammle haughtily replies, without stopping, and without looking back. 'The meanness.'

He is at her side again in a pace or two, and he retorts, 'That is not what you said. You said disingenuousness.'

'What if I did?'

'There is no "if" in the case. You did.'

'I did, then. And what of it?'

'What of it?' says Mr Lammle. 'Have you the face to utter the word to me?'

'The face, too!' replied Mrs Lammle, staring at him with cold scorn. 'Pray, how dare you, sir, utter the word to me?'

'I never did.'

As this happens to be true, Mrs Lammle is thrown on the feminine resource of saying, 'I don't care what you uttered or did not utter.'

After a little more walking and a little more silence, Mr Lammle breaks the latter.

'You shall proceed in your own way. You claim a right to ask me do I mean to tell you. Do I mean to tell you what?'

'That you are a man of property?'

'No.'

'Then you married me on false pretences?'

'So be it. Next comes what you mean to say. Do you mean to say you are a woman of property?'

'No.'

'Then you married me on false pretences.'

'If you were so dull a fortune-hunter that you deceived yourself, or if you were so greedy and grasping that you were over-willing to be deceived by appearances, is it my fault, you adventurer?' the lady demands, with great asperity.

'I asked Veneering, and he told me you were rich.'

'Veneering!' with great contempt. 'And what does Veneering know about me!'

'Was he not your trustee?'

'No. I have no trustee, but the one you saw on the day when you fraudulently married me. And his trust is not a very difficult one, for it is only an annuity of a hundred and fifteen pounds. I think there are some odd shillings or pence, if you are very particular.'

Mr Lammle bestows a by no means loving look upon the partner of his joys and sorrows, and he mutters something; but checks himself.

'Question for question. It is my turn again, Mrs Lammle. What made you suppose me a man of property?'

'You made me suppose you so. Perhaps you will deny that you always presented yourself to me in that character?'

'But you asked somebody, too. Come, Mrs Lammle, admission for admission. You asked somebody?'

'I asked Veneering.'

'And Veneering knew as much of me as he knew of you, or as anybody knows of him.'

After more silent walking, the bride stops short, to say in a passionate manner:

'I never will forgive the Veneerings for this!'

'Neither will I,' returns the bridegroom.

With that, they walk again; she, making those angry spirts in the sand; he, dragging that dejected tail. The tide is low, and seems to have thrown them together high on the bare shore. A gull comes sweeping by their heads and flouts them. There was a golden surface on the brown cliffs but now, and behold they are only damp earth. A taunting roar comes from the sea, and the far-out rollers mount upon one another, to look at the entrapped impostors, and to join in impish and exultant gambols.

'Do you pretend to believe,' Mrs Lammle resumes, sternly, 'when you talk of my marrying you for worldly advantages, that it was within the bounds of reasonable probability that I would have married you for yourself?'

'Again there are two sides to the question, Mrs Lammle. What do you pretend to believe?'

'So you first deceive me and then insult me!' cries the lady, with a heaving bosom.

'Not at all. I have originated nothing. The double-edged question was yours.'

'Was mine!' the bride repeats, and her parasol breaks in her angry hand.

His colour has turned to a livid white, and ominous marks have come to light about his nose, as if the finger of the very devil himself had, within the last few moments, touched it here and there. But he has repressive power, and she has none.

'Throw it away,' he coolly recommends as to the parasol; 'you have made it useless; you look ridiculous with it.'

Whereupon she calls him in her rage, 'A deliberate villain,' and so casts the broken thing from her as that it strikes him in falling. The finger-marks are something whiter for the instant, but he walks on at her side.

She bursts into tears, declaring herself the wretchedest, the most deceived, the worst-used, of women. Then she says that if she had the courage to kill herself, she would do it. Then she calls him vile impostor. Then she asks him, why, in the disappointment of his base speculation, he does not take her life with his own hand, under the present favourable circumstances. Then she cries again. Then she is enraged again, and makes some mention of swindlers. Finally, she sits down crying on a block of stone, and is in all the known and unknown humours of her sex at once. Pending her changes, those aforesaid marks in his face have come and gone, now here now there, like white steps of a pipe on which the diabolical performer has played a tune. Also his livid lips are parted at last, as if he were breathless with running. Yet he is not.

'Now, get up, Mrs Lammle, and let us speak reasonably.'

She sits upon her stone, and takes no heed of him.

'Get up, I tell you.'

Raising her head, she looks contemptuously in his face, and repeats, 'You tell me! Tell me, forsooth!'

She affects not to know that his eyes are fastened on her as she droops her head again; but her whole figure reveals that she knows it uneasily.

'Enough of this. Come! Do you hear? Get up.'

Yielding to his hand, she rises, and they walk again; but this time with their faces turned towards their place of residence.

'Mrs Lammle, we have both been deceiving, and we have both been deceived. We have both been biting, and we have both been bitten. In a nut-shell, there's the state of the case.'

'You sought me out—'

'Tut! Let us have done with that. *We* know very well how it was. Why should you and I talk about it, when you and I can't disguise it? To proceed. I am disappointed and cut a poor figure.'

'Am I no one?'

'Some one—and I was coming to you, if you had waited a moment. You, too, are disappointed and cut a poor figure.'

'An injured figure!'

'You are now cool enough, Sophronia, to see that you can't be injured without my being equally injured; and that therefore the mere word is not to the purpose. When I look back, I wonder how I can have been such a fool as to take you to so great an extent upon trust.'

'And when I look back—' the bride cries, interrupting.

'And when you look back, you wonder how you can have been—you'll excuse the word?'

'Most certainly, with so much reason.'

'—Such a fool as to take *me* to so great an extent upon trust. But the folly is committed on both sides. I cannot get rid of you; you cannot get rid of me. What follows?'

'Shame and misery,' the bride bitterly replies.

'I don't know. A mutual understanding follows, and I think it may carry us through. Here I split my discourse (give me your arm, Sophronia), into three heads, to make it shorter and plainer. Firstly, it's enough to have been done, without the mortification of being known to have been done. So we agree to keep the fact to ourselves. You agree?'

'If it is possible, I do.'

'Possible! We have pretended well enough to one another. Can't we, united, pretend to the world? Agreed. Secondly, we owe the Veneerings a grudge, and we owe all other people the grudge of wishing them to be taken in, as we ourselves have been taken in. Agreed?'

'Yes. Agreed.'

'We come smoothly to thirdly. You have called me an adventurer, Sophronia. So I am. In plain uncomplimentary English, so I am. So are you, my dear. So are many people. We agree to keep our own secret, and to work together in furtherance of our own schemes.'

'What schemes?'

'Any scheme that will bring us money. By our own schemes, I mean our joint interest. Agreed?'

She answers, after a little hesitation, 'I suppose so. Agreed.'

'Carried at once, you see! Now, Sophronia, only half a dozen words more. We know one another perfectly. Don't be tempted into twitting me with the past knowledge that you have of me, because it is identical with the past knowledge that I have of you, and in twitting me, you twit yourself, and I don't want to hear you do it. With this good understanding established between us, it is better never done. To wind up all:—You have shown temper today, Sophronia. Don't be betrayed into doing so again, because I have a Devil of a temper myself.'

So, the happy pair, with this hopeful marriage contract thus signed, sealed, and delivered, repair homeward. If, when those infernal finger-marks were on the white and breathless countenance of Alfred Lammle, Esquire, they denoted that he conceived the purpose of subduing his dear wife Mrs Alfred Lammle, by at once divesting her of any lingering reality or pretence of self-respect, the purpose would seem to have been presently executed. The mature young lady has mighty little need of powder, now, for her downcast face, as he escorts her in the light of the setting sun to their abode of bliss.

Chapter 11
Podsnappery

MR PODSNAP was well to do, and stood very high in Mr Podsnap's opinion. Beginning with a good inheritance, he had married a good inheritance, and had thriven exceedingly in the Marine Insurance way, and was quite satisfied. He never could make out why everybody was not quite satisfied, and he felt conscious that he set a brilliant social example in being particularly well satisfied with most things, and, above all other things, with himself.

Thus happily acquainted with his own merit and importance, Mr Podsnap settled that whatever he put behind him he put out of existence. There was a dignified conclusiveness—not to add a grand convenience—in this way of getting rid of disagreeables which had done much towards establishing Mr Podsnap in his lofty place in Mr Podsnap's satisfaction. 'I don't want to know about it; I don't choose to discuss it; I don't admit it!' Mr

Podsnap had even acquired a peculiar flourish of his right arm in often clearing the world of its most difficult problems, by sweeping them behind him (and consequently sheer away) with those words and a flushed face. For they affronted him.

Mr Podsnap's world was not a very large world, morally; no, nor even geographically: seeing that although his business was sustained upon commerce with other countries, he considered other countries, with that important reservation, a mistake, and of their manners and customs would conclusively observe, 'Not English!' when, PRESTO! with a flourish of the arm, and a flush of the face, they were swept away. Elsewhere, the world got up at eight, shaved close at a quarter-past, breakfasted at nine, went to the City at ten, came home at half-past five, and dined at seven. Mr Podsnap's notions of the Arts in their integrity might have been stated thus. Literature; large print, respectfully descriptive of getting up at eight, shaving close at a quarter past, breakfasting at nine, going to the City at ten, coming home at half-past five, and dining at seven. Painting and Sculpture; models and portraits representing Professors of getting up at eight, shaving close at a quarter past, breakfasting at nine, going to the City at ten, coming home at half-past five, and dining at seven. Music; a respectable performance (without variations) on stringed and wind instruments, sedately expressive of getting up at eight, shaving close at a quarter past, breakfasting at nine, going to the City at ten, coming home at half-past five, and dining at seven. Nothing else to be permitted to those same vagrants the Arts, on pain of excommunication. Nothing else To Be—anywhere!

As a so eminently respectable man, Mr Podsnap was sensible of its being required of him to take Providence under his protection. Consequently he always knew exactly what Providence meant. Inferior and less respectable men might fall short of that mark, but Mr Podsnap was always up to it. And it was very remarkable (and must have been very comfortable) that what Providence meant, was invariably what Mr Podsnap meant.

These may be said to have been the articles of a faith and school which the present chapter takes the liberty of calling, after its representative man, Podsnappery. They were confined within close bounds, as Mr Podsnap's own head was confined by his shirt-collar; and they were enunciated with a sounding pomp that smacked of the creaking of Mr Podsnap's own boots.

There was a Miss Podsnap. And this young rocking-horse was being trained in her mother's art of prancing in a stately manner without ever getting on. But the high parental action was not yet imparted to her, and in truth she was but an undersized damsel, with high shoulders, low spirits, chilled elbows, and a rasped surface of nose, who seemed to take occasional frosty peeps out of childhood into womanhood, and to shrink back again, overcome by her mother's head-dress and her father from head to foot—crushed by the mere dead-weight of Podsnappery.

A certain institution in Mr Podsnap's mind which he called 'the young person' may be considered to have been embodied in Miss Podsnap, his daughter. It was an inconvenient and exacting institution, as requiring everything in the universe to be filed down and fitted to it. The question about everything was, would it bring a blush into the cheek of the young person? And the inconvenience of the young person was, that, according to Mr Podsnap, she seemed always liable to burst into blushes when there was no need at all. There appeared to be no line of demarcation between the young person's excessive innocence, and another person's guiltiest knowledge. Take Mr Podsnap's word for it, and the soberest tints of drab, white, lilac, and grey, were all flaming red to this troublesome Bull of a young person.

The Podsnaps lived in a shady angle adjoining Portman Square. They were a kind of people certain to dwell in the shade, wherever they dwelt. Miss Podsnap's life had been, from her first appearance on this planet, altogether of a shady order; for, Mr Podsnap's young person was likely to get little good out of association with other young persons, and had therefore been restricted to companionship with not very congenial older persons, and with massive furniture. Miss Podsnap's early views of life being principally derived from the reflections of it in her father's boots, and in the walnut and rosewood tables of the dim drawing-rooms, and in their swarthy giants of looking-glasses, were of a sombre cast; and it was not wonderful that now, when she was on most days solemnly tooled through the Park by the side of her mother in a great tall custard-coloured phaeton, she showed above the apron of that vehicle like a dejected young person sitting up in bed to take a startled look at things in general, and very strongly desiring to get her head under the counterpane again.

Said Mr Podsnap to Mrs Podsnap, 'Georgiana is almost eighteen.'

Said Mrs Podsnap to Mr Podsnap, assenting, 'Almost eighteen.'

Said Mr Podsnap then to Mrs Podsnap, 'Really I think we should have some people on Georgiana's birthday.'

Said Mrs Podsnap then to Mr Podsnap, 'Which will enable us to clear off all those people who are due.'

So it came to pass that Mr and Mrs Podsnap requested the honour of the company of seventeen friends of their souls at dinner; and that they substituted other friends of their souls for such of the seventeen original friends of their souls as deeply regretted that a prior engagement prevented their having the honour of dining with Mr and Mrs Podsnap, in pursuance of their kind invitation; and that Mrs Podsnap said of all these inconsolable personages, as she checked them off with a pencil in her list, 'Asked, at any rate, and got rid of;' and that they successfully disposed of a good many friends of their souls in this way, and felt their consciences much lightened.

There were still other friends of their souls who were not entitled to be asked to dinner, but had a claim to be invited to come and take a haunch of mutton vapour-bath at half-past nine. For the clearing off of these worthies, Mrs Podsnap added a small and early evening to the dinner, and looked in at the music-shop to bespeak a well-conducted automaton to come and play quadrilles for a carpet dance.

Mr and Mrs Veneering, and Mr and Mrs Veneering's bran-new bride and bridegroom, were of the dinner company; but the Podsnap establishment had nothing else in common with the Veneerings. Mr Podsnap could tolerate taste in a mushroom man who stood in need of that sort of thing, but was far above it himself. Hideous solidity was the characteristic of the Podsnap plate. Everything was made to look as heavy as it could, and to take up as much room as possible. Everything said boastfully, 'Here you have as much of me in my ugliness as if I were only lead; but I am so many ounces of precious metal worth so much an ounce;—wouldn't you like to melt me down?' A corpulent straddling epergne, blotched all over as if it had broken out in an eruption rather than been ornamented, delivered this address from un unsightly silver platform in the centre of the table. Four silver wine-coolers, each furnished with four staring heads, each head obtrusively carrying a big silver ring in each of its ears, conveyed the sentiment up and down the table, and handed it on to the pot-bellied silver salt-cellars. All the big silver spoons and forks widened the mouths of the company expressly for the purpose of thrusting the sentiment down their throats with every morsel they ate.

The majority of the guests were like the plate, and included several heavy articles weighing ever so much. But there was a foreign gentleman among them: whom Mr Podsnap had invited after much debate with himself—believing the whole European continent to be in mortal alliance against the young person—and there was a droll disposition, not only on the part of Mr Podsnap but of everybody else, to treat him as if he were a child who was hard of hearing.

As a delicate concession to this unfortunately-born foreigner, Mr Podsnap, in receiving him, had presented his wife as 'Madame Podsnap;' also his daughter as 'Mademoiselle Podsnap,' with some inclination to add 'ma fille,' in which bold venture, however, he checked himself. The Veneerings being at that time the only other arrivals, he had added (in a condescendingly explanatory manner), 'Monsieur Vey-nair-reeng,' and had then subsided into English.

'How Do You Like London?' Mr Podsnap now inquired from his station of host, as if he were administering something in the nature of a powder or potion to the deaf child; 'London, Londres, London?'

The foreign gentleman admired it.

'You find it Very Large?' said Mr Podsnap, spaciously.

The foreign gentleman found it very large.

'And Very Rich?'

The foreign gentleman found it, without doubt, enormément riche.

'Enormously Rich, We say,' returned Mr Podsnap, in a condescending manner. 'Our English adverbs do Not terminate in Mong, and We Pronounce the "ch" as if there were a "t" before it. We say Ritch.'

'Reetch,' remarked the foreign gentleman.

'And Do You Find, Sir,' pursued Mr Podsnap, with dignity, 'Many Evidences that Strike You, of our British Constitution in the Streets Of The World's Metropolis, London, Londres, London?'

The foreign gentleman begged to be pardoned, but did not altogether understand.

'The Constitution Britannique,' Mr Podsnap explained, as if he were teaching in an infant school. 'We Say British, But You Say Britannique, You Know' (forgivingly, as if that were not his fault). 'The Constitution, Sir.'

The foreign gentleman said, 'Mais, yees; I know eem.'

A youngish sallowish gentleman in spectacles, with a lumpy

forehead, seated in a supplementary chair at a corner of the table, here caused a profound sensation by saying, in a raised voice, 'ESKER,' and then stopping dead.

'Mais oui,' said the foreign gentleman, turning towards him. 'Est-ce que? Quoi donc?'

But the gentleman with the lumpy forehead having for the time delivered himself of all that he found behind his lumps, spake for the time no more.

'I Was Inquiring,' said Mr Podsnap, resuming the thread of his discourse, 'Whether You Have Observed in our Streets as We should say, Upon our Pavvy as You would say, any Tokens—'

The foreign gentleman, with patient courtesy entreated pardon; 'But what was a tokenz?'

'Marks,' said Mr Podsnap; 'Signs, you know, Appearances—Traces.'

'Ah! Of a Orse?' inquired the foreign gentleman.

'We call it Horse,' said Mr Podsnap, with forbearance. 'In England, Angleterre, England, We Aspirate the "H," and We Say "Horse." Only our Lower Classes Say "Orse!" '

'Pardon,' said the foreign gentleman; 'I am alwiz wrong!'

'Our Language,' said Mr Podsnap, with a gracious consciousness of being always right, 'is Difficult. Ours is a Copious Language, and Trying to Strangers. I will not Pursue my Question.'

But the lumpy gentleman, unwilling to give it up, again madly said, 'ESKER,' and again spake no more.

'It merely referred,' Mr Podsnap explained, with a sense of meritorious proprietorship, 'to Our Constitution, Sir. We Englishmen are Very Proud of our Constitution, Sir. It Was Bestowed Upon Us By Providence. No Other Country is so Favoured as This Country.'

'And ozer countries?—' the foreign gentleman was beginning, when Mr Podsnap put him right again.

'We do not say Ozer; we say Other: the letters are "T" and "H;" You say Tay and Aish, You Know; (still with clemency). The sound is "th"—"th!" '

'And o*ther* countries,' said the foreign gentleman. 'They do how?'

'They do, Sir,' returned Mr Podsnap, gravely shaking his head; 'they do—I am sorry to be obliged to say it—*as* they do.'

'It was a little particular of Providence,' said the foreign gentleman, laughing; 'for the frontier is not large.'

'Undoubtedly,' assented Mr Podsnap; 'But So it is. It was the Charter of the Land. This Island was Blest, Sir, to the Direct

Exclusion of such Other Countries as—as there may happen to be. And if we were all Englishmen present, I would say,' added Mr Podsnap, looking round upon his compatriots, and sounding solemnly with his theme, 'that there is in the Englishman a combination of qualities, a modesty, an independence, a responsibility, a repose, combined with an absence of everything calculated to call a blush into the cheek of a young person, which one would seek in vain among the Nations of the Earth.'

Having delivered this little summary, Mr Podsnap's face flushed, as he thought of the remote possibility of its being at all qualified by any prejudiced citizen of any other country; and, with his favourite right-arm flourish, he put the rest of Europe and the whole of Asia, Africa, and America nowhere.

The audience were much edified by this passage of words; and Mr Podsnap, feeling that he was in rather remarkable force to-day, became smiling and conversational.

'Has anything more been heard, Veneering,' he inquired, 'of the lucky legatee?'

'Nothing more,' returned Veneering, 'than that he has come into possession of the property. I am told people now call him The Golden Dustman. I mentioned to you some time ago, I think, that the young lady whose intended husband was murdered is daughter to a clerk of mine?'

'Yes, you told me that,' said Podsnap; 'and by-the-bye, I wish you would tell it again here, for it's a curious coincidence—curious that the first news of the discovery should have been brought straight to your table (when I was there), and curious that one of your people should have been so nearly interested in it. Just relate that, will you?'

Veneering was more than ready to do it, for he had prospered exceedingly upon the Harmon Murder, and had turned the social distinction it conferred upon him to the account of making several dozen of bran-new bosom-friends. Indeed, such another lucky hit would almost have set him up in that way to his satisfaction. So, addressing himself to the most desirable of his neighbours, while Mrs Veneering secured the next most desirable, he plunged into the case, and emerged from it twenty minutes afterwards with a Bank Director in his arms. In the mean time, Mrs Veneering had dived into the same waters for a wealthy Ship-Broker, and had brought him up, safe and sound, by the hair. Then Mrs Veneering had to relate, to a larger circle, how she had been to see the girl, and how she was really pretty, and (considering her station) presentable. And this she did with such a successful display of her eight aquiline fingers and their encircling jewels, that she happily laid hold of a drifting General Officer, his wife and daughter, and not only restored their animation which had become suspended, but made them lively friends within an hour.

Although Mr Podsnap would in a general way have highly disapproved of Bodies in rivers as ineligible topics with reference to the cheek of the young person, he had, as one may say, a share in this affair which made him a part proprietor. As its returns were immediate, too, in the way of restraining the company from speechless contemplation of the wine-coolers, it paid, and he was satisfied.

And now the haunch of mutton vapour-bath having received a gamey infusion, and a few last touches of sweets and coffee, was quite ready, and the bathers came; but not before the discreet automaton had got behind the bars of the piano music-desk, and there presented the appearance of a captive languishing in a rosewood jail. And who now so pleasant or so well assorted as Mr and Mrs Alfred Lammle, he all sparkle, she all gracious contentment, both at occasional intervals exchanging looks like partners at cards who played a game against All England.

There was not much youth among the bathers, but there was no youth (the young person always excepted) in the articles of Podsnappery. Bald bathers folded their arms and talked to Mr Podsnap on the hearthrug; sleek-whiskered bathers, with hats in their hands, lunged at Mrs Podsnap and retreated; prowling bathers, went about looking into ornamental boxes and bowls as if they had suspicions of larceny on the part of the Podsnaps, and expected to find something they had lost at the bottom; bathers of the gentler sex sat silently comparing ivory shoulders. All this time and always, poor little Miss Podsnap, whose tiny efforts (if she had made any) were swallowed up in the magnificence of her mother's rocking, kept herself as much out of sight and mind as she could, and appeared to be counting on many dismal returns of the day. It was somehow understood, as a secret article in the state proprieties of Podsnappery that nothing must be said about the day. Consequently this young damsel's nativity was hushed up and looked over, as if it were agreed on all hands that it would have been better that she had never been born.

The Lammles were so fond of the dear Veneerings that they could not for some time detach themselves from those excellent friends; but at length, either a very open smile on Mr Lammle's part, or a very secret elevation of one of his gingerous eyebrows—

certainly the one or the other—seemed to say to Mrs Lammle, 'Why don't you play?' And so, looking about her, she saw Miss Podsnap, and seeming to say responsively, 'That card?' and to be answered, 'Yes,' went and sat beside Miss Podsnap.

Mrs Lammle was overjoyed to escape into a corner for a little quiet talk.

It promised to be a very quiet talk, for Miss Podsnap replied in a flutter, 'Oh! Indeed, it's very kind of you, but I am afraid I *don't* talk.'

'Let us make a beginning,' said the insinuating Mrs Lammle, with her best smile.

'Oh! I am afraid you'll find me very dull. But Ma talks!'

That was plainly to be seen, for Ma was talking then at her usual canter, with arched head and mane, opened eyes and nostrils

'Fond of reading perhaps?'

'Yes. At least I—don't mind that so much,' returned Miss Podsnap.

'M-m-m-m-music.' So insinuating was Mrs Lammle that she got half a dozen ms into the word before she got it out.

'I haven't nerve to play even if I could. Ma plays.'

(At exactly the same canter, and with a certain flourishing appearance of doing something, Ma did, in fact, occasionally take a rock upon the instrument.)

'Of course you like dancing?'

'Oh no, I don't,' said Miss Podsnap.

'No? With your youth and attractions? Truly, my dear, you surprise me!'

'I can't say,' observed Miss Podsnap, after hesitating considerably, and stealing several timid looks at Mrs Lammle's carefully arranged face, 'how I might have liked it if I had been a—you won't mention it, *will* you?'

'My dear! Never!'

'No, I am sure you won't. I can't say then how I should have liked it, if I had been a chimney-sweep on May-day.'

'Gracious!' was the exclamation which amazement elicited from Mrs Lammle.

'There! I knew you'd wonder. But you won't mention it, will you?'

'Upon my word, my love,' said Mrs Lammle, 'you make me ten times more desirous, now I talk to you, to know you well than I was when I sat over yonder looking at you. How I wish we could be real friends! Try me as a real friend. Come! Don't fancy me a frumpy old married woman, my dear; I was married but the other day, you know; I am dressed as a bride now, you see. About the chimney-sweeps?'

'Hush! Ma'll hear.'

'She can't hear from where she sits.'

'Don't you be too sure of that,' said Miss Podsnap, in a lower voice. 'Well, what I mean is, that they seem to enjoy it.'

'And that perhaps you would have enjoyed it, if you had been one of them?'

Miss Podsnap nodded significantly.

'Then you don't enjoy it now?'

'How is it possible?' said Miss Podsnap. 'Oh it is such a dreadful thing! If I was wicked enough—and strong enough—to kill anybody, it should be my partner.'

This was such an entirely new view of the Terpsichorean art as socially practised, that Mrs Lammle looked at her young friend in some astonishment. Her young friend sat nervously twiddling her fingers in a pinioned attitude, as if she were trying to hide her elbows. But this latter Utopian object (in short sleeves) always appeared to be the great inoffensive aim of her existence.

'It sounds horrid, don't it?' said Miss Podsnap, with a penitential face.

Mrs Lammle, not very well knowing what to answer, resolved herself into a look of smiling encouragement.

'But it is, and it always has been,' pursued Miss Podsnap, 'such a trial to me! I so dread being awful. And it is so awful! No one knows what I suffered at Madame Sauteuse's, where I learnt to dance and make presentation-curtseys, and other dreadful things—or at least where they tried to teach me. Ma can do it.'

'At any rate, my love,' said Mrs Lammle, soothingly, 'that's over.'

'Yes, it's over,' returned Miss Podsnap, 'but there's nothing gained by that. It's worse here, than at Madame Sauteuse's. Ma was there, and Ma's here; but Pa wasn't there, and company wasn't there, and there were not real partners there. Oh there's Ma speaking to the man at the piano! Oh there's Ma going up to somebody! Oh I know she's going to bring him to me! Oh please don't, please don't, please don't! Oh keep away, keep away, keep away!' These pious ejaculations Miss Podsnap uttered with her eyes closed, and her head leaning back against the wall.

But the Ogre advanced under the pilotage of Ma, and Ma

said, 'Georgiana, Mr Grompus,' and the Ogre clutched his victim and bore her off to his castle in the top couple. Then the discreet automaton who had surveyed his ground, played a blossomless tuneless 'set,' and sixteen disciples of Podsnappery went through the figures of—1, Getting up at eight and shaving close at a quarter past—2, Breakfasting at nine—3, Going to the City at ten—4, Coming home at half-past five—5, Dining at seven, and the grand chain.

While these solemnities were in progress, Mr Alfred Lammle (most loving of husbands) approached the chair of Mrs Alfred Lammle (most loving of wives), and bending over the back of it, trifled for some few seconds with Mrs Lammle's bracelet. Slightly in contrast with this brief airy toying, one might have noticed a certain dark attention in Mrs Lammle's face as she said some words with her eyes on Mr Lammle's waistcoat, and seemed in return to receive some lesson. But it was all done as a breath passes from a mirror.

And now, the grand chain riveted to the last link, the discreet automaton ceased, and the sixteen, two and two, took a walk among the furniture. And herein the unconsciousness of the Ogre Grompus was pleasantly conspicuous; for, that complacent monster, believing that he was giving Miss Podsnap a treat, prolonged to the utmost stretch of possibility a peripatetic account of an archery meeting; while his victim, heading the procession of sixteen as it slowly circled about, like a revolving funeral, never raised her eyes except once to steal a glance at Mrs Lammle, expressive of intense despair.

At length the procession was dissolved by the violent arrival of a nutmeg, before which the drawing-room door bounced open as if it were a cannon-ball; and while that fragrant article, dispersed through several glasses of coloured warm water, was going the round of society, Miss Podsnap returned to her seat by her new friend.

'Oh my goodness,' said Miss Podsnap. '*That's* over! I hope you didn't look at me.'

'My dear, why not?'

'Oh I know all about myself,' said Miss Podsnap.

'I'll tell you something *I* know about you, my dear,' returned Mrs Lammle in her winning way, 'and that is, you are most unnecessarily shy.'

'Ma ain't,' said Miss Podsnap. '—I detest you! Go along!' This shot was levelled under her breath at the gallant Grompus for bestowing an insinuating smile upon her in passing.

'Pardon me if I scarcely see, my dear Miss Podsnap,' Mrs Lammle was beginning when the young lady interposed.

'If we are going to be real friends (and I suppose we are, for you are the only person who ever proposed it) don't let us be awful. It's awful enough to *be* Miss Podsnap, without being called so. Call me Georgiana.'

'Dearest Georgiana,' Mrs Lammle began again.

'Thank you,' said Miss Podsnap.

'Dearest Georgiana, pardon me if I scarcely see, my love, why your mamma's not being shy, is a reason why you should be.'

'Don't you really see that?' asked Miss Podsnap, plucking at her fingers in a troubled manner, and furtively casting her eyes now on Mrs Lammle, now on the ground. 'Then perhaps it isn't?'

'My dearest Georgiana, you defer much too readily to my poor opinion. Indeed it is not even an opinion, darling, for it is only a confession of my dullness.'

'Oh *you* are not dull,' returned Miss Podsnap. '*I* am dull, but you couldn't have made me talk if you were.'

Some little touch of conscience answering this perception of her having gained a purpose, called bloom enough into Mrs Lammle's face to make it look brighter as she sat smiling her best smile on her dear Georgiana, and shaking her head with an affectionate playfulness. Not that it meant anything, but that Georgiana seemed to like it.

'What I mean is,' pursued Georgiana, 'that Ma being so endowed with awfulness, and Pa being so endowed with awfulness, and there being so much awfulness everywhere—I mean, at least, everywhere where I am—perhaps it makes me who am so deficient in awfulness, and frightened at it—I say it very badly—I don't know whether you can understand what I mean?'

'Perfectly, dearest Georgiana!' Mrs Lammle was proceeding with every reassuring wile, when the head of that young lady suddenly went back against the wall again and her eyes closed.

'Oh there's Ma being awful with somebody with a glass in his eye! Oh I know she's going to bring him here! Oh don't bring him, don't bring him! Oh he'll be my partner with his glass in his eye! Oh what shall I do!' This time Georgiana accompanied her ejaculations with taps of her feet upon the floor, and was altogether in quite a desperate condition. But, there was no escape from the majestic Mrs Podsnap's production of an ambling stranger, with one eye screwed up into extinction and the other framed and glazed, who, having looked down out of that organ, as if he descried Miss Podsnap at the bottom of some perpendicular shaft, brought her to the surface, and ambled off with her. And then the captive at the piano played another 'set,' expressive of his mournful aspirations after freedom, and other sixteen went through the former melancholy motions, and the ambler took Miss Podsnap for a furniture walk, as if he had struck out an entirely original conception.

In the mean time a stray personage of a meek demeanour, who had wandered to the hearthrug and got among the heads of tribes assembled there in conference with Mr Podsnap, eliminated Mr Podsnap's flush and flourish by a highly unpolite remark; no less than a reference to the circumstance that some half-dozen people had lately died in the streets, of starvation. It was clearly ill-timed after dinner. It was not adapted to the cheek of the young person. It was not in good taste.

'I don't believe it,' said Mr Podsnap, putting it behind him.

The meek man was afraid we must take it as proved, because there were the Inquests and the Registrar's returns.

'Then it was their own fault,' said Mr Podsnap.

Veneering and other elders of tribes commended this way out of it. At once a short cut and a broad road.

The man of meek demeanour intimated that truly it would seem from the facts, as if starvation had been forced upon the culprits in question—as if, in their wretched manner, they had made their weak protests against it—as if they would have taken the liberty of staving it off if they could—as if they would rather not have been starved upon the whole, if perfectly agreeable to all parties.

'There is not,' said Mr Podsnap, flushing angrily, 'there is not a country in the world, sir, where so noble a provision is made for the poor as in this country.'

The meek man was quite willing to concede that, but perhaps it rendered the matter even worse, as showing that there must be something appallingly wrong somewhere.

'Where?' said Mr Podsnap.

The meek man hinted Wouldn't it be well to try, very seriously, to find out where?

'Ah!' said Mr Podsnap. 'Easy to say somewhere; not so easy to say where! But I see what you are driving at. I knew it from the first. Centralization. No. Never with my consent. Not English.'

An approving murmur arose from the heads of tribes; as saying, 'There you have him! Hold him!'

He was not aware (the meek man submitted of himself) that he was driving at any ization. He had no favourite ization that he knew of. But he certainly was more staggered by these terrible occurrences than he was by names, of howsoever so many syllables. Might he ask, was dying of destitution and neglect necessarily English?

'You know what the population of London is, I suppose,' said Mr Podsnap.

The meek man supposed he did, but supposed that had absolutely nothing to do with it, if its laws were well administered.

'And you know; at least I hope you know;' said Mr Podsnap, with severity, 'that Providence has declared that you shall have the poor always with you?'

The meek man also hoped he knew that.

'I am glad to hear it,' said Mr Podsnap with a portentous air. 'I am glad to hear it. It will render you cautious how you fly in the face of Providence.'

In reference to that absurd and irreverent conventional phrase, the meek man said, for which Mr Podsnap was not responsible, he the meek man had no fear of doing anything so impossible; but——

But Mr Podsnap felt that the time had come for flushing and flourishing this meek man down for good. So he said:

'I must decline to pursue this painful discussion. It is not pleasant to my feelings; it is repugnant to my feelings. I have said that I do not admit these things. I have also said that if they do occur (not that I admit it), the fault lies with the sufferers themselves. It is not for *me*'—Mr Podsnap pointed 'me' forcibly, as adding by implication though it may be all very well for *you*—'it is not for me to impugn the workings of Providence. I know better than that, I trust, and I have mentioned what the intentions of Providence are. Besides,' said Mr Podsnap, flushing high up among his hair-brushes, with a strong consciousness of personal affront, 'the subject is a very disagreeable one. I will go so far as to say it is an odious one. It is not one to be introduced among our wives and young persons, and I—' He finished with that flourish of his arm which added more expressively than any words, And I remove it from the face of the earth.

Simultaneously with this quenching of the meek man's ineffectual fire, Georgiana having left the ambler up a lane of sofa, in a No Thoroughfare of back drawing-room, to find his own way out, came back to Mrs Lammle. And who should be with Mrs Lammle, but Mr Lammle. So fond of her!

'Alfred, my love, here is my friend. Georgiana, dearest girl, you must like my husband next to me.'

Mr Lammle was proud to be so soon distinguished by this special commendation to Miss Podsnap's favour. But if Mr Lammle were prone to be jealous of his dear Sophronia's friendships, he would be jealous of her feeling towards Miss Podsnap.

'Say Georgiana, darling,' interposed his wife.

'Towards—shall I?—Georgiana.' Mr Lammle uttered the name, with a delicate curve of his right hand, from his lips outward. 'For never have I known Sophronia (who is not apt to take sudden likings) so attracted and so captivated as she is by—shall I once more?—Georgiana.'

The object of this homage sat uneasily enough in receipt of it, and then said, turning to Mrs Lammle, much embarrassed:

'I wonder what you like me for! I am sure I can't think.'

'Dearest Georgiana, for yourself. For your difference from all around you.'

'Well! That may be. For I think I like you for your difference from all around me,' said Georgiana with a smile of relief.

'We must be going with the rest,' observed Mrs Lammle, rising with a show of unwillingness, amidst a general dispersal. 'We are real friends, Georgiana dear?'

'Real.'

'Good night, dear girl!'

She had established an attraction over the shrinking nature upon which her smiling eyes were fixed, for Georgiana held her hand while she answered in a secret and half-frightened tone:

'Don't forget me when you are gone away. And come again soon. Good night!'

Charming to see Mr and Mrs Lammle taking leave so gracefully, and going down the stairs so lovingly and sweetly. Not quite so charming to see their smiling faces fall and brood as they dropped moodily into separate corners of their little carriage. But to be sure that was a sight behind the scenes, which nobody saw, and which nobody was meant to see.

Certain big, heavy vehicles, built on the model of the Podsnap plate, took away the heavy articles of guests weighing ever so much; and the less valuable articles got away after their various manners; and the Podsnap plate was put to bed. As Mr Podsnap stood with his back to the drawing-room fire, pulling up his shirt-collar, like a veritable cock of the walk literally pluming himself in the midst of his possessions, nothing would have astonished him more than an intimation that Miss Podsnap, or any other young person properly born and bred, could not be exactly put away like the plate, brought out like the plate, polished like the plate, counted, weighed, and valued like the plate. That such a young person could possibly have a morbid vacancy in the heart for anything younger than the plate, or less monotonous than the plate; or that such a young person's thoughts could try to scale the region bounded on the north, south, east, and west, by the plate; was a monstrous imagination which he would on the spot have flourished into space. This perhaps in some sort arose from Mr Podsnap's blushing young person being, so to speak, all cheek; whereas there is a possibility that there may be young persons of a rather more complex organization.

If Mr Podsnap, pulling up his shirt-collar, could only have heard himself called 'that fellow' in a certain short dialogue, which passed between Mr and Mrs Lammle in their opposite corners of their little carriage, rolling home!

'Sophronia, are you awake?'

'Am I likely to be asleep, sir?'

'Very likely, I should think, after that fellow's company. Attend to what I am going to say.'

'I have attended to what you have already said, have I not? What else have I been doing all to-night.'

'Attend, I tell you,' (in a raised voice) 'to what I am going to say. Keep close to that idiot girl. Keep her under your thumb. You have her fast, and you are not to let her go. Do you hear?'

'I hear you.'

'I foresee there is money to be made out of this, besides taking that fellow down a peg. We owe each other money, you know.'

Mrs Lammle winced a little at the reminder, but only enough to shake her scents and essences anew into the atmosphere of the little carriage, as she settled herself afresh in her own dark corner.

Chapter 12

The Sweat of an Honest Man's Brow

MR MORTIMER LIGHTWOOD and Mr Eugene Wrayburn took a coffee-house dinner together in Mr Lightwood's office. They had newly agreed to set up a joint establishment together. They had taken a bachelor cottage near Hampton, on the brink of the Thames, with a lawn, and a boat-house, and all things fitting, and were to float with the stream through the summer and the Long Vacation.

It was not summer yet, but spring; and it was not gentle spring ethereally mild, as in Thomson's Seasons, but nipping spring with an easterly wind, as in Johnson's, Jackson's, Dickson's, Smith's, and Jones's Seasons. The grating wind sawed rather than blew; and as it sawed, the sawdust whirled about the sawpit. Every street was a sawpit, and there were no top-sawyers; every passenger was an under-sawyer, with the sawdust blinding him and choking him.

That mysterious paper currency which circulates in London when the wind blows, gyrated here and there and everywhere. Whence can it come, whither can it go? It hangs on every bush, flutters in every tree, is caught flying by the electric wires, haunts every enclosure, drinks at every pump, cowers at every grating, shudders upon every plot of grass, seeks rest in vain behind the legions of iron rails. In Paris, where nothing is wasted, costly and luxurious city though it be, but where wonderful human ants creep out of holes and pick up every scrap, there is no such thing. There, it blows nothing but dust. There, sharp eyes and sharp stomachs reap even the east wind, and get something out of it.

The wind sawed, and the sawdust whirled. The shrubs wrung their many hands, bemoaning that they had been over-persuaded by the sun to bud; the young leaves pined; the sparrows repented of their early marriages, like men and women; the colours of the rainbow were discernible, not in floral spring, but in the faces of the people whom it nibbled and pinched. And ever the wind sawed, and the sawdust whirled.

When the spring evenings are too long and light to shut out, and such weather is rife, the city which Mr Podsnap so explanatorily called London, Londres, London, is at its worst. Such a black shrill city, combining the qualities of a smoky house and a scolding wife; such a gritty city; such a hopeless city, with no rent in the leaden canopy of its sky; such a beleaguered city, invested by the great Marsh Forces of Essex and Kent. So the two old schoolfellows felt it to be, as, their dinner done, they turned towards the fire to smoke. Young Blight was gone, the coffee-house waiter was gone, the plates and dishes were gone, the wine was going—but not in the same direction.

'The wind sounds up here,' quoth Eugene, stirring the fire, 'as if we were keeping a lighthouse. I wish we were.'

'Don't you think it would bore us?' Lightwood asked.

'Not more than any other place. And there would be no Circuit to go. But that's a selfish consideration, personal to me.'

'And no clients to come,' added Lightwood. 'Not that that's a selfish consideration at all personal to *me*.'

'If we were on an isolated rock in a stormy sea,' said Eugene, smoking with his eyes on the fire, 'Lady Tippins couldn't put off to visit us, or, better still, might put off and get swamped. People couldn't ask one to wedding breakfasts. There would be no Precedents to hammer at, except the plain-sailing Precedent of keeping the light up. It would be exciting to look out for wrecks.'

'But otherwise,' suggested Lightwood, 'there might be a degree of sameness in the life.'

'I have thought of that also,' said Eugene, as if he really had been considering the subject in its various bearings with an eye to the business; 'but it would be a defined and limited monotony. It would not extend beyond two people. Now, it's a question with me, Mortimer, whether a monotony defined with that precision and limited to that extent, might not be more endurable than the unlimited monotony of one's fellow-creatures.'

As Lightwood laughed and passed the wine, he remarked, 'We shall have an opportunity, in our boating summer, of trying the question.'

'An imperfect one,' Eugene acquiesced, with a sigh, 'but so we shall. I hope we may not prove too much for one another.'

'Now, regarding your respected father,' said Lightwood, bringing him to a subject they had expressly appointed to discuss: always the most slippery eel of eels of subjects to lay hold of.

'Yes, regarding my respected father,' assented Eugene, settling himself in his arm-chair. 'I would rather have approached my respected father by candlelight, as a theme requiring a little artificial brilliancy; but we will take him by twilight, enlivened with a glow of Wallsend.'

He stirred the fire again as he spoke, and having made it blaze, resumed.

'My respected father has found, down in the parental neighbourhood, a wife for his not-generally-respected son.'

'With some money, of course?'

'With some money, of course, or he would not have found her. My respected father—let me shorten the dutiful tautology by substituting in future M. R. F., which sounds military, and rather like the Duke of Wellington.'

'What an absurd fellow you are, Eugene!'

'Not at all, I assure you. M. R. F. having always in the clearest manner provided (as he calls it) for his children by pre-arranging from the hour of the birth of each, and sometimes from an earlier period, what the devoted little victim's calling and course in life should be, M. R. F. pre-arranged for myself that I was to be the barrister I am (with the slight addition of an enormous practice, which has not accrued), and also the married man I am not.'

'The first you have often told me.'

'The first I have often told you. Considering myself sufficiently incongruous on my legal eminence, I have until now suppressed my domestic destiny. You know M. R. F., but not as well as I do. If you knew him as well as I do, he would amuse you.'

'Filially spoken, Eugene!'

'Perfectly so, believe me; and with every sentiment of affectionate deference towards M. R. F. But if he amuses me, I can't help it. When my eldest brother was born, of course the rest of us knew (I mean the rest of us would have known, if we had been in existence) that he was heir to the Family Embarrassments—we call it before the company the Family Estate. But when my second brother was going to be born by-and-by, "this," says M. R. F., "is a little pillar of the church." *Was* born, and became a pillar of the church; a very shaky one. My third brother appeared, considerably in advance of his engagement to my mother; but M. R. F., not at all put out by surprise, instantly declared him a Circumnavigator. Was pitch-forked into the Navy, but has not circumnavigated. I announced myself, and was disposed of with the highly satisfactory results embodied before you. When my younger brother was half an hour old, it was settled by M. R. F. that he should have a mechanical genius. And so on. Therefore I say that M. R. F. amuses me.'

'Touching the lady, Eugene.'

'There M. R. F. ceases to be amusing, because my intentions are opposed to touching the lady.'

'Do you know her?'

'Not in the least.'

'Hadn't you better see her?'

'My dear Mortimer, you have studied my character. Could I possibly go down there, labelled "ELIGIBLE. ON VIEW," and meet the lady, similarly labelled? Anything to carry out M. R. F.'s arrangements, I am sure, with the greatest pleasure—except matrimony. Could I possibly support it? I, so soon bored, so constantly, so fatally?'

'But you are not a consistent fellow, Eugene.'

'In susceptibility to boredom,' returned that worthy, 'I assure you I am the most consistent of mankind.'

'Why, it was but now that you were dwelling on the advantages of a monotony of two.'

'In a lighthouse. Do me the justice to remember the condition. In a lighthouse.'

Mortimer laughed again, and Eugene, having laughed too for the first time, as if he found himself on reflection rather entertaining, relapsed into his usual gloom, and drowsily said, as he enjoyed his cigar, 'No, there is no help for it; one of the prophetic deliveries of M. R. F. must for ever remain unfulfilled. With every disposition to oblige him, he must submit to a failure.'

It had grown darker as they talked, and the wind was sawing and the sawdust was whirling outside paler windows. The underlying churchyard was already settling into deep dim shade, and the shade was creeping up to the housetops among which they sat. 'As if,' said Eugene, 'as if the churchyard ghosts were rising.'

He had walked to the window with his cigar in his mouth, to exalt its flavour by comparing the fireside with the outside, when he stopped midway on his return to his arm-chair, and said:

'Apparently one of the ghosts has lost its way, and dropped in to be directed. Look at this phantom!'

Lightwood, whose back was towards the door, turned his head, and there, in the darkness of the entry, stood a something in the likeness of a man: to whom he addressed the not irrelevant inquiry, 'Who the devil are you?'

'I ask your pardons, Governors,' replied the ghost, in a hoarse double-barrelled whisper, 'but might either on you be Lawyer Lightwood?'

'What do you mean by not knocking at the door?' demanded Mortimer.

'I ask your pardons, Governors,' replied the ghost, as before, 'but probable you was not aware your door stood open.'

'What do you want?'

Hereunto the ghost again hoarsely replied, in its double-barrelled manner, 'I ask your pardons, Governors, but might one on you be Lawyer Lightwood?'

'One of us is,' said the owner of that name.

'All right, Governors Both,' returned the ghost, carefully closing the room door; ' 'tickler business.'

Mortimer lighted the candles. They showed the visitor to be an ill-looking visitor with a squinting leer, who, as he spoke, fumbled at an old sodden fur cap, formless and mangey, that looked like a furry animal, dog or cat, puppy or kitten, drowned and decaying.

'Now,' said Mortimer, 'what is it?'

'Governors Both,' returned the man, in what he meant to be a wheedling tone, 'which on you might be Lawyer Lightwood?'

'I am.'

'Lawyer Lightwood,' ducking at him with a servile air, 'I am a man as gets my living, and as seeks to get my living, by the sweat of my brow. Not to risk being done out of the sweat of my brow, by any chances, I should wish afore going further to be swore in.'

'I am not a swearer in of people, man.'

The visitor, clearly anything but reliant on this assurance, doggedly muttered 'Alfred David.'

'Is that your name?' asked Lightwood.

'My name?' returned the man. 'No; I want to take a Alfred David.'

(Which Eugene, smoking and contemplating him, interpreted as meaning Affidavit.)

'I tell you, my good fellow,' said Lightwood, with his indolent laugh, 'that I have nothing to do with swearing.'

'He can swear *at* you,' Eugene explained; 'and so can I. But we can't do more for you.'

Much discomfited by this information, the visitor turned the drowned dog or cat, puppy or kitten, about and about, and looked from one of the Governors Both to the other of the Governors Both, while he deeply considered within himself. At length he decided:

'Then I must be took down.'

'Where?' asked Lightwood.

'Here,' said the man. 'In pen and ink.'

'First, let us know what your business is about.'

'It's about,' said the man, taking a step forward, dropping his hoarse voice, and shading it with his hand, 'it's about from five to ten thousand pound reward. That's what it's about. It's about Murder. That's what it's about.'

'Come nearer the table. Sit down. Will you have a glass of wine?'

'Yes, I will,' said the man; 'and I don't deceive you, Governors.'

It was given him. Making a stiff arm to the elbow, he poured the wine into his mouth, tilted it into his right cheek, as saying, 'What do you think of it?' tilted it into his left cheek, as saying, 'What do *you* think of it?' jerked it into his stomach, as saying, 'What do *you* think of it?' To conclude, smacked his lips, as if all three replied, 'We think well of it.'

'Will you have another?'

'Yes, I will,' he repeated, 'and I don't deceive you, Governors.' And also repeated the other proceedings.

'Now,' began Lightwood, 'what's your name?'

'Why, there you're rather fast, Lawyer Lightwood,' he replied, in a remonstrant manner. 'Don't you see, Lawyer Lightwood? There you're a little bit fast. I'm going to earn from five to ten thousand pound by the sweat of my brow; and as a poor man doing justice to the sweat of my brow, is it likely I can afford to part with so much as my name without its being took down?'

Deferring to the man's sense of the binding powers of pen and ink and paper, Lightwood nodded acceptance of Eugene's nodded proposal to take those spells in hand. Eugene, bringing them to the table, sat down as clerk or notary.

'Now,' said Lightwood, 'what's your name?'

But further precaution was still due to the sweat of this honest fellow's brow.

'I should wish, Lawyer Lightwood,' he stipulated, 'to have that T'other Governor as my witness that what I said I said. Consequent, will the T'other Governor be so good as chuck me his name and where he lives?'

Eugene, cigar in mouth and pen in hand, tossed him his card. After spelling it out slowly, the man made it into a little roll, and tied it up in an end of his neckerchief still more slowly.

'Now,' said Lightwood, for the third time, 'if you have quite completed your various preparations, my friend, and have fully ascertained that your spirits are cool and not in any way hurried, what's your name?'

'Roger Riderhood.'

'Dwelling-place?'

'Lime'us Hole.'

'Calling or occupation?'

Not quite so glib with this answer as with the previous two, Mr Riderhood gave in the definition, 'Waterside character.'

'Anything against you?' Eugene quietly put in, as he wrote.

Rather baulked, Mr Riderhood evasively remarked, with an innocent air, that he believed the T'other Governor had asked him summa't.

'Ever in trouble?' said Eugene.

'Once.' (Might happen to any man, Mr Riderhood added incidentally.)

'On suspicion of—?'

'Of seaman's pocket,' said Mr Riderhood. 'Whereby I was in reality the man's best friend, and tried to take care of him.'

'With the sweat of your brow?' asked Eugene.

'Till it poured down like rain,' said Roger Riderhood.

Eugene leaned back in his chair, and smoked with his eyes negligently turned on the informer, and his pen ready to reduce him to more writing. Lightwood also smoked, with his eyes negligently turned on the informer.

'Now let me be took down again,' said Riderhood, when he had turned the drowned cap over and under, and had brushed it the wrong way (if it had a right way) with his sleeve. 'I give information that the man that done the Harmon Murder is Gaffer Hexam, the man that found the body. The hand of Jesse Hexam, commonly called Gaffer on the river and along shore, is the hand that done that deed. His hand and no other.'

The two friends glanced at one another with more serious faces than they had shown yet.

'Tell us on what grounds you make this accusation,' said Mortimer Lightwood.

'On the grounds,' answered Riderhood, wiping his face with his sleeve, 'that I was Gaffer's pardner, and suspected of him many a long day and many a dark night. On the grounds that I knowed his ways. On the grounds that I broke the pardnership because I see the danger; which I warn you his daughter may tell you another story about that, for anythink I can say, but you know what it'll be worth, for she'd tell you lies, the world round and the heavens broad, to save her father. On the grounds that it's well understood along the cause'ays and the stairs that he done it. On the grounds that he's fell off from, because he done it. On the grounds that I will swear he done it. On the grounds that you may take me where you will, and get me sworn to it. *I* don't want to back out of the consequences. I have made up *my* mind. Take me anywheres.'

'All this is nothing,' said Lightwood.

'Nothing?' repeated Riderhood, indignantly and amazedly.

'Merely nothing. It goes to no more than that you suspect this man of the crime. You may do so with some reason, or you may do so with no reason, but he cannot be convicted on your suspicion.'

'Haven't I said—I appeal to the T'other Governor as my witness—haven't I said from the first minute that I opened my mouth in this here world-without-end-everlasting chair' (he evidently used that form of words as next in force to an affidavit), 'that I was willing to swear that he done it? Haven't I said, Take me and get me sworn to it? Don't I say so now? You won't deny it, Lawyer Lightwood?'

'Surely not; but you only offer to swear to your suspicion, and I tell you it is not enough to swear to your suspicion.'

'Not enough, ain't it, Lawyer Lightwood?' he cautiously demanded.

'Positively not.'

'And did I say it *was* enough? Now, I appeal to the T'other Governor. Now, fair! Did I say so?'

'He certainly has not said that he had no more to tell,' Eugene observed in a low voice without looking at him, 'whatever he seemed to imply.'

'Hah!' cried the informer, triumphantly perceiving that the remark was generally in his favour, though apparently not closely understanding it. '"Fort'nate for me I had a witness!'

'Go on, then,' said Lightwood. 'Say out what you have to say. No after-thought.'

'Let me be took down then!' cried the informer, eagerly and anxiously. 'Let me be took down, for by George and the Draggin I'm a coming to it now! Don't do nothing to keep back from a honest man the fruits of the sweat of his brow! I give information, then, that he told me that he done it. Is *that* enough?'

'Take care what you say, my friend,' returned Mortimer.

'Lawyer Lightwood, take care, you, what I say; for I judge you'll be answerable for follering it up!' Then, slowly and emphatically beating it all out with his open right hand on the palm of his left; 'I, Roger Riderhood, Lime'us Hole, Waterside character, tell you, Lawyer Lightwood, that the man Jesse Hexam, commonly called upon the river and along-shore Gaffer, told me that he done the deed. What's more, he told me with his own lips that he done the deed. What's more, he said that he done the deed. And I'll swear it!'

'Where did he tell you so?'

'Outside,' replied Riderhood, always beating it out, with his head determinedly set askew, and his eyes watchfully dividing their attention between his two auditors, 'outside the door of the Six Jolly Fellowships, towards a quarter after twelve o'clock at midnight—but I will not in my conscience undertake to swear to so fine a matter as five minutes—on the night when he picked up the body. The Six Jolly Fellowships won't run away. If it turns out that he warn't at the Six Jolly Fellowships that night at midnight, I'm a liar.'

'What did he say?'

'I'll tell you (take me down, T'other Governor, I ask no better). He come out first; I come out last. I might be a minute arter him; I might be half a minute, I might be a quarter of a minute; I cannot swear to that, and therefore I won't. That's knowing the obligations of a Alfred David, ain't it?'

'Go on.'

'I found him a waiting to speak to me. He says to me, "Rogue Riderhood"—for that's the name I'm mostly called by—not for any meaning in it, for meaning it has none, but because of its being similar to Roger.'

'Never mind that.'

' 'Scuse *me*, Lawyer Lightwood, it's a part of the truth, and as such I do mind it, and I must mind it and I will mind it. "Rogue Riderhood," he says, "words passed betwixt us on the river tonight." Which they had; ask his daughter! "I threatened you," he says, "to chop you over the fingers with my boat's stretcher, or take a aim at your brains with my boathook. I did so on accounts of your looking too hard at what I had in tow, as if you was suspicious, and on accounts of your holding on to the gunwale of my boat." I says to him, "Gaffer, I know it." He says to me, "Rogue Riderhood, you are a man in a dozen"—I think he said in a score, but of that I am not positive, so take the lowest figure, for precious be the obligations of a Alfred David. "And," he says, "when your fellow-men is up, be it their lives or be it their watches, sharp is ever the word with you. Had you suspicions?" I says, "'Gaffer, I had; and what's more, I have." He falls a shaking, and he says, "Of what?" I says, "Of foul play." He falls a shaking worse, and he says, "There *was* foul play then. I done it for his money. Don't betray me!" Those were the words as ever he used.'

There was a silence, broken only by the fall of the ashes in the grate. An opportunity which the informer improved by smearing himself all over the head and neck and face with his drowned cap, and not at all improving his own appearance.

'What more?' asked Lightwood.

'Of him, d'ye mean, Lawyer Lightwood?'

'Of anything to the purpose.'

'Now, I'm blest if I understand you, Governors Both,' said the informer, in a creeping manner: propitiating both, though only one had spoken. 'What? Ain't *that* enough?'

'Did you ask him how he did it, where he did it, when he did it?'

'Far be it from me, Lawyer Lightwood! I was so troubled in my mind, that I wouldn't have knowed more, no, not for the sum as I expect to earn from you by the sweat of my brow, twice told! I had put an end to the pardnership. I had cut the connexion. I couldn't undo what was done; and when he begs and prays, "Old pardner, on my knees, don't split upon me!" I only makes answer "Never speak another word to Roger Riderhood, nor look him in the face!" and I shuns that man.'

Having given these words a swing to make them mount the higher and go the further, Rogue Riderhood poured himself out another glass of wine unbidden, and seemed to chew it, as, with the half-emptied glass in his hand, he stared at the candles.

Mortimer glanced at Eugene, but Eugene sat glowering at his paper, and would give him no responsive glance. Mortimer again turned to the informer, to whom he said:

'You have been troubled in your mind a long time, man?'

Giving his wine a final chew, and swallowing it, the informer answered in a single word:

'Hages!'

'When all that stir was made, when the Government reward was offered, when the police were on the alert, when the whole country rang with the crime!' said Mortimer, impatiently.

'Hah!' Mr Riderhood very slowly and hoarsely chimed in, with several retrospective nods of his head. 'Warn't I troubled in my mind then!'

'When conjecture ran wild, when the most extravagant suspicions were afloat, when half a dozen innocent people might have been laid by the heels any hour in the day!' said Mortimer, almost warming.

'Hah!' Mr Riderhood chimed in, as before. 'Warn't I troubled in my mind through it all!'

'But he hadn't,' said Eugene, drawing a lady's head upon his writing-paper, and touching it at intervals, 'the opportunity then of earning so much money, you see.'

'The T'other Governor hits the nail, Lawyer Lightwood! It was that as turned me. I had many times and again struggled to relieve myself of the trouble on my mind, but I couldn't get it off. I had once very nigh got it off to Miss Abbey Potterson which keeps the Six Jolly Fellowships—there is the 'ouse, it won't run away,—there lives the lady, she ain't likely to be struck dead afore you get there—ask her!—but I couldn't do it. At last, out comes the new bill with your own lawful name, Lawyer Lightwood, printed to it, and then I asks the question of my own intellects, Am I to have this trouble on my mind for ever? Am I never to throw it off? Am I always to think more of Gaffer than of my own self? If he's got a daughter, ain't *I* got a daughter?'

'And echo answered—?' Eugene suggested.

' "You have," ' said Mr Riderhood, in a firm tone.

'Incidentally mentioning, at the same time, her age?' inquired Eugene.

'Yes, governor. Two-and-twenty last October. And then I put it to myself, "Regarding the money. It is a pot of money." For it *is* a pot,' said Mr Riderhood, with candour, 'and why deny it?'

'Hear!' from Eugene as he touched his drawing.

' "It is a pot of money; but is it a sin for a labouring man that moistens every crust of bread he earns, with his tears—or if not with them, with the colds he catches in his head—is it a sin for that man to earn it? Say there is anything again earning it." This I put to myself strong, as in duty bound; "how can it be said without blaming Lawyer Lightwood for offering it to be earned?'' And was it for *me* to blame Lawyer Lightwood? No.'

'No,' said Eugene.

'Certainly not, Governor,' Mr Riderhood acquiesced. 'So I made up my mind to get my trouble off my mind, and to earn by the sweat of my brow what was held out to me. And what's more,' he added, suddenly turning bloodthirsty, 'I mean to have it! And now I tell you, once and away, Lawyer Lightwood, that Jesse Hexam, commonly called Gaffer, his hand and no other, done the deed, on his own confession to me. And I give him up to you, and I want him took. This night!'

After another silence, broken only by the fall of the ashes in the grate, which attracted the informer's attention as if it were the chinking of money, Mortimer Lightwood leaned over his friend, and said in a whisper:

'I suppose I must go with this fellow to our imperturbable friend at the police-station.'

'I suppose,' said Eugene, 'there is no help for it.'

'Do you believe him?'

'I believe him to be a thorough rascal. But he may tell the truth, for his own purpose, and for this occasion only.'

'It doesn't look like it.'

'*He* doesn't,' said Eugene. 'But neither is his late partner, whom he denounces, a prepossessing person. The firm are cut-throat Shepherds both, in appearance. I should like to ask him one thing.'

The subject of this conference sat leering at the ashes, trying with all his might to overhear what was said, but feigning abstraction as the 'Governors Both' glanced at him.

'You mentioned (twice, I think) a daughter of this Hexam's,' said Eugene, aloud. 'You don't mean to imply that she had any guilty knowledge of the crime?'

The honest man, after considering—perhaps considering how his answer might affect the fruits of the sweat of his brow—replied, unreservedly, 'No, I don't.'

'And you implicate no other person?'

'It ain't what I implicate, it's what Gaffer implicated,' was the dogged and determined answer. 'I don't pretend to know more than that his words to me was, "I done it." Those was his words.'

'I must see this out, Mortimer,' whispered Eugene, rising. 'How shall we go?'

'Let us walk,' whispered Lightwood, 'and give this fellow time to think of it.'

Having exchanged the question and answer, they prepared themselves for going out, and Mr Riderhood rose. While extinguishing the candles, Lightwood, quite as a matter of course took up the glass from which that honest gentleman had drunk, and coolly tossed it under the grate, where it fell shivering into fragments.

'Now, if you will take the lead,' said Lightwood, 'Mr Wrayburn and I will follow. You know where to go, I suppose?'

'I suppose I do, Lawyer Lightwood.'

'Take the lead, then.'

The waterside character pulled his drowned cap over his ears with both hands, and making himself more round-shouldered than nature had made him, by the sullen and persistent slouch with which he went, went down the stairs, round by the Temple Church, across the Temple into Whitefriars, and so on by the waterside streets.

'Look at his hang-dog air,' said Lightwood, following.

'It strikes me rather as a hang-*man* air,' returned Eugene. 'He has undeniable intentions that way.'

They said little else as they followed. He went on before them as an ugly Fate might have done, and they kept him in view, and would have been glad enough to lose sight of him. But on he went before them, always at the same distance, and the same rate. Aslant against the hard implacable weather and the rough wind, he was no more to be driven back than hurried forward, but held on like an advancing Destiny. There came, when they were about midway on their journey, a heavy rush of hail, which in a few minutes pelted the streets clear, and whitened them. It made no difference to him. A man's life being to be taken and the price of it got, the hailstones to arrest the purpose must lie larger and deeper than those. He crushed through them, leaving marks in the fast-melting slush that were mere shapeless holes; one might have fancied, following, that the very fashion of humanity had departed from his feet.

The blast went by, and the moon contended with the fast-flying clouds, and the wild disorder reigning up there made the pitiful little tumults in the streets of no account. It was not that the wind swept all the brawlers into places of shelter, as it had swept the hail still lingering in heaps wherever there was refuge for it; but that it seemed as if the streets were absorbed by the sky, and the night were all in the air.

'If he has had time to think of it,' said Eugene, 'he has not had time to think better of it—or differently of it, if that's better.

There is no sign of drawing back in him; and as I recollect this place, we must be close upon the corner where we alighted that night.'

In fact, a few abrupt turns brought them to the river side, where they had slipped about among the stones, and where they now slipped more; the wind coming against them in slants and flaws, across the tide and the windings of the river, in a furious way. With that habit of getting under the lee of any shelter which waterside characters acquire, the waterside character at present in question led the way to the leeside of the Six Jolly Fellowship Porters before he spoke.

'Look round here, Lawyer Lightwood, at them red curtains. It's the Fellowships, the 'ouse as I told you wouldn't run away. And has it run away?'

Not showing himself much impressed by this remarkable confirmation of the informer's evidence, Lightwood inquired what other business they had there?

'I wished you to see the Fellowships for yourself, Lawyer Lightwood, that you might judge whether I'm a liar; and now I'll see Gaffer's window for myself, that we may know whether he's at home.'

With that, he crept away.

'He'll come back, I suppose?' murmured Lightwood.

'Ay! and go through with it,' murmured Eugene.

He came back after a very short interval indeed.

'Gaffer's out, and his boat's out. His daughter's at home, sitting a-looking at the fire. But there's some supper getting ready, so Gaffer's expected. I can find what move he's upon, easy enough, presently.'

Then he beckoned and led the way again, and they came to the police-station, still as clean and cool and steady as before, saving that the flame of its lamp—being but a lamp-flame, and only attached to the Force as an outsider—flickered in the wind.

Also, within doors, Mr Inspector was at his studies as of yore. He recognized the friends the instant they reappeared, but their reappearance had no effect on his composure. Not even the circumstance that Riderhood was their conductor moved him, otherwise than that as he took a dip of ink he seemed, by a settlement of his chin in his stock, to propound to that personage, without looking at him, the question, 'What have *you* been up to, last?'

Mortimer Lightwood asked him, would he be so good as look at those notes? Handing him Eugene's.

Having read the first few lines, Mr Inspector mounted to that (for him) extraordinary pitch of emotion that he said, 'Does either of you two gentlemen happen to have a pinch of snuff about him?' Finding that neither had, he did quite as well without it, and read on.

'Have you heard these read?' he then demanded of the honest man.

'No,' said Riderhood.

'Then you had better hear them.' And so read them aloud, in an official manner.

'Are these notes correct, now, as to the information you bring here and the evidence you mean to give?' he asked, when he had finished reading.

'They are. They are as correct,' returned Mr Riderhood, 'as I am. I can't say more than that for 'em.'

'I'll take this man myself, sir,' said Mr Inspector to Lightwood. Then to Riderhood, 'Is he at home? Where is he? What's he doing? You have made it your business to know all about him, no doubt.'

Riderhood said what he did know, and promised to find out in a few minutes what he didn't know.

'Stop,' said Mr Inspector; 'not till I tell you. We mustn't look like business. Would you two gentlemen object to making a pretence of taking a glass of something in my company at the Fellowships? Well-conducted house, and highly respectable landlady.'

They replied that they would be happy to substitute a reality for the pretence, which, in the main, appeared to be as one with Mr Inspector's meaning.

'Very good,' said he, taking his hat from its peg, and putting a pair of handcuffs in his pocket as if they were his gloves. 'Reserve!' Reserve saluted. 'You know where to find me?' Reserve again saluted. 'Riderhood, when you have found out concerning his coming home, come round to the window of Cosy, tap twice at it, and wait for me. Now, gentlemen.'

As the three went out together, and Riderhood slouched off from under the trembling lamp his separate way, Lightwood asked the officer what he thought of this?

Mr Inspector replied, with due generality and reticence, that it was always more likely that a man had done a bad thing than that he hadn't. That he himself had several times 'reckoned up' Gaffer, but had never been able to bring him to a satisfactory criminal total. That if this story was true, it was only in part true.

That the two men, very shy characters, would have been jointly and pretty equally 'in it;' but that this man had 'spotted' the other, to save himself and get the money.

'And I think,' added Mr Inspector, in conclusion, 'that if all goes well with him, he's in a tolerable way of getting it. But as this is the Fellowships, gentlemen, where the lights are, I recommend dropping the subject. You can't do better than be interested in some lime works anywhere down about Northfleet, and doubtful whether some of your lime don't get into bad company as it comes up in barges.'

'You hear Eugene?' said Lightwood, over his shoulder. 'You are deeply interested in lime.'

'Without lime,' returned that unmoved barrister-at-law, 'my existence would be unilluminated by a ray of hope.'

Chapter 13
Tracking the Bird of Prey

THE two lime merchants, with their escort, entered the dominions of Miss Abbey Potterson, to whom their escort (presenting them and their pretended business over the half-door of the bar, in a confidential way) preferred his figurative request that 'a mouthful of fire' might be lighted in Cosy. Always well disposed to assist the constituted authorities, Miss Abbey bade Bob Gliddery attend the gentlemen to that retreat, and promptly enliven it with fire and gaslight. Of this commission the bare-armed Bob, leading the way with a flaming wisp of paper, so speedily acquitted himself, that Cosy seemed to leap out of a dark sleep and embrace them warmly, the moment they passed the lintels of its hospitable door.

'They burn sherry very well here,' said Mr Inspector, as a piece of local intelligence. 'Perhaps you gentlemen might like a bottle?'

The answer being By all means, Bob Gliddery received his instructions from Mr Inspector, and departed in a becoming state of alacrity engendered by reverence for the majesty of the law.

'It's a certain fact,' said Mr Inspector, 'that this man we have received our information from,' indicating Riderhood with his thumb over his shoulder, 'has for some time past given the other man a bad name arising out of your lime barges, and that the other man has been avoided in consequence. I don't say what it means or proves, but it's a certain fact. I had it first from one of the opposite sex of my acquaintance,' vaguely indicating Miss Abbey with his thumb over his shoulder, 'down away at a distance, over yonder.'

Then probably Mr Inspector was not quite unprepared for their visit that evening? Lightwood hinted.

'Well you see,' said Mr Inspector, 'it was a question of making a move. It's of no use moving if you don't know what your move is. You had better by far keep still. In the matter of this lime, I certainly had an idea that it might lie betwixt the two men; I always had that idea. Still I was forced to wait for a start, and I wasn't so lucky as to get a start. This man that we have received our information from, has got a start, and if he don't meet with a check he may make the running and come in first. There may turn out to be something considerable for him that comes in second, and I don't mention who may or who may not try for that place. There's duty to do, and I shall do it, under any circumstances, to the best of my judgment and ability.'

'Speaking as a shipper of lime—' began Eugene.

'Which no man has a better right to do than yourself, you know,' said Mr Inspector.

'I hope not,' said Eugene; 'my father having been a shipper of lime before me, and my grandfather before him—in fact we having been a family immersed to the crowns of our heads in lime during several generations—I beg to observe that if this missing lime could be got hold of without any young female relative of any distinguished gentleman engaged in the lime trade (which I cherish next to my life) being present, I think it might be a more agreeable proceeding to the assisting bystanders, that is to say, lime-burners.'

'I also,' said Lightwood, pushing his friend aside with a laugh, 'should much prefer that.'

'It shall be done, gentlemen, if it can be done conveniently,' said Mr Inspector, with coolness. 'There is no wish on my part to cause any distress in that quarter. Indeed, I am sorry for that quarter.'

'There was a boy in that quarter,' remarked Eugene. 'He is still there?'

'No,' said Mr Inspector. 'He has quitted those works. He is otherwise disposed of.'

'Will she be left alone then?' asked Eugene.

'She will be left,' said Mr Inspector, 'alone.'

Bob's reappearance with a steaming jug broke off the conversation. But although the jug steamed forth a delicious perfume, its contents had not received that last happy touch which the surpassing finish of the Six Jolly Fellowship Porters imparted on such momentous occasions. Bob carried in his left hand one of those iron models of sugar-loaf hats, before mentioned, into which he emptied the jug, and the pointed end of which he thrust deep down into the fire, so leaving it for a few moments while he disappeared and reappeared with three bright drinking-glasses. Placing these on the table and bending over the fire, meritoriously sensible of the trying nature of his duty, he watched the wreaths of steam, until at the special instant of projection he caught up the iron vessel and gave it one delicate twirl, causing it to send forth one gentle hiss. Then he restored the contents to the jug; held over the steam of the jug, each of the three bright glasses in succession; finally filled them all, and with a clear conscience awaited the applause of his fellow-creatures.

It was bestowed (Mr Inspector having proposed as an appropriate sentiment 'The lime trade!') and Bob withdrew to report the commendations of the guests to Miss Abbey in the bar. It may be here in confidence admitted that, the room being close shut in his absence, there had not appeared to be the slightest reason for the elaborate maintenance of this same lime fiction. Only it had been regarded by Mr Inspector as so uncommonly satisfactory, and so fraught with mysterious virtues, that neither of his clients had presumed to question it.

Two taps were now heard on the outside of the window. Mr Inspector, hastily fortifying himself with another glass, strolled out with a noiseless foot and an unoccupied countenance. As one might go to survey the weather and the general aspect of the heavenly bodies.

'This is becoming grim, Mortimer,' said Eugene, in a low voice. 'I don't like this.'

'Nor I,' said Lightwood. 'Shall we go?'

'Being here, let us stay. You ought to see it out, and I won't leave you. Besides, that lonely girl with the dark hair runs in my head. It was little more than a glimpse we had of her that last time, and yet I almost see her waiting by the fire to-night.

Do you feel like a dark combination of traitor and pickpocket when you think of that girl?'

'Rather,' returned Lightwood. 'Do you?'

'Very much so.'

Their escort strolled back again, and reported. Divested of its various lime-lights and shadows, his report went to the effect that Gaffer was away in his boat, supposed to be on his old look-out; that he had been expected last high-water; that having missed it for some reason or other, he was not, according to his usual habits at night, to be counted on before next high-water, or it might be an hour or so later; that his daughter, surveyed through the window, would seem to be so expecting him, for the supper was not cooking, but set out ready to be cooked; that it would be high-water at about one, and that it was now barely ten; that there was nothing to be done but watch and wait; that the informer was keeping watch at the instant of that present reporting, but that two heads were better than one (especially when the second was Mr Inspector's); and that the reporter meant to share the watch. And forasmuch as crouching under the lee of a hauled-up boat on a night when it blew cold and strong, and when the weather was varied with blasts of hail at times, might be wearisome to amateurs, the reporter closed with the recommendation that the two gentlemen should remain, for a while at any rate, in their present quarters, which were weather-tight and warm.

They were not inclined to dispute this recommendation, but they wanted to know where they could join the watchers when so disposed. Rather than trust to a verbal description of the place, which might mislead, Eugene (with a less weighty sense of personal trouble on him than he usually had) would go out with Mr Inspector, note the spot, and come back.

On the shelving bank of the river, among the slimy stones of a causeway—not the special causeway of the Six Jolly Fellowships, which had a landing-place of its own, but another, a little removed, and very near to the old windmill which was the denounced man's dwelling-place—were a few boats; some, moored and already beginning to float; others, hauled up above the reach of the tide. Under one of these latter, Eugene's companion disappeared. And when Eugene had observed its position with reference to the other boats, and had made sure that he could not miss it, he turned his eyes upon the building where, as he had been told, the lonely girl with the dark hair sat by the fire.

He could see the light of the fire shining through the

window. Perhaps it drew him on to look in. Perhaps he had come out with the express intention. That part of the bank having rank grass growing on it, there was no difficulty in getting close, without any noise of footsteps: it was but to scramble up a ragged face of pretty hard mud some three or four feet high and come upon the grass and to the window. He came to the window by that means.

She had no other light than the light of the fire. The unkindled lamp stood on the table. She sat on the ground, looking at the brazier, with her face leaning on her hand. There was a kind of film or flicker on her face, which at first he took to be the fitful firelight; but, on a second look, he saw that she was weeping. A sad and solitary spectacle, as shown him by the rising and the falling of the fire.

It was a little window of but four pieces of glass, and was not curtained; he chose it because the larger window near it was. It showed him the room, and the bills upon the wall respecting the drowned people starting out and receding by turns. But he glanced slightly at them, though he looked long and steadily at her. A deep rich piece of colour, with the brown flush of her cheek and the shining lustre of her hair, though sad and solitary, weeping by the rising and the falling of the fire.

She started up. He had been so very still that he felt sure it was not he who had disturbed her, so merely withdrew from the window and stood near it in the shadow of the wall. She opened the door, and said in an alarmed tone, 'Father, was that you calling me?' And again, 'Father!' And once again, after listening, 'Father! I thought I heard you call me twice before!'

No response. As she re-entered at the door, he dropped over the bank and made his way back, among the ooze and near the hiding-place, to Mortimer Lightwood: to whom he told what he had seen of the girl, and how this was becoming very grim indeed.

'If the real man feels as guilty as I do,' said Eugene, 'he is remarkably uncomfortable.'

'Influence of secrecy,' suggested Lightwood.

'I am not at all obliged to it for making me Guy Fawkes in the vault and a Sneak in the area both at once,' said Eugene. 'Give me some more of that stuff.'

Lightwood helped him to some more of that stuff, but it had been cooling, and didn't answer now.

'Pooh,' said Eugene, spitting it out among the ashes. 'Tastes like the wash of the river.'

'Are you so familiar with the flavour of the wash of the river?'

'I seem to be to-night. I feel as if I had been half drowned, and swallowing a gallon of it.'

'Influence of locality,' suggested Lightwood.

'You are mighty learned to-night, you and your influences,' returned Eugene. 'How long shall we stay here?'

'How long do you think?'

'If I could choose, I should say a minute,' replied Eugene, 'for the Jolly Fellowship Porters are not the jolliest dogs I have known. But I suppose we are best here until they turn us out with the other suspicious characters, at midnight.'

Thereupon he stirred the fire, and sat down on one side of it. It struck eleven, and he made believe to compose himself patiently. But gradually he took the fidgets in one leg, and then in the other leg, and then in one arm, and then in the other arm, and then in his chin, and then in his back, and then in his forehead, and then in his hair, and then in his nose; and then he stretched himself recumbent on two chairs, and groaned; and then he started up.

'Invisible insects of diabolical activity swarm in this place. I am tickled and twitched all over. Mentally, I have now committed a burglary under the meanest circumstances, and the myrmidons of justice are at my heels.'

'I am quite as bad,' said Lightwood, sitting up facing him, with a tumbled head, after going through some wonderful evolutions, in which his head had been the lowest part of him. 'This restlessness began with me, long ago. All the time you were out, I felt like Gulliver with the Lilliputians firing upon him.'

'It won't do, Mortimer. We must get into the air; we must join our dear friend and brother, Riderhood. And let us tranquillize ourselves by making a compact. Next time (with a view to our peace of mind) we'll commit the crime, instead of taking the criminal. You swear it?'

'Certainly.'

'Sworn! Let Tippins look to it. Her life's in danger.'

Mortimer rang the bell to pay the score, and Bob appeared to transact that business with him: whom Eugene, in his careless extravagance, asked if he would like a situation in the lime-trade?

'Thankee sir, no sir,' said Bob. 'I've a good sitiwation here, sir.'

'If you change your mind at any time,' returned Eugene,

'come to me at my works, and you'll always find an opening in the lime-kiln.'

'Thankee sir,' said Bob.

'This is my partner,' said Eugene, 'who keeps the books and attends to the wages. A fair day's wages for a fair day's work is ever my partner's motto.'

'And a very good 'un it is, gentlemen,' said Bob, receiving his fee, and drawing a bow out of his head with his right hand, very much as he would have drawn a pint of beer out of the beer engine.

'Eugene,' Mortimer apostrophized him, laughing quite heartily when they were alone again, 'how *can* you be so ridiculous?'

'I am in a ridiculous humour,' quoth Eugene; 'I am a ridiculous fellow. Everything is ridiculous. Come along!'

It passed into Mortimer Lightwood's mind that a change of some sort, best expressed perhaps as an intensification of all that was wildest and most negligent and reckless in his friend, had come upon him in the last half-hour or so. Thoroughly used to him as he was, he found something new and strained in him that was for the moment perplexing. This passed into his mind, and passed out again; but he remembered it afterwards.

'There's where she sits, you see,' said Eugene, when they were standing under the bank, roared and riven at by the wind. 'There's the light of her fire.'

'I'll take a peep through the window,' said Mortimer.

'No, don't!' Eugene caught him by the arm. 'Best not make a show of her. Come to our honest friend.'

He led him to the post of watch, and they both dropped down and crept under the lee of the boat; a better shelter than it had seemed before, being directly contrasted with the blowing wind and the bare night.

'Mr Inspector at home?' whispered Eugene.

'Here I am, sir.'

'And our friend of the perspiring brow is at the far corner there? Good. Anything happened?'

'His daughter has been out, thinking she heard him calling, unless it was a sign to him to keep out of the way. It might have been.'

'It might have been Rule Britannia,' muttered Eugene, 'but it wasn't. Mortimer!'

'Here!' (On the other side of Mr Inspector.)

'Two burglaries now, and a forgery!'

With this indication of his depressed state of mind, Eugene fell silent.

They were all silent for a long while. As it got to be flood-tide, and the water came nearer to them, noises on the river became more frequent, and they listened more. To the turning of steam-paddles, to the clinking of iron chain, to the creaking of blocks, to the measured working of oars, to the occasional violent barking of some passing dog on shipboard, who seemed to scent them lying in their hiding-place. The night was not so dark but that, besides the lights at bows and mast-heads gliding to and fro, they could discern some shadowy bulk attached; and now and then a ghostly lighter with a large dark sail, like a warning arm, would start up very near them, pass on, and vanish. At this time of their watch, the water close to them would be often agitated by some impulsion given it from a distance. Often they believed this beat and plash to be the boat they lay in wait for, running in ashore; and again and again they would have started up, but for the immobility with which the informer, well used to the river, kept quiet in his place.

The wind carried away the striking of the great multitude of city church clocks, for those lay to leeward of them; but there were bells to windward that told them of its being One—Two—Three. Without that aid they would have known how the night wore, by the falling of the tide, recorded in the appearance of an ever-widening black wet strip of shore, and the emergence of the paved causeway from the river, foot by foot.

As the time so passed, this slinking business became a more and more precarious one. It would seem as if the man had had some intimation of what was in hand against him, or had taken fright? His movements might have been planned to gain for him, in getting beyond their reach, twelve hours' advantage? The honest man who had expended the sweat of his brow became uneasy, and began to complain with bitterness of the proneness of man-kind to cheat him—him invested with the dignity of Labour!

Their retreat was so chosen that while they could watch the river, they could watch the house. No one had passed in or out, since the daughter thought she heard the father calling. No one could pass in or out without being seen.

'But it will be light at five,' said Mr Inspector, 'and then *we* shall be seen.'

'Look here,' said Riderhood, 'what do you say to this? He may have been lurking in and out, and just holding his own betwixt two or three bridges, for hours back.'

'What do you make of that?' said Mr Inspector. Stoical, but contradictory.

'He may be doing so at this present time.'

'What do you make of *that*?' said Mr Inspector.

'My boat's among them boats here at the cause'ay.'

'And what do you make of your boat?' said Mr Inspector.

'What if I put off in her and take a look round? I know his ways, and the likely nooks he favours. I know where he'd be at such a time of the tide, and where he'd be at such another time. Ain't I been his pardner? None of you need show. None of you need stir. I can shove her off without help; and as to me being seen, I'm about at all times.'

'You might have given a worse opinion,' said Mr Inspector, after brief consideration. 'Try it.'

'Stop a bit. Let's work it out. If I want you, I'll drop round under the Fellowships and tip you a whistle.'

'If I might so far presume as to offer a suggestion to my honourable and gallant friend, whose knowledge of naval matters far be it from me to impeach,' Eugene struck in with great deliberation, 'it would be, that to tip a whistle is to advertise mystery and invite speculation. My honourable and gallant friend will, I trust, excuse me, as an independent member, for throwing out a remark which I feel to be due to this house and the country.'

'Was that the T'other Governor, or Lawyer Lightwood?' asked Riderhood. For, they spoke as they crouched or lay, without seeing one another's faces.

'In reply to the question put by my honourable and gallant friend,' said Eugene, who was lying on his back with his hat on his face, as an attitude highly expressive of watchfulness, 'I can have no hesitation in replying (it not being inconsistent with the public service) that those accents were the accents of the T'other Governor.'

'You've tolerable good eyes, ain't you, Governor? You've all tolerable good eyes, ain't you?' demanded the informer.

All.

'Then if I row up under the Fellowship and lay there, no need to whistle. You'll make out that there's a speck of something or another there, and you'll know it's me, and you'll come down that cause'ay to me. Understood all?'

Understood all.

'Off she goes then!'

In a moment, with the wind cutting keenly at him sideways,

he was staggering down to his boat; in a few moments he was clear, and creeping up the river under their own shore.

Eugene had raised himself on his elbow to look into the darkness after him. 'I wish the boat of my honourable and gallant friend,' he murmured, lying down again and speaking into his hat, 'may be endowed with philanthropy enough to turn bottom-upward and extinguish him!—Mortimer.'

'My honourable friend.'

'Three burglaries, two forgeries, and a midnight assassination.'

Yet in spite of having those weights on his conscience, Eugene was somewhat enlivened by the late slight change in the circumstances of affairs. So were his two companions. Its being a change was everything. The suspense seemed to have taken a new lease, and to have begun afresh from a recent date. There was something additional to look for. They were all three more sharply on the alert, and less deadened by the miserable influences of the place and time.

More than an hour had passed, and they were even dozing, when one of the three—each said it was he, and he had *not* dozed—made out Riderhood in his boat at the spot agreed on. They sprang up, came out from their shelter, and went down to him. When he saw them coming, he dropped alongside the causeway; so that they, standing on the causeway, could speak with him in whispers, under the shadowy mass of the Six Jolly Fellowship Porters fast asleep.

'Blest if I can make it out!' said he, staring at them.

'Make what out? Have you seen him?'

'No.'

'What *have* you seen?' asked Lightwood. For, he was staring at them in the strangest way.

'I've seen his boat.'

'Not empty?'

'Yes, empty. And what's more,—adrift. And what's more, —with one scull gone. And what's more,—with t'other scull jammed in the thowels and broke short off. And what's more, —the boat's drove tight by the tide 'atwixt two tiers of barges. And what's more,—he's in luck again, by George if he ain't!'

Chapter 14

The Bird of Prey Brought Down

COLD on the shore, in the raw cold of that leaden crisis in the four-and-twenty hours when the vital force of all the noblest and prettiest things that live is at its lowest, the three watchers looked each at the blank faces of the other two, and all at the blank face of Riderhood in his boat.

'Gaffer's boat, Gaffer in luck again, and yet no Gaffer!' So spake Riderhood, staring disconsolate.

As if with one accord, they all turned their eyes towards the light of the fire shining through the window. It was fainter and duller. Perhaps fire, like the higher animal and vegetable life it helps to sustain, has its greatest tendency towards death, when the night is dying and the day is not yet born.

'If it was me that had the law of this here job in hand,' growled Riderhood with a threatening shake of his head, 'blest if I wouldn't lay hold of *her,* at any rate!'

'Ay, but it is not you,' said Eugene. With something so suddenly fierce in him that the informer returned submissively; 'Well, well, well, t'other governor, I didn't say it was. A man may speak.'

'And vermin may be silent,' said Eugene. 'Hold your tongue, you water-rat!'

Astonished by his friend's unusual heat, Lightwood stared too, and then said: 'What can have become of this man?'

'Can't imagine. Unless he dived overboard.' The informer wiped his brow ruefully as he said it, sitting in his boat and always staring disconsolate.

'Did you make his boat fast?'

'She's fast enough till the tide runs back. I couldn't make her faster than she is. Come aboard of mine, and see for your own-selves.'

There was a little backwardness in complying, for the freight looked too much for the boat; but on Riderhood's protesting 'that he had had half a dozen, dead and alive, in her afore now, and she was nothing deep in the water nor down in the stern even then, to speak of,' they carefully took their places, and trimmed the crazy thing. While they were doing so, Riderhood still sat staring disconsolate.

'All right. Give way!' said Lightwood.

'Give way, by George!' repeated Riderhood, before shoving off. 'If he's gone and made off any how Lawyer Lightwood, it's enough to make me give way in a different manner. But he always *was* a cheat, con-found him! He always was a infernal cheat, was Gaffer. Nothing straightfor'ard, nothing on the square. So mean, so underhanded. Never going through with a thing, nor carrying it out like a man!'

'Hallo! Steady!' cried Eugene (he had recovered immediately on embarking), as they bumped heavily against a pile; and then in a lower voice reversed his late apostrophe by remarking ('I wish the boat of my honourable and gallant friend may be endowed with philanthropy enough *not* to turn bottom-upward and extinguish us!) Steady, steady! Sit close, Mortimer. Here's the hail again. See how it flies, like a troop of wild cats, at Mr Riderhood's eyes!'

Indeed he had the full benefit of it, and it so mauled him, though he bent his head low and tried to present nothing but the mangy cap to it, that he dropped under the lee of a tier of shipping, and they lay there until it was over. The squall had come up, like a spiteful messenger before the morning; there followed in its wake a ragged tear of light which ripped the dark clouds until they showed a great grey hole of day.

They were all shivering, and everything about them seemed to be shivering; the river itself, craft, rigging, sails, such early smoke as there yet was on the shore. Black with wet, and altered to the eye by white patches of hail and sleet, the huddled buildings looked lower than usual, as if they were cowering, and had shrunk with the cold. Very little life was to be seen on either bank, windows and doors were shut, and the staring black and white letters upon wharves and warehouses 'looked,' said Eugene to Mortimer, 'like inscriptions over the graves of dead businesses.'

As they glided slowly on, keeping under the shore and sneaking in and out among the shipping by back-alleys of water, in a pilfering way that seemed to be their boatman's normal manner of progression, all the objects among which they crept were so huge in contrast with their wretched boat, as to threaten to crush it. Not a ship's hull, with its rusty iron links of cable run out of hawse-holes long discoloured with the iron's rusty tears, but seemed to be there with a fell intention. Not a figure-head but had the menacing look of bursting forward to run them down. Not a sluice gate, or a painted scale upon a post or wall, showing the depth of water, but seemed to hint, like the dreadfully facetious Wolf in bed in Grandmamma's cottage, 'That's to drown *you* in, my dears!' Not a lumbering black barge, with its cracked and blistered side impending over them, but seemed to suck at the river with a thirst for sucking them under. And everything so vaunted the spoiling influences of water—discoloured copper, rotten wood, honey-combed stone, green dank deposit— that the after-consequences of being crushed, sucked under, and drawn down, looked as ugly to the imagination as the main event.

Some half-hour of this work, and Riderhood unshipped his sculls, stood holding on to a barge, and hand over hand long-wise along the barge's side gradually worked his boat under her head into a secret little nook of scummy water. And driven into that nook, and wedged as he had described, was Gaffer's boat; that boat with the stain still in it, bearing some resemblance to a muffled human form.

'Now tell me I'm a liar!' said the honest man.

('With a morbid expectation,' murmured Eugene to Lightwood, 'that somebody is always going to tell him the truth.')

'This is Hexam's boat,' said Mr Inspector. 'I know her well.'

'Look at the broken scull. Look at the t'other scull gone. *Now* tell me I am a liar!' said the honest man.

Mr Inspector stepped into the boat. Eugene and Mortimer looked on.

'And see now!' added Riderhood, creeping aft, and showing a stretched rope made fast there and towing overboard. 'Didn't I tell you he was in luck again?'

'Haul in,' said Mr Inspector.

'Easy to say haul in,' answered Riderhood. 'Not so easy done. His luck's got fouled under the keels of the barges. I tried to haul in last time, but I couldn't. See how taut the line is!'

'I must have it up,' said Mr Inspector. 'I am going to take this boat ashore, and his luck along with it. Try easy now.'

He tried easy now; but the luck resisted; wouldn't come.

'I mean to have it, and the boat too,' said Mr Inspector, playing the line.

But still the luck resisted; wouldn't come.

'Take care,' said Riderhood. 'You'll disfigure. Or pull asunder perhaps.'

'I am not going to do either, not even to your Grandmother,' said Mr Inspector; 'but I mean to have it. Come!' he added, at once persuasively and with authority to the hidden object in the water, as he played the line again; 'it's no good this sort of game, you know. You *must* come up. I mean to have you.'

There was so much virtue in this distinctly and decidedly meaning to have it, that it yielded a little, even while the line was played.

'I told you so,' quoth Mr Inspector, pulling off his outer coat, and leaning well over the stern with a will. 'Come!'

It was an awful sort of fishing, but it no more disconcerted Mr Inspector than if he had been fishing in a punt on a summer evening by some soothing weir high up the peaceful river. After certain minutes, and a few directions to the rest to 'ease her a little for'ard,' and 'now ease her a trifle aft,' and the like, he said composedly, 'All clear!' and the line and the boat came free together.

Accepting Lightwood's proffered hand to help him up, he then put on his coat, and said to Riderhood, 'Hand me over those spare sculls of yours, and I'll pull this in to the nearest stairs. Go ahead you, and keep out in pretty open water, that I mayn't get fouled again.'

His directions were obeyed, and they pulled ashore directly; two in one boat, two in the other.

'Now,' said Mr Inspector, again to Riderhood, when they were all on the slushy stones; 'you have had more practice in this than I have had, and ought to be a better workman at it. Undo the tow-rope, and we'll help you haul in.'

Riderhood got into the boat accordingly. It appeared as if he had scarcely had a moment's time to touch the rope or look over the stern, when he came scrambling back, as pale as the morning, and gasped out:

'By the Lord, he's done me!'

'What do you mean?' they all demanded.

He pointed behind him at the boat, and gasped to that degree that he dropped upon the stones to get his breath.

'Gaffer's done me. It's Gaffer!'

They ran to the rope, leaving him gasping there. Soon, the form of the bird of prey, dead some hours, lay stretched upon the shore, with a new blast storming at it and clotting the wet hair with hailstones.

Father, was that you calling me? Father! I thought I heard you call me twice before! Words never to be answered, those, upon the earth-side of the grave. The wind sweeps jeeringly over Father, whips him with the frayed ends of his dress and his jagged hair, tries to turn him where he lies stark on his back, and force his face towards the rising sun, that he may be shamed the more. A lull, and the wind is secret and prying with him; lifts and lets falls a rag; hides palpitating under another rag; runs nimbly through his hair and beard. Then, in a rush, it cruelly taunts him. Father, was that you calling me? Was it you, the voiceless and the dead? Was it you, thus buffeted as you lie here in a heap? Was it you, thus baptized unto Death, with these flying impurities now flung upon your face? Why not speak, Father? Soaking into this filthy ground as you lie here, is your own shape. Did you never see such a shape soaked into your boat? Speak, Father. Speak to us, the winds, the only listeners left you!

'Now see,' said Mr Inspector, after mature deliberation: kneeling on one knee beside the body, when they had stood looking down on the drowned man, as he had many a time looked down on many another man: 'the way of it was this. Of course you gentlemen hardly failed to observe that he was towing by the neck and arms.'

They had helped to release the rope, and of course not.

'And you will have observed before, and you will observe now, that this knot, which was drawn chock-tight round his neck by the strain of his own arms, is a slip-knot': holding it up for demonstration.

Plain enough.

'Likewise you will have observed how he had run the other end of this rope to his boat.'

It had the curves and indentations in it still, where it had been twined and bound.

'Now see,' said Mr Inspector, 'see how it works round upon him. It's a wild tempestuous evening when this man that was,' stooping to wipe some hailstones out of his hair with an end of his own drowned jacket, '—there! Now he's more like himself, though he's badly bruised,—when this man that was, rows out upon the river on his usual lay. He carries with him this coil of rope. He always carries with him this coil of rope. It's as well known to me as he was himself. Sometimes it lay in the bottom of his boat. Sometimes he hung it loose round his neck. He was a light-dresser was this man;—you see?' lifting the loose neckerchief over his breast, and taking the opportunity of wiping the dead lips with it—'and when it was wet, or freezing, or blew cold, he would hang this coil of line round his neck. Last evening he does this. Worse for him! He dodges about in his boat, does this man, till he gets chilled. His hands,' taking up one of them, which dropped like a leaden weight, 'get numbed. He sees some object that's in his way of business, floating. He makes ready to secure that object. He unwinds the end of his coil that he wants to take some turns on in his boat, and he takes turns enough on it to secure that it shan't run out. He makes it too secure, as it happens. He is a little longer about this than usual, his hands being numbed. His object drifts up, before he is quite ready for it. He catches at it, thinks he'll make sure of the contents of the pockets anyhow, in case he should be parted from it, bends right over the stern, and in one of these heavy squalls, or in the cross-swell of two steamers, or in not being quite prepared, or through all or most or some, gets a lurch, overbalances and goes head-foremost overboard. Now see! He can swim, can this man, and instantly he strikes out. But in such striking-out he tangles his arms, pulls strong on the slip-knot, and it runs home. The object he had expected to take in tow, floats by, and his own boat tows him dead, to where we found him, all entangled in his own line. You'll ask me how I make out about the pockets? First, I'll tell you more; there was silver in 'em. How do I make that out? Simple and satisfactory. Because he's got it here.' The lecturer held up the tightly clenched right hand.

'What is to be done with the remains?' asked Lightwood.

'If you wouldn't object to standing by him half a minute, sir,' was the reply, 'I'll find the nearest of our men to come and take charge of him;—I still call it *him,* you see,' said Mr Inspector, looking back as he went, with a philosophical smile upon the force of habit.

'Eugene,' said Lightwood—and was about to add 'we may wait at a little distance,' when turning his head he found that no Eugene was there.

He raised his voice and called 'Eugene! Holloa!' But no Eugene replied.

It was broad daylight now, and he looked about. But no Eugene was in all the view.

Mr Inspector speedily returning down the wooden stairs, with a police constable, Lightwood asked him if he had seen his friend leave them? Mr Inspector could not exactly say that he had seen him go, but had noticed that he was restless.

'Singular and entertaining combination, sir, your friend.'

'I wish it had not been a part of his singular entertaining combination to give me the slip under these dreary circumstances at this time of the morning,' said Lightwood. 'Can we get anything hot to drink?'

We could, and we did. In a public-house kitchen with a large fire. We got hot brandy and water, and it revived us wonderfully. Mr Inspector having to Mr Riderhood announced his official intention of 'keeping his eye upon him', stood him in a corner of the fireplace, like a wet umbrella, and took no further outward and visible notice of that honest man, except ordering a separate service of brandy and water for him: apparently out of the public funds.

As Mortimer Lightwood sat before the blazing fire, conscious of drinking brandy and water then and there in his sleep, and yet at one and the same time drinking burnt sherry at the Six Jolly Fellowships, and lying under the boat on the river shore, and sitting in the boat that Riderhood rowed, and listening to the lecture recently concluded, and having to dine in the Temple with an unknown man, who described himself as M. R. F. Eugene Gaffer Harmon, and said he lived at Hailstorm,—as he passed through these curious vicissitudes of fatigue and slumber, arranged upon the scale of a dozen hours to the second, he became aware of answering aloud a communication of pressing importance that had never been made to him, and then turned it into a cough on beholding Mr Inspector. For, he felt, with some natural indignation, that that functionary might otherwise suspect him of having closed his eyes, or wandered in his attention.

'Here just before us, you see,' said Mr Inspector.

'*I* see,' said Lightwood, with dignity.

'And had hot brandy and water too, you see,' said Mr Inspector, 'and then cut off at a great rate.'

'Who?' said Lightwood.

'Your friend, you know.'

'*I* know,' he replied, again with dignity.

After hearing, in a mist through which Mr Inspector loomed vague and large, that the officer took upon himself to prepare the dead man's daughter for what had befallen in the night, and generally that he took everything upon himself, Mortimer Lightwood stumbled in his sleep to a cab-stand, called a cab, and had entered the army and committed a capital military offence and been tried by court martial and found guilty and had arranged his affairs and been marched out to be shot, before the door banged.

Hard work rowing the cab through the City to the Temple, for a cup of from five to ten thousand pounds value, given by Mr Boffin; and hard work holding forth at that immeasurable length to Eugene (when he had been rescued with a rope from the running pavement) for making off in that extraordinary manner! But he offered such ample apologies, and was so very penitent, that when Lightwood got out of the cab, he gave the driver a particular charge to be careful of him. Which the driver (knowing there was no other fare left inside) stared at prodigiously.

In short, the night's work had so exhausted and worn out this actor in it, that he had become a mere somnambulist. He was too tired to rest in his sleep, until he was even tired out of being too tired, and dropped into oblivion. Late in the afternoon he awoke, and in some anxiety sent round to Eugene's lodging hard by, to inquire if he were up yet?

Oh yes, he was up. In fact, he had not been to bed. He had just come home. And here he was, close following on the heels of the message.

'Why what bloodshot, draggled, dishevelled spectacle is this!' cried Mortimer.

'Are my feathers so very much rumpled?' said Eugene, coolly going up to the looking-glass. 'They *are* rather out of sorts. But consider. Such a night for plumage!'

'Such a night?' repeated Mortimer. 'What became of you in the morning?'

'My dear fellow,' said Eugene, sitting on his bed, 'I felt that we had bored one another so long, that an unbroken continuance of those relations must inevitably terminate in our flying to opposite points of the earth. I also felt that I had committed every crime in the Newgate Calendar. So, for mingled considerations of friendship and felony, I took a walk.'

Chapter 15
Two New Servants

MR and Mrs Boffin sat after breakfast, in the Bower, a prey to prosperity. Mr Boffin's face denoted Care and Complication. Many disordered papers were before him, and he looked at them about as hopefully as an innocent civilian might look at a crowd of troops whom he was required at five minutes' notice to manœuvre and review. He had been engaged in some attempts to make notes of these papers; but being troubled (as men of his stamp often are) with an exceedingly distrustful and corrective thumb, that busy member had so often interposed to smear his notes, that they were little more legible than the various impressions of itself, which blurred his nose and forehead. It is curious to consider, in such a case as Mr Boffin's, what a cheap article ink is, and how far it may be made to go. As a grain of musk will scent a drawer for many years, and still lose nothing appreciable of its original weight, so a halfpenny-worth of ink would blot Mr Boffin to the roots of his hair and the calves of his legs, without inscribing a line on the paper before him, or appearing to diminish in the inkstand.

Mr Boffin was in such severe literary difficulties that his eyes were prominent and fixed, and his breathing was stertorous, when, to the great relief of Mrs Boffin, who observed these symptoms with alarm, the yard bell rang.

'Who's that, I wonder!' said Mrs Boffin.

Mr Boffin drew a long breath, laid down his pen, looked at his notes as doubting whether he had the pleasure of their acquaintance, and appeared, on a second perusal of their countenances, to be confirmed in his impression that he had not, when there was announced by the hammer-headed young man:

'Mr Rokesmith.'

'Oh!' said Mr Boffin. 'Oh indeed! Our and the Wilfers' Mutual Friend, my dear. Yes. Ask him to come in.'

Mr Rokesmith appeared.

'Sit down, sir,' said Mr Boffin, shaking hands with him. 'Mrs Boffin you're already acquainted with. Well, sir, I am rather unprepared to see you, for, to tell you the truth, I've been so busy with one thing and another, that I've not had time to turn your offer over.'

'That's apology for both of us: for Mr Boffin, and for me as well,' said the smiling Mrs Boffin. 'But Lor! we can talk it over now; can't us?'

Mr Rokesmith bowed, thanked her, and said he hoped so.

'Let me see then,' resumed Mr Boffin, with his hand to his chin. 'It was Secretary that you named; wasn't it?'

'I said Secretary,' assented Mr Rokesmith.

'It rather puzzled me at the time,' said Mr Boffin, 'and it rather puzzled me and Mrs Boffin when we spoke of it after-wards, because (not to make a mystery of our belief) we have always believed a Secretary to be a piece of furniture, mostly of mahogany, lined with green baize or leather, with a lot of little drawers in it. Now, you won't think I take a liberty when I mention that you certainly ain't *that*.'

Certainly not, said Mr Rokesmith. But he had used the word in the sense of Steward.

'Why, as to Steward, you see,' returned Mr Boffin, with his hand still to his chin, 'the odds are that Mrs Boffin and me may never go upon the water. Being both bad sailors, we should want a Steward if we did; but there's generally one provided.'

Mr Rokesmith again explained; defining the duties he sought to undertake, as those of general superintendent, or manager, or overlooker, or man of business.

'Now, for instance—come!' said Mr Boffin, in his pouncing way. 'If you entered my employment, what would you do?'

'I would keep exact accounts of all the expenditure you sanctioned, Mr Boffin. I would write your letters, under your direction. I would transact your business with people in your pay or employment. I would,' with a glance and a half-smile at the table, 'arrange your papers—'

Mr Boffin rubbed his inky ear, and looked at his wife.

'—And so arrange them as to have them always in order for immediate reference, with a note of the contents of each outside it.'

'I tell you what,' said Mr Boffin, slowly crumpling his own blotted note in his hand; 'if you'll turn to at these present papers, and see what you can make of 'em, I shall know better what I can make of you.'

No sooner said than done. Relinquishing his hat and gloves, Mr Rokesmith sat down quietly at the table, arranged the open papers into an orderly heap, cast his eyes over each in succession, folded it, docketed it on the outside, laid it in a second heap, and, when that second heap was complete and the first gone, took from his pocket a piece of string and tied it together with a remarkably dexterous hand at a running curve and a loop.

'Good!' said Mr Boffin. 'Very good! Now let us hear what they're all about; will you be so good?'

John Rokesmith read his abstracts aloud. They were all about the new house. Decorator's estimate, so much. Furniture estimate, so much. Estimate for furniture of offices, so much. Coach-maker's estimate, so much. Horse-dealer's estimate, so much. Harness-maker's estimate, so much. Goldsmith's estimate, so much. Total, so very much. Then came correspondence. Acceptance of Mr Boffin's offer of such a date, and to such an effect. Rejection of Mr Boffin's proposal of such a date and to such an effect. Concerning Mr Boffin's scheme of such another date to such another effect. All compact and methodical.

'Apple-pie order!' said Mr Boffin, after checking off each inscription with his hand, like a man beating time. 'And whatever you do with your ink, *I* can't think, for you're as clean as a whistle after it. Now, as to a letter. Let's,' said Mr Boffin, rubbing his hands in his pleasantly childish admiration, 'let's try a letter next.'

'To whom shall it be addressed, Mr Boffin?'

'Anyone. Yourself.'

Mr Rokesmith quickly wrote, and then read aloud:

' "Mr Boffin presents his compliments to Mr John Rokesmith, and begs to say that he has decided on giving Mr John Rokesmith a trial in the capacity he desires to fill. Mr Boffin takes Mr John Rokesmith at his word, in postponing to some indefinite period, the consideration of salary. It is quite understood that Mr Boffin is in no way committed on that point. Mr Boffin has merely to add, that he relies on Mr John Rokesmith's assurance that he will be faithful and serviceable. Mr John Rokesmith will please enter on his duties immediately." '

'Well! Now, Noddy!' cried Mrs Boffin, clapping her hands, 'That *is* a good one!'

Mr Boffin was no less delighted; indeed, in his own bosom, he regarded both the composition itself and the device that had given birth to it, as a very remarkable monument of human ingenuity.

'And I tell you, my deary,' said Mrs Boffin, 'that if you don't close with Mr Rokesmith now at once, and if you ever go a muddling yourself again with things never meant nor made for you, you'll have an apoplexy—besides iron-moulding your linen—and you'll break my heart.'

Mr Boffin embraced his spouse for these words of wisdom, and then, congratulating John Rokesmith on the brilliancy of his achievements, gave him his hand in pledge of their new relations. So did Mrs Boffin.

'Now,' said Mr Boffin, who, in his frankness, felt that it did not become him to have a gentleman in his employment five minutes, without reposing some confidence in him, 'you must be let a little more into our affairs, Rokesmith. I mentioned to you, when I made your acquaintance, or I might better say when you made mine, that Mrs Boffin's inclinations was setting in the way of Fashion, but that I didn't know how fashionable we might or might not grow. Well! Mrs Boffin has carried the day, and we're going in neck and crop for Fashion.'

'I rather inferred that, sir,' replied John Rokesmith, 'from the scale on which your new establishment is to be maintained.'

'Yes,' said Mr Boffin, 'it's to be a Spanker. The fact is, my literary man named to me that a house with which he is, as I may say, connected—in which he has an interest—'

'As property?' inquired John Rokesmith.

'Why no,' said Mr Boffin, 'not exactly that; a sort of a family tie.'

'Association?' the Secretary suggested.

'Ah!' said Mr Boffin. 'Perhaps. Anyhow, he named to me that the house had a board up, "This Eminently Aristocratic Mansion to be let or sold." Me and Mrs Boffin went to look at it, and finding it beyond a doubt Eminently Aristocratic (though a trifle high and dull, which after all may be part of the same thing) took it. My literary man was so friendly as to drop into a charming piece of poetry on that occasion, in which he complimented Mrs Boffin on coming into possession of—how did it go, my dear?'

Mrs Boffin replied:

> ' "The gay, the gay and festive scene,
>   The halls, the halls of dazzling light." '

'That's it! And it was made neater by there really being two halls in the house, a front 'un and a back 'un, besides the servants'. He likewise dropped into a very pretty piece of poetry to be sure, respecting the extent to which he would be willing to put himself out of the way to bring Mrs Boffin round, in case she should ever get low in her spirits in the house. Mrs Boffin has a wonderful memory. Will you repeat it, my dear?'

Mrs Boffin complied, by reciting the verses in which this obliging offer had been made, exactly as she had received them.

' "I'll tell thee how the maiden wept, Mrs Boffin,
When her true love was slain ma'am,
And how her broken spirit slept, Mrs Boffin,
And never woke again ma'am.
I'll tell thee (if agreeable to Mr Boffin) how the steed drew nigh,
And left his lord afar;
And if my tale (which I hope Mr Boffin might excuse) should make you sigh,
I'll strike the light guitar." '

'Correct to the letter!' said Mr Boffin. 'And I consider that the poetry brings us both in, in a beautiful manner.'

The effect of the poem on the Secretary being evidently to astonish him, Mr Boffin was confirmed in his high opinion of it, and was greatly pleased.

'Now, you see, Rokesmith,' he went on, 'a literary man— *with* a wooden leg—is liable to jealousy. I shall therefore cast about for comfortable ways and means of not calling up Wegg's jealousy, but of keeping you in your department, and keeping him in his.'

'Lor!' cried Mrs Boffin. 'What I say is, the world's wide enough for all of us!'

'So it is, my dear,' said Mr Boffin, 'when not literary. But when so, not so. And I am bound to bear in mind that I took Wegg on, at a time when I had no thought of being fashionable or of leaving the Bower. To let him feel himself anyways slighted now, would be to be guilty of a meanness, and to act like having one's head turned by the halls of dazzling light. Which Lord forbid! Rokesmith, what shall we say about your living in the house?'

'In this house?'

'No, no. I have got other plans for this house. In the new house?'

'That will be as you please, Mr Boffin. I hold myself quite at your disposal. You know where I live at present.'

'Well!' said Mr Boffin, after considering the point; 'suppose you keep as you are for the present, and we'll decide by-and-by. You'll begin to take charge at once, of all that's going on in the new house, will you?'

'Most willingly. I will begin this very day. Will you give me the address?'

Mr Boffin repeated it, and the Secretary wrote it down in his pocket-book. Mrs Boffin took the opportunity of his being so engaged, to get a better observation of his face than she had yet taken. It impressed her in his favour, for she nodded aside to Mr Boffin, 'I like him.'

'I will see directly that everything is in train, Mr Boffin.'

'Thank'ee. Being here, would you care at all to look round the Bower?'

'I should greatly like it. I have heard so much of its story.'

'Come!' said Mr Boffin. And he and Mrs Boffin led the way.

A gloomy house the Bower, with sordid signs on it of having been, through its long existence as Harmony Jail, in miserly holding. Bare of paint, bare of paper on the walls, bare of furniture, bare of experience of human life. Whatever is built by man for man's occupation, must, like natural creations, fulfil the intention of its existence, or soon perish. This old house had wasted more from desuetude than it would have wasted from use, twenty years for one.

A certain leanness falls upon houses not sufficiently imbued with life (as if they were nourished upon it), which was very noticeable here. The staircase, balustrades, and rails, had a spare look—an air of being denuded to the bone—which the panels of the walls and the jambs of the doors and windows also bore. The scanty moveables partook of it; save for the cleanliness of the place, the dust into which they were all resolving would have lain thick on the floors; and those, both in colour and in grain, were worn like old faces that had kept much alone.

The bedroom where the clutching old man had lost his grip on life, was left as he had left it. There was the old grisly four-post bedstead, without hangings, and with a jail-like upper rim of iron and spikes; and there was the old patch-work counterpane. There was the tight-clenched old bureau, receding atop like a bad and secret forehead; there was the cumbersome old table with twisted legs, at the bed-side; and there was the box upon it, in which the will had lain. A few old chairs with patch-work covers, under which the more precious stuff to be preserved had slowly lost its quality of colour without imparting pleasure to any eye, stood against the wall. A hard family likeness was on all these things.

'The room was kept like this, Rokesmith,' said Mr Boffin, 'against the son's return. In short, everything in the house was kept exactly as it came to us, for him to see and approve. Even now, nothing is changed but our own room below-stairs that you have just left. When the son came home for the last time in his life, and for the last time in his life saw his father, it was most likely in this room that they met.'

As the Secretary looked all round it, his eyes rested on a side door in a corner.

'Another staircase,' said Mr Boffin, unlocking the door, 'leading down into the yard. We'll go down this way, as you may like to see the yard, and it's all in the road. When the son was a little child, it was up and down these stairs that he mostly came and went to his father. He was very timid of his father. I've seen him sit on these stairs, in his shy way, poor child, many a time. Mr and Mrs Boffin have comforted him, sitting with his little book on these stairs, often.'

'Ah! And his poor sister too,' said Mrs Boffin. 'And here's the sunny place on the white wall where they one day measured one another. Their own little hands wrote up their names here, only with a pencil; but the names are here still, and the poor dears gone for ever.'

'We must take care of the names, old lady,' said Mr Boffin. 'We must take care of the names. They shan't be rubbed out in our time, nor yet, if we can help it, in the time after us. Poor little children!'

'Ah, poor little children!' said Mrs Boffin.

They had opened the door at the bottom of the staircase giving on the yard, and they stood in the sunlight, looking at the scrawl of the two unsteady childish hands two or three steps up the staircase. There was something in this simple memento of a blighted childhood, and in the tenderness of Mrs Boffin, that touched the Secretary.

Mr Boffin then showed his new man of business the Mounds, and his own particular Mound which had been left him as his legacy under the will before he acquired the whole estate.

'It would have been enough for us,' said Mr Boffin, 'in case it had pleased God to spare the last of those two young lives and sorrowful deaths. We didn't want the rest.'

At the treasures of the yard, and at the outside of the house, and at the detached building which Mr Boffin pointed out as the residence of himself and his wife during the many years of their service, the Secretary looked with interest. It was not until Mr Boffin had shown him every wonder of the Bower twice over, that he remembered his having duties to discharge elsewhere.

'You have no instructions to give me, Mr Boffin, in reference to this place?'

'Not any, Rokesmith. No.'

'Might I ask, without seeming impertinent, whether you have any intention of selling it?'

'Certainly not. In remembrance of our old master, our old master's children, and our old service, me and Mrs Boffin mean to keep it up as it stands.'

The Secretary's eyes glanced with so much meaning in them at the Mounds, that Mr Boffin said, as if in answer to a remark:

'Ay, ay, that's another thing. I may sell *them,* though I should be sorry to see the neighbourhood deprived of 'em too. It'll look but a poor dead flat without the Mounds. Still I don't say that I'm going to keep 'em always there, for the sake of the beauty of the landscape. There's no hurry about it; that's all I say at present. I ain't a scholar in much, Rokesmith, but I'm a pretty fair scholar in dust. I can price the Mounds to a fraction, and I know how they can be best disposed of, and likewise that they take no harm by standing where they do. You'll look in to-morrow, will you be so kind?'

'Every day. And the sooner I can get you into your new house, complete, the better you will be pleased, sir?'

'Well, it ain't that I'm in a mortal hurry,' said Mr Boffin; 'only when you *do* pay people for looking alive, it's as well to know that they *are* looking alive. Ain't that your opinion?'

'Quite!' replied the Secretary; and so withdrew.

'Now,' said Mr Boffin to himself, subsiding into his regular series of turns in the yard, 'if I can make it comfortable with Wegg, my affairs will be going smooth.'

The man of low cunning had, of course, acquired a mastery over the man of high simplicity. The mean man had, of course, got the better of the generous man. How long such conquests last, is another matter; that they are achieved, is every-day experience, not even to be flourished away by Podsnappery itself. The undesigning Boffin had become so far immeshed by the wily Wegg that his mind misgave him he was a very designing man indeed in purposing to do more for Wegg. It seemed to him (so skilful was Wegg) that he was plotting darkly, when he was contriving to do the very thing that Wegg was plotting to get him to do. And thus, while he was mentally turning the kindest of kind faces on Wegg this morning, he was not absolutely sure but that he might somehow deserve the charge of turning his back on him.

For these reasons Mr Boffin passed but anxious hours until evening came, and with it Mr Wegg, stumping leisurely to the Roman Empire. At about this period Mr Boffin had become profoundly interested in the fortunes of a great military leader known to him as Bully Sawyers, but perhaps better known to fame and easier of identification by the classical student, under the less Britannic name of Belisarius. Even this general's career paled in interest for Mr Boffin before the clearing of his conscience with Wegg; and hence, when that literary gentleman had according to custom eaten and drunk until he was all a-glow, and when he took up his book with the usual chirping introduction, 'And now, Mr Boffin, sir, we'll decline and we'll fall!' Mr Boffin stopped him.

'You remember, Wegg, when I first told you that I wanted to make a sort of offer to you?'

'Let me get on my considering cap, sir,' replied that gentleman, turning the open book face downward. 'When you first told me that you wanted to make a sort of offer to me? Now let me think.' (as if there were the least necessity) 'Yes, to be sure I do, Mr Boffin. It was at my corner. To be sure it was! You had first asked me whether I liked your name, and Candour had compelled a reply in the negative case. I little thought then, sir, how familiar that name would come to be!'

'I hope it will be more familiar still, Wegg.'

'Do you, Mr Boffin? Much obliged to you, I'm sure. Is it your pleasure, sir, that we decline and we fall?' with a feint of taking up the book.

'Not just yet awhile, Wegg. In fact, I have got another offer to make you.'

Mr Wegg (who had had nothing else in his mind for several nights) took off his spectacles with an air of bland surprise.

'And I hope you'll like it, Wegg.'

'Thank you, sir,' returned that reticent individual. 'I hope it may prove so. On all accounts, I am sure.' (This, as a philanthropic aspiration.)

'What do you think,' said Mr Boffin, 'of not keeping a stall, Wegg?'

'I think, sir,' replied Wegg, 'that I should like to be shown the gentleman prepared to make it worth my while!'

'Here he is,' said Mr Boffin.

Mr Wegg was going to say, My Benefactor, and had said My Bene, when a grandiloquent change came over him.

'No, Mr Boffin, not you sir. Anybody but you. Do not fear, Mr Boffin, that I shall contaminate the premises which your gold has bought, with *my* lowly pursuits. I am aware, sir, that it would not become me to carry on my little traffic under the windows of your mansion. I have already thought of that, and taken my measures. No need to be bought out, sir. Would Stepney Fields be considered intrusive? If not remote enough, I can go remoter. In the words of the poet's song, which I do not quite remember:

Thrown on the wide world, doom'd to wander and roam,
Bereft of my parents, bereft of a home,
A stranger to something and what's his name joy,
Behold little Edmund the poor Peasant boy.

—And equally,' said Mr Wegg, repairing the want of direct application in the last line, 'behold myself on a similar footing!'

'Now, Wegg, Wegg, Wegg,' remonstrated the excellent Boffin. 'You are too sensitive.'

'I know I am, sir,' returned Wegg, with obstinate magnanimity. 'I am acquainted with my faults. I always was, from a child, too sensitive.'

'But listen,' pursued the Golden Dustman; 'hear me out, Wegg. You have taken it into your head that I mean to pension you off.'

'True, sir,' returned Wegg, still with an obstinate magnanimity. 'I am acquainted with my faults. Far be it from me to deny them. I *have* taken it into my head.'

'But I *don't* mean it.'

The assurance seemed hardly as comforting to Mr Wegg, as Mr Boffin intended it to be. Indeed, an appreciable elongation of his visage might have been observed as he replied:

'Don't you, indeed, sir?'

'No,' pursued Mr Boffin; 'because that would express, as I understand it, that you were not going to do anything to deserve your money. But you are; you are.'

'That, sir,' replied Mr Wegg, cheering up bravely, 'is quite another pair of shoes. Now, my independence as a man is again elevated. Now, I no longer

Weep for the hour,
When to Boffinses bower,
The Lord of the valley with offers came;
Neither does the moon hide her light
From the heavens to-night,
And weep behind her clouds o'er any individual in the present Company's shame.

—Please to proceed, Mr Boffin.'

'Thank'ee, Wegg, both for your confidence in me and for your frequent dropping into poetry; both of which is friendly. Well, then; my idea is, that you should give up your stall, and that I should put you into the Bower here, to keep it for us. It's a pleasant spot; and a man with coals and candles and a pound a week might be in clover here.'

'Hem! Would that man, sir—we will say that man, for the purposes of argueyment;' Mr Wegg made a smiling demonstration of great perspicuity here; 'would that man, sir, be expected to throw any other capacity in, or would any other capacity be considered extra? Now let us (for the purposes of argueyment) suppose that man to be engaged as a reader: say (for the purposes of argueyment) in the evening. Would that man's pay as a reader in the evening, be added to the other amount, which, adopting your language, we will call clover; or would it merge into that amount, or clover?'

'Well,' said Mr Boffin, 'I suppose it would be added.'

'I suppose it would, sir. You are right, sir. Exactly my own views, Mr Boffin.' Here Wegg rose, and balancing himself on his wooden leg, fluttered over his prey with extended hand. 'Mr Boffin, consider it done. Say no more, sir, not a word more. My stall and I are for ever parted. The collection of ballads will in future be reserved for private study, with the object of making poetry tributary'—Wegg was so proud of having found this word, that he said it again, with a capital letter—'Tributary, to friendship. Mr Boffin, don't allow yourself to be made uncomfortable by the pang it gives me to part from my stock and stall.

Similar emotion was undergone by my own father when promoted for his merits from his occupation as a waterman to a
situation under Government. His Christian name was Thomas.
His words at the time (I was then an infant, but so deep was their
impression on me, that I committed them to memory) were:

> Then farewell my trim-built wherry,
> Oars and coat and badge farewell!
> Never more at Chelsea Ferry,
> Shall your Thomas take a spell!

—My father got over it, Mr Boffin, and so shall I.'

While delivering these valedictory observations, Wegg continually disappointed Mr Boffin of his hand by flourishing it in
the air. He now darted it at his patron, who took it, and felt his
mind relieved of a great weight: observing that as they had
arranged their joint affairs so satisfactorily, he would now be
glad to look into those of Bully Sawyers. Which, indeed, had
been left over-night in a very unpromising posture, and for
whose impending expedition against the Persians the weather had
been by no means favourable all day.

Mr Wegg resumed his spectacles therefore. But Sawyers
was not to be of the party that night; for, before Wegg had found
his place, Mrs Boffin's tread was heard upon the stairs, so
unusually heavy and hurried, that Mr Boffin would have started
up at the sound, anticipating some occurrence much out of the
common course, even though she had not also called to him in
an agitated tone.

Mr Boffin hurried out, and found her on the dark staircase,
panting, with a lighted candle in her hand.

'What's the matter, my dear?'

'I don't know; I don't know; but I wish you'd come up-
stairs.'

Much surprised, Mr Boffin went upstairs and accompanied
Mrs Boffin into their own room: a second large room on the
same floor as the room in which the late proprietor had died. Mr
Boffin looked all round him, and saw nothing more unusual than
various articles of folded linen on a large chest, which Mrs
Boffin had been sorting.

'What is it, my dear? Why, you're frightened! *You* frightened?'

'I am not one of that sort certainly,' said Mrs Boffin, as she
sat down in a chair to recover herself, and took her husband's
arm; 'but it's very strange!'

'What is, my dear?'

'Noddy, the faces of the old man and the two children are all over the house to-night.'

'My dear?' exclaimed Mr Boffin. But not without a certain uncomfortable sensation gliding down his back.

'I know it must sound foolish, and yet it is so.'

'Where did you think you saw them?'

'I don't know that I think I saw them anywhere. I felt them.'

'Touched them?'

'No. Felt them in the air. I was sorting those things on the chest, and not thinking of the old man or the children, but singing to myself, when all in a moment I felt there was a face growing out of the dark.'

'What face?' asked her husband, looking about him.

'For a moment it was the old man's, and then it got younger. For a moment it was both the children's, and then it got older. For a moment it was a strange face, and then it was all the faces.'

'And then it was gone?'

'Yes; and then it was gone.'

'Where were you then, old lady?'

'Here, at the chest. Well; I got the better of it, and went on sorting, and went on singing to myself. "Lor!" I says, "I'll think of something else—something comfortable—and put it out of my head." So I thought of the new house and Miss Bella Wilfer, and was thinking at a great rate with that sheet there in my hand, when all of a sudden, the faces seemed to be hidden in among the folds of it and I let it drop.'

As it still lay on the floor where it had fallen, Mr Boffin picked it up and laid it on the chest.

'And then you ran down stairs?'

'No. I thought I'd try another room, and shake it off. I says to myself, "I'll go and walk slowly up and down the old man's room three times, from end to end, and then I shall have conquered it." I went in with the candle in my hand; but the moment I came near the bed, the air got thick with them.'

'With the faces?'

'Yes, and I even felt that they were in the dark behind the side-door, and on the little staircase, floating away into the yard. Then, I called you.'

Mr Boffin, lost in amazement, looked at Mrs Boffin. Mrs

Boffin, lost in her own fluttered inability to make this out, looked at Mr Boffin.

'I think, my dear,' said the Golden Dustman, 'I'll at once get rid of Wegg for the night, because he's coming to inhabit the Bower, and it might be put into his head or somebody else's, if he heard this and it got about that the house is haunted. Whereas we know better. Don't we?'

'I never had the feeling in the house before,' said Mrs Boffin; 'and I have been about it alone at all hours of the night. I have been in the house when Death was in it, and I have been in the house when Murder was a new part of its adventures, and I never had a fright in it yet.'

'And won't again, my dear,' said Mr Boffin. 'Depend upon it, it comes of thinking and dwelling on that dark spot.'

'Yes; but why didn't it come before?' asked Mrs Boffin.

This draft on Mr Boffin's philosophy could only be met by that gentleman with the remark that everything that is at all, must begin at some time. Then, tucking his wife's arm under his own, that she might not be left by herself to be troubled again, he descended to release Wegg. Who, being something drowsy after his plentiful repast, and constitutionally of a shirking temperament, was well enough pleased to stump away, without doing what he had come to do, and was paid for doing.

Mr Boffin then put on his hat, and Mrs Boffin her shawl; and the pair, further provided with a bunch of keys and a lighted lantern, went all over the dismal house—dismal everywhere, but in their own two rooms—from cellar to cock-loft. Not resting satisfied with giving that much chance to Mrs Boffin's fancies, they pursued them into the yard and outbuildings, and under the Mounds. And setting the lantern, when all was done, at the foot of one of the Mounds, they comfortably trotted to and fro for an evening walk, to the end that the murky cobwebs in Mrs Boffin's brain might be blown away.

'There, my dear!' said Mr Boffin when they came in to supper. 'That was the treatment, you see. Completely worked round, haven't you?'

'Yes, deary,' said Mrs Boffin, laying aside her shawl. 'I'm not nervous any more. I'm not a bit troubled now. I'd go anywhere about the house the same as ever. But—'

'Eh!' said Mr Boffin.

'But I've only to shut my eyes.'

'And what then?'

'Why then,' said Mrs Boffin, speaking with her eyes

closed, and her left hand thoughtfully touching her brow, 'then, there they are! The old man's face, and it gets younger. The two children's faces, and they get older. A face that I don't know. And then all the faces!'

Opening her eyes again, and seeing her husband's face across the table, she leaned forward to give it a pat on the cheek, and sat down to supper, declaring it to be the best face in the world.

Chapter 16
Minders and Re-Minders

THE Secretary lost no time in getting to work, and his vigilance and method soon set their mark on the Golden Dustman's affairs. His earnestness in determining to understand the length and breadth and depth of every piece of work submitted to him by his employer, was as special as his despatch in transacting it. He accepted no information or explanation at second hand, but made himself the master of everything confided to him.

One part of the Secretary's conduct, underlying all the rest, might have been mistrusted by a man with a better knowledge of men than the Golden Dustman had. The Secretary was as far from being inquisitive or intrusive as Secretary could be, but nothing less than a complete understanding of the whole of the affairs would content him. It soon became apparent (from the knowledge with which he set out) that he must have been to the office where the Harmon will was registered, and must have read the will. He anticipated Mr Boffin's consideration whether he should be advised with on this or that topic, by showing that he already knew of it and understood it. He did this with no attempt at concealment, seeming to be satisfied that it was part of his duty to have prepared himself at all attainable points for its utmost discharge.

This might—let it be repeated—have awakened some little vague mistrust in a man more worldly-wise than the Golden

Dustman. On the other hand, the Secretary was discerning, discreet, and silent, though as zealous as if the affairs had been his own. He showed no love of patronage or the command of money, but distinctly preferred resigning both to Mr Boffin. If, in his limited sphere, he sought power, it was the power of knowledge; the power derivable from a perfect comprehension of his business.

As on the Secretary's face there was a nameless cloud, so on his manner there was a shadow equally indefinable. It was not that he was embarrassed, as on that first night with the Wilfer family; he was habitually unembarrassed now, and yet the something remained. It was not that his manner was bad, as on that occasion; it was now very good, as being modest, gracious, and ready. Yet the something never left it. It has been written of men who have undergone a cruel captivity, or who have passed through a terrible strait, or who in self-preservation have killed a defenceless fellow-creature, that the record thereof has never faded from their countenances until they died. Was there any such record here?

He established a temporary office for himself in the new house, and all went well under his hand, with one singular exception. He manifestly objected to communicate with Mr Boffin's solicitor. Two or three times, when there was some slight occasion for his doing so, he transferred the task to Mr Boffin; and his evasion of it soon became so curiously apparent, that Mr Boffin spoke to him on the subject of his reluctance.

'It is so,' the Secretary admitted. 'I would rather not.'

Had he any personal objection to Mr Lightwood?

'I don't know him.'

Had he suffered from law-suits?

'Not more than other men,' was his short answer.

Was he prejudiced against the race of lawyers?

'No. But while I am in your employment, sir, I would rather be excused from going between the lawyer and the client. Of course if you press it, Mr Boffin, I am ready to comply. But I should take it as a great favour if you would not press it without urgent occasion.'

Now, it could not be said that there *was* urgent occasion, for Lightwood retained no other affairs in his hands than such as still lingered and languished about the undiscovered criminal, and such as arose out of the purchase of the house. Many other matters that might have travelled to him, now stopped short at the Secretary, under whose administration they were far more expeditiously and satisfactorily disposed of than they would have been if they had got into Young Blight's domain. This the Golden Dustman quite understood. Even the matter immediately in hand was of very little moment as requiring personal appearance on the Secretary's part, for it amounted to no more than this:—The death of Hexam rendering the sweat of the honest man's brow unprofitable, the honest man had shufflingly decided to moisten his brow for nothing, with that severe exertion which is known in legal circles as swearing your way through a stone wall. Consequently, that new light had gone sputtering out. But, the airing of the old facts had led some one concerned to suggest that it would be well before they were reconsigned to their gloomy shelf—now probably for ever—to induce or compel that Mr Julius Handford to reappear and be questioned. And all traces of Mr Julius Handford being lost, Lightwood now referred to his client for authority to seek him through public advertisement.

'Does your objection go to writing to Lightwood, Rokesmith?'

'Not in the least, sir.'

'Then perhaps you'll write him a line, and say he is free to do what he likes. I don't think it promises.'

'*I* don't think it promises,' said the Secretary.

'Still, he may do what he likes.'

'I will write immediately. Let me thank you for so considerately yielding to my disinclination. It may seem less unreasonable, if I avow to you that although I don't know Mr Lightwood, I have a disagreeable association connected with him. It is not his fault; he is not at all to blame for it, and does not even know my name.'

Mr Boffin dismissed the matter with a nod or two. The letter was written, and next day Mr Julius Handford was advertised for. He was requested to place himself in communication with Mr Mortimer Lightwood, as a possible means of furthering the ends of justice, and a reward was offered to any one acquainted with his whereabout who would communicate the same to the said Mr Mortimer Lightwood at his office in the Temple. Every day for six weeks this advertisement appeared at the head of all the newspapers, and every day for six weeks the Secretary, when he saw it, said to himself, in the tone in which he had said to his employer,—'*I* don't think it promises!'

Among his first occupations the pursuit of that orphan wanted by Mrs Boffin held a conspicuous place. From the earliest moment of his engagement he showed a particular desire to please her, and, knowing her to have this object at heart, he followed it up with unwearying alacrity and interest.

Mr and Mrs Milvey had found their search a difficult one. Either an eligible orphan was of the wrong sex (which almost always happened) or was too old, or too young, or too sickly, or too dirty, or too much accustomed to the streets, or too likely to run away; or, it was found impossible to complete the philanthropic transaction without buying the orphan. For, the instant it became known that anybody wanted the orphan, up started some affectionate relative of the orphan who put a price upon the orphan's head. The suddenness of an orphan's rise in the market was not to be paralleled by the maddest records of the Stock Exchange. He would be at five thousand per cent discount out at nurse making a mud pie at nine in the morning, and (being inquired for) would go up to five thousand per cent premium before noon. The market was 'rigged' in various artful ways. Counterfeit stock got into circulation. Parents boldly represented themselves as dead, and brought their orphans with them. Genuine orphan-stock was surreptitiously withdrawn from the market. It being announced, by emissaries posted for the purpose, that Mr and Mrs Milvey were coming down the court, orphan scrip would be instantly concealed, and production refused, save on a condition usually stated by the brokers as 'a gallon of beer'. Likewise, fluctuations of a wild and South-Sea nature were occasioned, by orphan-holders keeping back, and then rushing into the market a dozen together. But, the uniform principle at the root of all these various operations was bargain and sale; and that principle could not be recognized by Mr and Mrs Milvey.

At length, tidings were received by the Reverend Frank of a charming orphan to be found at Brentford. One of the deceased parents (late his parishioners) had a poor widowed grandmother in that agreeable town, and she, Mrs Betty Higden, had carried off the orphan with maternal care, but could not afford to keep him.

The Secretary proposed to Mrs Boffin, either to go down himself and take a preliminary survey of this orphan, or to drive her down, that she might at once form her own opinion. Mrs Boffin preferring the latter course, they set off one morning in a hired phaeton, conveying the hammer-headed young man behind them.

The abode of Mrs Betty Higden was not easy to find, lying in such complicated back settlements of muddy Brentford that they left their equipage at the sign of the Three Magpies, and went in search of it on foot. After many inquiries and defeats, there was pointed out to them in a lane, a very small cottage residence, with a board across the open doorway, hooked on to which board by the armpits was a young gentleman of tender years, angling for mud with a headless wooden horse and line. In this young sportsman, distinguished by a crisply curling auburn head and a bluff countenance, the Secretary descried the orphan.

It unfortunately happened as they quickened their pace, that the orphan, lost to considerations of personal safety in the ardour of the moment, overbalanced himself and toppled into the street. Being an orphan of a chubby conformation, he then took to rolling, and had rolled into the gutter before they could come up. From the gutter he was rescued by John Rokesmith, and thus the first meeting with Mrs Higden was inaugurated by the awkward circumstance of their being in possession—one would say at first sight unlawful possession—of the orphan, upside down and purple in the countenance. The board across the doorway too, acting as a trap equally for the feet of Mrs Higden coming out, and the feet of Mrs Boffin and John Rokesmith going in, greatly increased the difficulty of the situation: to which the cries of the orphan imparted a lugubrious and inhuman character.

At first, it was impossible to explain, on account of the orphan's 'holding his breath': a most terrific proceeding, superinducing in the orphan lead-colour rigidity and a deadly silence, compared with which his cries were music yielding the height of enjoyment. But as he gradually recovered, Mrs Boffin gradually introduced herself, and smiling peace was gradually wooed back to Mrs Betty Higden's home.

It was then perceived to be a small home with a large mangle in it, at the handle of which machine stood a very long boy, with a very little head, and an open mouth of disproportionate capacity that seemed to assist his eyes in staring at the visitors. In a corner below the mangle, on a couple of stools, sat two very little children: a boy and a girl; and when the very long boy, in an interval of staring, took a turn at the mangle, it was alarming to see how it lunged itself at those two innocents, like a catapult designed for their destruction, harmlessly retiring when within an inch of their heads. The room was clean and neat. It had a brick floor, and a window of diamond panes, and a flounce hanging below the chimney-piece, and strings nailed from bottom to top outside the window on which scarlet-beans were to grow in the coming season if the Fates were propitious. However propitious they might have been in the seasons that were gone, to Betty Higden in the matter of beans, they had not been very favourable in the matter of coins; for it was easy to see that she was poor.

She was one of those old women, was Mrs Betty Higden, who by dint of an indomitable purpose and a strong constitution fight out many years, though each year has come with its new knock-down blows fresh to the fight against her, wearied by it; an active old woman, with a bright dark eye and a resolute face, yet quite a tender creature too; not a logically-reasoning woman, but God is good, and hearts may count in Heaven as high as heads.

'Yes sure!' said she, when the business was opened, 'Mrs Milvey had the kindness to write to me, ma'am, and I got Sloppy to read it. It was a pretty letter. But she's an affable lady.'

The visitors glanced at the long boy, who seemed to indicate by a broader stare of his mouth and eyes that in him Sloppy stood confessed.

'For I aint, you must know,' said Betty, 'much of a hand at reading writing-hand, though I can read my Bible and most print. And I do love a newspaper. You mightn't think it, but Sloppy is a beautiful reader of a newspaper. He do the Police in different voices.'

The visitors again considered it a point of politeness to look at Sloppy, who, looking at them, suddenly threw back his head, extended his mouth to its utmost width, and laughed loud and long. At this the two innocents, with their brains in that apparent danger, laughed, and Mrs Higden laughed, and the orphan laughed, and then the visitors laughed. Which was more cheerful than intelligible.

Then Sloppy seeming to be seized with an industrious mania or fury, turned to at the mangle, and impelled it at the heads of the innocents with such a creaking and rumbling, that Mrs Higden stopped him.

'The gentlefolks can't hear themselves speak, Sloppy. Bide a bit, bide a bit!'

'Is that the dear child in your lap?' said Mrs Boffin.

'Yes, ma'am, this is Johnny.'

'Johnny, too!' cried Mrs Boffin, turning to the Secretary; 'already Johnny! Only one of the two names left to give him! He's a pretty boy.'

With his chin tucked down in his shy childish manner, he was looking furtively at Mrs Boffin out of his blue eyes, and reaching his fat dimpled hand up to the lips of the old woman, who was kissing it by times.

'Yes, ma'am, he's a pretty boy, he's a dear darling boy, he's the child of my own last left daughter's daughter. But she's gone the way of all the rest.'

'Those are not his brother and sister?' said Mrs Boffin.

'Oh, dear no, ma'am. Those are Minders.'

'Minders?' the Secretary repeated,

'Left to be Minded, sir. I keep a Minding-School. I can take only three, on account of the Mangle. But I love children, and Four-pence a week is Four-pence. Come here, Toddles and Poddles.'

Toddles was the pet-name of the boy; Poddles of the girl. At their little unsteady pace, they came across the floor, hand-in-hand, as if they were traversing an extremely difficult road intersected by brooks, and, when they had had their heads patted by Mrs Betty Higden, made lunges at the orphan, dramatically representing an attempt to bear him, crowing, into captivity and slavery. All the three children enjoyed this to a delightful extent, and the sympathetic Sloppy again laughed long and loud. When it was discreet to stop the play, Betty Higden said 'Go to your seats Toddles and Poddles,' and they returned hand-in-hand across country, seeming to find the brooks rather swollen by late rains.

'And Master—or Mister—Sloppy?' said the Secretary, in doubt whether he was man, boy, or what.

'A love-child,' returned Betty Higden, dropping her voice; 'parents never known; found in the street. He was brought up in the—' with a shiver of repugnance, '—the House.'

'The Poor-house?' said the Secretary.

Mrs Higden set that resolute old face of hers, and darkly nodded yes.

'You dislike the mention of it.'

'Dislike the mention of it?' answered the old woman. 'Kill me sooner than take me there. Throw this pretty child under cart-horses' feet and a loaded waggon, sooner than take him there. Come to us and find us all a-dying, and set a light to us all where we lie, and let us all blaze away with the house into a heap of cinders, sooner than move a corpse of us there!'

A surprising spirit in this lonely woman after so many years of hard working, and hard living, my Lords and Gentlemen and Honourable Boards! What is it that we call it in our grandiose speeches? British independence, rather perverted? Is that, or something like it, the ring of the cant?

'Do I never read in the newspapers,' said the dame, fondling the child—'God help me and the like of me!—how the worn-out people that do come down to that, get driven from post to pillar and pillar to post, a-purpose to tire them out! Do I never read how they are put off, put off, put off—how they are grudged, grudged, grudged, the shelter, or the doctor, or the drop of physic, or the bit of bread? Do I never read how they grow heartsick of it and give it up, after having let themselves drop so low, and how they after all die out for want of help? Then I say, I hope I can die as well as another, and I'll die without that disgrace.'

Absolutely impossible my Lords and Gentlemen and Honourable Boards, by any stretch of legislative wisdom to set these perverse people right in their logic?

'Johnny, my pretty,' continued old Betty, caressing the child, and rather mourning over it than speaking to it, 'your old Granny Betty is nigher fourscore year than threescore and ten. She never begged nor had a penny of the Union money in all her life. She paid scot and she paid lot when she had money to pay; she worked when she could, and she starved when she must. You pray that your Granny may have strength enough left her at the last (she's strong for an old one, Johnny), to get up from her bed and run and hide herself, and swoon to death in a hole, sooner than fall into the hands of those Cruel Jacks we read of, that dodge and drive, and worry and weary, and scorn and shame, the decent poor.'

A brilliant success, my Lords and Gentlemen and Honourable Boards to have brought it to this in the minds of the best of the poor! Under submission, might it be worth thinking of, at any odd time?

The fright and abhorrence that Mrs Betty Higden smoothed out of her strong face as she ended this diversion, showed how seriously she had meant it.

'And does he work for you?' asked the Secretary, gently bringing the discourse back to Master or Mister Sloppy.

'Yes,' said Betty with a good-humoured smile and nod of the head. 'And well too.'

'Does he live here?'

'He lives more here than anywhere. He was thought to be no better than a Natural, and first come to me as a Minder. I made interest with Mr Blogg the Beadle to have him as a Minder, seeing him by chance up at church, and thinking I might do something with him. For he was a weak ricketty creetur then.'

'Is he called by his right name?'

'Why, you see, speaking quite correctly, he has no right name. I always understood he took his name from being found on a Sloppy night.'

'He seems an amiable fellow.'

'Bless you, sir, there's not a bit of him,' returned Betty, 'that's not amiable. So you may judge how amiable he is, by running your eye along his heighth.'

Of an ungainly make was Sloppy. Too much of him longwise, too little of him broadwise, and too many sharp angles of him angle-wise. One of those shambling male human creatures, born to be indiscreetly candid in the revelation of buttons; every button he had about him glaring at the public to a quite preternatural extent. A considerable capital of knee and elbow and wrist and ankle, had Sloppy, and he didn't know how to dispose of it to the best advantage, but was always investing it in wrong securities, and so getting himself into embarrassed circumstances. Full-Private Number One in the Awkward Squad of the rank and file of life, was Sloppy, and yet had his glimmering notions of standing true to the Colours.

'And now,' said Mrs Boffin, 'concerning Johnny.'

As Johnny, with his chin tucked in and lips pouting, reclined in Betty's lap, concentrating his blue eyes on the visitors and shading them from observation with a dimpled arm, old Betty took one of his fresh fat hands in her withered right, and fell to gently beating it on her withered left.

'Yes, ma'am. Concerning Johnny.'

'If you trust the dear child to me,' said Mrs Boffin, with a face inviting trust, 'he shall have the best of homes, the best of care, the best of education, the best of friends. Please God I will be a true good mother to him!'

'I am thankful to you, ma'am, and the dear child would be thankful if he was old enough to understand.' Still lightly beating the little hand upon her own. 'I wouldn't stand in the dear child's light, not if I had all my life before me instead of a very little of it. But I hope you won't take it ill that I cleave to the child closer than words can tell, for he's the last living thing left me.'

'Take it ill, my dear soul? Is it likely? And you so tender of him as to bring him home here!'

'I have seen,' said Betty, still with that light beat upon her hard rough hand, 'so many of them on my lap. And they are all gone but this one! I am ashamed to seem so selfish, but I don't really mean it. It'll be the making of his fortune, and he'll be a gentleman when I am dead. I—I—don't know what comes over me. I—try against it. Don't notice me!' The light beat stopped, the resolute mouth gave way, and the fine strong old face broke up into weakness and tears.

Now, greatly to the relief of the visitors, the emotional Sloppy no sooner beheld his patroness in this condition, than, throwing back his head and throwing open his mouth, he lifted up his voice and bellowed. This alarming note of something wrong instantly terrified Toddles and Poddles, who were no sooner heard to roar surprisingly, than Johnny, curving himself the wrong way and striking out at Mrs Boffin with a pair of indifferent shoes, became a prey to despair. The absurdity of the situation put its pathos to the rout. Mrs Betty Higden was herself in a moment, and brought them all to order with that speed, that Sloppy, stopping short in a poly-syllabic bellow, transferred his energy to the mangle, and had taken several penitential turns before he could be stopped.

'There, there, there!' said Mrs Boffin, almost regarding her kind self as the most ruthless of women. 'Nothing is going to be done. Nobody need be frightened. We're all comfortable; ain't we, Mrs Higden?'

'Sure and certain we are,' returned Betty.

'And there really is no hurry, you know,' said Mrs Boffin in a lower voice. 'Take time to think of it, my good creature!'

'Don't you fear *me* no more, ma'am,' said Betty; 'I thought of it for good yesterday. I don't know what come over me just now, but it'll never come again.'

'Well, then, Johnny shall have more time to think of it,' returned Mrs Boffin; 'the pretty child shall have time to get used to it. And you'll get him more used to it, if you think well of it; won't you?'

Betty undertook that, cheerfully and readily.

'Lor,' cried Mrs Boffin, looking radiantly about her, 'we want to make everybody happy, not dismal!—And perhaps you wouldn't mind letting me know how used to it you begin to get, and how it all goes on?'

'I'll send Sloppy,' said Mrs Higden.

'And this gentleman who has come with me will pay him for his trouble,' said Mrs Boffin. 'And Mr Sloppy, whenever you come to my house, be sure you never go away without having had a good dinner of meat, beer, vegetables, and pudding.'

This still further brightened the face of affairs; for, the highly sympathetic Sloppy, first broadly staring and grinning,

and then roaring with laughter, Toddles and Poddles followed
suit, and Johnny trumped the trick. T and P considering these
favourable circumstances for the resumption of that dramatic
descent upon Johnny, again came across-country hand-in-hand
upon a buccaneering expedition; and this having been fought out
in the chimney corner behind Mrs Higden's chair, with great
valour on both sides, those desperate pirates returned hand-in-
hand to their stools, across the dry bed of a mountain torrent.

'You must tell me what I can do for you, Betty my friend,'
said Mrs Boffin confidentially, 'if not to-day, next time.'

'Thank you all the same, ma'am, but I want nothing for
myself. I can work. I'm strong. I can walk twenty mile if I'm
put to it.' Old Betty was proud, and said it with a sparkle in her
bright eyes.

'Yes, but there are some little comforts that you wouldn't
be the worse for,' returned Mrs Boffin. 'Bless ye, I wasn't born
a lady any more than you.'

'It seems to me,' said Betty, smiling, 'that you were born a
lady, and a true one, or there never was a lady born. But I
couldn't take anything from you, my dear. I never did take
anything from any one. It ain't that I'm not grateful, but I love to
earn it better.'

'Well, well!' returned Mrs Boffin. 'I only spoke of little
things, or I wouldn't have taken the liberty.'

Betty put her visitor's hand to her lips, in acknowledgment
of the delicate answer. Wonderfully upright her figure was, and
wonderfully self-reliant her look, as, standing facing her visitor,
she explained herself further.

'If I could have kept the dear child, without the dread that's
always upon me of his coming to that fate I have spoken of, I
could never have parted with him, even to you. For I love him, I
love him, I love him! I love my husband long dead and gone, in
him; I love my children dead and gone, in him; I love my young
and hopeful days dead and gone, in him. I couldn't sell that
love, and look you in your bright kind face. It's a free gift. I am
in want of nothing. When my strength fails me, if I can but die
out quick and quiet, I shall be quite content. I have stood
between my dead and that shame I have spoken of, and it has
been kept off from every one of them. Sewed into my gown,'
with her hand upon her breast, 'is just enough to lay me in the
grave. Only see that it's rightly spent, so as I may rest free to the
last from that cruelty and disgrace, and you'll have done much

more than a little thing for me, and all that in this present world my heart is set upon.'

Mrs Betty Higden's visitor pressed her hand. There was no more breaking up of the strong old face into weakness. My Lords and Gentlemen and Honourable Boards, it really was as composed as our own faces, and almost as dignified.

And now, Johnny was to be inveigled into occupying a temporary position on Mrs Boffin's lap. It was not until he had been piqued into competition with the two diminutive Minders, by seeing them successively raised to that post and retire from it without injury, that he could be by any means induced to leave Mrs Betty Higden's skirts; towards which he exhibited, even when in Mrs Boffin's embrace, strong yearnings, spiritual and bodily; the former expressed in a very gloomy visage, the latter in extended arms. However, a general description of the toy-wonders lurking in Mr Boffin's house, so far conciliated this worldly-minded orphan as to induce him to stare at her frowningly, with a fist in his mouth, and even at length to chuckle when a richly-caparisoned horse on wheels, with a miraculous gift of cantering to cake-shops, was mentioned. This sound being taken up by the Minders, swelled into a rapturous trio which gave general satisfaction.

So, the interview was considered very successful, and Mrs Boffin was pleased, and all were satisfied. Not least of all, Sloppy, who undertook to conduct the visitors back by the best way to the Three Magpies, and whom the hammer-headed young man much despised.

This piece of business thus put in train, the Secretary drove Mrs Boffin back to the Bower, and found employment for himself at the new house until evening. Whether, when evening came, he took a way to his lodgings that led through fields, with any design of finding Miss Bella Wilfer in those fields, is not so certain as that she regularly walked there at that hour.

And, moreover, it is certain that there she was.

No longer in mourning, Miss Bella was dressed in as pretty colours as she could muster. There is no denying that she was as pretty as they, and that she and the colours went very prettily together. She was reading as she walked, and of course it is to be inferred, from her showing no knowledge of Mr Rokesmith's approach, that she did not know he was approaching.

'Eh?' said Miss Bella, raising her eyes from her book, when he stopped before her. 'Oh! It's you.'

'Only I. A fine evening!'

'Is it?' said Bella, looking coldly round. 'I suppose it is, now you mention it. I have not been thinking of the evening.'

'So intent upon your book?'

'Ye-e-es,' replied Bella, with a drawl of indifference.

'A love story, Miss Wilfer?'

'Oh dear no, or I shouldn't be reading it. It's more about money than anything else.'

'And does it say that money is better than anything?'

'Upon my word,' returned Bella, 'I forget what it says, but you can find out for yourself, if you like, Mr Rokesmith. I don't want it any more.'

The Secretary took the book—she had fluttered the leaves as if it were a fan—and walked beside her.

'I am charged with a message for you, Miss Wilfer.'

'Impossible, I think!' said Bella, with another drawl.

'From Mrs Boffin. She desired me to assure you of the pleasure she has in finding that she will be ready to receive you in another week or two at furthest.'

Bella turned her head towards him, with her prettily-insolent eyebrows raised, and her eyelids drooping. As much as to say, 'How did *you* come by the message, pray?'

'I have been waiting for an opportunity of telling you that I am Mr Boffin's Secretary.'

'I am as wise as ever,' said Miss Bella, loftily, 'for I don't know what a Secretary is. Not that it signifies.'

'Not at all.'

A covert glance at her face, as he walked beside her, showed him that she had not expected his ready assent to that proposition.

'Then are you going to be always there, Mr Rokesmith?' she inquired, as if that would be a drawback.

'Always? No. Very much there? Yes.'

'Dear me!' drawled Bella, in a tone of mortification.

'But my position there as Secretary, will be very different from yours as guest. You will know little or nothing about me. I shall transact the business: you will transact the pleasure. I shall have my salary to earn; you will have nothing to do but to enjoy and attract.'

'Attract, sir?' said Bella, again with her eyebrows raised, and her eyelids drooping. 'I don't understand you.'

Without replying on this point, Mr Rokesmith went on.

'Excuse me; when I first saw you in your black dress—'

('There!' was Miss Bella's mental exclamation. 'What did I say to them at home? Everybody noticed that ridiculous mourning.')

'When I first saw you in your black dress, I was at a loss to account for that distinction between yourself and your family. I hope it was not impertinent to speculate upon it?'

'I hope not, I am sure,' said Miss Bella, haughtily. 'But you ought to know best how you speculated upon it.'

Mr Rokesmith inclined his head in a deprecatory manner, and went on.

'Since I have been entrusted with Mr Boffin's affairs, I have necessarily come to understand the little mystery. I venture to remark that I feel persuaded that much of your loss may be repaired. I speak, of course, merely of wealth, Miss Wilfer. The loss of a perfect stranger, whose worth, or worthlessness, I cannot estimate—nor you either—is beside the question. But this excellent gentleman and lady are so full of simplicity, so full of generosity, so inclined towards you, and so desirous to—how shall I express it?—to make amends for their good fortune, that you have only to respond.'

As he watched her with another covert look, he saw a certain ambitious triumph in her face which no assumed coldness could conceal.

'As we have been brought under one roof by an accidental combination of circumstances, which oddly extends itself to the new relations before us, I have taken the liberty of saying these few words. You don't consider them intrusive I hope?' said the Secretary with deference.

'Really, Mr Rokesmith, I can't say what I consider them,' returned the young lady. 'They are perfectly new to me, and may be founded altogether on your own imagination.'

'You will see.'

These same fields were opposite the Wilfer premises. The discreet Mrs Wilfer now looking out of window and beholding her daughter in conference with her lodger, instantly tied up her head and came out for a casual walk.

'I have been telling Miss Wilfer,' said John Rokesmith, as the majestic lady came stalking up, 'that I have become, by a curious chance, Mr Boffin's Secretary or man of business.'

'I have not,' returned Mrs Wilfer, waving her gloves in her chronic state of dignity, and vague ill-usage, 'the honour of any intimate acquaintance with Mr Boffin, and it is not for me to congratulate that gentleman on the acquisition he has made.'

'A poor one enough,' said Rokesmith.

'Pardon me,' returned Mrs Wilfer, 'the merits of Mr Boffin may be highly distinguished—may be more distinguished than the countenance of Mrs Boffin would imply—but it were the insanity of humility to deem him worthy of a better assistant.'

'You are very good. I have also been telling Miss Wilfer that she is expected very shortly at the new residence in town.'

'Having tacitly consented,' said Mrs Wilfer, with a grand shrug of her shoulders, and another wave of her gloves, 'to my child's acceptance of the proffered attentions of Mrs Boffin, I interpose no objection.'

Here Miss Bella offered the remonstrance: 'Don't talk nonsense, ma, please.'

'Peace!' said Mrs Wilfer.

'No, ma, I am not going to be made so absurd. Interposing objections!'

'I say,' repeated Mrs Wilfer, with a vast access of grandeur, 'that I am *not* going to interpose objections. If Mrs Boffin (to whose countenance no disciple of Lavater could possibly for a single moment subscribe),' with a shiver, 'seeks to illuminate her new residence in town with the attractions of a child of mine, I am content that she should be favoured by the company of a child of mine.'

'You use the word, ma'am, I have myself used,' said Rokesmith, with a glance at Bella, 'when you speak of Miss Wilfer's attractions there.'

'Pardon me,' returned Mrs Wilfer, with dreadful solemnity, 'but I had not finished.'

'Pray excuse me.'

'I was about to say,' pursued Mrs Wilfer, who clearly had not had the faintest idea of saying anything more: 'that when I use the term attractions, I do so with the qualification that I do not mean it in any way whatever.'

The excellent lady delivered this luminous elucidation of her views with an air of greatly obliging her hearers, and greatly distinguishing herself. Whereat Miss Bella laughed a scornful little laugh and said:

'Quite enough about this, I am sure, on all sides. Have the goodness, Mr Rokesmith, to give my love to Mrs Boffin—'

'Pardon me!' cried Mrs Wilfer. 'Compliments.'

'Love!' repeated Bella, with a little stamp of her foot.

'No!' said Mrs Wilfer, monotonously. 'Compliments.'

('Say Miss Wilfer's love, and Mrs Wilfer's compliments,' the Secretary proposed, as a compromise.)

'And I shall be very glad to come when she is ready for me. The sooner, the better.'

'One last word, Bella,' said Mrs Wilfer, 'before descending to the family apartment. I trust that as a child of mine you will ever be sensible that it will be graceful in you, when associating with Mr and Mrs Boffin upon equal terms, to remember that the Secretary, Mr Rokesmith, as your father's lodger, has a claim on your good word.'

The condescension with which Mrs Wilfer delivered this proclamation of patronage, was as wonderful as the swiftness with which the lodger had lost caste in the Secretary. He smiled as the mother retired down stairs; but his face fell, as the daughter followed.

'So insolent, so trivial, so capricious, so mercenary, so careless, so hard to touch, so hard to turn!' he said, bitterly.

And added as he went upstairs. 'And yet so pretty, so pretty!'

And added presently, as he walked to and fro in his room. 'And if she knew!'

She knew that he was shaking the house by his walking to and fro; and she declared it another of the miseries of being poor, that you couldn't get rid of a haunting Secretary, stump—stump—stumping overhead in the dark, like a Ghost.

Chapter 17

A Dismal Swamp

AND now, in the blooming summer days, behold Mr and Mrs Boffin established in the eminently aristocratic family mansion, and behold all manner of crawling, creeping, fluttering, and buzzing creatures, attracted by the gold dust of the Golden Dustman!

Foremost among those leaving cards at the eminently aristocratic door before it is quite painted, are the Veneerings: out of breath, one might imagine, from the impetuosity of their rush to the eminently aristocratic steps. One copper-plate Mrs Veneering, two copper-plate Mr Veneerings, and a connubial copper-plate Mr and Mrs Veneering, requesting the honour of Mr and Mrs Boffin's company at dinner with the utmost Analytical solemnities. The enchanting Lady Tippins leaves a card. Twemlow leaves cards. A tall custard-colored phaeton tooling up in a solemn manner leaves four cards, to wit, a couple of Mr Podsnaps, a Mrs Podsnap, and a Miss Podsnap. All the world and his wife and daughter leave cards. Sometimes the world's wife has so many daughters, that her card reads rather like a Miscellaneous Lot at an Auction; comprising Mrs Tapkins, Miss Tapkins, Miss Frederica Tapkins, Miss Antonina Tapkins, Miss Malvina Tapkins, and Miss Euphemia Tapkins; at the same time, the same lady leaves the card of Mrs Henry George Alfred Swoshle, *née* Tapkins; also, a card, Mrs Tapkins at Home, Wednesdays, Music, Portland Place.

Miss Bella Wilfer becomes an inmate, for an indefinite period, of the eminently aristocratic dwelling. Mrs Boffin bears Miss Bella away to her Milliner's and Dressmaker's, and she gets beautifully dressed. The Veneerings find with swift remorse that they have omitted to invite Miss Bella Wilfer. One Mrs Veneering and one Mr and Mrs Veneering requesting that additional honour, instantly do penance in white cardboard on the hall table. Mrs Tapkins likewise discovers her omission, and with promptitude repairs it; for herself, for Miss Tapkins, for Miss Frederica Tapkins, for Miss Antonina Tapkins, for Miss Malvina Tapkins, and for Miss Euphemia Tapkins. Likewise, for Mrs Henry George Alfred Swoshle *née* Tapkins. Likewise, for Mrs Tapkins at Home, Wednesdays, Music, Portland Place.

Tradesmen's books hunger, and tradesmen's mouths water, for the gold dust of the Golden Dustman. As Mrs Boffin and Miss Wilfer drive out, or as Mr Boffin walks out at his jog-trot pace, the fishmonger pulls off his hat with an air of reverence founded on conviction. His men cleanse their fingers on their woollen aprons before presuming to touch their foreheads to Mr Boffin or Lady. The gaping salmon and the golden mullet lying on the slab seem to turn up their eyes sideways, as they would turn up their hands if they had any, in worshipping admiration. The butcher, though a portly and prosperous man, doesn't know what to do with himself, so anxious is he to express humility when discovered by the passing Boffins taking the air in a mutton grove. Presents are made to the Boffin servants, and bland strangers with business-cards meeting said servants in the street, offer hypothetical corruption. As, 'Supposing I was to be favoured with an order from Mr Boffin, my dear friend, it would be worth my while'—to do a certain thing that I hope might not prove wholly disagreeable to your feelings.

But no one knows so well as the Secretary, who opens and

reads the letters, what a set is made at the man marked by a stroke of notoriety. Oh the varieties of dust for ocular use, offered in exchange for the gold dust of the Golden Dustman! Fifty-seven churches to be erected with half-crowns, forty-two parsonage houses to be repaired with shillings, seven-and-twenty organs to be built with halfpence, twelve hundred children to be brought up on postage stamps. Not that a half-crown, shilling, halfpenny, or postage stamp, would be particularly acceptable from Mr Boffin, but that it is so obvious he is the man to make up the deficiency. And then the charities, my Christian brother! And mostly in difficulties, yet mostly lavish, too, in the expensive articles of print and paper. Large fat private double letter, sealed with ducal coronet. 'Nicodemus Boffin, Esquire. My Dear Sir,—Having consented to preside at the forthcoming Annual Dinner of the Family Party Fund, and feeling deeply impressed with the immense usefulness of that noble Institution and the great importance of its being supported by a List of Stewards that shall prove to the public the interest taken in it by popular and distinguished men, I have undertaken to ask you to become a Steward on that occasion. Soliciting your favourable reply before the 14th instant, I am, My Dear Sir, Your faithful Servant, LINSEED. P.S. The Steward's fee is limited to three Guineas.' Friendly this, on the part of the Duke of Linseed (and thoughtful in the postscript), only lithographed by the hundred and presenting but a pale individuality of an address to Nicodemus Boffin, Esquire, in quite another hand. It takes two noble Earls and a Viscount, combined, to inform Nicodemus Boffin, Esquire, in an equally flattering manner, that an estimable lady in the West of England has offered to present a purse containing twenty pounds, to the Society for Granting Annuities to Unassuming Members of the Middle Classes, if twenty individuals will previously present purses of one hundred pounds each. And those benevolent noblemen very kindly point out that if Nicodemus Boffin, Esquire, should wish to present two or more purses, it will not be inconsistent with the design of the estimable lady in the West of England, provided each purse be coupled with the name of some member of his honoured and respected family.

These are the corporate beggars. But there are, besides, the individual beggars; and how does the heart of the Secretary fail him when he has to cope with *them*! And they must be coped with to some extent, because they all enclose documents (they call their scraps documents; but they are, as to papers deserving the name, what minced veal is to a calf), the non-return of which would be their ruin. That is to say, they are utterly ruined now, but they would be more utterly ruined then. Among these correspondents are several daughters of general officers, long accustomed to every luxury of life (except spelling), who little thought, when their gallant fathers waged war in the Peninsula, that they would ever have to appeal to those whom Providence, in its inscrutable wisdom, has blessed with untold gold, and from among whom they select the name of Nicodemus Boffin, Esquire, for a maiden effort in this wise, understanding that he has such a heart as never was. The Secretary learns, too, that confidence between man and wife would seem to obtain but rarely when virtue is in distress, so numerous are the wives who take up their pens to ask Mr Boffin for money without the knowledge of their devoted husbands, who would never permit it; while, on the other hand, so numerous are the husbands who take up their pens to ask Mr Boffin for money without the knowledge of their devoted wives, who would instantly go out of their senses if they had the least suspicion of the circumstance. There are the inspired beggars, too. These were sitting, only yesterday evening, musing over a fragment of candle which must soon go out and leave them in the dark for the rest of their nights, when surely some Angel whispered the name of Nicodemus Boffin, Esquire, to their souls, imparting rays of hope, nay confidence, to which they had long been strangers! Akin to these are the suggestively-befriended beggars. They were partaking of a cold potato and water by the flickering and gloomy light of a lucifer-match in their lodgings (rent considerably in arrear, and heartless landlady threatening expulsion 'like a dog' into the streets), when a gifted friend happening to look in, said, 'Write immediately to Nicodemus Boffin, Esquire,' and would take no denial. There are the nobly independent beggars too. These, in the days of their abundance, ever regarded gold as dross, and have not yet got over that only impediment in the way of their amassing wealth, but they want no dross from Nicodemus Boffin, Esquire; No, Mr Boffin; the world may term it pride, paltry pride if you will, but they wouldn't take it if you offered it; a loan, sir—for fourteen weeks to the day, interest calculated at the rate of five per cent per annum, to be bestowed upon any charitable institution you may name—is all they want of you, and if you have the meanness to refuse it, count on being despised by these great spirits. There are the beggars of punctual business-habits too. These will make an end of themselves at a quarter to one P.M. on Tuesday, if no Post-office order is in the interim received from Nicodemus Boffin,

Esquire; arriving after a quarter to one P.M. on Tuesday, it need not be sent, as they will then (having made an exact memorandum of the heartless circumstances) be 'cold in death.' There are the beggars on horseback too, in another sense from the sense of the proverb. These are mounted and ready to start on the highway to affluence. The goal is before them, the road is in the best condition, their spurs are on, the steed is willing, but, at the last moment, for want of some special thing—a clock, a violin, an astronomical telescope, an electrifying machine—they must dismount for ever, unless they receive its equivalent in money from Nicodemus Boffin, Esquire. Less given to detail are the beggars who make sporting ventures. These, usually to be addressed in reply under initials at a country post-office, inquire in feminine hands, Dare one who cannot disclose herself to Nicodemus Boffin, Esquire, but whose name might startle him were it revealed, solicit the immediate advance of two hundred pounds from unexpected riches exercising their noblest privilege in the trust of a common humanity?

In such a Dismal Swamp does the new house stand, and through it does the Secretary daily struggle breast-high. Not to mention all the people alive who have made inventions that won't act, and all the jobbers who job in all the jobberies jobbed; though these may be regarded as the Alligators of the Dismal Swamp, and are always lying by to drag the Golden Dustman under.

But the old house. There are no designs against the Golden Dustman there? There are no fish of the shark tribe in the Bower waters? Perhaps not. Still, Wegg is established there, and would seem, judged by his secret proceedings, to cherish a notion of making a discovery. For, when a man with a wooden leg lies prone on his stomach to peep under bedsteads; and hops up ladders, like some extinct bird, to survey the tops of presses and cupboards; and provides himself an iron rod which he is always poking and prodding into dust-mounds; the probability is that he expects to find something.

BOOK THE SECOND
BIRDS OF A FEATHER

———•••———

Chapter 1
Of an Educational Character

THE school at which young Charley Hexam had first learned from a book—the streets being, for pupils of his degree, the great Preparatory Establishment in which very much that is never unlearned is learned without and before book—was a miserable loft in an unsavoury yard. Its atmosphere was oppressive and disagreeable; it was crowded, noisy, and confusing; half the pupils dropped asleep, or fell into a state of waking stupefaction; the other half kept them in either condition by maintaining a monotonous droning noise, as if they were performing, out of time and tune, on a ruder sort of bagpipe. The teachers, animated solely by good intentions, had no idea of execution, and a lamentable jumble was the upshot of their kind endeavours.

It was a school for all ages, and for both sexes. The latter were kept apart, and the former were partitioned off into square assortments. But, all the place was pervaded by a grimly ludicrous pretence that every pupil was childish and innocent. This pretence, much favoured by the lady-visitors, led to the ghastliest absurdities. Young women old in the vices of the commonest and worst life, were expected to profess themselves enthralled by the good child's book, the Adventures of Little Margery, who resided in the village cottage by the mill; severely reproved and morally squashed the miller, when she was five and he was fifty; divided her porridge with singing birds; denied herself a new nankeen bonnet, on the ground that the turnips did not wear nankeen bonnets, neither did the sheep who ate them; who plaited straw and delivered the dreariest orations to all comers, at all sorts of unseasonable times. So, unwieldy young dredgers and hulking mudlarks were referred to the experiences of Thomas Twopence, who, having resolved not to rob (under circumstances of uncommon atrocity) his particular friend and benefactor, of eighteenpence, presently came into supernatural possession of three and sixpence, and lived a shining light ever afterwards. (Note, that the benefactor came to no good.) Several swaggering sinners had written their own biographies in the same strain; it always appearing from the lessons of those very boastful persons, that you were to do good, not because it *was* good, but because you were to make a good thing of it. Contrariwise, the adult pupils were taught to read (if they could learn) out of the New Testament; and by dint of stumbling over the syllables and keeping their bewildered eyes on the particular syllables coming round to their turn, were as absolutely ignorant of the sublime history, as if they had never seen or heard of it. An exceedingly and confoundingly perplexing jumble of a school, in fact, where black spirits and grey, red spirits and white, jumbled jumbled jumbled jumbled, jumbled every night. And particularly every Sunday night. For then, an inclined plane of unfortunate infants would be handed over to the prosiest and worst of all the teachers with good intentions, whom nobody older would endure. Who, taking his stand on the floor before them as chief executioner, would be attended by a conventional volunteer boy as executioner's assistant. When and where it first became the conventional system that a weary or inattentive infant in a class must have its face smoothed downward with a hot hand, or when and where the conventional volunteer boy first beheld such system in operation, and became inflamed with a sacred zeal to administer it, matters not. It was the function of the chief executioner to hold forth, and it was the function of the acolyte to dart at sleeping infants, yawning infants, restless infants, whimpering infants, and smooth their wretched faces; sometimes with one hand, as if he were anointing them for a whisker; sometimes with both hands, applied after the fashion of blinkers. And so the jumble would be in action in this department for a mortal hour; the exponent drawling on to My Dearerr Childerrenerr, let us say, for example, about the beautiful coming to the Sepulchre; and repeating the word Sepulchre (commonly used among infants) five hundred times, and never once hinting what it meant; the conventional boy smoothing away right and left, as an infallible commentary; the whole hot-bed of flushed and exhausted infants exchanging measles, rashes, whooping-cough, fever, and stomach disorders, as if they were assembled in High Market for the purpose.

Even in this temple of good intentions, an exceptionally sharp boy exceptionally determined to learn, could learn something, and, having learned it, could impart it much better than the teachers; as being more knowing than they, and not at the disadvantage in which they stood towards the shrewder pupils. In this way it had come about that Charley Hexam had risen in the jumble, taught in the jumble, and been received from the jumble into a better school.

'So you want to go and see your sister, Hexam?'

'If you please, Mr Headstone.'

'I have half a mind to go with you. Where does your sister live?'

'Why, she is not settled yet, Mr Headstone. I'd rather you didn't see her till she is settled, if it was all the same to you.'

'Look here, Hexam.' Mr Bradley Headstone, highly certificated stipendiary schoolmaster, drew his right forefinger through one of the buttonholes of the boy's coat, and looked at it attentively. 'I hope your sister may be good company for you?'

'Why do you doubt it, Mr Headstone?'

'I did not say I doubted it.'

'No, sir; you didn't say so.'

Bradley Headstone looked at his finger again, took it out of the buttonhole and looked at it closer, bit the side of it and looked at it again.

'You see, Hexam, you will be one of us. In good time you are sure to pass a creditable examination and become one of us. Then the question is—'

The boy waited so long for the question, while the schoolmaster looked at a new side of his finger, and bit it, and looked at it again, that at length the boy repeated:

'The question is, sir—?'

'Whether you had not better leave well alone.'

'Is it well to leave my sister alone, Mr Headstone?'

'I do not say so, because I do not know. I put it to you. I ask you to think of it. I want you to consider. You know how well you are doing here.'

'After all, she got me here,' said the boy, with a struggle.

'Perceiving the necessity of it,' acquiesced the schoolmaster, 'and making up her mind fully to the separation. Yes.'

The boy, with a return of that former reluctance or struggle or whatever it was, seemed to debate with himself. At length he said, raising his eyes to the master's face:

'I wish you'd come with me and see her, Mr Headstone, though she is not settled. I wish you'd come with me, and take her in the rough, and judge her for yourself.'

'You are sure you would not like,' asked the schoolmaster, 'to prepare her?'

'My sister Lizzie,' said the boy, proudly, 'wants no preparing, Mr Headstone. What she is, she is, and shows herself to be. There's no pretending about my sister.'

His confidence in her, sat more easily upon him than the indecision with which he had twice contended. It was his better nature to be true to her, if it were his worse nature to be wholly selfish. And as yet the better nature had the stronger hold.

'Well, I can spare the evening,' said the schoolmaster. 'I am ready to walk with you.'

'Thank you, Mr Headstone. And I am ready to go.'

Bradley Headstone, in his decent black coat and waistcoat, and decent white shirt, and decent formal black tie, and decent pantaloons of pepper and salt, with his decent silver watch in his pocket and its decent hair-guard round his neck, looked a thoroughly decent young man of six-and-twenty. He was never seen in any other dress, and yet there was a certain stiffness in his manner of wearing this, as if there were a want of adaption between him and it, recalling some mechanics in their holiday clothes. He had acquired mechanically a great store of teacher's knowledge. He could do mental arithmetic mechanically, sing at sight mechanically, blow various wind instruments mechanically, even play the great church organ mechanically. From his early childhood up, his mind had been a place of mechanical stowage. The arrangement of his wholesale warehouse, so that it might be always ready to meet the demands of retail dealers— history here, geography there, astronomy to the right, political economy to the left—natural history, the physical sciences, figures, music, the lower mathematics, and what not, all in their several places—this care had imparted to his countenance a look of care; while the habit of questioning and being questioned had given him a suspicious manner, or a manner that would be better described as one of lying in wait. There was a kind of settled trouble in the face. It was the face belonging to a naturally slow or inattentive intellect that had toiled hard to get what it had won, and that had to hold it now that it was gotten. He always seemed to be uneasy lest anything should be missing from his mental warehouse, and taking stock to assure himself.

Suppression of so much to make room for so much, had given him a constrained manner, over and above. Yet there was enough of what was animal, and of what was fiery (though smouldering), still visible in him, to suggest that if young Bradley Headstone, when a pauper lad, had chanced to be told off for the sea, he would not have been the last man in a ship's crew. Regarding that origin of his, he was proud, moody, and sullen, desiring it to be forgotten. And few people knew of it.

In some visits to the Jumble his attention had been attracted to this boy Hexam. An undeniable boy for a pupil-teacher; an undeniable boy to do credit to the master who should bring him on. Combined with this consideration, there may have been some thought of the pauper lad now never to be mentioned. Be that how it might, he had with pains gradually worked the boy into his own school, and procured him some offices to discharge there, which were repaid with food and lodging. Such were the circumstances that had brought together Bradley Headstone and young Charley Hexam that autumn evening. Autumn, because full half a year had come and gone since the bird of prey lay dead upon the river-shore.

The schools—for they were twofold, as the sexes—were down in that district of the flat country tending to the Thames, where Kent and Surrey meet, and where the railways still bestride the market-gardens that will soon die under them. The schools were newly built, and there were so many like them all over the country, that one might have thought the whole were but one restless edifice with the locomotive gift of Aladdin's palace. They were in a neighbourhood which looked like a toy neighbourhood taken in blocks out of a box by a child of particularly incoherent mind, and set up anyhow; here, one side of a new street; there, a large solitary public-house facing nowhere; here, another unfinished street already in ruins; there, a church; here, an immense new warehouse; there, a dilapidated old country villa; then, a medley of black ditch, sparkling cucumber-frame, rank field, richly cultivated kitchen-garden, brick viaduct, arch-spanned canal, and disorder of frowziness and fog. As if the child had given the table a kick, and gone to sleep.

But, even among school-buildings, school-teachers, and school-pupils, all according to pattern and all engendered in the light of the latest Gospel according to Monotony, the older pattern into which so many fortunes have been shaped for good and evil, comes out. It came out in Miss Peecher the schoolmistress, watering her flowers, as Mr Bradley Headstone walked forth. It came out in Miss Peecher the schoolmistress, watering the flowers in the little dusty bit of garden attached to her small official residence, with little windows like the eyes in needles, and little doors like the covers of school-books.

Small, shining, neat, methodical, and buxom was Miss Peecher; cherry-cheeked and tuneful of voice. A little pincushion, a little housewife, a little book, a little workbox, a little set of tables and weights and measures, and a little woman, all in one. She could write a little essay on any subject, exactly a slate long, beginning at the left-hand top of one side and ending at the right-hand bottom of the other, and the essay should be strictly according to rule. If Mr Bradley Headstone had addressed a written proposal of marriage to her, she would probably have replied in a complete little essay on the theme exactly a slate long, but would certainly have replied Yes. For she loved him. The decent hair-guard that went round his neck and took care of his decent silver watch was an object of envy to her. So would Miss Peecher have gone round his neck and taken care of him. Of him, insensible. Because he did not love Miss Peecher.

Miss Peecher's favourite pupil, who assisted her in her little household, was in attendance with a can of water to replenish her little watering-pot, and sufficiently divined the state of Miss Peecher's affections to feel it necessary that she herself should love young Charley Hexam. So, there was a double palpitation among the double stocks and double wall-flowers, when the master and the boy looked over the little gate.

'A fine evening, Miss Peecher,' said the Master.

'A very fine evening, Mr Headstone,' said Miss Peecher. 'Are you taking a walk?'

'Hexam and I are going to take a long walk.'

'Charming weather,' remarked Miss Peecher, '*for* a long walk.'

'Ours is rather on business than mere pleasure,' said the Master.

Miss Peecher inverting her watering-pot, and very carefully shaking out the few last drops over a flower, as if there were some special virtue in them which would make it a Jack's beanstalk before morning, called for replenishment to her pupil, who had been speaking to the boy.

'Good-night, Miss Peecher,' said the Master.

'Good-night, Mr Headstone,' said the Mistress.

The pupil had been, in her state of pupilage, so imbued with the class-custom of stretching out an arm, as if to hail a cab or omnibus, whenever she found she had an observation on hand to offer to Miss Peecher, that she often did it in their domestic relations; and she did it now.

'Well, Mary Anne?' said Miss Peecher.

'If you please, ma'am, Hexam said they were going to see his sister.'

'But that can't be, I think,' returned Miss Peecher: 'because Mr Headstone can have no business with *her*.'

Mary Anne again hailed.

'Well, Mary Anne?'

'If you please, ma'am, perhaps it's Hexam's business?'

'That may be,' said Miss Peecher. 'I didn't think of that. Not that it matters at all.'

Mary Anne again hailed.

'Well, Mary Anne?'

'They say she's very handsome.'

'Oh, Mary Anne, Mary Anne!' returned Miss Peecher, slightly colouring and shaking her head, a little out of humour; 'how often have I told you not to use that vague expression, not to speak in that general way? When you say *they* say, what do you mean? Part of speech They?'

Mary Anne hooked her right arm behind her in her left hand, as being under examination, and replied:

'Personal pronoun.'

'Person, They?'

'Third person.'

'Number, They?'

'Plural number.'

'Then how many do you mean, Mary Anne? Two? Or more?'

'I beg your pardon, ma'am,' said Mary Anne, disconcerted now she came to think of it; 'but I don't know that I mean more than her brother himself.' As she said it, she unhooked her arm.

'I felt convinced of it,' returned Miss Peecher, smiling again. 'Now pray, Mary Anne, be careful another time. He says is very different from they say, remember. Difference between he says and they say? Give it me.'

Mary Anne immediately hooked her right arm behind her in her left hand—an attitude absolutely necessary to the situation—and replied: 'One is indicative mood, present tense, third person singular, verb active to say. Other is indicative mood, present tense, third person plural, verb active to say.'

'Why verb active, Mary Anne?'

'Because it takes a pronoun after it in the objective case, Miss Peecher.'

'Very good indeed,' remarked Miss Peecher, with encouragement. 'In fact, could not be better. Don't forget to apply it, another time, Mary Anne.' This said, Miss Peecher finished the watering of her flowers, and went into her little official residence, and took a refresher of the principal rivers and mountains of the world, their breadths, depths, and heights, before settling the measurements of the body of a dress for her own personal occupation.

Bradley Headstone and Charley Hexam duly got to the Surrey side of Westminster Bridge, and crossed the bridge, and made along the Middlesex shore towards Millbank. In this region are a certain little street called Church Street, and a certain little blind square, called Smith Square, in the centre of which last retreat is a very hideous church with four towers at the four corners, generally resembling some petrified monster, frightful and gigantic, on its back with its legs in the air. They found a tree near by in a corner, and a blacksmith's forge, and a timber yard, and a dealer's in old iron. What a rusty portion of a boiler and a great iron wheel or so meant by lying half-buried in the dealer's fore-court, nobody seemed to know or to want to know. Like the Miller of questionable jollity in the song, They cared for Nobody, no not they, and Nobody cared for them.

After making the round of this place, and noting that there was a deadly kind of repose on it, more as though it had taken laudanum than fallen into a natural rest, they stopped at the point where the street and the square joined, and where there were some little quiet houses in a row. To these Charley Hexam finally led the way, and at one of these stopped.

"This must be where my sister lives, sir. This is where she came for a temporary lodging, soon after father's death.'

'How often have you seen her since?'

'Why, only twice, sir,' returned the boy, with his former reluctance; 'but that's as much her doing as mine.'

'How does she support herself?'

'She was always a fair needlewoman, and she keeps the stockroom of a seaman's outfitter.'

'Does she ever work at her own lodging here?'

'Sometimes; but her regular hours and regular occupation are at their place of business, I believe, sir. This is the number.'

The boy knocked at a door, and the door promptly opened with a spring and a click. A parlour door within a small entry stood open, and disclosed a child—a dwarf—a girl—a something—sitting on a little low old-fashioned arm-chair, which had a kind of little working bench before it.

'I can't get up,' said the child, 'because my back's bad, and my legs are queer. But I'm the person of the house.'

'Who else is at home?' asked Charley Hexam, staring.

'Nobody's at home at present,' returned the child, with a glib assertion of her dignity, 'except the person of the house. What did you want, young man?'

'I wanted to see my sister.'

'Many young men have sisters,' returned the child. 'Give me your name, young man?'

The queer little figure, and the queer but not ugly little face, with its bright grey eyes, were so sharp, that the sharpness of the manner seemed unavoidable. As if, being turned out of that mould, it must be sharp.

'Hexam is my name.'

'Ah, indeed?' said the person of the house. 'I thought it might be. Your sister will be in, in about a quarter of an hour. I am very fond of your sister. She's my particular friend. Take a seat. And this gentleman's name?'

'Mr Headstone, my schoolmaster.'

'Take a seat. And would you please to shut the street door first? I can't very well do it myself, because my back's so bad, and my legs are so queer.'

They complied in silence, and the little figure went on with its work of gumming or gluing together with a camel's-hair brush certain pieces of cardboard and thin wood, previously cut into various shapes. The scissors and knives upon the bench showed that the child herself had cut them; and the bright scraps of velvet and silk and ribbon also strewn upon the bench showed that when duly stuffed (and stuffing too was there), she was to cover them smartly. The dexterity of her nimble fingers was remarkable, and, as she brought two thin edges accurately together by giving them a little bite, she would glance at the visitors out of the corners of her gray eyes with a look that out-sharpened all her other sharpness.

'You can't tell me the name of my trade, I'll be bound,' she said, after taking several of these observations.

'You make pincushions,' said Charley.

'What else do I make?'

'Pen-wipers,' said Bradley Headstone.

'Ha! ha! What else do I make? You're a schoolmaster, but you can't tell me.'

'You do something,' he returned, pointing to a corner of the little bench, 'with straw; but I don't know what.'

'Well done you!' cried the person of the house. 'I only make pincushions and pen-wipers, to use up my waste. But my straw

really does belong to my business. Try again. What do I make
with my straw?'

'Dinner-mats?'

'A schoolmaster, and says dinner-mats! I'll give you a clue to
my trade, in a game of forfeits. I love my love with a B because
she's Beautiful; I hate my love with a B because she is Brazen; I
took her to the sign of the Blue Boar, and I treated her with
Bonnets; her name's Bouncer, and she lives in Bedlam.—Now,
what do I make with my straw?'

'Ladies' bonnets?'

'Fine ladies',' said the person of the house, nodding assent.
'Dolls'. I'm a Doll's Dressmaker.'

'I hope it's a good business?'

The person of the house shrugged her shoulders and shook
her head. 'No. Poorly paid. And I'm often so pressed for time! I
had a doll married, last week, and was obliged to work all night.
And it's not good for me, on account of my back being so bad
and my legs so queer.'

They looked at the little creature with a wonder that did not
diminish, and the schoolmaster said: 'I am sorry your fine ladies
are so inconsiderate.'

'It's the way with them,' said the person of the house,
shrugging her shoulders again. 'And they take no care of their
clothes, and they never keep to the same fashions a month. I
work for a doll with three daughters. Bless you, she's enough to
ruin her husband!' The person of the house gave a weird little
laugh here, and gave them another look out of the corners of her
eyes. She had an elfin chin that was capable of great expression;
and whenever she gave this look, she hitched this chin up. As if
her eyes and her chin worked together on the same wires.

'Are you always as busy as you are now?'

'Busier. I'm slack just now. I finished a large mourning order
the day before yesterday. Doll I work for, lost a canary-bird.' The
person of the house gave another little laugh, and then nodded
her head several times, as who should moralize, 'Oh this world,
this world!'

'Are you alone all day?' asked Bradley Headstone. 'Don't
any of the neighbouring children—?'

'Ah, lud!' cried the person of the house, with a little scream,
as if the word had pricked her. 'Don't talk of children. I can't
bear children. I know their tricks and their manners.' She said
this with an angry little shake of her right fist close before her
eyes.

Perhaps it scarcely required the teacher-habit, to perceive that the doll's dressmaker was inclined to be bitter on the difference between herself and other children. But both master and pupil understood it so.

'Always running about and screeching, always playing and fighting, always skip-skip-skipping on the pavement and chalking it for their games! Oh! *I* know their tricks and their manners!' Shaking the little fist as before. 'And that's not all. Ever so often calling names in through a person's keyhole, and imitating a person's back and legs. Oh! *I* know their tricks and their manners. And I'll tell you what I'd do, to punish 'em. There's doors under the church in the Square—black doors, leading into black vaults. Well! I'd open one of those doors, and I'd cram 'em all in, and then I'd lock the door and through the keyhole I'd blow in pepper.'

'What would be the good of blowing in pepper?' asked Charley Hexam.

'To set 'em sneezing,' said the person of the house, 'and make their eyes water. And when they were all sneezing and inflamed, I'd mock 'em through the keyhole. Just as they, with their tricks and their manners, mock a person through a person's keyhole!'

An uncommonly emphatic shake of her little fist close before her eyes, seemed to ease the mind of the person of the house; for she added with recovered composure, 'No, no, no. No children for me. Give me grown-ups.'

It was difficult to guess the age of this strange creature, for her poor figure furnished no clue to it, and her face was at once so young and so old. Twelve, or at the most thirteen, might be near the mark.

'I always did like grown-ups,' she went on, 'and always kept company with them. So sensible. Sit so quiet. Don't go prancing and capering about! And I mean always to keep among none but grown-ups till I marry. I suppose I must make up my mind to marry, one of these days.'

She listened to a step outside that caught her ear, and there was a soft knock at the door. Pulling at a handle within her reach, she said, with a pleased laugh: 'Now here, for instance, is a grown-up that's my particular friend!' and Lizzie Hexam in a black dress entered the room.

'Charley! You!'

Taking him to her arms in the old way—of which he seemed a little ashamed—she saw no one else.

'There, there, there, Liz, all right my dear. See! Here's Mr Headstone come with me.'

Her eyes met those of the schoolmaster, who had evidently expected to see a very different sort of person, and a murmured word or two of salutation passed between them. She was a little flurried by the unexpected visit, and the schoolmaster was not at his ease. But he never was, quite.

'I told Mr Headstone you were not settled, Liz, but he was so kind as to take an interest in coming, and so I brought him. How well you look!'

Bradley seemed to think so.

'Ah! Don't she, don't she?' cried the person of the house, resuming her occupation, though the twilight was falling fast. 'I believe you she does! But go on with your chat, one and all:

> You one two three,
> My com-pa-nie,
> And don't mind me.'

—pointing this impromptu rhyme with three points of her thin fore-finger.

'I didn't expect a visit from you, Charley,' said his sister. 'I supposed that if you wanted to see me you would have sent to me, appointing me to come somewhere near the school, as I did last time. I saw my brother near the school, sir,' to Bradley Headstone, 'because it's easier for me to go there, than for him to come here. I work about midway between the two places.'

'You don't see much of one another,' said Bradley, not improving in respect of ease.

'No.' With a rather sad shake of her head. 'Charley always does well, Mr Headstone?'

'He could not do better. I regard his course as quite plain before him.'

'I hope so. I am so thankful. So well done of you, Charley dear! It is better for me not to come (except when he wants me) between him and his prospects. You think so, Mr Headstone?'

Conscious that his pupil-teacher was looking for his answer, that he himself had suggested the boy's keeping aloof from this sister, now seen for the first time face to face, Bradley Headstone stammered:

'Your brother is very much occupied, you know. He has to work hard. One cannot but say that the less his attention is diverted from his work, the better for his future. When he shall have established himself, why then—it will be another thing then.'

Lizzie shook her head again, and returned, with a quiet smile: 'I always advised him as you advise him. Did I not, Charley?'

'Well, never mind that now,' said the boy. 'How are you getting on?'

'Very well, Charley. I want for nothing.'

'You have your own room here?'

'Oh yes. Upstairs. And it's quiet, and pleasant, and airy.'

'And she always has the use of this room for visitors,' said the person of the house, screwing up one of her little bony fists, like an opera-glass, and looking through it, with her eyes and her chin in that quaint accordance. 'Always this room for visitors; haven't you, Lizzie dear?'

It happened that Bradley Headstone noticed a very slight action of Lizzie Hexam's hand, as though it checked the doll's dressmaker. And it happened that the latter noticed him in the same instant; for she made a double eyeglass of her two hands, looked at him through it, and cried, with a waggish shake of her head: 'Aha! Caught you spying, did I?'

It might have fallen out so, any way; but Bradley Headstone also noticed that immediately after this, Lizzie, who had not taken off her bonnet, rather hurriedly proposed that as the room was getting dark they should go out into the air. They went out; the visitors saying good-night to the doll's dressmaker, whom they left, leaning back in her chair with her arms crossed, singing to herself in a sweet thoughtful little voice.

'I'll saunter on by the river,' said Bradley. 'You will be glad to talk together.'

As his uneasy figure went on before them among the evening shadows, the boy said to his sister, petulantly:

'When are you going to settle yourself in some Christian sort of place, Liz? I thought you were going to do it before now.'

'I am very well where I am, Charley.'

'Very well where you are! I am ashamed to have brought Mr Headstone with me. How came you to get into such company as that little witch's?'

'By chance at first, as it seemed, Charley. But I think it must have been by something more than chance, for that child— You remember the bills upon the walls at home?'

'Confound the bills upon the walls at home! I want to forget the bills upon the walls at home, and it would be better for you to do the same,' grumbled the boy. 'Well; what of them?'

'This child is the grandchild of the old man.'

'What old man?'

'The terrible drunken old man, in the list slippers and the nightcap.'

The boy asked, rubbing his nose in a manner that half expressed vexation at hearing so much, and half curiosity to hear more: 'How came you to make that out? What a girl you are!'

'The child's father is employed by the house that employs me; that's how I came to know it, Charley. The father is like his own father, a weak wretched trembling creature, falling to pieces, never sober. But a good workman too, at the work he does. The mother is dead. This poor ailing little creature has come to be what she is, surrounded by drunken people from her cradle—if she ever had one, Charley.'

'I don't see what you have to do with her, for all that,' said the boy.

'Don't you, Charley?'

The boy looked doggedly at the river. They were at Millbank, and the river rolled on their left. His sister gently touched him on the shoulder, and pointed to it.

'Any compensation—restitution—never mind the word, you know my meaning. Father's grave.'

But he did not respond with any tenderness. After a moody silence he broke out in an ill-used tone:

'It'll be a very hard thing, Liz, if, when I am trying my best to get up in the world, you pull me back.'

'I, Charley?'

'Yes, you, Liz. Why can't you let bygones be bygones? Why can't you, as Mr Headstone said to me this very evening about another matter, leave well alone? What we have got to do, is, to turn our faces full in our new direction, and keep straight on.'

'And never look back? Not even to try to make some amends?'

'You are such a dreamer,' said the boy, with his former petulance. 'It was all very well when we sat before the fire— when we looked into the hollow down by the flare—but we are looking into the real world, now.'

'Ah, we were looking into the real world then, Charley!'

'I understand what you mean by that, but you are not justified in it. I don't want, as I raise myself, to shake you off, Liz. I want to carry you up with me. That's what I want to do, and mean to do. I know what I owe you. I said to Mr Headstone this very evening, "After all, my sister got me here." Well, then. Don't pull me back, and hold me down. That's all I ask, and surely that's not unconscionable.'

She had kept a steadfast look upon him, and she answered with composure:

'I am not here selfishly, Charley. To please myself, I could not be too far from that river.'

'Nor could you be too far from it to please me. Let us get quit of it equally. Why should you linger about it any more than I? I give it a wide berth.'

'I can't get away from it, I think,' said Lizzie, passing her hand across her forehead. 'It's no purpose of mine that I live by it still.'

'There you go, Liz! Dreaming again! You lodge yourself of your own accord in a house with a drunken—tailor, I suppose—or something of the sort, and a little crooked antic of a child, or old person, or whatever it is, and then you talk as if you were drawn or driven there. Now, do be more practical.'

She had been practical enough with him, in suffering and striving for him; but she only laid her hand upon his shoulder—not reproachfully—and tapped it twice or thrice. She had been used to do so, to soothe him when she carried him about, a child as heavy as herself. Tears started to his eyes.

'Upon my word, Liz,' drawing the back of his hand across them, 'I mean to be a good brother to you, and to prove that I know what I owe you. All I say is, that I hope you'll control your fancies a little, on my account. I'll get a school, and then you must come and live with me, and you'll have to control your fancies then, so why not now? Now, say I haven't vexed you.'

'You haven't, Charley, you haven't.'

'And say I haven't hurt you.'

'You haven't, Charley.' But this answer was less ready.

'Say you are sure I didn't mean to. Come! There's Mr Headstone stopping and looking over the wall at the tide, to hint that it's time to go. Kiss me, and tell me that you know I didn't mean to hurt you.'

She told him so, and they embraced, and walked on and came up with the schoolmaster.

'But we go your sister's way,' he remarked, when the boy told him he was ready. And with his cumbrous and uneasy action he stiffly offered her his arm. Her hand was just within it, when she drew it back. He looked round with a start, as if he thought she had detected something that repelled her, in the momentary touch.

'I will not go in just yet,' said Lizzie. 'And you have a distance before you, and will walk faster without me.'

Being by this time close to Vauxhall Bridge, they resolved, in consequence, to take that way over the Thames, and they left her; Bradley Headstone giving her his hand at parting, and she thanking him for his care of her brother.

The master and the pupil walked on, rapidly and silently. They had nearly crossed the bridge, when a gentleman came coolly sauntering towards them, with a cigar in his mouth, his coat thrown back, and his hands behind him. Something in the careless manner of this person, and in a certain lazily arrogant air with which he approached, holding possession of twice as much pavement as another would have claimed, instantly caught the boy's attention. As the gentleman passed the boy looked at him narrowly, and then stood still, looking after him.

'Who is it that you stare after?' asked Bradley.

'Why!' said the boy, with a confused and pondering frown upon his face, 'It *is* that Wrayburn one!'

Bradley Headstone scrutinized the boy as closely as the boy had scrutinized the gentleman.

'I beg your pardon, Mr Headstone, but I couldn't help wondering what in the world brought *him* here!'

Though he said it as if his wonder were past—at the same time resuming the walk—it was not lost upon the master that he looked over his shoulder after speaking, and that the same perplexed and pondering frown was heavy on his face.

'You don't appear to like your friend, Hexam?'

'I DON'T like him,' said the boy.

'Why not?'

'He took hold of me by the chin in a precious impertinent way, the first time I ever saw him,' said the boy.

'Again, why?'

'For nothing. Or—it's much the same—because something I happened to say about my sister didn't happen to please him.'

'Then he knows your sister?'

'He didn't at that time,' said the boy, still moodily pondering.

'Does now?'

The boy had so lost himself that he looked at Mr Bradley Headstone as they walked on side by side, without attempting to reply until the question had been repeated; then he nodded and answered, 'Yes, sir.'

'Going to see her, I dare say.'

'It can't be!' said the boy, quickly. 'He doesn't know her well enough. I should like to catch him at it!'

When they had walked on for a time, more rapidly than before, the master said, clasping the pupil's arm between the elbow and the shoulder with his hand:

'You were going to tell me something about that person. What did you say his name was?'

'Wrayburn. Mr Eugene Wrayburn. He is what they call a barrister, with nothing to do. The first time he came to our old place was when my father was alive. He came on business; not that it was *his* business—*he* never had any business—he was brought by a friend of his.'

'And the other times?'

'There was only one other time that I know of. When my father was killed by accident, he chanced to be one of the finders. He was mooning about, I suppose, taking liberties with people's chins; but there he was, somehow. He brought the news home to my sister early in the morning, and brought Miss Abbey Potterson, a neighbour, to help break it to her. He was mooning about the house when I was fetched home in the afternoon— they didn't know where to find me till my sister could be brought round sufficiently to tell them—and then he mooned away.'

'And is that all?'

'That's all, sir.'

Bradley Headstone gradually released the boy's arm, as if he were thoughtful, and they walked on side by side as before. After a long silence between them, Bradley resumed the talk.

'I suppose—your sister—' with a curious break both before and after the words, 'has received hardly any teaching, Hexam?'

'Hardly any, sir.'

'Sacrificed, no doubt, to her father's objections. I remember them in your case. Yet—your sister—scarcely looks or speaks like an ignorant person.'

'Lizzie has as much thought as the best, Mr Headstone. Too much, perhaps, without teaching. I used to call the fire at home, her books, for she was always full of fancies—sometimes quite wise fancies, considering—when she sat looking at it.'

'I don't like that,' said Bradley Headstone.

His pupil was a little surprised by this striking in with so sudden and decided and emotional an objection, but took it as a proof of the master's interest in himself. It emboldened him to say:

'I have never brought myself to mention it openly to you, Mr Headstone, and you're my witness that I couldn't even make up my mind to take it from you before we came out to-night; but it's a painful thing to think that if I get on as well as you hope, I shall be—I won't say disgraced, because I don't mean disgraced—but—rather put to the blush if it was known—by a sister who has been very good to me.'

'Yes,' said Bradley Headstone in a slurring way, for his mind scarcely seemed to touch that point, so smoothly did it glide to another, 'and there is this possibility to consider. Some man who had worked his way might come to admire—your sister—and might even in time bring himself to think of marrying—your sister—and it would be a sad drawback and a heavy penalty upon him, if, overcoming in his mind other inequalities of condition and other considerations against it, this inequality and this consideration remained in full force.'

'That's much my own meaning, sir.'

'Ay, ay,' said Bradley Headstone, 'but you spoke of a mere brother. Now, the case I have supposed would be a much stronger case; because an admirer, a husband, would form the connexion voluntarily, besides being obliged to proclaim it: which a brother is not. After all, you know, it must be said of you that you couldn't help yourself: while it would be said of him, with equal reason, that he could.'

'That's true, sir. Sometimes since Lizzie was left free by father's death, I have thought that such a young woman might soon acquire more than enough to pass muster. And sometimes I have even thought that perhaps Miss Peecher—'

'For the purpose, I would advise NOT Miss Peecher,' Bradley Headstone struck in with a recurrence of his late decision of manner.

'Would you be so kind as to think of it for me, Mr Headstone?'

'Yes, Hexam, yes. I'll think of it. I'll think maturely of it. I'll think well of it.'

Their walk was almost a silent one afterwards, until it ended at the school-house. There, one of neat Miss Peecher's little windows, like the eyes in needles, was illuminated, and in a corner near it sat Mary Anne watching, while Miss Peecher at the table stitched at the neat little body she was making up by brown paper pattern for her own wearing. N.B. Miss Peecher and Miss Peecher's pupils were not much encouraged in the unscholastic art of needlework, by Government.

Mary Anne with her face to the window, held her arm up.

'Well, Mary Anne?'

'Mr Headstone coming home, ma'am.'

In about a minute, Mary Anne again hailed.

'Yes, Mary Anne?'

'Gone in and locked his door, ma'am.'

Miss Peecher repressed a sigh as she gathered her work together for bed, and transfixed that part of her dress where her heart would have been if she had had the dress on, with a sharp, sharp needle.

Chapter 2
Still Educational

THE person of the house, doll's dressmaker and manufacturer of ornamental pincushions and pen-wipers, sat in her quaint little low arm-chair, singing in the dark, until Lizzie came back. The person of the house had attained that dignity while yet of very tender years indeed, through being the only trustworthy person *in* the house.

'Well Lizzie-Mizzie-Wizzie,' said she, breaking off in her song. 'What's the news out of doors?'

'What's the news in doors?' returned Lizzie, playfully smoothing the bright long fair hair which grew very luxuriant and beautiful on the head of the doll's dressmaker.

'Let me see, said the blind man. Why the last news is, that I don't mean to marry your brother.'

'No?'

'No-o,' shaking her head and her chin. 'Don't like the boy.'

'What do you say to his master?'

'I say that I think he's bespoke.'

Lizzie finished putting the hair carefully back over the misshapen shoulders, and then lighted a candle. It showed the little parlour to be dingy, but orderly and clean. She stood it on the mantelshelf, remote from the dressmaker's eyes, and then put the room door open, and the house door open, and turned the little low chair and its occupant towards the outer air. It was a sultry night, and this was a fine-weather arrangement when the day's work was done. To complete it, she seated herself in a chair by the side of the little chair, and protectingly drew under her arm the spare hand that crept up to her.

'This is what your loving Jenny Wren calls the best time in the day and night,' said the person of the house. Her real name was Fanny Cleaver; but she had long ago chosen to bestow upon herself the appellation of Miss Jenny Wren.

'I have been thinking,' Jenny went on, 'as I sat at work to-day, what a thing it would be, if I should be able to have your company till I am married, or at least courted. Because when I am courted, I shall make Him do some of the things that you do for me. He couldn't brush my hair like you do, or help me up and down stairs like you do, and he couldn't do anything like you do; but he could take my work home, and he could call for orders in his clumsy way. And he shall too. *I'll* trot him about, I can tell him!'

Jenny Wren had her personal vanities—happily for her—and no intentions were stronger in her breast than the various trials and torments that were, in the fulness of time, to be inflicted upon 'him.'

'Wherever he may happen to be just at present, or whoever he may happen to be,' said Miss Wren, '*I* know his tricks and his manners, and I give him warning to look out.'

'Don't you think you are rather hard upon him?' asked her friend, smiling, and smoothing her hair.

'Not a bit,' replied the sage Miss Wren, with an air of vast experience. 'My dear, they don't care for you, those fellows, if you're *not* hard upon 'em. But I was saying If I should be able to have your company. Ah! What a large If! Ain't it?'

'I have no intention of parting company, Jenny.'

'Don't say that, or you'll go directly.'

'Am I so little to be relied upon?'

'You're more to be relied upon than silver and gold.' As she said it, Miss Wren suddenly broke off, screwed up her eyes and her chin, and looked prodigiously knowing. 'Aha!

> Who comes here?
> A Grenadier.
> What does he want?
> A pot of beer.

And nothing else in the world, my dear!'

A man's figure paused on the pavement at the outer door. 'Mr Eugene Wrayburn, ain't it?' said Miss Wren.

'So I am told,' was the answer.

'You may come in, if you're good.'

'I am not good,' said Eugene, 'but I'll come in.'

He gave his hand to Jenny Wren, and he gave his hand to Lizzie, and he stood leaning by the door at Lizzie's side. He had been strolling with his cigar, he said, (it was smoked out and gone by this time,) and he had strolled round to return in that direction that he might look in as he passed. Had she not seen her brother to-night?

'Yes,' said Lizzie, whose manner was a little troubled.

Gracious condescension on our brother's part! Mr Eugene Wrayburn thought he had passed my young gentleman on the bridge yonder. Who was his friend with him?

'The schoolmaster.'

'To be sure. Looked like it.'

Lizzie sat so still, that one could not have said wherein the fact of her manner being troubled was expressed; and yet one could not have doubted it. Eugene was as easy as ever; but perhaps, as she sat with her eyes cast down, it might have been rather more perceptible that his attention was concentrated upon her for certain moments, than its concentration upon any subject for any short time ever was, elsewhere.

'I have nothing to report, Lizzie,' said Eugene. 'But, having promised you that an eye should be always kept on Mr Riderhood through my friend Lightwood, I like occasionally to renew my assurrance that I keep my promise, and keep my friend up to the mark.'

'I should not have doubted it, sir.'

'Generally, I confess myself a man to be doubted,' returned Eugene, coolly, 'for all that.'

'Why are you?' asked the sharp Miss Wren.

'Because, my dear,' said the airy Eugene, 'I am a bad idle dog.'

'Then why don't you reform and be a good dog?' inquired Miss Wren.

'Because, my dear,' returned Eugene, 'there's nobody who makes it worth my while. Have you considered my suggestion, Lizzie?' This in a lower voice, but only as if it were a graver matter; not at all to the exclusion of the person of the house.

'I have thought of it, Mr Wrayburn, but I have not been able to make up my mind to accept it.'

'False pride!' said Eugene.

'I think not, Mr Wrayburn. I hope not.'

'False pride!' repeated Eugene. 'Why, what else is it? The thing is worth nothing in itself. The thing is worth nothing to me. What can it be worth to me? You know the most I make of it. I propose to be of some use to somebody—which I never was in this world, and never shall be on any other occasion—by paying some qualified person of your own sex and age, so many (or rather so few) contemptible shillings, to come here, certain nights in the week, and give you certain instruction which you wouldn't want if you hadn't been a self-denying daughter and sister. You know that it's good to have it, or you would never have so devoted yourself to your brother's having it. Then why not have it: especially when our friend Miss Jenny here would profit by it too? If I proposed to be the teacher, or to attend the lessons—obviously incongruous!—but as to that, I might as well be on the other side of the globe, or not on the globe at all. False pride, Lizzie. Because true pride wouldn't shame, or be shamed by, your thankless brother. True pride wouldn't have schoolmasters brought here, like doctors, to look at a bad case. True pride would go to work and do it. You know that, well enough, for you know that your own true pride would do it to-morrow, if you had the ways and means which false pride won't let me supply. Very well. I add no more than this. Your false pride does wrong to yourself and does wrong to your dead father.'

'How to my father, Mr Wrayburn?' she asked, with an anxious face.

'How to your father? Can you ask! By perpetuating the consequences of his ignorant and blind obstinacy. By resolving not to set right the wrong he did you. By determining that the deprivation to which he condemned you, and which he forced upon you, shall always rest upon his head.'

It chanced to be a subtle string to sound, in her who had so spoken to her brother within the hour. It sounded far more forcibly, because of the change in the speaker for the moment; the passing appearance of earnestness, complete conviction, injured resentment of suspicion, generous and unselfish interest. All these qualities, in him usually so light and careless, she felt to be inseparable from some touch of their opposites in her own breast. She thought, had she, so far below him and so different, rejected this disinterestedness, because of some vain misgiving that he sought her out, or heeded any personal attractions that he might descry in her? The poor girl, pure of heart and purpose, could not bear to think it. Sinking before her own eyes, as she suspected herself of it, she drooped her head as though she had done him some wicked and grievous injury, and broke into silent tears.

'Don't be distressed,' said Eugene, very, very kindly. 'I hope it is not I who have distressed you. I meant no more than to put the matter in its true light before you; though I acknowledge I did it selfishly enough, for I am disappointed.'

Disappointed of doing her a service. How else *could* he be disappointed?

'It won't break my heart,' laughed Eugene; 'it won't stay by me eight-and-forty hours; but I am genuinely disappointed. I had set my fancy on doing this little thing for you and for our friend Miss Jenny. The novelty of my doing anything in the least useful, had its charms. I see, now, that I might have managed it better. I might have affected to do it wholly for our friend Miss J. I might have got myself up, morally, as Sir Eugene Bountiful. But upon my soul I can't make flourishes, and I would rather be disappointed than try.'

If he meant to follow home what was in Lizzie's thoughts, it was skillfully done. If he followed it by mere fortuitous coincidence, it was done by an evil chance.

'It opened out so naturally before me,' said Eugene. 'The ball seemed so thrown into my hands by accident! I happen to be originally brought into contact with you, Lizzie, on those two occasions that you know of. I happen to be able to promise you that a watch shall be kept upon that false àccuser, Riderhood. I happen to be able to give you some little consolation in the darkest hour of your distress, by assuring you that I don't believe him. On the same occasion I tell you that I am the idlest and least of lawyers, but that I am better than none, in a case I have noted down with my own hand, and that you may be always sure of my best help, and incidentally of Lightwood's too, in your efforts to clear your father. So, it gradually takes my fancy that I may help you—so easily!—to clear your father of that other blame which I mentioned a few minutes ago, and which is a just and real one. I hope I have explained myself, for I am heartily sorry to have distressed you. I hate to claim to mean well, but I really did mean honestly and simply well, and I want you to know it.'

'I have never doubted that, Mr Wrayburn,' said Lizzie; the more repentant, the less he claimed.

'I am very glad to hear it. Though if you had quite understood my whole meaning at first, I think you would not have refused. Do you think you would?'

'I—don't know that I should, Mr Wrayburn.'

'Well! Then why refuse now you do understand it?'

'It's not easy for me to talk to you,' returned Lizzie, in some confusion, 'for you see all the consequences of what I say, as soon as I say it.'

'Take all the consequences,' laughed Eugene, 'and take away my disappointment. Lizzie Hexam, as I truly respect you, and as I am your friend and a poor devil of a gentleman, I protest I don't even now understand why you hesitate.'

There was an appearance of openness, trustfulness, unsuspecting generosity, in his words and manner, that won the poor girl over; and not only won her over, but again caused her to feel as though she had been influenced by the opposite qualities, with vanity at their head.

'I will not hesitate any longer, Mr Wrayburn. I hope you will not think the worse of me for having hesitated at all. For myself and for Jenny—you let me answer for you, Jenny dear?'

The little creature had been leaning back, attentive, with her elbows resting on the elbows of her chair, and her chin upon her hands. Without changing her attitude, she answered, 'Yes!' so suddenly that it rather seemed as if she had chopped the monosyllable than spoken it.

'For myself and for Jenny, I thankfully accept your kind offer.'

'Agreed! Dismissed!' said Eugene, giving Lizzie his hand before lightly waving it, as if he waved the whole subject away. 'I hope it may not be often that so much is made of so little!'

Then he fell to talking playfully with Jenny Wren. 'I think of setting up a doll, Miss Jenny,' he said.

'You had better not,' replied the dressmaker.

'Why not?'

'You are sure to break it. All you children do.'

'But that makes good for trade, you know, Miss Wren,' returned Eugene. 'Much as people's breaking promises and contracts and bargains of all sorts, makes good for *my* trade.'

'I don't know about that,' Miss Wren retorted; 'but you had better by half set up a pen-wiper, and turn industrious, and use it.'

'Why, if we were all as industrious as you, little Busy-Body, we should begin to work as soon as we could crawl, and there would be a bad thing!'

'Do you mean,' returned the little creature, with a flush suffusing her face, 'bad for your backs and your legs?'

'No, no, no,' said Eugene; shocked—to do him justice—at the thought of trifling with her infirmity. 'Bad for business, bad for business. If we all set to work as soon as we could use our hands, it would be all over with the dolls' dressmakers.'

'There's something in that,' replied Miss Wren; 'you have a sort of an idea in your noddle sometimes.' Then, in a changed tone; 'Talking of ideas, my Lizzie,' they were sitting side by side as they had sat at first, 'I wonder how it happens that when I am work, work, working here, all alone in the summer-time, I smell flowers.'

'As a commonplace individual, I should say,' Eugene suggested languidly—for he was growing weary of the person of the house—'that you smell flowers because you *do* smell flowers.'

'No I don't,' said the little creature, resting one arm upon the elbow of her chair, resting her chin upon that hand, and looking vacantly before her; 'this is not a flowery neighbourhood. It's anything but that. And yet as I sit at work, I smell miles of flowers. I smell roses, till I think I see the rose-leaves lying in heaps, bushels, on the floor. I smell fallen leaves, till I put down my hand—so—and expect to make them rustle. I smell the white and the pink May in the hedges, and all sorts of flowers that I never was among. For I have seen very few flowers indeed, in my life.'

'Pleasant fancies to have, Jenny dear!' said her friend: with a glance towards Eugene as if she would have asked him whether they were given the child in compensation for her losses.

'So I think, Lizzie, when they come to me. And the birds I hear! Oh!' cried the little creature, holding out her hand and looking upward, 'how they sing!'

There was something in the face and action for the moment, quite inspired and beautiful. Then the chin dropped musingly upon the hand again.

'I dare say my birds sing better than other birds, and my flowers smell better than other flowers. For when I was a little child,' in a tone as though it were ages ago, 'the children that I used to see early in the morning were very different from any others that I ever saw. They were not like me; they were not chilled, anxious, ragged, or beaten; they were never in pain. They were not like the children of the neighbours; they never made me tremble all over, by setting up shrill noises, and they never mocked me. Such numbers of them too! All in white dresses, and with something shining on the borders, and on their heads, that I have never been able to imitate with my work, though I know it so well. They used to come down in long bright slanting rows, and say all together, "Who is this in pain! Who is this in pain!" When I told them who it was, they answered, "Come and play with us!" When I said "I never play! I can't play!" they swept about me and took me up, and made me light. Then it was all delicious ease and rest till they laid me down, and said, all together, "Have patience, and we will come again." Whenever they came back, I used to know they were coming before I saw the long bright rows, by hearing them ask, all together a long way off, "Who is this in pain! who is this in pain!" And I used to cry out, "O my blessed children, it's poor me. Have pity on me. Take me up and make me light!" '

By degrees, as she progressed in this remembrance, the hand was raised, the late ecstatic look returned, and she became quite beautiful. Having so paused for a moment, silent, with a listening smile upon her face, she looked round and recalled herself.

'What poor fun you think me; don't you, Mr Wrayburn? You may well look tired of me. But it's Saturday night, and I won't detain you.'

'That is to say, Miss Wren,' observed Eugene, quite ready to profit by the hint, 'you wish me to go?'

'Well, it's Saturday night,' she returned, 'and my child's coming home. And my child is a troublesome bad child, and costs me a world of scolding. I would rather you didn't see my child.'

'A doll?' said Eugene, not understanding, and looking for an explanation.

But Lizzie, with her lips only, shaping the two words, 'Her father,' he delayed no longer. He took his leave immediately. At the corner of the street he stopped to light another cigar, and possibly to ask himself what he was doing otherwise. If so, the answer was indefinite and vague. Who knows what he is doing, who is careless what he does!

A man stumbled against him as he turned away, who mumbled some maudlin apology. Looking after this man, Eugene saw him go in at the door by which he himself had just come out.

On the man's stumbling into the room, Lizzie rose to leave it.

'Don't go away, Miss Hexam,' he said in a submissive man-

ner, speaking thickly and with difficulty. 'Don't fly from unfortunate man in shattered state of health. Give poor invalid honour
of your company. It ain't—ain't catching.'

Lizzie murmured that she had something to do in her own
room, and went away upstairs.

'How's my Jenny?' said the man, timidly. 'How's my Jenny
Wren, best of children, object dearest affections broken-hearted
invalid?'

To which the person of the house, stretching out her arm in
an attitude of command, replied with irresponsive asperity: 'Go
along with you! Go along into your corner! Get into your corner
directly!'

The wretched spectacle made as if he would have offered
some remonstrance; but not venturing to resist the person of the
house, thought better of it, and went and sat down on a particular chair of disgrace.

'Oh-h-h!' cried the person of the house, pointing her little
finger, 'You bad old boy! Oh-h-h you naughty, wicked creature!
What do you mean by it?'

The shaking figure, unnerved and disjointed from head to
foot, put out its two hands a little way, as making overtures of
peace and reconciliation. Abject tears stood in its eyes, and
stained the blotched red of its cheeks. The swollen lead-coloured
under lip trembled with a shameful whine. The whole indeco-
rous threadbare ruin, from the broken shoes to the prematurely-
grey scanty hair, grovelled. Not with any sense worthy to be
called a sense, of this dire reversal of the places of parent and
child, but in a pitiful expostulation to be let off from a scolding.

'*I* know your tricks and your manners,' cried Miss Wren. '*I*
know where you've been to!' (which indeed it did not require
discernment to discover). 'Oh, you disgraceful old chap!'

The very breathing of the figure was contemptible, as it
laboured and rattled in that operation, like a blundering clock.

'Slave, slave, slave, from morning to night,' pursued the
person of the house, 'and all for this! *What* do you mean by it?'

There was something in that emphasized 'What,' which ab-
surdly frightened the figure. As often as the person of the house
worked her way round to it—even as soon as he saw that it was
coming—he collapsed in an extra degree.

'I wish you had been taken up, and locked up,' said the
person of the house. 'I wish you had been poked into cells and
black holes, and run over by rats and spiders and beetles. *I* know

their tricks and their manners, and they'd have tickled you nicely. Ain't you ashamed of yourself?'

'Yes, my dear,' stammered the father.

'Then,' said the person of the house, terrifying him by a grand muster of her spirits and forces before recurring to the emphatic word, '*What* do you mean by it?'

'Circumstances over which had no control,' was the miserable creature's plea in extenuation.

'*I*'ll circumstance you and control you too,' retorted the person of the house, speaking with vehement sharpness, 'if you talk in that way. I'll give you in charge to the police, and have you fined five shillings when you can't pay, and then I won't pay the money for you, and you'll be transported for life. How should you like to be transported for life?'

'Shouldn't like it. Poor shattered invalid. Trouble nobody long,' cried the wretched figure.

'Come, come!' said the person of the house, tapping the table near her in a business-like manner, and shaking her head and her chin; 'you know what you've got to do. Put down your money this instant.'

The obedient figure began to rummage in its pockets.

'Spent a fortune out of your wages, I'll be bound!' said the person of the house. 'Put it here! All you've got left! Every farthing!'

Such a business as he made of collecting it from his dog's-eared pockets; of expecting it in this pocket, and not finding it; of not expecting it in that pocket, and passing it over; of finding no pocket where that other pocket ought to be!

'Is this all?' demanded the person of the house, when a confused heap of pence and shillings lay on the table.

'Got no more,' was the rueful answer, with an accordant shake of the head.

'Let me make sure. You know what you've got to do. Turn all your pockets inside out, and leave 'em so!' cried the person of the house.

He obeyed. And if anything could have made him look more abject or more dismally ridiculous than before, it would have been his so displaying himself.

'Here's but seven and eightpence halfpenny!' exclaimed Miss Wren, after reducing the heap to order. 'Oh, you prodigal old son! Now you shall be starved.'

'No, don't starve me,' he urged, whimpering.

'If you were treated as you ought to be,' said Miss Wren,

'you'd be fed upon the skewers of cats' meat;—only the skewers, after the cats had had the meat. As it is, go to bed.'

When he stumbled out of the corner to comply, he again put out both his hands, and pleaded: 'Circumstances over which no control—'

'Get along with you to bed!' cried Miss Wren, snapping him up. 'Don't speak to me. I'm not going to forgive you. Go to bed this moment!'

Seeing another emphatic 'What' upon its way, he evaded it by complying and was heard to shuffle heavily up stairs, and shut his door, and throw himself on his bed. Within a little while afterwards, Lizzie came down.

'Shall we have our supper, Jenny dear?'

'Ah! bless us and save us, we need have something to keep us going,' returned Miss Jenny, shrugging her shoulders.

Lizzie laid a cloth upon the little bench (more handy for the person of the house than an ordinary table), and put upon it such plain fare as they were accustomed to have, and drew up a stool for herself.

'Now for supper! What are you thinking of, Jenny darling?'

'I was thinking,' she returned, coming out of a deep study, 'what I would do to Him, if he should turn out a drunkard.'

'Oh, but he won't,' said Lizzie. 'You'll take care of that, beforehand.'

'I shall try to take care of it beforehand, but he might deceive me. Oh, my dear, all those fellows with their tricks and their manners do deceive!' With the little fist in full action. 'And if so, I tell you what I think I'd do. When he was asleep, I'd make a spoon red hot, and I'd have some boiling liquor bubbling in a saucepan, and I'd take it out hissing, and I'd open his mouth with the other hand—or perhaps he'd sleep with his mouth ready open—and I'd pour it down his throat, and blister it and choke him.'

'I am sure you would do no such horrible thing,' said Lizzie.

'Shouldn't I? Well; perhaps I shouldn't. But I should like to!'

'I am equally sure you would not.'

'Not even like to? Well, you generally know best. Only you haven't always lived among it as I have lived—and your back isn't bad and your legs are not queer.'

As they went on with their supper, Lizzie tried to bring her round to that prettier and better state. But, the charm was broken. The person of the house was the person of a house full of sordid shames and cares, with an upper room in which that abased figure was infecting even innocent sleep with sensual brutality and degradation. The doll's dressmaker had become a little quaint shrew; of the world, worldly; of the earth, earthy.

Poor doll's dressmaker! How often so dragged down by hands that should have raised her up; how often so misdirected when losing her way on the eternal road, and asking guidance! Poor, poor little doll's dressmaker!

Chapter 3
A Piece of work

BRITANNIA, sitting meditating one fine day (perhaps in the attitude in which she is presented on the copper coinage), discovers all of a sudden that she wants Veneering in Parliment. It occurs to her that Veneering is 'a representative man'—which cannot in these times be doubted—and that Her Majesty's faithful Commons are incomplete without him. So, Britannia mentions to a legal gentleman of her acquaintance that if Veneering will 'put down' five thousand pounds, he may write a couple of initial letters after his name at the extremely cheap rate of two thousand five hundred per letter. It is clearly understood between Britannia and the legal gentleman that nobody is to take up the five thousand pounds, but that being put down they will disappear by magical conjuration and enchantment.

The legal gentleman in Britannia's confidence going straight from that lady to Veneering, thus commissioned, Veneering declares himself highly flattered, but requires breathing time to ascertain 'whether his friends will rally round him.' Above all things, he says, it behoves him to be clear, at a crisis of this importance, 'whether his friends will rally round him.' The legal gentleman, in the interests of his client cannot allow much time for this purpose, as the lady rather thinks she knows somebody prepared to put down six thousand pounds; but he says he will give Veneering four hours.

Veneering than says to Mrs Veneering, 'We must work,' and

throws himself into a Hansom cab. Mrs Veneering in the same moment relinquishes baby to Nurse; presses her aquiline hands upon her brow, to arrange the throbbing intellect within; orders out the carriage; and repeats in a distracted and devoted manner, compounded of Ophelia and any self-immolating female of antiquity you may prefer, 'We must work.'

Veneering having instructed his driver to charge at the Public in the streets, like the Life-Guards at Waterloo, is driven furiously to Duke Street, Saint James's. There, he finds Twemlow in his lodgings, fresh from the hands of a secret artist who has been doing something to his hair with yolks of eggs. The process requiring that Twemlow shall, for two hours after the application, allow his hair to stick upright and dry gradually, he is in an appropriate state for the receipt of startling intelligence; looking equally like the Monument on Fish Street Hill, and King Priam on a certain incendiary occasion not wholly unknown as a neat point from the classics.

'My dear Twemlow,' says Veneering, grasping both his hands, 'as the dearest and oldest of my friends—'

('Then there can be no more doubt about it in future,' thinks Twemlow, 'and I AM!'')

'—Are you of opinion that your cousin, Lord Snigsworth, would give his name as a Member of my Committee? I don't go so far as to ask for his lordship; I only ask for his name. Do you think he would give me his name?'

In sudden low spirits, Twemlow replies, 'I don't think he would.'

'My political opinions,' says Veneering, not previously aware of having any, 'are identical with those of Lord Snigsworth, and perhaps as a matter of public feeling and public principle, Lord Snigsworth would give me his name.'

'It might be so,' says Twemlow; 'but—' And perplexedly scratching his head, forgetful of the yolks of eggs, is the more discomfited by being reminded how stickey he is.

'Between such old and intimate friends as ourselves,' pursues Veneering, 'there should in such a case be no reserve. Promise me that if I ask you to do anything for me which you don't like to do, or feel the slightest difficulty in doing, you will freely tell me so.'

This, Twemlow is so kind as to promise, with every appearance of most heartily intending to keep his word.

'Would you have any objection to write down to Snigsworthy Park, and ask this favour of Lord Snigsworth? Of course if it

were granted I should know that I owed it solely to you; while at
the same time you would put it to Lord Snigsworth entirely upon
public grounds. Would you have any objection?'

Says Twemlow, with his hand to his forehead, 'You have
exacted a promise from me.'

'I have, my dear Twemlow.'

'And you expect me to keep it honourably.'

'I do, my dear Twemlow.'

'*On* the whole, then;—observe me,' urges Twemlow with
great nicety, as if, in the case of its having been off the whole, he
would have done it directly—'*on* the whole, I must beg you to
excuse me from addressing any communication to Lord Snigsworth.'

'Bless you, bless you!' says Veneering; horribly disappointed,
but grasping him by both hands again, in a particularly fervent
manner.

It is not to be wondered at that poor Twemlow should
decline to inflict a letter on his noble cousin (who has gout in the
temper), inasmuch as his noble cousin, who allows him a small
annuity on which he lives, takes it out of him, as the phrase
goes, in extreme severity; putting him, when he visits at
Snigsworthy Park, under a kind of martial law; ordaining that he
shall hang his hat on a particular peg, sit on a particular chair,
talk on particular subjects to particular people, and perform particular exercises: such as sounding the praises of the Family
Varnish (not to say Pictures), and abstaining from the choicest of
the Family Wines unless expressly invited to partake.

'One thing, however, I *can* do for you,' says Twemlow; 'and
that is, work for you.'

Veneering blesses him again.

'I'll go,' says Twemlow, in a rising hurry of spirits, 'to the
club;—let us see now; what o'clock is it?'

'Twenty minutes to eleven.'

'I'll be,' says Twemlow, 'at the club by ten minutes to twelve,
and I'll never leave it all day.'

Veneering feels that his friends are rallying round him, and
says, 'Thank you, thank you. I knew I could rely upon you. I
said to Anastatia before leaving home just now to come to you—of
course the first friend I have seen on a subject so momentous to
me, my dear Twemlow—I said to Anastatia, "We must work." '

'You were right, you were right,' replies Twemlow. 'Tell me.
Is *she* working?'

'She is,' says Veneering.

'Good!' cried Twemlow, polite little gentleman that he is. 'A woman's tact is invaluable. To have the dear sex with us, is to have everything with us.'

'But you have not imparted to me,' remarks Veneering, 'what you think of my entering the House of Commons?'

'I think,' rejoins Twemlow, feelingly, 'that it is the best club in London.'

Veneering again blesses him, plunges down stairs, rushes into his Hansom, and directs the driver to be up and at the British Public, and to charge into the City.

Meanwhile Twemlow, in an increasing hurry of spirits, gets his hair down as well as he can—which is not very well; for, after these glutinous applications it is restive, and has a surface on it somewhat in the nature of pastry—and gets to the club by the appointed time. At the club he promptly secures a large window, writing materials, and all the newspapers, and establishes himself, immoveable, to be respectfully contemplated by Pall Mall. Sometimes, when a man enters who nods to him, Twemlow says, 'Do you know Veneering?' Man says, 'No; member of the club?' Twemlow says, 'Yes. Coming in for Pocket-Breaches.' Man says, 'Ah! Hope he may find it worth the money!' yawns, and saunters out. Towards six o'clock of the afternoon, Twemlow begins to persuade himself that he is positively jaded with work, and thinks it much to be regretted that he was not brought up as a Parliamentary agent.

From Twemlow's, Veneering dashes at Podsnap's place of business. Finds Podsnap reading the paper, standing, and inclined to be oratorical over the astonishing discovery he has made, that Italy is not England. Respectfully entreats Podsnap's pardon for stopping the flow of his words of wisdom, and informs him what is in the wind. Tells Podsnap that their political opinions are identical. Gives Podsnap to understand that he, Veneering, formed his political opinions while sitting at the feet of him, Podsnap. Seeks earnestly to know whether Podsnap 'will rally round him?'

Says Podsnap, something sternly, 'Now, first of all, Veneering, do you ask my advice?'

Veneering falters that as so old and so dear a friend—

'Yes, yes, that's all very well,' says Podsnap; 'but have you made up your mind to take this borough of Pocket-Breaches on its own terms, or do you ask my opinion whether you shall take it or leave it alone?'

Veneering repeats that his heart's desire and his soul's thirst are, that Podsnap shall rally round him.

'Now, I'll be plain with you, Veneering,' says Podsnap, knitting his brows. 'You will infer that *I* don't care about Parliament, from the fact of my not being there?'

Why, of course Veneering knows that! Of course Veneering knows that if Podsnap chose to go there, he would be there, in a space of time that might be stated by the light and thoughtless as a jiffy.

'It is not worth my while,' pursues Podsnap, becoming handsomely mollified, 'and it is the reverse of important to my position. But it is not my wish to set myself up as law for another man, differently situated. You think it *is* worth *your* while, and *is* important to *your* position. Is that so?'

Always with the proviso that Podsnap will rally round him, Veneering thinks it is so.

'Then you don't ask my advice,' says Podsnap. 'Good. Then I won't give it you. But you do ask my help. Good. Then I'll work for you.'

Veneering instantly blesses him, and apprises him that Twemlow is already working. Podsnap does not quite approve that anybody should be already working—regarding it rather in the light of a liberty—but tolerates Twemlow, and says he is a well-connected old female who will do no harm.

'I have nothing very particular to do to-day,' adds Podsnap, 'and I'll mix with some influential people. I had engaged myself to dinner, but I'll send Mrs Podsnap and get off going myself, and I'll dine with you at eight. It's important we should report progress and compare notes. Now, let me see. You ought to have a couple of active energetic fellows, of gentlemanly manners, to go about.'

Veneering, after cogitation, thinks of Boots and Brewer.

'Whom I have met at your house,' says Podsnap. 'Yes. They'll do very well. Let them each have a cab, and go about.'

Veneering immediately mentions what a blessing he feels it, to possess a friend capable of such grand administrative suggestions, and really is elated at this going about of Boots and Brewer, as an idea wearing an electioneering aspect and looking desperately like business. Leaving Podsnap, at a hand-gallop, he descends upon Boots and Brewer, who enthusiastically rally round him by at once bolting off in cabs, taking opposite directions. Then Veneering repairs to the legal gentleman in Britannia's confidence, and with him transacts some delicate affairs of business, and issues an address to the independent electors of Pocket-Breaches, announcing that he is coming among them for their suffrages, as the mariner returns to the home of his early child-hood: a phrase which is none the worse for his never having been near the place in his life, and not even now distinctly knowing where it is.

Mrs Veneering, during the same eventful hours, is not idle. No sooner does the carriage turn out, all complete, than she turns into it, all complete, and gives the word 'To Lady Tippins's.' That charmer dwells over a staymaker's in the Belgravian Borders, with a life-size model in the window on the ground floor of a distinguished beauty in a blue petticoat, stay-lace in hand, looking over her shoulder at the town in innocent surprise. As well she may, to find herself dressing under the circumstances.

Lady Tippins at home? Lady Tippins at home, with the room darkened, and her back (like the lady's at the ground-floor window, though for a different reason) cunningly turned towards the light. Lady Tippins is so surprised by seeing her dear Mrs Veneering so early—in the middle of the night, the pretty creature calls it—that her eyelids almost go up, under the influence of that emotion.

To whom Mrs Veneering incoherently communicates, how that Veneering has been offered Pocket-Breaches; how that it is the time for rallying round; how that Veneering has said 'We must work'; how that she is here, as a wife and mother, to entreat Lady Tippins to work; how that the carriage is at Lady Tippins's disposal for purposes of work; how that she, proprietress of said bran-new elegant equipage, will return home on foot—on bleeding feet if need be—to work (not specifying how), until she drops by the side of baby's crib.

'My love,' says Lady Tippins, 'compose yourself; we'll bring him in.' And Lady Tippins really does work, and work the Veneering horses too; for she clatters about town all day, calling upon everybody she knows, and showing her entertaining powers and green fan to immense advantage, by rattling on with, My dear soul, what do you think? What do you suppose me to be? You'll never guess. I'm pretending to be an electioneering agent. And for what place of all places? Pocket-Breaches. And why? Because the dearest friend I have in the world has bought it. And who is the dearest friend I have in the world? A man of the name of Veneering. Not omitting his wife, who is the other dearest friend I have in the world; and I positively declare I forgot their baby, who is the other. And we are carrying on this little farce to keep up appearances, and isn't it refreshing! Then, my precious child, the fun of it is that nobody knows who these Veneerings are, and that they know nobody, and that they have a house out of the Tales of the Genii, and give dinners out of the Arabian Nights. Curious to see 'em, my dear? Say you'll know 'em. Come and dine with 'em. They shan't bore you. Say who shall meet you. We'll make up a party of our own, and I'll engage that they shall not interfere with you for one single moment. You really ought to see their gold and silver camels. I call their dinner-table, the Caravan. Do come and dine with my Veneerings, my own Veneerings, my exclusive property, the dearest friends I have in the world! And above all, my dear, be sure you promise me your vote and interest and all sorts of plumpers for Pocket-Breaches; for we couldn't think of spending sixpence on it, my love, and can only consent to be brought in by the spontaneous thingummies of the incorruptible whatdoyoucallums.

Now, the point of view seized by the bewitching Tippins, that this same working and rallying round is to keep up appearances, may have something in it, but not all the truth. More is done, or considered to be done—which does as well—by taking cabs, and 'going about,' than the fair Tippins knew of. Many vast vague reputations have been made, solely by taking cabs and going about. This particularly obtains in all Parliamentary affairs. Whether the business in hand be to get a man in, or get a man out, or get a man over, or promote a railway, or jockey a railway, or what else, nothing is understood to be so effectual as scouring nowhere in a violent hurry—in short, as taking cabs and going about.

Probably because this reason is in the air, Twemlow, far from being singular in his persuasion that he works like a Trojan, is capped by Podsnap, who in his turn is capped by Boots and Brewer. At eight o'clock when all these hard workers assemble to dine at Veneering's, it is understood that the cabs of Boots and Brewer mustn't leave the door, but that pails of water must be brought from the nearest baiting-place, and cast over the horses' legs on the very spot, lest Boots and Brewer should have instant occasion to mount and away. Those fleet messengers require the Analytical to see that their hats are deposited where they can be laid hold of at an instant's notice; and they dine (remarkably well though) with the air of firemen in charge of an engine, expecting intelligence of some tremendous conflagration.

Mrs Veneering faintly remarks, as dinner opens, that many such days would be too much for her.

'Many such days would be too much for all of us,' says Podsnap; 'but we'll bring him in!'

'We'll bring him in,' says Lady Tippins, sportively waving her green fan. 'Veneering for ever!'

'We'll bring him in!' says Twemlow.

'We'll bring him in!' says Boots and Brewer.

Strictly speaking, it would be hard to show cause why they should not bring him in, Pocket-Breaches having closed its little bargain, and there being no opposition. However, it is agreed that they must 'work' to the last, and that if they did not work, something indefinite would happen. It is likewise agreed that they are all so exhausted with the work behind them, and need to be so fortified for the work before them, as to require peculiar strengthening from Veneering's cellar. Therefore, the Analytical has orders to produce the cream of the cream of his binns, and therefore it falls out that rallying becomes rather a trying word for the occasion; Lady Tippins being observed gamely to inculcate the necessity of rearing round their dear Veneering; Podsnap advocating roaring round him; Boots and Brewer declaring their intention of reeling round him; and Veneering thanking his devoted friends one and all, with great emotion, for rarullarulling round him.

In these inspiring moments, Brewer strikes out an idea which is the great hit of the day. He consults his watch, and says (like Guy Fawkes), he'll now go down to the House of Commons and see how things look.

'I'll keep about the lobby for an hour or so,' says Brewer, with a deeply mysterious countenance, 'and if things look well, I won't come back, but will order my cab for nine in the morning.'

'You couldn't do better,' says Podsnap.

Veneering expresses his inability ever to acknowledge this last service. Tears stand in Mrs Veneering's affectionate eyes. Boots shows envy, loses ground, and is regarded as possessing a second-rate mind. They all crowd to the door, to see Brewer off. Brewer says to his driver, 'Now, is your horse pretty fresh?' eyeing the animal with critical scrutiny. Driver says he's as fresh as butter. 'Put him along then,' says Brewer; 'House of Commons.' Driver darts up, Brewer leaps in, they cheer him as he departs, and Mr Podsnap says, 'Mark my words, sir. That's a man of resource; that's a man to make his way in life.'

When the time comes for Veneering to deliver a neat and appropriate stammer to the men of Pocket-Breaches, only Podsnap and Twemlow accompany him by railway to that sequestered spot. The legal gentleman is at the Pocket-Breaches Branch Station, with an open carriage with a printed bill 'Veneering for ever' stuck upon it, as if it were a wall; and they gloriously proceed, amidst the grins of the populace, to a feeble little town hall on crutches, with some onions and bootlaces under it, which the legal gentleman says are a Market; and from the front window of that edifice Veneering speaks to the listening earth. In the moment of his taking his hat off, Podsnap, as per agreement made with Mrs Veneering, telegraphs to that wife and mother, 'He's up.'

Veneering loses his way in the usual No Thoroughfares of speech, and Podsnap and Twemlow say Hear hear! and sometimes, when he can't by any means back himself out of some very unlucky No Thoroughfare, 'He-a-a-r He-a-a-r!' with an air of facetious conviction, as if the ingenuity of the thing gave them a sensation of exquisite pleasure. But Veneering makes two remarkably good points; so good, that they are supposed to have been suggested to him by the legal gentleman in Britannia's confidence, while briefly conferring on the stairs.

Point the first is this. Veneering institutes an original comparison between the country, and a ship; pointedly calling the ship, the Vessel of the State, and the Minister the Man at the Helm. Veneering's object is to let Pocket-Breaches know that his friend on his right (Podsnap) is a man of wealth. Consequently says he, 'And, gentlemen, when the timbers of the Vessel of the State are unsound and the Man at the Helm is unskilful, would those great Marine Insurers, who rank among our world-famed merchant-princes—would they insure her, gentlemen? Would they underwrite her? Would they incur a risk in her? Would they have confidence in her? Why, gentlemen, if I appealed to my honourable friend upon my right, himself among the greatest and most respected of that great and much respected class, he would answer No!'

Point the second is this. The telling fact that Twemlow is related to Lord Snigsworth, must be let off. Veneering supposes a state of public affairs that probably never could by any possibility exist (though this is not quite certain, in consequence of his picture being unintelligible to himself and everybody else), and thus proceeds. 'Why, gentlemen, if I were to indicate such a programme to any class of society, I say it would be received with derision, would be pointed at by the finger of scorn. If I indicated such a programme to any worthy and intelligent tradesman of your town—nay, I will here be personal, and say Our town—what would he reply? He would reply, "Away with it!" That's what *he* would reply, gentlemen. In his honest indignation he would reply, "Away with it!" But suppose I mounted higher in the social scale. Suppose I drew my arm through the arm of my respected friend upon my left, and, and, walking with him through the ancestral woods of his family, and under the spreading beeches of Snigsworthy Park, approached the noble hall, crossed the courtyard, entered by the door, went up the staircase, and, passing from room to room, found myself at last in the august presence of my friend's near kinsman, Lord Snigsworth. And suppose I said to that venerable earl, "My Lord, I am here before your lordship, presented by your lordship's near kinsman, my friend upon my left, to indicate that programme;" what would his lordship answer? Why, he would answer, "Away with it!" That's what he would answer, gentlemen. "Away with it!" Unconsciously using, in his exalted sphere, the exact language of the worthy and intelligent tradesman of our town, the near and dear kinsman of my friend upon my left would answer in his wrath, "Away with it!" '

Veneering finishes with this last success, and Mr Podsnap telegraphs to Mrs Veneering, 'He's down.'

Then, dinner is had at the Hotel with the legal gentleman, and then there are in due succession, nomination, and declaration. Finally Mr Podsnap telegraphs to Mrs Veneering, 'We have brought him in.'

Another gorgeous dinner awaits them on their return to the Veneering halls, and Lady Tippins awaits them, and Boots and Brewer await them. There is a modest assertion on everybody's part that everybody single-handed 'brought him in'; but in the main it is conceded by all, that that stroke of business on Brewer's part, in going down to the house that night to see how things looked, was the master-stroke.

A touching little incident is related by Mrs Veneering, in the course of the evening. Mrs Veneering is habitually disposed to be tearful, and has an extra disposition that way after her late excitement. Previous to withdrawing from the dinner-table with Lady Tippins, she says, in a pathetic and physically weak manner:

'You will all think it foolish of me, I know, but I must mention it. As I sat by Baby's crib, on the night before the election, Baby was very uneasy in her sleep.'

The Analytical chemist, who is gloomily looking on, has diabolical impulses to suggest 'Wind' and throw up his situation; but represses them.

'After an interval almost convulsive, Baby curled her little hands in one another and smiled.'

Mrs Veneering stopping here, Mr Podsnap deems it incumbent on him to say: 'I wonder why!'

'Could it be, I asked myself,' says Mrs Veneering, looking about her for her pocket-handkerchief, 'that the Fairies were telling Baby that her papa would shortly be an M.P.?'

So overcome by the sentiment is Mrs Veneering, that they all get up to make a clear stage for Veneering, who goes round the table to the rescue, and bears her out backward, with her feet impressively scraping the carpet: after remarking that her work has been too much for her strength. Whether the fairies made any mention of the five thousand pounds, and it disagreed with Baby, is not speculated upon.

Poor little Twemlow, quite done up, is touched, and still continues touched after he is safely housed over the livery-stable yard in Duke Street, Saint James's. But there, upon his sofa, a tremendous consideration breaks in upon the mild gentleman, putting all softer considerations to the rout.

'Gracious heavens! Now I have time to think of it, he never saw one of his constituents in all his days, until we saw them together!'

After having paced the room in distress of mind, with his hand to his forehead, the innocent Twemlow returns to his sofa and moans:

'I shall either go distracted, or die, of this man. He comes upon me too late in life. I am not strong enough to bear him!'

Chapter 4
Cupid Prompted

To USE the cold language of the world, Mrs Alfred Lammle rapidly improved the acquaintance of Miss Podsnap. To use the warm language of Mrs Lammle, she and her sweet Georgiana soon became one: in heart, in mind, in sentiment, in soul.

Whenever Georgiana could escape from the thraldom of Podsnappery; could throw off the bedclothes of the custard-coloured phaeton, and get up; could shrink out of the range of her mother's rocking, and (so to speak) rescue her poor little frosty toes from being rocked over; she repaired to her friend,

Mrs Alfred Lammle. Mrs Podsnap by no means objected. As a consciously 'splendid woman,' accustomed to overhear herself so denominated by elderly osteologists pursuing their studies in dinner society, Mrs Podsnap could dispense with her daughter. Mr Podsnap, for his part, on being informed where Georgiana was, swelled with patronage of the Lammles. That they, when unable to lay hold of him, should respectfully grasp at the hem of his mantle; that they, when they could not bask in the glory of him the sun, should take up with the pale reflected light of the watery young moon his daughter; appeared quite natural, becoming, and proper. It gave him a better opinion of the discretion of the Lammles than he had heretofore held, as showing that they appreciated the value of the connexion. So, Georgiana repairing to her friend, Mr Podsnap went out to dinner, and to dinner, and yet to dinner, arm in arm with Mrs Podsnap: settling his obstinate head in his cravat and shirt-collar, much as if he were performing on the Pandean pipes, in his own honour, the triumphal march, See the conquering Podsnap comes, Sound the trumpets, beat the drums!

It was a trait in Mr Podsnap's character (and in one form or other it will be generally seen to pervade the depths and shallows of Podsnappery), that he could not endure a hint of disparagement of any friend or acquaintance of his. 'How dare you?' he would seem to say, in such a case. 'What do you mean? I have licensed this person. This person has taken out *my* certificate. Through this person you strike at me, Podsnap the Great. And it is not that I particularly care for the person's dignity, but that I do most particularly care for Podsnap's.' Hence, if any one in his presence had presumed to doubt the responsibility of the Lammles, he would have been mightily huffed. Not that any one did, for Veneering, M.P., was always the authority for their being very rich, and perhaps believed it. As indeed he might, if he chose, for anything he knew of the matter.

Mr and Mrs Lammle's house in Sackville Street, Piccadilly, was but a temporary residence. It has done well enough, they informed their friends, for Mr Lammle when a bachelor, but it would not do now. So, they were always looking at palatial residences in the best situations, and always very nearly taking or buying one, but never quite concluding the bargain. Hereby they made for themselves a shining little reputation apart. People said, on seeing a vacant palatial residence, 'The very thing for the Lammles!' and wrote to the Lammles about it, and the Lammles always went to look at it, but unfortunately it never exactly answered. In short, they suffered so many disappointments, that they began to think it would be necessary to build a palatial residence. And hereby they made another shining reputation; many persons of their acquaintance becoming by anticipation dissatisfied with their own houses, and envious of the non-existent Lammle structure.

The handsome fittings and furnishings of the house in Sackville Street were piled thick and high over the skeleton up-stairs, and if it ever whispered from under its load of uphol-stery, 'Here I am in the closet!' it was to very few ears, and certainly never to Miss Podsnap's. What Miss Podsnap was par-ticularly charmed with, next to the graces of her friend, was the happiness of her friend's married life. This was frequently their theme of conversation.

'I am sure,' said Miss Podsnap, 'Mr Lammle is like a lover. At least I—I should think he was.'

'Georgiana, darling!' said Mrs Lammle, holding up a forefin-ger, 'Take care!'

'Oh my goodness me!' exclaimed Miss Podsnap, reddening. 'What have I said now?'

'Alfred, you know,' hinted Mrs Lammle, playfully shaking her head. 'You were never to say Mr Lammle any more, Georgiana.'

'Oh! Alfred, then. I am glad it's no worse. I was afraid I had said something shocking. I am always saying something wrong to ma.'

'To me, Georgiana dearest?'

'No, not to you; you are not ma. I wish you were.'

Mrs Lammle bestowed a sweet and loving smile upon her friend, which Miss Podsnap returned as she best could. They sat at lunch in Mrs Lammle's own boudoir.

'And so, dearest Georgiana, Alfred is like your notion of a lover?'

'I don't say that, Sophronia,' Georgiana replied, beginning to conceal her elbows. 'I haven't any notion of a lover. The dreadful wretches that ma brings up at places to torment me, are not lovers. I only mean that Mr—'

'Again, dearest Georgiana?'

'That Alfred—'

'Sounds much better, darling.'

'—Loves you so. He always treats you with such delicate gallantry and attention. Now, don't he?'

'Truly, my dear,' said Mrs Lammle, with a rather singular

expression crossing her face. 'I believe that he loves me, fully as much as I love him.'

'Oh, what happiness!' exclaimed Miss Podsnap.

'But do you know, my Georgiana,' Mrs Lammle resumed presently, 'that there is something suspicious in your enthusiastic sympathy with Alfred's tenderness?'

'Good gracious no, I hope not!'

'Doesn't it rather suggest,' said Mrs Lammle archly, 'that my Georgiana's little heart is—'

'Oh don't!' Miss Podsnap blushingly besought her. 'Please don't! I assure you, Sophronia, that I only praise Alfred, because he is your husband and so fond of you.'

Sophronia's glance was as if a rather new light broke in upon her. It shaded off into a cool smile, as she said, with her eyes upon her lunch, and her eyebrows raised:

'You are quite wrong, my love, in your guess at my meaning. What I insinuated was, that my Georgiana's little heart was growing conscious of a vacancy.'

'No, no, no,' said Georgiana. 'I wouldn't have anybody say anything to me in that way for I don't know how many thousand pounds.'

'In what way, my Georgiana?' inquired Mrs Lammle, still smiling coolly with her eyes upon her lunch, and her eyebrows raised.

'*You* know,' returned poor little Miss Podsnap. 'I think I should go out of my mind, Sophronia, with vexation and shyness and detestation, if anybody did. It's enough for me to see how loving you and your husband are. That's a different thing. I couldn't bear to have anything of that sort going on with myself. I should beg and pray to—to have the person taken away and trampled upon.'

Ah! here was Alfred. Having stolen in unobserved, he playfully leaned on the back of Sophronia's chair, and, as Miss Podsnap saw him, put one of Sophronia's wandering locks to his lips, and waved a kiss from it towards Miss Podsnap.

'What is this about husbands and detestations?' inquired the captivating Alfred.

'Why, they say,' returned his wife, 'that listeners never hear any good of themselves; though you—but pray how long have you been here, sir?'

'This instant arrived, my own.'

'Then I may go on—though if you had been here but a moment or two sooner, you would have heard your praises sounded by Georgiana.'

'Only, if they were to be called praises at all which I really don't think they were,' explained Miss Podsnap in a flutter, 'for being so devoted to Sophronia.'

'Sophronia!' murmured Alfred. 'My life!' and kissed her hand. In return for which she kissed his watch-chain.

'But it was not I who was to be taken away and trampled upon, I hope?' said Alfred, drawing a seat between them.

'Ask Georgiana, my soul,' replied his wife.

Alfred touchingly appealed to Georgiana.

'Oh, it was nobody,' replied Miss Podsnap. 'It was nonsense.'

'But if you are determined to know, Mr Inquisitive Pet, as I suppose you are,' said the happy and fond Sophronia, smiling, 'it was any one who should venture to aspire to Georgiana.'

'Sophronia, my love,' remonstrated Mr Lammle, becoming graver, 'you are not serious?'

'Alfred, my love,' returned his wife, 'I dare say Georgiana was not, but I am.'

'Now this,' said Mr Lammle, 'shows the accidental combinations that there are in things! Could you believe, my Ownest, that I came in here with the name of an aspirant to our Georgiana on my lips?'

'Of course I could believe, Alfred,' said Mrs Lammle, 'anything that *you* told me.'

'You dear one! And I anything that *you* told me.'

How delightful those interchanges, and the looks accompanying them! Now, if the skeleton up-stairs had taken that opportunity, for instance, of calling out 'Here I am, suffocating in the closet!'

'I give you my honour, my dear Sophronia—'

'And I know what that is, love,' said she.

'You do, my darling—that I came into the room all but uttering young Fledgeby's name. Tell Georgiana, dearest, about young Fledgeby.'

'Oh no, don't! Please don't!' cried Miss Podsnap, putting her fingers in her ears. 'I'd rather not.'

Mrs Lammle laughed in her gayest manner, and, removing her Georgiana's unresisting hands, and playfully holding them in her own at arms' length, sometimes near together and sometimes wide apart, went on:

'You must know, you dearly beloved little goose, that once upon a time there was a certain person called young Fledgeby. And this young Fledgeby, who was of an excellent family and rich, was known to two other certain persons, dearly attached to one another and called Mr and Mrs Alfred Lammle. So this young Fledgeby, being one night at the play, there sees with Mr and Mrs Alfred Lammle, a certain heroine called—'

'No, don't say Georgiana Podsnap!' pleaded that young lady almost in tears. 'Please don't. Oh do do do say somebody else! Not Georgiana Podsnap. Oh don't, don't, don't!'

'No other,' said Mrs Lammle, laughing airily, and, full of affectionate blandishments, opening and closing Georgiana's arms like a pair of compasses, 'than my little Georgiana Podsnap. So this young Fledgeby goes to that Alfred Lammle and says—'

'Oh ple-e-e-ease don't!' Georgiana, as if the supplication were being squeezed out of her by powerful compression. 'I so hate him for saying it!'

'For saying what, my dear?' laughed Mrs Lammle.

'Oh, I don't know what he said,' cried Georgiana wildly, 'but I hate him all the same for saying it.'

'My dear,' said Mrs Lammle, always laughing in her most captivating way, 'the poor young fellow only says that he is stricken all of a heap.'

'Oh, what shall I ever do!' interposed Georgiana. 'Oh my goodness what a Fool he must be!'

'—And implores to be asked to dinner, and to make a fourth at the play another time. And so he dines to-morrow and goes to the Opera with us. That's all. Except, my dear Georgiana— and what will you think of this!—that he is infinitely shyer than you, and far more afraid of you than you ever were of any one in all your days!'

In perturbation of mind Miss Podsnap still fumed and plucked at her hands a little, but could not help laughing at the notion of anybody's being afraid of her. With that advantage, Sophronia flattered her and rallied her more successfully, and then the insinuating Alfred flattered her and rallied her, and promised that at any moment when she might require that service at his hands, he would take young Fledgeby out and trample on him. Thus it remained amicably understood that young Fledgeby was to come to admire, and that Georgiana was to come to be admired; and Georgiana with the entirely new sensation in her breast of having that prospect before her, and with many kisses from her dear Sophronia in present possession, preceded six feet one of discontented footman (an amount of the article that always came for her when she walked home) to her father's dwelling.

The happy pair being left together, Mrs Lammle said to her husband:

'If I understand this girl, sir, your dangerous fascinations have produced some effect upon her. I mention the conquest in good time because I apprehend your scheme to be more important to you than your vanity.'

There was a mirror on the wall before them, and her eyes just caught him smirking in it. She gave the reflected image a look of the deepest disdain, and the image received it in the glass. Next moment they quietly eyed each other, as if they, the principals, had had no part in that expressive transaction.

It may have been that Mrs Lammle tried in some manner to excuse her conduct to herself by depreciating the poor little victim of whom she spoke with acrimonious contempt. It may have been too that in this she did not quite succeed, for it is very difficult to resist confidence, and she knew she had Georgiana's.

Nothing more was said between the happy pair. Perhaps conspirators who have once established an understanding, may not be over-fond of repeating the terms and objects of their conspiracy. Next day came; came Georgiana; and came Fledgeby.

Georgiana had by this time seen a good deal of the house and its frequenters. As there was a certain handsome room with a billiard table in it—on the ground floor, eating out a backyard—which might have been Mr Lammle's office, or library, but was called by neither name, but simply Mr Lammle's room, so it would have been hard for stronger female heads than Georgiana's to determine whether its frequenters were men of pleasure or men of business. Between the room and the men there were strong points of general resemblance. Both were too gaudy, too slangey, too odorous of cigars, and too much given to horseflesh; the latter characteristic being exemplified in the room by its decorations, and in the men by their conversation. High-stepping horses seemed necessary to all Mr Lammle's friends—as necessary as their transaction of business together in a gipsy way at untimely hours of the morning and evening, and in rushes and snatches. There were friends who seemed to be always coming and going across the Channel, on errands about the Bourse, and Greek and Spanish and India and Mexican and par and premium and discount and three quarters and seven eighths. There were other friends who seemed to be always lolling and lounging in and out of the City, on questions of the Bourse, and Greek and Spanish and India and Mexican and par and premium and discount and three quarters and seven eighths. They were all feverish, boastful, and indefinably loose; and they all ate and drank a great deal; and made bets in eating and drinking. They all spoke of sums of money, and only mentioned the sums and left the money to be understood; as 'five and forty thousand Tom,' or 'Two hundred and twenty-two on every individual share in the lot Joe.' They seemed to divide the world into two classes of people; people who were making enormous fortunes, and people who were being enormously ruined. They were always in a hurry, and yet seemed to have nothing tangible to do; except a few of them (these, mostly asthmatic and thick-lipped) who were for ever demonstrating to the rest, with gold pencil-cases which they could hardly hold because of the big rings on their forefingers, how money was to be made. Lastly, they all swore at their grooms, and the grooms were not quite as respectful or complete as other men's grooms; seeming somehow to fall short of the groom point as their masters fell short of the gentleman point.

Young Fledgeby was none of these. Young Fledgeby had a peachy cheek, or a cheek compounded of the peach and the red red red wall on which it grows, and was an awkward, sandy-haired, small-eyed youth, exceeding slim (his enemies would have said lanky), and prone to self-examination in the articles of whisker and moustache. While feeling for the whisker that he anxiously expected, Fledgeby underwent remarkable fluctuations of spirits, ranging along the whole scale from confidence to despair. There were times when he started, as exclaiming 'By Jupiter here it is at last!' There were other times when, being equally depressed, he would be seen to shake his head, and give up hope. To see him at those periods leaning on a chimneypiece, like as on an urn containing the ashes of his ambition, with the cheek that would not sprout, upon the hand on which that cheek had forced conviction, was a distressing sight.

Not so was Fledgeby seen on this occasion. Arrayed in superb raiment, with his opera hat under his arm, he concluded his self-examination hopefully, awaited the arrival of Miss Podsnap, and talked small-talk with Mrs Lammle. In facetious homage to the smallness of his talk, and the jerky nature of his manners, Fledgeby's familiars had agreed to confer upon him (behind his back) the honorary title of Fascination Fledgeby.

'Warm weather, Mrs Lammle,' said Fascination Fledgeby. Mrs Lammle thought it scarcely as warm as it had been yesterday. 'Perhaps not,' said Fascination Fledgeby, with great quickness of repartee; 'but I expect it will be devilish warm to-morrow.'

He threw off another little scintillation. 'Been out to-day, Mrs Lammle?'

Mrs Lammle answered, for a short drive.

'Some people,' said Fascination Fledgeby, 'are accustomed to take long drives; but it generally appears to me that if they make 'em too long, they overdo it.'

Being in such feather, he might have surpassed himself in his next sally, had not Miss Podsnap been announced. Mrs Lammle flew to embrace her darling little Georgy, and when the first transports were over, presented Mr Fledgeby. Mr Lammle came on the scene last, for he was always late, and so were the frequenters always late; all hands being bound to be made late, by private information about the Bourse, and Greek and Spanish and India and Mexican and par and premium and discount and three quarters and seven eighths.

A handsome little dinner was served immediately, and Mr Lammle sat sparkling at his end of the table, with his servant behind his chair, and *his* ever-lingering doubts upon the subject of his wages behind himself. Mr Lammle's utmost powers of sparkling were in requisition to-day, for Fascination Fledgeby and Georgiana not only struck each other speechless, but struck each other into astonishing attitudes; Georgiana, as she sat facing Fledgeby, making such efforts to conceal her elbows as were totally incompatible with the use of a knife and fork; and Fledgeby, as he sat facing Georgiana, avoiding her countenance by every possible device, and betraying the discomposure of his mind in feeling for his whiskers with his spoon, his wine glass, and his bread.

So, Mr and Mrs Alfred Lammle had to prompt, and this is how they prompted.

'Georgiana,' said Mr Lammle, low and smiling, and sparkling all over, like a harlequin; 'you are not in your usual spirits. Why are you not in your usual spirits, Georgiana?'

Georgiana faltered that she was much the same as she was in general; she was not aware of being different.

'Not aware of being different!' retorted Mr Alfred Lammle. 'You, my dear Georgiana! who are always so natural and unconstrained with us! who are such a relief from the crowd that are all alike! who are the embodiment of gentleness, simplicity, and reality!'

Miss Podsnap looked at the door, as if she entertained confused thoughts of taking refuge from these compliments in flight.

'Now, I will be judged,' said Mr Lammle, raising his voice a little, 'by my friend Fledgeby.'

'Oh DON'T!' Miss Podsnap faintly ejaculated: when Mrs Lammle took the prompt-book.

'I beg your pardon, Alfred, my dear, but I cannot part with

Mr Fledgeby quite yet; you must wait for him a moment. Mr Fledgeby and I are engaged in a personal discussion.'

Fledgeby must have conducted it on his side with immense art, for no appearance of uttering one syllable had escaped him.

'A personal discussion, Sophronia, my love? What discussion? Fledgeby, I am jealous. What discussion, Fledgeby?'

'Shall I tell him, Mr Fledgeby?' asked Mrs Lammle.

Trying to look as if he knew anything about it, Fascination replied, 'Yes, tell him.'

'We were discussing then,' said Mrs Lammle, 'if you *must* know, Alfred, whether Mr Fledgeby was in his usual flow of spirits.'

'Why, that is the very point, Sophronia, that Georgiana and I were discussing as to herself! What did Fledgeby say?'

'Oh, a likely thing, sir, that I am going to tell you everything, and be told nothing! What did Georgiana say?'

'Georgiana said she was doing her usual justice to herself to-day, and I said she was not.'

'Precisely,' exclaimed Mrs Lammle, 'what I said to Mr Fledgeby.'

Still, it wouldn't do. They would not look at one another. No, not even when the sparkling host proposed that the quartette should take an appropriately sparkling glass of wine. Georgiana looked from her wine glass at Mr Lammle and at Mrs Lammle; but mightn't, couldn't, shouldn't, wouldn't, look at Mr Fledgeby. Fascination looked from his wine glass at Mrs Lammle and at Mr Lammle; but mightn't, couldn't, shouldn't, wouldn't, look at Georgiana.

More prompting was necessary. Cupid must be brought up to the mark. The manager had put him down in the bill for the part, and he must play it.

'Sophronia, my dear,' said Mr Lammle, 'I don't like the colour of your dress.'

'I appeal,' said Mrs Lammle, 'to Mr Fledgeby.'

'And I,' said Mr Lammle, 'to Georgiana.'

'Georgy, my love,' remarked Mrs Lammle aside to her dear girl, 'I rely upon you not to go over to the opposition. Now, Mr Fledgeby.'

Fascination wished to know if the colour were not called rose-colour? Yes, said Mr Lammle; actually he knew everything; it was really rose-colour. Fascination took rose-colour to mean the colour of roses. (In this he was very warmly supported by Mr and Mrs Lammle.) Fascination had heard the term Queen of

Flowers applied to the Rose. Similarly, it might be said that the dress was the Queen of Dresses. ('Very happy, Fledgeby!' from Mr Lammle.) Notwithstanding, Fascination's opinion was that we all had our eyes—or at least a large majority of us—and that—and—and his further opinion was several ands, with nothing beyond them.

'Oh, Mr Fledgeby,' said Mrs Lammle, 'to desert me in that way! Oh, Mr Fledgeby, to abandon my poor dear injured rose and declare for blue!'

'Victory, victory!' cried Mr Lammle; 'your dress is condemned, my dear.'

'But what,' said Mrs Lammle, stealing her affectionate hand towards her dear girl's, 'what does Georgy say?'

'She says,' replied Mr Lammle, interpreting for her, 'that in her eyes you look well in any colour, Sophronia, and that if she had expected to be embarrassed by so pretty a compliment as she has received, she would have worn another colour herself. Though I tell her, in reply, that it would not have saved her, for whatever colour she had worn would have been Fledgeby's colour. But what does Fledgeby say?'

'He says,' replied Mrs Lammle, interpreting for him, and patting the back of her dear girl's hand, as if it were Fledgeby who was patting it, 'that it was no compliment, but a little natural act of homage that he couldn't resist. And,' expressing more feeling as if it were more feeling on the part of Fledgeby, 'he is right, he is right!'

Still, no not even now, would they look at one another. Seeming to gnash his sparkling teeth, studs, eyes, and buttons, all at once, Mr Lammle secretly bent a dark frown on the two, expressive of an intense desire to bring them together by knocking their heads together.

'Have you heard this opera of to-night, Fledgeby?' he asked, stopping very short, to prevent himself from running on into 'confound you.'

'Why no, not exactly,' said Fledgeby. 'In fact I don't know a note of it.'

'Neither do you know it, Georgy?' said Mrs Lammle.

'N-no,' replied Georgiana, faintly, under the sympathetic coincidence.

'Why, then,' said Mrs Lammle, charmed by the discovery which flowed from the premises, 'you neither of you know it! How charming!'

Even the craven Fledgeby felt that the time was now come

when he must strike a blow. He struck it by saying, partly to Mrs Lammle and partly to the circumambient air, 'I consider myself very fortunate in being reserved by—'

As he stopped dead, Mr Lammle, making that gingerous bush of his whiskers to look out of, offered him the word 'Destiny.'

'No, I wasn't going to say that,' said Fledgeby. 'I was going to say Fate. I consider it very fortunate that Fate has written in the book of—in the book which is its own property—that I should go to that opera for the first time under the memorable circumstances of going with Miss Podsnap.'

To which Georgiana replied, hooking her two little fingers in one another, and addressing the tablecloth, 'Thank you, but I generally go with no one but you, Sophronia, and I like that very much.'

Content perforce with this success for the time, Mr Lammle let Miss Podsnap out of the room, as if he were opening her cage door, and Mrs Lammle followed. Coffee being presently served up stairs, he kept a watch on Fledgeby until Miss Podsnap's cup was empty, and then directed him with his finger (as if that young gentleman was a slow Retriever) to go and fetch it. This feat he performed, not only without failure, but even with the original embellishment of informing Miss Podsnap that green tea was considered bad for the nerves. Though there Miss Podsnap unintentionally threw him out by faltering, 'Oh, is it indeed? How does it act?' Which he was not prepared to elucidate.

The carriage announced, Mrs Lammle said, 'Don't mind me, Mr Fledgeby, my skirts and cloak occupy both my hands, take Miss Podsnap.' And he took her, and Mrs Lammle went next, and Mr Lammle went last, savagely following his little flock, like a drover.

But he was all sparkle and glitter in the box at the Opera, and there he and his dear wife made a conversation between Fledgeby and Georgiana in the following ingenious and skilful manner. They sat in this order: Mrs Lammle, Fascination Fledgeby, Georgiana, Mr Lammle. Mrs Lammle made leading remarks to Fledgeby, only requiring monosyllabic replies. Mr Lammle did the like with Georgiana. At times Mrs Lammle would lean forward to address Mr Lammle to this purpose.

'Alfred, my dear, Mr Fledgeby very justly says, apropos of the last scene, that true constancy would not require any such stimulant as the stage deems necessary.' To which Mr Lammle would reply, 'Ay, Sophronia, my love, but as Georgiana has observed to me, the lady had no sufficient reason to know the state of the gentleman's affections.' To which Mrs Lammle would rejoin, 'Very true, Alfred; but Mr Fledgeby points out,' this. To which Alfred would demur: 'Undoubtedly, Sophronia, but Georgiana acutely remarks,' that. Through this device the two young people conversed at great length and committed themselves to a variety of delicate sentiments, without having once opened their lips, save to say yes or no, and even that not to one another.

Fledgeby took his leave of Miss Podsnap at the carriage door, and the Lammles dropped her at her own home, and on the way Mrs Lammle archly rallied her, in her fond and protecting manner, by saying at intervals, 'Oh little Georgiana, little Georgiana!' Which was not much; but the tone added, 'You have enslaved your Fledgeby.'

And thus the Lammles got home at last, and the lady sat down moody and weary, looking at her dark lord engaged in a deed of violence with a bottle of soda-water as though he were wringing the neck of some unlucky creature and pouring its blood down his throat. As he wiped his dripping whiskers in an ogreish way, he met her eyes, and pausing, said, with no very gentle voice:

'Well?'

'Was such an absolute Booby necessary to the purpose?'

'I know what I am doing. He is no such dolt as you suppose.'

'A genius, perhaps?'

'You sneer, perhaps; and you take a lofty air upon yourself, perhaps! But I tell you this:—when that young fellow's interest is concerned, he holds as tight as a horse-leech. When money is in question with that young fellow, he is a match for the Devil.'

'Is he a match for you?'

'He is. Almost as good a one as you thought me for you. He has no quality of youth in him, but such as you have seen to-day. Touch him upon money, and you touch no booby then. He really is a dolt, I suppose, in other things; but it answers his one purpose very well.'

'Has she money in her own right in any case?'

'Ay! she has money in her own right in any case. You have done so well to-day, Sophronia, that I answer the question, though you know I object to any such questions. You have done so well to-day, Sophronia, that you must be tired. Get to bed.'

Chapter 5
Mercury Prompting

FLEDGEBY deserved Mr Alfred Lammle's eulogium. He was the meanest cur existing, with a single pair of legs. And instinct (a word we all clearly understand) going largely on four legs, and reason always on two, meanness on four legs never attains the perfection of meanness on two.

The father of this young gentleman had been a money-lender, who had transacted professional business with the mother of this young gentleman, when he, the latter, was waiting in the vast dark ante-chambers of the present world to be born. The lady, a widow, being unable to pay the money-lender, married him; and in due course, Fledgeby was summoned out of the vast dark ante-chambers to come and be presented to the Registrar-General. Rather a curious speculation how Fledgeby would otherwise have disposed of his leisure until Doomsday.

Fledgeby's mother offended her family by marrying Fledgeby's father. It is one of the easiest achievements in life to offend your family when your family want to get rid of you. Fledgeby's mother's family had been very much offended with her for being poor, and broke with her for becoming comparatively rich. Fledgeby's mother's family was the Snigsworth family. She had even the high honour to be cousin to Lord Snigsworth—so many times removed that the noble Earl would have had no compunction in removing her one time more and dropping her clean outside the cousinly pale; but cousin for all that.

Among her pre-matrimonial transactions with Fledgeby's father, Fledgeby's mother had raised money of him at a great disadvantage on a certain reversionary interest. The reversion falling in soon after they were married, Fledgeby's father laid hold of the cash for his separate use and benefit. This led to subjective differences of opinion, not to say objective interchanges of boot-jacks, backgammon boards, and other such domestic missiles, between Fledgeby's father and Fledgeby's mother, and those led to Fledgeby's mother spending as much money as she could, and to Fledgeby's father doing all he couldn't to restrain her. Fledgeby's childhood had been, in consequence, a stormy one; but the winds and the waves had gone down in the grave, and Fledgeby flourished alone.

He lived in chambers in the Albany, did Fledgeby, and maintained a spruce appearance. But his youthful fire was all composed of sparks from the grindstone; and as the sparks flew off, went out, and never warmed anything, be sure that Fledgeby had his tools at the grindstone, and turned it with a wary eye.

Mr Alfred Lammle came round to the Albany to breakfast with Fledgeby. Present on the table, one scanty pot of tea, one scanty loaf, two scanty pats of butter, two scanty rashers of bacon, two pitiful eggs, and an abundance of handsome china bought a second-hand bargain.

'What did you think of Georgiana?' asked Mr Lammle.

'Why, I'll tell you,' said Fledgeby, very deliberately.

'Do, my boy.'

'You misunderstand me,' said Fledgeby. 'I don't mean I'll tell you that. I mean I'll tell you something else.'

'Tell me anything, old fellow!'

'Ah, but there you misunderstand me again,' said Fledgeby. 'I mean I'll tell you nothing.'

Mr Lammle sparkled at him, but frowned at him too.

'Look here,' said Fledgeby. 'You're deep and you're ready. Whether I am deep or not, never mind. I am not ready. But I can do one thing, Lammle, I can hold my tongue. And I intend always doing it.'

'You are a long-headed fellow, Fledgeby.'

'May be, or may not be. If I am a short-tongued fellow, it may amount to the same thing. Now, Lammle, I am never going to answer questions.'

'My dear fellow, it was the simplest question in the world.'

'Never mind. It seemed so, but things are not always what they seem. I saw a man examined as a witness in Westminster Hall. Questions put to him seemed the simplest in the world, but turned out to be anything rather than that, after he had answered 'em. Very well. Then he should have held his tongue. If he had held his tongue he would have kept out of scrapes that he got into.'

'If I had held my tongue, you would never have seen the subject of my question,' remarked Lammle, darkening.

'Now, Lammle,' said Fascination Fledgeby, calmly feeling for his whisker, 'it won't do. I won't be led on into a discussion. I can't manage a discussion. But I can manage to hold my tongue.'

'Can?' Mr Lammle fell back upon propitiation. 'I should think you could! Why, when these fellows of our acquaintance drink and you drink with them, the more talkative they get, the more silent you get. The more they let out, the more you keep in.'

'I don't object, Lammle,' returned Fledgeby, with an internal chuckle, 'to being understood, though I object to being questioned. That certainly *is* the way I do it.'

'And when all the rest of us are discussing our ventures, none of us ever know what a single venture of yours is!'

'And none of you ever will from me, Lammle,' replied Fledgeby, with another internal chuckle; 'that certainly *is* the way I do it.'

'Why of course it is, I know!' rejoined Lammle, with a flourish of frankness, and a laugh, and stretching out his hands as if to show the universe a remarkable man in Fledgeby. 'If I hadn't known it of my Fledgeby, should I have proposed our little compact of advantage, to my Fledgeby?'

'Ah!' remarked Fascination, shaking his head slyly. 'But I am not to be got at in that way. I am not vain. That sort of vanity don't pay, Lammle. No, no, no. Compliments only make me hold my tongue the more.'

Alfred Lammle pushed his plate away (no great sacrifice under the circumstances of there being so little in it), thrust his hands in his pockets, leaned back in his chair, and contemplated Fledgeby in silence. Then he slowly released his left hand from its pocket, and made that bush of his whiskers, still contemplating him in silence. Then he slowly broke silence, and slowly said: 'What—the—Dev-il is this fellow about this morning?'

'Now, look here, Lammle,' said Fascination Fledgeby, with the meanest of twinkles in his meanest of eyes: which were too near together, by the way: 'look here, Lammle; I am very well aware that I didn't show to advantage last night, and that you and your wife—who, I consider, is a very clever woman and an agreeable woman—did. I am not calculated to show to advantage under that sort of circumstances. I know very well you two did show to advantage, and managed capitally. But don't you on that account come talking to me as if I was your doll and puppet, because I am not.'

'And all this,' cried Alfred, after studying with a look the meanness that was fain to have the meanest help, and yet was so mean as to turn upon it: 'all this because of one simple natural question!'

'You should have waited till I thought proper to say something about it of myself. I don't like your coming over me with your Georgianas, as if you was her proprietor and mine too.'

'Well, when you are in the gracious mind to say anything about it of yourself,' retorted Lammle, 'pray do.'

'I have done it. I have said you managed capitally. You and your wife both. If you'll go on managing capitally, I'll go on doing my part. Only don't crow.'

'I crow!' exclaimed Lammle, shrugging his shoulders.

'Or,' pursued the other—'or take it in your head that people are your puppets because they don't come out to advantage at the particular moments when you do, with the assistance of a very clever and agreeable wife. All the rest keep on doing, and let Mrs Lammle keep on doing. Now, I have held my tongue when I thought proper, and I have spoken when I thought proper, and there's an end of that. And now the question is,' proceeded Fledgeby, with the greatest reluctance, 'will you have another egg?'

'No, I won't,' said Lammle, shortly.

'Perhaps you're right and will find yourself better without it,' replied Fascination, in greatly improved spirits. 'To ask you if you'll have another rasher would be unmeaning flattery, for it would make you thirsty all day. Will you have some more bread and butter?'

'No, I won't,' repeated Lammle.

'Then I will,' said Fascination. And it was not a mere retort for the sound's sake, but was a cheerful cogent consequence of the refusal; for if Lammle had applied himself again to the loaf, it would have been so heavily visited, in Fledgeby's opinion, as to demand abstinence from bread, on his part, for the remainder of that meal at least, if not for the whole of the next.

Whether this young gentleman (for he was but three-and-twenty) combined with the miserly vice of an old man, any of the open-handed vices of a young one, was a moot point; so very honourably did he keep his own counsel. He was sensible of the value of appearances as an investment, and liked to dress well; but he drove a bargain for every moveable about him, from the coat on his back to the china on his breakfast-table; and every bargain by representing somebody's ruin or somebody's loss, acquired a peculiar charm for him. It was a part of his avarice to take, within narrow bounds, long odds at races; if he won, he drove harder bargains; if he lost, he half starved himself until next time. Why money should be so precious to an Ass too dull and mean to exchange it for any other satisfaction, is strange; but there is no animal so sure to get laden with it, as the Ass who sees nothing written on the face of the earth and sky but the three letters L. S. D.—not Luxury, Sensuality, Dissoluteness, which they often stand for, but the three dry letters. Your concentrated Fox is seldom comparable to your concentrated Ass in money-breeding.

Fascination Fledgeby feigned to be a young gentleman living on his means, but was known secretly to be a kind of outlaw in the bill-broking line, and to put money out at high interest in various ways. His circle of familiar acquaintance, from Mr Lammle round, all had a touch of the outlaw, as to their rovings in the merry greenwood of Jobbery Forest, lying on the outskirts of the Share-Market and the Stock Exchange.

'I suppose you, Lammle,' said Fledgeby, eating his bread and butter, 'always did go in for female society?'

'Always,' replied Lammle, glooming considerably under his late treatment.

'Came natural to you, eh?' said Fledgeby.

'The sex were pleased to like me, sir,' said Lammle sulkily, but with the air of a man who had not been able to help himself.

'Made a pretty good thing of marrying, didn't you?' asked Fledgeby.

The other smiled (an ugly smile), and tapped one tap upon his nose.

'My late governor made a mess of it,' said Fledgeby. 'But Geor—is the right name Georgina or Georgiana?'

'Georgiana.'

'I was thinking yesterday, I didn't know there was such a name. I thought it must end in ina.'

'Why?'

'Why, you play—if you can—the Concertina, you know,' replied Fledgeby, meditating very slowly. 'And you have—when you catch it—the Scarlatina. And you can come down from a balloon in a parach—no you can't though. Well, say Georgeute—I mean Georgiana.'

'You were going to remark of Georgiana—?' Lammle moodily hinted, after waiting in vain.

'I was going to remark of Georgiana, sir,' said Fledgeby, not at all pleased to be reminded of his having forgotten it, 'that she don't seem to be violent. Don't seem to be of the pitching-in order.'

'She has the gentleness of the dove, Mr Fledgeby.'

'Of course you'll say so,' replied Fledgeby, sharpening, the moment his interest was touched by another. 'But you know, the real look-out is this:—what I say, not what you say. I say—having my late governor and my late mother in my eye—that Georgiana don't seem to be of the pitching-in order.'

The respected Mr Lammle was a bully, by nature and by usual practice. Perceiving, as Fledgeby's affronts cumulated, that conciliation by no means answered the purpose here, he now directed a scowling look into Fledgeby's small eyes for the effect of the opposite treatment. Satisfied by what he saw there, he burst into a violent passion and struck his hand upon the table, making the china ring and dance.

'You are a very offensive fellow, sir,' cried Mr Lammle, rising. 'You are a highly offensive scoundrel. What do you mean by this behaviour?'

'I say!' remonstrated Fledgeby. 'Don't break out.'

'You are a very offensive fellow sir,' repeated Mr Lammle. 'You are a highly offensive scoundrel!'

'I *say,* you know!' urged Fledgeby, quailing.

'Why, you coarse and vulgar vagabond!' said Mr Lammle, looking fiercely about him, 'if your servant was here to give me sixpence of your money to get my boots cleaned afterwards—for you are not worth the expenditure—I'd kick you.'

'No you wouldn't,' pleaded Fledgeby. 'I am sure you'd think better of it.'

'I tell you what, Mr Fledgeby,' said Lammle advancing on him. 'Since you presume to contradict me, I'll assert myself a little. Give me your nose!'

Fledgeby covered it with his hand instead, and said, retreating, 'I beg you won't!'

'Give me your nose, sir,' repeated Lammle.

Still covering that feature and backing, Mr Fledgeby reiterated (apparently with a severe cold in his head), 'I beg, I beg, you won't.'

'And this fellow,' exclaimed Lammle, stopping and making the most of his chest—'This fellow presumes on my having selected him out of all the young fellows I know, for an advantageous opportunity! This fellow presumes on my having in my desk round the corner, his dirty note of hand for a wretched sum payable on the occurrence of a certain event, which event can only be of my and my wife's bringing about! This fellow, Fledgeby, presumes to be impertinent to me, Lammle. Give me your nose sir!'

'No! Stop! I beg your pardon,' said Fledgeby, with humility.

'What do you say, sir?' demanded Mr Lammle, seeming too furious to understand.

'I beg your pardon,' repeated Fledgeby.

'Repeat your words louder, sir. The just indignation of a gentleman has sent the blood boiling to my head. I don't hear you.'

'I say,' repeated Fledgeby, with laborious explanatory politeness, 'I beg your pardon.'

Mr Lammle paused. 'As a man of honour,' said he, throwing himself into a chair, 'I am disarmed.'

Mr Fledgeby also took a chair, though less demonstratively, and by slow approaches removed his hand from his nose. Some natural diffidence assailed him as to blowing it, so shortly after its having assumed a personal and delicate, not to say public, character; but he overcame his scruples by degrees, and modestly took that liberty under an implied protest.

'Lammle,' he said sneakingly, when that was done, 'I hope we are friends again?'

'Mr Fledgeby,' returned Lammle, 'say no more.'

'I must have gone too far in making myself disagreeable,' said Fledgeby, 'but I never intended it.'

'Say no more, say no more!' Mr Lammle repeated in a magnificent tone. 'Give me your'—Fledgeby started—'hand.'

They shook hands, and on Mr Lammle's part, in particular, there ensued great geniality. For, he was quite as much of a dastard as the other, and had been in equal danger of falling into the second place for good, when he took heart just in time, to act upon the information conveyed to him by Fledgeby's eye.

The breakfast ended in a perfect understanding. Incessant machinations were to be kept at work by Mr and Mrs Lammle; love was to be made for Fledgeby, and conquest was to be insured to him; he on his part very humbly admitting his defects as to the softer social arts, and entreating to be backed to the utmost by his two able coadjutors.

Little recked Mr Podsnap of the traps and toils besetting his Young Person. He regarded her as safe within the Temple of Podsnappery, biding the fulness of time when she, Georgiana, should take him, Fitz-Podsnap, who with all his worldly goods should her endow. It would call a blush into the cheek of his standard Young Person to have anything to do with such matters save to take as directed, and with worldly goods as per settlement to be endowed. Who giveth this woman to be married to this man? I, Podsnap. Perish the daring thought that any smaller creation should come between!

It was a public holiday, and Fledgeby did not recover his spirits or his usual temperature of nose until the afternoon. Walking into the City in the holiday afternoon, he walked against a living stream setting out of it; and thus, when he turned into the precincts of St Mary Axe, he found a prevalent repose and quiet there. A yellow overhanging plaster-fronted house at which he stopped was quiet too. The blinds were all drawn down, and the inscription Pubsey and Co. seemed to doze in the counting-house window on the ground-floor giving on the sleepy street.

Fledgeby knocked and rang, and Fledgeby rang and knocked, but no one came. Fledgeby crossed the narrow street and looked up at the house-windows, but nobody looked down at Fledgeby. He got out of temper, crossed the narrow street again, and pulled the housebell as if it were the house's nose, and he were taking a hint from his late experience. His ear at the keyhole seemed then, at last, to give him assurance that something stirred within. His eye at the keyhole seemed to confirm his ear, for he angrily pulled the house's nose again, and pulled and pulled and continued to pull, until a human nose appeared in the dark doorway.

'Now you sir!' cried Fledgeby. 'These are nice games!'

He addressed an old Jewish man in an ancient coat, long of skirt, and wide of pocket. A venerable man, bald and shining at the top of his head, and with long grey hair flowing down at its sides and mingling with his beard. A man who with a graceful Eastern action of homage bent his head, and stretched out his hands with the palms downward, as if to deprecate the wrath of a superior.

'What have you been up to?' said Fledgeby, storming at him.

'Generous Christian master,' urged the Jewish man, 'it being holiday, I looked for no one.'

'Holiday be blowed!' said Fledgeby, entering. 'What have *you* got to do with holidays? Shut the door.'

With his former action the old man obeyed. In the entry hung his rusty large-brimmed low-crowned hat, as long out of date as his coat; in the corner near it stood his staff—no walking-stick but a veritable staff. Fledgeby turned into the counting-house, perched himself on a business stool, and cocked his hat. There were light boxes on shelves in the counting-house, and strings of mock beads hanging up. There were samples of cheap clocks, and samples of cheap vases of flowers. Foreign toys, all.

Perched on the stool with his hat cocked on his head and one of his legs dangling, the youth of Fledgeby hardly contrasted to advantage with the age of the Jewish man as he stood with his bare head bowed, and his eyes (which he only raised in speaking) on the ground. His clothing was worn down to the rusty hue of the hat in the entry, but though he looked shabby he did not look mean. Now, Fledgeby, though not shabby, did look mean.

'You have not told me what you were up to, you sir,' said Fledgeby, scratching his head with the brim of his hat.

'Sir, I was breathing the air.'

'In the cellar, that you didn't hear?'

'On the house-top.'

'Upon my soul! That's a way of doing business.'

'Sir,' the old man represented with a grave and patient air, 'there must be two parties to the transaction of business, and the holiday has left me alone.'

'Ah! Can't be buyer and seller too. That's what the Jews say; ain't it?'

'At least we say truly, if we say so,' answered the old man with a smile.

'Your people need speak the truth sometimes, for they lie enough,' remarked Fascination Fledgeby.

'Sir, there is,' returned the old man with quiet emphasis, 'too much untruth among all denominations of men.'

Rather dashed, Fascination Fledgeby took another scratch at his intellectual head with his hat, to gain time for rallying.

'For instance,' he resumed, as though it were he who had spoken last, 'who but you and I ever heard of a poor Jew?'

'The Jews,' said the old man, raising his eyes from the ground with his former smile. 'They hear of poor Jews often, and are very good to them.'

'Bother that!' returned Fledgeby. 'You know what I mean. You'd persuade me if you could, that you are a poor Jew. I wish you'd confess how much you really did make out of my late governor. I should have a better opinion of you.'

The old man only bent his head, and stretched out his hands as before.

'Don't go on posturing like a Deaf and Dumb School,' said the ingenious Fledgeby, 'but express yourself like a Christian—or as nearly as you can.'

'I had had sickness and misfortunes, and was so poor,' said the old man, 'as hopelessly to owe the father, principal and interest. The son inheriting, was so merciful as to forgive me both, and place me here.'

He made a little gesture as though he kissed the hem of an imaginary garment worn by the noble youth before him. It was humbly done, but picturesquely, and was not abasing to the doer.

'You won't say more, I see,' said Fledgeby, looking at him as if he would like to try the effect of extracting a double-tooth or two, 'and so it's of no use my putting it to you. But confess this, Riah; who believes you to be poor now?'

'No one,' said the old man.

'There you're right,' assented Fledgeby.

'No one,' repeated the old man with a grave slow wave of his head. 'All scout it as a fable. Were I to say "This little fancy business is not mine";' with a lithe sweep of his easily-turning hand around him, to comprehend the various objects on the shelves; ' "it is the little business of a Christian young gentleman who places me, his servant, in trust and charge here, and to whom I am accountable for every single bead," they would laugh. When, in the larger money-business, I tell the borrowers—'

'I say, old chap!' interposed Fledgeby, 'I hope you mind what you *do* tell 'em?'

'Sir, I tell them no more than I am about to repeat. When I tell them, "I cannot promise this, I cannot answer for the other, I must see my principal, I have not the money, I am a poor man and it does not rest with me," they are so unbelieving and so impatient, that they sometimes curse me in Jehovah's name.'

'That's deuced good, that is!' said Fascination Fledgeby.

'And at other times they say, "Can it never be done without these tricks, Mr Riah? Come, come, Mr Riah, we know the arts of your people"—my people!—"If the money is to be lent, fetch it, fetch it; if it is not to be lent, keep it and say so." They never believe me.'

'*That*'s all right,' said Fascination Fledgeby.

'They say, "We know, Mr Riah, we know. We have but to look at you, and we know." '

'Oh, a good 'un are you for the post,' thought Fledgeby, 'and a good 'un was I to mark you out for it! I may be slow, but I am precious sure.'

Not a syllable of this reflection shaped itself in any scrap of Mr Fledgeby's breath, lest it should tend to put his servant's price up. But looking at the old man as he stood quiet with his head bowed and his eyes cast down, he felt that to relinquish an inch of his baldness, an inch of his grey hair, an inch of his coat-skirt, an inch of his hat-brim, an inch of his walking-staff, would be to relinquish hundreds of pounds.

'Look here, Riah,' said Fledgeby, mollified by these self-approving considerations. 'I want to go a little more into buying-up queer bills. Look out in that direction.'

'Sir, it shall be done.'

'Casting my eye over the accounts, I find that branch of business pays pretty fairly, and I am game for extending it. I like to know people's affairs likewise. So look out.'

'Sir, I will, promptly.'

'Put it about in the right quarters, that you'll buy queer bills by the lump—by the pound weight if that's all—supposing you see your way to a fair chance on looking over the parcel. And there's one thing more. Come to me with the books for periodical inspection as usual, at eight on Monday morning.'

Riah drew some folding tablets from his breast and noted it down.

'That's all I wanted to say at the present time,' continued Fledgeby in a grudging vein, as he got off the stool, 'except that I wish you'd take the air where you can hear the bell, or the knocker, either one of the two or both. By-the-by how *do* you take the air at the top of the house? Do you stick your head out of a chimney-pot?'

'Sir, there are leads there, and I have made a little garden there.'

'To bury your money in, you old dodger?'

'A thumbnail's space of garden would hold the treasure *I* bury, master,' said Riah. 'Twelve shillings a week, even when they are an old man's wages, bury themselves.'

'I should like to know what you really are worth,' returned Fledgeby, with whom his growing rich on that stipend and gratitude was a very convenient fiction. 'But come! Let's have a look at your garden on the tiles, before I go!'

The old man took a step back, and hesitated.

'Truly, sir, I have company there.'

'Have you, by George!' said Fledgeby; 'I suppose you happen to know whose premises these are?'

'Sir, they are yours, and I am your servant in them.'

'Oh! I thought you might have overlooked that,' retorted Fledgeby, with his eyes on Riah's beard as he felt for his own; 'having company on my premises, you know!'

'Come up and see the guests, sir. I hope for your admission that they can do no harm.'

Passing him with a courteous reverence, specially unlike any action that Mr Fledgeby could for his life have imparted to his own head and hands, the old man began to ascend the stairs. As he toiled on before, with his palm upon the stair-rail, and his long black skirt, a very gaberdine, overhanging each successive step, he might have been the leader in some pilgrimage of devotional ascent to a prophet's tomb. Not troubled by any such weak imagining, Fascination Fledgeby merely speculated on the time of life at which his beard had begun, and thought once more what a good 'un he was for the part.

Some final wooden steps conducted them, stooping under a low penthouse roof, to the house-top. Riah stood still, and, turning to his master, pointed out his guests.

Lizzie Hexam and Jenny Wren. For whom, perhaps with some old instinct of his race, the gentle Jew had spread a carpet. Seated on it, against no more romantic object than a blackened chimney-stack over which some humble creeper had been trained, they both pored over one book; both with attentive faces; Jenny with the sharper; Lizzie with the more perplexed. Another little book or two were lying near, and a common basket of common fruit, and another basket full of strings of beads and tinsel scraps. A few boxes of humble flowers and evergreens completed the garden; and the encompassing wilderness of dowager old chimneys twirled their cowls and fluttered their smoke, rather as if they were bridling, and fanning themselves, and looking on in a state of airy surprise.

Taking her eyes off the book, to test her memory of something in it, Lizzie was the first to see herself observed. As she rose, Miss Wren likewise became conscious, and said, irreverently addressing the great chief of the premises: 'Whoever you are, *I* can't get up, because my back's bad and my legs are queer.'

'This is my master,' said Riah, stepping forward.

('Don't look like anybody's master,' observed Miss Wren to herself, with a hitch of her chin and eyes.)

'This, sir,' pursued the old man, 'is a little dressmaker for little people. Explain to the master, Jenny.'

'Dolls; that's all,' said Jenny, shortly. 'Very difficult to fit too, because their figures are so uncertain. You never know where to expect their waists.'

'Her friend,' resumed the old man, motioning towards Lizzie;

'and as industrious as virtuous. But that they both are. They are busy early and late, sir, early and late; and in bye-times, as on this holiday, they go to book-learning.'

'Not much good to be got out of that,' remarked Fledgeby.

'Depends upon the person!' quoth Miss Wren, snapping him up.

'I made acquaintance with my guests, sir,' pursued the Jew, with an evident purpose of drawing out the dressmaker, 'through their coming here to buy of our damage and waste for Miss Jenny's millinery. Our waste goes into the best of company, sir, on her rosy-cheeked little customers. They wear it in their hair, and on their ball-dresses, and even (so she tells me) are presented at Court with it.'

'Ah!' said Fledgeby, on whose intelligence this doll-fancy made rather strong demands; 'she's been buying that basketful to-day, I suppose?'

'I suppose she has,' Miss Jenny interposed; 'and paying for it too, most likely!'

'Let's have a look at it,' said the suspicious chief. Riah handed it to him. 'How much for this now?'

'Two precious silver shillings,' said Miss Wren.

Riah confirmed her with two nods, as Fledgeby looked to him. A nod for each shilling.

'Well,' said Fledgeby, poking into the contents of the basket with his forefinger, 'the price is not so bad. You have got good measure, Miss What-is-it.'

'Try Jenny,' suggested that young lady with great calmness.

'You have got good measure, Miss Jenny; but the price is not so bad.—And you,' said Fledgeby, turning to the other visitor, 'do you buy anything here, miss?'

'No, sir.'

'Nor sell anything neither, miss?'

'No, sir.'

Looking askew at the questioner, Jenny stole her hand up to her friend's, and drew her friend down, so that she bent beside her on her knee.

'We are thankful to come here for rest, sir,' said Jenny. 'You see, you don't know what the rest of this place is to us; does he, Lizzie? It's the quiet, and the air.'

'The quiet!' repeated Fledgeby, with a contemptuous turn of his head towards the City's roar. 'And the air!' with a 'Poof!' at the smoke.

'Ah!' said Jenny. 'But it's so high. And you see the clouds

rushing on above the narrow streets, not minding them, and you see the golden arrows pointing at the mountains in the sky from which the wind comes, and you feel as if you were dead.'

The little creature looked above her, holding up her slight transparent hand.

'How do you feel when you are dead?' asked Fledgeby, much perplexed.

'Oh, so tranquil!' cried the little creature, smiling. 'Oh, so peaceful and so thankful! And you hear the people who are alive, crying, and working, and calling to one another down in the close dark streets, and you seem to pity them so! And such a chain has fallen from you, and such a strange good sorrowful happiness comes upon you!'

Her eyes fell on the old man, who, with his hands folded, quietly looked on.

'Why it was only just now,' said the little creature, pointing at him, 'that I fancied I saw him come out of his grave! He toiled out at that low door so bent and worn, and then he took his breath and stood upright, and looked all round him at the sky, and the wind blew upon him, and his life down in the dark was over!—Till he was called back to life,' she added, looking round at Fledgeby with that lower look of sharpness. 'Why did you call him back?'

'He was long enough coming, anyhow,' grumbled Fledgeby.

'But *you* are not dead, you know,' said Jenny Wren. 'Get down to life!'

Mr Fledgeby seemed to think it rather a good suggestion, and with a nod turned round. As Riah followed to attend him down the stairs, the little creature called out to the Jew in a silvery tone, 'Don't be long gone. Come back, and be dead!' And still as they went down they heard the little sweet voice, more and more faintly, half calling and half singing, 'Come back and be dead, Come back and be dead!'

When they got down into the entry, Fledgeby, pausing under the shadow of the broad old hat, and mechanically poising the staff, said to the old man:

'That's a handsome girl, that one in her senses.'

'And as good as handsome,' answered Riah.

'At all events,' observed Fledgeby, with a dry whistle, 'I hope she ain't bad enough to put any chap up to the fastenings, and get the premises broken open. You look out. Keep your weather eye awake, and don't make any more acquaintances,

however handsome. Of course you always keep my name to
yourself?'

'Sir, assuredly I do.'

'If they ask it, say it's Pubsey, or say it's Co, or say it's
anything you like, but what it is.'

His grateful servant—in whose race gratitude is deep, strong,
and enduring—bowed his head, and actually did now put the hem
of his coat to his lips: though so lightly that the wearer knew
nothing of it.

Thus, Fascination Fledgeby went his way, exulting in the
artful cleverness with which he had turned his thumb down on a
Jew, and the old man went his different way up-stairs. As he
mounted, the call or song began to sound in his ears again, and,
looking above, he saw the face of the little creature looking down
out of a Glory of her long bright radiant hair, and muscially
repeating to him, like a vision:

'Come up and be dead! Come up and be dead!'

Chapter 6

A Riddle Without an Answer

AGAIN Mr Mortimer Lightwood and Mr Eugene Wrayburn sat
together in the Temple. This evening, however, they were not
together in the place of business of the eminent solicitor, but in
another dismal set of chambers facing it on the same second-
floor; on whose dungeon-like black outer-door appeared the legend:

PRIVATE

MR EUGENE WRAYBURN

MR MORTIMER LIGHTWOOD

(☞*Mr Lightwood's Offices opposite.*)

Appearances indicated that this establishment was a very
recent institution. The white letters of the inscription were ex-

tremely white and extremely strong to the sense of smell, the complexion of the tables and chairs was (like Lady Tippins's) a little too blooming to be believed in, and the carpets and floor-cloth seemed to rush at the beholder's face in the unusual prominency of their patterns. But the Temple, accustomed to tone down both the still life and the human life that has much to do with it, would soon get the better of all that.

'Well!' said Eugene, on one side of the fire, 'I feel tolerably comfortable. I hope the upholsterer may do the same.'

'Why shouldn't he?' asked Lightwood, from the other side of the fire.

'To be sure,' pursued Eugene, reflecting, 'he is not in the secret of our pecuniary affairs, so perhaps he may be in an easy frame of mind.'

'We shall pay him,' said Mortimer.

'Shall we, really?' returned Eugene, indolently surprised. 'You don't say so!'

'I mean to pay him, Eugene, for my part,' said Mortimer, in a slightly injured tone.

'Ah! I mean to pay him too,' retorted Eugene. 'But then I mean so much that I—that I don't mean.'

'Don't mean?'

'So much that I only mean and shall always only mean and nothing more, my dear Mortimer. It's the same thing.'

His friend, lying back in his easy chair, watched him lying back in his easy chair, as he stretched out his legs on the hearth-rug, and said, with the amused look that Eugene Wrayburn could always awaken in him without seeming to try or care:

'Anyhow, your vagaries have increased the bill.'

'Calls the domestic virtues vagaries!' exclaimed Eugene, raising his eyes to the ceiling.

'This very complete little kitchen of ours,' said Mortimer, 'in which nothing will ever be cooked—'

'My dear, dear Mortimer,' returned his friend, lazily lifting his head a little to look at him, 'how often have I pointed out to you that its moral influence is the important thing?'

'Its moral influence on this fellow!' exclaimed Lightwood, laughing.

'Do me the favour,' said Eugene, getting out of his chair with much gravity, 'to come and inspect that feature of our establishment which you rashly disparage.' With that, taking up a candle, he conducted his chum into the fourth room of the set of chambers—a little narrow room—which was very completely and neatly fitted as a kitchen. 'See!' said Eugene, 'miniature flour-barrel, rolling-pin, spice-box, shelf of brown jars, chopping-board, coffee-mill, dresser elegantly furnished with crockery, sauce-pans and pans, roasting jack, a charming kettle, an armoury of dish-covers. The moral influence of these objects, in forming the domestic virtues, may have an immense influence upon me; not upon you, for you are a hopeless case, but upon me. In fact, I have an idea that I feel the domestic virtues already forming. Do me the favour to step into my bedroom. Secrétaire, you see, and abstruse set of solid mahogany pigeon-holes, one for every letter of the alphabet. To what use do I devote them? I receive a bill—say from Jones. I docket it neatly at the secrétaire, JONES, and I put it into pigeon-hole J. It's the next thing to a receipt and is quite as satisfactory to *me*. And I very much wish, Mortimer,' sitting on his bed, with the air of a philosopher lecturing a disciple, 'that my example might induce *you* to cultivate habits of punctuality and method; and, by means of the moral influences with which I have surrounded you, to encourage the formation of the domestic virtues.'

Mortimer laughed again, with his usual commentaries of 'How *can* you be so ridiculous, Eugene!' and 'What an absurd fellow you are!' but when his laugh was out, there was something serious, if not anxious, in his face. Despite that pernicious assumption of lassitude and indifference, which had become his second nature, he was strongly attached to his friend. He had founded himself upon Eugene when they were yet boys at school; and at this hour imitated him no less, admired him no less, loved him no less, than in those departed days.

'Eugene,' said he, 'if I could find you in earnest for a minute, I would try to say an earnest word to you.'

'An earnest word?' repeated Eugene. 'The moral influences are beginning to work. Say on.'

'Well, I will,' returned the other, 'though you are not earnest yet.'

'In this desire for earnestness,' murmured Eugene, with the air of one who was meditating deeply, 'I trace the happy influences of the little flour-barrel and the coffee-mill. Gratifying.'

'Eugene,' resumed Mortimer, disregarding the light interruption, and laying a hand upon Eugene's shoulder, as he, Mortimer, stood before him seated on his bed, 'you are withholding something from me.'

Eugene looked at him, but said nothing.

'All this past summer, you have been withholding something from me. Before we entered on our boating vacation, you were as bent upon it as I have seen you upon anything since we first rowed together. But you cared very little for it when it came, often found it a tie and a drag upon you, and were constantly away. Now it was well enough half-a-dozen times, a dozen times, twenty times, to say to me in your own odd manner, which I know so well and like so much, that your disappearances were precautions against our boring one another; but of course after a short while I began to know that they covered something. I don't ask what it is, as you have not told me; but the fact is so. Say, is it not?'

'I give you my word of honour, Mortimer,' returned Eugene, after a serious pause of a few moments, 'that I don't know.'

'Don't know, Eugene?'

'Upon my soul, don't know. I know less about myself than about most people in the world, and I don't know.'

'You have some design in your mind?'

'Have I? I don't think I have.'

'At any rate, you have some subject of interest there which used not to be there?'

'I really can't say,' replied Eugene, shaking his head blankly, after pausing again to reconsider. 'At times I have thought yes; at other times I have thought no. Now, I have been inclined to pursue such a subject; now I have felt that it was absurd, and that it tired and embarrassed me. Absolutely, I can't say. Frankly and faithfully, I would if I could.'

So replying, he clapped a hand, in his turn, on his friend's shoulder, as he rose from his seat upon the bed, and said:

'You must take your friend as he is. You know what I am, my dear Mortimer. You know how dreadfully susceptible I am to boredom. You know that when I became enough of a man to find myself an embodied conundrum, I bored myself to the last degree by trying to find out what I meant. You know that at length I gave it up, and declined to guess any more. Then how can I possibly give you the answer that I have not discovered? The old nursery form runs, "Riddle-me-riddle-me-ree, p'raps you can't tell me what this may be?" My reply runs, "No. Upon my life, I can't." '

So much of what was fantastically true to his own knowledge of this utterly careless Eugene, mingled with the answer, that Mortimer could not receive it as a mere evasion. Besides, it was given with an engaging air of openness, and of special exemption of the one friend he valued, from his reckless indifference.

'Come, dear boy!' said Eugene. 'Let us try the effect of smoking. If it enlightens me at all on this question, I will impart unreservedly.'

They returned to the room they had come from, and, finding it heated, opened a window. Having lighted their cigars, they leaned out of this window, smoking, and looking down at the moonlight, as it shone into the court below.

'No enlightenment,' resumed Eugene, after certain minutes of silence. 'I feel sincerely apologetic, my dear Mortimer, but nothing comes.'

'If nothing comes,' returned Mortimer, 'nothing can come from it. So I shall hope that this may hold good throughout, and that there may be nothing on foot. Nothing injurious to you, Eugene, or—'

Eugene stayed him for a moment with his hand on his arm, while he took a piece of earth from an old flowerpot on the window-sill and dexterously shot it at a little point of light opposite; having done which to his satisfaction, he said, 'Or?'

'Or injurious to any one else.'

'How,' said Eugene, taking another little piece of earth, and shooting it with great precision at the former mark, 'how injurious to any one else?'

'I don't know.'

'And,' said Eugene, taking, as he said the word, another shot, 'to whom else?'

'I don't know.'

Checking himself with another piece of earth in his hand, Eugene looked at his friend inquiringly and a little suspiciously. There was no concealed or half-expressed meaning in his face.

'Two belated wanderers in the mazes of the law,' said Eugene, attracted by the sound of footsteps, and glancing down as he spoke, 'stray into the court. They examine the doorposts of number one, seeking the name they want. Not finding it at number one, they come to number two. On the hat of wanderer number two, the shorter one, I drop this pellet. Hitting him on the hat, I smoke serenely, and become absorbed in contemplation of the sky.'

Both the wanderers looked up towards the window; but, after interchanging a muttter or two, soon applied themselves to the door-posts below. There they seemed to discover what they wanted, for they disappeared from view by entering at the doorway. 'When they emerge,' said Eugene, 'you shall see me bring them both down'; and so prepared two pellets for the purpose.

He had not reckoned on their seeking his name, or Lightwood's. But either the one or the other would seem to be in question, for now there came a knock at the door. 'I am on duty to-night,' said Mortimer, 'stay you where you are, Eugene.' Requiring no persuasion, he stayed there, smoking quietly, and not at all curious to know who knocked, until Mortimer spoke to him from within the room, and touched him. Then, drawing in his head, he found the visitors to be young Charley Hexam and the schoolmaster; both standing facing him, and both recognized at a glance.

'You recollect this young fellow, Eugene?' said Mortimer.

'Let me look at him,' returned Wrayburn, coolly. 'Oh, yes, yes. I recollect him!'

He had not been about to repeat that former action of taking him by the chin, but the boy had suspected him of it, and had thrown up his arm with an angry start. Laughingly, Wrayburn looked to Lightwood for an explanation of this odd visit.

'He says he has something to say.'

'Surely it must be to you, Mortimer.'

'So I thought, but he says no. He says it is to you.'

'Yes, I do say so,' interposed the boy. 'And I mean to say what I want to say, too, Mr Eugene Wrayburn!'

Passing him with his eyes as if there were nothing where he stood, Eugene looked on to Bradley Headstone. With consummate indolence, he turned to Mortimer, inquiring: 'And who may this other person be?'

'I am Charles Hexam's friend,' said Bradley; 'I am Charles Hexam's schoolmaster.'

'My good sir, you should teach your pupils better manners,' returned Eugene.

Composedly smoking, he leaned an elbow on the chimneypiece, at the side of the fire, and looked at the schoolmaster. It was a cruel look, in its cold disdain of him, as a creature of no worth. The schoolmaster looked at him, and that, too, was a cruel look, though of the different kind, that it had a raging jealousy and fiery wrath in it.

Very remarkably, neither Eugene Wrayburn nor Bradley Headstone looked at all at the boy. Through the ensuing dialogue, those two, no matter who spoke, or whom was addressed, looked at each other. There was some secret, sure perception between them, which set them against one another in all ways.

'In some high respects, Mr Eugene Wrayburn,' said Bradley, answering him with pale and quivering lips, 'the natural feelings of my pupils are stronger than my teaching.'

'In most respects, I dare say,' replied Eugene, enjoying his cigar, 'though whether high or low is of no importance. You have my name very correctly. Pray what is yours?'

'It cannot concern you much to know, but—'

'True,' interposed Eugene, striking sharply and cutting him short at his mistake, 'it does not concern me at all to know. I can say Schoolmaster, which is a most respectable title. You are right, Schoolmaster.'

It was not the dullest part of this goad in its galling of Bradley Headstone, that he had made it himself in a moment of incautious anger. He tried to set his lips so as to prevent their quivering, but they quivered fast.

'Mr Eugene Wrayburn,' said the boy, 'I want a word with you. I have wanted it so much, that we have looked out your address in the book, and we have been to your office, and we have come from your office here.'

'You have given yourself much trouble, Schoolmaster,' observed Eugene, blowing the feathery ash from his cigar. 'I hope it may prove remunerative.'

'And I am glad to speak,' pursued the boy, 'in presence of Mr Lightwood, because it was through Mr Lightwood that you ever saw my sister.'

For a mere moment, Wrayburn turned his eyes aside from the schoolmaster to note the effect of the last word on Mortimer, who, standing on the opposite side of the fire, as soon as the word was spoken, turned his face towards the fire and looked down into it.

'Similarly, it was through Mr Lightwood that you ever saw her again, for you were with him on the night when my father was found, and so I found you with her on the next day. Since then, you have seen my sister often. You have seen my sister oftener and oftener. And I want to know why?'

'Was this worth while, Schoolmaster?' murmured Eugene, with the air of a disinterested adviser. 'So much trouble for nothing? You should know best, but I think not.'

'I don't know, Mr Wrayburn,' answered Bradley, with his passion rising, 'why you address me—'

'Don't you?' said Eugene. 'Then I won't.'

He said it so tauntingly in his perfect placidity, that the respectable right-hand clutching the respectable hair-guard of the

respectable watch could have wound it round his throat and
strangled him with it. Not another word did Eugene deem it
worth while to utter, but stood leaning his head upon his hand,
smoking, and looking imperturbably at the chafing Bradley Headstone with his clutching right-hand, until Bradley was wellnigh
mad.

'Mr Wrayburn,' proceeded the boy, 'we not only know this
that I have charged upon you, but we know more. It has not yet
come to my sister's knowledge that we have found it out, but we
have. We had a plan, Mr Headstone and I, for my sister's education, and for its being advised and overlooked by Mr Headstone,
who is a much more competent authority, whatever you may
pretend to think, as you smoke, than you could produce, if you
tried. Then, what do we find? What do we find, Mr Lightwood?
Why, we find that my sister is already being taught, without our
knowing it. We find that while my sister gives an unwilling and
cold ear to our schemes for her advantage—I, her brother, and
Mr Headstone, the most competent authority, as his certificates
would easily prove, that could be produced—she is wilfully and
willingly profiting by other schemes. Ay, and taking pains, too,
for I know what such pains are. And so does Mr Headstone!
Well! Somebody pays for this, is a thought that naturally occurs
to us; who pays? We apply ourselves to find out, Mr Lightwood,
and we find that your friend, this Mr Eugene Wrayburn, here,
pays. Then I ask him what right has he to do it, and what does
he mean by it, and how comes he to be taking such a liberty
without my consent, when I am raising myself in the scale of
society by my own exertions and Mr Headstone's aid, and have
no right to have any darkness cast upon my prospects, or any
imputation upon my respectability, through my sister?'

The boyish weakness of this speech, combined with its great
selfishness, made it a poor one indeed. And yet Bradley Headstone, used to the little audience of a school, and unused to the
larger ways of men, showed a kind of exultation in it.

'Now I tell Mr Eugene Wrayburn,' pursued the boy, forced
into the use of the third person by the hopelessness of addressing him in the first, 'that I object to his having any acquaintance
at all with my sister, and that I request him to drop it altogether.
He is not to take it into his head that I am afraid of my sister's
caring for *him*—'

(As the boy sneered, the Master sneered, and Eugene blew
off the feathery ash again.)

—'But I object to it, and that's enough. I am more important to my sister than he thinks. As I raise myself, I intend to raise her; she knows that, and she has to look to me for her prospects. Now I understand all this very well, and so does Mr Headstone. My sister is an excellent girl, but she has some romantic notions; not about such things as your Mr Eugene Wrayburn, but about the death of my father and other matters of that sort. Mr Wrayburn encourages those notions to make himself of importance, and so she thinks she ought to be grateful to him, and perhaps even likes to be. Now I don't choose her to be grateful to him, or to be grateful to anybody but me, except Mr Headstone. And I tell Mr Wrayburn that if he don't take heed of what I say, it will be worse for her. Let him turn that over in his memory, and make sure of it. Worse for her!'

A pause ensued, in which the schoolmaster looked very awkward.

'May I suggest, Schoolmaster,' said Eugene, removing his fast-waning cigar from his lips to glance at it, 'that you can now take your pupil away.'

'And Mr Lightwood,' added the boy, with a burning face, under the flaming aggravation of getting no sort of answer or attention, 'I hope you'll take notice of what I have said to your friend, and of what your friend has heard me say, word by word, whatever he pretends to the contrary. You are bound to take notice of it, Mr Lightwood, for, as I have already mentioned, you first brought your friend into my sister's company, and but for you we never should have seen him. Lord knows none of us ever wanted him, any more than any of us will ever miss him. Now Mr Headstone, as Mr Eugene Wrayburn has been obliged to hear what I had to say, and couldn't help himself, and as I have said it out to the last word, we have done all we wanted to do, and may go.'

'Go down-stairs, and leave me a moment, Hexam,' he returned. The boy complying with an indignant look and as much noise as he could make, swung out of the room; and Lightwood went to the window, and leaned there, looking out.

'You think me of no more value than the dirt under your feet,' said Bradley to Eugene, speaking in a carefully weighed and measured tone, or he could not have spoken at all.

'I assure you, Schoolmaster,' replied Eugene, 'I don't think about you.'

'That's not true,' returned the other; 'you know better.'

'That's coarse,' Eugene retorted; 'but you *don't* know better.'

'Mr Wrayburn, at least I know very well that it would be idle to set myself against you in insolent words or overbearing manners. That lad who has just gone out could put you to shame in half-a-dozen branches of knowledge in half an hour, but you can throw him aside like an inferior. You can do as much by me, I have no doubt, beforehand.'

'Possibly,' remarked Eugene.

'But I am more than a lad,' said Bradley, with his clutching hand, 'and I WILL be heard, sir.'

'As a schoolmaster,' said Eugene, 'you are always being heard. That ought to content you.'

'But it does not content me,' replied the other, white with passion. 'Do you suppose that a man, in forming himself for the duties I discharge, and in watching and repressing himself daily to discharge them well, dismisses a man's nature?'

'I suppose you,' said Eugene, 'judging from what I see as I look at you, to be rather too passionate for a good schoolmaster.' As he spoke, he tossed away the end of his cigar.

'Passionate with you, sir, I admit I am. Passionate with you, sir, I respect myself for being. But I have not Devils for my pupils.'

'For your Teachers, I should rather say,' replied Eugene.

'Mr Wrayburn.'

'Schoolmaster.'

'Sir, my name is Bradley Headstone.'

'As you justly said, my good sir, your name cannot concern me. Now, what more?'

'This more. Oh, what a misfortune is mine,' cried Bradley, breaking off to wipe the starting perspiration from his face as he shook from head to foot, 'that I cannot so control myself as to appear a stronger creature than this, when a man who has not felt in all his life what I have felt in a day can so command himself!' He said it in a very agony, and even followed it with an errant motion of his hands as if he could have torn himself.

Eugene Wrayburn looked on at him, as if he found him beginning to be rather an entertaining study.

'Mr Wrayburn, I desire to say something to you on my own part.'

'Come, come, Schoolmaster,' returned Eugene, with a languid approach to impatience as the other again struggled with himself; 'say what you have to say. And let me remind you that the door is standing open, and your young friend waiting for you on the stairs.'

'When I accompanied that youth here, sir, I did so with the

purpose of adding, as a man whom you should not be permitted to put aside, in case you put him aside as a boy, that his instinct is correct and right.' Thus Bradley Headstone, with great effort and difficulty.

'Is that all?' asked Eugene.

'No, sir,' said the other, flushed and fierce. 'I strongly support him in his disapproval of your visits to his sister, and in his objection to your officiousness—and worse—in what you have taken upon yourself to do for her.'

'Is *that* all?' asked Eugene.

'No, sir. I determined to tell you that you are not justified in these proceedings, and that they are injurious to his sister.'

'Are you her schoolmaster as well as her brother's?—Or perhaps you would like to be?' said Eugene.

It was a stab that the blood followed, in its rush to Bradley Headstone's face, as swiftly as if it had been dealt with a dagger. 'What do you mean by that?' was as much as he could utter.

'A natural ambition enough,' said Eugene, coolly. 'Far be it from me to say otherwise. The sister—who is something too much upon your lips, perhaps—is so very different from all the associations to which she had been used, and from all the low obscure people about her, that it is a very natural ambition.'

'Do you throw my obscurity in my teeth, Mr Wrayburn?'

'That can hardly be, for I know nothing concerning it, Schoolmaster, and seek to know nothing.'

'You reproach me with my origin,' said Bradley Headstone; 'you cast insinuations at my bringing-up. But I tell you, sir, I have worked my way onward, out of both and in spite of both, and have a right to be considered a better man than you, with better reasons for being proud.'

'How I can reproach you with what is not within my knowledge, or how I can cast stones that were never in my hand, is a problem for the ingenuity of a schoolmaster to prove,' returned Eugene. 'Is *that* all?'

'No, sir. If you suppose that boy—'

'Who really will be tired of waiting,' said Eugene, politely.

'If you suppose that boy to be friendless, Mr Wrayburn, you deceive yourself. I am his friend, and you shall find me so.'

'And you will find *him* on the stairs,' remarked Eugene.

'You may have promised yourself, sir, that you could do what you chose here, because you had to deal with a mere boy, inexperienced, friendless, and unassisted. But I give you warning that this mean calculation is wrong. You have to do with a man also. You have to do with me. I will support him, and, if need be, require reparation for him. My hand and heart are in this cause, and are open to him.'

'And—quite a coincidence—the door is open,' remarked Eugene.

'I scorn your shifty evasions, and I scorn you,' said the schoolmaster. 'In the meanness of your nature you revile me with the meanness of my birth. I hold you in contempt for it. But if you don't profit by this visit, and act accordingly, you will find me as bitterly in earnest against you as I could be if I deemed you worth a second thought on my own account.'

With a consciously bad grace and stiff manner, as Wrayburn looked so easily and calmly on, he went out with these words, and the heavy door closed like a furnace-door upon his red and white heats of rage.

'A curious monomaniac,' said Eugene. 'The man seems to believe that everybody was acquainted with his mother!'

Mortimer Lightwood being still at the window, to which he had in delicacy withdrawn, Eugene called to him, and he fell to slowly pacing the room.

'My dear fellow,' said Eugene, as he lighted another cigar, 'I fear my unexpected visitors have been troublesome. If as a set-off (excuse the legal phrase from a barrister-at-law) you would like to ask Tippins to tea, I pledge myself to make love to her.'

'Eugene, Eugene, Eugene,' replied Mortimer, still pacing the room, 'I am sorry for this. And to think that I have been so blind!'

'How blind, dear boy?' inquired his unmoved friend.

'What were your words that night at the river-side public-house?' said Lightwood, stopping. 'What was it that you asked me? Did I feel like a dark combination of traitor and pickpocket when I thought of that girl?'

'I seem to remember the expression,' said Eugene.

'How do *you* feel when you think of her just now?'

His friend made no direct reply, but observed, after a few whiffs of his cigar, 'Don't mistake the situation. There is no better girl in all this London than Lizzie Hexam. There is no better among my people at home; no better among your people.'

'Granted. What follows?'

'There,' said Eugene, looking after him dubiously as he paced away to the other end of the room, 'you put me again upon guessing the riddle that I have given up.'

'Eugene, do you design to capture and desert this girl?'

'My dear fellow, no.'

'Do you design to marry her?'

'My dear fellow, no.'

'Do you design to pursue her?'

'My dear fellow, I don't design anything. I have no design whatever. I am incapable of designs. If I conceived a design, I should speedily abandon it, exhausted by the operation.'

'Oh Eugene, Eugene!'

'My dear Mortimer, not that tone of melancholy reproach, I entreat. What can I do more than tell you all I know, and acknowledge my ignorance of all I don't know! How does that little old song go, which, under pretence of being cheerful, is by far the most lugubrious I ever heard in my life?

> "Away with melancholy,
>   Nor doleful changes ring
>   On life and human folly,
>   But merrily merrily sing
>   Fal la!"

Don't let us sing Fal la, my dear Mortimer (which is comparatively unmeaning), but let us sing that we give up guessing the riddle altogether.'

'Are you in communication with this girl, Eugene, and is what these people say true?'

'I concede both admissions to my honourable and learned friend.'

'Then what is to come of it? What are you doing? Where are you going?'

'My dear Mortimer, one would think the schoolmaster had left behind him a catechizing infection. You are ruffled by the want of another cigar. Take one of these, I entreat. Light it at mine, which is in perfect order. So! Now do me the justice to observe that I am doing all I can towards self-improvement, and that you have a light thrown on those household implements which, when you only saw them as in a glass darkly, you were hastily—I must say hastily—inclined to depreciate. Sensible of my deficiencies, I have surrounded myself with moral influences expressly meant to promote the formation of the domestic virtues. To those influences, and to the improving society of my friend from boyhood, commend me with your best wishes.'

'Ah, Eugene!' said Lightwood, affectionately, now standing near him, so that they both stood in one little cloud of smoke; 'I would that you answered my three questions! What is to come of it? What are you doing? Where are you going?'

'And my dear Mortimer,' returned Eugene, lightly fanning away the smoke with his hand for the better exposition of his frankness of face and manner, 'believe me, I would answer them instantly if I could. But to enable me to do so, I must first have found out the troublesome conundrum long abandoned. Here it is. Eugene Wrayburn.' Tapping his forehead and breast. 'Riddle-me, riddle-me-ree, perhaps you can't tell me what this may be?— No, upon my life I can't. I give it up!'

Chapter 7

In Which a Friendly Move is Originated

THE arrangement between Mr Boffin and his literary man, Mr Silas Wegg, so far altered with the altered habits of Mr Boffin's life, as that the Roman Empire usually declined in the morning and in the eminently aristocratic family mansion, rather than in the evening, as of yore, and in Boffin's Bower. There were occasions, however, when Mr Boffin, seeking a brief refuge from the blandishments of fashion, would present himself at the Bower after dark, to anticipate the next sallying forth of Wegg, and would there, on the old settle, pursue the downward fortunes of those enervated and corrupted masters of the world who were by this time on their last legs. If Wegg had been worse paid for his office, or better qualified to discharge it, he would have considered these visits complimentary and agreeable; but, hold-ing the position of a handsomely-remunerated humbug, he re-sented them. This was quite according to rule, for the incompetent servant, by whomsoever employed, is always against his em-ployer. Even those born governors, noble and right honourable creatures, who have been the most imbecile in high places, have uniformly shown themselves the most opposed (sometimes in belying distrust, sometimes in vapid insolence) to *their* employer. What is in such wise true of the public master and servant, is equally true of the private master and servant all the world over.

When Mr Silas Wegg did at last obtain free access to 'Our House', as he had been wont to call the mansion outside which he had sat shelterless so long, and when he did at last find it in all particulars as different from his mental plans of it as according to the nature of things it well could be, that far-seeing and far-reaching character, by way of asserting himself and making out a case for compensation, affected to fall into a melancholy strain of musing over the mournful past; as if the house and he had had a fall in life together.

'And this, sir,' Silas would say to his patron, sadly nodding his head and musing, 'was once Our House! This, sir, is the building from which I have so often seen those great creatures, Miss Elizabeth, Master George, Aunt Jane, and Uncle Parker' —whose very names were of his own inventing—'pass and repass! And has it come to this, indeed! Ah dear me, dear me!'

So tender were his lamentations, that the kindly Mr Boffin was quite sorry for him, and almost felt mistrustful that in buying the house he had done him an irreparable injury.

Two or three diplomatic interviews, the result of great subtlety on Mr Wegg's part, but assuming the mask of careless yielding to a fortuitous combination of circumstances impelling him towards Clerkenwell, had enabled him to complete his bargain with Mr Venus.

'Bring me round to the Bower,' said Silas, when the bargain was closed, 'next Saturday evening, and if a sociable glass of old Jamaikey warm should meet your views, I am not the man to begrudge it.'

'You are aware of my being poor company, sir,' replied Mr Venus, 'but be it so.'

It being so, here is Saturday evening come, and here is Mr Venus come, and ringing at the Bower-gate.

Mr Wegg opens the gate, descries a sort of brown paper truncheon under Mr Venus's arm, and remarks, in a dry tone: 'Oh! I thought perhaps you might have come in a cab.'

'No, Mr Wegg,' replies Venus. 'I am not above a parcel.'

'Above a parcel! No!' says Wegg, with some dissatisfaction. But does not openly growl, 'a certain sort of parcel might be above you.'

'Here is your purchase, Mr Wegg,' says Venus, politely handing it over, 'and I am glad to restore it to the source from whence it—flowed.'

'Thankee,' says Wegg. 'Now this affair is concluded, I may mention to you in a friendly way that I've my doubts whether, if

I had consulted a lawyer, you could have kept this article back from me. I only throw it out as a legal point.'

'Do you think so, Mr Wegg? I bought you in open contract.'

'You can't buy human flesh and blood in this country, sir; not alive, you can't,' says Wegg, shaking his head. 'Then query, bone?'

'As a legal point?' asks Venus.

'As a legal point.'

'I am not competent to speak upon that, Mr Wegg,' says Venus, reddening and growing something louder; 'but upon a point of fact I think myself competent to speak; and as a point of fact I would have seen you—will you allow me to say, further?'

'I wouldn't say more than further, if I was you,' Mr Wegg suggests, pacifically.

—'Before I'd have given that packet into your hand without being paid my price for it. I don't pretend to know how the point of law may stand, but I'm thoroughly confident upon the point of fact.'

As Mr Venus is irritable (no doubt owing to his disappointment in love), and as it is not the cue of Mr Wegg to have him out of temper, the latter gentleman soothingly remarks, 'I only put it as a little case; I only put it ha'porthetically.'

'Then I'd rather, Mr Wegg, you put it another time, penn'orthetically,' is Mr Venus's retort, 'for I tell you candidly I don't like your little cases.'

Arrived by this time in Mr Wegg's sitting-room, made bright on the chilly evening by gaslight and fire, Mr Venus softens and compliments him on his abode; profiting by the occasion to remind Wegg that he (Venus) told him he had got into a good thing.

'Tolerable,' Wegg rejoins. 'But bear in mind, Mr Venus, that there's no gold without its alloy. Mix for yourself and take a seat in the chimbley-corner. Will you perform upon a pipe, sir?'

'I am but an indifferent performer, sir,' returns the other; 'but I'll accompany you with a whiff or two at intervals.'

So, Mr Venus mixes, and Wegg mixes; and Mr Venus lights and puffs, and Wegg lights and puffs.

'And there's alloy even in this metal of yours, Mr Wegg, you was remarking?'

'Mystery,' returns Wegg. ''I don't like it, Mr Venus. I don't like to have the life knocked out of former inhabitants of this house, in the gloomy dark, and not know who did it.'

'Might you have any suspicions, Mr Wegg?'

'No,' returns that gentleman. 'I know who profits by it. But I've no suspicions.'

Having said which, Mr Wegg smokes and looks at the fire with a most determined expression of Charity; as if he had caught that cardinal virtue by the skirts as she felt it her painful duty to depart from him, and held her by main force.

'Similarly,' resumes Wegg, 'I have observations as I can offer upon certain points and parties; but I make no objections, Mr Venus. Here is an immense fortune drops from the clouds upon a person that shall be nameless. Here is a weekly allowance, with a certain weight of coals, drops from the clouds upon me. Which of us is the better man? Not the person that shall be nameless. That's an observation of mine, but I don't make it an objection. I take my allowance and my certain weight of coals. He takes his fortune. That's the way it works.'

'It would be a good thing for me, if I could see things in the calm light you do, Mr Wegg.'

'Again look here,' pursues Silas, with an oratorical flourish of his pipe and his wooden leg: the latter having an undignified tendency to tilt him back in his chair; 'here's another observation, Mr Venus, unaccompanied with an objection. Him that shall be nameless is liable to be talked over. He gets talked over. Him that shall be nameless, having me at his right hand, naturally looking to be promoted higher, and you may perhaps say meriting to be promoted higher—'

(Mr Venus murmurs that he does say so.)

'—Him that shall be nameless, under such circumstances passes me by, and puts a talking-over stranger above my head. Which of us two is the better man? Which of us two can repeat most poetry? Which of us two has, in the service of him that shall be nameless, tackled the Romans, both civil and military, till he has got as husky as if he'd been weaned and ever since brought up on sawdust? Not the talking-over stranger. Yet the house is as free to him as if it was his, and he has his room, and is put upon a footing, and draws about a thousand a year. I am banished to the Bower, to be found in it like a piece of furniture whenever wanted. Merit, therefore, don't win. That's the way it works. I observe it, because I can't help observing it, being accustomed to take a powerful sight of notice; but I don't object. Ever here before, Mr Venus?'

'Not inside the gate, Mr Wegg.'

'You've been as far as the gate then, Mr Venus?'

'Yes, Mr Wegg, and peeped in from curiosity.'

'Did you see anything?'

'Nothing but the dust-yard.'

Mr Wegg rolls his eyes all round the room, in that ever unsatisfied quest of his, and then rolls his eyes all round Mr Venus; as if suspicious of his having something about him to be found out.

'And yet, sir,' he pursues, 'being acquainted with old Mr Harmon, one would have thought it might have been polite in you, too, to give him a call. And you're naturally of a polite disposition, you are.' This last clause as a softening compliment to Mr Venus.

'It is true, sir,' replies Venus, winking his weak eyes, and running his fingers through his dusty shock of hair, 'that I was so, before a certain observation soured me. You understand to what I allude, Mr Wegg? To a certain written statement respecting not wishing to be regarded in a certain light. Since that, all is fled, save gall.'

'Not all,' says Mr Wegg, in a tone of sentimental condolence.

'Yes, sir,' returns Venus, 'all! The world may deem it harsh, but I'd quite as soon pitch into my best friend as not. Indeed, I'd sooner!'

Involuntarily making a pass with his wooden leg to guard himself as Mr Venus springs up in the emphasis of this unsociable declaration, Mr Wegg tilts over on his back, chair and all, and is rescued by that harmless misanthrope, in a disjointed state and ruefully rubbing his head.

'Why, you lost your balance, Mr Wegg,' says Venus, handing him his pipe.

'And about time to do it,' grumbles Silas, 'when a man's visitors, without a word of notice, conduct themselves with the sudden wiciousness of Jacks-in-boxes! Don't come flying out of your chair like that, Mr Venus!'

'I ask your pardon, Mr Wegg. I am so soured.'

'Yes, but hang it,' says Wegg argumentatively, 'a well-governed mind can be soured sitting! And as to being regarded in lights, there's bumpey lights as well as bony. *In* which,' again rubbing his head, 'I object to regard myself.'

'I'll bear it in memory, sir.'

'If you'll be so good.' Mr Wegg slowly subdues his ironical tone and his lingering irritation, and resumes his pipe. 'We were talking of old Mr Harmon being a friend of yours.'

'Not a friend, Mr Wegg. Only known to speak to, and to have a little deal with now and then. A very inquisitive character, Mr Wegg, regarding what was found in the dust. As inquisitive as secret.'

'Ah! You found him secret?' returns Wegg, with a greedy relish.

'He had always the look of it, and the manner of it.'

'Ah!' with another roll of his eyes. 'As to what was found in the dust now. Did you ever hear him mention how he found it, my dear friend? Living on the mysterious premises, one would like to know. For instance, where he found things? Or, for instance, how he set about it? Whether he began at the top of the mounds, or whether he began at the bottom. Whether he prodded'; Mr Wegg's pantomime is skilful and expressive here; 'or whether he scooped? Should you say scooped, my dear Mr Venus; or should you—as a man—say prodded?'

'I should say neither, Mr Wegg.'

'As a fellow-man, Mr Venus—mix again—why neither?'

'Because I suppose, sir, that what was found, was found in the sorting and sifting. All the mounds are sorted and sifted?'

'You shall see 'em and pass your opinion. Mix again.'

On each occasion of his saying 'mix again', Mr Wegg, with a hop on his wooden leg, hitches his chair a little nearer; more as if he were proposing that himself and Mr Venus should mix again, that they should replenish their glasses.

'Living (as I said before) on the mysterious premises,' says Wegg when the other has acted on his hospitable entreaty, 'one likes to know. Would you be inclined to say now—as a brother—that he ever hid things in the dust, as well as found 'em?'

'Mr Wegg, on the whole I should say he might.'

Mr Wegg claps on his spectacles, and admiringly surveys Mr Venus from head to foot.

'As a mortal equally with myself, whose hand I take in mine for the first time this day, having unaccountably overlooked that act so full of boundless confidence binding a fellow-creetur *to* a fellow-creetur,' says Wegg, holding Mr Venus's palm out, flat and ready for smiting, and now smiting it; 'as such—and no other—for I scorn all lowlier ties betwixt myself and the man walking with his face erect that alone I call my Twin—regarded and regarding in this trustful bond—what do you think he might have hid?'

'It is but a supposition, Mr Wegg.'

'As a Being with his hand upon his heart,' cries Wegg; and the apostrophe is not the less impressive for the Being's hand being actually upon his rum and water; 'put your supposition into language, and bring it out, Mr Venus!'

'He was the species of old gentleman, sir,' slowly returns that practical anatomist, after drinking, 'that I should judge likely to take such opportunities as this place offered, of stowing away money, valuables, maybe papers.'

'As one that was ever an ornament to human life,' says Mr Wegg, again holding out Mr Venus's palm as if he were going to tell his fortune by chiromancy, and holding his own up ready for smiting it when the time should come; 'as one that the poet might have had his eye on, in writing the national naval words:

> Helm a-weather, now lay her close,
>   Yard arm and yard arm she lies;
> Again, cried I, Mr Venus, give her t'other dose,
>   Man shrouds and grapple, sir, or she flies!

—that is to say, regarded in the light of true British Oak, for such you are—explain, Mr Venus, the expression "papers"!'

'Seeing that the old gentleman was generally cutting off some near relation, or blocking out some natural affection,' Mr Venus rejoins, 'he most likely made a good many wills and codicils.'

The palm of Silas Wegg descends with a sounding smack upon the palm of Venus, and Wegg lavishly exclaims, 'Twin in opinion equally with feeling! Mix a little more!'

Having now hitched his wooden leg and his chair close in front of Mr Venus, Mr Wegg rapidly mixes for both, gives his visitor his glass, touches its rim with the rim of his own, puts his own to his lips, puts it down, and spreading his hands on his visitor's knees thus addresses him:

'Mr Venus. It ain't that I object to being passed over for a stranger, though I regard the stranger as a more than doubtful customer. It ain't for the sake of making money, though money is ever welcome. It ain't for myself, though I am not so haughty as to be above doing myself a good turn. It's for the cause of the right.'

Mr Venus, passively winking his weak eyes both at once, demands: 'What is, Mr Wegg?'

'The friendly move, sir, that I now propose. You see the move, sir?'

'Till you have pointed it out, Mr Wegg, I can't say whether I do or not.'

'If there *is* anything to be found on these premises, let us find it together. Let us make the friendly move of agreeing to look for it together. Let us make the friendly move of agreeing to share the profits of it equally betwixt us. In the cause of the right.' Thus Silas assuming a noble air.

'Then,' says Mr Venus, looking up, after meditating with his hair held in his hands, as if he could only fix his attention by fixing his head; 'if anything was to be unburied from under the dust, it would be kept a secret by you and me? Would that be it, Mr Wegg?'

'That would depend upon what it was, Mr Venus. Say it was money, or plate, or jewellery, it would be as much ours as anybody else's.'

Mr Venus rubs an eyebrow, interrogatively.

'In the cause of the right it would. Because it would be unknowingly sold with the mounds else, and the buyer would get what he was never meant to have, and never bought. And what would that be, Mr Venus, but the cause of the wrong?'

'Say it was papers,' Mr Venus propounds.

'According to what they contained we should offer to dispose of 'em to the parties most interested,' replied Wegg, promptly.

'In the cause of the right, Mr Wegg?'

'Always so, Mr Venus. If the parties should use them in the cause of the wrong, that would be their act and deed. Mr Venus, I have an opinion of you, sir, to which it is not easy to give mouth. Since I called upon you that evening when you were, as I may say, floating your powerful mind in tea, I have felt that you required to be roused with an object. In this friendly move, sir, you will have a glorious object to rouse you.'

Mr Wegg then goes on to enlarge upon what throughout has been uppermost in his crafty mind:—the qualifications of Mr Venus for such a search. He expatiates on Mr Venus's patient habits and delicate manipulation; on his skill in piecing little things together; on his knowledge of various tissues and textures; on the likelihood of small indications leading him on to the discovery of great concealments. 'While as to myself,' says Wegg, 'I am not good at it. Whether I gave myself up to prodding, or whether I gave myself up to scooping, I couldn't do it with that delicate touch so as not to show that I was disturbing the mounds. Quite different with *you*, going to work (as *you* would) in the light of a fellow-man, holily pledged in a friendly move to his brother man.' Mr Wegg next modestly remarks on the want of adaptation in a wooden leg to ladders and such like airy perches, and also hints at an inherent tendency in that timber fiction, when called into action for the purposes of a promenade on an ashey slope, to stick itself into the yielding foothold, and peg its owner to one spot. Then, leaving this part of the subject, he remarks on the special phenomenon that before his installation in the Bower, it was from Mr Venus that he first heard of the legend of hidden wealth in the Mounds: 'which', he observes with a vaguely pious air, 'was surely never meant for nothing.' Lastly, he returns to the cause of the right, gloomily foreshadowing the possibility of something being unearthed to criminate Mr Boffin (of whom he once more candidly admits it cannot be denied that he profits by a murder), and anticipating his denunciation by the friendly movers to avenging justice. And this, Mr Wegg expressly points out, not at all for the sake of the reward— though it would be a want of principle not to take it.

To all this, Mr Venus, with his shock of dusty hair cocked after the manner of a terrier's ears, attends profoundly. When Mr Wegg, having finished, opens his arms wide, as if to show Mr Venus how bare his breast is, and then folds them pending a reply, Mr Venus winks at him with both eyes some little time before speaking.

'I see you have tried it by yourself, Mr Wegg,' he says when he does speak. 'You have found out the difficulties by experience.'

'No, it can hardly be said that I have tried it,' replies Wegg, a little dashed by the hint. 'I have just skimmed it. Skimmed it.'

'And found nothing besides the difficulties?'

Wegg shakes his head.

'I scarcely know what to say to this, Mr Wegg,' observes Venus, after ruminating for a while.

'Say yes,' Wegg naturally urges.

'If I wasn't soured, my answer would be no. But being soured, Mr Wegg, and driven to reckless madness and desperation, I suppose it's Yes.'

Wegg joyfully reproduces the two glasses, repeats the ceremony of clinking their rims, and inwardly drinks with great heartiness to the health and success in life of the young lady who has reduced Mr Venus to his present convenient state of mind.

The articles of the friendly move are then severally recited and agreed upon. They are but secrecy, fidelity, and perseverance. The Bower to be always free of access to Mr Venus for his researches, and every precaution to be taken against their attracting observation in the neighbourhood.

'There's a footstep!' exclaims Venus.

'Where?' cries Wegg, starting.

'Outside. St!'

They are in the act of ratifying the treaty of friendly move, by shaking hands upon it. They softly break off, light their pipes which have gone out, and lean back in their chairs. No doubt, a footstep. It approaches the window, and a hand taps at the glass. 'Come in!' calls Wegg; meaning come round by the door. But the heavy old-fashioned sash is slowly raised, and a head slowly looks in out of the dark background of night.

'Pray is Mr Silas Wegg here? Oh! I see him!'

The friendly movers might not have been quite at their ease, even though the visitor had entered in the usual manner. But, leaning on the breast-high window, and staring in out of the darkness, they find the visitor extremely embarrassing. Especially Mr Venus: who removes his pipe, draws back his head, and stares at the starer, as if it were his own Hindoo baby come to fetch him home.

'Good evening, Mr Wegg. The yard gate-lock should be looked to, if you please; it don't catch.'

'Is it Mr Rokesmith?' falters Wegg.

'It is Mr Rokesmith. Don't let me disturb you. I am not coming in. I have only a message for you, which I undertook to deliver on my way home to my lodgings. I was in two minds about coming beyond the gate without ringing: not knowing but you might have a dog about.'

'I wish I had,' mutters Wegg, with his back turned as he rose from his chair. 'St! Hush! The talking-over stranger, Mr Venus.'

'Is that any one I know?' inquires the staring Secretary.

'No, Mr Rokesmith. Friend of mine. Passing the evening with me.'

'Oh! I beg his pardon. Mr Boffin wishes you to know that he does not expect you to stay at home any evening, on the chance of his coming. It has occurred to him that he may, without intending it, have been a tie upon you. In future, if he should come without notice, he will take his chance of finding you, and it will be all the same to him if he does not. I undertook to tell you on my way. That's all.'

With that, and 'Good night,' the Secretary lowers the window, and disappears. They listen, and hear his footsteps go back to the gate, and hear the gate close after him.

'And for that individual, Mr Venus,' remarks Wegg, when he is fully gone, '*I* have been passed over! Let me ask you what you think of him?'

Apparently, Mr Venus does not know what to think of him, for he makes sundry efforts to reply, without delivering himself of any other articulate utterance than that he has 'a singular look'.

'A double look, you mean, sir,' rejoins Wegg, playing bitterly upon the word. 'That's *his* look. Any amount of singular look for me, but not a double look! That's an underhanded mind, sir.'

'Do you say there's something against him?' Venus asks.

'Something against him?' repeats Wegg. 'Something? What would the relief be to my feelings—as a fellow-man—if I wasn't the slave of truth, and didn't feel myself compelled to answer, Everything!'

See into what wonderful maudlin refuges, featherless ostriches plunge their heads! It is such unspeakable moral compensation to Wegg, to be overcome by the consideration that Mr Rokesmith has an underhanded mind!

'On this starlight night, Mr Venus,' he remarks, when he is showing that friendly mover out across the yard, and both are something the worse for mixing again and again: 'on this starlight night to think that talking-over strangers, and underhanded minds, can go walking home under the sky, as if they was all square!'

'The spectacle of those orbs,' says Mr Venus, gazing upward with his hat tumbling off, 'brings heavy on me her crushing words that she did not wish to regard herself nor yet to be regarded in that—'

'I know! I know! You needn't repeat 'em,' says Wegg, pressing his hand. 'But think how those stars steady me in the cause of the right against some that shall be nameless. It isn't that I bear malice. But see how they glisten with old remembrances! Old remembrances of what, sir?'

Mr Venus begins drearily replying, 'Of her words, in her own handwriting, that she does not wish to regard herself, nor yet—' when Silas cuts him short with dignity.

'No, sir! Remembrances of Our House, of Master George, of Aunt Jane, of Uncle Parker, all laid waste! All offered up sacrifices to the minion of fortune and the worm of the hour!'

Chapter 8
In Which an Innocent Elopement Occurs

THE minion of fortune and the worm of the hour, or in less cutting language, Nicodemus Boffin, Esquire, the Golden Dustman, had become as much at home in his eminently aristocratic family mansion as he was likely ever to be. He could not but feel that, like an eminently aristocratic family cheese, it was much too large for his wants, and bred an infinite amount of parasites; but he was content to regard this drawback on his property as a sort of perpetual Legacy Duty. He felt the more resigned to it, forasmuch as Mrs Boffin enjoyed herself completely, and Miss Bella was delighted.

That young lady was, no doubt, an acquisition to the Boffins. She was far too pretty to be unattractive anywhere, and far too quick of perception to be below the tone of her new career. Whether it improved her heart might be a matter of taste that was open to question; but as touching another matter of taste, its improvement of her appearance and manner, there could be no question whatever.

And thus it soon came about that Miss Bella began to set Mrs Boffin right; and even further, that Miss Bella began to feel ill at ease, and as it were responsible, when she saw Mrs Boffin going wrong. Not that so sweet a disposition and so sound a nature could ever go very wrong even among the great visiting authorities who agreed that the Boffins were 'charmingly vulgar' (which for certain was not their own case in saying so), but that when she made a slip on the social ice on which all the children of Podsnappery, with genteel souls to be saved, are required to skate in circles, or to slide in long rows, she inevitably tripped Miss Bella up (so that young lady felt), and caused her to experience great confusion under the glances of the more skilful performers engaged in those ice-exercises.

At Miss Bella's time of life it was not to be expected that she should examine herself very closely on the congruity or stability of her position in Mr Boffin's house. And as she had never been sparing of complaints of her old home when she had no other to compare it with, so there was no novelty of ingratitude or disdain in her very much preferring her new one.

'An invaluable man is Rokesmith,' said Mr Boffin, after some two or three months. 'But I can't quite make him out.'

Neither could Bella, so she found the subject rather interesting.

'He takes more care of my affairs, morning, noon, and night,' said Mr Boffin, 'than fifty other men put together either could or would; and yet he has ways of his own that are like tying a scaffolding-pole right across the road, and bringing me up short when I am almost a-walking arm in arm with him.'

'May I ask how so, sir?' inquired Bella.

'Well, my dear,' said Mr Boffin, 'he won't meet any company here, but you. When we have visitors, I should wish him to have his regular place at the table like ourselves; but no, he won't take it.'

'If he considers himself above it,' said Miss Bella, with an airy toss of her head, 'I should leave him alone.'

'It ain't that, my dear,' replied Mr Boffin, thinking it over. 'He don't consider himself above it.'

'Perhaps he considers himself beneath it,' suggested Bella. 'If so, he ought to know best.'

'No, my dear; nor it ain't that, neither. No,' repeated Mr Boffin, with a shake of his head, after again thinking it over; 'Rokesmith's a modest man, but he don't consider himself beneath it.'

'Then what does he consider, sir?' asked Bella.

'Dashed if I know!' said Mr Boffin. 'It seemed at first as if it was only Lightwood that he objected to meet. And now it seems to be everybody, except you.'

'Oho!' thought Miss Bella. 'In–deed! *That's* it, is it!' For Mr Mortimer Lightwood had dined there two or three times, and she had met him elsewhere, and he had shown her some attention. 'Rather cool in a Secretary—and Pa's lodger—to make me the subject of his jealousy!'

That Pa's daughter should be so contemptuous of Pa's lodger was odd; but there were odder anomalies than that in the mind of the spoilt girl: the doubly spoilt girl: spoilt first by poverty, and then by wealth. Be it this history's part, however, to leave them to unravel themselves.

'A little too much, I think,' Miss Bella reflected scornfully, 'to have Pa's lodger laying claim to me, and keeping eligible people off! A little too much, indeed, to have the opportunities opened to me by Mr and Mrs Boffin, appropriated by a mere Secretary and Pa's lodger!'

Yet it was not so very long ago that Bella had been fluttered by the discovery that this same Secretary and lodger seem to like her. Ah! but the eminently aristocratic mansion and Mrs Boffin's dressmaker had not come into play then.

In spite of his seemingly retiring manners a very intrusive person, this Secretary and lodger, in Miss Bella's opinion. Always a light in his office-room when we came home from the play or Opera, and he always at the carriage-door to hand us out. Always a provoking radiance too on Mrs Boffin's face, and an abominably cheerful reception of him, as if it were possible seriously to approve what the man had in his mind!

'You never charge me, Miss Wilfer,' said the Secretary, encountering her by chance alone in the great drawing-room, 'with commissions for home. I shall always be happy to execute any commands you may have in that direction.'

'Pray what may you mean, Mr Rokesmith?' inquired Miss Bella, with languidly drooping eyelids.

'By home? I mean your father's house at Holloway.'

She coloured under the retort—so skilfully thrust, that the words seemed to be merely a plain answer, given in plain good faith—and said, rather more emphatically and sharply:

'What commissions and commands are you speaking of?'

'Only such little words of remembrance as I assume you send somehow or other,' replied the Secretary with his former air. 'It would be a pleasure to me if you would make me the bearer of them. As you know, I come and go between the two houses every day.'

'You needn't remind me of that, sir.'

She was too quick in this petulant sally against 'Pa's lodger'; and she felt that she had been so when she met his quiet look.

'They don't send many—what was your expression?—words of remembrance to *me*,' said Bella, making haste to take refuge in ill-usage.

'They frequently ask me about you, and I give them such slight intelligence as I can.'

'I hope it's truly given,' exclaimed Bella.

'I hope you cannot doubt it, for it would be very much against you, if you could.'

'No, I do not doubt it. I deserve the reproach, which is very just indeed. I beg your pardon, Mr Rokesmith.'

'I should beg you not to do so, but that it shows you to such admirable advantage,' he replied with earnestness. 'Forgive me; I could not help saying that. To return to what I have digressed from, let me add that perhaps they think I report them to you, deliver little messages, and the like. But I forbear to trouble you, as you never ask me.'

'I am going, sir,' said Bella, looking at him as if he had reproved her 'to see them to-morrow.'

'Is that,' he asked, hesitating, 'said to me, or to them?'

'To which you please.'

'To both? Shall I make it a message?'

'You can if you like, Mr Rokesmith. Message or no message, I am going to see them to-morrow.'

'Then I will tell them so.'

He lingered a moment, as though to give her the opportunity of prolonging the conversation if she wished. As she remained silent, he left her. Two incidents of the little interview were felt by Miss Bella herself, when alone again, to be very curious. The first was, that he unquestionably left her with a penitent air upon her, and a penitent feeling in her heart. The second was, that she had not had an intention or a thought of going home, until she had announced it to him as a settled design.

'What can I mean by it, or what can he mean by it?' was her mental inquiry: 'He has no right to any power over me, and how do I come to mind him when I don't care for him?'

Mrs Boffin, insisting that Bella should make to-morrow's expedition in the chariot, she went home in great grandeur. Mrs Wilfer and Miss Lavinia had speculated much on the probabilities and improbabilities of her coming in this gorgeous state, and, on beholding the chariot from the window at which they were secreted to look out for it, agreed that it must be detained at the door as long as possible, for the mortification and confusion of the neighbours. Then they repaired to the usual family room, to receive Miss Bella with a becoming show of indifference.

The family room looked very small and very mean, and the downward staircase by which it was attained looked very narrow and very crooked. The little house and all its arrangements were a poor contrast to the eminently aristocratic dwelling. 'I can hardly believe,' thought Bella, 'that I ever did endure life in this place!'

Gloomy majesty on the part of Mrs Wilfer, and native pertness on the part of Lavvy, did not mend the matter. Bella really stood in natural need of a little help, and she got none.

'This,' said Mrs Wilfer, presenting a cheek to be kissed, as sympathetic and responsive as the back of the bowl of a spoon, 'is quite an honour! You will probably find your sister Lavvy grown, Bella.'

'Ma,' Miss Lavinia interposed, 'there can be no objection to your being aggravating, because Bella richly deserves it; but I really must request that you will not drag in such ridiculous nonsense as my having grown when I am past the growing age.'

'I grew, myself,' Mrs Wilfer sternly proclaimed, 'after I was married.'

'Very well, Ma,' returned Lavvy, 'then I think you had much better have left it alone.'

The lofty glare with which the majestic woman received this answer, might have embarrassed a less pert opponent, but it had no effect upon Lavinia: who, leaving her parent to the enjoyment of any amount of glaring that she might deem desirable under the circumstances, accosted her sister, undismayed.

'I suppose you won't consider yourself quite disgraced, Bella, if I give you a kiss? Well! And how do you do, Bella? And how are your Boffins?'

'Peace!' exclaimed Mrs Wilfer. 'Hold! I will not suffer this tone of levity.'

'My goodness me! How are your Spoffins, then?' said Lavvy, 'since Ma so very much objects to your Boffins.'

'Impertinent girl! Minx!' said Mrs Wilfer, with dread severity.

'I don't care whether I am a Minx, or a Sphinx,' returned Lavinia, coolly, tossing her head; 'it's exactly the same thing to me, and I'd every bit as soon be one as the other; but I know this—I'll not grow after I am married!'

'You will not? *You* will not?' repeated Mrs Wilfer, solemnly.

'No, Ma, I will not. Nothing shall induce me.'

Mrs Wilfer, having waved her gloves, became loftily pathetic.

'But it was to be expected;' thus she spake. 'A child of mine deserts me for the proud and prosperous, and another child of mine despises me. It is quite fitting.'

'Ma,' Bella struck in, 'Mr and Mrs Boffin are prosperous, no doubt; but you have no right to say they are proud. You must know very well that they are not.'

'In short, Ma,' said Lavvy, bouncing over to the enemy without a word of notice, 'you must know very well—or if you don't, more shame for you!—that Mr and Mrs Boffin are just absolute perfection.'

'Truly,' returned Mrs Wilfer, courteously receiving the deserter, 'it would seem that we are required to think so. And this, Lavinia, is my reason for objecting to a tone of levity. Mrs Boffin (of whose physiognomy I can never speak with the composure I would desire to preserve), and your mother, are not on terms of intimacy. It is not for a moment to be supposed that she and her husband dare to presume to speak of this family as the Wilfers. I cannot therefore condescend to speak of them as the Boffins. No; for such a tone—call it familiarity, levity, equality, or what you will—would imply those social interchanges which do not exist. Do I render myself intelligible?'

Without taking the least notice of this inquiry, albeit delivered in an imposing and forensic manner, Lavinia reminded her sister, 'After all, you know, Bella, you haven't told us how your Whatshisnames are.'

'I don't want to speak of them here,' replied Bella, suppressing indignation, and tapping her foot on the floor. 'They are much too kind and too good to be drawn into these discussions.'

'Why put it so?' demanded Mrs Wilfer, with biting sarcasm. 'Why adopt a circuitous form of speech? It is polite and it is obliging; but why do it? Why not openly say that they are much too kind and too good for *us*? We understand the allusion. Why disguise the phrase?'

'Ma,' said Bella, with one beat of her foot, 'you are enough to drive a saint mad, and so is Lavvy.'

'Unfortunate Lavvy!' cried Mrs Wilfer, in a tone of commiseration. 'She always comes in for it. My poor child!' But Lavvy, with the suddenness of her former desertion, now bounced over to the other enemy: very sharply remarking, 'Don't patronise *me*, Ma, because I can take care of myself.'

'I only wonder,' resumed Mrs Wilfer, directing her observations to her elder daughter, as safer on the whole than her utterly unmanageable younger, 'that you found time and inclination to tear yourself from Mr and Mrs Boffin, and come to see us at all. I only wonder that our claims, contending against the superior claims of Mr and Mrs Boffin, had any weight. I feel I ought to be thankful for gaining so much, in competition with Mr and Mrs Boffin.' (The good lady bitterly emphasized the first letter of the word Boffin, as if it represented her chief objection to the owners of that name, and as if she could have borne Doffin, Moffin, or Poffin much better.)

'Ma,' said Bella, angrily, 'you force me to say that I am truly sorry I did come home, and that I never will come home again, except when poor dear Pa is here. For, Pa is too magnanimous to feel envy and spite towards my generous friends, and Pa is delicate and gentle enough to remember the sort of little claim they thought I had upon them and the unusually trying position in which, through no act of my own, I had been placed. And I always did love poor dear Pa better than all the rest of you put together, and I always do and I always shall!'

Here Bella, deriving no comfort from her charming bonnet and her elegant dress, burst into tears.

'I think, R.W.,' cried Mrs Wilfer, lifting up her eyes and apostrophising the air, 'that if you were present, it would be a trial to your feelings to hear your wife and the mother of your family depreciated in your name. But Fate has spared you this, R.W., whatever it may have thought proper to inflict upon her!'

Here Mrs Wilfer burst into tears.

'I hate the Boffins!' protested Miss Lavinia. 'I don't care who objects to their being called the Boffins. I WILL call 'em the Boffins. The Boffins, the Boffins, the Boffins! And I say they are mischief-making Boffins, and I say the Boffins have set Bella against me, and I tell the Boffins to their faces:' which was not strictly the fact, but the young lady was excited: 'that they are detestable Boffins, disreputable Boffins, odious Boffins, beastly Boffins. There!'

Here Miss Lavinia burst into tears.

The front garden-gate clanked, and the Secretary was seen coming at a brisk pace up the steps. 'Leave Me to open the door to him,' said Mrs Wilfer, rising with stately resignation as she shook her head and dried her eyes; 'we have at present no stipendiary girl to do so. We have nothing to conceal. If he sees these traces of emotion on our cheeks, let him construe them as he may.'

With those words she stalked out. In a few moments she stalked in again, proclaiming in her heraldic manner, 'Mr Rokesmith is the bearer of a packet for Miss Bella Wilfer.'

Mr Rokesmith followed close upon his name, and of course saw what was amiss. But he discreetly affected to see nothing, and addressed Miss Bella.

'Mr Boffin intended to have placed this in the carriage for you this morning. He wished you to have it, as a little keepsake he had prepared—it is only a purse, Miss Wilfer—but as he was disappointed in his fancy, I volunteered to come after you with it.'

Bella took it in her hand, and thanked him.

'We have been quarrelling here a little, Mr Rokesmith, but not more than we used; you know our agreeable ways among ourselves. You find me just going. Good-bye, mamma. Good-bye, Lavvy!' and with a kiss for each Miss Bella turned to the door. The Secretary would have attended her, but Mrs Wilfer advancing and saying with dignity, 'Pardon me! Permit me to assert my natural right to escort my child to the equipage which is in waiting for her,' he begged pardon and gave place. It was a very magnificent spectacle indeed, to see Mrs Wilfer throw open the house-door, and loudly demand with extended gloves, 'The male domestic of Mrs Boffin!' To whom presenting himself, she delivered the brief but majestic charge, 'Miss Wilfer. Coming out!' and so delivered her over, like a female Lieutenant of the Tower relinquishing a State Prisoner. The effect of this ceremonial was for some quarter of an hour afterwards perfectly paralysing on the neighbours, and was much enhanced by the worthy lady airing herself for that term in a kind of splendidly serene trance on the top step.

When Bella was seated in the carriage, she opened the little packet in her hand. It contained a pretty purse, and the purse contained a bank note for fifty pounds. 'This shall be a joyful surprise for poor dear Pa,' said Bella, 'and I'll take it myself into the City!'

As she was uninformed respecting the exact locality of the place of business of Chicksey Veneering and Stobbles, but knew it to be near Mincing Lane, she directed herself to be driven to the corner of that darksome spot. Thence she despatched 'the male domestic of Mrs Boffin,' in search of the counting-house of Chicksey Veneering and Stobbles, with a message importing that if R. Wilfer could come out, there was a lady waiting who would be glad to speak with him. The delivery of these mysterious words from the mouth of a footman caused so great an excitement in the counting-house, that a youthful scout was instantly appointed to follow Rumty, observe the lady, and come in with his report. Nor was the agitation by any means diminished, when the scout rushed back with the intelligence that the lady was 'a slap-up gal in a bang-up chariot'.

Rumty himself, with his pen behind his ear under his rusty hat, arrived at the carriage-door in a breathless condition, and had been fairly lugged into the vehicle by his cravat and embraced almost unto choking, before he recognised his daughter. 'My dear child!' he then panted, incoherently. 'Good gracious me! What a lovely woman you are! I thought you had been unkind and forgotten your mother and sister.'

'I have just been to see them, Pa dear.'

'Oh! and how—how did you find your mother?' asked R. W., dubiously.

'Very disagreeable, Pa, and so was Lavvy.'

'They are sometimes a little liable to it,' observed the patient cherub; 'but I hope you made allowances, Bella, my dear?'

'No. I was disagreeable too, Pa; we were all of us disagreeable together. But I want you to come and dine with me somewhere, Pa.'

'Why, my dear, I have already partaken of a—if one might mention such an article in this superb chariot—of a—Saveloy,' replied R. Wilfer, modestly dropping his voice on the word, as he eyed the canary-coloured fittings.

'Oh! That's nothing, Pa!'

'Truly, it ain't as much as one could sometimes wish it to be, my dear,' he admitted, drawing his hand across his mouth. 'Still, when circumstances over which you have no control, interpose obstacles between yourself and Small Germans, you can't do better than bring a contented mind to bear on'—again dropping his voice in deference to the chariot—'Saveloys!'

'You poor good Pa! Pa, do, I beg and pray, get leave for the rest of the day, and come and pass it with me!'

'Well, my dear, I'll cut back and ask for leave.'

'But before you cut back,' said Bella, who had already taken him by the chin, pulled his hat off, and begun to stick up his hair in her old way, 'do say that you are sure I am giddy and inconsiderate, but have never really slighted you, Pa.'

'My dear, I say it with all my heart. And might I likewise observe,' her father delicately hinted, with a glance out at window, 'that perhaps it might be calculated to attract attention, having one's hair publicly done by a lovely woman in an elegant turn-out in Fenchurch Street?'

Bella laughed and put on his hat again. But when his boyish figure bobbed away, its shabbiness and cheerful patience smote the tears out of her eyes. 'I hate that Secretary for thinking it of me,' she said to herself, 'and yet it seems half true!'

Back came her father, more like a boy than ever, in his release from school. 'All right, my dear. Leave given at once. Really very handsomely done!'

'Now where can we find some quiet place, Pa, in which I

can wait for you while you go on an errand for me, if I send the carriage away?'

It demanded cogitation. 'You see, my dear,' he explained, 'you really have become such a very lovely woman, that it ought to be a very quiet place.' At length he suggested, 'Near the garden up by the Trinity House on Tower Hill.' So, they were driven there, and Bella dismissed the chariot; sending a pencilled note by it to Mrs Boffin, that she was with her father.

'Now, Pa, attend to what I am going to say, and promise and vow to be obedient.'

'I promise and vow, my dear.'

'You ask no questions. You take this purse; you go to the nearest place where they keep everything of the very very best, ready made; you buy and put on, the most beautiful suit of clothes, the most beautiful hat, and the most beautiful pair of bright boots (patent leather, Pa, mind!) that are to be got for money; and you come back to me.'

'But, my dear Bella—'

'Take care, Pa!' pointing her forefinger at him, merrily. 'You have promised and vowed. It's perjury, you know.'

There was water in the foolish little fellow's eyes, but she kissed them dry (though her own were wet), and he bobbed away again. After half an hour, he came back, so brilliantly transformed, that Bella was obliged to walk round him in ecstatic admiration twenty times, before she could draw her arm through his, and delightedly squeeze it.

'Now, Pa,' said Bella, hugging him close, 'take this lovely woman out to dinner.'

'Where shall we go, my dear?'

'Greenwich!' said Bella, valiantly. 'And be sure you treat this lovely woman with everything of the best.'

While they were going along to take boat, 'Don't you wish, my dear,' said R. W., timidly, 'that your mother was here?'

'No, I don't, Pa, for I like to have you all to myself to-day. I was always your little favourite at home, and you were always mine. We have run away together often, before now; haven't we, Pa?'

'Ah, to be sure we have! Many a Sunday when your mother was—was a little liable to it,' repeating his former delicate expression after pausing to cough.

'Yes, and I am afraid I was seldom or never as good as I ought to have been, Pa. I made you carry me, over and over again, when you should have made me walk; and I often drove you in harness, when you would much rather have sat down and read your newspaper: didn't I?'

'Sometimes, sometimes. But Lor, what a child you were! What a companion you were!'

'Companion? That's just what I want to be to-day, Pa.'

'You are safe to succeed, my love. Your brothers and sisters have all in their turns been companions to me, to a certain extent, but only to a certain extent. Your mother has, throughout life, been a companion that any man might—might look up to—and—and commit the sayings of, to memory—and—form himself upon—if he—'

'If he liked the model?' suggested Bella.

'We-ell, ye-es,' he returned, thinking about it, not quite satisfied with the phrase: 'or perhaps I might say, if it was in him. Supposing, for instance, that a man wanted to be always marching, he would find your mother an inestimable companion. But if he had any taste for walking, or should wish at any time to break into a trot, he might sometimes find it a little difficult to keep step with your mother. Or take it this way, Bella,' he added, after a moment's reflection; 'Supposing that a man had to go through life, we won't say with a companion, but we'll say to a tune. Very good. Supposing that the tune allotted to him was the Dead March in Saul. Well. It would be a very suitable tune for particular occasions—none better—but it would be difficult to keep time with in the ordinary run of domestic transactions. For instance, if he took his supper after a hard day, to the Dead March in Saul, his food might be likely to sit heavy on him. Or, if he was at any time inclined to relieve his mind by singing a comic song or dancing a hornpipe, and was obliged to do it to the Dead March in Saul, he might find himself put out in the execution of his lively intentions.'

'Poor Pa!' thought Bella, as she hung upon his arm.

'Now, what I will say for you, my dear,' the cherub pursued mildly and without a notion of complaining, 'is, that you are so adaptable. So adaptable.'

'Indeed I am afraid I have shown a wretched temper, Pa. I am afraid I have been very complaining, and very capricious. I seldom or never thought of it before. But when I sat in the carriage just now and saw you coming along the pavement, I reproached myself.'

'Not at all, my dear. Don't speak of such a thing.'

A happy and a chatty man was Pa in his new clothes that day. Take it for all in all, it was perhaps the happiest day he had

ever known in his life; not even excepting that on which his
heroic partner had approached the nuptial altar to the tune of the
Dead March in Saul.

The little expedition down the river was delightful, and the
little room overlooking the river into which they were shown for
dinner was delightful. Everything was delightful. The park was
delightful, the punch was delightful, the dishes of fish were
delightful, the wine was delightful. Bella was more delightful
than any other item in the festival; drawing Pa out in the gayest
manner; making a point of always mentioning herself as the
lovely woman; stimulating Pa to order things, by declaring that
the lovely woman insisted on being treated with them; and in
short causing Pa to be quite enraptured with the consideration
that he *was* the Pa of such a charming daughter.

And then, as they sat looking at the ships and steamboats
making their way to the sea with the tide that was running down,
the lovely woman imagined all sorts of voyages for herself and
Pa. Now, Pa, in the character of owner of a lumbering square-
sailed collier, was tacking away to Newcastle, to fetch black
diamonds to make his fortune with; now, Pa was going to China
in that handsome three-masted ship, to bring home opium, with
which he would for ever cut out Chicksey Veneering and Stobbles,
and to bring home silks and shawls without end for the decoration of his charming daughter. Now, John Harmon's disastrous
fate was all a dream, and he had come home and found the
lovely woman just the article for him, and the lovely woman had
found him just the article for her, and they were going away on a
trip, in their gallant bark, to look after their vines, with streamers
flying at all points, a band playing on deck, and Pa established in
the great cabin. Now, John Harmon was consigned to his grave
again, and a merchant of immense wealth (name unknown) had
courted and married the lovely woman, and he was so enormously rich that everything you saw upon the river sailing or
steaming belonged to him, and he kept a perfect fleet of yachts
for pleasure, and that little impudent yacht which you saw over
there, with the great white sail, was called The Bella, in honour
of his wife, and she held her state abroad when it pleased her,
like a modern Cleopatra. Anon, there would embark in that
troop-ship when she got to Gravesend, a mighty general, of large
property (name also unknown), who wouldn't hear of going to
victory without his wife, and whose wife was the lovely woman,
and she was destined to become the idol of all the red coats and
blue jackets alow and aloft. And then again: you saw that ship

being towed out by a steam-tug? Well! where did you suppose she was going to? She was going among the coral reefs and cocoa-nuts and all that sort of thing, and she was chartered for a fortunate individual of the name of Pa (himself on board, and much respected by all hands), and she was going, for his sole profit and advantage, to fetch a cargo of sweet-smelling woods, the most beautiful that ever were seen, and the most profitable that ever were heard of, and her cargo would be a great fortune, as indeed it ought to be: the lovely woman who had purchased her and fitted her expressly for this voyage, being married to an Indian Prince, who was a Something-or-Other, and who wore Cashmere shawls all over himself, and diamonds and emeralds blazing in his turban, and was beautifully coffee-coloured and excessively devoted, though a little too jealous. Thus Bella ran on merrily, in a manner perfectly enchanting to Pa, who was as willing to put his head into the Sultan's tub of water as the beggar-boys below the window were to put *their* heads in the mud.

'I suppose, my dear,' said Pa after dinner, 'we may come to the conclusion at home, that we have lost you for good?'

Bella shook her head. Didn't know. Couldn't say. All she was able to report was, that she was most handsomely supplied with everything she could possibly want, and that whenever she hinted at leaving Mr and Mrs Boffin, they wouldn't hear of it.

'And now, Pa,' pursued Bella, 'I'll make a confession to you. I am the most mercenary little wretch that ever lived in the world.'

'I should hardly have thought it of you, my dear,' returned her father, first glancing at himself, and then at the dessert.

'I understand what you mean, Pa, but it's not that. It's not that I care for money to keep as money, but I do care so much for what it will buy!'

'Really I think most of us do,' returned R. W.

'But not to the dreadful extent that I do, Pa. O-o!' cried Bella, screwing the exclamation out of herself with a twist of her dimpled chin. 'I AM so mercenary!'

With a wistful glance R. W. said, in default of having anything better to say: 'About when did you begin to feel it coming on, my dear?'

'That's it, Pa. That's the terrible part of it. When I was at home, and only knew what it was to be poor, I grumbled but didn't so much mind. When I was at home expecting to be rich, I thought vaguely of all the great things I would do. But when I

had been disappointed of my splendid fortune, and came to see it
from day to day in other hands, and to have before my eyes what
it could really do, then I became the mercenary little wretch I
am.'

'It's your fancy, my dear.'

'I can assure you it's nothing of the sort, Pa!' said Bella,
nodding at him, with her very pretty eyebrows raised as high as
they would go, and looking comically frightened. 'It's a fact. I
am always avariciously scheming.'

'Lor! But how?'

'I'll tell you, Pa. I don't mind telling *you*, because we have
always been favourites of each other's, and because you are not
like a Pa, but more like a sort of a younger brother with a dear
venerable chubbiness on him. And besides,' added Bella, laughing as she pointed a rallying finger at his face, 'because I have
got you in my power. This is a secret expedition. If ever you tell
of me, I'll tell of you. I'll tell Ma that you dined at Greenwich.'

'Well; seriously, my dear,' observed R. W., with some
trepidation of manner, 'it might be as well not to mention it.'

'Aha!' laughed Bella. 'I knew you wouldn't like it, sir! So
you keep my confidence, and I'll keep yours. But betray the
lovely woman, and you shall find her a serpent. Now, you may
give me a kiss, Pa, and I should like to give your hair a turn,
because it has been dreadfully neglected in my absence.'

R. W. submitted his head to the operator, and the operator
went on talking; at the same time putting separate locks of his
hair through a curious process of being smartly rolled over her
two revolving forefingers, which were then suddenly pulled out
of it in opposite lateral directions. On each of these occasions the
patient winced and winked.

'I have made up my mind that I must have money, Pa. I
feel that I can't beg it, borrow it, or steal it; and so I have
resolved that I must marry it.'

R. W. cast up his eyes towards her, as well as he could
under the operating circumstances, and said in a tone of remonstrance, 'My de-ar Bella!'

'Have resolved, I say, Pa, that to get money I must marry
money. In consequence of which, I am always looking out for
money to captivate.'

'My de-a-r Bella!'

'Yes, Pa, that is the state of the case. If ever there was a
mercenary plotter whose thoughts and designs were always in
her mean occupation, I am the amiable creature. But I don't

care. I hate and detest being poor, and I won't be poor if I can marry money. Now you are deliciously fluffy, Pa, and in a state to astonish the waiter and pay the bill.'

'But, my dear Bella, this is quite alarming at your age.'

'I told you so, Pa, but you wouldn't believe it,' returned Bella, with a pleasant childish gravity. 'Isn't it shocking?'

'It would be quite so, if you fully knew what you said, my dear, or meant it.'

'Well, Pa, I can only tell you that I mean nothing else. Talk to me of love!' said Bella, contemptuously: though her face and figure certainly rendered the subject no incongruous one. 'Talk to me of fiery dragons! But talk to me of poverty and wealth, and there indeed we touch upon realities.'

'My De-ar, this is becoming Awful—' her father was emphatically beginning: when she stopped him.

'Pa, tell me. Did *you* marry money?'

'You know I didn't, my dear.'

Bella hummed the Dead March in Saul, and said, after all it signified very little! But seeing him look grave and downcast, she took him round the neck and kissed him back to cheerfulness again.

'I didn't mean that last touch, Pa; it was only said in joke. Now mind! You are not to tell of me, and I'll not tell of you. And more than that; I promise to have no secrets from you, Pa, and you may make certain that, whatever mercenary things go on, I shall always tell you all about them in strict confidence.'

Fain to be satisfied with this concession from the lovely woman, R. W. rang the bell, and paid the bill. 'Now, all the rest of this, Pa,' said Bella, rolling up the purse when they were alone again, hammering it small with her little fist on the table, and cramming it into one of the pockets of his new waistcoat, 'is for you, to buy presents with for them at home, and to pay bills with, and to divide as you like, and spend exactly as you think proper. Last of all take notice, Pa, that it's not the fruit of any avaricious scheme. Perhaps if it was, your little mercenary wretch of a daughter wouldn't make so free with it!'

After which, she tugged at his coat with both hands, and pulled him all askew in buttoning that garment over the precious waistcoat pocket, and then tied her dimples into her bonnet-strings in a very knowing way, and took him back to London. Arrived at Mr Boffin's door, she set him with his back against it, tenderly took him by the ears as convenient handles for her purpose, and kissed him until he knocked muffled double knocks at the door with the back of his head. That done, she once more reminded him of their compact and gaily parted from him.

Not so gaily, however, but that tears filled her eyes as he went away down the dark street. Not so gaily, but that she several times said, 'Ah, poor little Pa! Ah, poor dear struggling shabby little Pa!' before she took heart to knock at the door. Not so gaily, but that the brilliant furniture seemed to stare her out of countenance as if it insisted on being compared with the dingy furniture at home. Not so gaily, but that she fell into very low spirits sitting late in her own room, and very heartily wept, as she wished, now that the deceased old John Harmon had never made a will about her, now that the deceased young John Harmon had lived to marry her. 'Contradictory things to wish,' said Bella, 'but my life and fortunes are so contradictory altogether that what can I expect myself to be!'

Chapter 9
In Which the Orphan Makes His Will

THE Secretary, working in the Dismal Swamp betimes next morning, was informed that a youth waited in the hall who gave the name of Sloppy. The footman who communicated this intelligence made a decent pause before uttering the name, to express that it was forced on his reluctance by the youth in question, and that if the youth had had the good sense and good taste to inherit some other name it would have spared the feelings of him the bearer.

'Mrs Boffin will be very well pleased,' said the Secretary in a perfectly composed way. 'Show him in.'

Mr Sloppy being introduced, remained close to the door: revealing in various parts of his form many surprising, confounding, and incomprehensible buttons.

'I am glad to see you,' said John Rokesmith, in a cheerful tone of welcome. 'I have been expecting you.'

Sloppy explained that he had meant to come before, but that

the Orphan (of whom he made mention as Our Johnny) had been ailing, and he had waited to report him well.

'Then he is well now?' said the Secretary.

'No he ain't,' said Sloppy.

Mr Sloppy having shaken his head to a considerable extent, proceeded to remark that he thought Johnny 'must have took 'em from the Minders.' Being asked what he meant, he answered, them that come out upon him and partickler his chest. Being requested to explain himself, he stated that there was some of 'em wot you couldn't kiver with a sixpence. Pressed to fall back upon a nominative case, he opined that they wos about as red as ever red could be. 'But as long as they strikes out'ards, sir,' continued Sloppy, 'they ain't so much. It's their striking in'ards that's to be kep off.'

John Rokesmith hoped the child had had medical attendance? Oh yes, said Sloppy, he had been took to the doctor's shop once. And what did the doctor call it? Rokesmith asked him. After some perplexed reflection, Sloppy answered, brightening, 'He called it something as wos wery long for spots.' Rokesmith suggested measles. 'No,' said Sloppy with confidence, 'ever so much longer than *them*, sir!' (Mr Sloppy was elevated by this fact, and seemed to consider that it reflected credit on the poor little patient.)

'Mrs Boffin will be sorry to hear this,' said Rokesmith.

'Mrs Higden said so, sir, when she kep it from her, hoping as Our Johnny would work round.'

'But I hope he will?' said Rokesmith, with a quick turn upon the messenger.

'I hope so,' answered Sloppy. 'It all depends on their striking in'ards.' He then went on to say that whether Johnny had 'took 'em' from the Minders, or whether the Minders had 'took 'em' from Johnny, the Minders had been sent home and had 'got 'em.' Furthermore, that Mrs Higden's days and nights being devoted to Our Johnny, who was never out of her lap, the whole of the mangling arrangements had devolved upon himself, and he had had 'rayther a tight time'. The ungainly piece of honesty beamed and blushed as he said it, quite enraptured with the remembrance of having been serviceable.

'Last night,' said Sloppy, 'when I was a-turning at the wheel pretty late, the mangle seemed to go like Our Johnny's breathing. It begun beautiful, then as it went out it shook a little and got unsteady, then as it took the turn to come home it had a rattle-like and lumbered a bit, then it come smooth, and so it went on till I scarce know'd which was mangle and which was Our Johnny. Nor Our Johnny, he scarce know'd either, for sometimes when the mangle lumbers he says, "Me choking, Granny!" and Mrs Higden holds him up in her lap and says to me "Bide a bit, Sloppy," and we all stops together. And when Our Johnny gets his breathing again, I turns again, and we all goes on together.'

Sloppy had gradually expanded with his description into a stare and a vacant grin. He now contracted, being silent, into a half-repressed gush of tears, and, under pretence of being heated, drew the under part of his sleeve across his eyes with a singularly awkward, laborious, and roundabout smear.

'This is unfortunate,' said Rokesmith. 'I must go and break it to Mrs Boffin. Stay you here, Sloppy.'

Sloppy stayed there, staring at the pattern of the paper on the wall, until the Secretary and Mrs Boffin came back together. And with Mrs Boffin was a young lady (Miss Bella Wilfer by name) who was better worth staring at, it occurred to Sloppy, than the best of wall-papering.

'Ah, my poor dear pretty little John Harmon!' exclaimed Mrs Boffin.

'Yes mum,' said the sympathetic Sloppy.

'You don't think he is in a very, very bad way, do you?' asked the pleasant creature with her wholesome cordiality.

Put upon his good faith, and finding it in collision with his inclinations, Sloppy threw back his head and uttered a mellifluous howl, rounded off with a sniff.

'So bad as that!' cried Mrs Boffin. 'And Betty Higden not to tell me of it sooner!'

'I think she might have been mistrustful, mum,' answered Sloppy, hesitating.

'Of what, for Heaven's sake?'

'I think she might have been mistrustful, mum,' returned Sloppy with submission, 'of standing in Our Johnny's light. There's so much trouble in illness, and so much expense, and she's seen such a lot of its being objected to.'

'But she never can have thought,' said Mrs Boffin, 'that I would grudge the dear child anything?'

'No mum, but she might have thought (as a habit-like) of its standing in Johnny's light, and might have tried to bring him through it unbeknownst.'

Sloppy knew his ground well. To conceal herself in sickness, like a lower animal; to creep out of sight and coil herself away and die; had become this woman's instinct. To catch up in her arms the sick child who was dear to her, and hide it as if it were a criminal, and keep off all ministration but such as her own ignorant tenderness and patience could supply, had become this woman's idea of maternal love, fidelity, and duty. The shameful accounts we read, every week in the Christian year, my lords and gentlemen and honourable boards, the infamous records of small official inhumanity, do not pass by the people as they pass by us. And hence these irrational, blind, and obstinate prejudices, so astonishing to our magnificence, and having no more reason in them—God save the Queen and Con-found their politics—no, than smoke has in coming from fire!

'It's not a right place for the poor child to stay in,' said Mrs Boffin. 'Tell us, dear Mr Rokesmith, what to do for the best.'

He had already thought what to do, and the consultation was very short. He could pave the way, he said, in half an hour, and then they would go down to Brentford. 'Pray take me,' said Bella. Therefore a carriage was ordered, of capacity to take them all, and in the meantime Sloppy was regaled, feasting alone in the Secretary's room, with a complete realization of that fairy vision—meat, beer, vegetables, and pudding. In consequence of which his buttons became more importunate of public notice than before, with the exception of two or three about the region of the waistband, which modestly withdrew into a creasy retirement.

Punctual to the time, appeared the carriage and the Secretary. He sat on the box, and Mr Sloppy graced the rumble. So, to the Three Magpies as before: where Mrs Boffin and Miss Bella were handed out, and whence they all went on foot to Mrs Betty Higden's.

But, on the way down, they had stopped at a toy-shop, and had bought that noble charger, a description of whose points and trappings had on the last occasion conciliated the then worldly-minded orphan, and also a Noah's ark, and also a yellow bird with an artificial voice in him, and also a military doll so well dressed that if he had only been of life-size his brother-officers in the Guards might never have found him out. Bearing these gifts, they raised the latch of Betty Higden's door, and saw her sitting in the dimmest and furthest corner with poor Johnny in her lap.

'And how's my boy, Betty?' asked Mrs Boffin, sitting down beside her.

'He's bad! He's bad!' said Betty. 'I begin to be afeerd he'll not be yours any more than mine. All others belonging to him have gone to the Power and the Glory, and I have a mind that they're drawing him to them—leading him away.'

'No, no, no,' said Mrs Boffin.

'I don't know why else he clenches his little hand as if it had hold of a finger that I can't see. Look at it,' said Betty, opening the wrappers in which the flushed child lay, and showing his small right hand lying closed upon his breast. 'It's always so. It don't mind me.'

'Is he asleep?'

'No, I think not. You're not asleep, my Johnny?'

'No,' said Johnny, with a quiet air of pity for himself, and without opening his eyes.

'Here's the lady, Johnny. And the horse.'

Johnny could bear the lady, with complete indifference, but not the horse. Opening his heavy eyes, he slowly broke into a smile on beholding that splendid phenomenon, and wanted to take it in his arms. As it was much too big, it was put upon a chair where he could hold it by the mane and contemplate it. Which he soon forgot to do.

But, Johnny murmuring something with his eyes closed, and Mrs Boffin not knowing what, old Betty bent her ear to listen and took pains to understand. Being asked by her to repeat what he had said, he did so two or three times, and then it came out that he must have seen more than they supposed when he looked up to see the horse, for the murmur was, 'Who is the boofer lady?' Now, the boofer, or beautiful, lady was Bella; and whereas this notice from the poor baby would have touched her of itself, it was rendered more pathetic by the late melting of her heart to her poor little father, and their joke about the lovely woman. So, Bella's behaviour was very tender and very natural when she kneeled on the brick floor to clasp the child, and when the child, with a child's admiration of what is young and pretty, fondled the boofer lady.

'Now, my good dear Betty,' said Mrs Boffin, hoping that she saw her opportunity, and laying her hand persuasively on her arm; 'we have come to remove Johnny from this cottage to where he can be taken better care of.'

Instantly, and before another word could be spoken, the old woman started up with blazing eyes, and rushed at the door with the sick child.

'Stand away from me every one of ye!' she cried out wildly. 'I see what ye mean now. Let me go my way, all of ye. I'd sooner kill the Pretty, and kill myself!'

'Stay, stay!' said Rokesmith, soothing her. 'You don't understand.'

'I understand too well. I know too much about it, sir. I've run from it too many a year. No! Never for me, nor for the child, while there's water enough in England to cover us!'

The terror, the shame, the passion of horror and repugnance, firing the worn face and perfectly maddening it, would have been a quite terrible sight, if embodied in one old fellow-creature alone. Yet it 'crops up'—as our slang goes—my lords and gentlemen and honourable boards, in other fellow-creatures, rather frequently!

'It's been chasing me all my life, but it shall never take me nor mine alive!' cried old Betty. 'I've done with ye. I'd have fastened door and window and starved out, afore I'd ever have let ye in, if I had known what ye came for!'

But, catching sight of Mrs Boffin's wholesome face, she relented, and crouching down by the door and bending over her burden to hush it, said humbly: 'Maybe my fears has put me wrong. If they have so, tell me, and the good Lord forgive me! I'm quick to take this fright, I know, and my head is summ'at light with wearying and watching.'

'There, there, there!' returned Mrs Boffin. 'Come, come! Say no more of it, Betty. It was a mistake, a mistake. Any one of us might have made it in your place, and felt just as you do.'

'The Lord bless ye!' said the old woman, stretching out her hand.

'Now, see, Betty,' pursued the sweet compassionate soul, holding the hand kindly, 'what I really did mean, and what I should have begun by saying out, if I had only been a little wiser and handier. We want to move Johnny to a place where there are none but children; a place set up on purpose for sick children; where the good doctors and nurses pass their lives with children, talk to none but children, touch none but children, comfort and cure none but children.'

'Is there really such a place?' asked the old woman, with a gaze of wonder.

'Yes, Betty, on my word, and you shall see it. If my home was a better place for the dear boy, I'd take him to it; but indeed indeed it's not.'

'You shall take him,' returned Betty, fervently kissing the comforting hand, 'where you will, my deary. I am not so hard, but that I believe your face and voice, and I will, as long as I can see and hear.'

This victory gained, Rokesmith made haste to profit by it, for he saw how wofully time had been lost. He despatched Sloppy to bring the carriage to the door; caused the child to be carefully wrapped up; bade old Betty get her bonnet on; collected the toys, enabling the little fellow to comprehend that his treasures were to be transported with him; and had all things prepared so easily that they were ready for the carriage as soon as it appeared, and in a minute afterwards were on their way. Sloppy they left behind, relieving his overcharged breast with a paroxysm of mangling.

At the Children's Hospital, the gallant steed, the Noah's ark, yellow bird, and the officer in the Guards, were made as welcome as their child-owner. But the doctor said aside to Rokesmith, 'This should have been days ago. Too late!'

However, they were all carried up into a fresh airy room, and there Johnny came to himself, out of a sleep or a swoon or whatever it was, to find himself lying in a little quiet bed, with a little platform over his breast, on which were already arranged, to give him heart and urge him to cheer up, the Noah's ark, the noble steed, and the yellow bird; with the officer in the Guards doing duty over the whole, quite as much to the satisfaction of his country as if he had been upon Parade. And at the bed's head was a coloured picture beautiful to see, representing as it were another Johnny seated on the knee of some Angel surely who loved little children. And, marvellous fact, to lie and stare at: Johnny had become one of a little family, all in little quiet beds (except two playing dominoes in little arm-chairs at a little table on the hearth): and on all the little beds were little platforms whereon were to be seen dolls' houses, woolly dogs with mechanical barks in them not very dissimilar from the artificial voice pervading the bowels of the yellow bird, tin armies, Moorish tumblers, wooden tea things, and the riches of the earth.

As Johnny murmured something in his placid admiration, the ministering women at his bed's head asked him what he said. It seemed that he wanted to know whether all these were brothers and sisters of his? So they told him yes. It seemed then, that he wanted to know whether God had brought them all together there? So they told him yes again. They made out then, that he wanted to know whether they would all get out of pain? So they answered yes to that question likewise, and made him understand that the reply included himself.

Johnny's powers of sustaining conversation were as yet so very imperfectly developed, even in a state of health, that in sickness they were little more than monosyllabic. But, he had to be washed and tended, and remedies were applied, and though those offices were far, far more skilfully and lightly done than ever anything had been done for him in his little life, so rough and short, they would have hurt and tired him but for an amazing circumstance which laid hold of his attention. This was no less than the appearance on his own little platform in pairs, of All Creation, on its way into his own particular ark: the elephant leading, and the fly, with a diffident sense of his size, politely bringing up the rear. A very little brother lying in the next bed with a broken leg, was so enchanted by this spectacle that his delight exalted its enthralling interest; and so came rest and sleep.

'I see you are not afraid to leave the dear child here, Betty,' whispered Mrs Boffin.

'No, ma'am. Most willingly, most thankfully, with all my heart and soul.'

So, they kissed him, and left him there, and old Betty was to come back early in the morning, and nobody but Rokesmith knew for certain how that the doctor had said, 'This should have been days ago. Too late!'

But, Rokesmith knowing it, and knowing that his bearing it in mind would be acceptable thereafter to that good woman who had been the only light in the childhood of desolate John Harmon dead and gone, resolved that late at night he would go back to the bedside of John Harmon's namesake, and see how it fared with him.

The family whom God had brought together were not all asleep, but were all quiet. From bed to bed, a light womanly tread and a pleasant fresh face passed in the silence of the night. A little head would lift itself up into the softened light here and there, to be kissed as the face went by—for these little patients are very loving—and would then submit itself to be composed to rest again. The mite with the broken leg was restless, and moaned; but after a while turned his face towards Johnny's bed, to fortify himself with a view of the ark, and fell asleep. Over most of the beds, the toys were yet grouped as the children had left them when they last laid themselves down, and, in their innocent grotesqueness and incongruity, they might have stood for the children's dreams.

The doctor came in too, to see how it fared with Johnny. And he and Rokesmith stood together, looking down with compassion on him.

'What is it, Johnny?' Rokesmith was the questioner, and put an arm round the poor baby as he made a struggle.

'Him!' said the little fellow. 'Those!'

The doctor was quick to understand children, and, taking the horse, the ark, the yellow bird, and the man in the Guards, from Johnny's bed, softly placed them on that of his next neighbour, the mite with the broken leg.

With a weary and yet a pleased smile, and with an action as if he stretched his little figure out to rest, the child heaved his body on the sustaining arm, and seeking Rokesmith's face with his lips, said:

'A kiss for the boofer lady.'

Having now bequeathed all he had to dispose of, and arranged his affairs in this world, Johnny, thus speaking, left it.

Chapter 10
A Successor

SOME of the Reverend Frank Milvey's brethren had found themselves exceedingly uncomfortable in their minds, because they were required to bury the dead too hopefully. But, the Reverend Frank, inclining to the belief that they were required to do one or two other things (say out of nine-and-thirty) calculated to trouble their consciences rather more if they would think as much about them, held his peace.

Indeed, the Reverend Frank Milvey was a forbearing man, who noticed many sad warps and blights in the vineyard wherein he worked, and did not profess that they made him savagely wise. He only learned that the more he himself knew, in his little limited human way, the better he could distantly imagine what Omniscience might know.

Wherefore, if the Reverend Frank had had to read the words that troubled some of his brethren, and profitably touched innumerable hearts, in a worse case than Johnny's, he would have done so out of the pity and humility of his soul. Reading them over Johnny, he thought of his own six children, but not of his poverty, and read them with dimmed eyes. And very seriously did he and his bright little wife, who had been listening, look down into the small grave and walk home arm-in-arm.

There was grief in the aristocratic house, and there was joy in the Bower. Mr Wegg argued, if an orphan were wanted, was he not an orphan himself, and could a better be desired? And why go beating about Brentford bushes, seeking orphans forsooth who had established no claims upon you and made no sacrifices for you, when here was an orphan ready to your hand who had given up in your cause, Miss Elizabeth, Master George, Aunt Jane, and Uncle Parker?

Mr Wegg chuckled, consequently, when he heard the tidings. Nay, it was afterwards affirmed by a witness who shall at present be nameless, that in the seclusion of the Bower he poked out his wooden leg, in the stage-ballet manner, and executed a taunting or triumphant pirouette on the genuine leg remaining to him.

John Rokesmith's manner towards Mrs Boffin at this time, was more the manner of a young man towards a mother, than that of a Secretary towards his employer's wife. It had always been marked by a subdued affectionate deference that seemed to have sprung up on the very day of his engagement; whatever was odd in her dress or her ways had seemed to have no oddity for him; he had sometimes borne a quietly-amused face in her company, but still it had seemed as if the pleasure her genial temper and radiant nature yielded him, could have been quite as naturally expressed in a tear as in a smile. The completeness of his sympathy with her fancy for having a little John Harmon to protect and rear, he had shown in every act and word, and now that the kind fancy was disappointed, he treated it with a manly tenderness and respect for which she could hardly thank him enough.

'But I do thank you, Mr Rokesmith,' said Mrs Boffin, 'and I thank you most kindly. You love children.'

'I hope everybody does.'

'They ought,' said Mrs Boffin; 'but we don't all of us do what we ought; do us?'

John Rokesmith replied, 'Some among us supply the shortcomings of the rest. You have loved children well, Mr Boffin has told me.'

'Not a bit better than he has, but that's his way; he puts all the good upon me. You speak rather sadly, Mr Rokesmith.'

'Do I?'

'It sounds to me so. Were you one of many children?'

He shook his head.

'An only child?'

'No, there was another. Dead long ago.'

'Father or mother alive?'

'Dead.'

'And the rest of your relations?'

'Dead—if I ever had any living. I never heard of any.'

At this point of the dialogue Bella came in with a light step. She paused at the door a moment, hesitating whether to remain or retire; perplexed by finding that she was not observed.

'Now, don't mind an old lady's talk,' said Mrs Boffin, 'but tell me. Are you quite sure, Mr Rokesmith, that you have never had a disappointment in love?'

'Quite sure. Why do you ask me?'

'Why, for this reason. Sometimes you have a kind of kept-down manner with you, which is not like your age. You can't be thirty?'

'I am not yet thirty.'

Deeming it high time to make her presence known, Bella coughed here to attract attention, begged pardon, and said she would go, fearing that she interrupted some matter of business.

'No, don't go,' rejoined Mrs Boffin, 'because we are coming to business, instead of having begun it, and you belong to it as much now, my dear Bella, as I do. But I want my Noddy to consult with us. Would somebody be so good as find my Noddy for me?'

Rokesmith departed on that errand, and presently returned accompanied by Mr Boffin at his jog-trot. Bella felt a little vague trepidation as to the subject-matter of this same consultation, until Mrs Boffin announced it.

'Now, you come and sit by me, my dear,' said that worthy soul, taking her comfortable place on a large ottoman in the centre of the room, and drawing her arm through Bella's; 'and Noddy, you sit here, and Mr Rokesmith you sit there. Now, you see, what I want to talk about, is this. Mr and Mrs Milvey have sent me the kindest note possible (which Mr Rokesmith just now read to me out aloud, for I ain't good at handwritings), offering to find me another little child to name and educate and bring up. Well. This has set me thinking.'

('And she is a steam-ingein at it,' murmured Mr Boffin, in an admiring parenthesis, 'when she once begins. It mayn't be so easy to start her; but once started, she's a ingein.')

'—This has set me thinking, I say,' repeated Mrs Boffin,

cordially beaming under the influence of her husband's compliment, 'and I have thought two things. First of all, that I have grown timid of reviving John Harmon's name. It's an unfortunate name, and I fancy I should reproach myself if I gave it to another dear child, and it proved again unlucky.'

'Now, whether,' said Mr Boffin, gravely propounding a case for his Secretary's opinion; 'whether one might call that a superstition?'

'It is a matter of feeling with Mrs Boffin,' said Rokesmith, gently. 'The name has always been unfortunate. It has now this new unfortunate association connected with it. The name has died out. Why revive it? Might I ask Miss Wilfer what she thinks?'

'It has not been a fortunate name for me,' said Bella, colouring—'or at least it was not, until it led to my being here—but that is not the point in my thoughts. As we had given the name to the poor child, and as the poor child took so lovingly to me, I think I should feel jealous of calling another child by it. I think I should feel as if the name had become endeared to me, and I had no right to use it so.'

'And that's your opinion?' remarked Mr Boffin, observant of the Secretary's face and again addressing him.

'I say again, it is a matter of feeling,' returned the Secretary. 'I think Miss Wilfer's feeling very womanly and pretty.'

'Now, give us your opinion, Noddy,' said Mrs Boffin.

'My opinion, old lady,' returned the Golden Dustman, 'is your opinion.'

'Then,' said Mrs Boffin, 'we agree not to revive John Harmon's name, but to let it rest in the grave. It is, as Mr Rokesmith says, a matter of feeling, but Lor how many matters *are* matters of feeling! Well; and so I come to the second thing I have thought of. You must know, Bella, my dear, and Mr Rokesmith, that when I first named to my husband my thoughts of adopting a little orphan boy in remembrance of John Harmon, I further named to my husband that it was comforting to think that how the poor boy would be benefited by John's own money, and protected from John's own forlornness.'

'Hear, hear!' cried Mr Boffin. 'So she did. Ancoar!'

'No, not Ancoar, Noddy, my dear,' returned Mrs Boffin, 'because I am going to say something else. I meant that, I am sure, as much as I still mean it. But this little death has made me ask myself the question, seriously, whether I wasn't too bent upon pleasing myself. Else why did I seek out so much for a pretty child, and a child quite to my liking? Wanting to do good, why not do it for its own sake, and put my tastes and likings by?'

'Perhaps,' said Bella; and perhaps she said it with some little sensitiveness arising out of those old curious relations of hers towards the murdered man; 'perhaps, in reviving the name, you would not have liked to give it to a less interesting child than the original. He interested you very much.'

'Well, my dear,' returned Mrs Boffin, giving her a squeeze, 'it's kind of you to find that reason out, and I hope it may have been so, and indeed to a certain extent I believe it was so, but I am afraid not to the whole extent. However, that don't come in question now, because we have done with the name.'

'Laid it up as a remembrance,' suggested Bella, musingly.

'Much better said, my dear; laid it up as a remembrance. Well then; I have been thinking if I take any orphan to provide for, let it not be a pet and a plaything for me, but a creature to be helped for its own sake.'

'Not pretty then?' said Bella.

'No,' returned Mrs Boffin, stoutly.

'Nor prepossessing then?' said Bella.

'No,' returned Mrs Boffin. 'Not necessarily so. That's as it may happen. A well-disposed boy comes in my way who may be even a little wanting in such advantages for getting on in life, but is honest and industrious and requires a helping hand and deserves it. If I am very much in earnest and quite determined to be unselfish, let me take care of *him*.'

Here the footman whose feelings had been hurt on the former occasion, appeared, and crossing to Rokesmith apologetically announced the objectionable Sloppy.

The four members of Council looked at one another, and paused. 'Shall he be brought here, ma'am?' asked Rokesmith.

'Yes,' said Mrs Boffin. Whereupon the footman disappeared, reappeared presenting Sloppy, and retired much disgusted.

The consideration of Mrs Boffin had clothed Mr Sloppy in a suit of black, on which the tailor had received personal directions from Rokesmith to expend the utmost cunning of his art, with a view to the concealment of the cohering and sustaining buttons. But, so much more powerful were the frailties of Sloppy's form than the strongest resources of tailoring science, that he now stood before the Council, a perfect Argus in the way of buttons: shining and winking and gleaming and twinkling out of a hundred of those eyes of bright metal, at the dazzled spectators. The artistic taste of some unknown hatter had furnished him with a hatband of wholesale capacity which was fluted behind, from the crown of his hat to the brim, and terminated in a black bunch, from which the imagination shrunk discomfited and the reason revolted. Some special powers with which his legs were endowed, had already hitched up his glossy trousers at the ankles, and bagged them at the knees; while similar gifts in his arms had raised his coat-sleeves from his wrists and accumulated them at his elbows. Thus set forth, with the additional embellishments of a very little tail to his coat, and a yawning gulf at his waistband, Sloppy stood confessed.

'And how is Betty, my good fellow?' Mrs Boffin asked him.

'Thankee, mum,' said Sloppy, 'she do pretty nicely, and sending her dooty and many thanks for the tea and all faviours and wishing to know the family's healths.'

'Have you just come, Sloppy?'

'Yes, mum.'

'Then you have not had your dinner yet?'

'No, mum. But I mean to it. For I ain't forgotten your handsome orders that I was never to go away without having had a good 'un off of meat and beer and pudding—no: there was four of 'em, for I reckoned 'em up when I had 'em; meat one, beer two, vegetables three, and which was four?—Why, pudding, *he* was four!' Here Sloppy threw his head back, opened his mouth wide, and laughed rapturously.

'How are the two poor little Minders?' asked Mrs Boffin.

'Striking right out, mum, and coming round beautiful.'

Mrs Boffin looked on the other three members of Council, and then said, beckoning with her finger:

'Sloppy.'

'Yes, mum.'

'Come forward, Sloppy. Should you like to dine here every day?'

'Off of all four on 'em, mum? O mum!' Sloppy's feelings obliged him to squeeze his hat, and contract one leg at the knee.

'Yes. And should you like to be always taken care of here, if you were industrious and deserving?'

'Oh, mum!—But there's Mrs Higden,' said Sloppy, checking himself in his raptures, drawing back, and shaking his head with very serious meaning. 'There's Mrs Higden. Mrs Higden goes before all. None can ever be better friends to me than Mrs Higden's been. And she must be turned for, must Mrs Higden. Where would Mrs Higden be if she warn't turned for!' At the mere thought of Mrs Higden in this inconceivable affliction, Mr Sloppy's countenance became pale, and manifested the most distressful emotions.

'You are as right as right can be, Sloppy,' said Mrs Boffin 'and far be it from me to tell you otherwise. It shall be seen to. If Betty Higden can be turned for all the same, you shall come here and be taken care of for life, and be made able to keep her in other ways than the turning.'

'Even as to that, mum,' answered the ecstatic Sloppy, 'the turning might be done in the night, don't you see? I could be here in the day, and turn in the night. I don't want no sleep, *I* don't. Or even if I any ways should want a wink or two,' added Sloppy, after a moment's apologetic reflection, 'I could take 'em turning. I've took 'em turning many a time, and enjoyed 'em wonderful!'

On the grateful impulse of the moment, Mr Sloppy kissed Mrs Boffin's hand, and then detaching himself from that good creature that he might have room enough for his feelings, threw back his head, opened his mouth wide, and uttered a dismal howl. It was creditable to his tenderness of heart, but suggested that he might on occasion give some offence to the neighbours: the rather, as the footman looked in, and begged pardon, finding he was not wanted, but excused himself, on the ground 'that he thought it was Cats.'

Chapter 11
Some Affairs of the Heart

LITTLE Miss Peecher, from her little official dwelling-house, with its little windows like the eyes in needles, and its little doors like the covers of school-books, was very observant indeed of the object of her quiet affections. Love, though said to be afflicted with blindness, is a vigilant watchman, and Miss Peecher kept him on double duty over Mr Bradley Headstone. It was not that she was naturally given to playing the spy—it was not that she was at all secret, plotting, or mean—it was simply that she loved the irresponsive Bradley with all the primitive and homely stock of love that had never been examined or certificated out of her. If her faithful slate had had the latent qualities of sympathetic paper, and its pencil those of invisible ink, many a little treatise calculated to astonish the pupils would have come bursting through the dry sums in school-time under the warming influence of Miss Peecher's bosom. For, oftentimes when school was not, and her calm leisure and calm little house were her own, Miss Peecher would commit to the confidential slate an imaginary description of how, upon a balmy evening at dusk, two figures might have been observed in the market-garden ground round the corner, of whom one, being a manly form, bent over the other, being a womanly form of short stature and some compactness, and breathed in a low voice the words, 'Emma Peecher, wilt thou be my own?' after which the womanly form's head reposed upon the manly form's shoulder, and the nightingales tuned up. Though all unseen, and unsuspected by the pupils, Bradley Headstone even pervaded the school exercises. Was Geography in question? He would come triumphantly flying out of Vesuvius and Ætna ahead of the lava, and would boil unharmed in the hot springs of Iceland, and would float majestically down the Ganges and the Nile. Did History chronicle a king of men? Behold him in pepper-and-salt pantaloons, with his watchguard round his neck. Were copies to be written? In capital B's and H's most of the girls under Miss Peecher's tuition were half a year ahead of every other letter in the alphabet. And Mental Arithmetic, administered by Miss Peecher, often devoted itself to providing Bradley Headstone with a wardrobe of fabulous extent: fourscore and four neck-ties at two and ninepence-halfpenny, two gross of silver watches at four pounds fifteen and sixpence, seventy-four black hats at eighteen shillings; and many similar superfluities.

The vigilant watchman, using his daily opportunities of turning his eyes in Bradley's direction, soon apprized Miss Peecher that Bradley was more preoccupied than had been his wont, and more given to strolling about with a downcast and reserved face, turning something difficult in his mind that was not in the scholastic syllabus. Putting this and that together—combining under the head 'this,' present appearances and the intimacy with Charley Hexam, and ranging under the head 'that' the visit to his sister, the watchman reported to Miss Peecher his strong suspicions that the sister was at the bottom of it.

'I wonder,' said Miss Peecher, as she sat making up her weekly report on a half-holiday afternoon, 'what they call Hexam's sister?'

Mary Anne, at her needlework, attendant and attentive, held her arm up.

'Well, Mary Anne?'

'She is named Lizzie, ma'am.'

'She can hardly be named Lizzie, I think, Mary Anne,' returned Miss Peecher, in a tunefully instructive voice. 'Is Lizzie a Christian name, Mary Anne?'

Mary Anne laid down her work, rose, hooked herself behind, as being under catechization, and replied: 'No, it is a corruption, Miss Peecher.'

'Who gave her that name?' Miss Peecher was going on, from the mere force of habit, when she checked herself, on Mary Anne's evincing theological impatience to strike in with her godfathers and her godmothers, and said: 'I mean of what name is it a corruption?'

'Elizabeth, or Eliza, Miss Peecher.'

'Right, Mary Anne. Whether there were any Lizzies in the early Christian Church must be considered very doubtful, very doubtful.' Miss Peecher was exceedingly sage here. 'Speaking correctly, we say, then, that Hexam's sister is called Lizzie; not that she is named so. Do we not, Mary Anne?'

'We do, Miss Peecher.'

'And where,' pursued Miss Peecher, complacent in her little transparent fiction of conducting the examination in a semi-official manner for Mary Anne's benefit, not her own, 'where does this young woman, who is called but not named Lizzie, live? Think, now, before answering.'

'In Church Street, Smith Square, by Mill Bank, ma'am.'

'In Church Street, Smith Square, by Mill Bank,' repeated Miss Peecher, as if possessed beforehand of the book in which it was written. 'Exactly so. And what occupation does this young woman pursue, Mary Anne? Take time.'

'She has a place of trust at an outfitter's in the City, ma'am.'

'Oh!' said Miss Peecher, pondering on it; but smoothly added, in a confirmatory tone, 'At an outfitter's in the City. Ye-es?'

'And Charley—' Mary Anne was proceeding, when Miss Peecher stared.

'I mean Hexam, Miss Peecher.'

'I should think you did, Mary Anne. I am glad to hear you do. And Hexam—?'

'Says,' Mary Anne went on, 'that he is not pleased with his sister, and that his sister won't be guided by his advice, and persists in being guided by somebody else's; and that—'

'Mr Headstone coming across the garden!' exclaimed Miss Peecher, with a flushed glance at the looking-glass. 'You have answered very well, Mary Anne. You are forming an excellent habit of arranging your thoughts clearly. That will do.'

The discreet Mary Anne resumed her seat and her silence, and stitched, and stitched, and was stitching when the schoolmaster's shadow came in before him, announcing that he might be instantly expected.

'Good evening, Miss Peecher,' he said, pursuing the shadow, and taking its place.

'Good evening, Mr Headstone. Mary Anne, a chair.'

'Thank you,' said Bradley, seating himself in his constrained manner. 'This is but a flying visit. I have looked in, on my way, to ask a kindness of you as a neighbour.'

'Did you say on your way, Mr Headstone?' asked Miss Peecher.

'On my way to—where I am going.'

'Church Street, Smith Square, by Mill Bank,' repeated Miss Peecher, in her own thoughts.

'Charley Hexam has gone to get a book or two he wants, and will probably be back before me. As we leave my house empty, I took the liberty of telling him I would leave the key here. Would you kindly allow me to do so?'

'Certainly, Mr Headstone. Going for an evening walk, sir?'

'Partly for a walk, and partly for—on business.'

'Business in Church Street, Smith Square, by Mill Bank,' repeated Miss Peecher to herself.

'Having said which,' pursued Bradley, laying his door-key on the table, 'I must be already going. There is nothing I can do for you, Miss Peecher?'

'Thank you, Mr Headstone. In which direction?'

'In the direction of Westminster.'

'Mill Bank,' Miss Peecher repeated in her own thoughts once again. 'No, thank you, Mr Headstone; I'll not trouble you.'

'You couldn't trouble me,' said the schoolmaster.

'Ah!' returned Miss Peecher, though not aloud; 'but you can trouble *me*!' And for all her quiet manner, and her quiet smile, she was full of trouble as he went his way.

She was right touching his destination. He held as straight a course for the house of the dolls' dressmaker as the wisdom of his ancestors, exemplified in the construction of the intervening streets, would let him, and walked with a bent head hammering at one fixed idea. It had been an immoveable idea since he first set eyes upon her. It seemed to him as if all that he could suppress in himself he had suppressed, as if all that he could restrain in himself he had restrained, and the time had come—in a rush, in a moment—when the power of self-command had departed from him. Love at first sight is a trite expression quite sufficiently discussed; enough that in certain smouldering natures like this man's, that passion leaps into a blaze, and makes such head as fire does in a rage of wind, when other passions, but for its mastery, could be held in chains. As a multitude of weak, imitative natures are always lying by, ready to go mad upon the next wrong idea that may be broached—in these times, generally some form of tribute to Somebody for something that never was done, or, if ever done, that was done by Somebody Else—so these less ordinary natures may lie by for years, ready on the touch of an instant to burst into flame.

The schoolmaster went his way, brooding and brooding, and a sense of being vanquished in a struggle might have been pieced out of his worried face. Truly, in his breast there lingered a resentful shame to find himself defeated by this passion for Charley Hexam's sister, though in the very self-same moments he was concentrating himself upon the object of bringing the passion to a successful issue.

He appeared before the dolls' dressmaker, sitting alone at her work. 'Oho!' thought that sharp young personage, 'it's you, is it? *I* know your tricks and your manners, my friend!'

'Hexam's sister,' said Bradley Headstone, 'is not come home yet?'

'You are quite a conjuror,' returned Miss Wren.

'I will wait, if you please, for I want to speak to her.'

'Do you?' returned Miss Wren. 'Sit down. I hope it's mutual.'

Bradley glanced distrustfully at the shrewd face again bending over the work, and said, trying to conquer doubt and hesitation:

'I hope you don't imply that my visit will be unacceptable to Hexam's sister?'

'There! Don't call her that. I can't bear you to call her that,' returned Miss Wren, snapping her fingers in a volley of impatient snaps, 'for I don't like Hexam.'

'Indeed?'

'No.' Miss Wren wrinkled her nose, to express dislike. 'Selfish. Thinks only of himself. The way with all of you.'

'The way with all of us? Then you don't like *me*?'

'So-so,' replied Miss Wren, with a shrug and a laugh. 'Don't know much about you.'

'But I was not aware it was the way with all of us,' said Bradley, returning to the accusation, a little injured. 'Won't you say, some of us?'

'Meaning,' returned the little creature, 'every one of you, but you. Hah! Now look this lady in the face. This is Mrs Truth. The Honourable. Full-dressed.'

Bradley glanced at the doll she held up for his observation—which had been lying on its face on her bench, while with a needle and thread she fastened the dress on at the back—and looked from it to her.

'I stand the Honourable Mrs T. on my bench in this corner against the wall, where her blue eyes can shine upon you,' pursued Miss Wren, doing so, and making two little dabs at him in the air with her needle, as if she pricked him with it in his own eyes; 'and I defy you to tell me, with Mrs T. for a witness, what you have come here for.'

'To see Hexam's sister.'

'You don't say so!' retorted Miss Wren, hitching her chin. 'But on whose account?'

'Her own.'

'O Mrs T.!' exclaimed Miss Wren. 'You hear him!'

'To reason with her,' pursued Bradley, half humouring what was present, and half angry with what was not present; 'for her own sake.'

'Oh Mrs T.!' exclaimed the dressmaker.

'For her own sake,' repeated Bradley, warming, 'and for her brother's, and as a perfectly disinterested person.'

'Really, Mrs T.,' remarked the dressmaker, 'since it comes to this, we must positively turn you with your face to the wall.' She had hardly done so, when Lizzie Hexam arrived, and showed some surprise on seeing Bradley Headstone there, and Jenny shaking her little fist at him close before her eyes, and the Honourable Mrs T. with her face to the wall.

'Here's a perfectly disinterested person, Lizzie dear,' said the knowing Miss Wren, 'come to talk with you, for your own sake and your brother's. Think of that. I am sure there ought to be no third party present at anything so very kind and so very serious; and so, if you'll remove the third party upstairs, my dear, the third party will retire.'

Lizzie took the hand which the dolls' dressmaker held out to her for the purpose of being supported away, but only looked at her with an inquiring smile, and made no other movement.

'The third party hobbles awfully, you know, when she's left to herself,' said Miss Wren, 'her back being so bad, and her legs so queer; so she can't retire gracefully unless you help her, Lizzie.'

'She can do no better than stay where she is,' returned Lizzie, releasing the hand, and laying her own lightly on Miss Jenny's curls. And then to Bradley: 'From Charley, sir?'

In an irresolute way, and stealing a clumsy look at her, Bradley rose to place a chair for her, and then returned to his own.

'Strictly speaking,' said he, 'I come from Charley, because I left him only a little while ago; but I am not commissioned by Charley. I come of my own spontaneous act.'

With her elbows on her bench, and her chin upon her hands, Miss Jenny Wren sat looking at him with a watchful sidelong look. Lizzie, in her different way, sat looking at him too.

'The fact is,' began Bradley, with a mouth so dry that he had some difficulty in articulating his words: the consciousness of which rendered his manner still more ungainly and undecided; 'the truth is, that Charley, having no secrets from me (to the best of my belief), has confided the whole of this matter to me.'

He came to a stop, and Lizzie asked: 'What matter, sir?'

'I thought,' returned the schoolmaster, stealing another look at her, and seeming to try in vain to sustain it; for the look dropped as it lighted on her eyes, 'that it might be so superfluous as to be almost impertinent, to enter upon a definition of it. My allusion was to this matter of your having put aside your brother's plans for you, and given the preference to those of Mr—I believe the name is Mr Eugene Wrayburn.'

He made this point of not being certain of the name, with another uneasy look at her, which dropped like the last.

Nothing being said on the other side, he had to begin again, and began with new embarrassment.

'Your brother's plans were communicated to me when he first had them in his thoughts. In point of fact he spoke to me about them when I was last here—when we were walking back together, and when I—when the impression was fresh upon me of having seen his sister.'

There might have been no meaning in it, but the little dressmaker here removed one of her supporting hands from her chin, and musingly turned the Honourable Mrs T. with her face to the company. That done, she fell into her former attitude.

'I approved of his idea,' said Bradley, with his uneasy look wandering to the doll, and unconsciously resting there longer than it had rested on Lizzie, 'both because your brother ought naturally to be the originator of any such scheme, and because I hoped to be able to promote it. I should have had inexpressible pleasure, I should have taken inexpressible interest, in promoting it. Therefore I must acknowledge that when your brother was disappointed, I too was disappointed. I wish to avoid reservation or concealment, and I fully acknowledge that.'

He appeared to have encouraged himself by having got so far. At all events he went on with much greater firmness and force of emphasis: though with a curious disposition to set his teeth, and with a curious tight-screwing movement of his right hand in the clenching palm of his left, like the action of one who was being physically hurt, and was unwilling to cry out.

'I am a man of strong feelings, and I have strongly felt this disappointment. I do strongly feel it. I don't show what I feel; some of us are obliged habitually to keep it down. To keep it down. But to return to your brother. He has taken the matter so much to heart that he has remonstrated (in my presence he remonstrated) with Mr Eugene Wrayburn, if that be the name. He did so, quite ineffectually. As any one not blinded to the real character of Mr—Mr Eugene Wrayburn—would readily suppose.'

He looked at Lizzie again, and held the look. And his face turned from burning red to white, and from white back to burning red, and so for the time to lasting deadly white.

'Finally, I resolved to come here alone, and appeal to you. I resolved to come here alone, and entreat you to retract the course you have chosen, and instead of confiding in a mere stranger—a person of most insolent behaviour to your brother and others—to prefer your brother and your brother's friend.'

Lizzie Hexam had changed colour when those changes came over him, and her face now expressed some anger, more dislike, and even a touch of fear. But she answered him very steadily.

'I cannot doubt, Mr Headstone, that your visit is well meant. You have been so good a friend to Charley that I have no right to doubt it. I have nothing to tell Charley, but that I accepted the help to which he so much objects before he made any plans for me; or certainly before I knew of any. It was considerately and delicately offered, and there were reasons that had weight with me which should be as dear to Charley as to me. I have no more to say to Charley on this subject.'

His lips trembled and stood apart, as he followed this repudiation of himself, and limitation of her words to her brother.

'I should have told Charley, if he had come to me,' she resumed, as though it were an after-thought, 'that Jenny and I find our teacher very able and very patient, and that she takes great pains with us. So much so, that we have said to her we hope in a very little while to be able to go on by ourselves. Charley knows about teachers, and I should also have told him, for his satisfaction, that ours comes from an institution where teachers are regularly brought up.'

'I should like to ask you,' said Bradley Headstone, grinding his words slowly out, as though they came from a rusty mill; 'I should like to ask you, if I may without offence, whether you would have objected—no; rather, I should like to say, if I may without offence, that I wish I had had the opportunity of coming here with your brother and devoting my poor abilities and experience to your service.'

'Thank you, Mr Headstone.'

'But I fear,' he pursued, after a pause, furtively wrenching at the seat of his chair with one hand, as if he would have wrenched the chair to pieces, and gloomily observing her while her eyes were cast down, 'that my humble services would not have found much favour with you?'

She made no reply, and the poor stricken wretch sat contending with himself in a heat of passion and torment. After a while he took out his handkerchief and wiped his forehead and hands.

'There is only one thing more I had to say, but it is the most important. There is a reason against this matter, there is a personal relation concerned in this matter, not yet explained to you. It might—I don't say it would—it might—induce you to think differently. To proceed under the present circumstances is out of the question. Will you please come to the understanding that there shall be another interview on the subject?'

'With Charley, Mr Headstone?'

'With—well,' he answered, breaking off, 'yes! Say with him too. Will you please come to the understanding that there must be another interview under more favourable circumstances, before the whole case can be submitted?'

'I don't,' said Lizzie, shaking her head, 'understand your meaning, Mr Headstone.'

'Limit my meaning for the present,' he interrupted, 'to the whole case being submitted to you in another interview.'

'What case, Mr Headstone? What is wanting to it?'

'You—you shall be informed in the other interview.' Then he said, as if in a burst of irrepressible despair, 'I—I leave it all incomplete! There is a spell upon me, I think!' And then added, almost as if he asked for pity, 'Good-night!'

He held out his hand. As she, with manifest hesitation, not to say reluctance, touched it, a strange tremble passed over him, and his face, so deadly white, was moved as by a stroke of pain. Then he was gone.

The dolls' dressmaker sat with her attitude unchanged, eyeing the door by which he had departed, until Lizzie pushed her bench aside and sat down near her. Then, eyeing Lizzie as she had previously eyed Bradley and the door, Miss Wren chopped that very sudden and keen chop in which her jaws sometimes indulged, leaned back in her chair with folded arms, and thus expressed herself:

'Humph! If he—I mean, of course, my dear, the party who is coming to court me when the time comes—should be *that* sort of man, he may spare himself the trouble. *He* wouldn't do to be trotted about and made useful. He'd take fire and blow up while he was about it.'

'And so you would be rid of him,' said Lizzie, humouring her.

'Not so easily,' returned Miss Wren. 'He wouldn't blow up alone. He'd carry me up with him. *I* know his tricks and his manners.'

'Would he want to hurt you, do you mean?' asked Lizzie.

'Mightn't exactly want to do it, my dear,' returned Miss Wren; 'but a lot of gunpowder among lighted lucifer-matches in the next room might almost as well be here.'

'He is a very strange man,' said Lizzie, thoughtfully.

'I wish he was so very strange a man as to be a total stranger,' answered the sharp little thing.

It being Lizzie's regular occupation when they were alone of an evening to brush out and smooth the long fair hair of the dolls' dressmaker, she unfastened a ribbon that kept it back while the little creature was at her work, and it fell in a beautiful

shower over the poor shoulders that were much in need of such
adorning rain. 'Not now, Lizzie, dear,' said Jenny; 'let us have a
talk by the fire.' With those words, she in her turn loosened her
friend's dark hair, and it dropped of its own weight over her
bosom, in two rich masses. Pretending to compare the colours
and admire the contrast, Jenny so managed a mere touch or two
of her nimble hands, as that she herself laying a cheek on one of
the dark folds, seemed blinded by her own clustering curls to all
but the fire, while the fine handsome face and brow of Lizzie
were revealed without obstruction in the sombre light.

'Let us have a talk,' said Jenny, 'about Mr Eugene
Wrayburn.'

Something sparkled down among the fair hair resting on the
dark hair; and if it were not a star—which it couldn't be—it was
an eye; and if it were an eye, it was Jenny Wren's eye, bright
and watchful as the bird's whose name she had taken.

'Why about Mr Wrayburn?' Lizzie asked.

'For no better reason than because I'm in the humour. I
wonder whether he's rich!'

'No, not rich.'

'Poor?'

'I think so, for a gentleman.'

'Ah! To be sure! Yes, he's a gentleman. Not of our sort; is
he?'

A shake of the head, a thoughtful shake of the head, and the
answer, softly spoken, 'Oh no, oh no!'

The dolls' dressmaker had an arm round her friend's waist.
Adjusting the arm, she slyly took the opportunity of blowing at
her own hair where it fell over her face; then the eye down there,
under lighter shadows sparkled more brightly and appeared more
watchful.

'When He turns up, he shan't be a gentleman; I'll very soon
send him packing, if he is. However, he's not Mr Wrayburn; I
haven't captivated *him*. I wonder whether anybody has, Lizzie!'

'It is very likely.'

'Is it very likely? I wonder who!'

'Is it not very likely that some lady has been taken by him,
and that he may love her dearly?'

'Perhaps. I don't know. What would you think of him,
Lizzie, if you were a lady?'

'I a lady!' she repeated, laughing. 'Such a fancy!'

'Yes. But say: just as a fancy, and for instance.'

'I a lady! I, a poor girl who used to row poor father on the river. I, who had rowed poor father out and home on the very night when I saw him for the first time. I, who was made so timid by his looking at me, that I got up and went out!'

('He did look at you, even that night, though you were not a lady!' thought Miss Wren.)

'I a lady!' Lizzie went on in a low voice, with her eyes upon the fire. 'I, with poor father's grave not even cleared of undeserved stain and shame, and he trying to clear it for me! I a lady!'

'Only as a fancy, and for instance,' urged Miss Wren.

'Too much, Jenny, dear, too much! My fancy is not able to get that far.' As the low fire gleamed upon her, it showed her smiling, mournfully and abstractedly.

'But I am in the humour, and I must be humoured, Lizzie, because after all I am a poor little thing, and have had a hard day with my bad child. Look in the fire, as I like to hear you tell how you used to do when you lived in that dreary old house that had once been a windmill. Look in the—what was its name when you told fortunes with your brother that I *don't* like?'

'The hollow down by the flare?'

'Ah! That's the name! You can find a lady there, *I* know.'

'More easily than I can make one of such material as myself, Jenny.'

The sparkling eye looked steadfastly up, as the musing face looked thoughtfully down. 'Well?' said the dolls' dressmaker, 'We have found our lady?'

Lizzie nodded, and asked, 'Shall she be rich?'

'She had better be, as he's poor.'

'She is very rich. Shall she be handsome?'

'Even you can be that, Lizzie, so she ought to be.'

'She is very handsome.'

'What does she say about him?' asked Miss Jenny, in a low voice: watchful, through an intervening silence, of the face looking down at the fire.

'She is glad, glad, to be rich, that he may have the money. She is glad, glad, to be beautiful, that he may be proud of her. Her poor heart—'

'Eh? Her poor heart?' said Miss Wren.

'Her heart—is given him, with all its love and truth. She would joyfully die with him, or, better than that, die for him. She knows he has failings, but she thinks they have grown up through his being like one cast away, for the want of something to trust in, and care for, and think well of. And she says, that

lady rich and beautiful that I can never come near, ''Only put me
in that empty place, only try how little I mind myself, only prove
what a world of things I will do and bear for you, and I hope that
you might even come to be much better than you are, through
me who am so much worse, and hardly worth the thinking of
beside you.'' '

As the face looking at the fire had become exalted and
forgetful in the rapture of these words, the little creature, openly
clearing away her fair hair with her disengaged hand, had gazed
at it with earnest attention and something like alarm. Now that
the speaker ceased, the little creature laid down her head again,
and moaned, 'O me, O me, O me!'

'In pain, dear Jenny?' asked Lizzie, as if awakened.

'Yes, but not the old pain. Lay me down, lay me down.
Don't go out of my sight to-night. Lock the door and keep close
to me.' Then turning away her face, she said in a whisper to
herself, 'My Lizzie, my poor Lizzie! O my blessed children,
come back in the long bright slanting rows, and come for her,
not me. She wants help more than I, my blessed children!'

She had stretched her hands up with that higher and better
look, and now she turned again, and folded them round Lizzie's
neck, and rocked herself on Lizzie's breast.

Chapter 12
More Birds of Prey

ROGUE RIDERHOOD dwelt deep and dark in Limehouse Hole,
among the riggers, and the mast, oar and block makers, and the
boat-builders, and the sail-lofts, as in a kind of ship's hold stored
full of waterside characters, some no better than himself, some
very much better, and none much worse. The Hole, albeit in a
general way not over nice in its choice of company, was rather
shy in reference to the honour of cultivating the Rogue's acquaintance; more frequently giving him the cold shoulder than
the warm hand, and seldom or never drinking with him unless at

his own expense. A part of the Hole, indeed, contained so much public spirit and private virtue that not even this strong leverage could move it to good fellowship with a tainted accuser. But, there may have been the drawback on this magnanimous morality, that its exponents held a true witness before Justice to be the next unneighbourly and accursed character to a false one.

Had it not been for the daughter whom he often mentioned, Mr Riderhood might have found the Hole a mere grave as to any means it would yield him of getting a living. But Miss Pleasant Riderhood had some little position and connection in Limehouse Hole. Upon the smallest of small scales, she was an unlicensed pawnbroker, keeping what was popularly called a Leaving Shop, by lending insignificant sums on insignificant articles of property deposited with her as security. In her four-and-twentieth year of life, Pleasant was already in her fifth year of this way of trade. Her deceased mother had established the business, and on that parent's demise she had appropriated a secret capital of fifteen shillings to establishing herself in it; the existence of such capital in a pillow being the last intelligible confidential communication made to her by the departed, before succumbing to dropsical conditions of snuff and gin, incompatible equally with coherence and existence.

Why christened Pleasant, the late Mrs Riderhood might possibly have been at some time able to explain, and possibly not. Her daughter had no information on that point. Pleasant she found herself, and she couldn't help it. She had not been consulted on the question, any more than on the question of her coming into these terrestrial parts, to want a name. Similarly, she found herself possessed of what is colloquially termed a swivel eye (derived from her father), which she might perhaps have declined if her sentiments on the subject had been taken. She was not otherwise positively ill-looking, though anxious, meagre, of a muddy complexion, and looking as old again as she really was.

As some dogs have it in the blood, or are trained, to worry certain creatures to a certain point, so—not to make the comparison disrespectfully—Pleasant Riderhood had it in the blood, or had been trained, to regard seamen, within certain limits, as her prey. Show her a man in a blue jacket, and, figuratively speaking, she pinned him instantly. Yet, all things considered, she was not of an evil mind or an unkindly disposition. For, observe how many things were to be considered according to her own unfortunate experience. Show Pleasant Riderhood a Wedding in the street, and she only saw two people taking out a regular licence to quarrel and fight. Show her a Christening, and she saw a little heathen personage having a quite superfluous name bestowed upon it, inasmuch as it would be commonly addressed by some abusive epithet: which little personage was not in the least wanted by anybody, and would be shoved and banged out of everybody's way, until it should grow big enough to shove and bang. Show her a Funeral, and she saw an unremunerative ceremony in the nature of a black masquerade, conferring a temporary gentility on the performers, at an immense expense, and representing the only formal party ever given by the deceased. Show her a live father, and she saw but a duplicate of her own father, who from her infancy had been taken with fits and starts of discharging his duty to her, which duty was always incorporated in the form of a fist or a leathern strap, and being discharged hurt her. All things considered, therefore, Pleasant Riderhood was not so very, very bad. There was even a touch of romance in her—of such romance as could creep into Limehouse Hole—and maybe sometimes of a summer evening, when she stood with folded arms at her shop-door, looking from the reeking street to the sky where the sun was setting, she may have had some vaporous visions of far-off islands in the southern seas or elsewhere (not being geographically particular), where it would be good to roam with a congenial partner among groves of bread-fruit, waiting for ships to be wafted from the hollow ports of civilization. For, sailors to be got the better of, were essential to Miss Pleasant's Eden.

Not on a summer evening did she come to her little shop-door, when a certain man standing over against the house on the opposite side of the street took notice of her. That was on a cold shrewd windy evening, after dark. Pleasant Riderhood shared with most of the lady inhabitants of the Hole, the peculiarity that her hair was a ragged knot, constantly coming down behind, and that she never could enter upon any undertaking without first twisting it into place. At that particular moment, being newly come to the threshold to take a look out of doors, she was winding herself up with both hands after this fashion. And so prevalent was the fashion, that on the occasion of a fight or other disturbance in the Hole, the ladies would be seen flocking from all quarters universally twisting their back-hair as they came along, and many of them, in the hurry of the moment, carrying their back-combs in their mouths.

It was a wretched little shop, with a roof that any man

standing in it could touch with his hand; little better than a cellar or cave, down three steps. Yet in its ill-lighted window, among a flaring handkerchief or two, an old peacoat or so, a few value-less watches and compasses, a jar of tobacco and two crossed pipes, a bottle of walnut ketchup, and some horrible sweets— these creature discomforts serving as a blind to the main business of the Leaving Shop—was displayed the inscription SEAMAN'S BOARDING-HOUSE.

Taking notice of Pleasant Riderhood at the door, the man crossed so quickly that she was still winding herself up, when he stood close before here.

'Is your father at home?' said he.

'I think he is,' returned Pleasant, dropping her arms; 'come in.'

It was a tentative reply, the man having a seafaring appearance. Her father was not at home, and Pleasant knew it. 'Take a seat by the fire,' were her hospitable words when she had got him in; 'men of your calling are always welcome here.'

'Thankee,' said the man.

His manner was the manner of a sailor, and his hands were the hands of a sailor, except that they were smooth. Pleasant had an eye for sailors, and she noticed the unused colour and texture of the hands, sunburnt though they were, as sharply as she noticed their unmistakable looseness and suppleness, as he sat himself down with his left arm carelessly thrown across his left leg a little above the knee, and the right arm as carelessly thrown over the elbow of the wooden chair, with the hand curved, half open and half shut, as if it had just let go a rope.

'Might you be looking for a Boarding-House?' Pleasant inquired, taking her observant stand on one side of the fire.

'I don't rightly know my plans yet,' returned the man.

'You ain't looking for a Leaving Shop?'

'No,' said the man.

'No,' assented Pleasant, 'you've got too much of an outfit on you for that. But if you should want either, this is both.'

'Ay, ay!' said the man, glancing round the place. 'I know. I've been here before.'

'Did you Leave anything when you were here before?' asked Pleasant, with a view to principal and interest.

'No.' The man shook his head.

'I am pretty sure you never boarded here?'

'No.' The man again shook his head.

'What *did* you do here when you were here before?' asked Pleasant. 'For I don't remember you.'

'It's not at all likely you should. I only stood at the door, one night—on the lower step there—while a shipmate of mine looked in to speak to your father. I remember the place well.' Looking very curiously round it.

'Might that have been long ago?'

'Ay, a goodish bit ago. When I came off my last voyage.'

'Then you have not been to sea lately?'

'No. Been in the sick bay since then, and been employed ashore.'

'Then, to be sure, that accounts for your hands.'

The man with a keen look, a quick smile, and a change of manner, caught her up. 'You're a good observer. Yes. That accounts for my hands.'

Pleasant was somewhat disquieted by his look, and returned it suspiciously. Not only was his change of manner, though very sudden, quite collected, but his former manner, which he resumed, had a certain suppressed confidence and sense of power in it that were half threatening.

'Will your father be long?' he inquired.

'I don't know. I can't say.'

'As you supposed he was at home, it would seem that he has just gone out? How's that?'

'I supposed he had come home,' Pleasant explained.

'Oh! You supposed he had come home? Then he has been some time out? How's that?'

'I don't want to deceive you. Father's on the river in his boat.'

'At the old work?' asked the man.

'I don't know what you mean,' said Pleasant, shrinking a step back. 'What on earth d'ye want?'

'I don't want to hurt your father. I don't want to say I might, if I chose. I want to speak to him. Not much in that, is there? There shall be no secrets from you; you shall be by. And plainly, Miss Riderhood, there's nothing to be got out of me, or made of me. I am not good for the Leaving Shop, I am not good for the Boarding-House, I am not good for anything in your way to the extent of sixpenn'orth of halfpence. Put the idea aside, and we shall get on together.'

'But you're a seafaring man?' argued Pleasant, as if that were a sufficient reason for his being good for something in her way.

'Yes and no. I have been, and I may be again. But I am not for you. Won't you take my word for it?'

The conversation had arrived at a crisis to justify Miss Pleasant's hair in tumbling down. It tumbled down accordingly, and she twisted it up, looking from under her bent forehead at the man. In taking stock of his familiarly worn rough-weather nautical clothes, piece by piece, she took stock of a formidable knife in a sheath at his waist ready to his hand, and of a whistle hanging round his neck, and of a short jagged knotted club with a loaded head that peeped out of a pocket of his loose outer jacket or frock. He sat quietly looking at her; but, with these appendages partially revealing themselves, and with a quantity of bristling oakum-coloured head and whisker, he had a formidable appearance.

'Won't you take my word for it?' he asked again.

Pleasant answered with a short dumb nod. He rejoined with another short dumb nod. Then he got up and stood with his arms folded, in front of the fire, looking down into it occasionally, as she stood with her arms folded, leaning against the side of the chimney-piece.

'To wile away the time till your father comes,' he said, —'pray is there much robbing and murdering of seamen about the waterside now?'

'No,' said Pleasant.

'Any?'

'Complaints of that sort are sometimes made, about Ratcliffe and Wapping, and up that way. But who knows how many are true?'

'To be sure. And it don't seem necessary.'

'That's what I say,' observed Pleasant. 'Where's the reason for it? Bless the sailors, it ain't as if they ever could keep what they have, without it.'

'You're right. Their money may be soon got out of them, without violence,' said the man.

'Of course it may,' said Pleasant; 'and then they ship again and get more. And the best thing for 'em, too, to ship again as soon as ever they can be brought to it. They're never so well off as when they're afloat.'

'I'll tell you why I ask,' pursued the visitor, looking up from the fire. 'I was once beset that way myself, and left for dead.'

'No?' said Pleasant. 'Where did it happen?'

'It happened,' returned the man, with a ruminative air, as

he drew his right hand across his chin, and dipped the other in the pocket of his rough outer coat, 'it happened somewhere about here as I reckon. I don't think it can have been a mile from here.'

'Were you drunk?' asked Pleasant.

'I was muddled, but not with fair drinking. I had not been drinking, you understand. A mouthful did it.'

Pleasant with a grave look shook her head; importing that she understood the process, but decidedly disapproved.

'Fair trade is one thing,' said she, 'but that's another. No one has a right to carry on with Jack in *that* way.'

'The sentiment does you credit,' returned the man, with a grim smile; and added, in a mutter, 'the more so, as I believe it's not your father's.—Yes, I had a bad time of it, that time. I lost everything, and had a sharp struggle for my life, weak as I was.'

'Did you get the parties punished?' asked Pleasant.

'A tremendous punishment followed,' said the man, more seriously; 'but it was not of my bringing about.'

'Of whose, then?' asked Pleasant.

The man pointed upward with his forefinger, and, slowly recovering that hand, settled his chin in it again as he looked at the fire. Bringing her inherited eye to bear upon him, Pleasant Riderhood felt more and more uncomfortable, his manner was so mysterious, so stern, so self-possessed.

'Anyways,' said the damsel, 'I am glad punishment followed, and I say so. Fair trade with seafaring men gets a bad name through deeds of violence. I am as much against deeds of violence being done to seafaring men, as seafaring men can be themselves. I am of the same opinion as my mother was, when she was living. Fair trade, my mother used to say, but no robbery and no blows.' In the way of trade Miss Pleasant would have taken—and indeed did take when she could—as much as thirty shillings a week for board that would be dear at five, and likewise conducted the Leaving business upon correspondingly equitable principles; yet she had that tenderness of conscience and those feelings of humanity, that the moment her ideas of trade were overstepped, she became the seaman's champion, even against her father whom she seldom otherwise resisted.

But, she was here interrupted by her father's voice exclaiming angrily, 'Now, Poll Parrot!' and by her father's hat being heavily flung from his hand and striking her face. Accustomed to such occasional manifestations of his sense of parental duty, Pleasant merely wiped her face on her hair (which of course had tumbled down) before she twisted it up. This was another common procedure on the part of the ladies of the Hole, when heated by verbal or fistic altercation.

'Blest if I believe such a Poll Parrot as you was ever learned to speak!' growled Mr Riderhood, stooping to pick up his hat, and making a feint at her with his head and right elbow; for he took the delicate subject of robbing seamen in extraordinary dudgeon, and was out of humour too. 'What are you Poll Parroting at now? Ain't you got nothing to do but fold your arms and stand a Poll Parroting all night?'

'Let her alone,' urged the man. 'She was only speaking to me.'

'Let her alone too!' retorted Mr Riderhood, eyeing him all over. 'Do you know she's my daughter?'

'Yes.'

'And don't you know that I won't have no Poll Parroting on the part of my daughter? No, nor yet that I won't take no Poll Parroting from no man? And who may *you* be, and what may *you* want?'

'How can I tell you until you are silent?' returned the other fiercely.

'Well,' said Mr Riderhood, quailing a little, 'I am willing to be silent for the purpose of hearing. But don't Poll Parrot me.'

'Are you thirsty, you?' the man asked, in the same fierce short way, after returning his look.

'Why nat'rally,' said Mr Riderhood, 'ain't I always thirsty!' (Indignant at the absurdity of the question.)

'What will you drink?' demanded the man.

'Sherry wine,' returned Mr Riderhood, in the same sharp tone, 'if you're capable of it.'

The man put his hand in his pocket, took out half a sovereign, and begged the favour of Miss Pleasant that she would fetch a bottle. 'With the cork undrawn,' he added, emphatically, looking at her father.

'I'll take my Alfred David,' muttered Mr Riderhood, slowly relaxing into a dark smile, 'that you know a move. Do *I* know *you*? N–n–no, I don't know you.'

The man replied, 'No, you don't know me.' And so they stood looking at one another surlily enough, until Pleasant came back.

'There's small glasses on the shelf,' said Riderhood to his daughter. 'Give me the one without a foot. I gets my living by the sweat of my brow, and it's good enough for *me*.' This had a modest self-denying appearance; but it soon turned out that as, by reason of the impossibility of standing the glass upright while there was anything in it, it required to be emptied as soon as filled, Mr Riderhood managed to drink in the proportion of three to one.

With his Fortunatus's goblet ready in his hand, Mr Riderhood sat down on one side of the table before the fire, and the strange man on the other: Pleasant occupying a stool between the latter and the fireside. The background, composed of handkerchiefs, coats, shirts, hats, and other old articles 'On Leaving,' had a general dim resemblance to human listeners; especially where a shiny black sou'wester suit and hat hung, looking very like a clumsy mariner with his back to the company, who was so curious to overhear, that he paused for the purpose with his coat half pulled on, and his shoulders up to his ears in the uncompleted action.

The visitor first held the bottle against the light of the candle, and next examined the top of the cork. Satisfied that it had not been tampered with, he slowly took from his breastpocket a rusty clasp-knife, and, with a corkscrew in the handle, opened the wine. That done, he looked at the cork, unscrewed it from the corkscrew, laid each separately on the table, and, with the end of the sailor's knot of his neckerchief, dusted the inside of the neck of the bottle. All this with great deliberation.

At first Riderhood had sat with his footless glass extended at arm's length for filling, while the very deliberate stranger seemed absorbed in his preparations. But, gradually his arm reverted home to him, and his glass was lowered and lowered until he rested it upside down upon the table. By the same degrees his attention became concentrated on the knife. And now, as the man held out the bottle to fill all round, Riderhood stood up, leaned over the table to look closer at the knife, and stared from it to him.

'What's the matter?' asked the man.

'Why, I know that knife!' said Riderhood.

'Yes, I dare say you do.'

He motioned to him to hold up his glass, and filled it. Riderhood emptied it to the last drop and began again.

'That there knife—'

'Stop,' said the man, composedly. 'I was going to drink to your daughter. Your health, Miss Riderhood.'

'That knife was the knife of a seaman named George Radfoot.'

'It was.'

'That seaman was well beknown to me.'

'He was.'

'What's come to him?'

'Death has come to him. Death came to him in an ugly shape. He looked,' said the man, 'very horrible after it.'

'Arter what?' said Riderhood, with a frowning stare.

'After he was killed.'

'Killed? Who killed him?'

Only answering with a shrug, the man filled the footless glass, and Riderhood emptied it: looking amazedly from his daughter to his visitor.

'You don't mean to tell a honest man—' he was recommencing with his empty glass in his hand, when his eye became fascinated by the stranger's outer coat. He leaned across the table to see it nearer, touched the sleeve, turned the cuff to look at the sleeve-lining (the man, in his perfect composure, offering not the least objection), and exclaimed, 'It's my belief as this here coat was George Radfoot's too!'

'You are right. He wore it the last time you ever saw him, and the last time you ever will see him—in this world.'

'It's my belief you mean to tell me to my face you killed him!' exclaimed Riderhood; but, nevertheless, allowing his glass to be filled again.

The man only answered with another shrug, and showed no symptom of confusion.

'Wish I may die if I know what to be up to with this chap!' said Riderhood, after staring at him, and tossing his last glassful down his throat. 'Let's know what to make of you. Say something plain.'

'I will,' returned the other, leaning forward across the table, and speaking in a low impressive voice. 'What a liar you are!'

The honest witness rose, and made as though he would fling his glass in the man's face. The man not wincing, and merely shaking his forefinger half knowingly, half menacingly, the piece of honesty thought better of it and sat down again, putting the glass down too.

'And when you went to that lawyer yonder in the Temple with that invented story,' said the stranger, in an exasperatingly comfortable sort of confidence, 'you might have had your strong suspicions of a friend of your own, you know. I think you had, you know.'

'Me my suspicions? Of what friend?'

'Tell me again whose knife was this?' demanded the man.

'It was possessed by, and was the property of—him as I have made mention on,' said Riderhood, stupidly evading the actual mention of the name.

'Tell me again whose coat was this?'

'That there article of clothing likeways belonged to, and was wore by—him as I have made mention on,' was again the dull Old Bailey evasion.

'I suspect that you gave him the credit of the deed, and of keeping cleverly out of the way. But there was small cleverness in *his* keeping out of the way. The cleverness would have been, to have got back for one single instant to the light of the sun.'

'Things is come to a pretty pass,' growled Mr Riderhood, rising to his feet, goaded to stand at bay, 'when bullyers as is wearing dead men's clothes, and bullyers as is armed with dead men's knives, is to come into the houses of honest live men, getting their livings by the sweats of their brows, and is to make these here sort of charges with no rhyme and no reason, neither the one nor yet the other! Why should I have had my suspicions of him?'

'Because you knew him,' replied the man; 'because you had been one with him, and knew his real character under a fair outside; because on the night which you had afterwards reason to believe to be the very night of the murder, he came in here, within an hour of his having left his ship in the docks, and asked you in what lodgings he could find room. Was there no stranger with him?'

'I'll take my world-without-end everlasting Alfred David that YOU warn't with him,' answered Riderhood. 'You talk big, you do, but things look pretty black against yourself, to my thinking. You charge again' me that George Radfoot got lost sight of, and was no more thought of. What's that for a sailor? Why there's fifty such, out of sight and out of mind, ten times as long as him—through entering in different names, re-shipping when the out'ard voyage is made, and what not—a turning up to light every day about here, and no matter made of it. Ask my daughter. You could go on Poll Parroting enough with her, when I warn't come in: Poll Parrot a little with her on this pint. You and your suspicions of my suspicions of him! What are my suspicions of you? You tell me George Radfoot got killed. I ask you who done it and how you know it. You carry his knife and you wear his coat. I ask you how you come by 'em? Hand over that there bottle!' Here Mr Riderhood appeared to labour under a virtuous delusion that it was his own property. 'And you,' he added, turning to his daughter, as he filled the footless glass, 'if it warn't wasting good sherry wine on you, I'd chuck this at you, for Poll Parroting with this man. It's along of Poll Parroting that such like as him gets their suspicions, whereas I gets mine by argueyment, and being nat'rally a honest man, and sweating away at the brow as a honest man ought.' Here he filled the footless goblet again, and stood chewing one half of its contents and looking down into the other as he slowly rolled the wine about in the glass; while Pleasant, whose sympathetic hair had come down on her being apostrophised, rearranged it, much in the style of the tail of a horse when proceeding to market to be sold.

'Well? Have you finished?' asked the strange man.

'No,' said Riderhood, 'I ain't. Far from it. Now then! I want to know how George Radfoot come by his death, and how you come by his kit?'

'If you ever do know, you won't know now.'

'And next I want to know,' proceeded Riderhood 'whether you mean to charge that what-you-may-call-it-murder—'

'Harmon murder, father,' suggested Pleasant.

'No Poll Parroting!' he vociferated, in return. 'Keep your mouth shut!—I want to know, you sir, whether you charge that there crime on George Radfoot?'

'If you ever do know, you won't know now.'

'Perhaps you done it yourself?' said Riderhood, with a threatening action.

'I alone know,' returned the man, sternly shaking his head, 'the mysteries of that crime. I alone know that your trumped-up story cannot possibly be true. I alone know that it must be altogether false, and that you must know it to be altogether false. I come here to-night to tell you so much of what I know, and no more.'

Mr Riderhood, with his crooked eye upon his visitor, meditated for some moments, and then refilled his glass, and tipped the contents down his throat in three tips.

'Shut the shop-door!' he then said to his daughter, putting the glass suddenly down. 'And turn the key and stand by it! If you know all this, you sir,' getting, as he spoke, between the visitor and the door, 'why han't you gone to Lawyer Light-wood?'

'That, also, is alone known to myself,' was the cool answer.

'Don't you know that, if you didn't do the deed, what you say you could tell is worth from five to ten thousand pound?' asked Riderhood.

'I know it very well, and when I claim the money you shall share it.'

The honest man paused, and drew a little nearer to the visitor, and a little further from the door.

'I know it,' repeated the man, quietly, 'as well as I know that you and George Radfoot were one together in more than one dark business; and as well as I know that you, Roger Riderhood, conspired against an innocent man for blood-money; and as well as I know that I can—and that I swear I will!—give you up on both scores, and be the proof against you in my own person, if you defy me!'

'Father!' cried Pleasant, from the door. 'Don't defy him! Give way to him! Don't get into more trouble, father!'

'Will you leave off a Poll Parroting, I ask you?' cried Mr Riderhood, half beside himself between the two. Then, propitiatingly and crawlingly: 'You sir! You han't said what you want of me. Is it fair, is it worthy of yourself, to talk of my defying you afore ever you say what you want of me?'

'I don't want much,' said the man. 'This accusation of yours must not be left half made and half unmade. What was done for the blood-money must be thoroughly undone.'

'Well; but Shipmate—'

'Don't call me Shipmate,' said the man.

'Captain, then,' urged Mr Riderhood; 'there! You won't object to Captain. It's a honourable title, and you fully look it. Captain! Ain't the man dead? Now I ask you fair. Ain't Gaffer dead?'

'Well,' returned the other, with impatience, 'yes, he is dead. What then?'

'Can words hurt a dead man, Captain? I only ask you fair.'

'They can hurt the memory of a dead man, and they can hurt his living children. How many children had this man?'

'Meaning Gaffer, Captain?'

'Of whom else are we speaking?' returned the other, with a movement of his foot, as if Rogue Riderhood were beginning to sneak before him in the body as well as the spirit, and he spurned him off. 'I have heard of a daughter, and a son. I ask for information; I ask *your* daughter; I prefer to speak to her. What children did Hexam leave?'

Pleasant, looking to her father for permission to reply, that honest man exclaimed with great bitterness:

'Why the devil don't you answer the Captain? You can Poll Parrot enough when you ain't wanted to Poll Parrot, you perwerse jade!'

Thus encouraged, Pleasant explained that there were only Lizzie, the daughter in question, and the youth. Both very respectable, she added.

'It is dreadful that any stigma should attach to them,' said the visitor, whom the consideration rendered so uneasy that he rose, and paced to and fro, muttering, 'Dreadful! Unforeseen? How could it be foreseen!' Then he stopped, and asked aloud: 'Where do they live?'

Pleasant further explained that only the daughter had resided with the father at the time of his accidental death, and that she had immediately afterwards quitted the neighbourhood.

'I know that,' said the man, 'for I have been to the place they dwelt in, at the time of the inquest. Could you quietly find out for me where she lives now?'

Pleasant had no doubt she could do that. Within what time, did she think? Within a day. The visitor said that was well, and he would return for the information, relying on its being obtained. To this dialogue Riderhood had attended in silence, and he now obsequiously bespake the Captain.

'Captain! Mentioning them unfort'net words of mine respecting Gaffer, it is contrairily to be bore in mind that Gaffer always were a precious rascal, and that his line were a thieving line. Likeways when I went to them two Governors, Lawyer Lightwood and the t'other Governor, with my information, I may have been a little over-eager for the cause of justice, or (to put it another way) a little over-stimulated by them feelings which rouses a man up, when a pot of money is going about, to get his hand into that pot of money for his family's sake. Besides which, I think the wine of them two Governors was—I will not say a hocussed wine, but fur from a wine as was elthy for the mind. And there's another thing to be remembered, Captain. Did I stick to them words when Gaffer was no more, and did I say bold to them two Governors, "Governors both, wot I informed I still inform; wot was took down I hold to"? No. I says, frank and open—no shuffling, mind you, Captain!—"I may have been mistook, I've been a thinking of it, it mayn't have been took down correct on this and that, and I won't swear to thick and thin, I'd rayther forfeit your good opinions than do it." And so far as I know,' concluded Mr Riderhood, by way of proof and evidence to character, 'I *have* actiwally forfeited the good opinions of several persons—even your own, Captain, if I understand your words—but I'd sooner do it than be forswore. There; if that's conspiracy, call me conspirator.'

'You shall sign,' said the visitor, taking very little heed of this oration, 'a statement that it was all utterly false, and the poor girl shall have it. I will bring it with me for your signature, when I come again.'

'When might you be expected, Captain?' inquired Riderhood, again dubiously getting between him and door.

'Quite soon enough for you. I shall not disappoint you; don't be afraid.'

'Might you be inclined to leave any name, Captain?'

'No, not at all. I have no such intention.'

' ''Shall'' is summ'at of a hard word, Captain,' urged Riderhood, still feebly dodging between him and the door, as he advanced. 'When you say a man ''shall'' sign this and that and t'other, Captain, you order him about in a grand sort of a way. Don't it seem so to yourself?'

The man stood still, and angrily fixed him with his eyes.

'Father, father!' entreated Pleasant, from the door, with her disengaged hand nervously trembling at her lips; 'don't! Don't get into trouble any more!'

'Hear me out, Captain, hear me out! All I was wishing to mention, Captain, afore you took your departer,' said the sneaking Mr Riderhood, falling out of his path, 'was, your handsome words relating to the reward.'

'When I claim it,' said the man, in a tone which seemed to leave some such words as 'you dog,' very distinctly understood, 'you shall share it.'

Looking stedfastly at Riderhood, he once more said in a low voice, this time with a grim sort of admiration of him as a perfect piece of evil, 'What a liar you are!' and, nodding his head twice or thrice over the compliment, passed out of the shop. But, to Pleasant he said good-night kindly.

The honest man who gained his living by the sweat of his brow remained in a state akin to stupefaction, until the footless glass and the unfinished bottle conveyed themselves into his mind. From his mind he conveyed them into his hands, and so conveyed the last of the wine into his stomach. When that was done, he awoke to a clear perception that Poll Parroting was solely chargeable with what had passed. Therefore, not to be remiss in his duty as a father, he threw a pair of sea-boots at Pleasant, which she ducked to avoid, and then cried, poor thing, using her hair for a pocket-handkerchief.

Chapter 13
A Solo and a Duett

THE wind was blowing so hard when the visitor came out at the shop-door into the darkness and dirt of Limehouse Hole, that it almost blew him in again. Doors were slamming violently, lamps were flickering or blown out, signs were rocking in their frames, the water of the kennels, wind-dispersed, flew about in drops like rain. Indifferent to the weather, and even preferring it to better weather for its clearance of the streets, the man looked about him with a scrutinizing glance. 'Thus much I know,' he murmured. 'I have never been here since that night, and never was here before that night, but thus much I recognize. I wonder which way did we take when we came out of that shop. We turned to the right as I have turned, but I can recall no more. Did we go by this alley? Or down that little lane?'

He tried both, but both confused him equally, and he came straying back to the same spot. 'I remember there were poles pushed out of upper windows on which clothes were drying, and I remember a low public-house, and the sound flowing down a narrow passage belonging to it of the scraping of a fiddle and the shuffling of feet. But here are all these things in the lane, and here are all these things in the alley. And I have nothing else in my mind but a wall, a dark doorway, a flight of stairs, and a room.'

He tried a new direction, but made nothing of it; walls, dark doorways, flights of stairs and rooms, were too abundant. And, like most people so puzzled, he again and again described a circle, and found himself at the point from which he had begun. 'This is like what I have read in narratives of escape from prison,' said he, 'where the little track of the fugitives in the night always seems to take the shape of the great round world, on which they wander; as if it were a secret law.'

Here he ceased to be the oakum-headed, oakum-whiskered man on whom Miss Pleasant Riderhood had looked, and, allowing for his being still wrapped in a nautical overcoat, became as like that same lost wanted Mr Julius Handford, as never man was like another in this world. In the breast of the coat he stowed the bristling hair and whisker, in a moment, as the favouring wind went with him down a solitary place that it had swept clear of passengers. Yet in that same moment he was the Secretary also, Mr Boffin's Secretary. For John Rokesmith, too, was as like that same lost wanted Mr Julius Handford as never man was like another in this world.

'I have no clue to the scene of my death,' said he. 'Not that it matters now. But having risked discovery by venturing here at all, I should have been glad to track some part of the way.' With which singular words he abandoned his search, came up out of Limehouse Hole, and took the way past Limehouse Church. At the great iron gate of the churchyard he stopped and looked in. He looked up at the high tower spectrally resisting the wind, and he looked round at the white tombstones, like enough to the dead in their winding-sheets, and he counted the nine tolls of the clock-bell.

'It is a sensation not experienced by many mortals,' said he, 'to be looking into a churchyard on a wild windy night, and to feel that I no more hold a place among the living than these dead do, and even to know that I lie buried somewhere else, as they lie buried here. Nothing uses me to it. A spirit that was once a man could hardly feel stranger or lonelier, going unrecognized among mankind, than I feel.

'But this is the fanciful side of the situation. It has a real side, so difficult that, though I think of it every day, I never thoroughly think it out. Now, let me determine to think it out as I walk home. I know I evade it, as many men—perhaps most men—do evade thinking their way through their greatest perplexity. I will try to pin myself to mine. Don't evade it, John Harmon; don't evade it; think it out!

'When I came to England, attracted to the country with which I had none but most miserable associations, by the accounts of my fine inheritance that found me abroad, I came back, shrinking from my father's money, shrinking from my father's memory, mistrustful of being forced on a mercenary wife, mistrustful of my father's intention in thrusting that marriage on me, mistrustful that I was already growing avaricious, mistrustful that I was slackening in gratitude to the two dear noble honest friends who had made the only sunlight in my childish life or that of my heartbroken sister. I came back, timid, divided in my mind, afraid of myself and everybody here, knowing of nothing but wretchedness that my father's wealth had ever brought about. Now, stop, and so far think it out, John Harmon. Is that so? That is exactly so.

'On board serving as third mate was George Radfoot. I knew nothing of him. His name first became known to me about a week before we sailed, through my being accosted by one of the ship-agent's clerks as "Mr Radfoot." It was one day when I had gone aboard to look to my preparations, and the clerk, coming behind me as I stood on deck, tapped me on the shoulder, and said, "Mr Radfoot, look here," referring to some papers that he had in his hand. And my name first became known to Radfoot, through another clerk within a day or two, and while the ship was yet in port, coming up behind him, tapping him on the shoulder and beginning, "I beg your pardon, Mr Harmon—." I believe we were alike in bulk and stature but not otherwise, and that we were not strikingly alike, even in those respects, when we were together and could be compared.

'However, a sociable word or two on these mistakes became an easy introduction between us, and the weather was hot, and he helped me to a cool cabin on deck alongside his own, and his first school had been at Brussels as mine had been, and he had learnt French as I had learnt it, and he had a little history of himself to relate—God only knows how much of it true, and how much of it false—that had its likeness to mine. I had been a seaman too. So we got to be confidential together, and the more easily yet, because he and every one on board had known by general rumour what I was making the voyage to England for. By such degrees and means, he came to the knowledge of my uneasiness of mind, and of its setting at that time in the direction of desiring to see and form some judgment of my allotted wife, before she could possibly know me for myself; also to try Mrs Boffin and give her a glad surprise. So the plot was made out of our getting common sailors' dresses (as he was able to guide me about London), and throwing ourselves in Bella Wilfer's neighbourhood, and trying to put ourselves in her way, and doing whatever chance might favour on the spot, and seeing what came of it. If nothing came of it, I should be no worse off, and there would merely be a short delay in my presenting myself to Lightwood. I have all these facts right? Yes. They are all accurately right.

'His advantage in all this was, that for a time I was to be lost. It might be for a day or for two days, but I must be lost sight of on landing, or there would be recognition, anticipation, and failure. Therefore, I disembarked with my valise in my hand—as Potterson the steward and Mr Jacob Kibble my fellow-passenger afterwards remembered—and waited for him in the dark by that very Limehouse Church which is now behind me.

'As I had always shunned the port of London, I only knew the church through his pointing out its spire from on board. Perhaps I might recall, if it were any good to try, the way by which I went to it alone from the river; but how we two went from it to Riderhood's shop, I don't know—any more than I know what turns we took and doubles we made, after we left it. The way was purposely confused, no doubt.

'But let me go on thinking the facts out, and avoid confusing them with my speculations. Whether he took me by a straight way or a crooked way, what is that to the purpose now? Steady, John Harmon.

'When we stopped at Riderhood's, and he asked that scoundrel a question or two, purporting to refer only to the lodging-houses in which there was accommodation for us, had I the least suspicion of him? None. Certainly none until afterwards when I held the clue. I think he must have got from Riderhood in a paper, the drug, or whatever it was, that afterwards stupefied me, but I am far from sure. All I felt safe in charging on him to-night, was old companionship in villainy between them. Their undisguised intimacy, and the character I now know Riderhood to bear, made that not at all adventurous. But I am not clear about the drug. Thinking out the circumstances on which I found my suspicion, they are only two. One: I remember his changing a small folded paper from one pocket to another, after we came out, which he had not touched before. Two: I now know Riderhood to have been previously taken up for being concerned in the robbery of an unlucky seaman, to whom some such poison had been given.

'It is my conviction that we cannot have gone a mile from that shop, before we came to the wall, the dark doorway, the flight of stairs, and the room. The night was particularly dark and it rained hard. As I think the circumstances back, I hear the rain splashing on the stone pavement of the passage, which was not under cover. The room overlooked the river, or a dock, or a creek, and the tide was out. Being possessed of the time down to that point, I know by the hour that it must have been about low water; but while the coffee was getting ready, I drew back the curtain (a dark-brown curtain), and, looking out, knew by the kind of reflection below, of the few neighbouring lights, that they were reflected in tidal mud.

'He had carried under his arm a canvas bag, containing a suit of his clothes. I had no change of outer clothes with me, as I was to buy slops. "You are very wet, Mr Harmon,"—I can hear him saying—"and I am quite dry under this good waterproof coat. Put on these clothes of mine. You may find on trying them that they will answer your purpose to-morrow, as well as the slops you mean to buy, or better. While you change, I'll hurry the hot coffee." When he came back, I had his clothes on, and there was a black man with him, wearing a linen jacket, like a steward, who put the smoking coffee on the table in a tray and never looked at me. I am so far literal and exact? Literal and exact, I am certain.

'Now, I pass to sick and deranged impressions; they are so strong, that I rely upon them; but there are spaces between them that I know nothing about, and they are not pervaded by any idea of time.

'I had drank some coffee, when to my sense of sight he began to swell immensely, and something urged me to rush at him. We had a struggle near the door. He got from me, through my not knowing where to strike, in the whirling round of the room, and the flashing of flames of fire between us. I dropped down. Lying helpless on the ground, I was turned over by a foot. I was dragged by the neck into a corner. I heard men speak together. I was turned over by other feet. I saw a figure like myself lying dressed in my clothes on a bed. What might have been, for anything I knew, a silence of days, weeks, months, years, was broken by a violent wrestling of men all over the room. The figure like myself was assailed, and my valise was in its hand. I was trodden upon and fallen over. I heard a noise of blows, and thought it was a wood-cutter cutting down a tree. I could not have said that my name was John Harmon—I could not have thought it—I didn't know it—but when I heard the blows, I thought of the wood-cutter and his axe, and had some dead idea that I was lying in a forest.

'This is still correct? Still correct, with the exception that I cannot possibly express it to myself without using the word I. But it was not I. There was no such thing as I, within my knowledge.

'It was only after a downward slide through something like a tube, and then a great noise and a sparkling and crackling as of fires, that the consciousness came upon me, "This is John Harmon drowning! John Harmon, struggle for your life. John Harmon, call on Heaven and save yourself!" I think I cried it out aloud in a great agony, and then a heavy horrid unintelligible something vanished, and it was I who was struggling there alone in the water.

'I was very weak and faint, frightfully oppressed with drowsiness, and driving fast with the tide. Looking over the black water, I saw the lights racing past me on the two banks of the river, as if they were eager to be gone and leave me dying in the dark. The tide was running down, but I knew nothing of up or down then. When, guiding myself safely with Heaven's assistance before the fierce set of the water, I at last caught at a boat moored, one of a tier of boats at a causeway, I was sucked under her, and came up, only just alive, on the other side.

'Was I long in the water? Long enough to be chilled to the heart, but I don't know how long. Yet the cold was merciful, for it was the cold night air and the rain that restored me from a swoon on the stones of the causeway. They naturally supposed me to have toppled in, drunk, when I crept to the public-house it belonged to; for I had no notion where I was, and could not articulate—through the poison that had made me insensible having affected my speech—and I supposed the night to be the previous night, as it was still dark and raining. But I had lost twenty-four hours.

'I have checked the calculation often, and it must have been two nights that I lay recovering in that public-house. Let me see. Yes. I am sure it was while I lay in that bed there, that the thought entered my head of turning the danger I had passed through, to the account of being for some time supposed to have disappeared mysteriously, and of proving Bella. The dread of our being forced on one another, and perpetuating the fate that seemed to have fallen on my father's riches—the fate that they should lead to nothing but evil—was strong upon the moral timidity that dates from my childhood with my poor sister.

'As to this hour I cannot understand that side of the river where I recovered the shore, being the opposite side to that on which I was ensnared, I shall never understand it now. Even at this moment, while I leave the river behind me, going home, I cannot conceive that it rolls between me and that spot, or that the sea is where it is. But this is not thinking it out; this is making a leap to the present time.

'I could not have done it, but for the fortune in the water-proof belt round my body. Not a great fortune, forty and odd pounds for the inheritor of a hundred and odd thousand! But it was enough. Without it I must have disclosed myself. Without it, I could never have gone to that Exchequer Coffee House, or taken Mrs Wilfer's lodgings.

'Some twelve days I lived at that hotel, before the night when I saw the corpse of Radfoot at the Police Station. The inexpressible mental horror that I laboured under, as one of the consequences of the poison, makes the interval seem greatly longer, but I know it cannot have been longer. That suffering has gradually weakened and weakened since, and has only come upon me by starts, and I hope I am free from it now; but even now, I have sometimes to think, constrain myself, and stop before speaking, or I could not say the words I want to say.

'Again I ramble away from thinking it out to the end. It is not so far to the end that I need be tempted to break off. Now, on straight!

'I examined the newspapers every day for tidings that I was missing, but saw none. Going out that night to walk (for I kept retired while it was light), I found a crowd assembled round a placard posted at Whitehall. It described myself, John Harmon, as found dead and mutilated in the river under circumstances of strong suspicion, described my dress, described the papers in my pockets, and stated where I was lying for recognition. In a wild incautious way I hurried there, and there—with the horror of the death I had escaped, before my eyes in its most appalling shape, added to the inconceivable horror tormenting me at that time when the poisonous stuff was strongest on me—I perceived that Radfoot had been murdered by some unknown hands for the money for which he would have murdered me, and that probably we had both been shot into the river from the same dark place into the same dark tide, when the stream ran deep and strong.

'That night I almost gave up my mystery, though I sus-pected no one, could offer no information, knew absolutely nothing save that the murdered man was not I, but Radfoot. Next day while I hesitated, and next day while I hesitated, it seemed as if the whole country were determined to have me dead. The Inquest declared me dead, the Government proclaimed me dead;

I could not listen at my fireside for five minutes to the outer noises, but it was borne into my ears that I was dead.

'So John Harmon died, and Julius Handford disappeared, and John Rokesmith was born. John Rokesmith's intent to-night has been to repair a wrong that he could never have imagined possible, coming to his ears through the Lightwood talk related to him, and which he is bound by every consideration to remedy. In that intent John Rokesmith will persevere, as his duty is.

'Now, is it all thought out? All to this time? Nothing omitted? No, nothing. But beyond this time? To think it out through the future, is a harder though a much shorter task than to think it out through the past. John Harmon is dead. Should John Harmon come to life?

'If yes, why? If no, why?'

'Take yes, first. To enlighten human Justice concerning the offence of one far beyond it who may have a living mother. To enlighten it with the lights of a stone passage, a flight of stairs, a brown window-curtain, and a black man. To come into possession of my father's money, and with it sordidly to buy a beautiful creature whom I love—I cannot help it; reason has nothing to do with it; I love her against reason—but who would as soon love me for my own sake, as she would love the beggar at the corner. What a use for the money, and how worthy of its old misuses!

'Now, take no. The reasons why John Harmon should not come to life. Because he has passively allowed these dear old faithful friends to pass into possession of the property. Because he sees them happy with it, making a good use of it, effacing the old rust and tarnish on the money. Because they have virtually adopted Bella, and will provide for her. Because there is affection enough in her nature, and warmth enough in her heart, to develop into something enduringly good, under favourable conditions. Because her faults have been intensified by her place in my father's will, and she is already growing better. Because her marriage with John Harmon, after what I have heard from her own lips, would be a shocking mockery, of which both she and I must always be conscious, and which would degrade her in her mind, and me in mine, and each of us in the other's. Because if John Harmon comes to life and does not marry her, the property falls into the very hands that hold it now.

'What would I have? Dead, I have found the true friends of my lifetime still as true as tender and as faithful as when I was alive, and making my memory an incentive to good actions done in my name. Dead, I have found them when they might have slighted my name, and passed greedily over my grave to ease and wealth, lingering by the way, like single-hearted children, to recall their love for me when I was a poor frightened child. Dead, I have heard from the woman who would have been my wife if I had lived, the revolting truth that I should have purchased her, caring nothing for me, as a Sultan buys a slave.

'What would I have? If the dead could know, or do know, how the living use them, who among the hosts of dead has found a more disinterested fidelity on earth than I? Is not that enough for me? If I had come back, these noble creatures would have welcomed me, wept over me, given up everything to me with joy. I did not come back, and they have passed unspoiled into my place. Let them rest in it, and let Bella rest in hers.

'What course for me then? This. To live the same quiet Secretary life, carefully avoiding chances of recognition, until they shall have become more accustomed to their altered state, and until the great swarm of swindlers under many names shall have found newer prey. By that time, the method I am establishing through all the affairs, and with which I will every day take new pains to make them both familiar, will be, I may hope, a machine in such working order as that they can keep it going. I know I need but ask of their generosity, to have. When the right time comes, I will ask no more than will replace me in my former path of life, and John Rokesmith shall tread it as contentedly as he may. But John Harmon shall come back no more.

'That I may never, in the days to come afar off, have any weak misgiving that Bella might, in any contingency, have taken me for my own sake if I had plainly asked her, I *will* plainly ask her: proving beyond all question what I already know too well. And now it is all thought out, from the beginning to the end, and my mind is easier.'

So deeply engaged had the living-dead man been, in thus communing with himself, that he had regarded neither the wind nor the way, and had resisted the former instinctively as he had pursued the latter. But being now come into the City, where there was a coach-stand, he stood irresolute whether to go to his lodgings, or to go first to Mr Boffin's house. He decided to go round by the house, arguing, as he carried his overcoat upon his arm, that it was less likely to attract notice if left there, than if taken to Holloway: both Mrs Wilfer and Miss Lavinia being ravenously curious touching every article of which the lodger stood possessed.

Arriving at the house, he found that Mr and Mrs Boffin were out, but that Miss Wilfer was in the drawing-room. Miss Wilfer had remained at home, in consequence of not feeling very well, and had inquired in the evening if Mr Rokesmith were in his room.

'Make my compliments to Miss Wilfer, and say I am here now.'

Miss Wilfer's compliments came down in return, and, if it were not too much trouble, would Mr Rokesmith be so kind as to come up before he went?

It was not too much trouble, and Mr Rokesmith came up.

Oh she looked very pretty, she looked very, very pretty! If the father of the late John Harmon had but left his money unconditionally to his son, and if his son had but lighted on this loveable girl for himself, and had the happiness to make her loving as well as loveable!

'Dear me! Are you not well, Mr Rokesmith?'

'Yes, quite well. I was sorry to hear, when I came in, that *you* were not.'

'A mere nothing. I had a headache—gone now—and was not quite fit for a hot theatre, so I stayed at home. I asked you if you were not well, because you look so white.'

'Do I? I have had a busy evening.'

She was on a low ottoman before the fire, with a little shining jewel of a table, and her book and her work, beside her. Ah! what a different life the late John Harmon's, if it had been his happy privilege to take his place upon that ottoman, and draw his arm about that waist, and say, 'I hope the time has been long without me? What a Home Goddess you look, my darling!'

But, the present John Rokesmith, far removed from the late John Harmon, remained standing at a distance. A little distance in respect of space, but a great distance in respect of separation.

'Mr Rokesmith,' said Bella, taking up her work, and inspecting it all round the corners, 'I wanted to say something to you when I could have the opportunity, as an explanation why I was rude to you the other day. You have no right to think ill of me, sir.'

The sharp little way in which she darted a look at him, half sensitively injured, and half pettishly, would have been very much admired by the late John Harmon.

'You don't know how well I think of you, Miss Wilfer.'

'Truly, you must have a very high opinion of me, Mr Rokesmith, when you believe that in prosperity I neglect and forget my old home.'

'Do I believe so?'

'You *did*, sir, at any rate,' returned Bella.

'I took the liberty of reminding you of a little omission into which you had fallen—insensibly and naturally fallen. It was no more than that.'

'And I beg leave to ask you, Mr Rokesmith,' said Bella, 'why you took that liberty?—I hope there is no offence in the phrase; it is your own, remember.'

'Because I am truly, deeply, profoundly interested in you, Miss Wilfer. Because I wish to see you always at your best. Because I—shall I go on?'

'No, sir,' returned Bella, with a burning face, 'you have said more than enough. I beg that you will *not* go on. If you have any generosity, any honour, you will say no more.'

The late John Harmon, looking at the proud face with the downcast eyes, and at the quick breathing as it stirred the fall of bright brown hair over the beautiful neck, would probably have remained silent.

'I wish to speak to you, sir,' said Bella, 'once for all, and I don't know how to do it. I have sat here all this evening, wishing to speak to you, and determining to speak to you, and feeling that I must. I beg for a moment's time.'

He remained silent, and she remained with her face averted, sometimes making a slight movement as if she would turn and speak. At length she did so.

'You know how I am situated here, sir, and you know how I am situated at home. I must speak to you for myself, since there is no one about me whom I could ask to do so. It is not generous in you, it is not honourable in you, to conduct yourself towards me as you do.'

'Is it ungenerous or dishonourable to be devoted to you; fascinated by you?'

'Preposterous!' said Bella.

The late John Harmon might have thought it rather a contemptuous and lofty word of repudiation.

'I now feel obliged to go on,' pursued the Secretary, 'though it were only in self-explanation and self-defence. I hope, Miss Wilfer, that it is not unpardonable—even in me—to make an honest declaration of an honest devotion to you.'

'An honest declaration!' repeated Bella, with emphasis.

'Is it otherwise?'

'I must request, sir,' said Bella, taking refuge in a touch of timely resentment, 'that I may not be questioned. You must excuse me if I decline to be cross-examined.'

'Oh, Miss Wilfer, this is hardly charitable. I ask you nothing but what your own emphasis suggests. However, I waive even that question. But what I have declared, I take my stand by. I cannot recall the avowal of my earnest and deep attachment to you, and I do not recall it.'

'I reject it, sir,' said Bella.

'I should be blind and deaf if I were not prepared for the reply. Forgive my offence, for it carries its punishment with it.'

'What punishment?' asked Bella.

'Is my present endurance none? But excuse me; I did not mean to cross-examine you again.'

'You take advantage of a hasty word of mine,' said Bella with a little sting of self-reproach, 'to make me seem—I don't know what. I spoke without consideration when I used it. If that was bad, I am sorry; but you repeat it after consideration, and that seems to me to be at least no better. For the rest, I beg it may be understood, Mr Rokesmith, that there is an end of this between us, now and for ever.'

'Now and for ever,' he repeated.

'Yes. I appeal to you, sir,' proceeded Bella with increasing spirit, 'not to pursue me. I appeal to you not to take advantage of your position in this house to make my position in it distressing and disagreeable. I appeal to you to discontinue your habit of making your misplaced attentions as plain to Mrs Boffin as to me.'

'Have I done so?'

'I should think you have,' replied Bella. 'In any case it is not your fault if you have not, Mr Rokesmith.'

'I hope you are wrong in that impression. I should be very sorry to have justified it. I think I have not. For the future there is no apprehension. It is all over.'

'I am much relieved to hear it,' said Bella. 'I have far other views in life, and why should you waste your own?'

'Mine!' said the Secretary. 'My life!'

His curious tone caused Bella to glance at the curious smile with which he said it. It was gone as he glanced back. 'Pardon me, Miss Wilfer,' he proceeded, when their eyes met; 'you have used some hard words, for which I do not doubt you have a justification in your mind, that I do not understand. Ungenerous and dishonourable. In what?'

'I would rather not be asked,' said Bella, haughtily looking down.

'I would rather not ask, but the question is imposed upon me. Kindly explain; or if not kindly, justly.'

'Oh, sir!' said Bella, raising her eyes to his, after a little struggle to forbear, 'is it generous and honourable to use the power here which your favour with Mr and Mrs Boffin and your ability in your place give you, against me?'

'Against you?'

'Is it generous and honourable to form a plan for gradually bringing their influence to bear upon a suit which I have shown you that I do not like, and which I tell you that I utterly reject?'

The late John Harmon could have borne a good deal, but he would have been cut to the heart by such a suspicion as this.

'Would it be generous and honourable to step into your place—if you did so, for I don't know that you did, and I hope you did not—anticipating, or knowing beforehand, that I should come here, and designing to take me at this disadvantage?'

'This mean and cruel disadvantage,' said the Secretary.

'Yes,' assented Bella.

The Secretary kept silence for a little while; then merely said, 'You are wholly mistaken, Miss Wilfer; wonderfully mistaken. I cannot say, however, that it is your fault. If I deserve better things of you, you do not know it.'

'At least, sir,' retorted Bella, with her old indignation rising, 'you know the history of my being here at all. I have heard Mr Boffin say that you are master of every line and word of that will, as you are master of all his affairs. And was it not enough that I should have been willed away, like a horse, or a dog, or a bird; but must you too begin to dispose of me in your mind, and speculate in me, as soon as I had ceased to be the talk and the laugh of the town? Am I for ever to be made the property of strangers?'

'Believe me,' returned the Secretary, 'you are wonderfully mistaken.'

'I should be glad to know it,' answered Bella.

'I doubt if you ever will. Good-night. Of course I shall be careful to conceal any traces of this interview from Mr and Mrs Boffin, as long as I remain here. Trust me, what you have complained of is at an end for ever.'

'I am glad I have spoken, then, Mr Rokesmith. It has been painful and difficult, but it is done. If I have hurt you, I hope you will forgive me. I am inexperienced and impetuous, and I have been a little spoilt; but I really am not so bad as I dare say I appear, or as you think me.'

He quitted the room when Bella had said this, relenting in her wilful inconsistent way. Left alone, she threw herself back on her ottoman, and said, 'I didn't know the lovely woman was such a Dragon!' Then, she got up and looked in the glass, and said to her image, 'You have been positively swelling your features, you little fool!' Then, she took an impatient walk to the other end of the room and back, and said, 'I wish Pa was here to have a talk about an avaricious marriage; but he is better away, poor dear, for I know I should pull his hair if he *was* here.' And then she threw her work away, and threw her book after it, and sat down and hummed a tune, and hummed it out of tune, and quarrelled with it.

And John Rokesmith, what did he?

He went down to his room, and buried John Harmon many additional fathoms deep. He took his hat, and walked out, and, as he went to Holloway or anywhere else—not at all minding where—heaped mounds upon mounds of earth over John Harmon's grave. His walking did not bring him home until the dawn of day. And so busy had he been all night, piling and piling weights upon weights of earth above John Harmon's grave, that by that time John Harmon lay buried under a whole Alpine range; and still the Sexton Rokesmith accumulated mountains over him, lightening his labour with the dirge, 'Cover him, crush him, keep him down!'

Chapter 14
Strong of Purpose

THE sexton-task of piling earth above John Harmon all night long, was not conducive to sound sleep; but Rokesmith had some broken morning rest, and rose strengthened in his purpose. It was all over now. No ghost should trouble Mr and Mrs Boffin's peace; invisible and voiceless, the ghost should look on for a little while longer at the state of existence out of which it had departed, and then should for ever cease to haunt the scenes in which it had no place.

He went over it all again. He had lapsed into the condition in which he found himself, as many a man lapses into many a condition, without perceiving the accumulative power of its separate circumstances. When in the distrust engendered by his wretched childhood and the action for evil—never yet for good within his knowledge then—of his father and his father's wealth on all within their influence, he conceived the idea of his first deception, it was meant to be harmless, it was to last but a few hours or days, it was to involve in it only the girl so capriciously forced upon him and upon whom he was so capriciously forced, and it was honestly meant well towards her. For, if he had found her unhappy in the prospect of that marriage (through her heart inclining to another man or for any other cause), he would seriously have said: 'This is another of the old perverted uses of the misery-making money. I will let it go to my and my sister's only protectors and friends.' When the snare into which he fell so outstripped his first intention as that he found himself placarded by the police authorities upon the London walls for dead, he confusedly accepted the aid that fell upon him, without considering how firmly it must seem to fix the Boffins in their accession to the fortune. When he saw them, and knew them, and even from his vantage-ground of inspection could find no flaw in them, he asked himself, 'And shall I come to life to dispossess such people as these?' There was no good to set against the putting of them to that hard proof. He had heard from Bella's own lips when he stood tapping at the door on that night of his taking the lodgings, that the marriage would have been on her part thoroughly mercenary. He had since tried her, in his own unknown person and supposed station, and she not only rejected his advances but resented them. Was it for him to have the shame of buying her, or the meanness of punishing her? Yet, by coming to life and accepting the condition of the inheritance, he must do the former; and by coming to life and rejecting it, he must do the latter.

Another consequence that he had never foreshadowed, was the implication of an innocent man in his supposed murder. He would obtain complete retraction from the accuser, and set the wrong right; but clearly the wrong could never have been done if he had never planned a deception. Then, whatever inconvenience or distress of mind the deception cost him, it was manful repentantly to accept as among its consequences, and make no complaint.

Thus John Rokesmith in the morning, and it buried John Harmon still many fathoms deeper than he had been buried in the night.

Going out earlier than he was accustomed to do, he encountered the cherub at the door. The cherub's way was for a certain space his way, and they walked together.

It was impossible not to notice the change in the cherub's appearance. The cherub felt very conscious of it, and modestly remarked: 'A present from my daughter Bella, Mr Rokesmith.'

The words gave the Secretary a stroke of pleasure, for he remembered the fifty pounds, and he still loved the girl. No doubt it was very weak—it always *is* very weak, some authorities hold—but he loved the girl.

'I don't know whether you happen to have read many books of African Travel, Mr Rokesmith?' said R. W.

'I have read several.'

'Well, you know, there's usually a King George, or a King Boy, or a King Sambo, or a King Bill, or Bull, or Rum, or Junk, or whatever name the sailors may have happened to give him.'

'Where?' asked Rokesmith.

'Anywhere. Anywhere in Africa, I mean. Pretty well everywhere, I may say; for black kings are cheap—and *I* think' —said R. W., with an apologetic air, 'nasty'.

'I am much of your opinion, Mr Wilfer. You were going to say—?'

'I was going to say, the king is generally dressed in a London hat only, or a Manchester pair of braces, or one epaulette, or an uniform coat with his legs in the sleeves, or something of that kind.'

'Just so,' said the Secretary.

'In confidence, I assure you, Mr Rokesmith,' observed the cheerful cherub, 'that when more of my family were at home and to be provided for, I used to remind myself immensely of that king. You have no idea, as a single man, of the difficulty I have had in wearing more than one good article at a time.'

'I can easily believe it, Mr Wilfer.'

'I only mention it,' said R. W. in the warmth of his heart, 'as a proof of the amiable, delicate, and considerate affection of my daughter Bella. If she had been a little spoilt, I couldn't have thought so very much of it, under the circumstances. But no, not a bit. And she is so very pretty! I hope you agree with me in finding her very pretty, Mr Rokesmith?'

'Certainly I do. Every one must.'

'I hope so,' said the cherub. 'Indeed, I have no doubt of it. This is a great advancement for her in life, Mr Rokesmith. A great opening of her prospects?'

'Miss Wilfer could have no better friends than Mr and Mrs Boffin.'

'Impossible!' said the gratified cherub. 'Really I begin to think things are very well as they are. If Mr John Harmon had lived—'

'He is better dead,' said the Secretary.

'No, I won't go so far as to say that,' urged the cherub, a little remonstrant against the very decisive and unpitying tone; 'but he mightn't have suited Bella, or Bella mightn't have suited him, or fifty things, whereas now I hope she can choose for herself.'

'Has she—as you place the confidence in me of speaking on the subject, you will excuse my asking—has she—perhaps—chosen?' faltered the Secretary.

'Oh dear no!' returned R. W.

'Young ladies sometimes,' Rokesmith hinted, 'choose without mentioning their choice to their fathers.'

'Not in this case, Mr Rokesmith. Between my daughter Bella and me there is a regular league and covenant of confidence. It was ratified only the other day. The ratification dates from—these,' said the cherub, giving a little pull at the lappels of his coat and the pockets of his trousers. 'Oh no, she has not chosen. To be sure, young George Sampson, in the days when Mr John Harmon—'

'Who I wish had never been born!' said the Secretary, with a gloomy brow.

R. W. looked at him with surprise, as thinking he had contracted an unaccountable spite against the poor deceased, and continued: 'In the days when Mr John Harmon was being sought out, young George Sampson certainly was hovering about Bella, and Bella let him hover. But it never was seriously thought of, and it's still less than ever to be thought of now. For Bella is ambitious, Mr Rokesmith, and I think I may predict will marry fortune. This time, you see, she will have the person and the property before her together, and will be able to make her choice with her eyes open. This is my road. I am very sorry to part company so soon. Good morning, sir!'

The Secretary pursued his way, not very much elevated in spirits by this conversation, and, arriving at the Boffin mansion, found Betty Higden waiting for him.

'I should thank you kindly, sir,' said Betty, 'if I might make so bold as have a word or two wi' you.'

She should have as many words as she liked, he told her; and took her into his room, and made her sit down.

' 'Tis concerning Sloppy, sir,' said Betty. 'And that's how I come here by myself. Not wishing him to know what I'm a-going to say to you, I got the start of him early and walked up.'

'You have wonderful energy,' returned Rokesmith. 'You are as young as I am.'

Betty Higden gravely shook her head. 'I am strong for my time of life, sir, but not young, thank the Lord!'

'Are you thankful for not being young?'

'Yes, sir. If I was young, it would all have to be gone through again, and the end would be a weary way off, don't you see? But never mind me; 'tis concerning Sloppy.'

'And what about him, Betty?'

' 'Tis just this, sir. It can't be reasoned out of his head by any powers of mine but what that he can do right by your kind lady and gentleman and do his work for me, both together. Now he can't. To give himself up to being put in the way of arning a good living and getting on, he must give me up. Well; he won't.'

'I respect him for it,' said Rokesmith.

'*Do* ye, sir? I don't know but what I do myself. Still that don't make it right to let him have his way. So as he won't give me up, I'm a-going to give him up.'

'How, Betty?'

'I'm a-going to run away from him.'

With an astonished look at the indomitable old face and the bright eyes, the Secretary repeated, 'Run away from him?'

'Yes, sir,' said Betty, with one nod. And in the nod and in the firm set of her mouth, there was a vigour of purpose not to be doubted.

'Come, come!' said the Secretary. 'We must talk about this. Let us take our time over it, and try to get at the true sense of the case and the true course, by degrees.'

'Now, lookee here, by dear,' returned old Betty—'asking your excuse for being so familiar, but being of a time of life a'most to be your grandmother twice over. Now, lookee, here. 'Tis a poor living and a hard as is to be got out of this work that I'm a doing now, and but for Sloppy I don't know as I should have held to it this long. But it did just keep us on, the two together. Now that I'm alone—with even Johnny gone—I'd far sooner be upon my feet and tiring of myself out, than a sitting folding and folding by the fire. And I'll tell you why. There's a deadness steals over me at times, that the kind of life favours and

I don't like. Now, I seem to have Johnny in my arms—now, his mother—now, his mother's mother—now, I seem to be a child myself, a lying once again in the arms of my own mother—then I get numbed, thought and sense, till I start out of my seat, afeerd that I'm a growing like the poor old people that they brick up in the Unions, as you may sometimes see when they let 'em out of the four walls to have a warm in the sun, crawling quite scared about the streets. I was a nimble girl, and have always been a active body, as I told your lady, first time ever I see her good face. I can still walk twenty mile if I am put to it. I'd far better be a walking than a getting numbed and dreary. I'm a good fair knitter, and can make many little things to sell. The loan from your lady and gentleman of twenty shillings to fit out a basket with, would be a fortune for me. Trudging round the country and tiring of myself out, I shall keep the deadness off, and get my own bread by my own labour. And what more can I want?'

'And this is your plan,' said the Secretary, 'for running away?'

'Show me a better! My deary, show me a better! Why, I know very well,' said old Betty Higden, 'and you know very well, that your lady and gentleman would set me up like a queen for the rest of my life, if so be that we could make it right among us to have it so. But we can't make it right among us to have it so. I've never took charity yet, nor yet has any one belonging to me. And it would be forsaking of myself indeed, and forsaking of my children dead and gone, and forsaking of their children dead and gone, to set up a contradiction now at last.'

'It might come to be justifiable and unavoidable at last,' the Secretary gently hinted, with a slight stress on the word.

'I hope it never will! It ain't that I mean to give offence by being anyways proud,' said the old creature simply, 'but that I want to be of a piece like, and helpful of myself right through to my death.'

'And to be sure,' added the Secretary, as a comfort for here, 'Sloppy will be eagerly looking forward to his opportunity of being to you what you have been to him.'

'Trust him for that, sir!' said Betty, cheerfully. 'Though he had need to be something quick about it, for I'm a getting to be an old one. But I'm a strong one too, and travel and weather never hurt me yet! Now, be so kind as speak for me to your lady and gentleman, and tell 'em what I ask of their good friendliness to let me do, and why I ask it.'

The Secretary felt that there was no gainsaying what was

urged by this brave old heroine, and he presently repaired to Mrs Boffin and recommended her to let Betty Higden have her way, at all events for the time. 'It would be far more satisfactory to your kind heart, I know,' he said, 'to provide for her, but it may be a duty to respect this independent spirit.' Mrs Boffin was not proof against the consideration set before her. She and her husband had worked too, and had brought their simple faith and honour clean out of dustheaps. If they owed a duty to Betty Higden, of a surety that duty must be done.

'But, Betty,' said Mrs Boffin, when she accompanied John Rokesmith back to his room, and shone upon her with the light of her radiant face, 'granted all else, I think I wouldn't run away'.

' 'Twould come easier to Sloppy,' said Mrs Higden, shaking her head. ' 'Twould come easier to me too. But 'tis as you please.'

'When would you go?'

'Now,' was the bright and ready answer. 'To-day, my deary, to-morrow. Bless ye, I am used to it. I know many parts of the country well. When nothing else was to be done, I have worked in many a market-garden afore now, and in many a hop-garden too.'

'If I give my consent to your going, Betty—which Mr Rokesmith thinks I ought to do—'

Betty thanked him with a grateful curtsey.

'—We must not lose sight of you. We must not let you pass out of our knowledge. We must know all about you.'

'Yes, my deary, but not through letter-writing, because letter-writing—indeed, writing of most sorts—hadn't much come up for such as me when I was young. But I shall be to and fro. No fear of my missing a chance of giving myself a sight of your reviving face. Besides,' said Betty, with logical good faith, 'I shall have a debt to pay off, by littles, and naturally that would bring me back, if nothing else would.'

'*Must* it be done?' asked Mrs Boffin, still reluctant, of the Secretary.

'I think it must.'

After more discussion it was agreed that it should be done, and Mrs Boffin summoned Bella to note down the little purchases that were necessary to set Betty up in trade. 'Don't ye be timorous for me, my dear,' said the stanch old heart, observant of Bella's face: 'when I take my seat with my work, clean and busy and fresh, in a country market-place, I shall turn a sixpence as sure as ever a farmer's wife there.'

The Secretary took that opportunity of touching on the practical question of Mr Sloppy's capabilities. He would have made a wonderful cabinet-maker, said Mrs Higden, 'if there had been the money to put him to it.' She had seen him handle tools that he had borrowed to mend the mangle, or to knock a broken piece of furniture together, in a surprising manner. As to constructing toys for the Minders, out of nothing, he had done that daily. And once as many as a dozen people had got together in the lane to see the neatness with which he fitted the broken pieces of a foreign monkey's musical instrument. 'That's well,' said the Secretary. 'It will not be hard to find a trade for him.'

John Harmon being buried under mountains now, the Secretary that very same day set himself to finish his affairs and have done with him. He drew up an ample declaration, to be signed by Rogue Riderhood (knowing he could get his signature to it, by making him another and much shorter evening call), and then considered to whom should he give the document? To Hexam's son, or daughter? Resolved speedily, to the daughter. But it would be safer to avoid seeing the daughter, because the son had seen Julius Handford, and—he could not be too careful—there might possibly be some comparison of notes between the son and daughter, which would awaken slumbering suspicion, and lead to consequences. 'I might even,' he reflected, 'be apprehended as having been concerned in my own murder!' Therefore, best to send it to the daughter under cover by the post. Pleasant Riderhood had undertaken to find out where she lived, and it was not necessary that it should be attended by a single word of explanation. So far, straight.

But, all that he knew of the daughter he derived from Mrs Boffin's accounts of what she heard from Mr Lightwood, who seemed to have a reputation for his manner of relating a story, and to have made this story quite his own. It interested him, and he would like to have the means of knowing more—as, for instance, that she received the exonerating paper, and that it satisfied her—by opening some channel altogether independent of Lightwood: who likewise had seen Julius Handford, who had publicly advertised for Julius Handford, and whom of all men he, the Secretary, most avoided. 'But with whom the common course of things might bring me in a moment face to face, any day in the week or any hour in the day.'

Now, to cast about for some likely means of opening such a

channel. The boy, Hexam, was training for and with a school-master. The Secretary knew it, because his sister's share in that disposal of him seemed to be the best part of Lightwood's account of the family. This young fellow, Sloppy, stood in need of some instruction. If he, the Secretary, engaged that school-master to impart it to him, the channel might be opened. The next point was, did Mrs Boffin know the schoolmaster's name? No, but she knew where the school was. Quite enough. Promptly the Secretary wrote to the master of that school, and that very evening Bradley Headstone answered in person.

The Secretary stated to the schoolmaster how the object was, to send to him for certain occasional evening instruction, a youth whom Mr and Mrs Boffin wished to help to an industrious and useful place in life. The schoolmaster was willing to under-take the charge of such a pupil. The Secretary inquired on what terms? The schoolmaster stated on what terms. Agreed and disposed of.

'May I ask, sir,' said Bradley Headstone, 'to whose good opinion I owe a recommendation to you?'

'You should know that I am not the principal here. I am Mr Boffin's Secretary. Mr Boffin is a gentleman who inherited a property of which you may have heard some public mention; the Harmon property.'

'Mr Harmon,' said Bradley: who would have been a great deal more at a loss than he was, if he had known to whom he spoke: 'was murdered and found in the river.'

'Was murdered and found in the river.'

'It was not—'

'No,' interposed the Secretary, smiling, 'it was not he who recommended you. Mr Boffin heard of you through a certain Mr Lightwood. I think you know Mr Lightwood, or know of him?'

'I know as much of him as I wish to know, sir. I have no acquaintance with Mr Lightwood, and I desire none. I have no objection to Mr Lightwood, but I have a particular objection to some of Mr Lightwood's friends—in short, to one of Mr Light-wood's friends. His great friend.'

He could hardly get the words out, even then and there, so fierce did he grow (though keeping himself down with infinite pains of repression), when the careless and contemptuous bear-ing of Eugene Wrayburn rose before his mind.

The Secretary saw there was a strong feeling here on some sore point, and he would have made a diversion from it, but for Bradley's holding to it in his cumbersome way.

'I have no objection to mention the friend by name,' he said, doggedly. 'The person I object to, is Mr Eugene Wrayburn.'

The Secretary remembered him. In his disturbed recollection of that night when he was striving against the drugged drink, there was but a dim image of Eugene's person; but he remembered his name, and his manner of speaking, and how he had gone with them to view the body, and where he had stood, and what he had said.

'Pray, Mr Headstone, what is the name,' he asked, again trying to make a diversion, 'of young Hexam's sister?'

'Her name is Lizzie,' said the schoolmaster, with a strong contraction of his whole face.

'She is a young woman of a remarkable character; is she not?'

'She is sufficiently remarkable to be very superior to Mr Eugene Wrayburn—though an ordinary person might be that,' said the schoolmaster; 'and I hope you will not think it impertinent in me, sir, to ask why you put the two names together?'

'By mere accident,' returned the Secretary. 'Observing that Mr Wrayburn was a disagreeable subject with you, I tried to get away from it: though not very successfully, it would appear.'

'Do you know Mr Wrayburn, sir?'

'No.'

'Then perhaps the names cannot be put together on the authority of any representation of his?'

'Certainly not.'

'I took the liberty to ask,' said Bradley, after casting his eyes on the ground, 'because he is capable of making any representation, in the swaggering levity of his insolence. I—I hope you will not misunderstand me, sir. I—I am much interested in this brother and sister, and the subject awakens very strong feelings within me. Very, very, strong feelings.' With a shaking hand, Bradley took out his handkerchief and wiped his brow.

The Secretary thought, as he glanced at the schoolmaster's face, that he had opened a channel here indeed, and that it was an unexpectedly dark and deep and stormy one, and difficult to sound. All at once, in the midst of his turbulent emotions, Bradley stopped and seemed to challenge his look. Much as though he suddenly asked him, 'What do you see in me?'

'The brother, young Hexam, was your real recommendation here,' said the Secretary, quietly going back to the point; 'Mr and Mrs Boffin happening to know, through Mr Lightwood, that he was your pupil. Anything that I ask respecting the brother and sister, or either of them, I ask for myself, out of my own interest in the subject, and not in my official character, or on Mr Boffin's behalf. How I come to be interested, I need not explain. You know the father's connection with the discovery of Mr Harmon's body.'

'Sir,' replied Bradley, very restlessly indeed, 'I know all the circumstances of that case.'

'Pray tell me, Mr Headstone,' said the Secretary. 'Does the sister suffer under any stigma because of the impossible accusation—groundless would be a better word—that was made against the father, and substantially withdrawn?'

'No, sir,' returned Bradley, with a kind of anger.

'I am very glad to hear it.'

'The sister,' said Bradley, separating his words over-carefully, and speaking as if he were repeating them from a book, 'suffers under no reproach that repels a man of unimpeachable character who had made for himself every step of his way in life, from placing her in his own station. I will not say, raising her to his own station; I say, placing her in it. The sister labours under no reproach, unless she should unfortunately make it for herself. When such a man is not deterred from regarding her as his equal, and when he has convinced himself that there is no blemish on her, I think the fact must be taken to be pretty expressive.'

'And there is such a man?' said the Secretary.

Bradley Headstone knotted his brows, and squared his large lower jaw, and fixed his eyes on the ground with an air of determination that seemed unnecessary to the occasion, as he replied: 'And there is such a man.'

The Secretary had no reason or excuse for prolonging the conversation, and it ended here. Within three hours the oakum-headed apparition once more dived into the Leaving Shop, and that night Rogue Riderhood's recantation lay in the post office, addressed under cover to Lizzie Hexam at her right address.

All these proceedings occupied John Rokesmith so much, that it was not until the following day that he saw Bella again. It seemed then to be tacitly understood between them that they were to be as distantly easy as they could, without attracting the attention of Mr and Mrs Boffin to any marked change in their manner. The fitting out of old Betty Higden was favourable to this, as keeping Bella engaged and interested, and as occupying the general attention.

'I think,' said Rokesmith, when they all stood about her, while she packed her tidy basket—except Bella, who was busily helping on her knees at the chair on which it stood; 'that at least you might keep a letter in your pocket, Mrs Higden, which I would write for you and date from here, merely stating, in the names of Mr and Mrs Boffin, that they are your friends;—I won't say patrons, because they wouldn't like it.'

'No, no, no,' said Mr Boffin; 'no patronizing! Let's keep out of *that*, whatever we come to.'

'There's more than enough of that about, without us; ain't there, Noddy?' said Mrs Boffin.

'I believe you, old lady!' returned the Golden Dustman. 'Over-much indeed!'

'But people sometimes like to be patronized; don't they, sir?' asked Bella, looking up.

'*I* don't. And if *they* do, my dear, they ought to learn better,' said Mr Boffin. 'Patrons and Patronesses, and Vice-Patrons and Vice-Patronesses, and Deceased Patrons and Deceased Patronesses, and Ex-Vice-Patrons and Ex-Vice-Patronesses, what does it all mean in the books of the Charities that come pouring in on Rokesmith as he sits among 'em pretty well up to his neck! If Mr Tom Noakes gives his five shillings ain't he a Patron, and if Mrs Jack Styles gives her five shillings ain't she a Patroness? What the deuce is it all about? If it ain't stark staring impudence, what do you call it?'

'Don't be warm, Noddy,' Mrs Boffin urged.

'Warm!' cried Mr Boffin. 'It's enough to make a man smoking hot. I can't go anywhere without being Patronized. I don't want to be Patronized. If I buy a ticket for a Flower Show, or a Music Show, or any sort of Show, and pay pretty heavy for it, why am I to be Patroned and Patronessed as if the Patrons and Patronesses treated me? If there's a good thing to be done, can't it be done on its own merits? If there's a bad thing to be done, can it ever be Patroned and Patronessed right? Yet when a new Institution's going to be built, it seems to me that the bricks and mortar ain't made of half so much consequence as the Patrons and Patronesses; no, nor yet the objects. I wish somebody would tell me whether other countries get Patronized to anything like the extent of this one! And as to the Patrons and Patronesses themselves, I wonder they're not ashamed of themselves. They ain't Pills, or Hair-Washes, or Invigorating Nervous Essences, to be puffed in that way!'

Having delivered himself of these remarks, Mr Boffin took a trot, according to his usual custom, and trotted back to the spot from which he had started.

'As to the letter, Rokesmith,' said Mr Boffin, 'you're as right as a trivet. Give her the letter, make her take the letter, put it in her pocket by violence. She might fall sick.—You know you might fall sick,' said Mr Boffin. 'Don't deny it, Mrs Higden, in your obstinacy; you know you might.'

Old Betty laughed, and said that she would take the letter and be thankful.

'That's right!' said Mr Boffin. 'Come! That's sensible. And don't be thankful to us (for we never thought of it), but to Mr Rokesmith.'

The letter was written, and read to her, and given to her.

'Now, how do you feel?' said Mr Boffin. 'Do you like it?'

'The letter, sir?' said Betty. 'Ay, it's a beautiful letter!'

'No, no, no; not the letter,' said Mr Boffin; 'the idea. Are you sure you're strong enough to carry out the idea?'

'I shall be stronger, and keep the deadness off better, this way, than any way left open to me, sir.'

'Don't say than any way left open, you know,' urged Mr Boffin; 'because there are ways without end. A housekeeper would be acceptable over yonder at the Bower, for instance. Wouldn't you like to see the Bower, and know a retired literary man of the name of Wegg that lives there—*with* a wooden leg?'

Old Betty was proof even against this temptation, and fell to adjusting her black bonnet and shawl.

'I wouldn't let you go, now it comes to this, after all,' said Mr Boffin, 'if I didn't hope that it may make a man and a workman of Sloppy, in as short a time as ever a man and workman was made yet. Why, what have you got there, Betty? Not a doll?'

It was the man in the Guards who had been on duty over Johnny's bed. The solitary old woman showed what it was, and put it up quietly in her dress. Then, she gratefully took leave of Mrs Boffin, and of Mr Boffin, and of Rokesmith, and then put her old withered arms round Bella's young and blooming neck, and said, repeating Johnny's words: 'A kiss for the boofer lady.'

The Secretary looked on from a doorway at the boofer lady thus encircled, and still looked on at the boofer lady standing alone there, when the determined old figure with its steady bright eyes was trudging through the streets, away from paralysis and pauperism.

Chapter 15
The Whole Case So Far

BRADLEY HEADSTONE held fast by that other interview he was to have with Lizzie Hexam. In stipulating for it, he had been impelled by a feeling little short of desperation, and the feeling abided by him. It was very soon after his interview with the Secretary, that he and Charley Hexam set out one leaden evening, not unnoticed by Miss Peecher, to have this desperate interview accomplished.

'That dolls' dressmaker,' said Bradley, 'is favourable neither to me nor to you, Hexam.'

'A pert crooked little chit, Mr Headstone! I knew she would put herself in the way, if she could, and would be sure to strike in with something impertinent. It was on that account that I proposed our going to the City to-night and meeting my sister.'

'So I supposed,' said Bradley, getting his gloves on his nervous hands as he walked. 'So I supposed.'

'Nobody but my sister,' pursued Charley, 'would have found out such an extraordinary companion. She has done it in a ridiculous fancy of giving herself up to another. She told me so, that night when we went there.'

'Why should she give herself up to the dressmaker?' asked Bradley.

'Oh!' said the boy, colouring. 'One of her romantic ideas! I tried to convince her so, but I didn't succeed. However, what we have got to do, is, to succeed to-night, Mr Headstone, and then all the rest follows.'

'You are still sanguine, Hexam.'

'Certainly I am, sir. Why, we have everything on our side.'

'Except your sister, perhaps,' thought Bradley. But he only gloomily thought it, and said nothing.

'Everything on our side,' repeated the boy with boyish confidence. 'Respectability, an excellent connexion for me, common sense, everything!'

'To be sure, your sister has always shown herself a devoted sister,' said Bradley, willing to sustain himself on even that low ground of hope.

'Naturally, Mr Headstone, I have a good deal of influence with her. And now that you have honoured me with your confidence and spoken to me first, I say again, we have everything on our side.'

And Bradley thought again, 'Except your sister, perhaps.'

A grey dusty withered evening in London city has not a hopeful aspect. The closed warehouses and offices have an air of death about them, and the national dread of colour has an air of mourning. The towers and steeples of the many house-encompassed churches, dark and dingy as the sky that seems descending on them, are no relief to the general gloom; a sun-dial on a church-wall has the look, in its useless black shade, of having failed in its business enterprise and stopped payment for ever; melancholy waifs and strays of housekeepers and porter sweep melancholy waifs and strays of papers and pins into the kennels, and other more melancholy waifs and strays explore them, searching and stooping and poking for anything to sell. The set of humanity outward from the City is as a set of prisoners departing from gaol, and dismal Newgate seems quite as fit a stronghold for the mighty Lord Mayor as his own state-dwelling.

On such an evening, when the city grit gets into the hair and eyes and skin, and when the fallen leaves of the few unhappy city trees grind down in corners under wheels of wind, the schoolmaster and the pupil emerged upon the Leadenhall Street region, spying eastward for Lizzie. Being something too soon in their arrival, they lurked at a corner, waiting for her to appear. The best-looking among us will not look very well, lurking at a corner, and Bradley came out of that disadvantage very poorly indeed.

'Here she comes, Mr Headstone! Let us go forward and meet her.'

As they advanced, she saw them coming, and seemed rather troubled. But she greeted her brother with the usual warmth, and touched the extended hand of Bradley.

'Why, where are you going, Charley, dear?' she asked him then.

'Nowhere. We came on purpose to meet you.'

'To meet me, Charley?'

'Yes. We are going to walk with you. But don't let us take the great leading streets where every one walks, and we can't hear ourselves speak. Let us go by the quiet backways. Here's a large paved court by this church, and quiet, too. Let us go up here.'

'But it's not in the way, Charley.'

'Yes it is,' said the boy, petulantly. 'It's in my way, and my way is yours.'

She had not released his hand, and, still holding it, looked at him with a kind of appeal. He avoided her eyes, under pretence of saying, 'Come along, Mr Headstone.' Bradley walked at his side—not at hers—and the brother and sister walked hand in hand. The court brought them to a churchyard; a paved square court, with a raised bank of earth about breast high, in the middle, enclosed by iron rails. Here, conveniently and heathfully elevated above the level of the living, were the dead, and the tombstones; some of the latter droopingly inclined from the perpendicular, as if they were ashamed of the lies they told.

They paced the whole of this place once, in a constrained and uncomfortable manner, when the boy stopped and said:

'Lizzie, Mr Headstone has something to say to you. I don't wish to be an interruption either to him or to you, and so I'll go and take a little stroll and come back. I know in a general way what Mr Headstone intends to say, and I very highly approve of it, as I hope—and indeed I do not doubt—you will. I needn't tell you, Lizzie, that I am under great obligations to Mr Headstone, and that I am very anxious for Mr Headstone to succeed in all he undertakes. As I hope—and as, indeed, I don't doubt—you must be.'

'Charley,' returned his sister, detaining his hand as he withdrew it, 'I think you had better stay. I think Mr Headstone had better not say what he thinks of saying.'

'Why, how do you know what it is?' returned the boy.

'Perhaps I don't, but—'

'Perhaps you don't? No, Liz, I should think not. If you knew what it was, you would give me a very different answer. There; let go; be sensible. I wonder you don't remember that Mr Headstone is looking on.'

She allowed him to separate himself from her, and he, after saying, 'Now Liz, be a rational girl and a good sister,' walked away. She remained standing alone with Bradley Headstone, and it was not until she raised her eyes, that he spoke.

'I said,' he began, 'when I saw you last, that there was something unexplained, which might perhaps influence you. I have come this evening to explain it. I hope you will not judge of me by my hesitating manner when I speak to you. You see me at my greatest disadvantage. It is most unfortunate for me that I wish you to see me at my best, and that I know you see me at my worst.'

She moved slowly on when he paused, and he moved slowly on beside her.

'It seems egotistical to begin by saying so much about myself,' he resumed, 'but whatever I say to you seems, even in my own ears, below what I want to say, and different from what I want to say. I can't help it. So it is. You are the ruin of me.'

She started at the passionate sound of the last words, and at the passionate action of his hands, with which they were accompanied.

'Yes! you are the ruin—the ruin—the ruin—of me. I have no resources in myself, I have no confidence in myself, I have no government of myself when you are near me or in my thoughts. And you are always in my thoughts now. I have never been quit of you since I first saw you. Oh, that was a wretched day for me! That was a wretched, miserable day!'

A touch of pity for him mingled with her dislike of him, and she said: 'Mr Headstone, I am grieved to have done you any harm, but I have never meant it.'

'There!' he cried, despairingly. 'Now, I seem to have re-proached you, instead of revealing to you the state of my own mind! Bear with me. I am always wrong when you are in question. It is my doom.'

Struggling with himself, and by times looking up at the deserted windows of the houses as if there could be anything written in their grimy panes that would help him, he paced the whole pavement at her side, before he spoke again.

'I must try to give expression to what is in my mind; it shall and must be spoken. Though you see me so confounded—though you strike me so helpless—I ask you to believe that there are many people who think well of me; that there are some people who highly esteem me; that I have in my way won a station which is considered worth winning.'

'Surely, Mr Headstone, I do believe it. Surely I have al-ways known it from Charley.'

'I ask you to believe that if I were to offer my home such as it is, my station such as it is, my affections such as they are, to any one of the best considered, and best qualified, and most distinguished, among the young women engaged in my calling, they would probably be accepted. Even readily accepted.'

'I do not doubt it,' said Lizzie, with her eyes upon the ground.

'I have sometimes had it in my thoughts to make that offer and to settle down as many men of my class do: I on the one side of a school, my wife on the other, both of us interested in the same work.'

'Why have you not done so?' asked Lizzie Hexam. 'Why do you not do so?'

'Far better that I never did! The only one grain of comfort I have had these many weeks,' he said, always speaking passionately, and, when most emphatic, repeating that former action of his hands, which was like flinging his heart's blood down before her in drops upon the pavement-stones; 'the only one grain of comfort I have had these many weeks is, that I never did. For if I had, and if the same spell had come upon me for my ruin, I know I should have broken that tie asunder as if it had been thread.'

She glanced at him with a glance of fear, and a shrinking gesture. He answered, as if she had spoken.

'No! It would not have been voluntary on my part, any more than it is voluntary in me to be here now. You draw me to you. If I were shut up in a strong prison, you would draw me out. I should break through the wall to come to you. If I were lying on a sick bed, you would draw me up—to stagger to your feet and fall there.'

The wild energy of the man, now quite let loose, was absolutely terrible. He stopped and laid his hand upon a piece of the coping of the burial-ground enclosure, as if he would have dislodged the stone.

'No man knows till the time comes, what depths are within him. To some men it never comes; let them rest and be thankful! To me, you brought it; on me, you forced it; and the bottom of this raging sea,' striking himself upon the breast, 'has been heaved up ever since.'

'Mr Headstone, I have heard enough. Let me stop you here. It will be better for you and better for me. Let us find my brother.'

'Not yet. It shall and must be spoken. I have been in torments ever since I stopped short of it before. You are alarmed. It is another of my miseries that I cannot speak to you or speak of you without stumbling at every syllable, unless I let the check go altogether and run mad. Here is a man lighting the lamps. He will be gone directly. I entreat of you let us walk round this place again. You have no reason to look alarmed; I can restrain myself, and I will.'

She yielded to the entreaty—how could she do otherwise! —and they paced the stones in silence. One by one the lights leaped up making the cold grey church tower more remote, and they were alone again. He said no more until they had regained the spot where he had broken off; there, he again stood still, and again grasped the stone. In saying what he said then, he never looked at her; but looked at it and wrenched at it.

'You know what I am going to say. I love you. What other men may mean when they use that expression, I cannot tell; what *I* mean is, that I am under the influence of some tremendous attraction which I have resisted in vain, and which overmasters me. You could draw me to fire, you could draw me to water, you could draw me to the gallows, you could draw me to any death, you could draw me to anything I have most avoided, you could draw me to any exposure and disgrace. This and the confusion of my thoughts, so that I am fit for nothing, is what I mean by your being the ruin of me. But if you would return a favourable answer to my offer of myself in marriage, you could draw me to any good—every good—with equal force. My circumstances are quite easy, and you would want for nothing. My reputation stands quite high, and would be a shield for yours. If you saw me at my work, able to do it well and respected in it, you might even come to take a sort of pride in me;—I would try hard that you should. Whatever considerations I may have thought of against this offer, I have conquered, and I make it with all my heart. Your brother favours me to the utmost, and it is likely that we might live and work together; anyhow, it is certain that he would have my best influence and support. I don't know what I could say more if I tried. I might only weaken what is ill enough said as it is. I only add that if it is any claim on you to be in earnest, I am in thorough earnest, dreadful earnest.'

The powdered mortar from under the stone at which he wrenched, rattled on the pavement to confirm his words.

'Mr Headstone—'

'Stop! I implore you, before you answer me, to walk round this place once more. It will give you a minute's time to think, and me a minute's time to get some fortitude together.'

Again she yielded to the entreaty, and again they came back to the same place, and again he worked at the stone.

'Is it,' he said, with his attention apparently engrossed by it, 'yes, or no?'

'Mr Headstone, I thank you sincerely, I thank you gratefully, and hope you may find a worthy wife before long and be very happy. But it is no.'

'Is no short time necessary for reflection; no weeks or days?' he asked, in the same half-suffocated way.

'None whatever.'

'Are you quite decided, and is there no chance of any change in my favour?'

'I am quite decided, Mr Headstone, and I am bound to answer I am certain there is none.'

'Then,' said he, suddenly changing his tone and turning to her, and bringing his clenched hand down upon the stone with a force that laid the knuckles raw and bleeding; 'then I hope that I may never kill him!'

The dark look of hatred and revenge with which the words broke from his livid lips, and with which he stood holding out his smeared hand as if it held some weapon and had just struck a mortal blow, made her so afraid of him that she turned to run away. But he caught her by the arm.

'Mr Headstone, let me go. Mr Headstone, I must call for help!'

'It is I who should call for help,' he said; 'you don't know yet how much I need it.'

The working of his face as she shrank from it, glancing round for her brother and uncertain what to do, might have extorted a cry from her in another instant; but all at once he sternly stopped it and fixed it, as if Death itself had done so.

'There! You see I have recovered myself. Hear me out.'

With much of the dignity of courage, as she recalled her self-reliant life and her right to be free from accountability to this man, she released her arm from his grasp and stood looking full at him. She had never been so handsome, in his eyes. A shade came over them while he looked back at her, as if she drew the very light out of them to herself.

'This time, at least, I will leave nothing unsaid,' he went on, folding his hands before him, clearly to prevent his being betrayed into any impetuous gesture; 'this last time at least I will not be tortured with after-thoughts of a lost opportunity. Mr Eugene Wrayburn.'

'Was it of him you spoke in your ungovernable rage and violence?' Lizzie Hexam demanded with spirit.

He bit his lip, and looked at her, and said never a word.

'Was it Mr Wrayburn that you threatened?'

He bit his lip again, and looked at her, and said never a word.

'You asked me to hear you out, and you will not speak. Let me find my brother.'

'Stay! I threatened no one.'

Her look dropped for an instant to his bleeding hand. He lifted it to his mouth, wiped it on his sleeve, and again folded it over the other. 'Mr Eugene Wrayburn,' he repeated.

'Why do you mention that name again and again, Mr Headstone?'

'Because it is the text of the little I have left to say. Observe! There are no threats in it. If I utter a threat, stop me, and fasten it upon me. Mr Eugene Wrayburn.'

A worse threat than was conveyed in his manner of uttering the name, could hardly have escaped him.

'He haunts you. You accept favours from him. You are willing enough to listen to *him*. I know it, as well as he does.'

'Mr Wrayburn has been considerate and good to me, sir,' said Lizzie, proudly, 'in connexion with the death and with the memory of my poor father.'

'No doubt. He is of course a very considerate and a very good man, Mr Eugene Wrayburn.'

'He is nothing to you, I think,' said Lizzie, with an indignation she could not repress.

'Oh yes, he is. There you mistake. He is much to me.'

'What can he be to you?'

'He can be a rival to me among other things,' said Bradley.

'Mr Headstone,' returned Lizzie, with a burning face, 'it is cowardly in you to speak to me in this way. But it makes me able to tell you that I do not like you, and that I never have liked you from the first, and that no other living creature has anything to do with the effect you have produced upon me for yourself.'

His head bent for a moment, as if under a weight, and he then looked up again, moistening his lips. 'I was going on with the little I had left to say. I knew all this about Mr Eugene Wrayburn, all the while you were drawing me to you. I strove against the knowledge, but quite in vain. It made no difference in me. With Mr Eugene Wrayburn in my mind, I went on. With Mr Eugene Wrayburn in my mind, I spoke to you just now. With Mr Eugene Wrayburn in my mind, I have been set aside and I have been cast out.'

'If you give those names to my thanking you for your proposal and declining it, is it my fault, Mr Headstone?' said

Lizzie, compassionating the bitter struggle he could not conceal, almost as much as she was repelled and alarmed by it.

'I am not complaining,' he returned, 'I am only stating the case. I had to wrestle with my self-respect when I submitted to be drawn to you in spite of Mr Wrayburn. You may imagine how low my self-respect lies now.'

She was hurt and angry; but repressed herself in consideration of his suffering, and of his being her brother's friend.

'And it lies under his feet,' said Bradley, unfolding his hands in spite of himself, and fiercely motioning with them both towards the stones of the pavement. 'Remember that! It lies under that fellow's feet, and he treads upon it and exults above it.'

'He does not!' said Lizzie.

'He does!' said Bradley. ''I have stood before him face to face, and he crushed me down in the dirt of his contempt, and walked over me. Why? Because he knew with triumph what was in store for me to-night.'

'O, Mr Headstone, you talk quite wildly.'

'Quite collectedly. I know what I say too well. Now I have said all. I have used no threat, remember; I have done no more than show you how the case stands;—how the case stands, so far.'

At this moment her brother sauntered into view close by. She darted to him, and caught him by the hand. Bradley followed, and laid his heavy hand on the boy's opposite shoulder.

'Charley Hexam, I am going home. I must walk home by myself to-night, and get shut up in my room without being spoken to. Give me half an hour's start, and let me be, till you find me at my work in the morning. I shall be at my work in the morning just as usual.'

Clasping his hands, he uttered a short unearthly broken cry, and went his way. The brother and sister were left looking at one another near a lamp in the solitary churchyard, and the boy's face clouded and darkened, as he said in a rough tone: 'What is the meaning of this? What have you done to my best friend? Out with the truth!'

'Charley!' said his sister. 'Speak a little more considerately!'

'I am not in the humour for consideration, or for nonsense of any sort,' replied the boy. 'What have you been doing? Why has Mr Headstone gone from us in that way?'

'He asked me—you know he asked me—to be his wife, Charley.'

'Well?' said the boy, impatiently.

'And I was obliged to tell him that I could not be his wife.'

'You were obliged to tell him,' repeated the boy angrily, between his teeth, and rudely pushing her away. 'You were obliged to tell him! Do you know that he is worth fifty of you?'

'It may easily be so, Charley, but I cannot marry him.'

'You mean that you are conscious that you can't appreciate him, and don't deserve him, I suppose?'

'I mean that I do not like him, Charley, and that I will never marry him.'

'Upon my soul,' exclaimed the boy, 'you are a nice picture of a sister! Upon my soul, you are a pretty piece of disinterestedness! And so all my endeavours to cancel the past and to raise myself in the world, and to raise you with me, are to be beaten down by *your* low whims; are they?'

'I will not reproach you, Charley.'

'Hear her!' exclaimed the boy, looking round at the darkness. 'She won't reproach me! She does her best to destroy my fortunes and her own, and she won't reproach me! Why, you'll tell me, next, that you won't reproach Mr Headstone for coming out of the sphere to which he is an ornament, and putting himself at *your* feet, to be rejected by *you!*'

'No, Charley; I will only tell you, as I told himself, that I thank him for doing so, that I am sorry he did so, and that I hope he will do much better, and be happy.'

Some touch of compunction smote the boy's hardening heart as he looked upon her, his patient little nurse in infancy, his patient friend, adviser, and reclaimer in boyhood, the self-forgetting sister who had done everything for him. His tone relented, and he drew her arm through his.

'Now, come, Liz; don't let us quarrel: let us be reasonable and talk this over like brother and sister. Will you listen to me?'

'Oh, Charley!' she replied through her starting tears; 'do I not listen to you, and hear many hard things!'

'Then I am sorry. There, Liz! I am unfeignedly sorry. Only you do put me out so. Now see. Mr Headstone is perfectly devoted to you. He has told me in the strongest manner that he has never been his old self for one single minute since I first brought him to see you. Miss Peecher, our schoolmistress—pretty and young, and all that—is known to be very much attached to him, and he won't so much as look at her or hear of her. Now, his devotion to you must be a disinterested one; mustn't it? If he married Miss Peecher, he would be a great deal better off in all worldly respects, than in marrying you. Well then; he has nothing to get by it, has he?'

'Nothing, Heaven knows!'

'Very well then,' said the boy; 'that's something in his favour, and a great thing. Then *I* come in. Mr Headstone has always got me on, and he has a good deal in his power, and of course if he was my brother-in-law he wouldn't get me on less, but would get me on more. Mr Headstone comes and confides in me, in a very delicate way, and says, "I hope my marrying your sister would be agreeable to you, Hexam, and useful to you?" I say, "There's nothing in the world, Mr Headstone, that I could be better pleased with." Mr Headstone says, "Then I may rely upon your intimate knowledge of me for your good word with your sister, Hexam?" And I say, "Certainly, Mr Headstone, and naturally I have a good deal of influence with her." So I have; haven't I, Liz?'

'Yes, Charley.'

'Well said! Now, you see, we begin to get on, the moment we begin to be really talking it over, like brother and sister. Very well. Then *you* come in. As Mr Headstone's wife you would be occupying a most respectable station, and you would be holding a far better place in society than you hold now, and you would at length get quit of the river-side and the old disagreeables belonging to it, and you would be rid for good of dolls' dressmakers and their drunken fathers, and the like of that. Not that I want to disparage Miss Jenny Wren: I dare say she is all very well in her way; but her way is not your way as Mr Headstone's wife. Now, you see, Liz, on all three accounts—on Mr Headstone's, on mine, on yours—nothing could be better or more desirable.'

They were walking slowly as the boy spoke, and here he stood still, to see what effect he had made. His sister's eyes were fixed upon him; but as they showed no yielding, and as she remained silent, he walked her on again. There was some discomfiture in his tone as he resumed, though he tried to conceal it.

'Having so much influence with you, Liz, as I have, perhaps I should have done better to have had a little chat with you in the first instance, before Mr Headstone spoke for himself. But really all this in his favour seemed so plain and undeniable, and I knew you to have always been so reasonable and sensible, that I didn't consider it worth while. Very likely that was a mistake of mine. However, it's soon set right. All that need be done to set it right, is for you to tell me at once that I may go home and tell

Mr Headstone that what has taken place is not final, and that it will all come round by-and-by.'

He stopped again. The pale face looked anxiously and lovingly at him, but she shook her head.

'Can't you speak?' said the boy sharply.

'I am very unwilling to speak, Charley. If I must, I must. I cannot authorize you to say any such thing to Mr Headstone: I cannot allow you to say any such thing to Mr Headstone. Nothing remains to be said to him from me, after what I have said for good and all, to-night.'

'And this girl,' cried the boy, contemptuously throwing her off again, 'calls herself a sister!'

'Charley, dear, that is the second time that you have almost struck me. Don't be hurt by my words. I don't mean—Heaven forbid!—that you intended it; but you hardly know with what a sudden swing you removed yourself from me.'

'However!' said the boy, taking no heed of the remonstrance, and pursuing his own mortified disappointment, 'I know what this means, and you shall not disgrace me.'

'It means what I have told you, Charley, and nothing more.'

'That's not true,' said the boy in a violent tone, 'and you know it's not. It means your precious Mr Wrayburn; that's what it means.'

'Charley! If you remember any old days of ours together, forbear!'

'But you shall not disgrace me,' doggedly pursued the boy. 'I am determined that after I have climbed up out of the mire, you shall not pull me down. You can't disgrace me if I have nothing to do with you, and I *will* have nothing to do with you for the future.'

'Charley! On many a night like this, and many a worse night, I have sat on the stones of the street, hushing you in my arms. Unsay those words without even saying you are sorry for them, and my arms are open to you still, and so is my heart.'

'I'll not unsay them. I'll say them again. You are an inveterately bad girl, and a false sister, and I have done with you. For ever, I have done with you!'

He threw up his ungrateful and ungracious hand as if it set up a barrier between them, and flung himself upon his heel and left her. She remained impassive on the same spot, silent and motionless, until the striking of the church clock roused her, and she turned away. But then, with the breaking up of her immobility came the breaking up of the waters that the cold heart of the selfish boy had frozen. And 'O that I were lying here with the dead!' and 'O Charley, Charley, that this should be the end of our pictures in the fire!' were all the words she said, as she laid her face in her hands on the stone coping.

A figure passed by, and passed on, but stopped and looked round at her. It was the figure of an old man with a bowed head, wearing a large brimmed low-crowned hat, and a long-skirted coat. After hesitating a little, the figure turned back, and, advancing with an air of gentleness and compassion, said:

'Pardon me, young woman, for speaking to you, but you are under some distress of mind. I cannot pass upon my way and leave you weeping here alone, as if there was nothing in the place. Can I help you? Can I do anything to give you comfort?'

She raised her head at the sound of these kind words, and answered gladly, 'O, Mr Riah, is it you?'

'My daughter,' said the old man, 'I stand amazed! I spoke as to a stranger. Take my arm, take my arm. What grieves you? Who has done this? Poor girl, poor girl!'

'My brother has quarrelled with me,' sobbed Lizzie, 'and renounced me.'

'He is a thankless dog,' said the Jew, angrily. 'Let him go. Shake the dust from thy feet and let him go. Come, daughter! Come home with me—it is but across the road—and take a little time to recover your peace and to make your eyes seemly, and then I will bear you company through the streets. For it is past your usual time, and will soon be late, and the way is long, and there is much company out of doors to-night.'

She accepted the support he offered her, and they slowly passed out of the churchyard. They were in the act of emerging into the main thoroughfare, when another figure loitering discontentedly by, and looking up the street and down it, and all about, started and exclaimed, 'Lizzie! why, where have you been? Why, what's the matter?'

As Eugene Wrayburn thus addressed her, she drew closer to the Jew, and bent her head. The Jew having taken in the whole of Eugene at one sharp glance, cast his eyes upon the ground, and stood mute,

'Lizzie, what is the matter?'

'Mr Wrayburn, I cannot tell you now. I cannot tell you to-night, if I ever can tell you. Pray leave me.'

'But, Lizzie, I came expressly to join you. I came to walk home with you, having dined at a coffee-house in this neighbour-

hood and knowing your hour. And I have been lingering about,'
added Eugene, 'like a bailiff; or,' with a look at Riah, 'an old
clothesman.'

The Jew lifted up his eyes, and took in Eugene once more,
at another glance.

'Mr Wrayburn, pray, pray, leave me with this protector.
And one thing more. Pray, pray be careful of yourself.'

'Mysteries of Udolpho!' said Eugene, with a look of wonder. 'May I be excused for asking, in the elderly gentleman's
presence, who is this kind protector?'

'A trustworthy friend,' said Lizzie.

'I will relieve him of his trust,' returned Eugene. 'But you
must tell me, Lizzie, what is the matter?'

'Her brother is the matter,' said the old man, lifting up his
eyes again.

'Our brother the matter?' returned Eugene, with airy contempt. 'Our brother is not worth a thought, far less a tear. What
has our brother done?'

The old man lifted up his eyes again, with one grave look at
Wrayburn, and one grave glance at Lizzie, as she stood looking
down. Both were so full of meaning that even Eugene was
checked in his light career, and subsided into a thoughtful 'Humph!'

With an air of perfect patience the old man, remaining mute
and keeping his eyes cast down, stood, retaining Lizzie's arm, as
though in his habit of passive endurance, it would be all one to
him if he had stood there motionless all night.

'If Mr Aaron,' said Eugene, who soon found this fatiguing,
'will be good enough to relinquish his charge to me, he will be
quite free for any engagement he may have at the Synagogue.
Mr Aaron, will you have the kindness?'

But the old man stood stock still.

'Good evening, Mr Aaron,' said Eugene, politely; 'we need
not detain you.' Then turning to Lizzie, 'Is our friend Mr Aaron
a little deaf?'

'My hearing is very good, Christian gentleman,' replied the
old man, calmly; 'but I will hear only one voice to-night,
desiring me to leave this damsel before I have conveyed her to
her home. If she requests it, I will do it. I will do it for no one
else.'

'May I ask why so, Mr Aaron?' said Eugene, quite undisturbed in his ease.

'Excuse me. If she asks me, I will tell her,' replied the old
man. "I will tell no one else.'

'I do not ask you,' said Lizzie, 'and I beg you to take me home. Mr Wrayburn, I have had a bitter trial to-night, and I hope you will not think me ungrateful, or mysterious, or changeable. I am neither; I am wretched. Pray remember what I said to you. Pray, pray, take care.'

'My dear Lizzie,' he returned, in a low voice, bending over her on the other side; 'of what? Of whom?'

'Of any one you have lately seen and made angry.'

He snapped his fingers and laughed. 'Come,' said he, 'since no better may be, Mr Aaron and I will divide this trust, and see you home together. Mr Aaron on that side; I on this. If perfectly agreeable to Mr Aaron, the escort will now proceed.'

He knew his power over her. He knew that she would not insist upon his leaving her. He knew that, her fears for him being aroused, she would be uneasy if he were out of her sight. For all his seeming levity and carelessness, he knew whatever he chose to know of the thoughts of her heart.

And going on at her side, so gaily, regardless of all that had been urged against him; so superior in his sallies and self-possession to the gloomy constraint of her suitor and the selfish petulance of her brother; so faithful to her, as it seemed, when her own stock was faithless; what an immense advantage, what an overpowering influence, were his that night! Add to the rest, poor girl, that she had heard him vilified for her sake, and that she had suffered for his, and where the wonder that his occasional tones of serious interest (setting off his carelessness, as if it were assumed to calm her), that his lightest touch, his lightest look, his very presence beside her in the dark common street, were like glimpses of an enchanted world, which it was natural for jealousy and malice and all meanness to be unable to bear the brightness of, and to gird at as bad spirits might.

Nothing more being said of repairing to Riah's, they went direct to Lizzie's lodging. A little short of the house-door she parted from them, and went in alone.

'Mr Aaron,' said Eugene, when they were left together in the street, 'with many thanks for your company, it remains for me unwillingly to say Farewell.'

'Sir,' returned the other, 'I give you good night, and I wish that you were not so thoughtless.'

'Mr Aaron,' returned Eugene, 'I give you good night, and I wish (for you are a little dull) that you were not so thoughtful.'

But now, that his part was played out for the evening, and when in turning his back upon the Jew he came off the stage, he was thoughtful himself. 'How did Lightwood's catechism run?' he murmured, as he stopped to light his cigar. 'What is to come of it? What are you doing? Where are you going? We shall soon know now. Ah!' with a heavy sigh.

The heavy sigh was repeated as if by an echo, an hour afterwards, when Riah, who had been sitting on some dark steps in a corner over against the house, arose and went his patient way; stealing through the streets in his ancient dress, like the ghost of a departed Time.

Chapter 16
An Anniversary Occasion

THE estimable Twemlow, dressing himself in his lodgings over the stable-yard in Duke Street, Saint James's, and hearing the horses at their toilette below, finds himself on the whole in a disadvantageous position as compared with the noble animals at livery. For whereas, on the one hand, he has no attendant to slap him soundingly and require him in gruff accents to come up and come over, still, on the other hand, he has no attendant at all; and the mild gentleman's finger-joints and other joints working rustily in the morning, he could deem it agreeable even to be tied up by the countenance at his chamber-door, so he were there skilfully rubbed down and slushed and sluiced and polished and clothed, while himself taking merely a passive part in these trying transactions.

How the fascinating Tippins gets on when arraying herself for the bewilderment of the senses of men, is known only to the Graces and her maid; but perhaps even that engaging creature, though not reduced to the self-dependence of Twemlow could dispense with a good deal of the trouble attendant on the daily restoration of her charms, seeing that as to her face and neck this adorable divinity is, as it were, a diurnal species of lobster—throwing off a shell every forenoon, and needing to keep in a retired spot until the new crust hardens.

Howbeit, Twemlow doth at length invest himself with collar and cravat and wristbands to his knuckles, and goeth forth to breakfast. And to breakfast with whom but his near neighbours, the Lammles of Sackville Street, who have imparted to him that he will meet his distant kinsman, Mr Fledgeby. The awful Snigsworth might taboo and prohibit Fledgeby, but the peaceable Twemlow reasons, 'If he *is* my kinsman I didn't make him so, and to meet a man is not to know him.'

It is the first anniversary of the happy marriage of Mr and Mrs Lammle, and the celebration is a breakfast, because a dinner on the desired scale of sumptuosity cannot be achieved within less limits than those of the non-existent palatial residence of which so many people are madly envious. So, Twemlow trips with not a little stiffness across Piccadilly, sensible of having once been more upright in figure and less in danger of being knocked down by swift vehicles. To be sure that was in the days when he hoped for leave from the dread Snigsworth to do something, or be something, in life, and before that magnificent Tartar issued the ukase, 'As he will never distinguish himself, he must be a poor gentleman-pensioner of mine, and let him hereby consider himself pensioned.'

Ah! my Twemlow! Say, little feeble grey personage, what thoughts are in thy breast to-day, of the Fancy—so still to call her who bruised thy heart when it was green and thy head brown—and whether it be better or worse, more painful or less, to believe in the Fancy to this hour, than to know her for a greedy armour-plated crocodile, with no more capacity of imagining the delicate and sensitive and tender spot behind thy waistcoat, than of going straight at it with a knitting-needle. Say likewise, my Twemlow, whether it be the happier lot to be a poor relation of the great, or to stand in the wintry slush giving the hack horses to drink out of the shallow tub at the coach-stand, into which thou has so nearly set thy uncertain foot. Twemlow says nothing, and goes on.

As he approaches the Lammles' door, drives up a little one-horse carriage, containing Tippins the divine. Tippins, letting down the window, playfully extols the vigilance of her cavalier in being in waiting there to hand her out. Twemlow hands her out with as much polite gravity as if she were anything real, and they proceed upstairs. Tippins all abroad about the legs, and seeking to express that those unsteady articles are only skipping in their native buoyancy.

And dear Mrs Lammle and dear Mr Lammle, how do you

do, and when are you going down to what's-its-name place—
Guy, Earl of Warwick, you know—what is it?—Dun Cow—to
claim the flitch of bacon? And Mortimer, whose name is for ever
blotted out from my list of lovers, by reason first of fickleness
and then of base desertion, how do *you* do, wretch? And Mr
Wrayburn, *you* here! What can *you* come for, because we are all
very sure beforehand that you are not going to talk! And Veneering, M.P., how are things going on down at the house, and when
will you turn out those terrible people for us? And Mrs Veneering, my dear, can it positively be true that you go down to that
stifling place night after night, to hear those men prose? Talking
of which, Veneering, why don't *you* prose, for you haven't
opened your lips there yet, and we are dying to hear what you
have got to say to us! Miss Podsnap, charmed to see you. Pa,
here? No! Ma, neither? Oh! Mr Boots! Delighted. Mr Brewer!
This *is* a gathering of the clans. Thus Tippins, and surveys
Fledgeby and outsiders through golden glass, murmuring as she
turns about and about, in her innocent giddy way, Anybody else
I know? No, I think not. Nobody there. Nobody *there*. Nobody
anywhere!

Mr Lammle, all a-glitter, produces his friend Fledgeby, as
dying for the honour of presentation to Lady Tippins. Fledgeby
presented, has the air of going to say something, has the air of
going to say nothing, has an air successively of meditation, of
resignation, and of desolation, backs on Brewer, makes the tour
of Boots, and fades into the extreme background, feeling for his
whisker, as if it might have turned up since he was there five
minutes ago.

But Lammle has him out again before he has so much as
completely ascertained the bareness of the land. He would seem
to be in a bad way, Fledgeby; for Lammle represents him as
dying again. He is dying now, of want of presentation to
Twemlow.

Twemlow offers his hand. Glad to see him. 'Your mother,
sir, was a connexion of mine.'

'I believe so,' says Fledgeby, 'but my mother and her
family were two.'

'Are you staying in town?' asks Twemlow.

'I always am,' says Fledgeby.

'You like town,' says Twemlow. But is felled flat by
Fledgeby's taking it quite ill, and replying, No, he don't like
town. Lammle tries to break the force of the fall, by remarking
that some people do not like town. Fledgeby retorting that he

never heard of any such case but his own, Twemlow goes down again heavily.

'There is nothing new this morning, I suppose?' says Twemlow, returning to the mark with great spirit.

Fledgeby has not heard of anything.

'No, there's not a word of news,' says Lammle.

'Not a particle,' adds Boots.

'Not an atom,' chimes in Brewer.

Somehow the execution of this little concerted piece appears to raise the general spirits as with a sense of duty done, and sets the company a going. Everybody seems more equal than before, to the calamity of being in the society of everybody else. Even Eugene standing in a window, moodily swinging the tassel of a blind, gives it a smarter jerk now, as if he found himself in better case.

Breakfast announced. Everything on table showy and gaudy, but with a self-assertingly temporary and nomadic air on the decorations, as boasting that they will be much more showy and gaudy in the palatial residence. Mr Lammle's own particular servant behind his chair; the Analytical behind Veneering's chair; instances in point that such servants fall into two classes: one mistrusting the master's acquaintances, and the other mistrusting the master. Mr Lammle's servant, of the second class. Appearing to be lost in wonder and low spirits because the police are so long in coming to take his master up on some charge of the first magnitude.

Veneering, M.P., on the right of Mrs Lammle; Twemlow on her left; Mrs Veneering, W.M.P. (wife of Member of Parliament), and Lady Tippins on Mr Lammle's right and left. But be sure that well within the fascination of Mr Lammle's eye and smile sits little Georgiana. And be sure that close to little Georgiana, also under inspection by the same gingerous gentleman, sits Fledgeby.

Oftener than twice or thrice while breakfast is in progress, Mr Twemlow gives a little sudden turn towards Mrs Lammle, and then says to her, 'I beg your pardon!' This not being Twemlow's usual way, why is it his way to-day? Why, the truth is, Twemlow repeatedly labours under the impression that Mrs Lammle is going to speak to him, and turning finds that it is not so, and mostly that she has her eyes upon Veneering. Strange that this impression so abides by Twemlow after being corrected, yet so it is.

Lady Tippins partaking plentifully of the fruits of the earth (including grape-juice in the category) becomes livelier, and applies herself to elicit sparks from Mortimer Lightwood. It is always understood among the initiated, that that faithless lover must be planted at table opposite to Lady Tippins, who will then strike conversational fire out of him. In a pause of mastication and deglutition, Lady Tippins, contemplating Mortimer, recalls that it was at our dear Veneerings, and in the presence of a party who are surely all here, that he told them his story of the man from somewhere, which afterwards became so horribly interesting and vulgarly popular.

'Yes, Lady Tippins,' assents Mortimer; 'as they say on the stage, "Even so!" '

'Then we expect you,' retorts the charmer, 'to sustain your reputation, and tell us something else.'

'Lady Tippins, I exhausted myself for life that day, and there is nothing more to be got out of me.'

Mortimer parries thus, with a sense upon him that elsewhere it is Eugene and not he who is the jester, and that in these circles where Eugene persists in being speechless, he, Mortimer, is but the double of the friend on whom he has founded himself.

'But,' quoth the fascinating Tippins, 'I am resolved on getting something more out of you. Traitor! what is this I hear about another disappearance?'

'As it is you who have heard it,' returns Lightwood, 'perhaps you'll tell us.'

'Monster, away!' retorts Lady Tippins. 'Your own Golden Dustman referred me to you.'

Mr Lammle, striking in here, proclaims aloud that there is a sequel to the story of the man from somewhere. Silence ensues upon the proclamation.

'I assure you,' says Lightwood, glancing round the table, 'I have nothing to tell.' But Eugene adding in a low voice, 'There, tell it, tell it!' he corrects himself with the addition, 'Nothing worth mentioning.'

Boots and Brewer immediately perceive that it is immensely worth mentioning, and become politely clamorous. Veneering is also visited by a perception to the same effect. But it is understood that his attention is now rather used up, and difficult to hold, that being the tone of the House of Commons.

'Pray don't be at the trouble of composing yourselves to listen,' says Mortimer Lightwood, 'because I shall have finished long before you have fallen into comfortable attitudes. It's like—'

'It's like,' impatiently interrupts Eugene, 'the children's narrative:

> "I'll tell you a story
> Of Jack a Manory,
> And now my story's begun;
> I'll tell you another
> Of Jack and his brother,
> And now my story is done."

—Get on, and get it over!'

Eugene says this with a sound of vexation in his voice, leaning back in his chair and looking balefully at Lady Tippins, who nods to him as her dear Bear, and playfully insinuates that she (a self-evident proposition) is Beauty, and he Beast.

'The reference,' proceeds Mortimer, 'which I suppose to be made by my honourable and fair enslaver opposite, is to the following circumstance. Very lately, the young woman, Lizzie Hexam, daughter of the late Jesse Hexam, otherwise Gaffer, who will be remembered to have found the body of the man from somewhere, mysteriously received, she knew not from whom, an explicit retraction of the charges made against her father, by another waterside character of the name of Riderhood. Nobody believed them, because little Rogue Riderhood—I am tempted into the paraphrase by remembering the charming wolf who would have rendered society a great service if he had devoured Mr Riderhood's father and mother in their infancy—had previously played fast and loose with the said charges, and, in fact, abandoned them. However, the retraction I have mentioned found its way into Lizzie Hexam's hands, with a general flavour on it of having been favoured by some anonymous messenger in a dark cloak and slouched hat, and was by her forwarded, in her father's vindication, to Mr Boffin, my client. You will excuse the phraseology of the shop, but as I never had another client, and in all likelihood never shall have, I am rather proud of him as a natural curiosity probably unique.'

Although as easy as usual on the surface, Lightwood is not quite as easy as usual below it. With an air of not minding Eugene at all, he feels that the subject is not altogether a safe one in that connexion.

'The natural curiosity which forms the sole ornament of my professional museum,' he resumes, 'hereupon desires his Secretary—an individual of the hermit-crab or oyster species, and whose name, I think, is Chokesmith—but it doesn't in the least matter—say Artichoke—to put himself in communication with Lizzie Hexam. Artichoke professes his readiness so to do, endeavours to do so, but fails.'

'Why fails?' asks Boots.

'How fails?' asks Brewer.

'Pardon me,' returns Lightwood, 'I must postpone the reply for one moment, or we shall have an anti-climax. Artichoke failing signally, my client refers the task to me: his purpose being to advance the interests of the object of his search. I proceed to put myself in communication with her; I even happen to possess some special means,' with a glance at Eugene, 'of putting myself in communication with her; but I fail too, because she has vanished.'

'Vanished!' is the general echo.

'Disappeared,' says Mortimer. 'Nobody knows how, nobody knows when, nobody knows where. And so ends the story to which my honourable and fair enslaver opposite referred.'

Tippins, with a bewitching little scream, opines that we shall every one of us be murdered in our beds. Eugene eyes her as if some of us would be enough for him. Mrs Veneering, W.M.P., remarks that these social mysteries make one afraid of leaving Baby. Veneering, M.P., wishes to be informed (with something of a second-hand air of seeing the Right Honourable Gentleman at the head of the Home Department in his place) whether it is intended to be conveyed that the vanished person has been spirited away or otherwise harmed? Instead of Lightwood's answering, Eugene answers, and answers hastily and vexedly: 'No, no, no; he doesn't mean that; he means voluntarily vanished—but utterly—completely.'

However, the great subject of the happiness of Mr and Mrs Lammle must not be allowed to vanish with the other vanishments—with the vanishing of the murderer, the vanishing of Julius Handford, the vanishing of Lizzie Hexam,—and therefore Veneering must recall the present sheep to the pen from which they have strayed. Who so fit to discourse of the happiness of Mr and Mrs Lammle, they being the dearest and oldest friends he had in the world; or what audience so fit for him to take into his confidence as that audience, a noun of multitude or signifying many, who are all the oldest and dearest friends he has in the world? So Veneering, without the formality of rising, launches into a familiar oration, gradually toning into the Parliamentary sing-song, in which he sees at that board his dear friend Twemlow who on that day twelvemonth bestowed on his dear friend Lammle the fair hand of his dear friend Sophronia, and in which he also sees at that board his dear friends Boots and Brewer whose rallying round him at a period when his dear friend Lady Tippins likewise rallied round him—ay, and in the foremost rank—he can never forget while memory holds her seat. But he is free to confess that he misses from that board his dear old friend Podsnap, though he is well represented by his dear young friend Georgiana. And he further sees at that board (this he announces with pomp, as if exulting in the powers of an extraordinary telescope) his friend Mr Fledgeby, if he will permit him to call him so. For all of these reasons, and many more which he right well knows will have occurred to persons of your exceptional acuteness, he is here to submit to you that the time has arrived when, with our hearts in our glasses, with tears in our eyes, with blessings on our lips, and in a general way with a profusion of gammon and spinach in our emotional larders, we should one and all drink to our dear friends the Lammles, wishing them many years as happy as the last, and many many friends as congenially united as themselves. And this he will add; that Anastatia Veneering (who is instantly heard to weep) is formed on the same model as her old and chosen friend Sophronia Lammle, in respect that she is devoted to the man who wooed and won her, and nobly discharges the duties of a wife.

Seeing no better way out of it, Veneering here pulls up his oratorical Pegasus extremely short, and plumps down, clean over his head, with: 'Lammle, God bless you!'

Then Lammle. Too much of him every way; pervadingly too much nose of a coarse wrong shape, and his nose in his mind and his manners; too much smile to be real; too much frown to be false; too many large teeth to be visible at once without suggesting a bite. He thanks you, dear friends, for your kindly greeting, and hopes to receive you—it may be on the next of these delightful occasions—in a residence better suited to your claims on the rites of hospitality. He will never forget that at Veneering's he first saw Sophronia. Sophronia will never forget that at Veneering's she first saw him. They spoke of it soon after they were married, and agreed that they would never forget it. In fact, to Veneering they owe their union. They hope to show their sense of this some day ('No, no,' from Veneering)—oh yes, yes, and let him rely upon it, they will if they can! His marriage with Sophronia was not a marriage of interest on either side: she had her little fortune, he had his little fortune: they joined their little fortunes: it was a marriage of pure inclination and suitability. Thank you! Sophronia and he are fond of the society of young people; but he is not sure that their house would be a good house for young people proposing to remain single, since the contemplation of its domestic bliss might induce them to change their minds. He will not apply this to any one present; certainly not to their darling little Georgiana. Again thank you! Neither, by-the-by, will he apply it to his friend Fledgeby. He thanks Veneering for the feeling manner in which he referred to their common friend Fledgeby, for he holds that gentleman in the highest estimation. Thank you. In fact (returning unexpectedly to Fledgeby), the better you know him, the more you find in him that you desire to know. Again thank you! In his dear Sophronia's name and in his own, thank you!

Mrs Lammle has sat quite still, with her eyes cast down upon the table-cloth. As Mr Lammle's address ends, Twemlow once more turns to her involuntarily, not cured yet of that often recurring impression that she is going to speak to him. This time she really is going to speak to him. Veneering is talking with his other next neighbour, and she speaks in a low voice.

'Mr Twemlow.'

He answers, 'I beg your pardon? Yes?' Still a little doubtful, because of her not looking at him.

'You have the soul of a gentleman, and I know I may trust you. Will you give me the opportunity of saying a few words to you when you come up stairs?'

'Assuredly. I shall be honoured.'

'Don't seem to do so, if you please, and don't think it inconsistent if my manner should be more careless than my words. I may be watched.'

Intensely astonished, Twemlow puts his hand to his forehead, and sinks back in his chair meditating. Mrs Lammle rises. All rise. The ladies go up stairs. The gentlemen soon saunter after them. Fledgeby has devoted the interval to taking an observation of Boots's whiskers, Brewer's whiskers, and Lammle's whiskers, and considering which pattern of whisker he would prefer to produce out of himself by friction, if the Genie of the cheek would only answer to his rubbing.

In the drawing-room, groups form as usual. Lightwood, Boots, and Brewer, flutter like moths around that yellow wax candle—guttering down, and with some hint of a winding-sheet in it—Lady Tippins. Outsiders cultivate Veneering, M.P., and Mrs Veneering, W.M.P. Lammle stands with folded arms,

Mephistophelean in a corner, with Georgiana and Fledgeby. Mrs Lammle, on a sofa by a table, invites Mr Twemlow's attention to a book of portraits in her hand.

Mr Twemlow takes his station on a settee before her, and Mrs Lammle shows him a portrait.

'You have reason to be surprised,' she says softly, 'but I wish you wouldn't look so.'

Disturbed Twemlow, making an effort not to look so, looks much more so.

'I think, Mr Twemlow, you never saw that distant connexion of yours before to-day?'

'No, never.'

'Now that you do see him, you see what he is. You are not proud of him?'

'To say the truth, Mrs Lammle, no.'

'If you knew more of him, you would be less inclined to acknowledge him. Here is another portrait. What do you think of it?'

Twemlow has just presence of mind enough to say aloud: 'Very like! Uncommonly like!'

'You have noticed, perhaps, whom he favours with his attentions? You notice where he is now, and how engaged?'

'Yes. But Mr Lammle—'

She darts a look at him which he cannot comprehend, and shows him another portrait.

'Very good; is it not?'

'Charming!' says Twemlow.

'So like as to be almost a caricature?—Mr Twemlow, it is impossible to tell you what the struggle in my mind has been, before I could bring myself to speak to you as I do now. It is only in the conviction that I may trust you never to betray me, that I can proceed. Sincerely promise me that you never will betray my confidence—that you will respect it, even though you may no longer respect me,—and I shall be as satisfied as if you had sworn it.'

'Madam, on the honour of a poor gentleman—'

'Thank you. I can desire no more. Mr. Twemlow, I implore you to save that child!'

'That child?'

'Georgiana. She will be sacrificed. She will be inveigled and married to that connexion of yours. It is a partnership affair, a money-speculation. She has no strength of will or character to help herself, and she is on the brink of being sold into wretchedness for life.'

'Amazing! But what can *I* do to prevent it?' demands Twemlow, shocked and bewildered to the last degree.

'Here is another portrait. And not good, is it?'

Aghast at the light manner of her throwing her head back to look at it critically, Twemlow still dimly perceives the expediency of throwing his own head back, and does so. Though he no more sees the portrait than if it were in China.

'Decidedly not good,' says Mrs Lammle. 'Stiff and exaggerated!'

'And ex—' But Twemlow, in his demolished state, cannot command the word, and trails off into '—actly so.'

'Mr Twemlow, your word will have weight with her pompous, self-blinded father. You know how much he makes of your family. Warn him.'

'But warn him against whom?'

'Against me.'

By great good fortune Twemlow receives a stimulant at this critical instant. The stimulant is Lammle's voice.

'Sophronia, my dear, what portraits are you showing Twemlow?'

'Public characters, Alfred.'

'Show him the last of me.'

'Yes, Alfred.'

She puts the book down, takes another book up, turns the leaves, and presents the portrait to Twemlow.

'That is the last of Mr Lammle. Do you think it good?— Warn her father against me. I deserve it, for I have been in the scheme from the first. It is my husband's scheme, your connexion's, and mine. I tell you this, only to show you the necessity of the poor little foolish affectionate creature's being befriended and rescued. You will not repeat this to her father. You will spare me so far, and spare my husband. For, though this celebration of to-day is all a mockery, he is my husband, and we must live.—Do you think it like?'

Twemlow, in a stunned condition, feigns to compare the portrait in his hand with the original looking towards him from his Mephistophelean corner.

'Very well indeed!' are at length the words which Twemlow with great difficulty extracts from himself.

'I am glad you think so. On the whole, I myself consider it

the best. The others are so dark. Now here, for instance, is another of Mr Lammle—'

'But I don't understand; I don't see my way,' Twemlow stammers, as he falters over the book with his glass at his eye. 'How warn her father, and not tell him? Tell him how much? Tell him how little? I—I—am getting lost.'

'Tell him I am a match-maker; tell him I am an artful and designing woman; tell him you are sure his daughter is best out of my house and my company. Tell him any such things of me; they will all be true. You know what a puffed-up man he is, and how easily you can cause his vanity to take the alarm. Tell him as much as will give him the alarm and make him careful of her, and spare me the rest. Mr Twemlow, I feel my sudden degradation in your eyes; familiar as I am with my degradation in my own eyes, I keenly feel the change that must have come upon me in yours, in these last few moments. But I trust to your good faith with me as implicitly as when I began. If you knew how often I have tried to speak to you to-day, you would almost pity me. I want no new promise from you on my own account, for I am satisfied, and I always shall be satisfied, with the promise you have given me. I can venture to say no more, for I see that I am watched. If you would set my mind at rest with the assurance that you will interpose with the father and save this harmless girl, close that book before you return it to me, and I shall know what you mean, and deeply thank you in my heart.—Alfred, Mr Twemlow thinks the last one the best, and quite agrees with you and me.'

Alfred advances. The groups break up. Lady Tippins rises to go, and Mrs Veneering follows her leader. For the moment, Mrs Lammle does not turn to them, but remains looking at Twemlow looking at Alfred's portrait through his eyeglass. The moment past, Twemlow drops his eyeglass at its ribbon's length, rises, and closes the book with an emphasis which makes that fragile nursling of the fairies, Tippins, start.

Then good-bye and good-bye, and charming occasion worthy of the Golden Age, and more about the flitch of bacon, and the like of that; and Twemlow goes staggering across Piccadilly with his hand to his forehead, and is nearly run down by a flushed letter-cart, and at last drops safe in his easy-chair, innocent good gentleman, with his hand to his forehead still, and his head in a whirl.

BOOK THE THIRD
A LONG LANE

Chapter 1
Lodgers in Queer Street

It was a foggy day in London, and the fog was heavy and dark. Animate London, with smarting eyes and irritated lungs, was blinking, wheezing, and choking; inanimate London was a sooty spectre, divided in purpose between being visible and invisible, and so being wholly neither. Gaslights flared in the shops with a haggard and unblest air, as knowing themselves to be night-creatures that had no business abroad under the sun; while the sun itself, when it was for a few moments dimly indicated through circling eddies of fog, showed as if it had gone out and were collapsing flat and cold. Even in the surrounding country it was a foggy day, but there the fog was grey, whereas in London it was, at about the boundary line, dark yellow, and a little within it brown, and then browner, and then browner, until at the heart of the City—which call Saint Mary Axe—it was rusty-black. From any point of the high ridge of land northward, it might have been discerned that the loftiest buildings made an occasional struggle to get their heads above the foggy sea, and especially that the great dome of Saint Paul's seemed to die hard; but this was not perceivable in the streets at their feet, where the whole metropolis was a heap of vapour charged with muffled sound of wheels, and enfolding a gigantic catarrh.

At nine o'clock on such a morning, the place of business of Pubsey and Co. was not the liveliest object even in Saint Mary Axe—which is not a very lively spot—with a sobbing gaslight in the counting-house window, and a burglarious stream of fog creeping in to strangle it through the keyhole of the main door. But the light went out, and the main door opened, and Riah came forth with a bag under his arm.

Almost in the act of coming out at the door, Riah went into the fog, and was lost to the eyes of Saint Mary Axe. But the eyes of this history can follow him westward, by Cornhill, Cheapside,

Fleet Street, and the Strand, to Piccadilly and the Albany. Thither he went at his grave and measured pace, staff in hand, skirt at heel; and more than one head, turning to look back at his venerable figure already lost in the mist, supposed it to be some ordinary figure indistinctly seen, which fancy and the fog had worked into that passing likeness.

Arrived at the house in which his master's chambers were on the second floor, Riah proceeded up the stairs, and paused at Fascination Fledgeby's door. Making free with neither bell nor knocker, he struck upon the door with the top of his staff, and, having listened, sat down on the threshold. It was characteristic of his habitual submission, that he sat down on the raw dark staircase, as many of his ancestors had probably sat down in dungeons, taking what befell him as it might befall.

After a time, when he had grown so cold as to be fain to blow upon his fingers, he arose and knocked with his staff again, and listened again, and again sat down to wait. Thrice he repeated these actions before his listening ears were greeted by the voice of Fledgeby, calling from his bed, 'Hold your row!—I'll come and open the door directly!' But, in lieu of coming directly, he fell into a sweet sleep for some quarter of an hour more, during which added interval Riah sat upon the stairs and waited with perfect patience.

At length the door stood open, and Mr Fledgeby's retreating drapery plunged into bed again. Following it at a respectful distance, Riah passed into the bed-chamber, where a fire had been sometime lighted, and was burning briskly.

'Why, what time of night do you mean to call it?' inquired Fledgeby, turning away beneath the clothes, and presenting a comfortable rampart of shoulder to the chilled figure of the old man.

'Sir, it is full half-past ten in the morning.'

'The deuce it is! Then it must be precious foggy?'

'Very foggy, sir.'

'And raw, then?'

'Chill and bitter,' said Riah, drawing out a handkerchief, and wiping the moisture from his beard and long grey hair as he stood on the verge of the rug, with his eyes on the acceptable fire.

With a plunge of enjoyment, Fledgeby settled himself afresh.

'Any snow, or sleet, or slush, or anything of that sort?' he asked.

'No, sir, no. Not quite so bad as that. The streets are pretty clean.'

'You needn't brag about it,' returned Fledgeby, disappointed in his desire to heighten the contrast between his bed and the streets. 'But you're always bragging about something. Got the books there?'

'They are here, sir.'

'All right. I'll turn the general subject over in my mind for a minute or two, and while I'm about it you can empty your bag and get ready for me.'

With another comfortable plunge, Mr Fledgeby fell asleep again. The old man, having obeyed his directions, sat down on the edge of a chair, and, folding his hands before him, gradually yielded to the influence of the warmth, and dozed. He was roused by Mr Fledgeby's appearing erect at the foot of the bed, in Turkish slippers, rose-coloured Turkish trousers (got cheap from somebody who had cheated some other somebody out of them), and a gown and cap to correspond. In that costume he would have left nothing to be desired, if he had been further fitted out with a bottomless chair, a lantern, and a bunch of matches.

'Now, old 'un!' cried Fascination, in his light raillery, 'what dodgery are you up to next, sitting there with your eyes shut? You ain't asleep. Catch a weasel at it, and catch a Jew!'

'Truly, sir, I fear I nodded,' said the old man.

'Not you!' returned Fledgeby, with a cunning look. 'A telling move with a good many, I dare say, but it won't put *me* off my guard. Not a bad notion though, if you want to look indifferent in driving a bargain. Oh, you are a dodger!'

The old man shook his head, gently repudiating the imputation, and suppresed a sigh, and moved to the table at which Mr Fledgeby was now pouring out for himself a cup of steaming and fragrant coffee from a pot that had stood ready on the hob. It was an edifying spectacle, the young man in his easy chair taking his coffee, and the old man with his grey head bent, standing awaiting his pleasure.

'Now!' said Fledgeby. 'Fork out your balance in hand, and prove by figures how you make it out that it ain't more. First of all, light that candle.'

Riah obeyed, and then taking a bag from his breast, and referring to the sum in the accounts for which they made him responsible, told it out upon the table. Fledgeby told it again with great care, and rang every sovereign.

'I suppose,' he said, taking one up to eye it closely, 'you haven't been lightening any of these; but it's a trade of your people's, you know. *You* understand what sweating a pound means, don't you?'

'Much as you do, sir,' returned the old man, with his hands under opposite cuffs of his loose sleeves, as he stood at the table, deferentially observant of the master's face. 'May I take the liberty to say something?'

'You may,' Fledgeby graciously conceded.

'Do you not, sir—without intending it—of a surety without intending it—sometimes mingle the character I fairly earn in your employment, with the character which it is your policy that I should bear?'

'I don't find it worth my while to cut things so fine as to go into the inquiry,' Fascination coolly answered.

'Not in justice?'

'Bother justice!' said Fledgeby.

'Not in generosity?'

'Jews and generosity!' said Fledgeby. 'That's a good connexion! Bring out your vouchers, and don't talk Jerusalem palaver.'

The vouchers were produced, and for the next half-hour Mr Fledgeby concentrated his sublime attention on them. They and the accounts were all found correct, and the books and the papers resumed their places in the bag.

'Next,' said Fledgeby, 'concerning that bill-broking branch of the business; the branch I like best. What queer bills are to be bought, and at what prices? You have got your list of what's in the market?'

'Sir, a long list,' replied Riah, taking out a pocket-book, and selecting from its contents a folded paper, which, being unfolded, became a sheet of foolscap covered with close writing.

'Whew!' whistled Fledgeby, as he took it in his hand. 'Queer Street is full of lodgers just at present! These are to be disposed of in parcels; are they?'

'In parcels as set forth,' returned the old man, looking over his master's shoulder; 'or the lump.'

'Half the lump will be waste-paper, one knows beforehand,' said Fledgeby. 'Can you get it at waste-paper price? That's the question.'

Riah shook his head, and Fledgeby cast his small eyes down the list. They presently began to twinkle, and he no sooner became conscious of their twinkling, than he looked up over his shoulder at the grave face above him, and moved to the chimney-piece. Making a desk of it, he stood there with his back to the old man, warming his knees, perusing the list at his leisure, and often returning to some lines of it, as though they were particularly interesting. At those times he glanced in the chimney-glass to see what note the old man took of him. He took none that could be detected, but, aware of his employer's suspicions, stood with his eyes on the ground.

Mr Fledgeby was thus amiably engaged when a step was heard at the outer door, and the door was heard to open hastily. 'Hark! That's your doing, you Pump of Israel,' said Fledgeby; 'you can't have shut it.' Then the step was heard within, and the voice of Mr Alfred Lammle called aloud, 'Are you anywhere here, Fledgeby?' To which Fledgeby, after cautioning Riah in a low voice to take his cue as it should be given him, replied, 'Here I am!' and opened his bedroom door.

'Come in!' said Fledgeby. 'This gentleman is only Pubsey and Co. of Saint Mary Axe, that I am trying to make terms for an unfortunate friend with in a matter of some dishonoured bills. But really Pubsey and Co. are so strict with their debtors, and so hard to move, that I seem to be wasting my time. Can't I make *any* terms with you on my friend's part, Mr Riah?'

'I am but the representative of another, sir,' returned the Jew in a low voice. 'I do as I am bidden by my principal. It is not my capital that is invested in the business. It is not my profit that arises therefrom.'

'Ha ha!' laughed Fledgeby. 'Lammle?'

'Ha ha!' laughed Lammle. 'Yes. Of course. We know.'

'Devilish good, ain't it, Lammle?' said Fledgeby, unspeakably amused by his hidden joke.

'Always the same, always the same!' said Lammle. 'Mr—'

'Riah, Pubsey and Co. Saint Mary Axe,' Fledgeby put in, as he wiped away the tears that trickled from his eyes, so rare was his enjoyment of his secret joke.

'Mr Riah is bound to observe the invariable forms of such cases made and provided,' said Lammle.

'He is only the representative of another!' cried Fledgeby. 'Does as he is told by his principal! Not his capital that's invested in the business. Oh, that's good! Ha ha ha ha!' Mr Lammle joined in the laugh and looked knowing; and the more he did both, the more exquisite the secret joke became for Mr Fledgeby.

'However,' said that fascinating gentleman, wiping his eyes again, 'if we go on in this way, we shall seem to be almost making game of Mr Riah, or of Pubsey and Co. Saint Mary Axe, or of somebody: which is far from our intention. Mr Riah, if you would have the kindness to step into the next room for a few moments while I speak with Mr Lammle here, I should like to try to make terms with you once again before you go.'

The old man, who had never raised his eyes during the whole transaction of Mr Fledgeby's joke, silently bowed and passed out by the door which Fledgeby opened for him. Having closed it on him, Fledgeby returned to Lammle, standing with his back to the bedroom fire, with one hand under his coat-skirts, and all his whiskers in the other.

'Halloa!' said Fledgeby. 'There's something wrong!'

'How do you know it?' demanded Lammle.

'Because you show it,' replied Fledgeby in unintentional rhyme.

'Well then; there is,' said Lammle; 'there *is* something wrong; the whole thing's wrong.'

'I say!' remonstrated Fascination very slowly, and sitting down with his hands on his knees to stare at his glowering friend with his back to the fire.

'I tell you, Fledgeby,' repeated Lammle, with a sweep of his right arm, 'the whole thing's wrong. The game's up.'

'What game's up?' demanded Fledgeby, as slowly as before, and more sternly.

'THE game. OUR game. Read that.'

Fledgeby took a note from his extended hand and read it aloud. 'Alfred Lammle, Esquire. Sir: Allow Mrs Podsnap and myself to express our united sense of the polite attentions of Mrs Alfred Lammle and yourself towards our daughter, Georgiana. Allow us also, wholly to reject them for the future, and to communicate our final desire that the two families may become entire strangers. I have the honour to be, Sir, your most obedient and very humble servant, JOHN PODSNAP.' Fledgeby looked at the three blank sides of this note, quite as long and earnestly as at the first expressive side, and then looked at Lammle, who responded with another extensive sweep of his right arm.

'Whose doing is this?' said Fledgeby.

'Impossible to imagine,' said Lammle.

'Perhaps,' suggested Fledgeby, after reflecting with a very discontented brow, 'somebody has been giving you a bad character.'

'Or you,' said Lammle, with a deeper frown.

Mr Fledgeby appeared to be on the verge of some mutinous expressions, when his hand happened to touch his nose. A certain remembrance connected with that feature operating as a timely warning, he took it thoughtfully between his thumb and forefinger, and pondered; Lammle meanwhile eyeing him with furtive eyes.

'Well!' said Fledgeby. 'This won't improve with talking about. If we ever find out who did it, we'll mark that person. There's nothing more to be said, except that you undertook to do what circumstances prevent your doing.'

'And that you undertook to do what you might have done by this time, if you had made a prompter use of circumstances,' snarled Lammle.

'Hah! That,' remarked Fledgeby, with his hands in the Turkish trousers, 'is matter of opinion.'

'Mr Fledgeby,' said Lammle, in a bullying tone, 'am I to understand that you in any way reflect upon me, or hint dissatisfaction with me, in this affair?'

'No,' said Fledgeby; 'provided you have brought my promissory note in your pocket, and now hand it over.'

Lammle produced it, not without reluctance. Fledgeby looked at it, identified it, twisted it up, and threw it into the fire. They both looked at it as it blazed, went out, and flew in feathery ash up the chimney.

'*Now*, Mr Fledgeby,' said Lammle, as before; 'am I to understand that you in any way reflect upon me, or hint dissatisfaction with me, in this affair?'

'No,' said Fledgeby.

'Finally and unreservedly no?'

'Yes.'

'Fledgeby, my hand.'

Mr Fledgeby took it, saying, 'And if we ever find out who did this, we'll mark that person. And in the most friendly manner, let me mention one thing more. I don't know what your circumstances are, and I don't ask. You have sustained a loss here. Many men are liable to be involved at times, and you may be, or you may not be. But whatever you do, Lammle, don't—don't—don't, I beg of you—ever fall into the hands of Pubsey and Co. in the next room, for they are grinders. Regular flayers and grinders, my dear Lammle,' repeated Fledgeby with a peculiar relish, 'and they'll skin you by the inch, from the nape of your neck to the sole of your foot, and grind every inch of your skin to tooth-powder. You have seen what Mr Riah is. Never fall into his hands, Lammle, I beg of you as a friend!'

Mr Lammle, disclosing some alarm at the solemnity of this

affectionate adjuration, demanded why the devil he ever should fall into the hands of Pubsey and Co.?

'To confess the fact, I was made a little uneasy,' said the candid Fledgeby, 'by the manner in which that Jew looked at you when he heard your name. I didn't like his eye. But it may have been the heated fancy of a friend. Of course if you are sure that you have no personal security out, which you may not be quite equal to meeting, and which can have got into his hands, it must have been fancy. Still, I didn't like his eye.'

The brooding Lammle, with certain white dints coming and going in his palpitating nose, looked as if some tormenting imp were pinching it. Fledgeby, watching him with a twitch in his mean face which did duty there for a smile, looked very like the tormentor who was pinching.

'But I mustn't keep him waiting too long,' said Fledgeby, 'or he'll revenge it on my unfortunate friend. How's your very clever and agreeable wife? She knows we have broken down?'

'I showed her the letter.'

'Very much surprised?' asked Fledgeby.

'I think she would have been more so,' answered Lammle, 'if there had been more go in *you*?'

'Oh!—She lays it upon me, then?'

'Mr Fledgeby, I will not have my words misconstrued.'

'Don't break out, Lammle,' urged Fledgeby, in a submissive tone, 'because there's no occasion. I only asked a question. Then she don't lay it upon me? To ask another question.'

'No, sir.'

'Very good,' said Fledgeby, plainly seeing that she did. 'My compliments to her. Good-bye!'

They shook hands, and Lammle strode out pondering. Fledgeby saw him into the fog, and, returning to the fire and musing with his face to it, stretched the legs of the rose-coloured Turkish trousers wide apart, and meditatively bent his knees, as if he were going down upon them.

'You have a pair of whiskers, Lammle, which I never liked,' murmured Fledgeby, 'and which money can't produce; you are boastful of your manners and your conversation; you wanted to pull my nose, and you have let me in for a failure, and your wife says I am the cause of it. I'll bowl you down. I will, though I have no whiskers,' here he rubbed the places where they were due, 'and no manners, and no conversation!'

Having thus relieved his noble mind, he collected the legs of the Turkish trousers, straightened himself on his knees, and called out to Riah in the next room, 'Halloa, you sir!' At sight of the old man re-entering with a gentleness monstrously in contrast with the character he had given him, Mr Fledgeby was so tickled again, that he exclaimed, laughing, 'Good! Good! Upon my soul it is uncommon good!

'Now, old 'un,' proceeded Fledgeby, when he had had his laugh out, 'you'll buy up these lots that I mark with my pencil—there's a tick there, and a tick there, and a tick there—and I wager two-pence you'll afterwards go on squeezing those Christians like the Jew you are. Now, next you'll want a cheque—or you'll say you want it, though you've capital enough somewhere, if one only knew where, but you'd be peppered and salted and grilled on a gridiron before you'd own to it—and that cheque I'll write.'

When he had unlocked a drawer and taken a key from it to open another drawer, in which was another key that opened another drawer, in which was another key that opened another drawer, in which was the cheque book; and when he had written the cheque; and when, reversing the key and drawer process, he had placed his cheque book in safety again; he beckoned the old man, with the folded cheque, to come and take it.

'Old 'un,' said Fledgeby, when the Jew had put it in his pocketbook, and was putting that in the breast of his outer garment; 'so much at present for my affairs. Now a word about affairs that are not exactly mine. Where is she?'

With his hand not yet withdrawn from the breast of his garment, Riah started and paused.

'Oho!' said Fledgeby. 'Didn't expect it! Where have you hidden her?'

Showing that he was taken by surprise, the old man looked at his master with some passing confusion, which the master highly enjoyed.

'Is she in the house I pay rent and taxes for in Saint Mary Axe?' demanded Fledgeby.

'No, sir.'

'Is she in your garden up atop of that house—gone up to be dead, or whatever the game is?' asked Fledgeby.

'No, sir.'

'Where is she then?'

Riah bent his eyes upon the ground, as if considering whether he could answer the question without breach of faith, and then silently raised them to Fledgeby's face, as if he could not.

'Come!' said Fledgeby. 'I won't press that just now. But I want to know this, and I will know this, mind you. What are you up to?'

The old man, with an apologetic action of his head and hands, as not comprehending the master's meaning, addressed to him a look of mute inquiry.

'You can't be a gallivanting dodger,' said Fledgeby. 'For you're a "regular pity the sorrows", you know—if you *do* know any Christian rhyme—"whose trembling limbs have borne him to"—et cetrer. You're one of the Patriarchs; you're a shaky old card; and you can't be in love with this Lizzie?'

'O, sir!' expostulated Riah. 'O, sir, sir, sir!'

'Then why,' retorted Fledgeby, with some slight tinge of a blush, 'don't you out with your reason for having your spoon in the soup at all?'

'Sir, I will tell you the truth. But (your pardon for the stipulation) it is in sacred confidence; it is strictly upon honour.'

'Honour too!' cried Fledgeby, with a mocking lip. 'Honour among Jews. Well. Cut away.'

'It is upon honour, sir?' the other still stipulated, with respectful firmness.

'Oh, certainly. Honour bright,' said Fledgeby.

The old man, never bidden to sit down, stood with an earnest hand laid on the back of the young man's easy chair. The young man sat looking at the fire with a face of listening curiosity, ready to check him off and catch him tripping.

'Cut away,' said Fledgeby. 'Start with your motive.'

'Sir, I have no motive but to help the helpless.'

Mr Fledgeby could only express the feelings to which this incredible statement gave rise in his breast, by a prodigiously long derisive sniff.

'How I came to know, and much to esteem and to respect, this damsel, I mentioned when you saw her in my poor garden on the house-top,' said the Jew.

'Did you?' said Fledgeby, distrustfully. 'Well. Perhaps you did, though.'

'The better I knew her, the more interest I felt in her fortunes. They gathered to a crisis. I found her beset by a selfish and ungrateful brother, beset by an unacceptable wooer, beset by the snares of a more powerful lover, beset by the wiles of her own heart.'

'She took to one of the chaps then?'

'Sir, it was only natural that she should incline towards

him, for he had many and great advantages. But he was not of her station, and to marry her was not in his mind. Perils were closing round her, and the circle was fast darkening, when I—being as you have said, sir, too old and broken to be suspected of any feeling for her but a father's—stepped in, and counselled flight. I said, "My daughter, there are times of moral danger when the hardest virtuous resolution to form is flight, and when the most heroic bravery is flight." She answered, she had had this in her thoughts; but whither to fly without help she knew not, and there were none to help her. I showed her there was one to help her, and it was I. And she is gone.'

'What did you do with her?' asked Fledgeby, feeling his cheek.

'I placed her,' said the old man, 'at a distance;' with a grave smooth outward sweep from one another of his two open hands at arm's length; 'at a distance—among certain of our people, where her industry would serve her, and where she could hope to exercise it, unassailed from any quarter.'

Fledgeby's eyes had come from the fire to notice the action of his hands when he said 'at a distance.' Fledgeby now tried (very unsuccessfully) to imitate that action, as he shook his head and said, 'Placed her in that direction, did you? Oh you circular old dodger!'

With one hand across his breast and the other on the easy chair, Riah, without justifying himself, waited for further questioning. But, that it was hopeless to question him on that one reserved point, Fledgeby, with his small eyes too near together, saw full well.

'Lizzie,' said Fledgeby, looking at the fire again, and then looking up. 'Humph, Lizzie. You didn't tell me the other name in your garden atop of the house. I'll be more communicative with you. The other name's Hexam.'

Riah bent his head in assent.

'Look here, you sir,' said Fledgeby. 'I have a notion I know something of the inveigling chap, the powerful one. Has he anything to do with the law?'

'Nominally, I believe it his calling.'

'I thought so. Name anything like Lightwood?'

'Sir, not at all like.'

'Come, old 'un,' said Fledgeby, meeting his eyes with a wink, 'say the name.'

'Wrayburn.'

'By Jupiter!' cried Fledgeby. 'That one, is it? I thought it might be the other, but I never dreamt of that one! I shouldn't object to your baulking either of the pair, dodger, for they are both conceited enough; but that one is as cool a customer as ever I met with. Got a beard besides, and presumes upon it. Well done, old 'un! Go on and prosper!'

Brightened by this unexpected commendation, Riah asked were there more instructions for him?

'No,' said Fledgeby, 'you may toddle now, Judah, and grope about on the orders you have got.' Dismissed with those pleasing words, the old man took his broad hat and staff, and left the great presence: more as if he were some superior creature benignantly blessing Mr Fledgeby, than the poor dependent on whom he set his foot. Left alone, Mr Fledgeby locked his outer door, and came back to his fire.

'Well done you!' said Fascination to himself. 'Slow, you may be; sure, you are!' This he twice or thrice repeated with much complacency, as he again dispersed the legs of the Turkish trousers and bent the knees.

'A tidy shot that, I flatter myself,' he then soliloquised. 'And a Jew brought down with it! Now, when I heard the story told at Lammle's, I didn't make a jump at Riah. Not a bit of it; I got at him by degrees.' Herein he was quite accurate; it being his habit, not to jump, or leap, or make an upward spring, at anything in life, but to crawl at everything.

'I got at him,' pursued Fledgeby, feeling for his whisker, 'by degrees. If your Lammles or your Lightwoods had got at him anyhow, they would have asked him the question whether he hadn't something to do with that gal's disappearance. I knew a better way of going to work. Having got behind the hedge, and put him in the light, I took a shot at him and brought him down plump. Oh! It don't count for much, being a Jew, in a match against *me*!'

Another dry twist in place of a smile, made his face crooked here.

'As to Christians,' proceeded Fledgeby, 'look out, fellow-Christians, particularly you that lodge in Queer Street! I have got the run of Queer Street now, and you shall see some games there. To work a lot of power over you and you not know it, knowing as you think yourselves, would be almost worth laying out money upon. But when it comes to squeezing a profit out of you into the bargain, it's something like!'

With this apostrophe Mr Fledgeby appropriately proceeded to divest himself of his Turkish garments, and invest himself with Christian attire. Pending which operation, and his morning ablutions, and his anointing of himself with the last infallible preparation for the production of luxuriant and glossy hair upon the human countenance (quacks being the only sages he believed in besides usurers), the murky fog closed about him and shut him up in its sooty embrace. If it had never let him out any more, the world would have had no irreparable loss, but could have easily replaced him from its stock on hand.

Chapter 2
A Respected Friend in a New Aspect

IN the evening of this same foggy day when the yellow window-blind of Pubsey and Co. was drawn down upon the day's work, Riah the Jew once more went forth into Saint Mary Axe. But this time he carried no bag, and was not bound on his master's affairs. He passed over London Bridge, and returned to the Middlesex shore by that of Westminster, and so, ever wading through the fog, waded to the doorstep of the dolls' dressmaker.

Miss Wren expected him. He could see her through the window by the light of her low fire—carefully banked up with damp cinders that it might last the longer and waste the less when she was out—sitting waiting for him in her bonnet. His tap at the glass roused her from the musing solitude in which she sat, and she came to the door to open it; aiding her steps with a little crutch-stick.

'Good evening, godmother!' said Miss Jenny Wren.

The old man laughed, and gave her his arm to lean on.

'Won't you come in and warm yourself, godmother?' asked Miss Jenny Wren.

'Not if you are ready, Cinderella, my dear.'

'Well!' exclaimed Miss Wren, delighted. 'Now you ARE a clever old boy! If we gave prizes at this establishment (but we only keep blanks), you should have the first silver medal, for taking me up so quick.' As she spake thus, Miss Wren removed the key of the house-door from the keyhole and put it in her pocket, and then bustlingly closed the door, and tried it as they both stood on the step. Satisfied that her dwelling was safe, she drew one hand through the old man's arm and prepared to ply her crutch-stick with the other. But the key was an instrument of such gigantic proportions, that before they started Riah proposed to carry it.

'No, no, no! I'll carry it myself,' returned Miss Wren. 'I'm awfully lopsided, you know, and stowed down in my pocket it'll trim the ship. To let you into a secret, godmother, I wear my pocket on my high side, o' purpose.'

With that they began their plodding through the fog.

'Yes, it was truly sharp of you, godmother,' resumed Miss Wren with great approbation, 'to understand me. But, you see, you *are* so like the fairy godmother in the bright little books! You look so unlike the rest of people, and so much as if you had changed yourself into that shape, just this moment, with some benevolent object. Boh!' cried Miss Jenny, putting her face close to the old man's. 'I can see your features, godmother, behind the beard.'

'Does the fancy go to my changing other objects too, Jenny?'

'Ah! That it does! If you'd only borrow my stick and tap this piece of pavement—this dirty stone that my foot taps—it would start up a coach and six. I say! Let's believe so!'

'With all my heart,' replied the good old man.

'And I'll tell you what I must ask you to do, godmother. I must ask you to be so kind as give my child a tap, and change him altogether. O my child has been such a bad, bad child of late! It worries me nearly out of my wits. Not done a stroke of work these ten days. Has had the horrors, too, and fancied that four copper-coloured men in red wanted to throw him into a fiery furnace.'

'But that's dangerous, Jenny.'

'Dangerous, godmother? My child is always dangerous, more or less. He might'—here the little creature glanced back over her shoulder at the sky—'be setting the house on fire at this present moment. I don't know who would have a child, for my part! It's no use shaking him. I have shaken him till I have made myself giddy. "Why don't you mind your Commandments and honour your parent, you naughty old boy?" I said to him all the time. But he only whimpered and stared at me.'

'What shall be changed, after him?' asked Riah in a compassionately playful voice.

'Upon my word, godmother, I am afraid I must be selfish next, and get you to set me right in the back and the legs. It's a little thing to you with your power, godmother, but it's a great deal to poor weak aching me.'

There was no querulous complaining in the words, but they were not the less touching for that.

'And then?'

'Yes, and then—*you* know, godmother. We'll both jump up into the coach and six and go to Lizzie. This reminds me, godmother, to ask you a serious question. You are as wise as wise can be (having been brought up by the fairies), and you can tell me this: Is it better to have had a good thing and lost it, or never to have had it?'

'Explain, god-daughter.'

'I feel so much more solitary and helpless without Lizzie now, than I used to feel before I knew her.' (Tears were in her eyes as she said so.)

'Some beloved companionship fades out of most lives, my dear,' said the Jew,—'that of a wife, and a fair daughter, and a son of promise, has faded out of my own life—but the happiness was.'

'Ah!' said Miss Wren thoughtfully, by no means convinced, and chopping the exclamation with that sharp little hatchet of hers; 'then I tell you what change I think you had better begin with, godmother. You had better change Is into Was and Was into Is, and keep them so.'

'Would that suit your case? Would you not be always in pain then?' asked the old man tenderly.

'Right!' exclaimed Miss Wren with another chop. 'You have changed me wiser, godmother.—Not,' she added with the quaint hitch of her chin and eyes, 'that you need be a very wonderful godmother to do that deed.'

Thus conversing, and having crossed Westminster Bridge, they traversed the ground that Riah had lately traversed, and new ground likewise; for, when they had recrossed the Thames by way of London Bridge, they struck down by the river and held their still foggier course that way.

But previously, as they were going along, Jenny twisted her venerable friend aside to a brilliantly-lighted toy-shop window, and said: 'Now look at 'em! All my work!'

This referred to a dazzling semicircle of dolls in all the

colours of the rainbow, who were dressed for presentation at court, for going to balls, for going out driving, for going out on horseback, for going out walking, for going to get married, for going to help other dolls to get married, for all the gay events of life.

'Pretty, pretty, pretty!' said the old man with a clap of his hands. 'Most elegant taste!'

'Glad you like 'em,' returned Miss Wren, loftily. 'But the fun is, godmother, how I make the great ladies try my dresses on. Though it's the hardest part of my business, and would be, even if my back were not bad and my legs queer.'

He looked at her as not understanding what she had said.

'Bless you, godmother,' said Miss Wren, 'I have to scud about town at all hours. If it was only sitting at my bench, cutting out and sewing, it would be comparatively easy work; but it's the trying-on by the great ladies that takes it out of me.'

'How, the trying-on?' asked Riah.

'What a mooney godmother you are, after all!' returned Miss Wren. 'Look here. There's a Drawing Room, or a grand day in the Park, or a Show, or a Fête, or what you like. Very well. I squeeze among the crowd, and I look about me. When I see a great lady very suitable for my business, I say "You'll do, my dear!" and I take particular notice of her, and run home and cut her out and baste her. Then another day, I come scudding back again to try on, and then I take particular notice of her again. Sometimes she plainly seems to say, "How that little creature is staring!" and sometimes likes it and sometimes don't, but much more often yes than no. All the time I am only saying to myself, "I must hollow out a bit here; I must slope away there;" and I am making a perfect slave of her, with making her try on my doll's dress. Evening parties are severer work for me, because there's only a doorway for a full view, and what with hobbling among the wheels of the carriages and the legs of the horses, I full expect to be run over some night. However, there I have 'em, just the same. When they go bobbing into the hall from the carriage, and catch a glimpse of my little physiognomy poked out from behind a policeman's cape in the rain, I dare say they think I am wondering and admiring with all my eyes and heart, but they little think they're only working for my dolls! There was Lady Belinda Whitrose. I made her do double duty in one night. I said when she came out of the carriage, "*You*'ll do, my dear!" and I ran straight home and cut her out and basted her. Back I came again, and waited behind the men that called the carriages. Very bad night too. At last, "Lady Belinda Whitrose's carriage! Lady Belinda Whitrose coming down!" And I made her try on—oh! and take pains about it too—before she got seated. That's Lady Belinda hanging up by the waist, much too near the gaslight for a wax one, with her toes turned in.'

When they had plodded on for some time nigh the river, Riah asked the way to a certain tavern called the Six Jolly Fellowship Porters. Following the directions he received, they arrived, after two or three puzzled stoppages for consideration, and some uncertain looking about them, at the door of Miss Abbey Potterson's dominions. A peep through the glass portion of the door revealed to them the glories of the bar, and Miss Abbey herself seated in state on her snug throne, reading the newspaper. To whom, with deference, they presented themselves.

Taking her eyes off her newspaper, and pausing with a suspended expression of countenance, as if she must finish the paragraph in hand before undertaking any other business whatever, Miss Abbey demanded, with some slight asperity: 'Now then, what's for you?'

'Could we see Miss Potterson?' asked the old man, uncovering his head.

'You not only could, but you can and you do,' replied the hostess.

'Might we speak with you, madam?'

By this time Miss Abbey's eyes had possessed themselves of the small figure of Miss Jenny Wren. For the closer observation of which, Miss Abbey laid aside her newspaper, rose, and looked over the half-door of the bar. The crutch-stick seemed to entreat for its owner leave to come in and rest by the fire; so, Miss Abbey opened the half-door, and said, as though replying to the crutch-stick: 'Yes, come in and rest by the fire.'

'My name is Riah,' said the old man, with courteous action, 'and my avocation is in London city. This, my young companion—'

'Stop a bit,' interposed Miss Wren. 'I'll give the lady my card.' She produced it from her pocket with an air, after struggling with the gigantic door-key which had got upon the top of it and kept it down. Miss Abbey, with manifest tokens of astonishment, took the diminutive document, and found it to run concisely thus:—

> **MISS JENNY WREN**
> DOLLS' DRESSMAKER
> *Dolls attended at their own residences.*

'Lud!' exclaimed Miss Potterson, staring. And dropped the card.

'We take the liberty of coming, my young companion and I, madam,' said Riah, 'on behalf of Lizzie Hexam.'

Miss Potterson was stooping to loosen the bonnet-strings of the dolls' dressmaker. She looked round rather angrily, and said: 'Lizzie Hexam is a very proud young woman.'

'She would be so proud,' returned Riah, dexterously, 'to stand well in your good opinion, that before she quitted London for—'

'For where, in the name of the Cape of Good Hope?' asked Miss Potterson, as though supposing her to have emigrated.

'For the country,' was the cautious answer,—'she made us promise to come and show you a paper, which she left in our hands for that special purpose. I am an unserviceable friend of hers, who began to know her after her departure from this neighbourhood. She has been for some time living with my young companion, and has been a helpful and a comfortable friend to her. Much needed, madam,' he added, in a lower voice. 'Believe me; if you knew all, much needed.'

'I can believe that,' said Miss Abbey, with a softening glance at the little creature.

'And if it's proud to have a heart that never hardens, and a temper that never tires, and a touch that never hurts,' Miss Jenny struck in, flushed, 'she is proud. And if it's not, she is NOT.'

Her set purpose of contradicting Miss Abbey point blank, was so far from offending that dread authority, as to elicit a gracious smile. 'You do right, child,' said Miss Abbey, 'to speak well of those who deserve well of you.'

'Right or wrong,' muttered Miss Wren, inaudibly, with a visible hitch of her chin, 'I mean to do it, and you may make up your mind to *that*, old lady.'

'Here is the paper, madam,' said the Jew, delivering into Miss Potterson's hands the original document drawn up by Rokesmith, and signed by Riderhood. 'Will you please to read it?'

'But first of all,' said Miss Abbey, '—did you ever taste shrub, child?'

Miss Wren shook her head.

'Should you like to?'

'Should if it's good,' returned Miss Wren.

'You shall try. And, if you find it good, I'll mix some for you with hot water. Put your poor little feet on the fender. It's a cold, cold night, and the fog clings so.' As Miss Abbey helped her to turn her chair, her loosened bonnet dropped on the floor. 'Why, what lovely hair!' cried Miss Abbey. 'And enough to make wigs for all the dolls in the world. What a quantity!'

'Call *that* a quantity?' returned Miss Wren. 'Poof! What do you say to the rest of it?' As she spoke, she untied a band, and the golden stream fell over herself and over the chair, and flowed down to the ground. Miss Abbey's admiration seemed to increase her perplexity. She beckoned the Jew towards her, as she reached down the shrub-bottle from its niche, and whispered:

'Child, or woman?'

'Child in years,' was the answer; 'woman in self-reliance and trial.'

'You are talking about Me, good people,' thought Miss Jenny, sitting in her golden bower, warming her feet. 'I can't hear what you say, but *I* know your tricks and your manners!'

The shrub, when tasted from a spoon, perfectly harmonizing with Miss Jenny's palate, a judicious amount was mixed by Miss Potterson's skilful hands, whereof Riah too partook. After this preliminary, Miss Abbey read the document; and, as often as she raised her eyebrows in so doing, the watchful Miss Jenny accompanied the action with an expressive and emphatic sip of the shrub and water.

'As far as this goes,' said Miss Abbey Potterson, when she had read it several times, and thought about it, 'it proves (what didn't much need proving) that Rogue Riderhood is a villain. I have my doubts whether he is not the villain who solely did the deed; but I have no expectation of those doubts ever being cleared up now. I believe I did Lizzie's father wrong, but never Lizzie's self; because when things were at the worst I trusted her, had perfect confidence in her, and tried to persuade her to come to me for a refuge. I am very sorry to have done a man wrong, particularly when it can't be undone. Be kind enough to let Lizzie know what I say; not forgetting that if she will come to the Porters, after all, bygones being bygones, she will find a home at the Porters, and a friend at the Porters. She knows Miss Abbey of old, remind her, and she knows what-like the home, and what-like the friend, is likely to turn out. I am generally short and sweet—or short and sour, according as it may be and as opinions vary—' remarked Miss Abbey, 'and that's about all I have got to say, and enough too.'

But before the shrub and water was sipped out, Miss Abbey bethought herself that she would like to keep a copy of the paper by her. 'It's not long, sir,' said she to Riah, 'and perhaps you wouldn't mind just jotting it down.' The old man willingly put on his spectacles, and, standing at the little desk in the corner where Miss Abbey filed her receipts and kept her sample phials (customers' scores were interdicted by the strict administration of the Porters), wrote out the copy in a fair round character. As he stood there, doing his methodical penmanship, his ancient scribe-like figure intent upon the work, and the little dolls' dressmaker sitting in her golden bower before the fire, Miss Abbey had her doubts whether she had not dreamed those two rare figures into the bar of the Six Jolly Fellowships, and might not wake with a nod next moment and find them gone.

Miss Abbey had twice made the experiment of shutting her eyes and opening them again, still finding the figures there, when, dreamlike, a confused hubbub arose in the public room. As she started up, and they all three looked at one another, it became a noise of clamouring voices and of the stir of feet; then all the windows were heard to be hastily thrown up, and shouts and cries came floating into the house from the river. A moment more, and Bob Gliddery came clattering along the passage, with the noise of all the nails in his boots condensed into every separate nail.

'What is it?' asked Miss Abbey.

'It's summut run down in the fog, ma'am,' answered Bob. 'There's ever so many people in the river.'

'Tell 'em to put on all the kettles!' cried Miss Abbey. 'See that the boiler's full. Get a bath out. Hang some blankets to the fire. Heat some stone bottles. Have your senses about you, you girls down stairs, and use 'em.'

While Miss Abbey partly delivered these directions to Bob—whom she seized by the hair, and whose head she knocked against the wall, as a general injunction to vigilance and presence of mind—and partly hailed the kitchen with them—the company in the public room, jostling one another, rushed out to the causeway, and the outer noise increased.

'Come and look,' said Miss Abbey to her visitors. They all three hurried to the vacated public room, and passed by one of the windows into the wooden verandah overhanging the river.

'Does anybody down there know what has happened?' demanded Miss Abbey, in her voice of authority.

'It's a steamer, Miss Abbey,' cried one blurred figure in the fog.

'It always *is* a steamer, Miss Abbey,' cried another.

'Them's her lights, Miss Abbey, wot you see a-blinking yonder,' cried another.

'She's a-blowing off her steam, Miss Abbey, and that's what makes the fog and the noise worse, don't you see?' explained another.

Boats were putting off, torches were lighting up, people were rushing tumultuously to the water's edge. Some man fell in with a splash, and was pulled out again with a roar of laughter. The drags were called for. A cry for the life-buoy passed from mouth to mouth. It was impossible to make out what was going on upon the river, for every boat that put off sculled into the fog and was lost to view at a boat's length. Nothing was clear but that the unpopular steamer was assailed with reproaches on all sides. She was the Murderer, bound for Gallows Bay; she was the Manslaughterer, bound for Penal Settlement; her captain ought to be tried for his life; her crew ran down men in row-boats with a relish; she mashed up Thames lightermen with her paddles; she fired property with her funnels; she always was, and she always would be, wreaking destruction upon somebody or something, after the manner of all her kind. The whole bulk of the fog teemed with such taunts, uttered in tones of universal hoarseness. All the while, the steamer's lights moved spectrally a very little, as she lay-to, waiting the upshot of whatever accident had happened. Now, she began burning blue-lights. These made a luminous patch about her, as if she had set the fog on fire, and in the patch—the cries changing their note, and becoming more fitful and more excited—shadows of men and boats could be seen moving, while voices shouted: 'There!' 'There again!' 'A couple more strokes a-head!' 'Hurrah!' 'Look out!' 'Hold on!' 'Haul in!' and the like. Lastly, with a few tumbling clots of blue fire, the night closed in dark again, the wheels of the steamer were heard revolving, and her lights glided smoothly away in the direction of the sea.

It appeared to Miss Abbey and her two companions that a considerable time had been thus occupied. There was now as eager a set towards the shore beneath the house as there had been from it; and it was only on the first boat of the rush coming in that it was known what had occurred.

'If that's Tom Tootle,' Miss Abbey made proclamation, in her most commanding tones, 'let him instantly come underneath here.'

The submissive Tom complied, attended by a crowd.

'What is it, Tootle?' demanded Miss Abbey.

'It's a foreign steamer, miss, run down a wherry.'

'How many in the wherry?'

'One man, Miss Abbey.'

'Found?'

'Yes. He's been under water a long time, Miss; but they've grappled up the body.'

'Let 'em bring it here. You, Bob Gliddery, shut the house-door and stand by it on the inside, and don't you open till I tell you. Any police down there?'

'Here, Miss Abbey,' was official rejoinder.

'After they have brought the body in, keep the crowd out, will you? And help Bob Gliddery to shut 'em out.'

'All right, Miss Abbey.'

The autocratic landlady withdrew into the house with Riah and Miss Jenny, and disposed those forces, one on either side of her, within the half-door of the bar, as behind a breastwork.

'You two stand close here,' said Miss Abbey, 'and you'll come to no hurt, and see it brought in. Bob, you stand by the door.'

That sentinel, smartly giving his rolled shirt-sleeves an extra and a final tuck on his shoulders, obeyed.

Sound of advancing voices, sound of advancing steps. Shuffle and talk without. Momentary pause. Two peculiarly blunt knocks or pokes at the door, as if the dead man arriving on his back were striking at it with the soles of his motionless feet.

'That's the stretcher, or the shutter, whichever of the two they are carrying,' said Miss Abbey, with experienced ear. 'Open, you Bob!'

Door opened. Heavy tread of laden men. A halt. A rush. Stoppage of rush. Door shut. Baffled hoots from the vexed souls of disappointed outsiders.

'Come on, men!' said Miss Abbey; for so potent was she with her subjects that even then the bearers awaited her permission. 'First floor.'

The entry being low, and the staircase being low, they so took up the burden they had set down, as to carry that low. The recumbent figure, in passing, lay hardly as high as the half door.

Miss Abbey started back at sight of it. 'Why, good God!' said she, turning to her two companions, 'that's the very man who made the declaration we have just had in our hands. That's Riderhood!'

Chapter 3
The Same Respected Friend in More Aspects Than One

IN sooth, it is Riderhood and no other, or it is the outer husk and shell of Riderhood and no other, that is borne into Miss Abbey's first-floor bedroom. Supple to twist and turn as the Rogue has ever been, he is sufficiently rigid now; and not without much shuffling of attendant feet, and tilting of his bier this way and that way, and peril even of his sliding off it and being tumbled in a heap over the balustrades, can he be got up stairs.

'Fetch a doctor,' quoth Miss Abbey. And then, 'Fetch his daughter.' On both of which errands, quick messengers depart.

The doctor-seeking messenger meets the doctor halfway, coming under convoy of police. Doctor examines the dank carcase, and pronounces, not hopefully, that it is worth while trying to reanimate the same. All the best means are at once in action, and everybody present lends a hand, and a heart and soul. No one has the least regard for the man; with them all, he has been an object of avoidance, suspicion, and aversion; but the spark of life within him is curiously separable from himself now, and they have a deep interest in it, probably because it *is* life, and they are living and must die.

In answer to the doctor's inquiry how did it happen, and was anyone to blame, Tom Tootle gives in his verdict, unavoidable accident and no one to blame but the sufferer. 'He was slinking about in his boat,' says Tom, 'which slinking were, not to speak ill of the dead, the manner of the man, when he come right athwart the steamer's bows and she cut him in two.' Mr Tootle is so far figurative, touching the dismemberment, as that he means the boat, and not the man. For, the man lies whole before them.

Captain Joey, the bottle-nosed regular customer in the glazed hat, is a pupil of the much-respected old school, and (having insinuated himself into the chamber, in the execution of the important service of carrying the drowned man's neck-kerchief) favours the doctor with a sagacious old-scholastic suggestion that the body should be hung up by the heels, 'sim'lar', says Captain Joey, 'to mutton in a butcher's shop,' and should then, as a particularly choice manœuvre for promoting easy respiration, be rolled upon casks. These scraps of the wisdom of the captain's ancestors are received with such speechless indignation by Miss Abbey, that she instantly seizes the Captain by the collar, and without a single word ejects him, not presuming to remonstrate, from the scene.

There then remain, to assist the doctor and Tom, only those three other regular customers, Bob Glamour, William Williams, and Jonathan (family name of the latter, if any, unknown to mankind), who are quite enough. Miss Abbey having looked in to make sure that nothing is wanted, descends to the bar, and there awaits the result, with the gentle Jew and Miss Jenny Wren.

If you are not gone for good, Mr Riderhood, it would be something to know where you are hiding at present. This flabby lump of mortality that we work so hard at with such patient perseverance, yields no sign of you. If you are gone for good, Rogue, it is very solemn, and if you are coming back, it is hardly less so. Nay, in the suspense and mystery of the latter question, involving that of where you may be now, there is a solemnity even added to that of death, making us who are in attendance alike afraid to look on you and to look off you, and making those below start at the least sound of a creaking plank in the floor.

Stay! Did that eyelid tremble? So the doctor, breathing low, and closely watching, asks himself.

No.

Did that nostril twitch?

No.

This artificial respiration ceasing, do I feel any faint flutter under my hand upon the chest?

No.

Over and over again. No. No. But try over and over again, nevertheless.

See! A token of life! An indubitable token of life! The spark may smoulder and go out, or it may glow and expand, but see! The four rough fellows, seeing, shed tears. Neither Riderhood in this world, nor Riderhood in the other, could draw tears from them; but a striving human soul between the two can do it easily.

He is struggling to come back. Now, he is almost here, now he is far away again. Now he is struggling harder to get back. And yet—like us all, when we swoon—like us all, every day of our lives when we wake—he is instinctively unwilling to be restored to the consciousness of this existence, and would be left dormant, if he could.

Bob Gliddery returns with Pleasant Riderhood, who was out when sought for, and hard to find. She has a shawl over her head, and her first action, when she takes it off weeping, and curtseys to Miss Abbey, is to wind her hair up.

'Thank you, Miss Abbey, for having father here.'

'I am bound to say, girl, I didn't know who it was,' returns Miss Abbey; 'but I hope it would have been pretty much the same if I had known.'

Poor Pleasant, fortified with a sip of brandy, is ushered into the first-floor chamber. She could not express much sentiment about her father if she were called upon to pronounce his funeral oration, but she has a greater tenderness for him than he ever had for her, and crying bitterly when she sees him stretched unconscious, asks the doctor, with clasped hands: 'Is there no hope, sir? O poor father! Is poor father dead?'

To which the doctor, on one knee beside the body, busy and watchful, only rejoins without looking round: 'Now, my girl, unless you have the self-command to be perfectly quiet, I cannot allow you to remain in the room.'

Pleasant, consequently, wipes her eyes with her back-hair, which is in fresh need of being wound up, and having got it out of the way, watches with terrified interest all that goes on. Her natural woman's aptitude soon renders her able to give a little help. Anticipating the doctor's want of this or that, she quietly has it ready for him, and so by degrees is intrusted with the charge of supporting her father's head upon her arm.

It is something so new to Pleasant to see her father an object of sympathy and interest, to find any one very willing to tolerate his society in this world, not to say pressingly and soothingly entreating him to belong to it, that it gives her a sensation she never experienced before. Some hazy idea that if affairs could remain thus for a long time it would be a respectable change, floats in her mind. Also some vague idea that the old evil is drowned out of him, and that if he should happily come back to resume his occupation of the empty form that lies upon the bed, his spirit will be altered. In which state of mind she kisses the stony lips, and quite believes that the impassive hand she chafes will revive a tender hand, if it revive ever.

Sweet delusion for Pleasant Riderhood. But they minister to him with such extraordinary interest, their anxiety is so keen, their vigilance is so great, their excited joy grows so intense as the signs of life strengthen, that how can she resist it, poor thing! And now he begins to breathe naturally, and he stirs, and the doctor declares him to have come back from that inexplicable journey where he stopped on the dark road, and to be here.

Tom Tootle, who is nearest to the doctor when he says this, grasps the doctor fervently by the hand. Bob Glamour, William Williams, and Jonathan of the no surname, all shake hands with one another round, and with the doctor too. Bob Glamour blows his nose, and Jonathan of the no surname is moved to do likewise, but lacking a pocket handkerchief abandons that outlet for his emotion. Pleasant sheds tears deserving her own name, and her sweet delusion is at its height.

There is intelligence in his eyes. He wants to ask a question. He wonders where he is. Tell him.

'Father, you were run down on the river, and are at Miss Abbey Potterson's.'

He stares at his daughter, stares all around him, closes his eyes, and lies slumbering on her arm.

The short-lived delusion begins to fade. The low, bad, unimpressible face is coming up from the depths of the river, or what other depths, to the surface again. As he grows warm, the doctor and the four men cool. As his lineaments soften with life, their faces and their hearts harden to him.

'He will do now,' says the doctor, washing his hands, and looking at the patient with growing disfavour.

'Many a better man,' moralizes Tom Tootle with a gloomy shake of the head, 'ain't had his luck.'

'It's to be hoped he'll make a better use of his life,' says Bob Glamour, 'than I expect he will.'

'Or than he done afore,' adds William Williams.

'But no, not he!' says Jonathan of the no surname, clinching the quartette.

They speak in a low tone because of his daughter, but she sees that they have all drawn off, and that they stand in a group at the other end of the room, shunning him. It would be too much to suspect them of being sorry that he didn't die when he had done so much towards it, but they clearly wish that they had had a better subject to bestow their pains on. Intelligence is conveyed to Miss Abbey in the bar, who reappears on the scene, and contemplates from a distance, holding whispered discourse with the doctor. The spark of life was deeply interesting while it was in abeyance, but now that it has got established in Mr Riderhood, there appears to be a general desire that circumstances had admitted of its being developed in anybody else, rather than that gentleman.

'However,' says Miss Abbey, cheering them up, 'you have done your duty like good and true men, and you had better come down and take something at the expense of the Porters.'

This they all do, leaving the daughter watching the father. To whom, in their absence, Bob Gliddery presents himself.

'His gills looks rum; don't they?' says Bob, after inspecting the patient.

Pleasant faintly nods.

'His gills 'll look rummer when he wakes; won't they?' says Bob.

Pleasant hopes not. Why?

'When he finds himself here, you know,' Bob explains. 'Cause Miss Abbey forbid him the house and ordered him out of it. But what you may call the Fates ordered him into it again. Which is rumness; ain't it?'

'He wouldn't have come here of his own accord,' returns poor Pleasant, with an effort at a little pride.

'No,' retorts Bob. 'Nor he wouldn't have been let in, if he had.'

The short delusion is quite dispelled now. As plainly as she sees on her arm the old father, unimproved, Pleasant sees that everybody there will cut him when he recovers consciousness. 'I'll take him away ever so soon as I can,' thinks Pleasant with a sigh; 'he's best at home.'

Presently they all return, and wait for him to become conscious that they will all be glad to get rid of him. Some clothes are got together for him to wear, his own being saturated with water, and his present dress being composed of blankets.

Becoming more and more uncomfortable, as though the prevalent dislike were finding him out somewhere in his sleep and expressing itself to him, the patient at last opens his eyes wide, and is assisted by his daughter to sit up in bed.

'Well, Riderhood,' says the doctor, 'how do you feel?'

He replies gruffly, 'Nothing to boast on.' Having, in fact, returned to life in an uncommonly sulky state.

'I don't mean to preach; but I hope,' says the doctor, gravely shaking his head, 'that this escape may have a good effect upon you, Riderhood.'

The patient's discontented growl of a reply is not intelligible; his daughter, however, could interpret, if she would, that what he says is, he 'don't want no Poll-Parroting.'

Mr Riderhood next demands his shirt; and draws it on over his head (with his daughter's help) exactly as if he had just had a Fight.

'Warn't it a steamer?' he pauses to ask her.

'Yes, father.'

'I'll have the law on her, bust her! and make her pay for it.'

He then buttons his linen very moodily, twice or thrice stopping to examine his arms and hands, as if to see what punishment he has received in the Fight. He then doggedly demands his other garments, and slowly gets them on, with an appearance of great malevolence towards his late opponent and all the spectators. He has an impression that his nose is bleeding, and several times draws the back of his hand across it, and looks for the result, in a pugilistic manner, greatly strengthening that incongruous resemblance.

'Where's my fur cap?' he asks in a surly voice, when he has shuffled his clothes on.

'In the river,' somebody rejoins.

'And warn't there no honest man to pick it up? O' course there was though, and to cut off with it arterwards. You are a rare lot, all on you!'

Thus, Mr Riderhood: taking from the hands of his daughter, with special ill-will, a lent cap, and grumbling as he pulls it down over his ears. Then, getting on his unsteady legs, leaning heavily upon her, and growling, 'Hold still, can't you? What! You must be a staggering next, must you?' he takes his departure out of the ring in which he has had that little turn-up with Death.

Chapter 4

A Happy Return of the Day

MR AND MRS WILFER had seen a full quarter of a hundred more anniversaries of their wedding day than Mr and Mrs Lammle had seen of theirs, but they still celebrated the occasion in the bosom of their family. Not that these celebrations ever resulted in anything particularly agreeable, or that the family was ever disappointed by that circumstance on account of having looked forward to the return of the auspicious day with sanguine anticipations of enjoyment. It was kept morally, rather as a Fast than a Feast, enabling Mrs Wilfer to hold a sombre darkling state, which exhibited that impressive woman in her choicest colours.

The noble lady's condition on these delightful occasions was one compounded of heroic endurance and heroic forgiveness. Lurid indications of the better marriages she might have made, shone athwart the awful gloom of her composure, and fitfully revealed the cherub as a little monster unaccountably favoured by Heaven, who had possessed himself of a blessing for which many of his superiors had sued and contended in vain. So firmly had this his position towards his treasure become established, that when the anniversary arrived, it always found him in an apologetic state. It is not impossible that his modest penitence may have even gone the length of sometimes severely reproving him for that he ever took the liberty of making so exalted a character his wife.

As for the children of the union, their experience of these festivals had been sufficiently uncomfortable to lead them annually to wish, when out of their tenderest years, either that Ma had married somebody else instead of much-teased Pa, or that Pa had married somebody else instead of Ma. When there came to be but two sisters left at home, the daring mind of Bella on the next of these occasions scaled the height of wondering with droll vexation 'what on earth Pa ever could have seen in Ma, to induce him to make such a little fool of himself as to ask her to have him.'

The revolving year now bringing the day round in its orderly sequence, Bella arrived in the Boffin chariot to assist at the celebration. It was the family custom when the day recurred, to sacrifice a pair of fowls on the altar of Hymen; and Bella had sent a note beforehand, to intimate that she would bring the votive offering with her. So, Bella and the fowls, by the united energies of two horses, two men, four wheels, and a plum-pudding carriage dog with as uncomfortable a collar on as if he had been George the Fourth, were deposited at the door of the parental dwelling. They were there received by Mrs Wilfer in person, whose dignity on this, as on most special occasions, was heightened by a mysterious toothache.

'I shall not require the carriage at night,' said Bella. 'I shall walk back.'

The male domestic of Mrs Boffin touched his hat, and in the act of departure had an awful glare bestowed upon him by Mrs Wilfer, intended to carry deep into his audacious soul the assurance that, whatever his private suspicions might be, male domestics in livery were no rarity there.

'Well, dear Ma,' said Bella, 'and how do you do?'

'I am as well, Bella,' replied Mrs Wilfer, 'as can be expected.'

'Dear me, Ma,' said Bella; 'you talk as if one was just born!'

'That's exactly what Ma has been doing,' interposed Lavvy, over the maternal shoulder, 'ever since we got up this morning. It's all very well to laugh, Bella, but anything more exasperating it is impossible to conceive.'

Mrs Wilfer, with a look too full of majesty to be accompanied by any words, attended both her daughters to the kitchen, where the sacrifice was to be prepared.

'Mr Rokesmith,' said she, resignedly, 'has been so polite as to place his sitting-room at our disposal to-day. You will therefore, Bella, be entertained in the humble abode of your parents, so far in accordance with your present style of living, that there will be a drawing-room for your reception as well as a dining-room. Your papa invited Mr Rokesmith to partake of our lowly fare. In excusing himself on account of a particular engagement, he offered the use of his apartment.'

Bella happened to know that he had no engagement out of his own room at Mr Boffin's, but she approved of his staying away. 'We should only have put one another out of countenance,' she thought, 'and we do that quite often enough as it is.'

Yet she had sufficient curiosity about his room, to run up to it with the least possible delay, and make a close inspection of its contents. It was tastefully though economically furnished, and very neatly arranged. There were shelves and stands of books, English, French, and Italian; and in a portfolio on the writing-table there were sheets upon sheets of memoranda and calculations in figures, evidently referring to the Boffin property. On that table also, carefully backed with canvas, varnished, mounted, and rolled like a map, was the placard descriptive of the murdered man who had come from afar to be her husband. She shrank from this ghostly surprise, and felt quite frightened as she rolled and tied it up again. Peeping about here and there, she came upon a print, a graceful head of a pretty woman, elegantly framed, hanging in the corner by the easy chair. 'Oh, indeed, sir!' said Bella, after stopping to ruminate before it. 'Oh, indeed, sir! I fancy I can guess whom you think *that's* like. But I'll tell you what it's much more like—your impudence!' Having said which she decamped: not solely because she was offended, but because there was nothing else to look at.

'Now, Ma,' said Bella, reappearing in the kitchen with some remains of a blush, 'you and Lavvy think magnificent me fit for nothing, but I intend to prove the contrary. I mean to be Cook to-day.'

'Hold!' rejoined her majestic mother. 'I cannot permit it. Cook, in that dress!'

'As for my dress, Ma,' returned Bella, merrily searching in a dresser-drawer, 'I mean to apron it and towel it all over the front; and as to permission, I mean to do without.'

'*You* cook!' said Mrs Wilfer. '*You*, who never cooked when you were at home?'

'Yes, Ma,' returned Bella; 'that is precisely the state of the case.'

She girded herself with a white apron, and busily with knots and pins contrived a bib to it, coming close and tight under her chin, as if it had caught her round the neck to kiss her. Over this bib her dimples looked delightful, and under it her pretty figure not less so. 'Now, Ma,' said Bella, pushing back her hair from her temples with both hands, 'what's first?'

'First,' returned Mrs Wilfer solemnly, 'if you persist in what I cannot but regard as conduct utterly incompatible with the equipage in which you arrived—'

('Which I do, Ma.')

'First, then, you put the fowls down to the fire.'

'To—be—sure!' cried Bella; 'and flour them, and twirl them round, and there they go!' sending them spinning at a great rate. 'What's next, Ma?'

'Next,' said Mrs Wilfer with a wave of her gloves, expressive of abdication under protest from the culinary throne, 'I would recommend examination of the bacon in the saucepan on the fire, and also of the potatoes by the application of a fork. Preparation of the greens will further become necessary if you persist in this unseemly demeanour.'

'As of course I do, Ma.'

Persisting, Bella gave her attention to one thing and forgot the other, and gave her attention to the other and forgot the third, and remembering the third was distracted by the fourth, and made amends whenever she went wrong by giving the unfortunate fowls an extra spin, which made their chance of ever getting cooked exceedingly doubtful. But it was pleasant cookery too. Meantime Miss Lavinia, oscillating between the kitchen and the opposite room, prepared the dining-table in the latter chamber. This office she (always doing her household spiriting with unwillingness) performed in a startling series of whisks and bumps; laying the table-cloth as if she were raising the wind, putting down the glasses and salt-cellars as if she were knocking at the door, and clashing the knives and forks in a skirmishing manner suggestive of hand-to-hand conflict.

'Look at Ma,' whispered Lavinia to Bella when this was done, and they stood over the roasting fowls. 'If one was the most dutiful child in existence (of course on the whole one hopes one is), isn't she enough to make one want to poke her with something wooden, sitting there bolt upright in a corner?'

'Only suppose,' returned Bella, 'that poor Pa was to sit bolt upright in another corner.'

'My dear, he couldn't do it,' said Lavvy. 'Pa would loll directly. But indeed I do not believe there ever was any human creature who could keep so bolt upright as Ma, or put such an amount of aggravation into one back! What's the matter, Ma? Ain't you well, Ma?'

'Doubtless I am very well,' returned Mrs Wilfer, turning her eyes upon her youngest born, with scornful fortitude. 'What should be the matter with Me?'

'You don't seem very brisk, Ma,' retorted Lavvy the bold.

'Brisk?' repeated her parent, 'Brisk? Whence the low ex-

pression, Lavinia? If I am uncomplaining, if I am silently contented with my lot, let that suffice for my family.'

'Well, Ma,' returned Lavvy, 'since you will force it out of
me, I must respectfully take leave to say that your family are no
doubt under the greatest obligations to you for having an annual
toothache on your wedding day, and that it's very disinterested
in you, and an immense blessing to them. Still, on the whole, it
is possible to be too boastful even of that boon.'

'You incarnation of sauciness,' said Mrs Wilfer, 'do you
speak like that to me? On this day, of all days in the year? Pray
do you know what would have become of you, if I had not
bestowed my hand upon R. W., your father, on this day?'

'No, Ma,' replied Lavvy, 'I really do not; and, with the
greatest respect for your abilities and information, I very much
doubt if you do either.'

Whether or no the sharp vigour of this sally on a weak point
of Mrs Wilfer's entrenchments might have routed that heroine
for the time, is rendered uncertain by the arrival of a flag of truce
in the person of Mr George Sampson: bidden to the feast as a
friend of the family, whose affections were now understood to be
in course of transference from Bella to Lavinia, and whom
Lavinia kept—possibly in remembrance of his bad taste in having overlooked her in the first instance—under a course of
stinging discipline.

'I congratulate you, Mrs Wilfer,' said Mr George Sampson,
who had meditated this neat address while coming along, 'on
the day.' Mrs Wilfer thanked him with a magnanimous sigh,
and again became an unresisting prey to that inscrutable toothache.

'I am surprised,' said Mr Sampson feebly, 'that Miss Bella
condescends to cook.'

Here Miss Lavinia descended on the ill-starred young gentleman with a crushing supposition that at all events it was no
business of his. This disposed of Mr Sampson in a melancholy
retirement of spirit, until the cherub arrived, whose amazement at
the lovely woman's occupation was great.

However, she persisted in dishing the dinner as well as
cooking it, and then sat down, bibless and apronless, to partake
of it as an illustrious guest: Mrs Wilfer first responding to her
husband's cheerful 'For what we are about to receive—' with a
sepulchral Amen, calculated to cast a damp upon the stoutest
appetite.

'But what,' said Bella, as she watched the carving of the
fowls, 'makes them pink inside, I wonder, Pa! Is it the breed?'

'No, I don't think it's the breed, my dear,' returned Pa. 'I rather think it is because they are not done.'

'They ought to be,' said Bella.

'Yes, I am aware they ought to be, my dear,' rejoined her father, 'but they—ain't.'

So, the gridiron was put in requisition, and the good-tempered cherub, who was often as un-cherubically employed in his own family as if he had been in the employment of some of the Old Masters, undertook to grill the fowls. Indeed, except in respect of staring about him (a branch of the public service to which the pictorial cherub is much addicted), this domestic cherub discharged as many odd functions as his prototype; with the difference, say, that he performed with a blacking-brush on the family's boots, instead of performing on enormous wind instruments and double-bases, and that he conducted himself with cheerful alacrity to much useful purpose, instead of foreshortening himself in the air with the vaguest intentions.

Bella helped him with his supplemental cookery, and made him very happy, but put him in mortal terror too by asking him when they sat down at table again, how he supposed they cooked fowls at the Greenwich dinners, and whether he believed they really were such pleasant dinners as people said? His secret winks and nods of remonstrance, in reply, made the mischievous Bella laugh until she choked, and then Lavinia was obliged to slap her on the back, and then she laughed the more.

But her mother was a fine corrective at the other end of the table; to whom her father, in the innocence of his good-fellowship, at intervals appealed with: 'My dear, I am afraid you are not enjoying yourself?'

'Why so, R. W.?' she would sonorously reply.

'Because, my dear, you seem a little out of sorts.'

'Not at all,' would be the rejoinder, in exactly the same tone.

'Would you take a merry-thought, my dear?'

'Thank you. I will take whatever you please, R. W.'

'Well, but my dear, do you like it?'

'I like it as well as I like anything, R. W.' The stately woman would then, with a meritorious appearance of devoting herself to the general good, pursue her dinner as if she were feeding somebody else on high public grounds.

Bella had brought dessert and two bottles of wine, thus shedding unprecedented splendour on the occasion. Mrs Wilfer did the honours of the first glass by proclaiming: 'R. W. I drink to you.'

'Thank you, my dear. And I to you.'

'Pa and Ma!' said Bella.

'Permit me,' Mrs Wilfer interposed, with outstretched glove. 'No. I think not. I drank to your papa. If, however, you insist on including me, I can in gratitude offer no objection.'

'Why, Lor, Ma,' interposed Lavvy the bold, 'isn't it the day that made you and Pa one and the same? I have no patience!'

'By whatever other circumstance the day may be marked, it is not the day, Lavinia, on which I will allow a child of mine to pounce upon me. I beg—nay, command!—that you will not pounce. R. W., it is appropriate to recall that it is for you to command and for me to obey. It is your house, and you are master at your own table. Both our healths!' Drinking the toast with tremendous stiffness.

'I really am a little afraid, my dear,' hinted the cherub meekly, 'that you are not enjoying yourself?'

'On the contrary,' returned Mrs Wilfer, 'quite so. Why should I not?'

'I thought, my dear, that perhaps your face might—'

'My face might be a martyrdom, but what would that import, or who should know it, if I smiled?'

And she did smile; manifestly freezing the blood of Mr George Sampson by so doing. For that young gentleman, catching her smiling eye, was so very much appalled by its expression as to cast about in his thoughts concerning what he had done to bring it down upon himself.

'The mind naturally falls,' said Mrs Wilfer, 'shall I say into a reverie, or shall I say into a retrospect? on a day like this.'

Lavvy, sitting with defiantly folded arms, replied (but not audibly), 'For goodness' sake say whichever of the two you like best, Ma, and get it over.'

'The mind,' pursued Mrs Wilfer in an oratorical manner, 'naturally reverts to Papa and Mamma—I here allude to my parents—at a period before the earliest dawn of this day. I was considered tall; perhaps I was. Papa and Mamma were unquestionably tall. I have rarely seen a finer woman than my mother; never than my father.'

The irrepressible Lavvy remarked aloud, 'Whatever grandpapa was, he wasn't a female.'

'Your grandpapa,' retorted Mrs Wilfer, with an awful look, and in an awful tone, 'was what I describe him to have been, and would have struck any of his grandchildren to the earth who presumed to question it. It was one of mamma's cherished hopes

that I should become united to a tall member of society. It may
have been a weakness, but if so, it was equally the weakness, I
believe, of King Fredrick of Prussia.' These remarks being offered
to Mr George Sampson, who had not the courage to come out for
single combat, but lurked with his chest under the table and his
eyes cast down, Mrs Wilfer proceeded, in a voice of increasing
sternness and impressiveness, until she should force that skulker
to give himself up. 'Mamma would appear to have had an
indefinable foreboding of what afterwards happened, for she
would frequently urge upon me, "Not a little man. Promise me,
my child, not a little man. Never, never, never, marry a little
man!" Papa also would remark to me (he possessed extraordinary humour), "that a family of whales must not ally themselves
with sprats." His company was eagerly sought, as may be
supposed, by the wits of the day, and our house was their
continual resort. I have known as many as three copper-plate
engravers exchanging the most exquisite sallies and retorts there,
at one time.' (Here Mr Sampson delivered himself captive, and
said, with an uneasy movement on his chair, that three was a
large number, and it must have been highly entertaining.) 'Among
the most prominent members of that distinguished circle, was a
gentleman measuring six feet four in height. *He* was *not* an
engraver.' (Here Mr Sampson said, with no reason whatever, Of
course not.) 'This gentleman was so obliging as to honour me
with attentions which I could not fail to understand.' (Here Mr
Sampson murmured that when it came to that, you could always
tell.) 'I immediately announced to both my parents that those
attentions were misplaced, and that I could not favour his suit.
They inquired was he too tall? I replied it was not the stature, but
the intellect was too lofty. At our house, I said, the tone was too
brilliant, the pressure was too high, to be maintained by me, a
mere woman, in every-day domestic life. I well remember mamma's clasping her hands, and exclaiming "This will end in a
little man!" ' (Here Mr Sampson glanced at his host and shook
his head with despondency.) 'She afterwards went so far as to
predict that it would end in a little man whose mind would be
below the average, but that was in what I may denominate a
paroxysm of maternal disappointment. Within a month,' said
Mrs Wilfer, deepening her voice, as if she were relating a
terrible ghost story, 'within a month, I first saw R. W. my
husband. Within a year, I married him. It is natural for the mind
to recall these dark coincidences on the present day.'

Mr Sampson at length released from the custody of Mrs Wilfer's eye, now drew a long breath, and made the original and striking remark that there was no accounting for these sort of presentiments. R. W. scratched his head and looked apologetically all round the table until he came to his wife, when observing her as it were shrouded in a more sombre veil than before, he once more hinted, 'My dear, I am really afraid you are not altogether enjoying yourself?' To which she once more replied, 'On the contrary, R. W. Quite so.'

The wretched Mr Sampson's position at this agreeable entertainment was truly pitiable. For, not only was he exposed defenceless to the harangues of Mrs Wilfer, but he received the utmost contumely at the hands of Lavinia; who, partly to show Bella that she (Lavinia) could do what she liked with him, and partly to pay him off for still obviously admiring Bella's beauty, led him the life of a dog. Illuminated on the one hand by the stately graces of Mrs Wilfer's oratory, and shadowed on the other by the checks and frowns of the young lady to whom he had devoted himself in his destitution, the sufferings of this young gentleman were distressing to witness. If his mind for the moment reeled under them, it may be urged, in extenuation of its weakness, that it was constitutionally a knock-knee'd mind and never very strong upon its legs.

The rosy hours were thus beguiled until it was time for Bella to have Pa's escort back. The dimples duly tied up in the bonnet-strings and the leave-taking done, they got out into the air, and the cherub drew a long breath as if he found it refreshing.

'Well, dear Pa,' said Bella, 'the anniversary may be considered over.'

'Yes, my dear,' returned the cherub, 'there's another of 'em gone.'

Bella drew his arm closer through hers as they walked along, and gave it a number of consolatory pats. 'Thank you, my dear,' he said, as if she had spoken; 'I am all right, my dear. Well, and how do you get on, Bella?'

'I am not at all improved, Pa.'

'Ain't you really though?'

'No, Pa. On the contrary, I am worse.'

'Lor!' said the cherub.

'I am worse, Pa. I make so many calculations how much a year I must have when I marry, and what is the least I can manage to do with, that I am beginning to get wrinkles over my nose. Did you notice any wrinkles over my nose this evening, Pa?'

Pa laughing at this, Bella gave him two or three shakes.

'You won't laugh, sir, when you see your lovely woman turning haggard. You had better be prepared in time, I can tell you. I shall not be able to keep my greediness for money out of my eyes long, and when you see it there you'll be sorry, and serve you right for not being warned in time. Now, sir, we entered into a bond of confidence. Have you anything to impart?'

'I thought it was you who was to impart, my love.'

'Oh! did you indeed, sir? Then why didn't you ask me, the moment we came out? The confidences of lovely women are not to be slighted. However, I forgive you this once, and look here, Pa; that's'—Bella laid the little forefinger of her right glove on her lip, and then laid it on her father's lip—'that's a kiss for you. And now I am going seriously to tell you—let me see how many—four secrets. Mind! Serious, grave, weighty secrets. Strictly between ourselves.'

'Number one, my dear?' said her father, settling her arm comfortably and confidentially.

'Number one,' said Bella, 'will electrify you, Pa. Who do you think has'—she was confused here in spite of her merry way of beginning—'has made an offer to me?'

Pa looked in her face, and looked at the ground, and looked in her face again, and declared he could never guess.

'Mr Rokesmith.'

'You don't tell me so, my dear!'

'Mis—ter Roke—smith, Pa,' said Bella separating the syllables for emphasis. 'What do you say to *that*?'

Pa answered quietly with the counter-question, 'What did *you* say to that, my love?'

'I said No,' returned Bella sharply. 'Of course.'

'Yes. Of course,' said her father, meditating.

'And I told him why I thought it a betrayal of trust on his part, and an affront to me,' said Bella.

'Yes. To be sure. I am astonished indeed. I wonder he committed himself without seeing more of his way first. Now I think of it, I suspect he always has admired you though, my dear.'

'A hackney coachman may admire me,' remarked Bella, with a touch of her mother's loftiness.

'It's highly probable, my love. Number two, my dear?'

'Number two, Pa, is much to the same purpose, though not so preposterous. Mr Lightwood would propose to me, if I would let him.'

'Then I understand, my dear, that you don't intend to let him?'

Bella again saying, with her former emphasis, 'Why, of course not!' her father felt himself bound to echo, 'Of course not.'

'I don't care for him,' said Bella.

'That's enough,' her father interposed.

'No, Pa, it's *not* enough,' rejoined Bella, giving him another shake or two. 'Haven't I told you what a mercenary little wretch I am? It only becomes enough when he has no money, and no clients, and no expectations, and no anything but debts.'

'Hah!' said the cherub, a little depressed. 'Number three, my dear?'

'Number three, Pa, is a better thing. A generous thing, a noble thing, a delightful thing. Mrs Boffin has herself told me, as a secret, with her own kind lips—and truer lips never opened or closed in this life, I am sure—that they wish to see me well married; and that when I marry with their consent they will portion me most handsomely.' Here the grateful girl burst out crying very heartily.

'Don't cry, my darling,' said her father, with his hand to his eyes, 'it's excusable in me to be a little overcome when I find that my dear favourite child is, after all disappointments, to be so provided for and so raised in the world; but don't *you* cry, don't *you* cry. I am very thankful. I congratulate you with all my heart, my dear.' The good soft little fellow, drying his eyes, here, Bella put her arms round his neck and tenderly kissed him on the high road, passionately telling him he was the best of fathers and the best of friends, and that on her wedding-morning she would go down on her knees to him and beg his pardon for having ever teased him or seemed insensible to the worth of such a patient, sympathetic, genial, fresh young heart. At every one of her adjectives she redoubled her kisses, and finally kissed his hat off, and then laughed immoderately when the wind took it and he ran after it.

When he had recovered his hat and his breath, and they were going on again once more, said her father then: 'Number four, my dear?'

Bella's countenance fell in the midst of her mirth. 'After all, perhaps I had better put off number four, Pa. Let me try once more, if for never so short a time, to hope that it may not really be so.'

The change in her, strengthened the cherub's interest in

number four, and he said quietly: 'May not be so, my dear? May not be how, my dear?'

Bella looked at him pensively, and shook her head.

'And yet I know right well it is so, Pa. I know it only too well.'

'My love,' returned her father, 'you make me quite uncomfortable. Have you said No to anybody else, my dear?'

'No, Pa.'

'Yes to anybody?' he suggested, lifting up his eyebrows.

'No, Pa.'

'Is there anybody else who would take his chance between Yes and No, if you would let him, my dear?'

'Not that I know of, Pa.'

'There can't be somebody who won't take his chance when you want him to?' said the cherub, as a last resource.

'Why, of course not, Pa,' said Bella, giving him another shake or two.

'No, of course not,' he assented. 'Bella, my dear, I am afraid I must either have no sleep to-night, or I must press for number four.'

'Oh, Pa, there is no good in number four! I am so sorry for it, I am so unwilling to believe it, I have tried so earnestly not to see it, that it is very hard to tell, even to you. But Mr Boffin is being spoilt by prosperity, and is changing every day.'

'My dear Bella, I hope and trust not.'

'I have hoped and trusted not too, Pa; but every day he changes for the worse, and for the worse. Not to me—he is always much the same to me—but to others about him. Before my eyes he grows suspicious, capricious, hard, tyrannical, unjust. If ever a good man were ruined by good fortune, it is my benefactor. And yet, Pa, think how terrible the fascination of money is! I see this, and hate this, and dread this, and don't know but that money might make a much worse change in me. And yet I have money always in my thoughts and my desires; and the whole life I place before myself is money, money, money, and what money can make of life!'

Chapter 5

The Golden Dustman Falls Into Bad Company

WERE Bella Wilfer's bright and ready little wits at fault, or was the Golden Dustman passing through the furnace of proof and coming out dross? Ill news travels fast. We shall know full soon.

On that very night of her return from the Happy Return, something chanced which Bella closely followed with her eyes and ears. There was an apartment at the side of the Boffin mansion, known as Mr Boffin's room. Far less grand than the rest of the house, it was far more comfortable, being pervaded by a certain air of homely snugness, which upholstering despotism had banished to that spot when it inexorably set its face against Mr Boffin's appeals for mercy in behalf of any other chamber. Thus, although a room of modest situation—for its windows gave on Silas Wegg's old corner—and of no pretensions to velvet, satin, or gilding, it had got itself established in a domestic position analogous to that of an easy dressing-gown or pair of slippers; and whenever the family wanted to enjoy a particularly pleasant fireside evening, they enjoyed it, as an institution that must be, in Mr Boffin's room.

Mr and Mrs Boffin were reported sitting in this room, when Bella got back. Entering it, she found the Secretary there too; in official attendance it would appear, for he was standing with some papers in his hand by a table with shaded candles on it, at which Mr Boffin was seated thrown back in his easy chair.

'You are busy, sir,' said Bella, hesitating at the door.

'Not at all, my dear, not at all. You're one of ourselves. We never make company of you. Come in, come in. Here's the old lady in her usual place.'

Mrs Boffin adding her nod and smile of welcome to Mr Boffin's words, Bella took her book to a chair in the fireside corner, by Mrs Boffin's work-table. Mr Boffin's station was on the opposite side.

'Now, Rokesmith,' said the Golden Dustman, so sharply rapping the table to bespeak his attention as Bella turned the leaves of her book, that she started; 'where were we?'

'You were saying, sir,' returned the Secretary, with an air of some reluctance and a glance towards those others who were present, 'that you considered the time had come for fixing my salary.'

'Don't be above calling it wages, man,' said Mr Boffin, testily. 'What the deuce! I never talked of *my* salary when I was in service.'

'My wages,' said the Secretary, correcting himself.

'Rokesmith, you are not proud, I hope?' observed Mr Boffin, eyeing him askance.

'I hope not, sir.'

'Because I never was, when I was poor,' said Mr Boffin. 'Poverty and pride don't go at all well together. Mind that. How can they go well together? Why it stands to reason. A man, being poor, has nothing to be proud of. It's nonsense.'

With a slight inclination of his head, and a look of some surprise, the Secretary seemed to assent by forming the syllables of the word 'nonsense' on his lips.

'Now, concerning these same wages,' said Mr Boffin. 'Sit down.'

The Secretary sat down.

'Why didn't you sit down before?' asked Mr Boffin, distrustfully. 'I hope that wasn't pride? But about these wages. Now, I've gone into the matter, and I say two hundred a year. What do you think of it? Do you think it's enough?'

'Thank you. It is a fair proposal.'

'I don't say, you know,' Mr Boffin stipulated, 'but what it may be more than enough. And I'll tell you why, Rokesmith. A man of property, like me, is bound to consider the market-price. At first I didn't enter into that as much as I might have done; but I've got acquainted with other men of property since, and I've got acquainted with the duties of property. I mustn't go putting the market-price up, because money may happen not to be an object with me. A sheep is worth so much in the market, and I ought to give it and no more. A secretary is worth so much in the market, and I ought to give it and no more. However, I don't mind stretching a point with you.'

'Mr Boffin, you are very good,' replied the Secretary, with an effort.

'Then we put the figure,' said Mr Boffin, 'at two hundred a year. Then the figure's disposed of. Now, there must be no misunderstanding regarding what I buy for two hundred a year. If I pay for a sheep, I buy it out and out. Similarly, if I pay for a secretary, I buy *him* out and out.'

'In other words, you purchase my whole time?'

'Certainly I do. Look here,' said Mr Boffin, 'it ain't that I want to occupy your whole time; you can take up a book for a minute or two when you've nothing better to do, though I think you'll a'most always find something useful to do. But I want to keep you in attendance. It's convenient to have you at all times ready on the premises. Therefore, betwixt your breakfast and your supper,—on the premises I expect to find you.'

The Secretary bowed.

'In bygone days, when I was in service myself,' said Mr Boffin, 'I couldn't go cutting about at my will and pleasure, and you won't expect to go cutting about at your will and pleasure. You've rather got into a habit of that, lately; but perhaps it was for want of a right specification betwixt us. Now, let there be a right specification betwixt us, and let it be this. If you want leave, ask for it.'

Again the Secretary bowed. His manner was uneasy and astonished, and showed a sense of humiliation.

'I'll have a bell,' said Mr Boffin, 'hung from this room to yours, and when I want you, I'll touch it. I don't call to mind that I have anything more to say at the present moment.'

The Secretary rose, gathered up his papers, and withdrew. Bella's eyes followed him to the door, lighted on Mr Boffin complacently thrown back in his easy chair, and drooped over her book.

'I have let that chap, that young man of mine,' said Mr Boffin, taking a trot up and down the room, 'get above his work. It won't do. I must have him down a peg. A man of property owes a duty to other men of property, and must look sharp after his inferiors.'

Bella felt that Mrs Boffin was not comfortable, and that the eyes of that good creature sought to discover from her face what attention she had given to this discourse, and what impression it had made upon her. For which reason Bella's eyes drooped more engrossedly over her book, and she turned the page with an air of profound absorption in it.

'Noddy,' said Mrs Boffin, after thoughtfully pausing in her work.

'My dear,' returned the Golden Dustman, stopping short in his trot.

'Excuse my putting it to you, Noddy, but now really! Haven't you been a little strict with Mr Rokesmith to-night? Haven't you been a little—just a little little—not quite like your old self?'

'Why, old woman, I hope so,' returned Mr Boffin, cheerfully, if not boastfully.

'Hope so, deary?'

'Our old selves wouldn't do here, old lady. Haven't you found that out yet? Our old selves would be fit for nothing here but to be robbed and imposed upon. Our old selves weren't people of fortune; our new selves are; it's a great difference.'

'Ah!' said Mrs Boffin, pausing in her work again, softly to draw a long breath and to look at the fire. 'A great difference.'

'And we must be up to the difference,' pursued her husband; 'we must be equal to the change; that's what we must be. We've got to hold our own now, against everybody (for everybody's hand is stretched out to be dipped into our pockets), and we have got to recollect that money makes money, as well as makes everything else.'

'Mentioning recollecting,' said Mrs Boffin, with her work abandoned, her eyes upon the fire, and her chin upon her hand, 'do you recollect, Noddy, how you said to Mr Rokesmith when he first came to see us at the Bower, and you engaged him—how you said to him that if it had pleased Heaven to send John Harmon to his fortune safe, we could have been content with the one Mound which was our legacy, and should never have wanted the rest?'

'Ay, I remember, old lady. But we hadn't tried what it was to have the rest then. Our new shoes had come home, but we hadn't put 'em on. We're wearing 'em now, we're wearing 'em, and must step out accordingly.'

Mrs Boffin took up her work again, and plied her needle in silence.

'As to Rokesmith, that young man of mine,' said Mr Boffin, dropping his voice and glancing towards the door with an apprehension of being overheard by some eavesdropper there, 'it's the same with him as with the footmen. I have found out that you must either scrunch them, or let them scrunch you. If you ain't imperious with 'em, they won't believe in your being any better than themselves, if as good, after the stories (lies mostly) that they have heard of your beginnings. There's nothing betwixt stiffening yourself up, and throwing yourself away; take my word for that, old lady.'

Bella ventured for a moment to look stealthily towards him under her eyelashes, and she saw a dark cloud of suspicion, covetousness, and conceit, overshadowing the once open face.

'Hows'ever,' said he, 'this isn't entertaining to Miss Bella. Is it, Bella?'

A deceiving Bella she was, to look at him with that pensively abstracted air, as if her mind were full of her book, and she had not heard a single word!

'Hah! Better employed than to attend to it,' said Mr Boffin. 'That's right, that's right. Especially as you have no call to be told how to value yourself, my dear.'

Colouring a little under this compliment, Bella returned, 'I hope sir, you don't think me vain?'

'Not a bit, my dear,' said Mr Boffin. 'But I think it's very creditable in you, at your age, to be so well up with the pace of the world, and to know what to go in for. You are right. Go in for money, my love. Money's the article. You'll make money of your good looks, and of the money Mrs Boffin and me will have the pleasure of settling upon you, and you'll live and die rich. That's the state to live and die in!' said Mr Boffin, in an unctuous manner. 'R–r–rich!'

There was an expression of distress in Mrs Boffin's face, as, after watching her husband's, she turned to their adopted girl, and said: 'Don't mind him, Bella, my dear.'

'Eh?' cried Mr Boffin. 'What! Not mind him?'

'I don't mean that,' said Mrs Boffin, with a worried look, 'but I mean, don't believe him to be anything but good and generous, Bella, because he is the best of men. No, I must say that much, Noddy. You are always the best of men.'

She made the declaration as if he were objecting to it: which assuredly he was not in any way.

'And as to you, my dear Bella,' said Mrs Boffin, still with that distressed expression, 'he is so much attached to you, whatever he says, that your own father has not a truer interest in you and can hardly like you better than he does.'

'Says too!' cried Mr Boffin. 'Whatever he says! Why, I say so, openly. Give me a kiss, my dear child, in saying Good Night, and let me confirm what my old lady tells you. I am very fond of you, my dear, and I am entirely of your mind, and you and I will take care that you shall be rich. These good looks of yours (which you have some right to be vain of, my dear, though you are not, you know) are worth money, and you shall make money of 'em. The money you will have, will be worth money, and you shall make money of that too. There's a golden ball at your feet. Good night, my dear.'

Somehow, Bella was not so well pleased with this assurance and this prospect as she might have been. Somehow, when she put her arms round Mrs Boffin's neck and said Good Night, she derived a sense of unworthiness from the still anxious face of that good woman and her obvious wish to excuse her husband. 'Why, what need to excuse him?' thought Bella, sitting down in her own room. 'What he said was very sensible, I am sure, and very true, I am sure. It is only what I often say to myself. Don't I like it then? No, I don't like it, and, though he is my liberal benefactor, I disparage him for it. Then pray,' said Bella, sternly putting the question to herself in the looking-glass as usual, 'what do you mean by this, you inconsistent little Beast?'

The looking-glass preserving a discreet ministerial silence when thus called upon for explanation, Bella went to bed with a weariness upon her spirit which was more than the weariness of want of sleep. And again in the morning, she looked for the cloud, and for the deepening of the cloud, upon the Golden Dustman's face.

She had begun by this time to be his frequent companion in his morning strolls about the streets, and it was at this time that he made her a party to his engaging in a curious pursuit. Having been hard at work in one dull enclosure all his life, he had a child's delight in looking at shops. It had been one of the first novelties and pleasures of his freedom, and was equally the delight of his wife. For many years their only walks in London had been taken on Sundays when the shops were shut; and when every day in the week became their holiday, they derived an enjoyment from the variety and fancy and beauty of the display in the windows, which seemed incapable of exhaustion. As if the principal streets were a great Theatre and the play were childishly new to them, Mr and Mrs Boffin, from the beginning of Bella's intimacy in their house, had been constantly in the front row, charmed with all they saw and applauding vigorously. But now, Mr Boffin's interest began to centre in book-shops; and more than that—for that of itself would not have been much—in one exceptional kind of book.

'Look in here, my dear,' Mr Boffin would say, checking

Bella's arm at a bookseller's window; 'you can read at sight, and your eyes are as sharp as they're bright. Now, look well about you, my dear, and tell me if you see any book about a Miser.'

If Bella saw such a book, Mr Boffin would instantly dart in and buy it. And still, as if they had not found it, they would seek out another book-shop, and Mr Boffin would say, 'Now, look well all round, my dear, for a Life of a Miser, or any book of that sort; any Lives of odd characters who may have been Misers.'

Bella, thus directed, would examine the window with the greatest attention, while Mr Boffin would examine her face. The moment she pointed out any book as being entitled Lives of eccentric personages, Anecdotes of strange characters, Records of remarkable individuals, or anything to that purpose, Mr Boffin's countenance would light up, and he would instantly dart in and buy it. Size, price, quality, were of no account. Any book that seemed to promise a chance of miserly biography, Mr Boffin purchased without a moment's delay and carried home. Happening to be informed by a bookseller that a portion of the Annual Register was devoted to 'Characters', Mr Boffin at once bought a whole set of that ingenious compilation, and began to carry it home piecemeal, confiding a volume to Bella, and bearing three himself. The completion of this labour occupied them about a fortnight. When the task was done, Mr Boffin, with his appetite for Misers whetted instead of satiated, began to look out again.

It very soon became unnecessary to tell Bella what to look for, and an understanding was established between her and Mr Boffin that she was always to look for Lives of Misers. Morning after morning they roamed about the town together, pursuing this singular research. Miserly literature not being abundant, the proportion of failures to successes may have been as a hundred to one; still Mr Boffin, never wearied, remained as avaricious for misers as he had been at the first onset. It was curious that Bella never saw the books about the house, nor did she ever hear from Mr Boffin one word of reference to their contents. He seemed to save up his Misers as they had saved up their money. As they had been greedy for it, and secret about it, and had hidden it, so he was greedy for them, and secret about them, and hid them. But beyond all doubt it was to be noticed, and was by Bella very clearly noticed, that, as he pursued the acquisition of those dismal records with the ardour of Don Quixote for his books of chivalry, he began to spend his money with a more sparing hand.

And often when he came out of a shop with some new account of one of those wretched lunatics, she would almost shrink from the sly dry chuckle with which he would take her arm again and trot away. It did not appear that Mrs Boffin knew of this taste. He made no allusion to it, except in the morning walks when he and Bella were always alone; and Bella, partly under the impression that he took her into his confidence by implication, and partly in remembrance of Mrs Boffin's anxious face that night, held the same reserve.

While these occurrences were in progress, Mrs Lammle made the discovery that Bella had a fascinating influence over her. The Lammles, originally presented by the dear Veneerings, visited the Boffins on all grand occasions, and Mrs Lammle had not previously found this out; but now the knowledge came upon her all at once. It was a most extraordinary thing (she said to Mrs Boffin); she was foolishly susceptible of the power of beauty, but it wasn't altogether that; she never had been able to resist a natural grace of manner, but it wasn't altogether that; it was more than that, and there was no name for the indescribable extent and degree to which she was captivated by this charming girl.

This charming girl having the words repeated to her by Mrs Boffin (who was proud of her being admired, and would have done anything to give her pleasure), naturally recognized in Mrs Lammle a woman of penetration and taste. Responding to the sentiments, by being very gracious to Mrs Lammle, she gave that lady the means of so improving her opportunity, as that the captivation became reciprocal, though always wearing an appearance of greater sobriety on Bella's part than on the enthusiastic Sophronia's. Howbeit, they were so much together that, for a time, the Boffin chariot held Mrs Lammle oftener than Mrs Boffin: a preference of which the latter worthy soul was not in the least jealous, placidly remarking, 'Mrs Lammle is a younger companion for her than I am, and Lor! she's more fashionable.'

But between Bella Wilfer and Georgiana Podsnap there was this one difference, among many others, that Bella was in no danger of being captivated by Alfred. She distrusted and disliked him. Indeed, her perception was so quick, and her observation so sharp, that after all she mistrusted his wife too, though with her giddy vanity and wilfulness she squeezed the mistrust away into a corner of her mind, and blocked it up there.

Mrs Lammle took the friendliest interest in Bella's making a good match. Mrs Lammle said, in a sportive way, she really must show her beautiful Bella what kind of wealthy creatures she and Alfred had on hand, who would as one man fall at her feet enslaved. Fitting occasion made, Mrs Lammle accordingly produced the most passable of those feverish, boastful, and indefinably loose gentlemen who were always lounging in and out of the City on questions of the Bourse and Greek and Spanish and India and Mexican and par and premium and discount and three-quarters and seven-eighths. Who in their agreeable manner did homage to Bella as if she were a compound of fine girl, thorough-bred horse, well-built drag, and remarkable pipe. But without the least effect, though even Mr Fledgeby's attractions were cast into the scale.

'I fear, Bella dear,' said Mrs Lammle one day in the chariot, 'that you will be very hard to please.'

'I don't expect to be pleased, dear,' said Bella, with a languid turn of her eyes.

'Truly, my love,' returned Sophronia, shaking her head, and smiling her best smile, 'it would not be very easy to find a man worthy of your attractions.'

'The question is not a man, my dear,' said Bella, coolly, 'but an establishment.'

'My love,' returned Mrs Lammle, 'your prudence amazes me—where *did* you study life so well!—you are right. In such a case as yours, the object is a fitting establishment. You could not descend to an inadequate one from Mr Boffin's house, and even if your beauty alone could not command it, it is to be assumed that Mr and Mrs Boffin will—'

'Oh! they have already,' Bella interposed.

'No! Have they really?'

A little vexed by a suspicion that she had spoken precipitately, and withal a little defiant of her own vexation, Bella determined not to retreat.

'That is to say,' she explained, 'they have told me they mean to portion me as their adopted child, if you mean that. But don't mention it.'

'Mention it!' replied Mrs Lammle, as if she were full of awakened feeling at the suggestion of such an impossibility. 'Men-tion it!'

'I don't mind telling you, Mrs Lammle—' Bella began again.

'My love, say Sophronia, or I must not say Bella.'

With a little short, petulant 'Oh!' Bella complied. 'Oh!—Sophronia then—I don't mind telling you, Sophronia, that I am convinced I have no heart, as people call it; and that I think that sort of thing is nonsense.'

'Brave girl!' murmured Mrs Lammle.

'And so,' pursued Bella, 'as to seeking to please myself, I don't; except in the one respect I have mentioned. I am indifferent otherwise.'

'But you can't help pleasing, Bella,' said Mrs Lammle, rallying her with an arch look and her best smile, 'you can't help making a proud and an admiring husband. You may not care to please yourself, and you may not care to please him, but you are not a free agent as to pleasing: you are forced to do that, in spite of yourself, my dear; so it may be a question whether you may not as well please yourself too, if you can.'

Now, the very grossness of this flattery put Bella upon proving that she actually did please in spite of herself. She had a misgiving that she was doing wrong—though she had an indistinct foreshadowing that some harm might come of it thereafter, she little thought what consequences it would really bring about— but she went on with her confidence.

'Don't talk of pleasing in spite of one's self, dear,' said Bella. 'I have had enough of that.'

'Ay?' cried Mrs Lammle. 'Am I already corroborated, Bella?'

'Never mind, Sophronia, we will not speak of it any more. Don't ask me about it.'

This plainly meaning Do ask me about it, Mrs Lammle did as she was requested.

'Tell me, Bella. Come, my dear. What provoking burr has been inconveniently attracted to the charming skirts, and with difficulty shaken off?'

'Provoking indeed,' said Bella, 'and no burr to boast of! But don't ask me.'

'Shall I guess?'

'You would never guess. What would you say to our Secretary?'

'My dear! The hermit Secretary, who creeps up and down the back stairs, and is never seen!'

'I don't know about his creeping up and down the back stairs,' said Bella, rather contemptuously, 'further than knowing that he does no such thing; and as to his never being seen, I should be content never to have seen him, though he is quite as visible as you are. But I pleased *him* (for my sins) and he had the presumption to tell me so.'

'The man never made a declaration to you, my dear Bella!'

'Are you sure of that, Sophronia?' said Bella. '*I* am not. In fact, I am sure of the contrary.'

'The man must be mad,' said Mrs Lammle, with a kind of resignation.

'He appeared to be in his senses,' returned Bella, tossing her head, 'and he had plenty to say for himself. I told him my opinion of his declaration and his conduct, and dismissed him. Of course this has all been very inconvenient to me, and very disagreeable. It has remained a secret, however. That word reminds me to observe, Sophronia, that I have glided on into telling you the secret, and that I rely upon you never to mention it.'

'Mention it!' repeated Mrs Lammle with her former feeling. 'Men-tion it!'

This time Sophronia was so much in earnest that she found it necessary to bend forward in the carriage and give Bella a kiss. A Judas order of kiss; for she thought, while she yet pressed Bella's hand after giving it, 'Upon your own showing, you vain heartless girl, puffed up by the doting folly of a dustman, I need have no relenting towards *you*. If my husband, who sends me here, should form any schemes for making *you* a victim, I should certainly not cross him again.' In those very same moments, Bella was thinking, 'Why am I always at war with myself? Why have I told, as if upon compulsion, what I knew all along I ought to have withheld? Why am I making a friend of this woman beside me, in spite of the whispers against her that I hear in my heart?'

As usual, there was no answer in the looking-glass when she got home and referred these questions to it. Perhaps if she had consulted some better oracle, the result might have been more satisfactory; but she did not, and all things consequent marched the march before them.

On one point connected with the watch she kept on Mr Boffin, she felt very inquisitive, and that was the question whether the Secretary watched him too, and followed the sure and steady change in him, as she did? Her very limited intercourse with Mr Rokesmith rendered this hard to find out. Their communication now, at no time extended beyond the preservation of commonplace appearances before Mr and Mrs Boffin; and if Bella and the Secretary were ever left alone together by any chance, he immediately withdrew. She consulted his face when she could do so covertly, as she worked or read, and could make nothing of it. He looked subdued; but he had acquired a strong command of feature, and, whenever Mr Boffin spoke to him in Bella's presence, or whatever revelation of himself Mr Boffin made, the Secretary's face changed no more than a wall. A slightly knitted brow, that expressed nothing but an almost mechanical attention, and a compression of the mouth, that might have been a guard against a scornful smile—these she saw from morning to night, from day to day, from week to week, monotonous, unvarying, set, as in a piece of sculpture.

The worst of the matter was, that it thus fell out insensibly— and most provokingly, as Bella complained to herself, in her impetuous little manner—that her observation of Mr Boffin in- volved a continual observation of Mr Rokesmith. 'Won't *that* extract a look from him?'—'Can it be possible *that* makes no impression on him?' Such questions Bella would propose to herself, often as many times in a day as there were hours in it. Impossible to know. Always the same fixed face.

'Can he be so base as to sell his very nature for two hundred a year?' Bella would think. And then, 'But why not? It's a mere question of price with others besides him. I suppose I would sell mine, if I could get enough for it.' And so she would come round again to the war with herself.

A kind of illegibility, though a different kind, stole over Mr Boffin's face. Its old simplicity of expression got masked by a certain craftiness that assimilated even his good-humour to itself. His very smile was cunning, as if he had been studying smiles among the portraits of his misers. Saving an occasional burst of impatience, or coarse assertion of his mastery, his good-humour remained to him, but it had now a sordid alloy of distrust; and though his eyes should twinkle and all his face should laugh, he would sit holding himself in his own arms, as if he had an inclination to hoard himself up, and must always grudgingly stand on the defensive.

What with taking heed of these two faces, and what with feeling conscious that the stealthy occupation must set some mark on her own, Bella soon began to think that there was not a candid or a natural face among them all but Mrs Boffin's. None the less because it was far less radiant than of yore, faithfully reflecting in its anxiety and regret every line of change in the Golden Dustman's.

'Rokesmith,' said Mr Boffin one evening when they were all in his room again, and he and the Secretary had been going over some accounts, 'I am spending too much money. Or least- ways, you are spending too much for me.'

'You are rich, sir.'

'I am not,' said Mr Boffin.

The sharpness of the retort was next to telling the Secretary that he lied. But it brought no change of expression into the set face.

'I tell you I am not rich,' repeated Mr Boffin, 'and I won't have it.'

'You are not rich, sir?' repeated the Secretary, in measured words.

'Well,' returned Mr Boffin, 'if I am, that's my business. I am not going to spend at this rate, to please you, or anybody. You wouldn't like it, if it was your money.'

'Even in that impossible case, sir, I—'

'Hold your tongue!' said Mr Boffin. 'You oughtn't to like it in any case. There! I didn't mean to be rude, but you put me out so, and after all I'm master. I didn't intend to tell you to hold your tongue. I beg your pardon. Don't hold your tongue. Only, don't contradict. Did you ever come across the life of Mr Elwes?' referring to his favourite subject at last.

'The miser?'

'Ah, people called him a miser. People are always calling other people something. Did you ever read about him?'

'I think so.'

'He never owned to being rich, and yet he might have bought me twice over. Did you ever hear of Daniel Dancer?'

'Another miser? Yes.'

'He was a good 'un,' said Mr Boffin, 'and he had a sister worthy of him. They never called themselves rich neither. If they *had* called themselves rich, most likely they wouldn't have been so.'

'They lived and died very miserably. Did they not, sir?'

'No, I don't know that they did,' said Mr Boffin, curtly.

'Then they are not the Misers I mean. Those abject wretches—'

'Don't call names, Rokesmith,' said Mr Boffin.

'—That exemplary brother and sister—lived and died in the foulest and filthiest degradation.'

'They pleased themselves,' said Mr Boffin, 'and I suppose they could have done no more if they had spent their money. But however, I ain't going to fling mine away. Keep the expenses down. The fact is, you ain't enough here, Rokesmith. It wants constant attention in the littlest things. Some of us will be dying in a work-house next.'

'As the persons you have cited,' quietly remarked the Secretary, 'thought they would, if I remember, sir.'

'And very creditable in 'em too,' said Mr Boffin. 'Very independent in 'em! But never mind them just now. Have you given notice to quit your lodgings?'

'Under your direction, I have, sir.'

'Then I tell you what,' said Mr Boffin; 'pay the quarter's rent—pay the quarter's rent, it'll be the cheapest thing in the end—and come here at once, so that you may be always on the spot, day and night, and keep the expenses down. You'll charge the quarter's rent to me, and we must try and save it somewhere. You've got some lovely furniture; haven't you?'

'The furniture in my rooms is my own.'

'Then we shan't have to buy any for you. In case you was to think it,' said Mr Boffin, with a look of peculiar shrewdness, 'so honourably independent in you as to make it a relief to your mind, to make that furniture over to me in the light of a set-off against the quarter's rent, why ease your mind, ease your mind. I don't ask it, but I won't stand in your way if you should consider it due to yourself. As to your room, choose any empty room at the top of the house.'

'Any empty room will do for me,' said the Secretary.

'You can take your pick,' said Mr Boffin, 'and it'll be as good as eight or ten shillings a week added to your income. I won't deduct for it; I look to you to make it up handsomely by keeping the expenses down. Now, if you'll show a light, I'll come to your office-room and dispose of a letter or two.'

On that clear, generous face of Mrs Boffin's, Bella had seen such traces of a pang at the heart while this dialogue was being held, that she had not the courage to turn her eyes to it when they were left alone. Feigning to be intent on her embroidery, she sat plying her needle until her busy hand was stopped by Mrs Boffin's hand being lightly laid upon it. Yielding to the touch, she felt her hand carried to the good soul's lips, and felt a tear fall on it.

'Oh my loved husband!' said Mrs Boffin. 'This is hard to see and hear. But my dear Bella, believe me that in spite of all the change in him, he is the best of men.'

He came back, at the moment when Bella had taken the hand comfortingly between her own.

'Eh?' said he, mistrustfully looking in at the door. 'What's she telling you?'

'She is only praising you, sir,' said Bella.

'Praising me? You are sure? Not blaming me for standing on my own defence against a crew of plunderers, who could suck me dry by driblets? Not blaming me for getting a little hoard together?'

He came up to them, and his wife folded her hands upon his shoulder, and shook her head as she laid it on her hands.

'There, there, there!' urged Mr Boffin, not unkindly. 'Don't take on, old lady.'

'But I can't bear to see you so, my dear.'

'Nonsense! Recollect we are not our old selves. Recollect, we must scrunch or be scrunched. Recollect, we must hold our own. Recollect, money makes money. Don't you be uneasy, Bella, my child; don't you be doubtful. The more I save, the more you shall have.'

Bella thought it was well for his wife that she was musing with her affectionate face on his shoulder; for there was a cunning light in his eyes as he said all this, which seemed to cast a disagreeable illumination on the change in him, and make it morally uglier.

Chapter 6

The Golden Dustman
Falls Into Worse Company

IT had come to pass that Mr Silas Wegg now rarely attended the minion of fortune and the worm of the hour, at his (the worm's and minion's) own house, but lay under general instructions to await him within a certain margin of hours at the Bower. Mr Wegg took this arrangement in great dudgeon, because the appointed hours were evening hours, and those he considered precious to the progress of the friendly move. But it was quite in character, he bitterly remarked to Mr Venus, that the upstart who had trampled on those eminent creatures, Miss Elizabeth, Master George, Aunt Jane, and Uncle Parker, should oppress his literary man.

The Roman Empire having worked out its destruction, Mr

Boffin next appeared in a cab with Rollin's Ancient History, which valuable work being found to possess lethargic properties, broke down, at about the period when the whole of the army of Alexander the Macedonian (at that time about forty thousand strong) burst into tears simultaneously, on his being taken with a shivering fit after bathing. The Wars of the Jews, likewise languishing under Mr Wegg's generalship, Mr Boffin arrived in another cab with Plutarch: whose Lives he found in the sequel extremely entertaining, though he hoped Plutarch might not expect him to believe them all. What to believe, in the course of his reading, was Mr Boffin's chief literary difficulty indeed; for some time he was divided in his mind between half, all, or none; at length, when he decided, as a moderate man, to compound with half, the question still remained, which half? And that stumbling-block he never got over.

One evening, when Silas Wegg had grown accustomed to the arrival of his patron in a cab, accompanied by some profane historian charged with unutterable names of incomprehensible peoples, of impossible descent, waging wars any number of years and syllables long, and carrying illimitable hosts and riches about, with the greatest ease, beyond the confines of geography—one evening the usual time passed by, and no patron appeared. After half an hour's grace, Mr Wegg proceeded to the outer gate, and there executed a whistle, conveying to Mr Venus, if perchance within hearing, the tidings of his being at home and disengaged. Forth from the shelter of a neighbouring wall, Mr Venus then emerged.

'Brother in arms,' said Mr Wegg, in excellent spirits, 'welcome!'

In return, Mr Venus gave him a rather dry good evening.

'Walk in, brother,' said Silas, clapping him on the shoulder, 'and take your seat in my chimley corner; for what says the ballad?

> "No malice to dread, sir,
>   And no falsehood to fear,
>   But truth to delight me, Mr Venus,
>   And I forgot what to cheer.
>   Li toddle de om dee.
>   And something to guide,
>   My ain fireside, sir,
>   My ain fireside." '

With this quotation (depending for its neatness rather on the spirit than the words), Mr Wegg conducted his guest to his hearth.

'And you come, brother,' said Mr Wegg, in a hospitable glow, 'you come like I don't know what—exactly like it—I shouldn't know you from it—shedding a halo all around you.'

'What kind of halo?' asked Mr Venus.

' 'Ope sir,' replied Silas. 'That's *your* halo.'

Mr Venus appeared doubtful on the point, and looked rather discontentedly at the fire.

'We'll devote the evening, brother,' exclaimed Wegg, 'to prosecute our friendly move. And arterwards, crushing a flowing wine-cup—which I allude to brewing rum and water—we'll pledge one another. For what says the Poet?

> "And you needn't Mr Venus be your black bottle,
>   For surely I'll be mine,
> And we'll take a glass with a slice of lemon in it
>   to which you're partial,
> For auld lang syne." '

This flow of quotation and hospitality in Wegg indicated his observation of some little querulousness on the part of Venus.

'Why, as to the friendly move,' observed the last-named gentleman, rubbing his knees peevishly, 'one of my objections to it is, that it *don't* move.'

'Rome, brother,' returned Wegg: 'a city which (it may not be generally known) originated in twins and a wolf, and ended in Imperial marble: wasn't built in a day.'

'Did I say it was?' asked Venus.

'No, you did not, brother. Well-inquired.'

'But I do say,' proceeded Venus, 'that I am taken from among my trophies of anatomy, am called upon to exchange my human warious for mere coal-ashes warious, and nothing comes of it. I think I must give up.'

'No, sir!' remonstrated Wegg, enthusiastically. 'No, sir!

> "Charge, Chester, charge,
>   On, Mr Venus, on!"

Never say die, sir! A man of your mark!'

'It's not so much saying it that I object to,' returned Mr Venus, 'as doing it. And having got to do it whether or no, I can't afford to waste my time on groping for nothing in cinders.'

'But think how little time you have given to the move, sir, after all,' urged Wegg. 'Add the evenings so occupied together, and what do they come to? And you, sir, harmonizer with myself in opinions, views, and feelings, you with the patience to fit together on wires the whole framework of society—I allude to the human skelinton—you to give in so soon!'

'I don't like it,' returned Mr Venus moodily, as he put his head between his knees and stuck up his dusty hair. 'And there's no encouragement to go on.'

'Not them Mounds without,' said Mr Wegg, extending his right hand with an air of solemn reasoning, 'encouragement? Not them Mounds now looking down upon us?'

'They're too big,' grumbled Venus. 'What's a scratch here and a scrape there, a poke in this place and a dig in the other, to them. Besides; what have we found?'

'What *have* we found?' cried Wegg, delighted to be able to acquiesce. 'Ah! There I grant you, comrade. Nothing. But on the contrary, comrade, what *may* we find? There you'll grant me. Anything.'

'I don't like it,' pettishly returned Venus as before. 'I came into it without enough consideration. And besides again. Isn't your own Mr Boffin well acquainted with the Mounds? And wasn't he well acquainted with the deceased and his ways? And has he ever showed any expectation of finding anything?'

At that moment wheels were heard.

'Now, I should be loth,' said Mr Wegg, with an air of patient injury, 'to think so ill of him as to suppose him capable of coming at this time of night. And yet it sounds like him.'

A ring at the yard bell.

'It *is* him,' said Mr Wegg, 'and he *is* capable of it. I am sorry, because I could have wished to keep up a little lingering fragment of respect for him.'

Here Mr Boffin was heard lustily calling at the yard gate, 'Halloa! Wegg! Halloa!'

'Keep your seat, Mr Venus,' said Wegg. 'He may not stop.' And then called out, 'Halloa, sir! Halloa! I'm with you directly, sir! Half a minute, Mr Boffin. Coming, sir, as fast as my leg will bring me!' And so with a show of much cheerful alacrity stumped out to the gate with a light, and there, through the window of a cab, descried Mr Boffin inside, blocked up with books.

'Here! lend a hand, Wegg,' said Mr Boffin excitedly, 'I

can't get out till the way is cleared for me. This is the Annual Register, Wegg, in a cab-full of wollumes. Do you know him?'

'Know the Animal Register, sir?' returned the Impostor, who had caught the name imperfectly. 'For a trifling wager, I think I could find any Animal in him, blindfold, Mr Boffin.'

'And here's Kirby's Wonderful Museum,' said Mr Boffin, 'and Caulfield's Characters, and Wilson's. Such Characters, Wegg, such Characters! I must have one or two of the best of 'em to-night. It's amazing what places they used to put the guineas in, wrapped up in rags. Catch hold of that pile of wollumes, Wegg, or it'll bulge out and burst into the mud. Is there anyone about, to help?'

'There's a friend of mine, sir, that had the intention of spending the evening with me when I gave you up—much against my will—for the night.'

'Call him out,' cried Mr Boffin in a bustle; 'get him to bear a hand. Don't drop that one under your arm. It's Dancer. Him and his sister made pies of a dead sheep they found when they were out a walking. Where's your friend? Oh, here's your friend. Would you be so good as help Wegg and myself with these books? But don't take Jemmy Taylor of Southwark, nor yet Jemmy Wood of Gloucester. These are the two Jemmys. I'll carry them myself.'

Not ceasing to talk and bustle, in a state of great excitement, Mr Boffin directed the removal and arrangement of the books, appearing to be in some sort beside himself until they were all deposited on the floor, and the cab was dismissed.

'There!' said Mr Boffin, gloating over them. 'There they are, like the four-and-twenty fiddlers—all of a row. Get on your spectacles, Wegg; I know where to find the best of 'em, and we'll have a taste at once of what we have got before us. What's your friend's name?'

Mr Wegg presented his friend as Mr Venus.

'Eh?' cried Mr Boffin, catching at the name. 'Of Clerkenwell?'

'Of Clerkenwell, sir,' said Mr Venus.

'Why, I've heard of you,' cried Mr Boffin, 'I heard of you in the old man's time. You knew him. Did you ever buy anything of him?' With piercing eagerness.

'No, sir,' returned Venus.

'But he showed you things; didn't he?'

Mr Venus, with a glance at his friend, replied in the affirmative.

'What did he show you?' asked Mr Boffin, putting his

hands behind him, and eagerly advancing his head. 'Did he show you boxes, little cabinets, pocket-books, parcels, anything locked or sealed, anything tied up?'

Mr Venus shook his head.

'Are you a judge of china?'

Mr Venus again shook his head.

'Because if he had ever showed you a teapot, I should be glad to know of it,' said Mr Boffin. And then, with his right hand at his lips, repeated thoughtfully, 'a Teapot, a Teapot', and glanced over the books on the floor, as if he knew there was something interesting connected with a teapot, somewhere among them.

Mr Wegg and Mr Venus looked at one another wonderingly: and Mr Wegg, in fitting on his spectacles, opened his eyes wide, over their rims, and tapped the side of his nose: as an admonition to Venus to keep himself generally wide awake.

'A Teapot,' repeated Mr Boffin, continuing to muse and survey the books; 'a Teapot, a Teapot. Are you ready, Wegg?'

'I am at your service, sir,' replied that gentleman, taking his usual seat on the usual settle, and poking his wooden leg under the table before it. 'Mr Venus, would you make yourself useful, and take a seat beside me, sir, for the conveniency of snuffing the candles?'

Venus complying with the invitation while it was yet being given, Silas pegged at him with his wooden leg, to call his particular attention to Mr Boffin standing musing before the fire, in the space between the two settles.

'Hem! Ahem!' coughed Mr Wegg to attract his employer's attention. 'Would you wish to commence with an Animal, sir— from the Register?'

'No,' said Mr Boffin, 'no, Wegg.' With that, producing a little book from his breast-pocket, he handed it with great care to the literary gentleman, and inquired, 'What do you call that, Wegg?'

'This, sir,' replied Silas, adjusting his spectacles, and referring to the title-page, 'is Merryweather's Lives and Anecdotes of Misers. Mr Venus, would you make yourself useful and draw the candles a little nearer, sir?' This is to have a special opportunity of bestowing a stare upon his comrade.

'Which of 'em have you got in that lot?' asked Mr Boffin. 'Can you find out pretty easy?'

'Well, sir,' replied Silas, turning to the table of contents and slowly fluttering the leaves of the book, 'I should say they must be pretty well all here, sir; here's a large assortment, sir; my eye catches John Overs, sir, John Little, sir, Dick Jarrel, John Elwes, the Reverend Mr Jones of Blewbury, Vulture Hopkins, Daniel Dancer—'

'Give us Dancer, Wegg,' said Mr Boffin.

With another stare at his comrade, Silas sought and found the place.

'Page a hundred and nine, Mr Boffin. Chapter eight. Contents of chapter, "His birth and estate. His garments and outward appearance. Miss Dancer and her feminine graces. The Miser's Mansion. The finding of a treasure. The Story of the Mutton Pies. A Miser's Idea of Death. Bob, the Miser's cur. Griffiths and his Master. How to turn a penny. A substitute for a Fire. The Advantages of keeping a Snuff-box. The Miser dies without a Shirt. The Treasures of a Dunghill—" '

'Eh? What's that?' demanded Mr Boffin.

' "The Treasures," sir,' repeated Silas, reading very distinctly, ' "of a Dunghill." Mr Venus, sir, would you obleege with the snuffers?' This, to secure attention to his adding with his lips only, 'Mounds!'

Mr Boffin drew an arm-chair into the space where he stood, and said, seating himself and slyly rubbing his hands:

'Give us Dancer.'

Mr Wegg pursued the biography of that eminent man through its various phases of avarice and dirt, through Miss Dancer's death on a sick regimen of cold dumpling, and through Mr Dancer's keeping his rags together with a hayband, and warming his dinner by sitting upon it, down to the consolatory incident of his dying naked in a sack. After which he read on as follows:

' "The house, or rather the heap of ruins, in which Mr Dancer lived, and which at his death devolved to the right of Captain Holmes, was a most miserable, decayed building, for it had not been repaired for more than half a century." '

(Here Mr Wegg eyes his comrade and the room in which they sat: which had not been repaired for a long time.)

' "But though poor in external structure, the ruinous fabric was very rich in the interior. It took many weeks to explore its whole contents; and Captain Holmes found it a very agreeable task to dive into the miser's secret hoards." '

(Here Mr Wegg repeated 'secret hoards', and pegged his comrade again.)

' "One of Mr Dancer's richest escretoires was found to be a dungheap in the cowhouse; a sum but little short of two thousand five hundred pounds was contained in this rich piece of manure; and in an old jacket, carefully tied, and strongly nailed down to the manger, in bank notes and gold were found five hundred pounds more." '

(Here Mr Wegg's wooden leg started forward under the table, and slowly elevated itself as he read on.)

' "Several bowls were discovered filled with guineas and half-guineas; and at different times on searching the corners of the house they found various parcels of bank notes. Some were crammed into the crevices of the wall" ';

(Here Mr Venus looked at the wall.)

' "Bundles were hid under the cushions and covers of the chairs" ';

(Here Mr Venus looked under himself on the settle.)

' "Some were reposing snugly at the back of the drawers; and notes amounting to six hundred pounds were found neatly doubled up in the inside of an old teapot. In the stable the Captain found jugs full of old dollars and shillings. The chimney was not left unsearched, and paid very well for the trouble; for in nineteen different holes, all filled with soot, were found various sums of money, mounting together to more than two hundred pounds." '

On the way to this crisis Mr Wegg's wooden leg had gradually elevated itself more and more, and he had nudged Mr Venus with his opposite elbow deeper and deeper, until at length the preservation of his balance became incompatible with the two actions, and he now dropped over sideways upon that gentleman, squeezing him against the settle's edge. Nor did either of the two, for some few seconds, make any effort to recover himself; both remaining in a kind of pecuniary swoon.

But the sight of Mr Boffin sitting in the arm-chair hugging himself, with his eyes upon the fire, acted as a restorative. Counterfeiting a sneeze to cover their movements, Mr Wegg, with a spasmodic 'Tish-ho!' pulled himself and Mr Venus up in a masterly manner.

'Let's have some more,' said Mr Boffin, hungrily.

'John Elwes is the next, sir. Is it your pleasure to take John Elwes?'

'Ah!' said Mr Boffin. 'Let's hear what John did.'

He did not appear to have hidden anything, so went off rather flatly. But an exemplary lady named Wilcocks, who had stowed away gold and silver in a pickle-pot in a clock-case, a canister-full of treasure in a hole under her stairs, and a quantity of money in an old rat-trap, revived the interest. To her suc-ceeded another lady, claiming to be a pauper, whose wealth was found wrapped up in little scraps of paper and old rag. To her, another lady, apple-woman by trade, who had saved a fortune of ten thousand pounds and hidden it 'here and there, in cracks and corners, behind bricks and under the flooring.' To her, a French gentleman, who had crammed up his chimney, rather to the detriment of its drawing powers, 'a leather valise, containing twenty thousand francs, gold coins, and a large quantity of precious stones,' as discovered by a chimneysweep after his death. By these steps Mr Wegg arrived at a concluding instance of the human Magpie:

' "Many years ago, there lived at Cambridge a miserly old couple of the name of Jardine: they had two sons: the father was a perfect miser, and at his death one thousand guineas were discovered secreted in his bed. The two sons grew up as parsi-monious as their sire. When about twenty years of age, they commenced business at Cambridge as drapers, and they contin-ued there until their death. The establishment of the Messrs Jardine was the most dirty of all the shops in Cambridge. Cus-tomers seldom went in to purchase, except perhaps out of curios-ity. The brothers were most disreputable-looking beings; for, although surrounded with gay apparel as their staple in trade, they wore the most filthy rags themselves. It is said that they had no bed, and, to save the expense of one, always slept on a bundle of packing-cloths under the counter. In their housekeeping they were penurious in the extreme. A joint of meat did not grace their board for twenty years. Yet when the first of the brothers died, the other, much to his surprise, found large sums of money which had been secreted even from him.'

'There!' cried Mr Boffin. 'Even from him, you see! There was only two of 'em, and yet one of 'em hid from the other.'

Mr Venus, who since his introduction to the French gentle-man, had been stooping to peer up the chimney, had his attention recalled by the last sentence, and took the liberty of repeating it.

'Do you like it?' asked Mr Boffin, turning suddenly.

'I beg your pardon, sir?'

'Do you like what Wegg's been a-reading?'

Mr Venus answered that he found it extremely interesting.

'Then come again,' said Mr Boffin, 'and hear some more. Come when you like; come the day after to-morrow, half an hour sooner. There's plenty more; there's no end to it.'

Mr Venus expressed his acknowledgments and accepted the invitation.

'It's wonderful what's been hid, at one time and another,' said Mr Boffin, ruminating; 'truly wonderful.'

'Meaning sir,' observed Wegg, with a propitiatory face to draw him out, and with another peg at his friend and brother, 'in the way of money?'

'Money,' said Mr Boffin. 'Ah! And papers.'

Mr Wegg, in a languid transport, again dropped over on Mr Venus, and again recovering himself, masked his emotions with a sneeze.

'Tish-ho! Did you say papers too, sir? Been hidden, sir?'

'Hidden and forgot,' said Mr Boffin. 'Why the bookseller that sold me the Wonderful Museum—where's the Wonderful Museum?' He was on his knees on the floor in a moment, groping eagerly among the books.

'Can I assist you, sir?' asked Wegg.

'No, I have got it; here it is,' said Mr Boffin, dusting it with the sleeve of his coat. 'Wollume four. I know it was the fourth wollume, that the bookseller read it to me out of. Look for it, Wegg.'

Silas took the book and turned the leaves.

'Remarkable petrefaction, sir?'

'No, that's not it,' said Mr Boffin. 'It can't have been a petrefaction.'

'Memoirs of General John Reid, commonly called The Walking Rushlight, sir? With portrait?'

'No, nor yet him,' said Mr Boffin.

'Remarkable case of a person who swallowed a crownpiece, sir?'

'To hide it?' asked Mr Boffin.

'Why, no, sir,' replied Wegg, consulting the text, 'it appears to have been done by accident. Oh! This next must be it. "Singular discovery of a will, lost twenty-one years." '

'That's it!' cried Mr Boffin. 'Read that.'

' "A most extraordinary case," ' read Silas Wegg aloud, ' "was tried at the last Maryborough assizes in Ireland. It was briefly this. Robert Baldwin, in March 1782, made his will, in which he devised the lands now in question, to the children of his youngest son; soon after which his faculties failed him, and he became altogether childish and died, above eighty years old. The defendant, the eldest son, immediately afterwards gave out that his father had destroyed the will; and no will being found, he entered into possession of the lands in question, and so matters remained for twenty-one years, the whole family during all that time believing that the father had died without a will. But after twenty-one years the defendant's wife died, and he very soon afterwards, at the age of seventy-eight, married a very young woman: which caused some anxiety to his two sons, whose poignant expressions of this feeling so exasperated their father, that he in his resentment executed a will to disinherit his eldest son, and in his fit of anger showed it to his second son, who instantly determined to get at it, and destroy it, in order to preserve the property to his brother. With this view, he broke open his father's desk, where he found—not his father's will which he sought after, but the will of his grandfather, which was then altogether forgotten in the family.'' '

'There!' said Mr Boffin. 'See what men put away and forget, or mean to destroy, and don't!' He then added in a slow tone, 'As–ton–ish–ing!' And as he rolled his eyes all round the room, Wegg and Venus likewise rolled their eyes all round the room. And then Wegg, singly, fixed his eyes on Mr Boffin looking at the fire again; as if he had a mind to spring upon him and demand his thoughts or his life.

'However, time's up for to-night,' said Mr Boffin, waving his hand after a silence. 'More, the day after to-morrow. Range the books upon the shelves, Wegg. I dare say Mr Venus will be so kind as help you.'

While speaking, he thrust his hand into the breast of his outer coat, and struggled with some object there that was too large to be got out easily. What was the stupefaction of the friendly movers when this object at last emerging, proved to be a much-dilapidated dark lantern!

Without at all noticing the effect produced by this little instrument, Mr Boffin stood it on his knee, and, producing a box of matches, deliberately lighted the candle in the lantern, blew out the kindled match, and cast the end into the fire. 'I'm going, Wegg,' he then announced, 'to take a turn about the place and round the yard. I don't want you. Me and this same lantern have taken hundreds—thousands—of such turns in our time together.'

'But I couldn't think, sir—not on any account, I couldn't,'— Wegg was politely beginning, when Mr Boffin, who had risen and was going towards the door, stopped:

'I have told you that I don't want you, Wegg.'

Wegg looked intelligently thoughtful, as if that had not occurred to his mind until he now brought it to bear on the circumstance. He had nothing for it but to let Mr Boffin go out and shut the door behind him. But, the instant he was on the other side of it, Wegg clutched Venus with both hands, and said in a choking whisper, as if he were being strangled:

'Mr Venus, he must be followed, he must be watched, he mustn't be lost sight of for a moment.'

'Why mustn't he?' asked Venus, also strangling.

'Comrade, you might have noticed I was a little elewated in spirits when you come in to-night. I've found something.'

'What have you found?' asked Venus, clutching him with both hands, so that they stood interlocked like a couple of preposterous gladiators.

'There's no time to tell you now. I think he must have gone to look for it. We must have an eye upon him instantly.'

Releasing each other, they crept to the door, opened it softly, and peeped out. It was a cloudy night, and the black shadow of the Mounds made the dark yard darker. 'If not a double swindler,' whispered Wegg, 'why a dark lantern? We could have seen what he was about, if he had carried a light one. Softly, this way.'

Cautiously along the path that was bordered by fragments of crockery set in ashes, the two stole after him. They could hear him at his peculiar trot, crushing the loose cinders as he went. 'He knows the place by heart,' muttered Silas, 'and don't need to turn his lantern on, confound him!' But he did turn it on, almost in that same instant, and flashed its light upon the first of the Mounds.

'Is that the spot?' asked Venus in a whisper.

'He's warm,' said Silas in the same tone. 'He's precious warm. He's close. I think he must be going to look for it. What's that he's got in his hand?'

'A shovel,' answered Venus. 'And he knows how to use it, remember, fifty times as well as either of us.'

'If he looks for it and misses it, partner,' suggested Wegg, 'what shall we do?'

'First of all, wait till he does,' said Venus.

Discreet advice too, for he darkened his lantern again, and the mound turned black. After a few seconds, he turned the light on once more, and was seen standing at the foot of the second mound, slowly raising the lantern little by little until he held it up at arm's length, as if he were examining the condition of the whole surface.

'That can't be the spot too?' said Venus.

'No,' said Wegg, 'he's getting cold.'

'It strikes me,' whispered Venus, 'that he wants to find out whether any one has been groping about there.'

'Hush!' returned Wegg, 'he's getting colder and colder. —Now he's freezing!'

This exclamation was elicited by his having turned the lantern off again, and on again, and being visible at the foot of the third mound.

'Why, he's going up it!' said Venus.

'Shovel and all!' said Wegg.

At a nimbler trot, as if the shovel over his shoulder stimulated him by reviving old associations. Mr Boffin ascended the 'serpentining walk', up the Mound which he had described to Silas Wegg on the occasion of their beginning to decline and fall. On striking into it he turned his lantern off. The two followed him, stooping low, so that their figures might make no mark in relief against the sky when he should turn his lantern on again. Mr Venus took the lead, towing Mr Wegg, in order that his refractory leg might be promptly extricated from any pitfalls it should dig for itself. They could just make out that the Golden Dustman stopped to breathe. Of course they stopped too, instantly.

'This is his own Mound,' whispered Wegg, as he recovered his wind, 'this one.'

'Why all three are his own,' returned Venus.

'So he thinks; but he's used to call this his own, because it's the one first left to him; the one that was his legacy: when it was all he took under the will.'

'When he shows his light,' said Venus, keeping watch upon his dusky figure all the time, 'drop lower and keep closer.'

He went on again, and they followed again. Gaining the top of the Mound, he turned on his light—but only partially—and stood it on the ground. A bare lopsided weatherbeaten pole was planted in the ashes there, and had been there many a year. Hard by this pole, his lantern stood: lighting a few feet of the lower part of it and a little of the ashy surface around, and then casting off a purposeless little clear trail of light into the air.

'He can never be going to dig up the pole!' whispered Venus as they dropped low and kept close.

'Perhaps it's holler and full of something,' whispered Wegg.

He was going to dig, with whatsoever object, for he tucked up his cuffs and spat on his hands, and then went at it like an old digger as he was. He had no design upon the pole, except that he measured a shovel's length from it before beginning, nor was it his purpose to dig deep. Some dozen or so of expert strokes sufficed. Then, he stopped, looked down into the cavity, bent over it, and took out what appeared to be an ordinary case-bottle: one of those squat, high-shouldered, short-necked glass bottles which the Dutchman is said to keep his Courage in. As soon as he had done this, he turned off his lantern, and they could hear that he was filling up the hole in the dark. The ashes being easily moved by a skilful hand, the spies took this as a hint to make off in good time. Accordingly, Mr Venus slipped past Mr Wegg and towed him down. But Mr Wegg's descent was not accomplished without some personal inconvenience, for his self-willed leg sticking into the ashes about half way down, and time pressing, Mr Venus took the liberty of hauling him from his tether by the collar: which occasioned him to make the rest of the journey on his back, with his head enveloped in the skirts of his coat, and his wooden leg coming last, like a drag. So flustered was Mr Wegg by this mode of travelling, that when he was set on the level ground with his intellectual developments uppermost, he was quite unconscious of his bearings, and had not the least idea where his place of residence was to be found, until Mr Venus shoved him into it. Even then he staggered round and round, weakly staring about him, until Mr Venus with a hard brush brushed his senses into him and the dust out of him.

Mr Boffin came down leisurely, for this brushing process had been well accomplished, and Mr Venus had had time to take his breath, before he reappeared. That he had the bottle somewhere about him could not be doubted; where, was not so clear. He wore a large rough coat, buttoned over, and it might be in any one of half a dozen pockets.

'What's the matter, Wegg?' said Mr Boffin. 'You are as pale as a candle.'

Mr Wegg replied, with literal exactness, that he felt as if he had had a turn.

'Bile,' said Mr Boffin, blowing out the light in the lantern, shutting it up, and stowing it away in the breast of his coat as before. 'Are you subject to bile, Wegg?'

Mr Wegg again replied, with strict adherence to truth, that he didn't think he had ever had a similar sensation in his head, to anything like the same extent.

'Physic yourself to-morrow, Wegg,' said Mr Boffin, 'to be in order for next night. By-the-by, this neighbourhood is going to have a loss, Wegg.'

'A loss, sir?'

'Going to lose the Mounds.'

The friendly movers made such an obvious effort not to look at one another, that they might as well have stared at one another with all their might.

'Have you parted with them, Mr Boffin?' asked Silas.

'Yes; they're going. Mine's as good as gone already.'

'You mean the little one of the three, with the pole atop, sir.'

'Yes,' said Mr Boffin, rubbing his ear in his old way, with that new touch of craftiness added to it. 'It has fetched a penny. It'll begin to be carted off to-morrow.'

'Have you been out to take leave of your old friend, sir?' asked Silas, jocosely.

'No,' said Mr Boffin. 'What the devil put that in your head?'

He was so sudden and rough, that Wegg, who had been hovering closer and closer to his skirts, despatching the back of his hand on exploring expeditions in search of the bottle's surface, retired two or three paces.

'No offence, sir,' said Wegg, humbly. 'No offence.'

Mr Boffin eyed him as a dog might eye another dog who wanted his bone; and actually retorted with a low growl, as the dog might have retorted.

'Good-night,' he said, after having sunk into a moody silence, with his hands clasped behind him, and his eyes suspiciously wandering about Wegg.—'No! stop there. I know the way out, and I want no light.'

Avarice, and the evening's legends of avarice, and the inflammatory effect of what he had seen, and perhaps the rush of his ill-conditioned blood to his brain in his descent, wrought Silas Wegg to such a pitch of insatiable appetite, that when the door closed he made a swoop at it and drew Venus along with him.

'He mustn't go,' he cried. 'We mustn't let him go. He has got that bottle about him. We must have that bottle.'

'Why, you wouldn't take it by force?' said Venus, restraining him.

'Wouldn't I? Yes I would. I'd take it by any force, I'd have it at any price! Are you so afraid of one old man as to let him go, you coward?'

'I am so afraid of you, as not to let *you* go,' muttered Venus, sturdily, clasping him in his arms.

'Did you hear him?' retorted Wegg. 'Did you hear him say that he was resolved to disappoint us? Did you hear him say, you cur, that he was going to have the Mounds cleared off, when no doubt the whole place will be rummaged? If you haven't the spirit of a mouse to defend your rights, I have. Let me go after him.'

As in his wildness he was making a strong struggle for it, Mr Venus deemed it expedient to lift him, throw him, and fall with him; well knowing that, once down, he would not be up again easily with his wooden leg. So they both rolled on the floor, and, as they did so, Mr Boffin shut the gate.

Chapter 7

The Friendly Move
Takes Up a Strong Position

THE friendly movers sat upright on the floor, panting and eyeing one another, after Mr Boffin had slammed the gate and gone away. In the weak eyes of Venus, and in every reddish dust-coloured hair in his shock of hair, there was a marked distrust of Wegg and an alertness to fly at him on perceiving the smallest occasion. In the hard-grained face of Wegg, and in his stiff knotty figure (he looked like a German wooden toy), there was expressed a politic conciliation, which had no spontaneity in it. Both were flushed, flustered, and rumpled, by the late scuffle; and Wegg, in coming to the ground, had received a humming knock on the back of his devoted head, which caused him still to rub it with an air of having been highly—but disagreeably—astonished. Each was silent for some time, leaving it to the other to begin.

'Brother,' said Wegg, at length breaking the silence, 'you were right, and I was wrong. I forgot myself.'

Mr Venus knowingly cocked his shock of hair, as rather thinking Mr Wegg had remembered himself, in respect of appearing without any disguise.

'But comrade,' pursued Wegg, 'it was never your lot to know Miss Elizabeth, Master George, Aunt Jane, nor Uncle Parker.'

Mr Venus admitted that he had never known those distinguished persons, and added, in effect, that he had never so much as desired the honour of their acquaintance.

'Don't say that, comrade!' retorted Wegg: 'No, don't say that! Because, without having known them, you never can fully know what it is to be stimulated to frenzy by the sight of the Usurper.'

Offering these excusatory words as if they reflected great credit on himself, Mr Wegg impelled himself with his hands towards a chair in a corner of the room, and there, after a variety of awkward gambols, attained a perpendicular position. Mr Venus also rose.

'Comrade,' said Wegg, 'take a seat. Comrade, what a speaking countenance is yours!'

Mr Venus involuntarily smoothed his countenance, and looked at his hand, as if to see whether any of its speaking properties came off.

'For clearly do I know, mark you,' pursued Wegg, pointing his words with his forefinger, 'clearly do I know what question your expressive features puts to me.'

'What question?' said Venus.

'The question,' returned Wegg, with a sort of joyful affability, 'why I didn't mention sooner, that I had found something. Says your speaking countenance to me: ''Why didn't you communicate that, when I first come in this evening? Why did you keep it back till you thought Mr Boffin had come to look for the article?'' Your speaking countenance,' said Wegg, 'puts it plainer than language. Now, you can't read in my face what answer I give?'

'No, I can't,' said Venus.

'I knew it! And why not?' returned Wegg, with the same joyful candour. 'Because I lay no claims to a speaking countenance. Because I am well aware of my deficiencies. All men are not gifted alike. But I can answer in words. And in what words? These. I wanted to give you a delightful sap–pur–IZE!'

Having thus elongated and emphasized the word Surprise, Mr Wegg shook his friend and brother by both hands, and then clapped him on both knees, like an affectionate patron who entreated him not to mention so small a service as that which it had been his happy privilege to render.

'Your speaking countenance,' said Wegg, 'being answered to its satisfaction, only asks then, ''What have you found?'' Why, I hear it say the words!'

'Well?' retorted Venus snappishly, after waiting in vain. 'If you hear it say the words, why don't you answer it?'

'Hear me out!' said Wegg. 'I'm a-going to. Hear me out! Man and brother, partner in feelings equally with undertakings and actions, I have found a cash-box.'

'Where?'

'—Hear me out!' said Wegg. (He tried to reserve whatever he could, and, whenever disclosure was forced upon him, broke into a radiant gush of Hear me out.) 'On a certain day, sir—'

'When?' said Venus bluntly.

'N–no,' returned Wegg, shaking his head at once observantly, thoughtfully, and playfully. 'No, sir! That's not your expressive countenance which asks that question. That's your voice; merely your voice. To proceed. On a certain day, sir, I happened to be walking in the yard—taking my lonely round—for in the words of a friend of my own family, the author of All's Well arranged as a duett:

"Deserted, as you will remember Mr Venus, by the
     waning moon,
   When stars, it will occur to you before I mention it,
     proclaim night's cheerless noon,
   On tower, fort, or tented ground,
   The sentry walks his lonely round,
   The sentry walks:"

—under those circumstances, sir, I happened to be walking in the yard early one afternoon, and happened to have an iron rod in my hand, with which I have been sometimes accustomed to beguile the monotony of a literary life, when I struck it against an object not necessary to trouble you by naming—'

'It *is* necessary. What object?' demanded Venus, in a wrathful tone.

'—Hear me out!' said Wegg. 'The Pump.—When I struck it against the Pump, and found, not only that the top was loose and opened with a lid, but that something in it rattled. That something, comrade, I discovered to be a small flat oblong cash-box. Shall I say it was disappointingly light?'

'There were papers in it,' said Venus.

'There your expressive countenance speaks indeed!' cried Wegg. '*A* paper. The box was locked, tied up, and sealed, and on the outside was a parchment label, with the writing, "MY WILL, JOHN HARMON, TEMPORARILY DEPOSITED HERE." '

'We must know its contents,' said Venus.

'—Hear me out!' cried Wegg. 'I said so, and I broke the box open.'

'Without coming to me!' exclaimed Venus.

'Exactly so, sir!' returned Wegg, blandly and buoyantly. 'I see I take you with me! Hear, hear, hear! Resolved, as your discriminating good sense perceives, that if you was to have a sap–pur–IZE, it should be a complete one! Well, sir. And so, as you have honoured me by anticipating, I examined the document. Regularly executed, regularly witnessed, very short. Inasmuch as he has never made friends, and has ever had a rebellious family, he, John Harmon, gives to Nicodemus Boffin the Little Mound, which is quite enough for him, and gives the whole rest and residue of his property to the Crown.'

'The date of the will that has been proved, must be looked to,' remarked Venus. 'It may be later than this one.'

'—Hear me out!' cried Wegg. 'I said so. I paid a shilling (never mind your sixpence of it) to look up that will. Brother, that will is dated months before this will. And now, as a fellow-man, and as a partner in a friendly move,' added Wegg, benignantly taking him by both hands again, and clapping him on both knees again, 'say have I completed my labour of love to your perfect satisfaction, and are you sap–pur–IZED?'

Mr Venus contemplated his fellow-man and partner with doubting eyes, and then rejoined stiffly:

'This is great news indeed, Mr Wegg. There's no denying it. But I could have wished you had told it me before you got your fright to-night, and I could have wished you had ever asked me as your partner what we were to do, before you thought you were dividing a responsibility.'

'—Hear me out!' cried Wegg. 'I knew you was a-going to say so. But alone I bore the anxiety, and alone I'll bear the blame!' This with an air of great magnanimity.

'No,' said Venus. 'Let's see this will and this box.'

'Do I understand, brother,' returned Wegg with considerable reluctance, 'that it is your wish to see this will and this—?'

Mr Venus smote the table with his hand.

'—Hear me out!' said Wegg. 'Hear me out! I'll go and fetch 'em.'

After being some time absent, as if in his covetousness he could hardly make up his mind to produce the treasure to his partner, he returned with an old leathern hat-box, into which he had put the other box, for the better preservation of commonplace appearances, and for the disarming of suspicion. 'But I

don't half like opening it here,' said Silas in a low voice, looking
around: 'he might come back, he may not be gone; we don't
know what he may be up to, after what we've seen.'

'There's something in that,' assented Venus. 'Come to my
place.'

Jealous of the custody of the box, and yet fearful of opening
it under the existing circumstances, Wegg hesitated. 'Come, I
tell you,' repeated Venus, chafing, 'to my place.' Not very well
seeing his way to a refusal, Mr Wegg then rejoined in a gush,
'— Hear me out!—Certainly.' So he locked up the Bower and
they set forth: Mr Venus taking his arm, and keeping it with
remarkable tenacity.

They found the usual dim light burning in the window of
Mr Venus's establishment, imperfectly disclosing to the public
the usual pair of preserved frogs, sword in hand, with their point
of honour still unsettled. Mr Venus had closed his shop door on
coming out, and now opened it with the key and shut it again as
soon as they were within; but not before he had put up and
barred the shutters of the shop window. 'No one can get in
without being let in,' said he then, 'and we couldn't be more
snug than here.' So he raked together the yet warm cinders in the
rusty grate, and made a fire, and trimmed the candle on the little
counter. As the fire cast its flickering gleams here and there upon
the dark greasy walls; the Hindoo baby, the African baby, the
articulated English baby, the assortment of skulls, and the rest of
the collection, came starting to their various stations as if they
had all been out, like their master and were punctual in a general
rendezvous to assist at the secret. The French gentleman had
grown considerably since Mr Wegg last saw him, being now
accommodated with a pair of legs and a head, though his arms
were yet in abeyance. To whomsoever the head had originally
belonged, Silas Wegg would have regarded it as a personal
favour if he had not cut quite so many teeth.

Silas took his seat in silence on the wooden box before the
fire, and Venus dropping into his low chair produced from
among his skeleton hands, his tea-tray and tea-cups, and put the
kettle on. Silas inwardly approved of these preparations, trusting
they might end in Mr Venus's diluting his intellect.

'Now, sir,' said Venus, 'all is safe and quiet. Let us see this
discovery.'

With still reluctant hands, and not without several glances
towards the skeleton hands, as if he mistrusted that a couple
of them might spring forth and clutch the document, Wegg opened

the hat-box and revealed the cash-box, opened the cash-box and revealed the will. He held a corner of it tight, while Venus, taking hold of another corner, searchingly and attentively read it.

'Was I correct in my account of it, partner?' said Mr Wegg at length.

'Partner, you were,' said Mr Venus.

Mr Wegg thereupon made an easy, graceful movement, as though he would fold it up; but Mr Venus held on by his corner.

'No, sir,' said Mr Venus, winking his weak eyes and shaking his head. 'No, partner. The question is now brought up, who is going to take care of this. Do you know who is going to take care of this, partner?'

'I am,' said Wegg.

'Oh dear no, partner,' retorted Venus. 'That's a mistake. I am. Now look here, Mr Wegg. I don't want to have any words with you, and still less do I want to have any anatomical pursuits with you.'

'What do you mean?' said Wegg, quickly.

'I mean, partner,' replied Venus, slowly, 'that it's hardly possible for a man to feel in a more amiable state towards another man than I do towards you at this present moment. But I am on my own ground, I am surrounded by the trophies of my art, and my tools is very handy.'

'What do you mean, Mr Venus?' asked Wegg again.

'I am surrounded, as I have observed,' said Mr Venus, placidly, 'by the trophies of my art. They are numerous, my stock of human warious is large, the shop is pretty well crammed, and I don't just now want any more trophies of my art. But I like my art, and I know how to exercise my art.'

'No man better,' assented Mr Wegg, with a somewhat staggered air.

'There's the Miscellanies of several human specimens,' said Venus, '(although you mightn't think it) in the box on which you're sitting. There's the Miscellanies of several human specimens, in the lovely compo-one behind the door'; with a nod towards the French gentleman. 'It still wants a pair of arms. I *don't* say that I'm in any hurry for 'em.'

'You must be wandering in your mind, partner,' Silas remonstrated.

'You'll excuse me if I wander,' returned Venus; 'I am sometimes rather subject to it. I like my art, and I know how to exercise my art, and I mean to have the keeping of this document.'

'But what has that got to do with your art, partner?' asked Wegg, in an insinuating tone.

Mr Venus winked his chronically-fatigued eyes both at once, and adjusting the kettle on the fire, remarked to himself, in a hollow voice, 'She'll bile in a couple of minutes.'

Silas Wegg glanced at the kettle, glanced at the shelves, glanced at the French gentleman behind the door, and shrank a little as he glanced at Mr Venus winking his red eyes, and feeling in his waistcoat pocket—as for a lancet, say—with his unoccupied hand. He and Venus were necessarily seated close together, as each held a corner of the document, which was but a common sheet of paper.

'Partner,' said Wegg, even more insinuatingly than before, 'I propose that we cut it in half, and each keep a half.'

Venus shook his shock of hair, as he replied, 'It wouldn't do to mutilate it, partner. It might seem to be cancelled.'

'Partner,' said Wegg, after a silence, during which they had contemplated one another, 'don't your speaking countenance say that you're a-going to suggest a middle course?'

Venus shook his shock of hair as he replied, 'Partner, you have kept this paper from me once. You shall never keep it from me again. I offer you the box and the label to take care of, but I'll take care of the paper.'

Silas hesitated a little longer, and then suddenly releasing his corner, and resuming his buoyant and benignant tone, exclaimed, 'What's life without trustfulness! What's a fellow-man without honour! You're welcome to it, partner, in a spirit of trust and confidence.'

Continuing to wink his red eyes both together—but in a self-communing way, and without any show of triumph—Mr Venus folded the paper now left in his hand, and locked it in a drawer behind him, and pocketed the key. He then proposed 'A cup of tea, partner?' To which Mr Wegg returned, 'Thank'ee, partner,' and the tea was made and poured out.

'Next,' said Venus, blowing at his tea in his saucer, and looking over it at his confidential friend, 'comes the question, What's the course to be pursued?'

On this head, Silas Wegg had much to say. Silas had to say That, he would beg to remind his comrade, brother, and partner, of the impressive passages they had read that evening; of the evident parallel in Mr Boffin's mind between them and the late owner of the Bower, and the present circumstances of the Bower; of the bottle; and of the box. That, the fortunes of his brother and comrade, and of himself, were evidently made, inasmuch as they had but to put their price upon this document, and get that price from the minion of fortune and the worm of the hour: who now appeared to be less of a minion and more of a worm than had been previously supposed. That, he considered it plain that such price was stateable in a single expressive word, and that the word was, 'Halves!' That, the question then arose when 'Halves!' should be called. That, here he had a plan of action to recommend, with a conditional clause. That, the plan of action was that they should lie by with patience; that, they should allow the Mounds to be gradually levelled and cleared away, while retaining to themselves their present opportunity of watching the process—which would be, he conceived, to put the trouble and cost of daily digging and delving upon somebody else, while they might nightly turn such complete disturbance of the dust to the account of their own private investigations—and that, when the Mounds were gone, and they had worked those chances for their own joint benefit solely, they should then, and not before, explode on the minion and worm. But here came the conditional clause, and to this he entreated the special attention of his comrade, brother, and partner. It was not to be borne that the minion and worm should carry off any of that property which was now to be regarded as their own property. When he, Mr Wegg, had seen the minion surreptitiously making off with that bottle, and its precious contents unknown, he had looked upon him in the light of a mere robber, and, as such, would have despoiled him of his ill-gotten gain, but for the judicious interference of his comrade, brother, and partner. Therefore, the conditional clause he proposed was, that, if the minion should return in his late sneaking manner, and if, being closely watched, he should be found to possess himself of anything, no matter what, the sharp sword impending over his head should be instantly shown him, he should be strictly examined as to what he knew or suspected, should be severely handled by them his masters, and should be kept in a state of abject moral bondage and slavery until the time when they should see fit to permit him to purchase his freedom at the price of half his possessions. If, said Mr Wegg by way of peroration, he had erred in saying only 'Halves!' he trusted to his comrade, brother, and partner not to hesitate to set him right, and to reprove his weakness. It might be more according to the rights of things, to say Two-thirds; it might be more according to the rights of things, to say Three-fourths. On those points he was ever open to correction.

Mr Venus, having wafted his attention to this discourse over three successive saucers of tea, signified his concurrence in the views advanced. Inspirited hereby, Mr Wegg extended his right hand, and declared it to be a hand which never yet. Without entering into more minute particulars. Mr Venus, sticking to his tea, briefly professed his belief, as polite forms required of him, that it *was* a hand which never yet. But contented himself with looking at it, and did not take it to his bosom.

'Brother,' said Wegg, when this happy understanding was established, 'I should like to ask you something. You remember the night when I first looked in here, and found you floating your powerful mind in tea?'

Still swilling tea, Mr Venus nodded assent.

'And there you sit, sir,' pursued Wegg with an air of thoughtful admiration, 'as if you had never left off! There you sit, sir, as if you had an unlimited capacity of assimilating the flagrant article! There you sit, sir, in the midst of your works, looking as if you'd been called upon for Home, Sweet Home, and was obleeging the company!

> "A exile from home splendour dazzles in vain,
>   O give you your lovely Preparations again,
>   The birds stuffed so sweetly that can't be expected
>   to come at your call,
>   Give you these with the peace of mind dearer than all.
>   Home, Home, Home, sweet Home!"

—Be it ever,' added Mr Wegg in prose as he glanced about the shop, 'ever so ghastly, all things considered there's no place like it.'

'You said you'd like to ask something; but you haven't asked it,' remarked Venus, very unsympathetic in manner.

'Your peace of mind,' said Wegg, offering condolence, 'your peace of mind was in a poor way that night. *How's* it going on? *Is* it looking up at all?'

'She does not wish,' replied Mr Venus with a comical mixture of indignant obstinacy and tender melancholy, 'to regard herself, nor yet to be regarded, in that particular light. There's no more to be said.'

'Ah, dear me, dear me!' exclaimed Wegg with a sigh, but eyeing him while pretending to keep him company in eyeing the fire, 'such is Woman! And I remember you said that night, sitting there as I sat here—said that night when your peace of mind was first laid low, that you had taken an interest in these very affairs. Such is coincidence!'

'Her father,' rejoined Venus, and then stopped to swallow more tea, 'her father was mixed up in them.'

'You didn't mention her name, sir, I think?' observed Wegg, pensively. 'No, you didn't mention her name that night.'

'Pleasant Riderhood.'

'In—deed!' cried Wegg. 'Pleasant Riderhood. There's something moving in the name. Pleasant. Dear me! Seems to express what she might have been, if she hadn't made that unpleasant remark—and what she ain't, in consequence of having made it. Would it at all pour balm into your wounds, Mr Venus, to inquire how you came acquainted with her?'

'I was down at the water-side,' said Venus, taking another gulp of tea and mournfully winking at the fire—'looking for parrots'—taking another gulp and stopping.

Mr Wegg hinted, to jog his attention: 'You could hardly have been out parrot-shooting, in the British climate, sir?'

'No, no, no,' said Venus fretfully. 'I was down at the water-side, looking for parrots brought home by sailors, to buy for stuffing.'

'Ay, ay, ay, sir!'

'—And looking for a nice pair of rattlesnakes, to articulate for a Museum—when I was doomed to fall in with her and deal with her. It was just at the time of that discovery in the river. Her father had seen the discovery being towed in the river. I made the popularity of the subject a reason for going back to improve the acquaintance, and I have never since been the man I was. My very bones is rendered flabby by brooding over it. If they could be brought to me loose, to sort, I should hardly have the face to claim 'em as mine. To such an extent have I fallen off under it.'

Mr Wegg, less interested than he had been, glanced at one particular shelf in the dark.

'Why I remember, Mr Venus,' he said in a tone of friendly commiseration '(for I remember every word that falls from you, sir), I remember that you said that night, you had got up there—and then your words was, "Never mind." '

'—The parrot that I bought of her,' said Venus, with a despondent rise and fall of his eyes. 'Yes; there it lies on its side, dried up; except for its plumage, very like myself. I've never had the heart to prepare it, and I never shall have now.'

With a disappointed face, Silas mentally consigned this

parrot to regions more than tropical, and, seeming for the time to have lost his power of assuming an interest in the woes of Mr Venus, fell to tightening his wooden leg as a preparation for departure: its gymnastic performances of that evening having severely tried its constitution.

After Silas had left the shop, hat-box in hand, and had left Mr Venus to lower himself to oblivion-point with the requisite weight of tea, it greatly preyed on his ingenuous mind that he had taken this artist into partnership at all. He bitterly felt that he had overreached himself in the beginning, by grasping at Mr Venus's mere straws of hints, now shown to be worthless for his purpose. Casting about for ways and means of dissolving the connexion without loss of money, reproaching himself for having been betrayed into an avowal of his secret, and complimenting himself beyond measure on his purely accidental good luck, he beguiled the distance between Clerkenwell and the mansion of the Golden Dustman.

For, Silas Wegg felt it to be quite out of the question that he could lay his head upon his pillow in peace, without first hovering over Mr Boffin's house in the superior character of its Evil Genius. Power (unless it be the power of intellect or virtue) has ever the greatest attraction for the lowest natures; and the mere defiance of the unconscious house-front, with his power to strip the roof off the inhabiting family like the roof of a house of cards, was a treat which had a charm for Silas Wegg.

As he hovered on the opposite side of the street, exulting, the carriage drove up.

'There'll shortly be an end of *you*,' said Wegg, threatening it with the hat-box. '*Your* varnish is fading.'

Mrs Boffin descended and went in.

'Look out for a fall, my Lady Dustwoman,' said Wegg.

Bella lightly descended, and ran in after her.

'How brisk we are!' said Wegg. 'You won't run so gaily to your old shabby home, my girl. You'll have to go there, though.'

A little while, and the Secretary came out.

'I was passed over for you,' said Wegg. 'But you had better provide yourself with another situation, young man.'

Mr Boffin's shadow passed upon the blinds of three large windows as he trotted down the room, and passed again as he went back.

'Yoop!' cried Wegg. 'You're there, are you? Where's the bottle? You would give your bottle for my box, Dustman!'

Having now composed his mind for slumber, he turned

homeward. Such was the greed of the fellow, that his mind had shot beyond halves, two-thirds, three-fourths, and gone straight to spoliation of the whole. 'Though that wouldn't quite do,' he considered, growing cooler as he got away. 'That's what would happen to him if he didn't buy us up. We should get nothing by that.'

We so judge others by ourselves, that it had never come into his head before, that he might not buy us up, and might prove honest, and prefer to be poor. It caused him a slight tremor as it passed; but a very slight one, for the idle thought was gone directly.

'He's grown too fond of money for that,' said Wegg; 'he's grown too fond of money.' The burden fell into a strain or tune as he stumped along the pavements. All the way home he stumped it out of the rattling streets, *piano* with his own foot, and *forte* with his wooden leg, 'He's GROWN TOO FOND of MONEY for THAT, he's GROWN TOO FOND of MONEY.'

Even next day Silas soothed himself with this melodious strain, when he was called out of bed at daybreak, to set open the yard-gate and admit the train of carts and horses that came to carry off the little Mound. And all day long, as he kept unwinking watch on the slow process which promised to protract itself through many days and weeks, whenever (to save himself from being choked with dust) he patrolled a little cinderous beat he established for the purpose, without taking his eyes from the diggers, he still stumped to the tune: He's GROWN TOO FOND of MONEY for THAT, he's GROWN TOO FOND of MONEY.'

Chapter 8
The End of a Long Journey

THE train of carts and horses came and went all day from dawn to nightfall, making little or no daily impression on the heap of ashes, though, as the days passed on, the heap was seen to be slowly melting. My lords and gentlemen and honourable boards, when you in the course of your dust-shovelling and cinder-raking have piled up a mountain of pretentious failure, you must off with your honourable coats for the removal of it, and fall to the work with the power of all the queen's horses and all the queen's men, or it will come rushing down and bury us alive.

Yes, verily, my lords and gentlemen and honourable boards, adapting your Catechism to the occasion, and by God's help so you must. For when we have got things to the pass that with an enormous treasure at disposal to relieve the poor, the best of the poor detest our mercies, hide their heads from us, and shame us by starving to death in the midst of us, it is a pass impossible of prosperity, impossible of continuance. It may not be so written in the Gospel according to Podsnappery; you may not 'find these words' for the text of a sermon, in the Returns of the Board of Trade; but they have been the truth since the foundations of the universe were laid, and they will be the truth until the foundations of the universe are shaken by the Builder. This boastful handiwork of ours, which fails in its terrors for the professional pauper, the sturdy breaker of windows and the rampant tearer of clothes, strikes with a cruel and a wicked stab at the stricken sufferer, and is a horror to the deserving and unfortunate. We must mend it, lords and gentlemen and honourable boards, or in its own evil hour it will mar every one of us.

Old Betty Higden fared upon her pilgrimage as many ruggedly honest creatures, women and men, fare on their toiling way along the roads of life. Patiently to earn a spare bare living, and quietly to die, untouched by workhouse hands—this was her highest sublunary hope.

Nothing had been heard of her at Mr Boffin's house since she trudged off. The weather had been hard and the roads had been bad, and her spirit was up. A less stanch spirit might have been subdued by such adverse influences; but the loan for her little outfit was in no part repaid, and it had gone worse with her than she had foreseen, and she was put upon proving her case and maintaining her independence.

Faithful soul! When she had spoken to the Secretary of that 'deadness that steals over me at times', her fortitude had made too little of it. Oftener and ever oftener, it came stealing over her; darker and ever darker, like the shadow of advancing Death. That the shadow should be deep as it came on, like the shadow of an actual presence, was in accordance with the laws of the physical world, for all the Light that shone on Betty Higden lay beyond Death.

The poor old creature had taken the upward course of the river Thames as her general track; it was the track in which her last home lay, and of which she had last had local love and knowledge. She had hovered for a little while in the near neighbourhood of her abandoned dwelling, and had sold, and knitted and sold, and gone on. In the pleasant towns of Chertsey, Walton, Kingston, and Staines, her figure came to be quite well known for some short weeks, and then again pressed on.

She would take her stand in market-places, where there were such things, on market days; at other times, in the busiest (that was seldom very busy) portion of the little quiet High Street; at still other times she would explore the outlying roads for great houses, and would ask leave at the Lodge to pass in with her basket, and would not often get it. But ladies in carriages would frequently make purchases from her trifling stock, and were usually pleased with her bright eyes and her hopeful speech. In these and her clean dress originated a fable that she was well to do in the world: one might say, for her station, rich. As making a comfortable provision for its subject which costs nobody anything, this class of fable has long been popular.

In those pleasant little towns on Thames, you may hear the fall of the water over the weirs, or even, in still weather, the rustle of the rushes; and from the bridge you may see the young river, dimpled like a young child, playfully gliding away among the trees, unpolluted by the defilements that lie in wait for it on its course, and as yet out of hearing of the deep summons of the sea. It were too much to pretend that Betty Higden made out such thoughts; no; but she heard the tender river whispering to many like herself, 'Come to me, come to me! When the cruel shame and terror you have so long fled from, most beset you, come to me! I am the Relieving Officer appointed by eternal ordinance to do my work; I am not held in estimation according as I shirk it. My breast is softer than the pauper-nurses's; death in my arms is peacefuller than among the pauper-wards. Come to me!'

There was abundant place for gentler fancies too, in her untutored mind. Those gentlefolks and their children inside those fine houses, could they think, as they looked out at her, what it was to be really hungry, really cold? Did they feel any of the wonder about her, that she felt about them? Bless the dear laughing children! If they could have seen sick Johnny in her arms, would they have cried for pity? If they could have seen dead Johnny on that little bed, would they have understood it? Bless the dear children for his sake, anyhow! So with the humbler houses in the little street, the inner firelight shining on the panes as the outer twilight darkened. When the families gathered in-doors there, for the night, it was only a foolish fancy to feel as if it were a little hard in them to close the shutter and blacken the flame. So with the lighted shops, and speculations whether their masters and mistresses taking tea in a perspective of back-parlour—not so far within but that the flavour of tea and toast came out, mingled with the glow of light, into the street—ate or drank or wore what they sold, with the greater relish because they dealt in it. So with the churchyard on a branch of the solitary way to the night's sleeping-place. 'Ah me! The dead and I seem to have it pretty much to ourselves in the dark and in this weather! But so much the better for all who are warmly housed at home.' The poor soul envied no one in bitterness, and grudged no one anything.

But, the old abhorrence grew stronger on her as she grew weaker, and it found more sustaining food than she did in her wanderings. Now, she would light upon the shameful spectacle of some desolate creature—or some wretched ragged groups of either sex, or of both sexes, with children among them, huddled together like the smaller vermin for a little warmth—lingering and lingering on a doorstep, while the appointed evader of the public trust did his dirty office of trying to weary them out and so get rid of them. Now, she would light upon some poor decent person, like herself, going afoot on a pilgrimage of many weary miles to see some worn-out relative or friend who had been charitably clutched off to a great blank barren Union House, as far from old home as the County Jail (the remoteness of which is always its worst punishment for small rural offenders), and in its dietary, and in its lodging, and in its tending of the sick, a much more penal establishment. Sometimes she would hear a newspaper read out, and would learn how the Registrar General cast up the units that had within the last week died of want and of exposure to the weather: for which that Recording Angel seemed to have a regular fixed place in his sum, as if they were its halfpence. All such things she would hear discussed, as we, my lords and gentlemen and honourable boards, in our unapproachable magnificence never hear them, and from all such things she would fly with the wings of raging Despair.

This is not to be received as a figure of speech. Old Betty Higden however tired, however footsore, would start up and be driven away by her awakened horror of falling into the hands of Charity. It is a remarkable Christian improvement, to have made a pursuing Fury of the Good Samaritan; but it was so in this case, and it is a type of many, many, many.

Two incidents united to intensify the old unreasoning abhorrence—granted in a previous place to be unreasoning, because the people always are unreasoning, and invariably make a point of producing all their smoke without fire.

One day she was sitting in a market-place on a bench outside an inn, with her little wares for sale, when the deadness that she strove against came over her so heavily that the scene departed from before her eyes; when it returned, she found herself on the ground, her head supported by some good-natured market-women, and a little crowd about her.

'Are you better now, mother?' asked one of the women. 'Do you think you can do nicely now?'

'Have I been ill then?' asked old Betty.

'You have had a faint like,' was the answer, 'or a fit. It ain't that you've been a-struggling, mother, but you've been stiff and numbed.'

'Ah!' said Betty, recovering her memory. 'It's the numbness. Yes. It comes over me at times.'

Was it gone? the women asked her.

'It's gone now,' said Betty. 'I shall be stronger than I was afore. Many thanks to ye, my dears, and when you come to be as old as I am, may others do as much for you!'

They assisted her to rise, but she could not stand yet, and they supported her when she sat down again upon the bench.

'My head's a bit light, and my feet are a bit heavy,' said old Betty, leaning her face drowsily on the breast of the woman who had spoken before. 'They'll both come nat'ral in a minute. There's nothing more the matter.'

'Ask her,' said some farmers standing by, who had come out from their market-dinner, 'who belongs to her.'

'Are there any folks belonging to you, mother?' said the woman.

'Yes, sure,' answered Betty. 'I heerd the gentleman say it, but I couldn't answer quick enough. There's plenty belonging to me. Don't ye fear for me, my dear.'

'But are any of 'em near here?' said the men's voices; the women's voices chiming in when it was said, and prolonging the strain.

'Quite near enough,' said Betty, rousing herself. 'Don't ye be afeard for me, neighbours.'

'But you are not fit to travel. Where are you going?' was the next compassionate chorus she heard.

'I'm a going to London when I've sold out all,' said Betty, rising with difficulty. 'I've right good friends in London. I want for nothing. I shall come to no harm. Thankye. Don't ye be afeard for me.'

A well-meaning bystander, yellow-legginged and purple-faced, said hoarsely over his red comforter, as she rose to her feet, that she 'oughtn't to be let to go'.

'For the Lord's love don't meddle with me!' cried old Betty, all her fears crowding on her. 'I am quite well now, and I must go this minute.'

She caught up her basket as she spoke and was making an unsteady rush away from them, when the same bystander checked her with his hand on her sleeve, and urged her to come with him and see the parish-doctor. Strengthening herself by the utmost exercise of her resolution, the poor trembling creature shook him off, almost fiercely, and took to flight. Nor did she feel safe until she had set a mile or two of by-road between herself and the market-place, and had crept into a copse, like a hunted animal, to hide and recover breath. Not until then for the first time did she venture to recall how she had looked over her shoulder before turning out of the town, and had seen the sign of the White Lion hanging across the road, and the fluttering market booths, and the old grey church, and the little crowd gazing after her but not attempting to follow her.

The second frightening incident was this. She had been again as bad, and had been for some days better, and was travelling along by a part of the road where it touched the river, and in wet seasons was so often overflowed by it that there were tall white posts set up to mark the way. A barge was being towed towards her, and she sat down on the bank to rest and watch it. As the tow-rope was slackened by a turn of the stream and dipped into the water, such a confusion stole into her mind that she thought she saw the forms of her dead children and dead grandchildren peopling the barge, and waving their hands to her in solemn measure; then, as the rope tightened and came up, dropping diamonds, it seemed to vibrate into two parallel ropes and strike her, with a twang, though it was far off. When she looked again, there was no barge, no river, no daylight, and a man whom she had never before seen held a candle close to her face.

'Now, Missis,' said he; 'where did you come from and where are you going to?'

The poor soul confusedly asked the counter-question where she was?

'I am the Lock,' said the man.

'The Lock?'

'I am the Deputy Lock, on job, and this is the Lock-house. (Lock or Deputy Lock, it's all one, while t'other man's in the hospital.) What's your Parish?'

'Parish!' She was up from the truckle-bed directly, wildly feeling about her for her basket, and gazing at him in affright.

'You'll be asked the question down town,' said the man. 'They won't let you be more than a Casual there. They'll pass you on to your settlement, Missis, with all speed. You're not in a state to be let come upon strange parishes 'ceptin as a Casual.'

' 'Twas the deadness again!' murmured Betty Higden, with her hand to her head.

'It was the deadness, there's not a doubt about it,' returned the man. 'I should have thought the deadness was a mild word for it, if it had been named to me when we brought you in. Have you got any friends, Missis?'

'The best of friends, Master.'

'I should recommend your looking 'em up if you consider 'em game to do anything for you,' said the Deputy Lock. 'Have you got any money?'

'Just a morsel of money, sir.'

'Do you want to keep it?'

'Sure I do!'

'Well, you know,' said the Deputy Lock, shrugging his shoulders with his hands in his pockets, and shaking his head in a sulkily ominous manner, 'the parish authorities down town will have it out of you, if you go on, you may take your Alfred David.'

'Then I'll not go on.'

'They'll make you pay, as fur as your money will go,' pursued the Deputy, 'for your relief as a Casual and for your being passed to your Parish.'

'Thank ye kindly, Master, for your warning, thank ye for your shelter, and good night.'

'Stop a bit,' said the Deputy, striking in between her and the door. 'Why are you all of a shake, and what's your hurry, Missis?'

'Oh, Master, Master,' returned Betty Higden, 'I've fought

against the Parish and fled from it, all my life, and I want to die free of it!'

'I don't know,' said the Deputy, with deliberation, 'as I ought to let you go. I'm a honest man as gets my living by the sweat of my brow, and I may fall into trouble by letting you go. I've fell into trouble afore now, by George, and I know what it is, and it's made me careful. You might be took with your deadness again, half a mile off—or half of half a quarter, for the matter of that—and then it would be asked, Why did that there honest Deputy Lock, let her go, instead of putting her safe with the Parish? That's what a man of his character ought to have done, it would be argueyfied,' said the Deputy Lock, cunningly harping on the strong string of her terror; 'he ought to have handed her over safe to the Parish. That was to be expected of a man of his merits.'

As he stood in the doorway, the poor old careworn way-worn woman burst into tears, and clasped her hands, as if in a very agony she prayed to him.

'As I've told you, Master, I've the best of friends. This letter will show how true I spoke, and they will be thankful for me.'

The Deputy Lock opened the letter with a grave face, which underwent no change as he eyed its contents. But it might have done, if he could have read them.

'What amount of small change, Missis,' he said, with an abstracted air, after a little meditation, 'might you call a morsel of money?'

Hurriedly emptying her pocket, old Betty laid down on the table, a shilling, and two sixpenny pieces, and a few pence.

'If I was to let you go instead of handing you over safe to the Parish,' said the Deputy, counting the money with his eyes, 'might it be your own free wish to leave that there behind you?'

'Take it, Master, take it, and welcome and thankful!'

'I'm a man,' said the Deputy, giving her back the letter, and pocketing the coins, one by one, 'as earns his living by the sweat of his brow;' here he drew his sleeve across his forehead, as if this particular portion of his humble gains were the result of sheer hard labour and virtuous industry; 'and I won't stand in your way. Go where you like.'

She was gone out of the Lock-house as soon as he gave her this permission, and her tottering steps were on the road again. But, afraid to go back and afraid to go forward; seeing what she fled from, in the sky-glare of the lights of the little town before her, and leaving a confused horror of it everywhere behind her, as if she had escaped it in every stone of every market-place; she struck off by side ways, among which she got bewildered and lost. That night she took refuge from the Samaritan in his latest accredited form, under a farmer's rick; and if—worth thinking of, perhaps, my fellow-Christians—the Samaritan had in the lonely night, 'passed by on the other side', she would have most devoutly thanked High Heaven for her escape from him.

The morning found her afoot again, but fast declining as to the clearness of her thoughts, though not as to the steadiness of her purpose. Comprehending that her strength was quitting her, and that the struggle of her life was almost ended, she could neither reason out the means of getting back to her protectors, nor even form the idea. The overmastering dread, and the proud stubborn resolution it engendered in her to die undegraded, were the two distinct impressions left in her failing mind. Supported only by a sense that she was bent on conquering in her life-long fight, she went on.

The time was come, now, when the wants of this little life were passing away from her. She could not have swallowed food, though a table had been spread for her in the next field. The day was cold and wet, but she scarcely knew it. She crept on, poor soul, like a criminal afraid of being taken, and felt little beyond the terror of falling down while it was yet daylight, and being found alive. She had no fear that she would live through another night.

Sewn in the breast of her gown, the money to pay for her burial was still intact. If she could wear through the day, and then lie down to die under cover of the darkness, she would die independent. If she were captured previously, the money would be taken from her as a pauper who had no right to it, and she would be carried to the accursed workhouse. Gaining her end, the letter would be found in her breast, along with the money, and the gentlefolks would say when it was given back to them, 'She prized it, did old Betty Higden; she was true to it; and while she lived, she would never let it be disgraced by falling into the hands of those that she held in horror.' Most illogical, inconsequential, and light-headed, this; but travellers in the valley of the shadow of death are apt to be light-headed; and worn-out old people of low estate have a trick of reasoning as indifferently as they live, and doubtless would appreciate our Poor Law more philosophically on an income of ten thousand a year.

So, keeping to byways, and shunning human approach, this

troublesome old woman hid herself, and fared on all through the dreary day. Yet so unlike was she to vagrant hiders in general, that sometimes, as the day advanced, there was a bright fire in her eyes, and a quicker beating at her feeble heart, as though she said exultingly, 'The Lord will see me through it!'

By what visionary hands she was led along upon that journey of escape from the Samaritan; by what voices, hushed in the grave, she seemed to be addressed; how she fancied the dead child in her arms again, and times innumerable adjusted her shawl to keep it warm; what infinite variety of forms of tower and roof and steeple the trees took; how many furious horsemen rode at her, crying, 'There she goes! Stop! Stop, Betty Higden!' and melted away as they came close; be these things left untold. Faring on and hiding, hiding and faring on, the poor harmless creature, as though she were a Murderess and the whole country were up after her, wore out the day, and gained the night.

'Water-meadows, or such like,' she had sometimes murmured, on the day's pilgrimage, when she had raised her head and taken any note of the real objects about her. There now arose in the darkness, a great building, full of lighted windows. Smoke was issuing from a high chimney in the rear of it, and there was the sound of a water-wheel at the side. Between her and the building, lay a piece of water, in which the lighted windows were reflected, and on its nearest margin was a plantation of trees. 'I humbly thank the Power and the Glory,' said Betty Higden, holding up her withered hands, 'that I have come to my journey's end!'

She crept among the trees to the trunk of a tree whence she could see, beyond some intervening trees and branches, the lighted windows, both in their reality and their reflection in the water. She placed her orderly little basket at her side, and sank upon the ground, supporting herself against the tree. It brought to her mind the foot of the Cross, and she committed herself to Him who died upon it. Her strength held out to enable her to arrange the letter in her breast, so as that it could be seen that she had a paper there. It had held out for this, and it departed when this was done.

'I am safe here,' was her last benumbed thought. 'When I am found dead at the foot of the Cross, it will be by some of my own sort; some of the working people who work among the lights yonder. I cannot see the lighted windows now, but they are there. I am thankful for all!'

* * *

The darkness gone, and a face bending down.

'It cannot be the boofer lady?'

'I don't understand what you say. Let me wet your lips again with this brandy. I have been away to fetch it. Did you think that I was long gone?'

It is as the face of a woman, shaded by a quantity of rich dark hair. It is the earnest face of a woman who is young and handsome. But all is over with me on earth, and this must be an Angel.

'Have I been long dead?'

'I don't understand what you say. Let me wet your lips again. I hurried all I could, and brought no one back with me, lest you should die of the shock of strangers.'

'Am I not dead?'

'I cannot understand what you say. Your voice is so low and broken that I cannot hear you. Do you hear me?'

'Yes.'

'Do you mean Yes?'

'Yes.'

'I was coming from my work just now, along the path outside (I was up with the night-hands last night), and I heard a groan, and found you lying here.'

'What work, deary?'

'Did you ask what work? At the paper-mill.'

'Where is it?'

'Your face is turned up to the sky, and you can't see it. It is close by. You can see my face, here, between you and the sky?'

'Yes.'

'Dare I lift you?'

'Not yet.'

'Not even lift your head to get it on my arm? I will do it by very gentle degrees. You shall hardly feel it.'

'Not yet. Paper. Letter.'

'This paper in your breast?'

'Bless ye!'

'Let me wet your lips again. Am I to open it? To read it?'

'Bless ye!'

She reads it with surprise, and looks down with a new expression and an added interest on the motionless face she kneels beside.

'I know these names. I have heard them often.'

'Will you send it, my dear?'

'I cannot understand you. Let me wet your lips again, and

your forehead. There. O poor thing, poor thing!' These words through her fast-dropping tears. 'What was it that you asked me? Wait till I bring my ear quite close.'

'Will you sent it, my dear?'

'Will I send it to the writers? Is that your wish? Yes, certainly.'

'You'll not give it up to any one but them?'

'No.'

'As you must grow old in time, and come to your dying hour, my dear, you'll not give it up to any one but them?'

'No. Most solemnly.'

'Never to the Parish!' with a convulsed struggle.

'No. Most solemnly.'

'Nor let the Parish touch me, not yet so much as look at me!' with another struggle.

'No. Faithfully.'

A look of thankfulness and triumph lights the worn old face. The eyes, which have been darkly fixed upon the sky, turn with meaning in them towards the compassionate face from which the tears are dropping, and a smile is on the aged lips as they ask:

'What is your name, my dear?'

'My name is Lizzie Hexam.'

'I must be sore disfigured. Are you afraid to kiss me?'

The answer is, the ready pressure of her lips upon the cold but smiling mouth.

'Bless ye! *Now* lift me, my love.'

Lizzie Hexam very softly raised the weather-stained grey head, and lifted her as high as Heaven.

Chapter 9
Somebody Becomes the Subject
of a Prediction

' "WE GIVE THEE HEARTY THANKS FOR THAT IT HATH PLEASED THEE
TO DELIVER THIS OUR SISTER OUT OF THE MISERIES OF THIS SINFUL
WORLD." ' So read the Reverend Frank Milvey in a not untroubled
voice, for his heart misgave him that all was not quite right
between us and our sister—or say our sister in Law—Poor
Law—and that we sometimes read these words in an awful
manner, over our Sister and our Brother too.

And Sloppy—on whom the brave deceased had never turned
her back until she ran away from him, knowing that otherwise he
would not be separated from her—Sloppy could not in his conscience as yet find the hearty thanks required of it. Selfish in
Sloppy, and yet excusable, it may be humbly hoped, because our
sister had been more than his mother.

The words were read above the ashes of Betty Higden, in a
corner of a churchyard near the river; in a churchyard so obscure
that there was nothing in it but grass-mounds, not so much as
one single tombstone. It might not be to do an unreasonably
great deal for the diggers and hewers, in a registering age, if we
ticketed their graves at the common charge; so that a new
generation might know which was which: so that the soldier,
sailor, emigrant, coming home, should be able to identify the
resting-place of father, mother, playmate, or betrothed. For, we
turn up our eyes and say that we are all alike in death, and we
might turn them down and work the saying out in this world, so
far. It would be sentimental, perhaps? But how say ye, my lords
and gentleman and honourable boards, shall we not find good
standing-room left for a little sentiment, if we look into our
crowds?

Near unto the Reverend Frank Milvey as he read, stood his
little wife, John Rokesmith the Secretary, and Bella Wilfer.
These, over and above Sloppy, were the mourners at the lowly

grave. Not a penny had been added to the money sewn in her dress: what her honest spirit had so long projected, was fulfilled.

'I've took it in my head,' said Sloppy, laying it, inconsolable, against the church door, when all was done: 'I've took it in my wretched head that I might have sometimes turned it a little harder for her, and it cuts me deep to think so now.'

The Reverend Frank Milvey, comforting Sloppy, expounded to him how the best of us were more or less remiss in our turnings at our respective Mangles—some of us very much so—and how we were all a halting, failing, feeble, and inconstant crew.

'*She* warn't, sir,' said Sloppy, taking this ghostly counsel rather ill, in behalf of his late benefactress. 'Let us speak for ourselves, sir. She went through with whatever duty she had to do. She went through with me, she went through with the Minders, she went through with herself, she went through with everythink. O Mrs Higden, Mrs Higden, you was a woman and a mother and a mangler in a million million!'

With those heartfelt words, Sloppy removed his dejected head from the church door, and took it back to the grave in the corner, and laid it down there, and wept alone. 'Not a very poor grave,' said the Reverend Frank Milvey, brushing his hand across his eyes, 'when it has that homely figure on it. Richer, I think, than it could be made by most of the sculpture in Westminster Abbey!'

They left him undisturbed, and passed out at the wicket-gate. The water-wheel of the paper-mill was audible there, and seemed to have a softening influence on the bright wintry scene. They had arrived but a little while before, and Lizzie Hexam now told them the little she could add to the letter in which she had enclosed Mr Rokesmith's letter and had asked for their instructions. This was merely how she had heard the groan, and what had afterwards passed, and how she had obtained leave for the remains to be placed in that sweet, fresh, empty store-room of the mill from which they had just accompanied them to the churchyard, and how the last requests had been religiously observed.

'I could not have done it all, or nearly all, of myself,' said Lizzie. 'I should not have wanted the will; but I should not have had the power, without our managing partner.'

'Surely not the Jew who received us?' said Mrs Milvey.

('My dear,' observed her husband in parenthesis, 'why not?')

'The gentleman certainly is a Jew,' said Lizzie, 'and the lady, his wife, is a Jewess, and I was first brought to their notice by a Jew. But I think there cannot be kinder people in the world.'

'But suppose they try to convert you!' suggested Mrs Milvey, bristling in her good little way, as a clergyman's wife.

'To do what, ma'am?' asked Lizzie, with a modest smile.

'To make you change your religion,' said Mrs Milvey.

Lizzie shook her head, still smiling. 'They have never asked me what my religion is. They asked me what my story was, and I told them. They asked me to be industrious and faithful, and I promised to be so. They most willingly and cheerfully do their duty to all of us who are employed here, and we try to do ours to them. Indeed they do much more than their duty to us, for they are wonderfully mindful of us in many ways.'

'It is easy to see you're a favourite, my dear,' said little Mrs Milvey, not quite pleased.

'It would be very ungrateful in me to say I am not,' returned Lizzie, 'for I have been already raised to a place of confidence here. But that makes no difference in their following their own religion and leaving all of us to ours. They never talk of theirs to us, and they never talk of ours to us. If I was the last in the mill, it would be just the same. They never asked me what religion that poor thing had followed.'

'My dear,' said Mrs Milvey, aside to the Reverend Frank, 'I wish you would talk to her.'

'My dear,' said the Reverend Frank aside to his good little wife, 'I think I will leave it to somebody else. The circumstances are hardly favourable. There are plenty of talkers going about, my love, and she will soon find one.'

While this discourse was interchanging, both Bella and the Secretary observed Lizzie Hexam with great attention. Brought face to face for the first time with the daughter of his supposed murderer, it was natural that John Harmon should have his own secret reasons for a careful scrutiny of her countenance and manner. Bella knew that Lizzie's father had been falsely accused of the crime which had had so great an influence on her own life and fortunes; and her interest, though it had no secret springs, like that of the Secretary, was equally natural. Both had expected to see something very different from the real Lizzie Hexam, and thus it fell out that she became the unconscious means of bringing them together.

For, when they had walked on with her to the little house in the clean village by the paper-mill, where Lizzie had a lodging with an elderly couple employed in the establishment, and when Mrs Milvey and Bella had been up to see her room and had come down, the mill bell rang. This called Lizzie away for the time, and left the Secretary and Bella standing rather awkwardly in the small street; Mrs Milvey being engaged in pursuing the village children, and her investigations whether they were in danger of becoming children of Israel; and the Reverend Frank being engaged—to say the truth—in evading that branch of his spiritual functions, and getting out of sight surreptitiously.

Bella at length said:

'Hadn't we better talk about the commission we have undertaken, Mr Rokesmith?'

'By all means,' said the Secretary.

'I suppose,' faltered Bella, 'that we *are* both commissioned, or we shouldn't both be here?'

'I suppose so,' was the Secretary's answer.

'When I proposed to come with Mr and Mrs Milvey,' said Bella, 'Mrs Boffin urged me to do so, in order that I might give her my small report—it's not worth anything, Mr Rokesmith, except for it's being a woman's—which indeed with you may be a fresh reason for it's being worth nothing—of Lizzie Hexam.'

'Mr Boffin,' said the Secretary, 'directed me to come for the same purpose.'

As they spoke they were leaving the little street and emerging on the wooded landscape by the river.

'You think well of her, Mr Rokesmith?' pursued Bella, conscious of making all the advances.

'I think highly of her.'

'I am so glad of that! Something quite refined in her beauty, is there not?'

'Her appearance is very striking.'

'There is a shade of sadness upon her that is quite touching. At least I—I am not setting up my own poor opinion, you know, Mr Rokesmith,' said Bella, excusing and explaining herself in a pretty shy way; 'I am consulting you.'

'I noticed that sadness. I hope it may not,' said the Secretary in a lower voice, 'be the result of the false accusation which has been retracted.'

When they had passed on a little further without speaking, Bella, after stealing a glance or two at the Secretary, suddenly said:

'Oh, Mr Rokesmith, don't be hard with me, don't be stern

with me; be magnanimous! I want to talk with you on equal terms.'

The Secretary as suddenly brightened, and returned: 'Upon my honour I had no thought but for you. I forced myself to be constrained, lest you might misinterpret my being more natural. There. It's gone.'

'Thank you,' said Bella, holding out her little hand. 'Forgive me.'

'No!' cried the Secretary, eagerly. 'Forgive *me*!' For there were tears in her eyes, and they were prettier in his sight (though they smote him on the heart rather reproachfully too) than any other glitter in the world.

When they had walked a little further:

'You were going to speak to me,' said the Secretary, with the shadow so long on him quite thrown off and cast away, 'about Lizzie Hexam. So was I going to speak to you, if I could have begun.'

'Now that you *can* begin, sir,' returned Bella, with a look as if she italicized the word by putting one of her dimples under it, 'what were you going to say?'

'You remember, of course, that in her short letter to Mrs Boffin—short, but containing everything to the purpose—she stipulated that either her name, or else her place of residence, must be kept strictly a secret among us.'

Bella nodded Yes.

'It is my duty to find out why she made that stipulation. I have it in charge from Mr Boffin to discover, and I am very desirous for myself to discover, whether that retracted accusation still leaves any stain upon her. I mean whether it places her at any disadvantage towards any one, even towards herself.'

'Yes,' said Bella, nodding thoughtfully; 'I understand. That seems wise, and considerate.'

'You may not have noticed, Miss Wilfer, that she has the same kind of interest in you, that you have in her. Just as you are attracted by her beaut—by her appearance and manner, she is attracted by yours.'

'I certainly have *not* noticed it,' returned Bella, again italicizing with the dimple, 'and I should have given her credit for—'

The Secretary with a smile held up his hand, so plainly interposing 'not for better taste', that Bella's colour deepened over the little piece of coquetry she was checked in.

'And so,' resumed the Secretary, 'if you would speak with

her alone before we go away from here, I feel quite sure that a natural and easy confidence would arise between you. Of course you would not be asked to betray it; and of course you would not, if you were. But if you do not object to put this question to her—to ascertain for us her own feeling in this one matter—you can do so at a far greater advantage than I or any one else could. Mr Boffin is anxious on the subject. And I am,' added the Secretary after a moment, 'for a special reason, very anxious.'

'I shall be happy, Mr Rokesmith,' returned Bella, 'to be of the least use; for I feel, after the serious scene of to-day, that I am useless enough in this world.'

'Don't say that,' urged the Secretary.

'Oh, but I mean that,' said Bella, raising her eyebrows.

'No one is useless in this world,' retorted the Secretary, 'who lightens the burden of it for any one else.'

'But I assure you I *don't*, Mr Rokesmith,' said Bella, half-crying.

'Not for your father?'

'Dear, loving, self-forgetting, easily-satisfied Pa! Oh, yes! He thinks so.'

'It is enough if he only thinks so,' said the Secretary. 'Excuse the interruption: I don't like to hear you depreciate yourself.'

'But *you* once depreciated *me*, sir,' thought Bella, pouting, 'and I hope you may be satisfied with the consequences you brought upon your head!' However, she said nothing to that purpose; she even said something to a different purpose.

'Mr Rokesmith, it seems so long since we spoke together naturally, that I am embarrassed in approaching another subject. Mr Boffin. You know I am very grateful to him; don't you? You know I feel a true respect for him, and am bound to him by the strong ties of his own generosity; now don't you?'

'Unquestionably. And also that you are his favourite companion.'

'That makes it,' said Bella, 'so very difficult so speak of him. But—. Does he treat you well?'

'You see how he treats me,' the Secretary answered, with a patient and yet proud air.

'Yes, and I see it with pain,' said Bella, very energetically.

The Secretary gave her such a radiant look, that if he had thanked her a hundred times, he could not have said as much as the look said.

'I see it with pain,' repeated Bella, 'and it often makes me miserable. Miserable, because I cannot bear to be supposed to approve of it, or have any indirect share in it. Miserable, because I cannot bear to be forced to admit to myself that Fortune is spoiling Mr Boffin.'

'Miss Wilfer,' said the Secretary, with a beaming face, 'if you could know with what delight I make the discovery that Fortune is not spoiling *you,* you would know that it more than compensates me for any slight at any other hands.'

'Oh, don't speak of *me,*' said Bella, giving herself an impatient little slap with her glove. 'You don't know me as well as—'

'As you know yourself?' suggested the Secretary, finding that she stopped. '*Do* you know yourself?'

'I know quite enough of myself,' said Bella, with a charming air of being inclined to give herself up as a bad job, 'and I don't improve upon acquaintance. But Mr Boffin.'

'That Mr Boffin's manner to me, or consideration for me, is not what it used to be,' observed the Secretary, 'must be admitted. It is too plain to be denied.'

'Are you disposed to deny it, Mr Rokesmith?' asked Bella, with a look of wonder.

'Ought I not to be glad to do so, if I could: though it were only for my own sake?'

'Truly,' returned Bella, 'it must try you very much, and—you must please promise me that you won't take ill what I am going to add, Mr Rokesmith?'

'I promise it with all my heart.'

'—And it must sometimes, I should think,' said Bella, hesitating, 'a little lower you in your own estimation?'

Assenting with a movement of his head, though not at all looking as if it did, the Secretary replied:

'I have very strong reasons, Miss Wilfer, for bearing with the drawbacks of my position in the house we both inhabit. Believe that they are not all mercenary, although I have, through a series of strange fatalities, faded out of my place in life. If what you see with such a gracious and good sympathy is calculated to rouse my pride, there are other considerations (and those you do not see) urging me to quiet endurance. The latter are by far the stronger.'

'I think I have noticed, Mr Rokesmith,' said Bella, looking at him with curiosity, as not quite making him out, 'that you repress yourself, and force yourself, to act a passive part.'

'You are right. I repress myself and force myself to act a

part. It is not in tameness of spirit that I submit. I have a settled purpose.'

'And a good one, I hope,' said Bella.

'And a good one, I hope,' he answered, looking steadily at her.

'Sometimes I have fancied, sir,' said Bella, turning away her eyes, 'that your great regard for Mrs Boffin is a very powerful motive with you.'

'You are right again; it is. I would do anything for her, bear anything for her. There are no words to express how I esteem that good, good woman.'

'As I do too! May I ask you one thing more, Mr Rokesmith?'

'Anything more.'

'Of course you see that she really suffers, when Mr Boffin shows how he is changing?'

'I see it, every day, as you see it, and am grieved to give her pain.'

'To give her pain?' said Bella, repeating the phrase quickly, with her eyebrows raised.

'I am generally the unfortunate cause of it.'

'Perhaps she says to you, as she often says to me, that he is the best of men, in spite of all.'

'I often overhear her, in her honest and beautiful devotion to him, saying so to you,' returned the Secretary, with the same steady look, 'but I cannot assert that she ever says so to me.'

Bella met the steady look for a moment with a wistful, musing little look of her own, and then, nodding her pretty head several times, like a dimpled philosopher (of the very best school) who was moralizing on Life, heaved a little sigh, and gave up things in general for a bad job, as she had previously been inclined to give up herself.

But, for all that, they had a very pleasant walk. The trees were bare of leaves, and the river was bare of water-lilies; but the sky was not bare of its beautiful blue, and the water reflected it, and a delicious wind ran with the stream, touching the surface crisply. Perhaps the old mirror was never yet made by human hands, which, if all the images it has in its time reflected could pass across its surface again, would fail to reveal some scene of horror or distress. But the great serene mirror of the river seemed as if it might have reproduced all it had ever reflected between those placid banks, and brought nothing to the light save what was peaceful, pastoral, and blooming.

So, they walked, speaking of the newly filled-up grave, and

of Johnny, and of many things. So, on their return, they met brisk Mrs Milvey coming to seek them, with the agreeable intelligence that there was no fear for the village children, there being a Christian school in the village, and no worse Judaical interference with it than to plant its garden. So, they got back to the village as Lizzie Hexam was coming from the paper-mill, and Bella detached herself to speak with her in her own home.

'I am afraid it is a poor room for you,' said Lizzie, with a smile of welcome, as she offered the post of honour by the fireside.

'Not so poor as you think, my dear,' returned Bella, 'if you knew all.' Indeed, though attained by some wonderful winding narrow stairs, which seemed to have been erected in a pure white chimney, and though very low in the ceiling, and very rugged in the floor, and rather blinking as to the proportions of its lattice window, it was a pleasanter room than that despised chamber once at home, in which Bella had first bemoaned the miseries of taking lodgers.

The day was closing as the two girls looked at one another by the fireside. The dusky room was lighted by the fire. The grate might have been the old brazier, and the glow might have been the old hollow down by the flare.

'It's quite new to me,' said Lizzie, 'to be visited by a lady so nearly of my own age, and so pretty, as you. It's a pleasure to me to look at you.'

'I have nothing left to begin with,' returned Bella, blushing, 'because I was going to say that it was a pleasure to me to look at you, Lizzie. But we can begin without a beginning, can't we?'

Lizzie took the pretty little hand that was held out in as pretty a little frankness.

'Now, dear,' said Bella, drawing her chair a little nearer, and taking Lizzie's arm as if they were going out for a walk, 'I am commissioned with something to say, and I dare say I shall say it wrong, but I won't if I can help it. It is in reference to your letter to Mr and Mrs Boffin, and this is what it is. Let me see. Oh yes! This is what it is.'

With this exordium, Bella set forth that request of Lizzie's touching secrecy, and delicately spoke of that false accusation and its retraction, and asked might she beg to be informed whether it had any bearing, near or remote, on such request. 'I feel, my dear,' said Bella, quite amazing herself by the business-like manner in which she was getting on, 'that the subject must be a painful one to you, but I am mixed up in it also; for—I don't know whether you may know it or suspect it—I am the willed-away girl who was to have been married to the unfortunate gentleman, if he had been pleased to approve of me. So I was dragged into the subject without my consent, and you were dragged into it without your consent, and there is very little to choose between us.'

'I had no doubt,' said Lizzie, 'that you were the Miss Wilfer I have often heard named. Can you tell me who my unknown friend is?'

'Unknown friend, my dear?' said Bella.

'Who caused the charge against poor father to be contradicted, and sent me the written paper.'

Bella had never heard of him. Had no notion who he was.

'I should have been glad to thank him,' returned Lizzie. 'He has done a great deal for me. I must hope that he will let me thank him some day. You asked me has it anything to do—'

'It or the accusation itself,' Bella put in.

'Yes. Has either anything to do with my wishing to live quite secret and retired here? No.'

As Lizzie Hexam shook her head in giving this reply and as her glance sought the fire, there was a quiet resolution in her folded hands, not lost on Bella's bright eyes.

'Have you lived much alone?' asked Bella.

'Yes. It's nothing new to me. I used to be always alone many hours together, in the day and in the night, when poor father was alive.'

'You have a brother, I have been told?'

'I have a brother, but he is not friendly with me. He is a very good boy though, and has raised himself by his industry. I don't complain of him.'

As she said it, with her eyes upon the fire-glow, there was an instantaneous escape of distress into her face. Bella seized the moment to touch her hand.

'Lizzie, I wish you would tell me whether you have any friend of your own sex and age.'

'I have lived that lonely kind of life, that I have never had one,' was the answer.

'Nor I neither,' said Bella. 'Not that my life has been lonely, for I could have sometimes wished it lonelier, instead of having Ma going on like the Tragic Muse with a face-ache in majestic corners, and Lavvy being spiteful—though of course I am very fond of them both. I wish you could make a friend of me, Lizzie. Do you think you could? I have no more of what they call character, my dear, than a canary-bird, but I know I am trustworthy.'

The wayward, playful, affectionate nature, giddy for want of the weight of some sustaining purpose, and capricious because it was always fluttering among little things, was yet a captivating one. To Lizzie it was so new, so pretty, at once so womanly and so childish, that it won her completely. And when Bella said again, 'Do you think you could, Lizzie?' with her eyebrows raised, her head inquiringly on one side, and an odd doubt about it in her own bosom, Lizzie showed beyond all question that she thought she could.

'Tell me, my dear,' said Bella, 'what is the matter, and why you live like this.'

Lizzie presently began, by way of prelude, 'You must have many lovers—' when Bella checked her with a little scream of astonishment.

'My dear, I haven't one!'

'Not one?'

'Well! Perhaps one,' said Bella. 'I am sure I don't know. I *had* one, but what he may think about it at the present time I can't say. Perhaps I have half a one (of course I don't count that Idiot, George Sampson). However, never mind me. I want to hear about you.'

'There is a certain man,' said Lizzie, 'a passionate and angry man, who says he loves me, and who I must believe does love me. He is the friend of my brother. I shrank from him within myself when my brother first brought him to me; but the last time I saw him he terrified me more than I can say.' There she stopped.

'Do you come here to escape from him, Lizzie?'

'I came here immediately after he so alarmed me.'

'Are you afraid of him here?'

'I am not timid generally, but I am always afraid of him. I am afraid to see a newspaper, or to hear a word spoken of what is done in London, lest he should have done some violence.'

'Then you are not afraid of him for yourself, dear?' said Bella, after pondering on the words.

'I should be even that, if I met him about here. I look round for him always, as I pass to and fro at night.'

'Are you afraid of anything he may do to himself in London, my dear?'

'No. He might be fierce enough even to do some violence to himself, but I don't think of that.'

'Then it would almost seem, dear,' said Bella quaintly, 'as if there must be somebody else?'

Lizzie put her hands before her face for a moment before replying: 'The words are always in my ears, and the blow he struck upon a stone wall as he said them is always before my eyes. I have tried hard to think it not worth remembering, but I cannot make so little of it. His hand was trickling down with blood as he said to me, "Then I hope that I may never kill him!"'

Rather startled, Bella made and clasped a girdle of her arms round Lizzie's waist, and then asked quietly, in a soft voice, as they both looked at the fire:

'Kill him! Is this man so jealous, then?'

'Of a gentleman,' said Lizzie. '—I hardly know how to tell you—of a gentleman far above me and my way of life, who broke father's death to me, and has shown an interest in me since.'

'Does he love you?'

Lizzie shook her head.

'Does he admire you?'

Lizzie ceased to shake her head, and pressed her hand upon her living girdle.

'Is it through his influence that you came here?'

'O no! And of all the world I wouldn't have him know that I am here, or get the least clue where to find me.'

'Lizzie, dear! Why?' asked Bella, in amazement at this burst. But then quickly added, reading Lizzie's face: 'No. Don't say why. That was a foolish question of mine. I see, I see.'

There was silence between them. Lizzie, with a drooping head, glanced down at the glow in the fire where her first fancies had been nursed, and her first escape made from the grim life out of which she had plucked her brother, foreseeing her reward.

'You know all now,' she said, raising her eyes to Bella's. 'There is nothing left out. This is my reason for living secret here, with the aid of a good old man who is my true friend. For a short part of my life at home with father, I knew of things—don't ask me what—that I set my face against, and tried to better. I don't think I could have done more, then, without letting my hold on father go; but they sometimes lie heavy on my mind. By doing all for the best, I hope I may wear them out.'

'And wear out too,' said Bella soothingly, 'this weakness, Lizzie, in favour of one who is not worthy of it.'

'No. I don't want to wear that out,' was the flushed reply,

'nor do I want to believe, nor do I believe, that he is not worthy of it. What should I gain by that, and how much should I lose!'

Bella's expressive little eyebrows remonstrated with the fire for some short time before she rejoined:

'Don't think that I press you, Lizzie; but wouldn't you gain in peace, and hope, and even in freedom? Wouldn't it be better not to live a secret life in hiding, and not to be shut out from your natural and wholesome prospects? Forgive my asking you, would that be no gain?'

'Does a woman's heart that—that has that weakness in it which you have spoken of,' returned Lizzie, 'seek to gain anything?'

The question was so directly at variance with Bella's views in life, as set forth to her father, that she said internally, 'There, you little mercenary wretch! Do you hear that? Ain't you ashamed of yourself?' and unclasped the girdle of her arms, expressly to give herself a penitential poke in the side.

'But you said, Lizzie,' observed Bella, returning to her subject when she had administered this chastisement, 'that you would lose, besides. Would you mind telling me what you would lose, Lizzie?'

'I should lose some of the best recollections, best encouragements, and best objects, that I carry through my daily life. I should lose my belief that if I had been his equal, and he had loved me, I should have tried with all my might to make him better and happier, as he would have made me. I should lose almost all the value that I put upon the little learning I have, which is all owing to him, and which I conquered the difficulties of, that he might not think it thrown away upon me. I should lose a kind of picture of him—or of what he might have been, if I had been a lady, and he had loved me—which is always with me, and which I somehow feel that I could not do a mean or a wrong thing before. I should leave off prizing the remembrance that he has done me nothing but good since I have known him, and that he has made a change within me, like—like the change in the grain of these hands, which were coarse, and cracked, and hard, and brown when I rowed on the river with father, and are softened and made supple by this new work as you see them now.'

They trembled, but with no weakness, as she showed them.

'Understand me, my dear;' thus she went on. 'I have never dreamed of the possibility of his being anything to me on this earth but the kind picture that I know I could not make you understand, if the understanding was not in your own breast already. I have no more dreamed of the possibility of *my* being his wife, than he ever has—and words could not be stronger than that. And yet I love him. I love him so much, and so dearly, that when I sometimes think my life may be but a weary one, I am proud of it and glad of it. I am proud and glad to suffer something for him, even though it is of no service to him, and he will never know of it or care for it.'

Bella sat enchained by the deep, unselfish passion of this girl or woman of her own age, courageously revealing itself in the confidence of her sympathetic perception of its truth. And yet she had never experienced anything like it, or thought of the existence of anything like it.

'It was late upon a wretched night,' said Lizzie, 'when his eyes first looked at me in my old river-side home, very different from this. His eyes may never look at me again. I would rather that they never did; I hope that they never may. But I would not have the light of them taken out of my life, for anything my life can give me. I have told you everything now, my dear. If it comes a little strange to me to have parted with it, I am not sorry. I had no thought of ever parting with a single word of it, a moment before you came in; but you came in, and my mind changed.'

Bella kissed her on the cheek, and thanked her warmly for her confidence. 'I only wish,' said Bella, 'I was more deserving of it.'

'More deserving of it?' repeated Lizzie, with an incredulous smile.

'I don't mean in respect of keeping it,' said Bella, 'because any one should tear me to bits before getting at a syllable of it—though there's no merit in that, for I am naturally as obstinate as a Pig. What I mean is, Lizzie, that I am a mere impertinent piece of conceit, and you shame me.'

Lizzie put up the pretty brown hair that came tumbling down, owing to the energy with which Bella shook her head; and she remonstrated while thus engaged, 'My dear!'

'Oh, it's all very well to call me your dear,' said Bella, with a pettish whimper, 'and I am glad to be called so, though I have slight enough claim to be. But I AM such a nasty little thing!'

'My dear!' urged Lizzie again.

'Such a shallow, cold, worldly, Limited little brute!' said Bella, bringing out her last adjective with culminating force.

'Do you think,' inquired Lizzie with her quiet smile, the hair being now secured, 'that I don't know better?'

'*Do* you know better though?' said Bella. 'Do you really believe you know better? Oh, I should be so glad if you did know better, but I am so very much afraid that I must know best!'

Lizzie asked her, laughing outright, whether she ever saw her own face or heard her own voice?

'I suppose so,' returned Bella; 'I look in the glass often enough, and I chatter like a Magpie.'

'I have seen your face, and heard your voice, at any rate,' said Lizzie, 'and they have tempted me to say to you—with a certainty of not going wrong—what I thought I should never say to any one. Does that look ill?'

'No, I hope it doesn't,' pouted Bella, stopping herself in something between a humoured laugh and a humoured sob.

'I used once to see pictures in the fire,' said Lizzie playfully, 'to please my brother. Shall I tell you what I see down there where the fire is glowing?'

They had risen, and were standing on the hearth, the time being come for separating; each had drawn an arm around the other to take leave.

'Shall I tell you,' asked Lizzie, 'what I see down there?'

'Limited little b?' suggested Bella with her eyebrows raised.

'A heart well worth winning, and well won. A heart that, once won, goes through fire and water for the winner, and never changes, and is never daunted.'

'Girl's heart?' asked Bella, with accompanying eyebrows.

Lizzie nodded. 'And the figure to which it belongs—'

'Is yours,' suggested Bella.

'No. Most clearly and distinctly yours.'

So the interview terminated with pleasant words on both sides, and with many reminders on the part of Bella that they were friends, and pledges that she would soon come down into that part of the country again. There with Lizzie returned to her occupation, and Bella ran over to the little inn to rejoin her company.

'You look rather serious, Miss Wilfer,' was the Secretary's first remark.

'I feel rather serious,' returned Miss Wilfer.

She had nothing else to tell him but that Lizzie Hexam's secret had no reference whatever to the cruel charge, or its withdrawal. Oh yes though! said Bella; she might as well men-

tion one other thing; Lizzie was very desirous to thank her
unknown friend who had sent her the written retractation. Was
she, indeed? observed the Secretary. Ah! Bella asked him, had
he any notion who that unknown friend might be? He had no
notion whatever.

They were on the borders of Oxfordshire, so far had poor
old Betty Higden strayed. They were to return by the train
presently, and, the station being near at hand, the Reverend
Frank and Mrs Frank, and Sloppy and Bella and the Secretary,
set out to walk to it. Few rustic paths are wide enough for five,
and Bella and the Secretary dropped behind.

'Can you believe, Mr Rokesmith,' said Bella, 'that I feel as
if whole years had passed since I went into Lizzie Hexam's
cottage?'

'We have crowded a good deal into the day,' he returned,
'and you were much affected in the churchyard. You are
over-tired.'

'No, I am not at all tired. I have not quite expressed what I
mean. I don't mean that I feel as if a great space of time had
gone by, but that I feel as if much had happened—to myself, you
know.'

'For good, I hope?'

'I hope so,' said Bella.

'You are cold; I felt you tremble. Pray let me put this
wrapper of mine about you. May I fold it over this shoulder
without injuring your dress? Now, it will be too heavy and too
long. Let me carry this end over my arm, as you have no arm to
give me.'

Yes she had though. How she got it out, in her muffled state,
Heaven knows; but she got it out somehow—there it was—and
slipped it through the Secretary's.

'I have had a long and interesting talk with Lizzie, Mr
Rokesmith, and she gave me her full confidence.'

'She could not withhold it,' said the Secretary.

'I wonder how you come,' said Bella, stopping short as she
glanced at him, 'to say to me just what she said about it!'

'I infer that it must be because I feel just as she felt about
it.'

'And how was that, do you mean to say, sir?' asked Bella,
moving again.

'That if you were inclined to win her confidence—anybody's
confidence—you were sure to do it.'

The railway, at this point, knowingly shutting a green eye

and opening a red one, they had to run for it. As Bella could not run easily so wrapped up, the Secretary had to help her. When she took her opposite place in the carriage corner, the brightness in her face was so charming to behold, that on her exclaiming, 'What beautiful stars and what a glorious night!' the Secretary said 'Yes,' but seemed to prefer to see the night and the stars in the light of her lovely little countenance, to looking out of window.

O boofer lady, fascinating boofer lady! If I were but legally executor of Johnny's will! If I had but the right to pay your legacy and to take your receipt!—Something to this purpose surely mingled with the blast of the train as it cleared the stations, all knowingly shutting up their green eyes and opening their red ones when they prepared to let the boofer lady pass.

Chapter 10
Scouts Out

'AND so, Miss Wren,' said Mr Eugene Wrayburn, 'I cannot persuade you to dress me a doll?'

'No,' replied Miss Wren snappishly; 'if you want one, go and buy one at the shop.'

'And my charming young goddaughter,' said Mr Wrayburn plaintively, 'down in Hertfordshire—'

('Humbugshire you mean, I think,' interposed Miss Wren.)

'—is to be put upon the cold footing of the general public, and is to derive no advantage from my private acquaintance with the Court Dressmaker?'

'If it's any advantage to your charming godchild—and oh, a precious godfather she has got!'—replied Miss Wren, pricking at him in the air with her needle, 'to be informed that the Court Dressmaker knows your tricks and your manners, you may tell her so by post, with my compliments.'

Miss Wren was busy at her work by candle-light, and Mr Wrayburn, half amused and half vexed, and all idle and shiftless,

stood by her bench looking on. Miss Wren's troublesome child
was in the corner in deep disgrace, and exhibiting great
wretchedness in the shivering stage of prostration from drink.

'Ugh, you disgraceful boy!' exclaimed Miss Wren, attracted
by the sound of his chattering teeth, 'I wish they'd all drop down
your throat and play at dice in your stomach! Boh, wicked child!
Bee-baa, black sheep!'

On her accompanying each of these reproaches with a threatening stamp of the foot, the wretched creature protested with a
whine.

'Pay five shillings for you indeed!' Miss Wren proceeded;
'how many hours do you suppose it costs me to earn five
shillings, you infamous boy?—Don't cry like that, or I'll throw a
doll at you. Pay five shillings fine for you indeed. Fine in more
ways than one, I think! I'd give the dustman five shillings, to
carry you off in the dust cart.'

'No, no,' pleaded the absurd creature. 'Please!'

'He's enough to break his mother's heart, is this boy,' said
Miss Wren, half appealing to Eugene. 'I wish I had never
brought him up. He'd be sharper than a serpent's tooth, if he
wasn't as dull as ditch water. Look at him. There's a pretty
object for a parent's eyes!'

Assuredly, in his worse than swinish state (for swine at least
fatten on their guzzling, and make themselves good to eat), he
was a pretty object for any eyes.

'A muddling and a swipey old child,' said Miss Wren,
rating him with great severity, 'fit for nothing but to be preserved in the liquor that destroys him, and put in a great glass
bottle as a sight for other swipey children of his own pattern,—if he
has no consideration for his liver, has he none for his mother?'

'Yes. Deration, oh don't!' cried the subject of these angry
remarks.

'Oh don't and oh don't,' pursued Miss Wren. 'It's oh do
and oh do. And why do you?'

'Won't do so any more. Won't indeed. Pray!'

'There!' said Miss Wren, covering her eyes with her hand.
'I can't bear to look at you. Go up stairs and get me my bonnet
and shawl. Make yourself useful in some way, bad boy, and let
me have your room instead of your company, for one half
minute.'

Obeying her, he shambled out, and Eugene Wrayburn saw
the tears exude from between the little creature's fingers as she
kept her hand before her eyes. He was sorry, but his sympathy

did not move his carelessness to do anything but feel sorry.

'I'm going to the Italian Opera to try on,' said Miss Wren, taking away her hand after a little while, and laughing satirically to hide that she had been crying; 'I must see your back before I go, Mr Wrayburn. Let me first tell you, once for all, that it's of no use your paying visits to me. You wouldn't get what you want, of me, no, not if you brought pincers with you to tear it out.'

'Are you so obstinate on the subject of a doll's dress for my godchild?'

'Ah!' returned Miss Wren with a hitch of her chin, 'I am so obstinate. And of course it's on the subject of a doll's dress—or *ad*dress—whichever you like. Get along and give it up!'

Her degraded charge had come back, and was standing behind her with the bonnet and shawl.

'Give 'em to me and get back into your corner, you naughty old thing!' said Miss Wren, as she turned and espied him. 'No, no, I won't have your help. Go into your corner, this minute!'

The miserable man, feebly rubbing the back of his faltering hands downward from the wrists, shuffled on to his post of disgrace; but not without a curious glance at Eugene in passing him, accompanied with what seemed as if it might have been an action of his elbow, if any action of any limb or joint he had, would have answered truly to his will. Taking no more particular notice of him than instinctively falling away from the disagreeable contact, Eugene, with a lazy compliment or so to Miss Wren, begged leave to light his cigar, and departed.

'Now you prodigal old son,' said Jenny, shaking her head and her emphatic little forefinger at her burden, 'you sit there till I come back. You dare to move out of your corner for a single instant while I'm gone, and I'll know the reason why.'

With this admonition, she blew her work candles out, leaving him to the light of the fire, and, taking her big door-key in her pocket and her crutch-stick in her hand, marched off.

Eugene lounged slowly towards the Temple, smoking his cigar, but saw no more of the dolls' dressmaker, through the accident of their taking opposite sides of the street. He lounged along moodily, and stopped at Charing Cross to look about him, with as little interest in the crowd as any man might take, and was lounging on again, when a most unexpected object caught his eyes. No less an object than Jenny Wren's bad boy trying to make up his mind to cross the road.

A more ridiculous and feeble spectacle than this tottering

wretch making unsteady sallies into the roadway, and as often
staggering back again, oppressed by terrors of vehicles that were
a long way off or were nowhere, the streets could not have
shown. Over and over again, when the course was perfectly
clear, he set out, got half way, described a loop, turned, and
went back again, when he might have crossed and re-crossed half
a dozen times. Then, he would stand shivering on the edge of the
pavement, looking up the street and looking down, while scores
of people jostled him, and crossed, and went on. Stimulated in
course of time by the sight of so many successes, he would make
another sally, make another loop, would all but have his foot on
the opposite pavement, would see or imagine something coming,
and would stagger back again. There, he would stand making
spasmodic preparations as if for a great leap, and at last would
decide on a start at precisely the wrong moment, and would be
roared at by drivers, and would shrink back once more, and
stand in the old spot shivering, with the whole of the proceedings
to go through again.

'It strikes me,' remarked Eugene coolly, after watching him
for some minutes, 'that my friend is likely to be rather behind
time if he has any appointment on hand.' With which remark he
strolled on, and took no further thought of him.

Lightwood was at home when he got to the Chambers, and
had dined alone there. Eugene drew a chair to the fire by which
he was having his wine and reading the evening paper, and
brought a glass, and filled it for good fellowship's sake.

'My dear Mortimer, you are the express picture of contented industry, reposing (on credit) after the virtuous labours of
the day.'

'My dear Eugene, you are the express picture of discontented idleness not reposing at all. Where have you been?'

'I have been,' replied Wrayburn, '—about town. I have
turned up at the present juncture, with the intention of consulting
my highly intelligent and respected solicitor on the position of
my affairs.'

'Your highly intelligent and respected solicitor is of opinion
that your affairs are in a bad way, Eugene.'

'Though whether,' said Eugene thoughtfully, 'that can be
intelligently said, now, of the affairs of a client who has nothing
to lose and who cannot possibly be made to pay, may be open to
question.'

'You have fallen into the hands of the Jews, Eugene.'

'My dear boy,' returned the debtor, very composedly taking

up his glass, 'having previously fallen into the hands of some of the Christians, I can bear it with philosophy.'

'I have had an interview to-day, Eugene, with a Jew, who seems determined to press us hard. Quite a Shylock, and quite a Patriarch. A picturesque grey-headed and grey-bearded old Jew, in a shovel-hat and gaberdine.'

'Not,' said Eugene, pausing in setting down his glass, 'surely not my worthy friend Mr. Aaron?'

'He calls himself Mr Riah.'

'By-the-by,' said Eugene, 'it comes into my mind that—no doubt with an instinctive desire to receive him into the bosom of our Church—*I* gave him the name of Aaron!'

'Eugene, Eugene,' returned Lightwood, 'you are more ridiculous than usual. Say what you mean.'

'Merely, my dear fellow, that I have the honour and pleasure of a speaking acquaintance with such a Patriarch as you describe, and that I address him as Mr Aaron, because it appears to me Hebraic, expressive, appropriate, and complimentary. Notwithstanding which strong reasons for its being his name, it may not be his name.'

'I believe you are the absurdest man on the face of the earth,' said Lightwood, laughing.

'Not at all, I assure you. Did he mention that he knew me?'

'He did not. He only said of you that he expected to be paid by you.'

'Which looks,' remarked Eugene with much gravity, 'like *not* knowing me. I hope it may not be my worthy friend Mr Aaron, for, to tell you the truth, Mortimer, I doubt he may have a prepossession against me. I strongly suspect him of having had a hand in spiriting away Lizzie.'

'Everything,' returned Lightwood impatiently, 'seems, by a fatality, to bring us round to Lizzie. ''About town'' meant about Lizzie, just now, Eugene.'

'My solicitor, do you know,' observed Eugene, turning round to the furniture, 'is a man of infinite discernment!'

'Did it not, Eugene?'

'Yes it did, Mortimer.'

'And yet, Eugene, you know you do not really care for her.'

Eugene Wrayburn rose, and put his hands in his pockets, and stood with a foot on the fender, indolently rocking his body and looking at the fire. After a prolonged pause, he replied: 'I don't know that. I must ask you not to say that, as if we took it for granted.'

'But if you do care for her, so much the more should you leave her to herself.'

Having again paused as before, Eugene said: 'I don't know that, either. But tell me. Did you ever see me take so much trouble about anything, as about this disappearance of hers? I ask, for information.'

'My dear Eugene, I wish I ever had!'

'Then you have not? Just so. You confirm my own impression. Does that look as if I cared for her? I ask, for information.'

'I asked *you* for information, Eugene,' said Mortimer reproachfully.

'Dear boy, I know it, but I can't give it. I thirst for information. What do I mean? If my taking so much trouble to recover her does not mean that I care for her, what does it mean? "If Peter Piper picked a peck of pickled pepper, where's the peck," &c.?'

Though he said this gaily, he said it with a perplexed and inquisitive face, as if he actually did not know what to make of himself. 'Look on to the end—' Lightwood was beginning to remonstrate, when he caught at the words:

'Ah! See now! That's exactly what I am incapable of doing. How very acute you are, Mortimer, in finding my weak place! When we were at school together, I got up my lessons at the last moment, day by day and bit by bit; now we are out in life together, I get up my lessons in the same way. In the present task I have not got beyond this:—I am bent on finding Lizzie, and I mean to find her, and I will take any means of finding her that offer themselves. Fair means or foul means, are all alike to me. I ask you—for information—what does that mean? When I have found her I may ask you—also for information—what do I mean now? But it would be premature in this stage, and it's not the character of my mind.'

Lightwood was shaking his head over the air with which his friend held forth thus—an air so whimsically open and argumentative as almost to deprive what he said of the appearance of evasion—when a shuffling was heard at the outer door, and then an undecided knock, as though some hand were groping for the knocker. 'The frolicsome youth of the neighbourhood,' said Eugene, 'whom I should be delighted to pitch from this elevation into the churchyard below, without any intermediate ceremonies, have probably turned the lamp out. I am on duty to-night, and will see to the door.'

His friend had barely had time to recall the unprecedented

gleam of determination with which he had spoken of finding this girl, and which had faded out of him with the breath of the spoken words, when Eugene came back, ushering in a most disgraceful shadow of a man, shaking from head to foot, and clothed in shabby grease and smear.

'This interesting gentleman,' said Eugene, 'is the son—the occasionally rather trying son, for he has his failings—of a lady of my acquaintance. My dear Mortimer—Mr Dolls.' Eugene had no idea what his name was, knowing the little dressmaker's to be assumed, but presented him with easy confidence under the first appellation that his associations suggested.

'I gather, my dear Mortimer,' pursued Eugene, as Lightwood stared at the obscene visitor, 'from the manner of Mr Dolls—which is occasionally complicated—that he desires to make some communication to me. I have mentioned to Mr Dolls that you and I are on terms of confidence, and have requested Mr Dolls to develop his views here.'

The wretched object being much embarrassed by holding what remained of his hat, Eugene airily tossed it to the door, and put him down in a chair.

'It will be necessary, I think,' he observed, 'to wind up Mr Dolls, before anything to any mortal purpose can be got out of him. Brandy, Mr Dolls, or—?'

'Threepenn'orth Rum,' said Mr Dolls.

A judiciously small quantity of the spirit was given him in a wine-glass, and he began to convey it to his mouth, with all kinds of falterings and gyrations on the road.

'The nerves of Mr Dolls,' remarked Eugene to Lightwood, 'are considerably unstrung. And I deem it on the whole expedient to fumigate Mr Dolls.'

He took the shovel from the grate, sprinkled a few live ashes on it, and from a box on the chimney-piece took a few pastiles, which he set upon them; then, with great composure began placidly waving the shovel in front of Mr Dolls, to cut him off from his company.

'Lord bless my soul, Eugene!' cried Lightwood, laughing again, 'what a mad fellow you are! Why does this creature come to see you?'

'We shall hear,' said Wrayburn, very observant of his face withal. 'Now then. Speak out. Don't be afraid. State your business, Dolls.'

'Mist Wrayburn!' said the visitor, thickly and huskily. '—'*Tis* Mist Wrayburn, ain't?' With a stupid stare.

'Of course it is. Look at me. What do you want?'

Mr Dolls collapsed in his chair, and faintly said 'Threepenn'orth Rum.'

'Will you do me the favour, my dear Mortimer, to wind up Mr Dolls again?' said Eugene. 'I am occupied with the fumigation.'

A similar quantity was poured into his glass, and he got it to his lips by similar circuitous ways. Having drunk it, Mr Dolls, with an evident fear of running down again unless he made haste, proceeded to business.

'Mist Wrayburn. Tried to nudge you, but you wouldn't. You want that drection. You want t'know where she lives. *Do* you Mist Wrayburn?'

With a glance at his friend, Eugene replied to the question sternly, 'I do.'

'I am er man,' said Mr Dolls, trying to smite himself on the breast, but bringing his hand to bear upon the vicinity of his eye, 'er do it. I am er man er do it.'

'What are you the man to do?' demanded Eugene, still sternly.

'Er give up that drection.'

'Have you got it?'

With a most laborious attempt at pride and dignity, Mr Dolls rolled his head for some time, awakening the highest expectations, and then answered, as if it were the happiest point that could possibly be expected of him: 'No.'

'What do you mean then?'

Mr Dolls, collapsing in the drowsiest manner after his late intellectual triumph, replied: 'Threepenn'orth Rum.'

'Wind him up again, my dear Mortimer,' said Wrayburn; 'wind him up again.'

'Eugene, Eugene,' urged Lightwood in a low voice, as he complied, 'can you stoop to the use of such an instrument as this?'

'I said,' was the reply, made with that former gleam of determination, 'that I would find her out by any means, fair or foul. These are foul, and I'll take them—if I am not first tempted to break the head of Mr Dolls with the fumigator. Can you get the direction? Do you mean that? Speak! If that's what you have come for, say how much you want.'

'Ten shillings—Threepenn'orths Rum,' said Mr Dolls.

'You shall have it.'

'Fifteen shillings—Threepenn'orths Rum,' said Mr Dolls, making an attempt to stiffen himself.

'You shall have it. Stop at that. How will you get the direction you talk of?'

'I am er man,' said Mr Dolls, with majesty, 'er get it, sir.'

'How will you get it, I ask you?'

'I am ill-used vidual,' said Mr Dolls. 'Blown up morning t'night. Called names. She makes Mint money, sir, and never stands Threepenn'orth Rum.'

'Get on,' rejoined Eugene, tapping his palsied head with the fire-shovel, as it sank on his breast. 'What comes next?'

Making a dignified attempt to gather himself together, but, as it were, dropping half a dozen pieces of himself while he tried in vain to pick up one, Mr Dolls, swaying his head from side to side, regarded his questioner with what he supposed to be a haughty smile and a scornful glance.

'She looks upon me as mere child, sir. I am NOT mere child, sir. Man. Man talent. Lerrers pass betwixt 'em. Postman lerrers. Easy for man talent er get drection, as get his own drection.'

'Get it then,' said Eugene; adding very heartily under his breath, '—You Brute! Get it, and bring it here to me, and earn the money for sixty threepenn'orths of rum, and drink them all, one a top of another, and drink yourself dead with all possible expedition.' The latter clauses of these special instructions he addressed to the fire, as he gave it back the ashes he had taken from it, and replaced the shovel.

Mr Dolls now struck out the highly unexpected discovery that he had been insulted by Lightwood, and stated his desire to 'have it out with him' on the spot, and defied him to come on, upon the liberal terms of a sovereign to a halfpenny. Mr Dolls then fell a crying, and then exhibited a tendency to fall asleep. This last manifestation as by far the most alarming, by reason of its threatening his prolonged stay on the premises, necessitated vigorous measures. Eugene picked up his worn-out hat with the tongs, clapped it on his head, and, taking him by the collar—all this at arm's length—conducted him down stairs and out of the precincts into Fleet Street. There, he turned his face westward, and left him.

When he got back, Lightwood was standing over the fire, brooding in a sufficiently low-spirited manner.

'I'll wash my hands of Mr Dolls—physically—' said Eugene, 'and be with you again directly, Mortimer.'

'I would much prefer,' retorted Mortimer, 'your washing your hands of Mr Dolls, morally, Eugene.'

'So would I,' said Eugene; 'but you see, dear boy, I can't do without him.'

In a minute or two he resumed his chair, as perfectly unconcerned as usual, and rallied his friend on having so narrowly escaped the prowess of their muscular visitor.

'I can't be amused on this theme,' said Mortimer, restlessly. 'You can make almost any theme amusing to me, Eugene, but not this.'

'Well!' cried Eugene, 'I am a little ashamed of it myself, and therefore let us change the subject.'

'It is so deplorably underhanded,' said Mortimer. 'It is so unworthy of you, this setting on of such a shameful scout.'

'We have changed the subject!' exclaimed Eugene, airily. 'We have found a new one in that word, scout. Don't be like Patience on a mantelpiece frowning at Dolls, but sit down, and I'll tell you something that you really will find amusing. Take a cigar. Look at this of mine. I light it—draw one puff—breathe the smoke out—there it goes—it's Dolls!—it's gone—and being gone you are a man again.'

'Your subject,' said Mortimer, after lighting a cigar, and comforting himself with a whiff or two, 'was scouts, Eugene.'

'Exactly. Isn't it droll that I never go out after dark, but I find myself attended, always by one scout, and often by two?'

Lightwood took his cigar from his lips in surprise, and looked at his friend, as if with a latent suspicion that there must be a jest or hidden meaning in his words.

'On my honour, no,' said Wrayburn, answering the look and smiling carelessly; 'I don't wonder at your supposing so, but on my honour, no. I say what I mean. I never go out after dark, but I find myself in the ludicrous situation of being followed and observed at a distance, always by one scout, and often by two.'

'Are you sure, Eugene?'

'Sure? My dear boy, they are always the same.'

'But there's no process out against you. The Jews only threaten. They have done nothing. Besides, they know where to find you, and I represent you. Why take the trouble?'

'Observe the legal mind!' remarked Eugene, turning round to the furniture again, with an air of indolent rapture. 'Observe the dyer's hand, assimilating itself to what it works in,—or would work in, if anybody would give it anything to do. Respected solicitor, it's not that. The schoolmaster's abroad.'

'The schoolmaster?'

'Ay! Sometimes the schoolmaster and the pupil are both

abroad. Why, how soon you rust in my absence! You don't understand yet? Those fellows who were here one night. They are the scouts I speak of, as doing me the honour to attend me after dark.'

'How long has this been going on?' asked Lightwood, opposing a serious face to the laugh of his friend.

'I apprehend it has been going on, ever since a certain person went off. Probably, it had been going on some little time before I noticed it: which would bring it to about that time.'

'Do you think they suppose you to have inveigled her away?'

'My dear Mortimer, you know the absorbing nature of my professional occupations; I really have not had leisure to think about it.'

'Have you asked them what they want? Have you objected?'

'Why should I ask them what they want, dear fellow, when I am indifferent what they want? Why should I express objection, when I don't object?'

'You are in your most reckless mood. But you called the situation just now, a ludicrous one; and most men object to that, even those who are utterly indifferent to everything else.'

'You charm me, Mortimer, with your reading of my weaknesses. (By-the-by, that very word, Reading, in its critical use, always charms me. An actress's Reading of a chambermaid, a dancer's Reading of a hornpipe, a singer's Reading of a song, a marine painter's Reading of the sea, the kettle-drum's Reading of an instrumental passage, are phrases ever youthful and delightful.) I was mentioning your perception of my weaknesses. I own to the weakness of objecting to occupy a ludicrous position, and therefore I transfer the position to the scouts.'

'I wish, Eugene, you would speak a little more soberly and plainly, if it were only out of consideration for my feeling less at ease than you do.'

'Then soberly and plainly, Mortimer, I goad the schoolmaster to madness. I make the schoolmaster so ridiculous, and so aware of being made ridiculous, that I see him chafe and fret at every pore when we cross one another. The amiable occupation has been the solace of my life, since I was baulked in the manner unnecessary to recall. I have derived inexpressible comfort from it. I do it thus: I stroll out after dark, stroll a little way, look in at a window and furtively look out for the schoolmaster. Sooner or later, I perceive the schoolmaster on the watch; sometimes accompanied by his hopeful pupil; oftener, pupil-less. Having made sure of his watching me, I tempt him on, all over London. One night I go east, another night north, in a few nights I go all round the compass. Sometimes, I walk; sometimes, I proceed in cabs, draining the pocket of the schoolmaster who then follows in cabs. I study and get up abstruse No Thoroughfares in the course of the day. With Venetian mystery I seek those No Thoroughfares at night, glide into them by means of dark courts, tempt the schoolmaster to follow, turn suddenly, and catch him before he can retreat. Then we face one another, and I pass him as unaware of his existence, and he undergoes grinding torments. Similarly, I walk at a great pace down a short street, rapidly turn the corner, and, getting out of his view, as rapidly turn back. I catch him coming on post, again pass him as unaware of his existence, and again he undergoes grinding torments. Night after night his disappointment is acute, but hope springs eternal in the scholastic breast, and he follows me again to-morrow. Thus I enjoy the pleasures of the chase, and derive great benefit from the healthful exercise. When I do not enjoy the pleasures of the chase, for anything I know he watches at the Temple Gate all night.'

'This is an extraordinary story,' observed Lightwood, who had heard it out with serious attention. 'I don't like it.'

'You are a little hipped, dear fellow,' said Eugene; 'you have been too sedentary. Come and enjoy the pleasures of the chase.'

'Do you mean that you believe he is watching now?'

'I have not the slightest doubt he is.'

'Have you seen him to-night?'

'I forgot to look for him when I was last out,' returned Eugene with the calmest indifference; 'but I dare say he was there. Come! Be a British sportsman and enjoy the pleasures of the chase. It will do you good.'

Lightwood hesitated; but, yielding to his curiosity, rose.

'Bravo!' cried Eugene, rising too. 'Or, if Yoicks would be in better keeping, consider that I said Yoicks. Look to your feet, Mortimer, for we shall try your boots. When you are ready, I am—need I say with a Hey Ho Chivey, and likewise with a Hark Forward, Hark Forward, Tantivy?'

'Will nothing make you serious?' said Mortimer, laughing through his gravity.

'I am always serious, but just now I am a little excited by the glorious fact that a southerly wind and a cloudy sky proclaim a hunting evening. Ready? So. We turn out the lamp and shut the door, and take the field.'

As the two friends passed out of the Temple into the public street, Eugene demanded with a show of courteous patronage in which direction Mortimer would like the run to be? 'There is a rather difficult country about Bethnal Green,' said Eugene, 'and we have not taken in that direction lately. What is your opinion of Bethnal Green?' Mortimer assented to Bethnal Green, and they turned eastward. 'Now, when we come to St Paul's churchyard,' pursued Eugene, 'we'll loiter artfully, and I'll show you the schoolmaster.' But, they both saw him, before they got there; alone, and stealing after them in the shadow of the houses, on the opposite side of the way.

'Get your wind,' said Eugene, 'for I am off directly. Does it occur to you that the boys of Merry England will begin to deteriorate in an educational light, if this lasts long? The schoolmaster can't attend to me and the boys too. Got your wind? I am off!'

At what a rate he went, to breathe the schoolmaster; and how he then lounged and loitered, to put his patience to another kind of wear; what preposterous ways he took, with no other object on earth than to disappoint and punish him; and how he wore him out by every piece of ingenuity that his eccentric humour could devise; all this Lightwood noted, with a feeling of astonishment that so careless a man could be so wary, and that so idle a man could take so much trouble. At last, far on in the third hour of the pleasures of the chase, when he had brought the poor dogging wretch round again into the City, he twisted Mortimer up a few dark entries, twisted him into a little square court, twisted him sharp round again, and they almost ran against Bradley Headstone.

'And you see, as I was saying, Mortimer,' remarked Eugene aloud with the utmost coolness, as though there were no one within hearing by themselves: 'and you see, as I was saying— undergoing grinding torments.'

It was not too strong a phrase for the occasion. Looking like the hunted and not the hunter, baffled, worn, with the exhaustion of deferred hope and consuming hate and anger in his face, white-lipped, wild-eyed, draggle-haired, seamed with jealousy and anger, and torturing himself with the conviction that he showed it all and they exulted in it, he went by them in the dark, like a haggard head suspended in the air: so completely did the force of his expression cancel his figure.

Mortimer Lightwood was not an extraordinarily impressible man, but this face impressed him. He spoke of it more than once on the remainder of the way home, and more than once when they got home.

They had been abed in their respective rooms two or three hours, when Eugene was partly awakened by hearing a footstep going about, and was fully awakened by seeing Lightwood standing at his beside.

'Nothing wrong, Mortimer?'

'No.'

'What fancy takes you, then, for walking about in the night?'

'I am horribly wakeful.'

'How comes that about, I wonder!'

'Eugene, I cannot lose sight of that fellow's face.'

'Odd!' said Eugene with a light laugh, '*I* can.' And turned over, and fell asleep again.

Chapter 11
In the Dark

THERE was no sleep for Bradley Headstone on that night when Eugene Wrayburn turned so easily in his bed; there was no sleep for little Miss Peecher. Bradley consumed the lonely hours, and consumed himself, in haunting the spot where his careless rival lay a dreaming; little Miss Peecher wore them away in listening for the return home of the master of her heart, and in sorrowfully presaging that much was amiss with him. Yet more was amiss with him than Miss Peecher's simply arranged little work-box of thoughts, fitted with no gloomy and dark recesses, could hold. For, the state of the man was murderous.

The state of the man was murderous, and he knew it. More; he irritated it, with a kind of perverse pleasure akin to that which a sick man sometimes has in irritating a wound upon his body. Tied up all day with his disciplined show upon him, subdued to the performance of his routine of educational tricks, encircled by a gabbling crowd, he broke loose at night like an ill-tamed wild animal. Under his daily restraint, it was his compensation, not his trouble, to give a glance towards his state at night, and to the freedom of its being indulged. If great criminals told the truth— which, being great criminals, they do not—they would very rarely tell of their struggles against the crime. Their struggles are towards it. They buffet with opposing waves, to gain the bloody shore, not to recede from it. This man perfectly comprehended that he hated his rival with his strongest and worst forces, and that if he tracked him to Lizzie Hexam, his so doing would never serve himself with her, or serve her. All his pains were taken, to the end that he might incense himself with the sight of the detested figure in her company and favour, in her place of concealment. And he knew as well what act of his would follow if he did, as he knew that his mother had borne him. Granted, that he may not have held it necessary to make express mention to himself of the one familiar truth any more than of the other.

He knew equally well that he fed his wrath and hatred, and that he accumulated provocation and self-justification, by being made the nightly sport of the reckless and insolent Eugene. Knowing all this, and still always going on with infinite endurance, pains, and perseverance, could his dark soul doubt whither he went?

Baffled, exasperated, and weary, he lingered opposite the Temple gate when it closed on Wrayburn and Lightwood, debating with himself should he go home for that time or should he watch longer. Possessed in his jealousy by the fixed idea that Wrayburn was in the secret, if it were not altogether of his contriving, Bradley was as confident of getting the better of him at last by sullenly sticking to him, as he would have been—and often had been—of mastering any piece of study in the way of his vocation, by the like slow persistent process. A man of rapid passions and sluggish intelligence, it had served him often and should serve him again.

The suspicion crossed him as he rested in a doorway with his eyes upon the Temple gate, that perhaps she was even concealed in that set of Chambers. It would furnish another reason for Wrayburn's purposeless walks, and it might be. He thought of it and thought of it, until he resolved to steal up the stairs, if the gatekeeper would let him through, and listen. So, the haggard head suspended in the air flitted across the road, like the spectre of one of the many heads erst hoisted upon neighbouring Temple Bar, and stopped before the watchman.

The watchman looked at it, and asked: 'Who for?'

'Mr. Wrayburn.'

'It's very late.'

'He came back with Mr.Lightwood, I know, near upon two hours ago. But if he has gone to bed, I'll put a paper in his letter-box. I am expected.'

The watchman said no more, but opened the gate, though rather doubtfully. Seeing, however, that the visitor went straight and fast in the right direction, he seemed satisfied.

The haggard head floated up the dark staircase, and softly descended nearer to the floor outside the outer door of the chambers. The doors of the rooms within, appeared to be standing open. There were rays of candlelight from one of them, and there was the sound of a footstep going about. There were two voices. The words they uttered were not distinguishable, but they were both the voices of men. In a few moments the voices were silent, and there was no sound of footstep, and the inner light went out. If Lightwood could have seen the face which kept him awake, staring and listening in the darkness outside the door as he spoke of it, he might have been less disposed to sleep, through the remainder of the night.

'Not there,' said Bradley; 'but she might have been.' The head arose to its former height from the ground, floated down the staircase again, and passed on to the gate. A man was standing there, in parley with the watchman.

'Oh!' said the watchman. 'Here he is!'

Perceiving himself to be the antecedent, Bradley looked from the watchman to the man.

'This man is leaving a letter for Mr Lightwood,' the watchman explained, showing it in his hand; 'and I was mentioning that a person had just gone up to Mr Lightwood's chambers. It might be the same business perhaps?'

'No,' said Bradley, glancing at the man, who was a stranger to him.

'No,' the man assented in a surly way; 'my letter—it's wrote by my daughter, but it's mine—is about my business, and my business ain't nobody else's business.'

As Bradley passed out at the gate with an undecided foot, he heard it shut behind him, and heard the footstep of the man coming after him.

' 'Scuse me,' said the man, who appeared to have been drinking and rather stumbled at him than touched him, to attract his attention: 'but might you be acquainted with the T'other Governor?'

'With whom?' asked Bradley.

'With,' returned the man, pointing backward over his right shoulder with his right thumb, 'the T'other Governor?'

'I don't know what you mean.'

'Why look here,' hooking his proposition on his left-hand fingers with the forefinger of his right. 'There's two Governors, ain't there? One and one, two—Lawyer Lightwood, my first finger, he's one, ain't he? Well; might you be acquainted with my middle finger, the T'other?'

'I know quite as much of him,' said Bradley, with a frown and a distant look before him, 'as I want to know.'

'Hooroar!' cried the man. 'Hooroar T'other t'other Governor. Hooroar T'otherest Governor! I am of your way of thinkin'.'

'Don't make such a noise at this dead hour of the night. What are you talking about?'

'Look here, T'otherest Governor,' replied the man, becoming hoarsely confidential. 'The T'other Governor he's always joked his jokes agin me, owing, as *I* believe, to my being a honest man as gets my living by the sweat of my brow. Which he ain't, and he don't.'

'What is that to me?'

'T'otherest Governor,' returned the man in a tone of injured innocence, 'if you don't care to hear no more, don't hear no more. You begun it. You said, and likeways showed pretty plain, as you warn't by no means friendly to him. But I don't seek to force my company nor yet my opinions on no man. I am a honest man, that's what I am. Put me in the dock anywhere—I don't care where—and I says, "My Lord, I am a honest man." Put me in the witness-box anywhere—I don't care where—and I says the same to his lordship, and I kisses the book. I don't kiss my coat-cuff; I kisses the book.'

It was not so much in deference to these strong testimonials to character, as in his restless casting about for any way or help towards the discovery on which he was concentrated, that Bradley Headstone replied: 'You needn't take offence. I didn't mean to stop you. You were too loud in the open street; that was all.'

' 'Totherest Governor,' replied Mr Riderhood, mollified and mysterious, 'I know wot it is to be loud, and I know wot it is to be soft. Nat'rally I do. It would be a wonder if I did not, being by the Chris'en name of Roger, which took it arter my own father, which took it from his own father, though which of our fam'ly fust took it nat'ral I will not in any ways mislead you by undertakin' to say. And wishing that your elth may be better than

your looks, which your inside must be bad indeed if it's on the
footing of your out.'

Startled by the implication that his face revealed too much
of his mind, Bradley made an effort to clear his brow. It might
be worth knowing what this strange man's business was with
Lightwood, or Wrayburn, or both, at such an unseasonable hour.
He set himself to find out, for the man might prove to be a
messenger between those two.

'You call at the Temple late,' he remarked, with a lumbering show of ease.

'Wish I may die,' cried Mr Riderhood, with a hoarse laugh,
'if I warn't a goin' to say the self-same words to you, T'otherest
Governor!'

'It chanced so with me,' said Bradley, looking disconcertedly
about him.

'And it chanced so with me,' said Riderhood. 'But I don't
mind telling you how. Why should I mind telling you? I'm a
Deputy Lock-keeper up the river, and I was off duty yes'day,
and I shall be on to-morrow.'

'Yes?'

'Yes, and I come to London to look arter my private affairs.
My private affairs is to get appinted to the Lock as reg'lar
keeper at fust hand, and to have the law of a busted B'low-
Bridge steamer which drownded of me. I ain't a goin' to be
drownded and not paid for it!'

Bradley looked at him, as though he were claiming to be a
Ghost.

'The steamer,' said Mr Riderhood, obstinately, 'run me
down and drownded of me. Interference on the part of other
parties brought me round; but I never asked 'em to bring me
round, nor yet the steamer never asked 'em to it. I mean to be
paid for the life as the steamer took.'

'Was that your business at Mr Lightwood's chambers in the
middle of the night?' asked Bradley, eyeing him with distrust.

'That and to get a writing to be fust-hand Lock Keeper. A
recommendation in writing being looked for, who else ought to
give it to me? As I says in the letter in my daughter's hand, with
my mark put to it to make it good in law, Who but you, Lawyer
Lightwood, ought to hand over this here stifficate, and who but
you ought to go in for damages on my account agin the Steamer?
For (as I says under my mark) I have had trouble enough along
of you and your friend. If you, Lawyer Lightwood, had backed
me good and true, and if the T'other Governor had took me

down correct (I says under my mark), I should have been worth money at the present time, instead of having a barge-load of bad names chucked at me, and being forced to eat my words, which is a unsatisfying sort of food wotever a man's appetite! And when you mention the middle of the night, T'otherest Governor,' growled Mr Riderhood, winding up his monotonous summary of his wrongs, 'throw your eye on this here bundle under my arm, and bear in mind that I'm a walking back to my Lock, and that the Temple laid upon my line of road.'

Bradley Headstone's face had changed during this latter recital, and he had observed the speaker with a more sustained attention.

'Do you know,' said he, after a pause, during which they walked on side by side, 'that I believe I could tell you your name, if I tried?'

'Prove your opinion,' was the answer, accompanied with a stop and a stare. 'Try.'

'Your name is Riderhood.'

'I'm blest if it ain't,' returned that gentleman. 'But I don't know your'n.'

'That's quite another thing,' said Bradley. 'I never supposed you did.'

As Bradley walked on meditating, the Rogue walked on at his side muttering. The purport of the muttering was: 'that Rogue Riderhood, by George! seemed to be made public property on, now, and that every man seemed to think himself free to handle his name as if it was a Street Pump.' The purport of the meditating was: 'Here is an instrument. Can I use it?'

They had walked along the Strand, and into Pall Mall, and had turned up-hill towards Hyde Park Corner; Bradley Headstone waiting on the pace and lead of Riderhood, and leaving him to indicate the course. So slow were the schoolmaster's thoughts, and so indistinct his purposes when they were but tributary to the one absorbing purpose—or rather when, like dark trees under a stormy sky, they only lined the long vista at the end of which he saw those two figures of Wrayburn and Lizzie on which his eyes were fixed—that at least a good half-mile was traversed before he spoke again. Even then, it was only to ask:

'Where is your Lock?'

'Twenty mile and odd—call it five-and-twenty mile and odd, if you like—up stream,' was the sullen reply.

'How is it called?'

'Plashwater Weir Mill Lock.'

'Suppose I was to offer you five shillings; what then?'

'Why, then, I'd take it,' said Mr Riderhood.

The schoolmaster put his hand in his pocket, and produced two half-crowns, and placed them in Mr Riderhood's palm: who stopped at a convenient doorstep to ring them both, before acknowledging their receipt.

'There's one thing about you, T'otherest Governor,' said Riderhood, faring on again, 'as looks well and goes fur. You're a ready-money man. Now;' when he had carefully pocketed the coins on that side of himself which was furthest from his new friend; 'what's this for?'

'For you.'

'Why, o' course I know *that*,' said Riderhood, as arguing something that was self-evident. 'O' course I know very well as no man in his right senses would suppose as anythink would make me give it up agin when I'd once got it. But what do you want for it?'

'I don't know that I want anything for it. Or if I do want anything for it, I don't know what it is.' Bradley gave this answer in a stolid, vacant, and self-communing manner, which Mr Riderhood found very extraordinary.

'You have no goodwill towards this Wrayburn,' said Bradley, coming to the name in a reluctant and forced way, as if he were dragged to it.

'No.'

'Neither have I.'

Riderhood nodded, and asked: 'Is it for that?'

'It's as much for that as anything else. It's something to be agreed with, on a subject that occupies so much of one's thoughts.'

'I don't agree with *you*,' returned Mr Riderhood, bluntly. 'No! It don't, T'otherest Governor, and it's no use a lookin' as if you wanted to make out that it did. I tell you it rankles in you. It rankles in you, rusts in you, and pisons you.'

'Say that it does so,' returned Bradley with quivering lips; 'is there no cause for it?'

'Cause enough, I'll bet a pound!' cried Mr Riderhood.

'Haven't you yourself declared that the fellow has heaped provocations, insults, and affronts on you, or something to that effect? He has done the same by me. He is made of venomous insults and affronts, from the crown of his head to the sole of his foot. Are you so hopeful or so stupid, as not to know that he and the other will treat your application with contempt, and light their cigars with it?'

'I shouldn't wonder if they did, by George!' said Riderhood, turning angry.

'If they did! They will. Let me ask you a question. I know something more than your name about you; I knew something about Gaffer Hexam. When did you last set eyes upon his daughter?'

'When did I last set eyes upon his daughter, T'otherest Governor?' repeated Mr Riderhood, growing intentionally slower of comprehension as the other quickened in his speech.

'Yes. Not to speak to her. To see her—anywhere?'

The Rogue had got the clue he wanted, though he held it with a clumsy hand. Looking perplexedly at the passionate face, as if he were trying to work out a sum in his mind, he slowly answered: 'I ain't set eyes upon her—never once—not since the day of Gaffer's death.'

'You know her well, by sight?'

'I should think I did! No one better.'

'And you know him as well?'

'Who's him?' asked Riderhood, taking off his hat and rubbing his forehead, as he directed a dull look at his questioner.

'Curse the name! Is it so agreeable to you that you want to hear it again?'

'Oh! *Him*!' said Riderhood, who had craftily worked the schoolmaster into this corner, then he might again take note of his face under its evil possession. 'I'd know *him* among a thousand.'

'Did you—' Bradley tried to ask it quietly; but, do what he might with his voice, he could not subdue his face;—'did you ever see them together?'

(The Rogue had got the clue in both hands now.)

'I see 'em together, T'otherest Governor, on the very day when Gaffer was towed ashore.'

Bradley could have hidden a reserved piece of information from the sharp eyes of a whole inquisitive class, but he could not veil from the eyes of the ignorant Riderhood the withheld question next in his breast. 'You shall put it plain if you want it answered,' thought the Rogue, doggedly; 'I ain't a'going a wolunteering.'

'Well! was he insolent to her too?' asked Bradley after a struggle. 'Or did he make a show of being kind to her?'

'He made a show of being most uncommon kind to her,' said Riderhood. 'By George! now I—'

His flying off at a tangent was indisputably natural. Bradley looked at him for the reason.

'Now I think of it,' said Mr Riderhood, evasively, for he was substituting those words for 'Now I see you so jealous,' which was the phrase really in his mind; 'P'r'aps he went and took me down wrong, a purpose, on account o' being sweet upon her!'

The baseness of confirming him in this suspicion or pretence of one (for he could not have really entertained it), was a line's breadth beyond the mark the schoolmaster had reached. The baseness of communing and intriguing with the fellow who would have set that stain upon her, and upon her brother too, was attained. The line's breadth further, lay beyond. He made no reply, but walked on with a lowering face.

What he might gain by this acquaintance, he could not work out in his slow and cumbrous thoughts. The man had an injury against the object of his hatred, and that was something; though it was less than he supposed, for there dwelt in the man no such deadly rage and resentment as burned in his own breast. The man knew her, and might by a fortunate chance see her, or hear of her; that was something, as enlisting one pair of eyes and ears the more. The man was a bad man, and willing enough to be in his pay. That was something, for his own state and purpose were as bad as bad could be, and he seemed to derive a vague support from the possession of a congenial instrument, though it might never be used.

Suddenly he stood still, and asked Riderhood point-blank if he knew where she was? Clearly, he did not know. He asked Riderhood if he would be willing, in case any intelligence of her, or of Wrayburn as seeking her or associating with her, should fall in his way, to communicate it if it were paid for? He would be very willing indeed. He was 'agin 'em both,' he said with an oath, and for why? 'Cause they had both stood betwixt him and his getting his living by the sweat of his brow.

'It will not be long then,' said Bradley Headstone, after some more discourse to this effect, 'before we see one another again. Here is the country road, and here is the day. Both have come upon me by surprise.'

'But, T'otherest Governor,' urged Mr Riderhood, 'I don't know where to find you.'

'It is of no consequence. I know where to find you, and I'll come to your Lock.'

'But, T'otherest Governor,' urged Mr Riderhood again, 'no luck never come yet of a dry acquaintance. Let's wet it, in a mouthful of rum and milk, T'otherest Governor.'

Bradley assenting, went with him into an early public-house, haunted by unsavoury smells of musty hay and stale straw, where returning carts, farmers' men, gaunt dogs, fowls of a beery breed, and certain human nightbirds fluttering home to roost, were solacing themselves after their several manners; and where not one of the nightbirds hovering about the sloppy bar failed to discern at a glance in the passion-wasted nightbird with respectable feathers, the worst nightbird of all.

An inspiration of affection for a half-drunken carter going his way led to Mr Riderhood's being elevated on a high heap of baskets on a waggon, and pursuing his journey recumbent on his back with his head on his bundle. Bradley then turned to retrace his steps, and by-and-by struck off through little-traversed ways, and by-and-by reached school and home. Up came the sun to find him washed and brushed, methodically dressed in decent black coat and waistcoat, decent formal black tie, and pepper-and-salt pantaloons, with his decent silver watch in its pocket, and its decent hair-guard round his neck: a scholastic huntsman clad for the field, with his fresh pack yelping and barking around him.

Yet more really bewitched than the miserable creatures of the much-lamented times, who accused themselves of impossibilities under a contagion of horror and the strongly suggestive influences of Torture, he had been ridden hard by Evil Spirits in the night that was newly gone. He had been spurred and whipped and heavily sweated. If a record of the sport had usurped the places of the peaceful texts from Scripture on the wall, the most advanced of the scholars might have taken fright and run away from the master.

Chapter 12
Meaning Mischief

Up came the sun, streaming all over London, and in its glorious impartiality even condescending to make prismatic sparkles in the whiskers of Mr Alfred Lammle as he sat at breakfast. In need of some brightening from without, was Mr Alfred Lammle, for he had the air of being dull enough within, and looked grievously discontented.

Mrs Alfred Lammle faced her lord. The happy pair of swindlers, with the comfortable tie between them that each had swindled the other, sat moodily observant of the tablecloth. Things looked so gloomy in the breakfast-room, albeit on the sunny side of Sackville Street, that any of the family tradespeople glancing through the blinds might have taken the hint to send in his account and press for it. But this, indeed, most of the family tradespeople had already done, without the hint.

'It seems to me,' said Mrs Lammle, 'that you have had no money at all, ever since we have been married.'

'What seems to you,' said Mr Lammle, 'to have been the case, may possibly have been the case. It doesn't matter.'

Was it the speciality of Mr and Mrs. Lammle, or does it ever obtain with other loving couples? In these matrimonial dialogues they never addressed each other, but always some invisible presence that appeared to take a station about midway between them. Perhaps the skeleton in the cupboard comes out to be talked to, on such domestic occasions?

'I have never seen any money in the house,' said Mrs Lammle to the skeleton, 'except my own annuity. That I swear.'

'You needn't take the trouble of swearing,' said Mr Lammle to the skeleton; 'once more, it doesn't matter. You never turned your annuity to so good an account.'

'Good an account! In what way?' asked Mrs Lammle.

'In the way of getting credit, and living well,' said Mr Lammle.

Perhaps the skeleton laughed scornfully on being intrusted with this question and this answer; certainly Mrs Lammle did, and Mr Lammle did.

'And what is to happen next?' asked Mrs Lammle of the skeleton.

'Smash is to happen next,' said Mr Lammle to the same authority.

After this, Mrs Lammle looked disdainfully at the skeleton—but without carrying the look on to Mr Lammle—and drooped her eyes. After that, Mr Lammle did exactly the same thing, and drooped *his* eyes. A servant then entering with toast, the skeleton retired into the closet, and shut itself up.

'Sophronia,' said Mr Lammle, when the servant had withdrawn. And then, very much louder: 'Sophronia!'

'Well?'

'Attend to me, if you please.' He eyed her sternly until she did attend, and then went on. 'I want to take counsel with you. Come, come; no more trifling. You know our league and convenant. We are to work together for our joint interest, and you are as knowing a hand as I am. We shouldn't be together, if you were not. What's to be done? We are hemmed into a corner. What shall we do?'

'Have you no scheme on foot that will bring in anything?'

Mr Lammle plunged into his whiskers for reflection, and came out hopeless: 'No; as adventurers we are obliged to play rash games for chances of high winnings, and there has been a run of luck against us.'

She was resuming, 'Have you nothing—' when he stopped her.

'We, Sophronia. We, we, we.'

'Have we nothing to sell?'

'Deuce a bit. I have given a Jew a bill of sale on this furniture, and he could take it to-morrow, to-day, now. He would have taken it before now, I believe, but for Fledgeby.'

'What has Fledgeby to do with him?'

'Knew him. Cautioned me against him before I got into his claws. Couldn't persuade him then, in behalf of somebody else.'

'Do you mean that Fledgeby has at all softened him towards you?'

'Us, Sophronia. Us, us, us.'

'Towards us?'

'I mean that the Jew has not yet done what he might have

done, and that Fledgeby takes the credit of having got him to hold his hand.'

'Do you believe Fledgeby?'

'Sophronia, I never believe anybody. I never have, my dear, since I believed you. But it looks like it.'

Having given her this back-handed reminder of her mutinous observations to the skeleton, Mr Lammle rose from table—perhaps, the better to conceal a smile, and a white dint or two about his nose—and took a turn on the carpet and came to the hearthrug.

'If we could have packed the brute off with Georgiana; —but however; that's spilled milk.'

As Lammle, standing gathering up the skirts of his dressing-gown with his back to the fire, said this, looking down at his wife, she turned pale and looked down at the ground. With a sense of disloyalty upon her, and perhaps with a sense of personal danger—for she was afraid of him—even afraid of his hand and afraid of his foot, though he had never done her violence—she hastened to put herself right in his eyes.

'If we could borrow money, Alfred—'

'Beg money, borrow money, or steal money. It would be all one to us, Sophronia,' her husband struck in.

'—Then, we could weather this?'

'No doubt. To offer another original and undeniable remark, Sophronia, two and two make four.'

But, seeing that she was turning something in her mind, he gathered up the skirts of his dressing-gown again, and, tucking them under one arm, and collecting his ample whiskers in his other hand, kept his eye upon her, silently.

'It is natural, Alfred,' she said, looking up with some timidity into his face, 'to think in such an emergency of the richest people we know, and the simplest.'

'Just so, Sophronia.'

'The Boffins.'

'Just so, Sophronia.'

'Is there nothing to be done with them?'

'What is there to be done with them, Sophronia?'

She cast about in her thoughts again, and he kept his eye upon her as before.

'Of course I have repeatedly thought of the Boffins, Sophronia,' he resumed, after a fruitless silence; 'but I have seen my way to nothing. They are well guarded. That infernal Secretary stands between them and—people of merit.'

'If he could be got rid of?' said she, brightening a little, after more casting about.

'Take time, Sophronia,' observed her watchful husband, in a patronizing manner.

'If working him out of the way could be presented in the light of a service to Mr Boffin?'

'Take time, Sophronia.'

'We have remarked lately, Alfred, that the old man is turning very suspicious and distrustful.'

'Miserly too, my dear; which is far the most unpromising for us. Nevertheless, take time, Sophronia, take time.'

She took time and then said:

'Suppose we should address ourselves to that tendency in him of which we have made ourselves quite sure. Suppose my conscience—'

'And we know what a conscience it is, my soul. Yes?'

'Suppose my conscience should not allow me to keep to myself any longer what that upstart girl told me of the Secretary's having made a declaration to her. Suppose my conscience should oblige me to repeat it to Mr Boffin.'

'I rather like that,' said Lammle.

'Suppose I so repeated it to Mr Boffin, as to insinuate that my sensitive delicacy and honour—'

'Very good words, Sophronia.'

'—As to insinuate that *our* sensitive delicacy and honour,' she resumed, with a bitter stress upon the phrase, 'would not allow us to be silent parties to so mercenary and designing a speculation on the Secretary's part, and so gross a breach of faith towards his confiding employer. Suppose I had imparted my virtuous uneasiness to my excellent husband, and he had said, in his integrity, "Sophronia, you must immediately disclose this to Mr Boffin." '

'Once more, Sophronia,' observed Lammle, changing the leg on which he stood, 'I rather like that.'

'You remark that he is well guarded,' she pursued. 'I think so too. But if this should lead to his discharging his Secretary, there would be a weak place made.'

'Go on expounding, Sophronia. I begin to like this very much.'

'Having, in our unimpeachable rectitude, done him the service of opening his eyes to the treachery of the person he trusted, we shall have established a claim upon him and a confidence with him. Whether it can be made much of, or little of, we must wait—because we can't help it—to see. Probably we shall make the most of it that is to be made.'

'Probably,' said Lammle.

'Do you think it impossible,' she asked, in the same cold plotting way, 'that you might replace the Secretary?'

'Not impossible, Sophronia. It might be brought about. At any rate it might be skilfully led up to.'

She nodded her understanding of the hint, as she looked at the fire. 'Mr Lammle,' she said, musingly: not without a slight ironical touch: 'Mr Lammle would be so delighted to do anything in his power. Mr Lammle, himself a man of business as well as a capitalist. Mr Lammle, accustomed to be intrusted with the most delicate affairs. Mr Lammle, who has managed my own little fortune so admirably, but who, to be sure, began to make his reputation with the advantage of being a man of property, above temptation, and beyond suspicion.'

Mr Lammle smiled, and even patted her on the head. In his sinister relish of the scheme, as he stood above her, making it the subject of his cogitations, he seemed to have twice as much nose on his face as he had ever had in his life.

He stood pondering, and she sat looking at the dusty fire without moving, for some time. But, the moment he began to speak again she looked up with a wince and attended to him, as if that double-dealing of hers had been in her mind, and the fear were revived in her of his hand or his foot.

'It appears to me, Sophronia, that you have omitted one branch of the subject. Perhaps not, for women understand women. We might oust the girl herself?'

Mrs Lammle shook her head. 'She has an immensely strong hold upon them both, Alfred. Not to be compared with that of a paid secretary.'

'But the dear child,' said Lammle, with a crooked smile, 'ought to have been open with her benefactor and benefactress. The darling love ought to have reposed unbounded confidence in her benefactor and benefactress.'

Sophronia shook her head again.

'Well! Women understand women,' said her husband, rather disappointed. 'I don't press it. It might be the making of our fortune to make a clean sweep of them both. With me to manage the property, and my wife to manage the people—Whew!'

Again shaking her head, she returned: 'They will never quarrel with the girl. They will never punish the girl. We must accept the girl, rely upon it.'

'Well!' cried Lammle, shrugging his shoulders, 'so be it: only always remember that we don't want her.'

'Now, the sole remaining question is,' said Mrs Lammle, 'when shall I begin?'

'You cannot begin too soon, Sophronia. As I have told you, the condition of our affairs is desperate, and may be blown upon at any moment.'

'I must secure Mr Boffin alone, Alfred. If his wife was present, she would throw oil upon the waters. I know I should fail to move him to an angry outburst, if his wife was there. And as to the girl herself—as I am going to betray her confidence, she is equally out of the question.'

'It wouldn't do to write for an appointment?' said Lammle.

'No, certainly not. They would wonder among themselves why I wrote, and I want to have him wholly unprepared.'

'Call, and ask to see him alone?' suggested Lammle.

'I would rather not do that either. Leave it to me. Spare me the little carriage for to-day, and for to-morrow (if I don't succeed to-day), and I'll lie in wait for him.'

It was barely settled when a manly form was seen to pass the windows and heard to knock and ring. 'Here's Fledgeby,' said Lammle. 'He admires you, and has a high opinion of you. I'll be out. Coax him to use his influence with the Jew. His name is Riah, of the House of Pubsey and Co.' Adding these words under his breath, lest he should be audible in the erect ears of Mr Fledgeby, through two keyholes and the hall, Lammle, making signals of discretion to his servant, went softly up stairs.

'Mr Fledgeby,' said Mrs Lammle, giving him a very gracious reception, 'so glad to see you! My poor dear Alfred, who is greatly worried just now about his affairs, went out rather early. Dear Mr Fledgeby, do sit down.'

Dear Mr Fledgeby did sit down, and satisfied himself (or, judging from the expression of his countenance, *dis*satisfied himself) that nothing new had occurred in the way of whisker-sprout since he came round the corner from the Albany.

'Dear Mr Fledgeby, it was needless to mention to you that my poor dear Alfred is much worried about his affairs at present, for he has told me what a comfort you are to him in his temporary difficulties, and what a great service you have rendered him.'

'Oh!' said Mr Fledgeby.

'Yes,' said Mrs Lammle.

'I didn't know,' remarked Mr. Fledgeby, trying a new part

of his chair, 'but that Lammle might be reserved about his affairs.'

'Not to me,' said Mrs Lammle, with deep feeling.

'Oh, indeed?' said Fledgeby.

'Not to me, dear Mr Fledgeby. I am his wife.'

'Yes. I—I always understood so,' said Mr Fledgeby.

'And as the wife of Alfred, may I, dear Mr Fledgeby, wholly without his authority or knowledge, as I am sure your discernment will perceive, entreat you to continue that great service, and once more use your well-earned influence with Mr Riah for a little more indulgence? The name I have heard Alfred mention, tossing in his dreams, *is* Riah; is it not?'

'The name of the Creditor is Riah,' said Mr Fledgeby, with a rather uncompromising accent on his noun-substantive. 'Saint Mary Axe. Pubsey and Co.'

'Oh yes!' exclaimed Mrs Lammle, clasping her hands with a certain gushing wildness. 'Pubsey and Co.!'

'The pleading of the feminine—' Mr Fledgeby began, and there stuck so long for a word to get on with, that Mrs Lammle offered him sweetly, 'Heart?'

'No,' said Mr Fledgeby, 'Gender—is ever what a man is bound to listen to, and I wish it rested with myself. But this Riah is a nasty one, Mrs Lammle; he really is.'

'Not if *you* speak to him, dear Mr. Fledgeby.'

'Upon my soul and body he is!' said Fledgeby.

'Try. Try once more, dearest Mr Fledgeby. What is there you cannot do, if you will!'

'Thank you,' said Fledgeby, 'you're very complimentary to say so. I don't mind trying him again, at your request. But of course I can't answer for the consequences. Riah is a tough subject, and when he says he'll do a thing, he'll do it.'

'Exactly so,' cried Mrs Lammle, 'and when he says to you he'll wait, he'll wait.'

('She is a devilish clever woman,' thought Fledgeby. 'I didn't see that opening, but she spies it out and cuts into it as soon as it's made.')

'In point of fact, dear Mr Fledgeby,' Mrs Lammle went on in a very interesting manner, 'not to affect concealment of Alfred's hopes, to you who are so much his friend, there is a distant break in his horizon.'

This figure of speech seemed rather mysterious to Fascination Fledgeby, who said, 'There's a what in his—eh?'

'Alfred, dear Mr Fledgeby, discussed with me this very

morning before he went out, some prospects he has, which might entirely change the aspect of his present troubles.'

'Really?' said Fledgeby.

'O yes!' Here Mrs Lammle brought her handkerchief into play. 'And you know, dear Mr. Fledgeby—you who study the human heart, and study the world—what an affliction it would be to lose position and to lose credit, when ability to tide over a very short time might save all appearances.'

'Oh!' said Fledgeby. 'Then you think, Mrs Lammle, that if Lammle got time, he wouldn't burst up?—To use an expression,' Mr Fledgeby apologetically explained, 'which is adopted in the Money Market.'

'Indeed yes. Truly, truly, yes!'

'That makes all the difference,' said Fledgeby. 'I'll make a point of seeing Riah at once.'

'Blessings on you, dearest Mr Fledgeby!'

'Not at all,' said Fledgeby. She gave him her hand. 'The hand,' said Mr Fledgeby, 'of a lovely and superior-minded female is ever the repayment of a—'

'Noble action!' said Mrs Lammle, extremely anxious to get rid of him.

'It wasn't what I was going to say,' returned Fledgeby, who never would, under any circumstances, accept a suggested expression, 'but you're very complimentary. May I imprint a—a one—upon it? Good morning!'

'I may depend upon your promptitude, dearest Mr Fledgeby?'

Said Fledgeby, looking back at the door and respectfully kissing his hand, 'You may depend upon it.'

In fact, Mr Fledgeby sped on his errand of mercy through the streets, at so brisk a rate that his feet might have been winged by all the good spirits that wait on Generosity. They might have taken up their station in his breast, too, for he was blithe and merry. There was quite a fresh trill in his voice, when, arriving at the counting-house in St Mary Axe, and finding it for the moment empty, he trolled forth at the foot of the staircase: 'Now, Judah, what are you up to there?'

The old man appeared, with his accustomed deference.

'Halloa!' said Fledgeby, falling back, with a wink. 'You mean mischief, Jerusalem!'

The old man raised his eyes inquiringly.

'Yes you do,' said Fledgeby. 'Oh, you sinner! Oh, you dodger! What! You're going to act upon that bill of sale at

Lammle's, are you? Nothing will turn you, won't it? You won't be put off for another single minute, won't you?'

Ordered to immediate action by the master's tone and look, the old man took up his hat from the little counter where it lay.

'You have been told that he might pull through it, if you didn't go in to win, Wide-Awake; have you?' said Fledgeby. 'And it's not your game that he should pull through it; ain't it? You having got security, and there being enough to pay you? Oh, you Jew!'

The old man stood irresolute and uncertain for a moment, as if there might be further instructions for him in reserve.

'Do I go, sir?' he at length asked in a low voice.

'Asks me if he is going!' exclaimed Fledgeby. 'Asks me, as if he didn't know his own purpose! Asks me, as if he hadn't got his hat on ready! Asks me, as if his sharp old eye—why, it cuts like a knife—wasn't looking at his walking-stick by the door!'

'Do I go, sir?'

'Do you go?' sneered Fledgeby. 'Yes, you do go. Toddle, Judah!'

Chapter 13
Give a Dog a Bad Name, and Hang Him

FASCINATION FLEDGEBY, left alone in the counting-house, strolled about with his hat on one side, whistling, and investigating the drawers, and prying here and there for any small evidences of his being cheated, but could find none. 'Not his merit that he don't cheat me,' was Mr Fledgeby's commentary delivered with a wink, 'but my precaution.' He then with a lazy grandeur asserted his rights as lord of Pubsey and Co. by poking his cane at the stools and boxes, and spitting in the fireplace, and so loitered royally to the window and looked out into the narrow street, with his small eyes just peering over the top of Pubsey and Co.'s blind. As a blind in more senses than one, it reminded him that he was alone in the counting-house with the front door open. He was moving away to shut it, lest he should be injudiciously identified with the establishment, when he was stopped by some one coming to the door.

This some one was the dolls' dressmaker, with a little basket on her arm, and her crutch stick in her hand. Her keen eyes had espied Mr Fledgeby before Mr. Fledgeby had espied her, and he was paralysed in his purpose of shutting her out, not so much by her approaching the door, as by her favouring him with a shower of nods, the instant he saw her. This advantage she improved by hobbling up the steps with such despatch that before Mr Fledgeby could take measures for her finding nobody at home, she was face to face with him in the counting-house.

'Hope I see you well, sir,' said Miss Wren. 'Mr Riah in?'

Fledgeby had dropped into a chair, in the attitude of one waiting wearily. 'I suppose he will be back soon,' he replied; 'he has cut out and left me expecting him back, in an odd way. Haven't I seen you before?'

'Once before—if you had your eyesight,' replied Miss Wren; the conditional clause in an under-tone.

'When you were carrying on some games up at the top of the house. I remember. How's your friend?'

'I have more friends than one, sir, I hope,' replied Miss Wren. 'Which friend?'

'Never mind,' said Mr Fledgeby, shutting up one eye, 'any of your friends, all your friends. Are they pretty tolerable?'

Somewhat confounded, Miss Wren parried the pleasantry, and sat down in a corner behind the door, with her basket in her lap. By-and-by, she said, breaking a long and patient silence:

'I beg your pardon, sir, but I am used to find Mr Riah at this time, and so I generally come at this time. I only want to buy my poor little two shillings' worth of waste. Perhaps you'll kindly let me have it, and I'll trot off to my work.'

'*I* let you have it?' said Fledgeby, turning his head towards her; for he had been sitting blinking at the light, and feeling his cheek. 'Why, you don't really suppose that I have anything to do with the place, or the business; do you?'

'Suppose?' exclaimed Miss Wren. 'He said, that day, you were the master!'

'The old cock in black said? Riah said? Why, he'd say anything.'

'Well; but you said so too,' returned Miss Wren. 'Or at least you took on like the master, and didn't contradict him.'

'One of his dodges,' said Mr. Fledgeby, with a cool and

contemptuous shrug. 'He's made of dodges. He said to me, "Come up to the top of the house, sir, and I'll show you a handsome girl. But I shall call you the master." So I went up to the top of the house and he showed me the handsome girl (very well worth looking at she was), and I was called the master. I don't know why. I dare say he don't. He loves a dodge for its own sake; being,' added Mr Fledgeby, after casting about for an expressive phrase, 'the dodgerest of all the dodgers.'

'Oh my head!' cried the dolls' dressmaker, holding it with both her hands, as if it were cracking. 'You can't mean what you say.'

'I can, my little woman,' retorted Fledgeby, 'and I do, I assure you.'

This repudiation was not only an act of deliberate policy on Fledgeby's part, in case of his being surprised by any other caller, but was also a retort upon Miss Wren for her over-sharpness, and a pleasant instance of his humour as regarded the old Jew. 'He has got a bad name as an old Jew, and he is paid for the use of it, and I'll have my money's worth out of him.' This was Fledgeby's habitual reflection in the way of business, and it was sharpened just now by the old man's presuming to have a secret from him: though of the secret itself, as annoying somebody else whom he disliked, he by no means disapproved.

Miss Wren with a fallen countenance sat behind the door looking thoughtfully at the ground, and the long and patient silence had again set in for some time, when the expression of Mr Fledgeby's face betokened that through the upper portion of the door, which was of glass, he saw some one faltering on the brink of the counting-house. Presently there was a rustle and a tap, and then some more rustling and another tap. Fledgeby taking no notice, the door was at length softly opened, and the dried face of a mild little elderly gentleman looked in.

'Mr Riah?' said this visitor, very politely.

'I am waiting for him, sir,' returned Mr Fledgeby. 'He went out and left me here. I expect him back every minute. Perhaps you had better take a chair.'

The gentleman took a chair, and put his hand to his forehead, as if he were in a melancholy frame of mind. Mr Fledgeby eyed him aside, and seemed to relish his attitude.

'A fine day, sir,' remarked Fledgeby.

The little dried gentleman was so occupied with his own depressed reflections that he did not notice the remark until the sound of Mr Fledgeby's voice had died out of the counting-house. Then he started, and said: 'I beg your pardon, sir. I fear you spoke to me?'

'I said,' remarked Fledgeby, a little louder than before, 'it was a fine day.'

'I beg your pardon. I beg your pardon. Yes.'

Again the little dried gentleman put his hand to his forehead, and again Mr Fledgeby seemed to enjoy his doing it. When the gentleman changed his attitude with a sigh, Fledgeby spake with a grin.

'Mr Twemlow, I think?'

The dried gentleman seemed much surprised.

'Had the pleasure of dining with you at Lammle's,' said Fledgeby. 'Even have the honour of being a connexion of yours. An unexpected sort of place this to meet in; but one never knows, when one gets into the City, what people one may knock up against. I hope you have your health, and are enjoying yourself.'

There might have been a touch of impertinence in the last words; on the other hand, it might have been but the native grace of Mr Fledgeby's manner. Mr Fledgeby sat on a stool with a foot on the rail of another stool, and his hat on. Mr Twemlow had uncovered on looking in at the door, and remained so.

Now the conscientious Twemlow, knowing what he had done to thwart the gracious Fledgeby, was particulary disconcerted by this encounter. He was as ill at ease as a gentleman well could be. He felt himself bound to conduct himself stiffly towards Fledgeby, and he made him a distant bow. Fledgeby made his small eyes smaller in taking special note of his manner. The dolls' dressmaker sat in her corner behind the door, with her eyes on the ground and her hands folded on her basket, holding her crutch-stick between them, and appearing to take no heed of anything.

'He's a long time,' muttered Mr Fledgeby, looking at his watch. 'What time may you make it, Mr Twemlow?'

Mr Twemlow made it ten minutes past twelve, sir.

'As near as a toucher,' assented Fledgeby. 'I hope, Mr Twemlow, your business here may be of a more agreeable character than mine.'

'Thank you, sir,' said Mr Twemlow.

Fledgeby again made his small eyes smaller, as he glanced with great complacency at Twemlow, who was timorously tapping the table with a folded letter.

'What I know of Mr Riah,' said Fledgeby, with a very

disparaging utterance of his name, 'leads me to believe that this is about the shop for disagreeable business. I have always found him the bitingest and tightest screw in London.'

Mr Twemlow acknowledged the remark with a little distant bow. It evidently made him nervous.

'So much so,' pursued Fledgeby, 'that if it wasn't to be true to a friend, nobody should catch me waiting here a single minute. But if you have friends in adversity, stand by them. That's what I say and act up to.'

The equitable Twemlow felt that this sentiment, irrespective of the utterer, demanded his cordial assent. 'You are very right, sir,' he rejoined with spirit. 'You indicate the generous and manly course.'

'Glad to have your approbation,' returned Fledgeby. 'It's a coincidence, Mr Twemlow;' here he descended from his perch, and sauntered towards him; 'that the friends I am standing by to-day are the friends at whose house I met you! The Lammles. She's a very taking and agreeable woman?'

Conscience smote the gentle Twemlow pale. 'Yes,' he said. 'She is.'

'And when she appealed to me this morning, to come and try what I could do to pacify their creditor, this Mr Riah—that I certainly have gained some little influence with in transacting business for another friend, but nothing like so much as she supposes—and when a woman like that spoke to me as her dearest Mr Fledgeby, and shed tears—why what could I do, you know?'

Twemlow gasped 'Nothing but come.'

'Nothing but come. And so I came. But why,' said Fledgeby, putting his hands in his pockets and counterfeiting deep meditation, 'why Riah should have started up, when I told him that the Lammles entreated him to hold over a Bill of Sale he has on all their effects; and why he should have cut out, saying he would be back directly; and why he should have left me here alone so long; I cannot understand.'

The chivalrous Twemlow, Knight of the Simple Heart, was not in a condition to offer any suggestion. He was too penitent, too remorseful. For the first time in his life he had done an underhanded action, and he had done wrong. He had secretly interposed against this confiding young man, for no better real reason than because the young man's ways were not his ways.

But, the confiding young man proceeded to heap coals of fire on his sensitive head.

'I beg your pardon, Mr Twemlow; you see I am acquainted with the nature of the affairs that are transacted here. Is there anything I can do for you here? You have always been brought up as a gentleman, and never as a man of business;' another touch of possible impertinence in this place; 'and perhaps you are but a poor man of business. What else is to be expected!'

'I am even a poorer man of business than I am a man, sir,' returned Twemlow, 'and I could hardly express my deficiency in a stronger way. I really do not so much as clearly understand my position in the matter on which I am brought here. But there are reasons which make me very delicate of accepting your assistance. I am greatly, greatly, disinclined to profit by it. I don't deserve it.'

Good childish creature! Condemned to a passage through the world by such narrow little dimly-lighted ways, and picking up so few specks or spots on the road!

'Perhaps,' said Fledgeby, 'you may be a little proud of entering on the topic,—having been brought up as a gentleman.'

'It's not that, sir,' returned Twemlow, 'it's not that. I hope I distinguish between true pride and false pride.'

'I have no pride at all, myself,' said Fledgeby, 'and perhaps I don't cut things so fine as to know one from t'other. But I know this is a place where even a man of business needs his wits about him; and if mine can be of any use to you here, you're welcome to them.'

'You are very good,' said Twemlow, faltering. 'But I am most unwilling—'

'I don't, you know,' proceeded Fledgeby with an ill-favoured glance, 'entertain the vanity of supposing that my wits could be of any use to you in society, but they might be here. You cultivate society and society cultivates you, but Mr Riah's not society. In society, Mr Riah is kept dark; eh, Mr Twemlow?'

Twemlow, much disturbed, and with his hand fluttering about his forehead, replied: 'Quite true.'

The confiding young man besought him to state his case. The innocent Twemlow, expecting Fledgeby to be astounded by what he should unfold, and not for an instant conceiving the possibility of its happening every day, but treating of it as a terrible phenomenon occurring in the course of ages, related how that he had had a deceased friend, a married civil officer with a family, who had wanted money for change of place on change of post, and how he, Twemlow, had 'given him his name,' with the usual, but in the eyes of Twemlow almost incredible result that he had been left to repay what he had never had. How, in the course of years, he had reduced the principal by trifling sums, 'having,' said Twemlow, 'always to observe great economy, being in the enjoyment of a fixed income limited in extent, and that depending on the munificence of a certain nobleman,' and had always pinched the full interest out of himself with punctual pinches. How he had come, in course of time, to look upon this one only debt of his life as a regular quarterly drawback, and no worse, when 'his name' had some way fallen into the possession of Mr Riah, who had sent him notice to redeem it by paying up in full, in one plump sum, or take tremendous consequences. This, with hazy remembrances of how he had been carried to some office to 'confess judgment' (as he recollected the phrase), and how he had been carried to another office where his life was assured for somebody not wholly unconnected with the sherry trade whom he remembered by the remarkable circumstance that he had a Straduarius violin to dispose of, and also a Madonna, formed the sum and substance of Mr Twemlow's narrative. Through which stalked the shadow of the awful Snigsworth, eyed afar off by money-lenders as Security in the Mist, and menacing Twemlow with his baronial truncheon.

To all, Mr. Fledgeby listened with the modest gravity becoming a confiding young man who knew it all beforehand, and, when it was finished, seriously shook his head. 'I don't like, Mr Twemlow,' said Fledgeby, 'I don't like Riah's calling in the principal. If he's determined to call it in, it must come.'

'But supposing, sir,' said Twemlow, downcast, 'that it can't come?'

'Then,' retorted Fledgeby, 'you must go, you know.'

'Where?' asked Twemlow, faintly.

'To prison,' returned Fledgeby. Whereat Mr Twemlow leaned his innocent head upon his hand, and moaned a little moan of distress and disgrace.

'However,' said Fledgeby, appearing to pluck up his spirits, 'we'll hope it's not so bad as that comes to. If you'll allow me, I'll mention to Mr Riah when he comes in, who you are, and I'll tell him you're my friend, and I'll say my say for you, instead of your saying it for yourself; I may be able to do it in a more businesslike way. You don't consider it a liberty?'

'I thank you again and again, sir,' said Twemlow. 'I am strong, strongly, disinclined to avail myself of your generosity, though my helplessness yields. For I cannot but feel that I—to put it in the mildest form of speech—that I have done nothing to deserve it.'

'Where *can* he be?' muttered Fledgeby, referring to his watch again. 'What *can* he have gone out for? Did you ever see him, Mr Twemlow?'

'Never.'

'He is a thorough Jew to look at, but he is a more thorough Jew to deal with. He's worst when he's quiet. If he's quiet, I shall take it as a very bad sign. Keep your eye upon him when he comes in, and, if he's quiet, don't be hopeful. Here he is!—He looks quiet.'

With these words, which had the effect of causing the harmless Twemlow painful agitation, Mr Fledgeby withdrew to his former post, and the old man entered the counting-house.

'Why, Mr Riah,' said Fledgeby, 'I thought you were lost!'

The old man, glancing at the stranger, stood stock-still. He perceived that his master was leading up to the orders he was to take, and he waited to understand them.

'I really thought,' repeated Fledgeby slowly, 'that you were lost, Mr Riah. Why, now I look at you—but no, you can't have done it; no, you can't have done it!'

Hat in hand, the old man lifted his head, and looked distressfully at Fledgeby as seeking to know what new moral burden he was to bear.

'You can't have rushed out to get the start of everybody else, and put in that bill of sale at Lammle's?' said Fledgeby. 'Say you haven't, Mr Riah.'

'Sir, I have,' replied the old man in a low voice.

'Oh my eye!' cried Fledgeby. 'Tut, tut, tut! Dear, dear, dear! Well! I knew you were a hard customer, Mr Riah, but I never thought you were as hard as that.'

'Sir,' said the old man, with great uneasiness, 'I do as I am directed. I am not the principal here. I am but the agent of a superior, and I have no choice, no power.'

'Don't say so,' retorted Fledgeby, secretly exultant as the old man stretched out his hands, with a shrinking action of defending himself against the sharp construction of the two observers. 'Don't play the tune of the trade, Mr Riah. You've a right to get in your debts, if you're determined to do it, but don't pretend what every one in your line regularly pretends. At least, don't do it to me. Why should you, Mr Riah? You know I know all about you.'

The old man clasped the skirt of his long coat with his

disengaged hand, and directed a wistful look at Fledgeby.

'And don't,' said Fledgeby, 'don't, I entreat you as a favour, Mr Riah, be so devilish meek, for I know what'll follow if you are. Look here, Mr Riah. This gentleman is Mr Twemlow.'

The Jew turned to him and bowed. That poor lamb bowed in return; polite, and terrified.

'I have made such a failure,' proceeded Fledgeby, 'in trying to do anything with you for my friend Lammle, that I've hardly a hope of doing anything with you for my friend (and connexion indeed) Mr Twemlow. But I do think that if you would do a favour for anybody, you would for me, and I won't fail for want of trying, and I've passed my promise to Mr Twemlow besides. Now, Mr Riah, here is Mr Twemlow. Always good for his interest, always coming up to time, always paying his little way. Now, why should you press Mr Twemlow? You can't have any spite against Mr Twemlow! Why not be easy with Mr Twemlow?'

The old man looked into Fledgeby's little eyes for any sign of leave to be easy with Mr Twemlow; but there was no sign in them.

'Mr Twemlow is no connexion of yours, Mr Riah,' said Fledgeby; 'you can't want to be even with him for having through life gone in for a gentleman and hung on to his Family. If Mr Twemlow has a contempt for business, what can it matter to you?'

'But pardon me,' interposed the gentle victim, 'I have not. I should consider it presumption.'

'There, Mr Riah!' said Fledgeby, 'isn't that handsomely said? Come! Make terms with me for Mr Twemlow.'

The old man looked again for any sign of permission to spare the poor little gentleman. No. Mr Fledgeby meant him to be racked.

'I am very sorry, Mr Twemlow,' said Riah. 'I have my instructions. I am invested with no authority for diverging from them. The money must be paid.'

'In full and slap down, do you mean, Mr Riah?' asked Fledgeby, to make things quite explicit.

'In full, sir, and at once,' was Riah's answer.

Mr Fledgeby shook his head deploringly at Twemlow, and mutely expressed in reference to the venerable figure standing before him with eyes upon the ground: 'What a Monster of an Israelite this is!'

'Mr Riah,' said Fledgeby.

The old man lifted up his eyes once more to the little eyes

in Mr Fledgeby's head, with some reviving hope that the sign might be coming yet.

'Mr Riah, it's of no use my holding back the fact. There's a certain great party in the background in Mr Twemlow's case, and you know it.'

'I know it,' the old man admitted.

'Now, I'll put it as a plain point of business, Mr Riah. Are you fully determined (as a plain point of business) either to have that said great party's security, or that said great party's money?'

'Fully determined,' answered Riah, as he read his master's face, and learnt the book.

'Not at all caring for, and indeed as it seems to me rather enjoying,' said Fledgeby, with peculiar unction, 'the precious kick-up and row that will come off between Mr Twemlow and the said great party?'

This required no answer, and received none. Poor Mr Twemlow, who had betrayed the keenest mental terrors since his noble kinsman loomed in the perspective, rose with a sigh to take his departure. 'I thank you very much, sir,' he said, offering Fledgeby his feverish hand. 'You have done me an unmerited service. Thank you, thank you!'

'Don't mention it,' answered Fledgeby. 'It's a failure so far, but I'll stay behind, and take another touch at Mr Riah.'

'Do not deceive yourself, Mr Twemlow,' said the Jew, then addressing him directly for the first time. 'There is no hope for you. You must expect no leniency here. You must pay in full, and you cannot pay too promptly, or you will be put to heavy charges. Trust nothing to me, sir. Money, money, money.' When he had said these words in an emphatic manner, he acknowledged Mr Twemlow's still polite motion of his head, and that amiable little worthy took his departure in the lowest spirits.

Fascination Fledgeby was in such a merry vein when the counting-house was cleared of him, that he had nothing for it but to go to the window, and lean his arms on the frame of the blind, and have his silent laugh out, with his back to his subordinate. When he turned round again with a composed countenance, his subordinate still stood in the same place, and the dolls' dressmaker sat behind the door with a look of horror.

'Halloa!' cried Mr Fledgeby, 'you're forgetting this young lady, Mr Riah, and she has been waiting long enough too. Sell her her waste, please, and give her good measure if you can make up your mind to do the liberal thing for once.'

He looked on for a time, as the Jew filled her little basket with such scraps as she was used to buy; but, his merry vein coming on again, he was obliged to turn round to the window once more, and lean his arms on the blind.

'There, my Cinderella dear,' said the old man in a whisper, and with a worn-out look, 'the basket's full now. Bless you! And get you gone!'

'Don't call me your Cinderella dear,' returned Miss Wren. 'O you cruel godmother!'

She shook that emphatic little forefinger of hers in his face at parting, as earnestly and reproachfully as she had ever shaken it at her grim old child at home.

'You are not the godmother at all!' said she. 'You are the Wolf in the Forest, the wicked Wolf! And if ever my dear Lizzie is sold and betrayed, I shall know who sold and betrayed her!'

Chapter 14
Mr Wegg Prepares a Grindstone for Mr Boffin's Nose

HAVING assisted at a few more expositions of the lives of Misers, Mr Venus became almost indispensable to the evenings at the Bower. The circumstance of having another listener to the wonders unfolded by Wegg, or, as it were, another calculator to cast up the guineas found in teapots, chimneys, racks and mangers, and other such banks of deposit, seemed greatly to heighten Mr Boffin's enjoyment; while Silas Wegg, for his part, though of a jealous temperament which might under ordinary circumstances have resented the anatomist's getting into favour, was so very anxious to keep his eye on that gentleman—lest, being too much left to himself, he should be tempted to play any tricks with the precious document in his keeping—that he never lost an opportunity of commending him to Mr Boffin's notice as a third party whose company was much to be desired. Another friendly demonstration towards him Mr Wegg now regularly gratified. After each sitting was over, and the patron had departed, Mr Wegg invariably saw Mr Venus home. To be sure, he as invariably requested to be refreshed with a sight of the paper in which he was a joint proprietor; but he never failed to remark that it was the great pleasure he derived from Mr Venus's improving society which had insensibly lured him round to Clerkenwell again, and that, finding himself once more attracted to the spot by the social powers of Mr V., he would beg leave to go through that little incidental procedure, as a matter of form. 'For well I know, sir,' Mr Wegg would add, 'that a man of your delicate mind would wish to be checked off whenever the opportunity arises, and it is not for me to baulk your feelings.'

A certain rustiness in Mr Venus, which never became so lubricated by the oil of Mr Wegg but that he turned under the screw in a creaking and stiff manner, was very noticeable at about this period. While assisting at the literary evenings, he even went so far, on two or three occasions, as to correct Mr Wegg when he grossly mispronounced a word, or made non-sense of a passage; insomuch that Mr Wegg took to surveying his course in the day, and to making arrangements for getting round rocks at night instead of running straight upon them. Of the slightest anatomical reference he became particularly shy, and, if he saw a bone ahead, would go any distance out of his way rather than mention it by name.

The adverse destinies ordained that one evening Mr Wegg's labouring bark became beset by polysyllables, and embarrassed among a perfect archipelago of hard words. It being necessary to take soundings every minute, and to feel the way with the greatest caution, Mr Wegg's attention was fully employed. Advantage was taken of this dilemma by Mr Venus, to pass a scrap of paper into Mr Boffin's hand, and lay his finger on his own lip.

When Mr Boffin got home at night he found that the paper contained Mr Venus's card and these words: 'Should be glad to be honoured with a call respecting business of your own, about dusk on an early evening.'

The very next evening saw Mr Boffin peeping in at the preserved frogs in Mr Venus's shop-window, and saw Mr Venus espying Mr Boffin with the readiness of one on the alert, and beckoning that gentleman into his interior. Responding, Mr Boffin was invited to seat himself on the box of human miscellanies before the fire, and did so, looking round the place with admiring eyes. The fire being low and fitful, and the dusk gloomy, the whole stock seemed to be winking and blinking with both eyes, as Mr Venus did. The French gentleman, though he had no eyes, was not at all behindhand, but appeared, as the flame rose and fell, to open and shut his no eyes, with the regularity of the glass-eyed dogs and ducks and birds. The big-headed babies were equally obliging in lending their grotesque aid to the general effect.

'You see, Mr Venus, I've lost no time,' said Mr Boffin. 'Here I am.'

'Here you are, sir,' assented Mr Venus.

'I don't like secrecy,' pursued Mr Boffin—'at least, not in a general way I don't—but I dare say you'll show me good reason for being secret so far.'

'I think I shall, sir,' returned Venus.

'Good,' said Mr Boffin. 'You don't expect Wegg, I take it for granted?'

'No, sir. I expect no one but the present company.'

Mr Boffin glanced about him, as accepting under that inclusive denomination the French gentleman and the circle in which he didn't move, and repeated, 'The present company.'

'Sir,' said Mr Venus, 'before entering upon business, I shall have to ask you for your word and honour that we are in confidence.'

'Let's wait a bit and understand what the expression means,' answered Mr Boffin. 'In confidence for how long? In confidence for ever and a day?'

'I take your hint, sir,' said Venus; 'you think you might consider the business, when you came to know it, to be of a nature incompatible with confidence on your part?'

'I might,' said Mr Boffin with a cautious look.

'True, sir. Well, sir,' observed Venus, after clutching at his dusty hair, to brighten his ideas, 'let us put it another way. I open the business with you, relying upon your honour not to do anything in it, and not to mention me in it, without my knowledge.'

'That sounds fair,' said Mr Boffin. 'I agree to that.'

'I have your word and honour, sir?'

'My good fellow,' retorted Mr Boffin, 'you have my word; and how you can have that, without my honour too, I don't know. I've sorted a lot of dust in my time, but I never knew the two things go into separate heaps.'

This remark seemed rather to abash Mr Venus. He hesitated, and said, 'Very true, sir;' and again, 'Very true, sir,' before resuming the thread of his discourse.

'Mr Boffin, if I confess to you that I fell into a proposal of which you were the subject, and of which you oughtn't to have been the subject, you will allow me to mention, and will please take into favourable consideration, that I was in a crushed state of mind at the time.'

The Golden Dustman, with his hands folded on the top of his stout stick, with his chin resting upon them, and with something leering and whimsical in his eyes, gave a nod, and said, 'Quite so, Venus.'

'That proposal, sir, was a conspiring breach of your confidence, to such an extent, that I ought at once to have made it known to you. But I didn't, Mr Boffin, and I fell into it.'

Without moving eye or finger, Mr Boffin gave another nod, and placidly repeated, 'Quite so, Venus.'

'Not that I was ever hearty in it, sir,' the penitent anatomist went on, 'or that I ever viewed myself with anything but reproach for having turned out of the paths of science into the paths of—' he was going to say 'villany,' but, unwilling to press too hard upon himself, substituted with great emphasis —'Weggery.'

Placid and whimsical of look as ever, Mr Boffin answered: 'Quite so, Venus.'

'And now, sir,' said Venus, 'having prepared your mind in the rough, I will articulate the details.' With which brief professional exordium, he entered on the history of the friendly move, and truly recounted it. One might have thought that it would have extracted some show of surprise or anger, or other emotion, from Mr Boffin, but it extracted nothing beyond his former comment: 'Quite so, Venus.'

'I have astonished you, sir, I believe?' said Mr Venus, pausing dubiously.

Mr Boffin simply answered as aforesaid: 'Quite so, Venus.'

By this time the astonishment was all on the other side. It did not, however, so continue. For, when Venus passed to Wegg's discovery, and from that to their having both seen Mr Boffin dig up the Dutch bottle, that gentleman changed colour, changed his attitude, became extremely restless, and ended (when Venus ended) by being in a state of manifest anxiety, trepidation, and confusion.

'Now, sir,' said Venus, finishing off; 'you best know what was in that Dutch bottle, and why you dug it up, and took it away. I don't pretend to know anything more about it than I saw. All I know is this: I am proud of my calling after all (though it has been attended by one dreadful drawback which has told upon my heart, and almost equally upon my skeleton), and I mean to live by my calling. Putting the same meaning into other words, I do not mean to turn a single dishonest penny by this affair. As the best amends I can make you for having ever gone into it, I make known to you, as a warning, what Wegg has found out. My opinion is, that Wegg is not to be silenced at a modest price, and I build that opinion on his beginning to dispose of your property the moment he knew his power. Whether it's worth your while to silence him at any price, you will decide for yourself, and take your measures accordingly. As far as I am concerned, I have no price. If I am ever called upon for the truth, I tell it, but I want to do no more than I have now done and ended.'

'Thank'ee, Venus!' said Mr Boffin, with a hearty grip of his hand; 'thank'ee, Venus, thank'ee, Venus!' And then walked up and down the little shop in great agitation. 'But look here, Venus,' he by-and-by resumed, nervously sitting down again; 'if I have to buy Wegg up, I shan't buy him any cheaper for your being out of it. Instead of his having half the money—it was to have been half, I suppose? Share and share alike?'

'It was to have been half, sir,' answered Venus.

'Instead of that, he'll now have all. I shall pay the same, if not more. For you tell me he's an unconscionable dog, a ravenous rascal.'

'He is,' said Venus.

'Don't you think, Venus,' insinuated Mr Boffin, after looking at the fire for a while—'don't you feel as if—you might like to pretend to be in it till Wegg was bought up, and then ease your mind by handing over to me what you had made believe to pocket?'

'No I don't, sir,' returned Venus, very positively.

'Not to make amends?' insinuated Mr Boffin.

'No, sir. It seems to me, after maturely thinking it over, that the best amends for having got out of the square is to get back into the square.'

'Humph!' mused Mr Boffin. 'When you say the square, you mean—'

'I mean,' said Venus, stoutly and shortly, 'the right.'

'It appears to me,' said Mr Boffin, grumbling over the fire in an injured manner, 'that the right is with me, if it's anywhere. I have much more right to the old man's money than the Crown can ever have. What was the Crown to him except the King's Taxes? Whereas, me and my wife, we was all in all to him.'

Mr Venus, with his head upon his hands, rendered melancholy by the contemplation of Mr Boffin's avarice, only murmured to steep himself in the luxury of that frame of mind: 'She did not wish so to regard herself, nor yet to be so regarded.'

'And how am I to live,' asked Mr Boffin, piteously, 'if I'm to be going buying fellows up out of the little that I've got? And how am I to set about it? When am I to get my money ready? When am I to make a bid? You haven't told me when he threatens to drop down upon me.'

Venus explained under what conditions, and with what views, the dropping down upon Mr Boffin was held over until the Mounds should be cleared away. Mr Boffin listened attentively. 'I suppose,' said he, with a gleam of hope, 'there's no doubt about the genuineness and date of this confounded will?'

'None whatever,' said Mr Venus.

'Where might it be deposited at present?' asked Mr Boffin, in a wheedling tone.

'It's in my possession, sir.'

'Is it?' he cried, with great eagerness. 'Now, for any liberal sum of money that could be agreed upon, Venus, would you put it in the fire?'

'No, sir, I wouldn't,' interrupted Mr Venus.

'Nor pass it over to me?'

'That would be the same thing. No, sir,' said Mr Venus.

The Golden Dustman seemed about to pursue these questions, when a stumping noise was heard outside, coming towards the door. 'Hush! here's Wegg!' said Venus. 'Get behind the young alligator in the corner, Mr Boffin, and judge him for yourself. I won't light a candle till he's gone; there'll only be the glow of the fire; Wegg's well acquainted with the alligator, and he won't take particular notice of him. Draw your legs in, Mr Boffin, at present I see a pair of shoes at the end of his tail. Get your head well behind his smile, Mr Boffin, and you'll lie comfortable there; you'll find plenty of room behind his smile. He's a little dusty, but he's very like you in tone. Are you right, sir?'

Mr Boffin had but whispered an affirmative response, when Wegg came stumping in. 'Partner,' said that gentleman in a sprightly manner, 'how's yourself?'

'Tolerable,' returned Mr Venus. 'Not much to boast of.'

'In-deed!' said Wegg: 'sorry, partner, that you're not picking up faster, but your soul's too large for your body, sir; that's where it is. And how's our stock in trade, partner? Safe bind, safe find, partner? Is that about it?'

'Do you wish to see it?' asked Venus.

'If you please, partner,' said Wegg, rubbing his hands. 'I wish to see it jintly with yourself. Or, in similar words to some that was set to music some time back:

> "I wish you to see it with your eyes,
>   And I will pledge with mine." '

Turning his back and turning a key, Mr Venus produced the document, holding on by his usual corner. Mr Wegg, holding on by the opposite corner, sat down on the seat so lately vacated by Mr Boffin, and looked it over. 'All right, sir,' he slowly and unwillingly admitted, in his reluctance to loose his hold, 'all right!' And greedily watched his partner as he turned his back again, and turned his key again.

'There's nothing new, I suppose?' said Venus, resuming his low chair behind the counter.

'Yes there is, sir,' replied Wegg; 'there was something new this morning. That foxey old grasper and griper—'

'Mr Boffin?' inquired Venus, with a glance towards the alligator's yard or two of smile.

'Mister be blowed!' cried Wegg, yielding to his honest indignation. 'Boffin. Dusty Boffin. That foxey old grunter and grinder, sir, turns into the yard this morning, to meddle with our property, a menial tool of his own, a young man by the name of Sloppy. Ecod, when I say to him, "What do you want here, young man? This is a private yard," he pulls out a paper from Boffin's other blackguard, the one I was passed over for. "This is to authorize Sloppy to overlook the carting and to watch the work." That's pretty strong, I think, Mr Venus?'

'Remember he doesn't know yet of our claim on the property,' suggested Venus.

'Then he must have a hint of it,' said Wegg, 'and a strong one that'll jog his terrors a bit. Give him an inch, and he'll take an ell. Let him alone this time, and what'll he do with our property next? I tell you what, Mr Venus; it comes to this; I must be overbearing with Boffin, or I shall fly into several pieces. I can't contain myself when I look at him. Every time I see him putting his hand in his pocket, I see him putting it into my pocket. Every time I hear him jingling his money, I hear him taking liberties with my money. Flesh and blood can't bear it. No,' said Mr Wegg, greatly exasperated, 'and I'll go further. A wooden leg can't bear it!'

'But, Mr Wegg,' urged Venus, 'it was your own idea that he should not be exploded upon, till the Mounds were carted away.'

'But it was likewise my idea, Mr Venus,' retorted Wegg, 'that if he came sneaking and sniffing about the property, he should be threatened, given to understand that he has no right to it, and be made our slave. Wasn't that my idea, Mr Venus?'

'It certainly was, Mr Wegg.'

'It certainly was, as you say, partner,' assented Wegg, put into a better humour by the ready admission. 'Very well. I consider his planting one of his menial tools in the yard, an act of sneaking and sniffing. And his nose shall be put to the grindstone for it.'

'It was not your fault, Mr Wegg, I must admit,' said Venus, 'that he got off with the Dutch bottle that night.'

'As you handsomely say again, partner! No, it was not my fault. I'd have had that bottle out of him. Was it to be borne that he should come, like a thief in the dark, digging among stuff that was far more ours than his (seeing that we could deprive him of every grain of it, if he didn't buy us at our own figure), and carrying off treasure from its bowels? No, it was not to be borne. And for that, too, his nose shall be put to the grindstone.'

'How do you propose to do it, Mr Wegg?'

'To put his nose to the grindstone? I propose,' returned that estimable man, 'to insult him openly. And, if looking into this eye of mine, he dares to offer a word in answer, to retort upon him before he can take his breath, "Add another word to that, you dusty old dog, and you're a beggar."'

'Suppose he says nothing, Mr Wegg?'

'Then,' replied Wegg, 'we shall have come to an understanding with very little trouble, and I'll break him and drive him, Mr Venus. I'll put him in harness, and I'll bear him up tight, and I'll break him and drive him. The harder the old Dust is driven, sir, the higher he'll pay. And I mean to be paid high, Mr Venus, I promise you.'

'You speak quite revengefully, Mr Wegg.'

'Revengefully, sir? Is it for him that I have declined and falled, night after night? Is it for his pleasure that I've waited at home of an evening, like a set of skittles, to be set up and knocked over, set up and knocked over, by whatever balls—or books—he chose to bring against me? Why, I'm a hundred times the man he is, sir; five hundred times!'

Perhaps it was with the malicious intent of urging him on to his worst that Mr Venus looked as if he doubted that.

'What? Was it outside the house at present ockypied, to its disgrace, by that minion of fortune and worm of the hour,' said Wegg, falling back upon his strongest terms of reprobation, and slapping the counter, 'that I, Silas Wegg, five hundred times the man he ever was, sat in all weathers, waiting for a errand or a customer? Was it outside that very house as I first set eyes upon him, rolling in the lap of luxury, when I was selling halfpenny ballads there for a living? And am I to grovel in the dust for *him* to walk over? No!'

There was a grin upon the ghastly countenance of the French gentleman under the influence of the firelight, as if he were computing how many thousand slanderers and traitors array themselves against the fortunate, on premises exactly answering to those of Mr Wegg. One might have fancied that the big-headed babies were toppling over with their hydrocephalic attempts to reckon up the children of men who transform their benefactors into their injurers by the same process. The yard or two of smile on the part of the alligator might have been invested with the meaning, 'All about this was quite familiar knowledge down in the depths of the slime, ages ago.'

'But,' said Wegg, possibly with some slight perception to the foregoing effect, 'your speaking countenance remarks, Mr Venus, that I'm duller and savager than usual. Perhaps I *have* allowed myself to brood too much. Begone, dull Care! 'Tis gone, sir. I've looked in upon you, and empire resumes her sway. For, as the song says—subject to your correction, sir—

"When the heart of a man is depressed with cares,
    The mist is dispelled if Venus appears.
    Like the notes of a fiddle, you sweetly, sir, sweetly,
    Raises our spirits and charms our ears."

Good-night, sir.'

'I shall have a word or two to say to you, Mr Wegg, before long,' remarked Venus, 'respecting my share in the project we've been speaking of.'

'My time, sir,' returned Wegg, 'is yours. In the meanwhile let it be fully understood that I shall not neglect bringing the grindstone to bear, nor yet bringing Dusty Boffin's nose to it. His nose once brought to it, shall be held to it by these hands, Mr Venus, till the sparks flies out in showers.'

With this agreeable promise Wegg stumped out, and shut the shop-door after him. 'Wait till I light a candle, Mr Boffin,' said Venus, 'and you'll come out more comfortable.' So, he lighting a candle and holding it up at arm's length, Mr Boffin disengaged himself from behind the alligator's smile, with an expression of countenance so very downcast that it not only appeared as if the alligator had the whole of the joke to himself, but further as if it had been conceived and executed at Mr Boffin's expense.

'That's a treacherous fellow,' said Mr Boffin, dusting his arms and legs as he came forth, the alligator having been but dusty company. 'That's a dreadful fellow.'

'The alligator, sir?' said Venus.

'No, Venus, no. The Serpent.'

'You'll have the goodness to notice, Mr Boffin,' remarked Venus, 'that I said nothing to him about my going out of the affair altogether, because I didn't wish to take you anyways by surprise. But I can't be too soon out of it for my satisfaction, Mr Boffin, and I now put it to you when it will suit your views for me to retire?'

'Thank'ee, Venus, thank'ee, Venus; but I don't know what to say,' returned Mr Boffin, 'I don't know what to do. He'll drop down on me any way. He seems fully determined to drop down; don't he?'

Mr Venus opined that such was clearly his intention.

'You might be a sort of protection for me, if you remained in it,' said Mr Boffin; 'you might stand betwixt him and me, and take the edge off him. Don't you feel as if you could make a show of remaining in it, Venus, till I had time to turn myself round?'

Venus naturally inquired how long Mr Boffin thought it might take him to turn himself round?

'I am sure I don't know,' was the answer, given quite at a loss. 'Everything is so at sixes and sevens. If I had never come into the property, I shouldn't have minded. But being in it, it would be very trying to be turned out; now, don't you acknowledge that it would, Venus?'

Mr Venus preferred, he said, to leave Mr Boffin to arrive at his own conclusions on that delicate question.

'I am sure I don't know what to do,' said Mr Boffin. 'If I ask advice of any one else, it's only letting in another person to be bought out, and then I shall be ruined that way, and might as well have given up the property and gone slap to the workhouse. If I was to take advice of my young man, Rokesmith, I should have to buy *him* out. Sooner or later, of course, he'd drop down upon me, like Wegg. I was brought into the world to be dropped down upon, it appears to me.'

Mr Venus listened to these lamentations in silence, while Mr Boffin jogged to and fro, holding his pockets as if he had a pain in them.

'After all, you haven't said what you mean to do yourself, Venus. When you do go out of it, how do you mean to go?'

Venus replied that as Wegg had found the document and handed it to him, it was his intention to hand it back to Wegg, with the declaration that he himself would have nothing to say to it, or do with it, and that Wegg must act as he chose, and take the consequences.

'And then he drops down with his whole weight upon *me*!' cried Mr Boffin, ruefully. 'I'd sooner be dropped upon by you than by him, or even by you jintly, than by him alone!'

Mr Venus could only repeat that it was his fixed intention to betake himself to the paths of science, and to walk in the same all the days of his life; not dropping down upon his fellow-creatures until they were deceased, and then only to articulate them to the best of his humble ability.

'How long could you be persuaded to keep up the appearance of remaining in it?' asked Mr Boffin, retiring on his other idea. 'Could you be got to do so, till the Mounds are gone?'

No. That would protract the mental uneasiness of Mr Venus too long, he said.

'Not if I was to show you reason now?' demanded Mr Boffin; 'not if I was to show you good and sufficient reason?'

If by good and sufficient reason Mr Boffin meant honest and unimpeachable reason, that might weigh with Mr Venus against his personal wishes and convenience. But he must add that he saw no opening to the possibility of such reason being shown him.

'Come and see me, Venus,' said Mr Boffin, 'at my house.'

'Is the reason there, sir?' asked Mr Venus, with an incredulous smile and blink.

'It may be, or may not be,' said Mr Boffin, 'just as you view it. But in the meantime don't go out of the matter. Look here. Do this. Give me your word that you won't take any steps with Wegg, without my knowledge, just as I have given you my word that I won't without yours.'

'Done, Mr Boffin!' said Venus, after brief consideration.

'Thank'ee, Venus, thank'ee, Venus! Done!'

'When shall I come to see you, Mr Boffin.'

'When you like. The sooner the better. I must be going now. Good-night, Venus.'

'Good-night, sir.'

'And good-night to the rest of the present company,' said Mr Boffin, glancing round the shop. 'They make a queer show, Venus, and I should like to be better acquainted with them some day. Good-night, Venus, good-night! Thankee, Venus, thankee, Venus!' With that he jogged out into the street, and jogged upon his homeward way.

'Now, I wonder,' he meditated as he went along, nursing his stick, 'whether it can be, that Venus is setting himself to get the better of Wegg? Whether it can be, that he means, when I have bought Wegg out, to have me all to himself and to pick me clean to the bones!'

It was a cunning and suspicious idea, quite in the way of his school of Misers, and he looked very cunning and suspicious as he went jogging through the streets. More than once or twice, more than twice or thrice, say half a dozen times, he took his stick from the arm on which he nursed it, and hit a straight sharp rap at the air with its head. Possibly the wooden countenance of Mr Silas Wegg was incorporeally before him at those moments, for he hit with intense satisfaction.

He was within a few streets of his own house, when a little private carriage, coming in the contrary direction, passed him, turned round, and passed him again. It was a little carriage of eccentric movement, for again he heard it stop behind him and turn round, and again he saw it pass him. Then it stopped, and then went on, out of sight. But, not far out of sight, for, when he came to the corner of his own street, there it stood again.

There was a lady's face at the window as he came up with this carriage, and he was passing it when the lady softly called to him by his name.

'I beg your pardon, Ma'am?' said Mr Boffin, coming to a stop.

'It is Mrs Lammle,' said the lady.

Mr Boffin went up to the window, and hoped Mrs Lammle was well.

'Not very well, dear Mr. Boffin; I have fluttered myself by being—perhaps foolishly—uneasy and anxious. I have been waiting for you some time. Can I speak to you?'

Mr Boffin proposed that Mrs Lammle should drive on to his house, a few hundred yards further.

'I would rather not, Mr Boffin, unless you particularly wish it. I feel the difficulty and delicacy of the matter so much that I would rather avoid speaking to you at your own home. You must think this very strange?'

Mr Boffin said no, but meant yes.

'It is because I am so grateful for the good opinion of all my friends, and am so touched by it, that I cannot bear to run the risk of forfeiting it in any case, even in the cause of duty. I have asked my husband (my dear Alfred, Mr Boffin) whether it *is* the cause of duty, and he has most emphatically said Yes. I wish I had asked him sooner. It would have spared me much distress.'

('Can this be more dropping down upon me!' thought Mr Boffin, quite bewildered.)

'It was Alfred who sent me to you, Mr Boffin. Alfred said, "Don't come back, Sophronia, until you have seen Mr Boffin, and told him all. Whatever he may think of it, he ought certainly to know it." Would you mind coming into the carriage?'

Mr Boffin answered, 'Not at all,' and took his seat at Mrs Lammle's side.

'Drive slowly anywhere,' Mrs Lammle called to her coachman, 'and don't let the carriage rattle.'

'It *must* be more dropping down, I think,' said Mr Boffin to himself. 'What next?'

Chapter 15
The Golden Dustman at his Worst

THE breakfast table at Mr Boffin's was usually a very pleasant one, and was always presided over by Bella. As though he began each new day in his healthy natural character, and some waking hours were necessary to his relapse into the corrupting influences of his wealth, the face and the demeanour of the Golden Dustman were generally unclouded at that meal. It would have been easy to believe then, that there was no change in him. It was as the day went on that the clouds gathered, and the brightness of the morning became obscured. One might have said that the shadows of avarice and distrust lengthened as his own shadow lengthened, and that the night closed around him gradually.

But, one morning long afterwards to be remembered, it was black midnight with the Golden Dustman when he first appeared. His altered character had never been so grossly marked. His bearing towards his Secretary was so charged with insolent distrust and arrogance, that the latter rose and left the table before breakfast was half done. The look he directed at the Secretary's retiring figure was so cunningly malignant, that Bella would have sat astounded and indignant, even though he had not gone the length of secretly threatening Rokesmith with his clenched fist as he closed the door. This unlucky morning, of all mornings in the year, was the morning next after Mr Boffin's interview with Mrs Lammle in her little carriage.

Bella looked to Mrs Boffin's face for comment on, or explanation of, this stormy humour in her husband, but none was there. An anxious and a distressed observation of her own face was all she could read in it. When they were left alone together— which was not until noon, for Mr Boffin sat long in his easy-chair, by turns jogging up and down the breakfast-room, clenching his fist and muttering—Bella, in consternation, asked her what had happened, what was wrong? 'I am forbidden to speak to you about it, Bella dear; I mustn't tell you,' was all the answer she could get. And still, whenever, in her wonder and dismay, she raised her eyes to Mrs Boffin's face, she saw in it the same anxious and distressed observation of her own.

Oppressed by her sense that trouble was impending, and lost in speculations why Mrs Boffin should look at her as if she had any part in it, Bella found the day long and dreary. It was far on in the afternoon when, she being in her own room, a servant brought her a message from Mr Boffin begging her to come to his.

Mrs Boffin was there, seated on a sofa, and Mr Boffin was jogging up and down. On seeing Bella he stopped, beckoned her to him, and drew her arm through his. 'Don't be alarmed, my dear,' he said, gently; 'I am not angry with you. Why you actually tremble! Don't be alarmed, Bella my dear. I'll see you righted.'

'See me righted?' thought Bella. And then repeated aloud in a tone of astonishment; 'see me righted, sir?'

'Ay, ay!' said Mr Boffin. 'See you righted. Send Mr Rokesmith here, you sir.'

Bella would have been lost in perplexity if there had been

pause enough; but the servant found Mr Rokesmith near at hand, and he almost immediately presented himself.

'Shut the door, sir!' said Mr Boffin. 'I have got something to say to you which I fancy you'll not be pleased to hear.'

'I am sorry to reply, Mr Boffin,' returned the Secretary, as, having closed the door, he turned and faced him, 'that I think that very likely.'

'What do you mean?' blustered Mr Boffin.

'I mean that it has become no novelty to me to hear from your lips what I would rather not hear.'

'Oh! Perhaps we shall change that,' said Mr Boffin with a threatening roll of his head.

'I hope so,' returned the Secretary. He was quiet and respectful; but stood, as Bella thought (and was glad to think), on his manhood too.

'Now, sir,' said Mr Boffin, 'look at this young lady on my arm.'

Bella involuntarily raising her eyes, when this sudden reference was made to herself, met those of Mr Rokesmith. He was pale and seemed agitated. Then her eyes passed on to Mrs Boffin's, and she met the look again. In a flash it enlightened her, and she began to understand what she had done.

'I say to you, sir,' Mr Boffin repeated, 'look at this young lady on my arm.'

'I do so,' returned the Secretary.

As his glance rested again on Bella for a moment, she thought there was reproach in it. But it is possible that the reproach was within herself.

'How dare you, sir' said Mr Boffin, 'tamper, unknown to me, with this young lady? How dare you come out of your station, and your place in my house, to pester this young lady with your impudent addresses?'

'I must decline to answer questions,' said the Secretary, 'that are so offensively asked.'

'You decline to answer?' retorted Mr Boffin. 'You decline to answer, do you? Then I'll tell you what it is, Rokesmith; I'll answer for you. There are two sides to this matter, and I'll take 'em separately. The first side is, sheer Insolence. That's the first side.'

The Secretary smiled with some bitterness, as though he would have said, 'So I see and hear.'

'It was sheer Insolence in you, I tell you,' said Mr Boffin, 'even to think of this young lady. This young lady was far above *you*. This young lady was no match for *you*. This young lady was lying in wait (as she was qualified to do) for money, and you had no money.'

Bella hung her head and seemed to shrink a little from Mr Boffin's protecting arm.

'What are you, I should like to know,' pursued Mr Boffin, 'that you were to have the audacity to follow up this young lady? This young lady was looking about the market for a good bid; she wasn't in it to be snapped up by fellows that had no money to lay out; nothing to buy with.'

'Oh, Mr Boffin! Mrs Boffin, pray say something for me!' murmured Bella, disengaging her arm, and covering her face with her hands.

'Old lady,' said Mr Boffin, anticipating his wife, 'you hold your tongue. Bella, my dear, don't you let yourself be put out. I'll right you.'

'But you don't, you don't right me!' exclaimed Bella, with great emphasis. 'You wrong me, wrong me!'

'Don't you be put out, my dear,' complacently retorted Mr Boffin. 'I'll bring this young man to book. Now, you Rokesmith! You can't decline to hear, you know, as well as to answer. You hear me tell you that the first side of your conduct was Insolence— Insolence and Presumption. Answer me one thing, if you can. Didn't this young lady tell you so herself?'

'Did I, Mr Rokesmith?' asked Bella with her face still covered. 'O say, Mr Rokesmith! Did I?'

'Don't be distressed, Miss Wilfer; it matters very little now.'

'Ah! You can't deny it, though!' said Mr Boffin, with a knowing shake of his head.

'But I have asked him to forgive me since,' cried Bella; 'and I would ask him to forgive me now again, upon my knees, if it would spare him!'

Here Mrs Boffin broke out a-crying.

'Old lady,' said Mr Boffin, 'stop that noise! Tender-hearted in you, Miss Bella; but I mean to have it out right through with this young man, having got him into a corner. Now, you Rokesmith. I tell you that's one side of your conduct—Insolence and Presumption. Now, I'm a-coming to the other, which is much worse. This was a speculation of yours.'

'I indignantly deny it.'

'It's of no use your denying it; it doesn't signify a bit whether you deny it or not; I've got a head upon my shoulders, and it ain't a baby's. What!' said Mr Boffin, gathering himself together in his most suspicious attitude, and wrinkling his face into a very map of curves and corners. 'Don't I know what grabs are made at a man with money? If I didn't keep my eyes open, and my pockets buttoned, shouldn't I be brought to the work-house before I knew where I was? Wasn't the experience of Dancer, and Elwes, and Hopkins, and Blewbury Jones, and ever so many more of 'em, similar to mine? Didn't everybody want to make grabs at what they'd got, and bring 'em to poverty and ruin? Weren't they forced to hide everything belonging to 'em, for fear it should be snatched from 'em? Of course they was. I shall be told next that they didn't know human natur!'

'They! Poor creatures,' murmured the Secretary.

'What do you say?' asked Mr Boffin, snapping at him. 'However, you needn't be at the trouble of repeating it, for it ain't worth hearing, and won't go down with *me*. I'm a-going to unfold your plan, before this young lady; I'm a-going to show this young lady the second view of you; and nothing you can say will stave it off. (Now, attend here, Bella, my dear.) Rokesmith, you're a needy chap. You're a chap that I pick up in the street. Are you, or ain't you?'

'Go on, Mr Boffin; don't appeal to me.'

'Not appeal to *you*,' retorted Mr Boffin as if he hadn't done so. 'No, I should hope not! Appealing to *you*, would be rather a rum course. As I was saying, you're a needy chap that I pick up in the street. You come and ask me in the street to take you for a Secretary, and I take you. Very good.'

'Very bad,' murmured the Secretary.

'What do you say?' asked Mr Boffin, snapping at him again.

He returned no answer. Mr Boffin, after eyeing him with a comical look of discomfited curiosity, was fain to begin afresh.

'This Rokesmith is a needy young man that I take for my Secretary out of the open street. This Rokesmith gets acquainted with my affairs, and gets to know that I mean to settle a sum of money on this young lady. "Oho!" says this Rokesmith;' here Mr Boffin clapped a finger against his nose, and tapped it several times with a sneaking air, as embodying Rokesmith confidentially confabulating with his own nose; ' "This will be a good haul; I'll go in for this!" And so this Rokesmith, greedy and hungering, begins a-creeping on his hands and knees towards the money. Not so bad a speculation either: for if this young lady had had less spirit, or had had less sense, through being at all in the romantic line, by George he might have worked it out and made it pay! But fortunately she was too many for him, and a pretty figure he cuts now he is exposed. There he stands!' said Mr Boffin, addressing Rokesmith himself with ridiculous inconsistency. 'Look at him!'

'Your unfortunate suspicions, Mr Boffin—' began the Secretary.

'Precious unfortunate for *you*, I can tell you,' said Mr Boffin.

'—are not to be combated by any one, and I address myself to no such hopeless task. But I will say a word upon the truth.'

'Yah! Much you care about the truth,' said Mr Boffin, with a snap of his fingers.

'Noddy! My dear love!' expostulated his wife.

'Old lady,' returned Mr Boffin, 'you keep still. I say to this Rokesmith here, much he cares about the truth. I tell him again, much he cares about the truth.'

'Our connexion being at an end, Mr Boffin,' said the Secretary, 'it can be of very little moment to me what you say.'

'Oh! You are knowing enough,' retorted Mr Boffin, with a sly look, 'to have found out that our connexion's at an end, eh? But you can't get beforehand with me. Look at this in my hand. This is your pay, on your discharge. You can only follow suit. You can't deprive me of the lead. Let's have no pretending that you discharge yourself. I discharge you.'

'So that I go,' remarked the Secretary, waving the point aside with his hand, 'it is all one to me.'

'Is it?' said Mr Boffin. 'But it's two to me, let me tell you. Allowing a fellow that's found out, to discharge himself, is one thing; discharging him for insolence and presumption, and likewise for designs upon his master's money, is another. One and one's two; not one. (Old lady, don't you cut in. You keep still.)'

'Have you said all you wish to say to me?' demanded the Secretary.

'I don't know whether I have or not,' answered Mr Boffin. 'It depends.'

'Perhaps you will consider whether there are any other strong expressions that you would like to bestow upon me?'

'I'll consider that,' said Mr Boffin, obstinately, 'at my convenience, and not at yours. You want the last word. It may not be suitable to let you have it.'

'Noddy! My dear, dear Noddy! You sound so hard!' cried poor Mrs Boffin, not to be quite repressed.

'Old lady,' said her husband, but without harshness, 'if you cut in when requested not, I'll get a pillow and carry you out of the room upon it. What do you want to say, you Rokesmith?'

'To you, Mr Boffin, nothing. But to Miss Wilfer and to your good kind wife, a word.'

'Out with it then,' replied Mr Boffin, 'and cut it short, for we've had enough of you.'

'I have borne,' said the Secretary, in a low voice, 'with my false position here, that I might not be separated from Miss Wilfer. To be near her, has been a recompense to me from day to day, even for the undeserved treatment I have had here, and for the degraded aspect in which she has often seen me. Since Miss Wilfer rejected me, I have never again urged my suit, to the best of my belief, with a spoken syllable or a look. But I have never changed in my devotion to her, except—if she will forgive my saying so—that it is deeper than it was, and better founded.'

'Now, mark this chap's saying Miss Wilfer, when he means £ s. d.!' cried Mr Boffin, with a cunning wink. 'Now, mark this chap's making Miss Wilfer stand for Pounds, Shillings, and Pence!'

'My feeling for Miss Wilfer,' pursued the Secretary, without deigning to notice him, 'is not one to be ashamed of. I avow it. I love her. Let me go where I may when I presently leave this house, I shall go into a blank life, leaving her.'

'Leaving £ s. d. behind me,' said Mr Boffin, by way of commentary, with another wink.

'That I am incapable,' the Secretary went on, still without heeding him, 'of a mercenary project, or a mercenary thought, in connexion with Miss Wilfer, is nothing meritorious in me, because any prize that I could put before my fancy would sink into insignificance beside her. If the greatest wealth or the highest rank were hers, it would only be important in my sight as removing her still farther from me, and making me more hopeless, if that could be. Say,' remarked the Secretary, looking full at his late master, 'say that with a word she could strip Mr Boffin of his fortune and take possession of it, she would be of no greater worth in my eyes than she is.'

'What do you think by this time, old lady,' asked Mr Boffin, turning to his wife in a bantering tone, 'about this Rokesmith here, and his caring for the truth? You needn't say what you think, my dear, because I don't want you to cut in, but you can think it all the same. As to taking possession of my property, I warrant you he wouldn't do that himself if he could.'

'No,' returned the Secretary, with another full look.

'Ha, ha, ha!' laughed Mr Boffin. 'There's nothing like a good 'un while you *are* about it.'

'I have been for a moment,' said the Secretary, turning from him and falling into his former manner, 'diverted from the little I have to say. My interest in Miss Wilfer began when I first saw her; even began when I had only heard of her. It was, in fact, the cause of my throwing myself in Mr Boffin's way, and entering his service. Miss Wilfer has never known this until now. I mention it now, only as a corroboration (though I hope it may be needless) of my being free from the sordid design attributed to me.'

'Now, this is a very artful dog,' said Mr Boffin, with a deep look. 'This is a longer-headed schemer than I thought him. See how patiently and methodically he goes to work. He gets to know about me and my property, and about this young lady, and her share in poor young John's story, and he puts this and that together, and he says to himself, "I'll get in with Boffin, and I'll get in with this young lady, and I'll work 'em both at the same time, and I'll bring my pigs to market somewhere." I hear him say it, bless you! I look at him, now, and I see him say it!'

Mr Boffin pointed at the culprit, as it were in the act, and hugged himself in his great penetration.

'But luckily he hadn't to deal with the people he supposed, Bella, my dear!' said Mr Boffin. 'No! Luckily he had to deal with you, and with me, and with Daniel and Miss Dancer, and with Elwes, and with Vulture Hopkins, and with Blewbury Jones and all the rest of us, one down t'other come on. And he's beat; that's what he is; regularly beat. He thought to squeeze money out of us, and he has done for himself instead, Bella my dear!'

Bella my dear made no response, gave no sign of acquiescence. When she had first covered her face she had sunk upon a chair with her hands resting on the back of it, and had never moved since. There was a short silence at this point, and Mrs Boffin softly rose as if to go to her. But, Mr Boffin stopped her with a gesture, and she obediently sat down again and stayed where she was.

'There's your pay, Mister Rokesmith,' said the Golden Dustman, jerking the folded scrap of paper he had in his hand, towards his late Secretary. 'I dare say you can stoop to pick it up, after what you have stooped to here.'

'I have stooped to nothing but this,' Rokesmith answered as he took it from the ground; 'and this is mine, for I have earned it by the hardest of hard labour.'

'You're a pretty quick packer, I hope,' said Mr Boffin; 'because the sooner you are gone, bag and baggage, the better for all parties.'

'You need have no fear of my lingering.'

'There's just one thing though,' said Mr Boffin, 'that I should like to ask you before we come to a good riddance, if it was only to show this young lady how conceited you schemers are, in thinking that nobody finds out how you contradict yourselves.'

'Ask me anything you wish to ask,' returned Rokesmith, 'but use the expedition that you recommend.'

'You pretend to have a mighty admiration for this young lady?' said Mr Boffin, laying his hand protectingly on Bella's head without looking down at her.

'I do not pretend.'

'Oh! Well. You *have* a mighty admiration for this young lady—since you are so particular?'

'Yes.'

'How do you reconcile that, with this young lady's being a weak-spirited, improvident idiot, not knowing what was due to herself, flinging up her money to the church-weathercocks, and racing off at a splitting pace for the workhouse?'

'I don't understand you.'

'Don't you? Or won't you? What else could you have made this young lady out to be, if she had listened to such addresses as yours?'

'What else, if I had been so happy as to win her affections and possess her heart?'

'Win her affections,' retorted Mr Boffin, with ineffable contempt, 'and possess her heart! Mew says the cat, Quack-quack says the duck, Bow-wow-wow says the dog! Win her affections and possess her heart! Mew, Quack-quack, Bow-wow!'

John Rokesmith stared at him in his outburst, as if with some faint idea that he had gone mad.

'What is due to this young lady,' said Mr Boffin, 'is Money, and this young lady right well knows it.'

'You slander the young lady.'

'*You* slander the young lady; you with your affections and hearts and trumpery,' returned Mr Boffin. 'It's of a piece with the rest of your behaviour. I heard of these doings of yours only last night, or you should have heard of 'em from me, sooner, take your oath of it. I heard of 'em from a lady with as good a headpiece as the best, and she knows this young lady, and I know this young lady, and we all three know that it's Money she makes a stand for—money, money, money—and that you and your affections and hearts are a Lie, sir!'

'Mrs Boffin,' said Rokesmith, quietly turning to her, 'for your delicate and unvarying kindness I thank you with the warmest gratitude. Good-bye! Miss Wilfer, good-bye!'

'And now, my dear;' said Mr Boffin, laying his hand on Bella's head again, 'you may begin to make yourself quite comfortable, and I hope you feel that you've been righted.'

But, Bella was so far from appearing to feel it, that she shrank from his hand and from the chair, and, starting up in an incoherent passion of tears, and stretching out her arms, cried, 'O Mr Rokesmith, before you go, if you could but make me poor again! O! Make me poor again, Somebody, I beg and pray, or my heart will break if this goes on! Pa, dear, make me poor again and take me home! I was bad enough there, but I have been so much worse here. Don't give me money, Mr Boffin, I won't have money. Keep it away from me, and only let me speak to good little Pa, and lay my head upon his shoulder, and tell him all my griefs. Nobody else can understand me, nobody else can comfort me, nobody else knows how unworthy I am, and yet can love me like a little child. I am better with Pa than any one—more innocent, more sorry, more glad!' So, crying out in a wild way that she could not bear this, Bella drooped her head on Mrs Boffin's ready breast.

John Rokesmith from his place in the room, and Mr Boffin from his, looked on at her in silence until she was silent herself. Then Mr Boffin observed in a soothing and comfortable tone, 'There, my dear, there; you are righted now, and it's *all* right. I don't wonder, I'm sure, at your being a little flurried by having a scene with this fellow, but it's all over, my dear, and you're righted, and it's—and it's *all* right!' Which Mr Boffin repeated with a highly satisfied air of completeness and finality.

'I hate you!' cried Bella, turning suddenly upon him, with a stamp of her little foot—'at least, I can't hate you, but I don't like you!'

'Hul—lo!' exclaimed Mr Boffin in an amazed under-tone.

'You're a scolding, unjust, abusive, aggravating, bad old creature!' cried Bella. 'I am angry with my ungrateful self for calling you names; but you are, you are; you know you are!'

Mr Boffin stared here, and stared there, as misdoubting that he must be in some sort of fit.

'I have heard you with shame,' said Bella. 'With shame for myself, and with shame for you. You ought to be above the base tale-bearing of a time-serving woman; but you are above nothing now.'

Mr Boffin, seeming to become convinced that this was a fit, rolled his eyes and loosened his neckcloth.

'When I came here, I respected you and honoured you, and I soon loved you,' cried Bella. 'And now I can't bear the sight of you. At least, I don't know that I ought to go so far as that—only you're a—you're a Monster!' Having shot this bolt out with a great expenditure of force, Bella hysterically laughed and cried together.

'The best wish I can wish you is,' said Bella, returning to the charge, 'that you had not one single farthing in the world. If any true friend and well-wisher could make you a bankrupt, you would be a Duck; but as a man of property you are a Demon!'

After despatching this second bolt with a still greater expenditure of force, Bella laughed and cried still more.

'Mr Rokesmith, pray stay one moment. Pray hear one word from me before you go! I am deeply sorry for the reproaches you have borne on my account. Out of the depths of my heart I earnestly and truly beg your pardon.'

As she stepped towards him, he met her. As she gave him her hand, he put it to his lips, and said, 'God bless you!' No laughing was mixed with Bella's crying then; her tears were pure and fervent.

'There is not an ungenerous word that I have heard addressed to you—heard with scorn and indignation, Mr Rokesmith—but it has wounded me far more than you, for I have deserved it, and you never have. Mr Rokesmith, it is to me you owe this perverted account of what passed between us that night. I parted with the secret, even while I was angry with myself for doing so. It was very bad in me, but indeed it was not wicked. I did it in a moment of conceit and folly—one of my many such moments—one of my many such hours—years. As I am punished for it severely, try to forgive it!'

'I do with all my soul.'

'Thank you. O thank you! Don't part from me till I have said one other word, to do you justice. The only fault you can be truly charged with, in having spoken to me as you did that night—with how much delicacy and how much forbearance no one but I can know or be grateful to you for—is, that you laid

yourself open to be slighted by a worldly shallow girl whose
head was turned, and who was quite unable to rise to the worth
of what you offered her. Mr Rokesmith, that girl has often seen
herself in a pitiful and poor light since, but never in so pitiful
and poor a light as now, when the mean tone in which she
answered you—sordid and vain girl that she was—has been
echoed in her ears by Mr Boffin.'

He kissed her hand again.

'Mr Boffin's speeches were detestable to me, shocking to
me,' said Bella, startling that gentleman with another stamp of
her little foot. 'It is quite true that there was a time, and very
lately, when I deserved to be so "righted," Mr. Rokesmith; but
I hope that I shall never deserve it again!'

He once more put her hand to his lips, and then relinquished
it, and left the room. Bella was hurrying back to the chair in
which she had hidden her face so long, when, catching sight of
Mrs Boffin by the way, she stopped at her. 'He is gone,' sobbed
Bella indignantly, despairingly, in fifty ways at once, with her
arms round Mrs Boffin's neck. 'He has been most shamefully
abused, and most unjustly and most basely driven away, and I
am the cause of it!'

All this time, Mr Boffin had been rolling his eyes over his
loosened neckerchief, as if his fit were still upon him. Appearing
now to think that he was coming to, he stared straight before him
for a while, tied his neckerchief again, took several long inspira-
tions, swallowed several times, and ultimately exclaimed with a
deep sigh, as if he felt himself on the whole better: 'Well!'

No word, good or bad, did Mrs Boffin say; but she tenderly
took care of Bella, and glanced at her husband as if for orders.
Mr Boffin, without imparting any, took his seat on a chair over
against them, and there sat leaning forward, with a fixed countenance, his legs apart, a hand on each knee, and his elbows
squared, until Bella should dry her eyes and raise her head,
which in the fulness of time she did.

'I must go home,' said Bella, rising hurriedly. 'I am very
grateful to you for all you have done for me, but I can't stay
here.'

'My darling girl!' remonstrated Mrs Boffin.

'No, I can't stay here,' said Bella; 'I can't indeed.—Ugh!
you vicious old thing!' (This to Mr Boffin.)

'Don't be rash, my love,' urged Mrs Boffin. 'Think well of
what you do.'

'Yes, you had better think well,' said Mr Boffin.

'I shall never more think well of *you*,' cried Bella, cutting him short, with intense defiance in her expressive little eyebrows, and championship of the late Secretary in every dimple. 'No! Never again! Your money has changed you to marble. You are a hard-hearted Miser. You are worse than Dancer, worse than Hopkins, worse than Blackberry Jones, worse than any of the wretches. And more!' proceeded Bella, breaking into tears again, 'you were wholly undeserving of the Gentleman you have lost.'

'Why, you don't mean to say, Miss Bella,' the Golden Dustman slowly remonstrated, 'that you set up Rokesmith against me?'

'I do!' said Bella. 'He is worth a Million of you.'

Very pretty she looked, though very angry, as she made herself as tall as she possibly could (which was not extremely tall), and utterly renounced her patron with a lofty toss of her rich brown head.

'I would rather he thought well of me,' said Bella, 'though he swept the street for bread, than that you did, though you splashed the mud upon him from the wheels of a chariot of pure gold.—There!'

'Well I'm sure!' cried Mr Boffin, staring.

'And for a long time past, when you have thought you set yourself above him, I have only seen you under his feet,' said Bella—'There! And throughout I saw in him the master, and I saw in you the man—There! And when you used him shamefully, I took his part and loved him—There! I boast of it!'

After which strong avowal Bella underwent reaction, and cried to any extent, with her face on the back of her chair.

'Now, look here,' said Mr Boffin, as soon as he could find an opening for breaking the silence and striking in. 'Give me your attention, Bella. I am not angry.'

'I *am*!' said Bella.

'I say,' resumed the Golden Dustman, 'I am not angry, and I mean kindly to you, and I want to overlook this. So you'll stay where you are, and we'll agree to say no more about it.'

'No, I can't stay here,' cried Bella, rising hurriedly again; 'I can't think of staying here. I must go home for good.'

'Now, don't be silly,' Mr Boffin reasoned. 'Don't do what you can't undo; don't do what you're sure to be sorry for.'

'I shall never be sorry for it,' said Bella; 'and I should always be sorry, and should every minute of my life despise myself, if I remained here after what has happened.'

'At least, Bella,' argued Mr Boffin, 'let there be no mistake about it. Look before you leap, you know. Stay where you are, and all's well, and all's as it was to be. Go away, and you can never come back.'

'I know that I can never come back, and that's what I mean,' said Bella.

'You mustn't expect,' Mr Boffin pursued, 'that I'm a-going to settle money on you, if you leave us like this, because I am not. No, Bella! Be careful! Not one brass farthing.'

'Expect!' said Bella, haughtily. 'Do you think that any power on earth could make me take it, if you did, sir?'

But there was Mrs Boffin to part from, and, in the full flush of her dignity, the impressible little soul collapsed again. Down upon her knees before that good woman, she rocked herself upon her breast, and cried, and sobbed, and folded her in her arms with all her might.

'You're a dear, a dear, the best of dears!' cried Bella. 'You're the best of human creatures. I can never be thankful enough to you, and I can never forget you. If I should live to be blind and deaf, I know I shall see and hear you, in my fancy, to the last of my dim old days!'

Mrs Boffin wept most heartily, and embraced her with all fondness; but said not one single word except that she was her dear girl. She said that often enough, to be sure, for she said it over and over again; but not one word else.

Bella broke from her at length, and was going weeping out of the room, when in her own little queer affectionate way, she half relented towards Mr Boffin.

'I am very glad,' sobbed Bella, 'that I called you names, sir, because you richly deserved it. But I am very sorry that I called you names, because you used to be so different. Say good-bye!'

'Good-bye,' said Mr Boffin, shortly.

'If I knew which of your hands was the least spoilt, I would ask you to let me touch it,' said Bella, 'for the last time. But not because I repent of what I have said to you. For I don't. It's true!'

'Try the left hand,' said Mr Boffin, holding it out in a stolid manner; 'it's the least used.'

'You have been wonderfully good and kind to me,' said Bella, 'and I kiss it for that. You have been as bad as bad could be to Mr Rokesmith, and I throw it away for that. Thank you for myself, and good-bye!'

'Good-bye,' said Mr Boffin as before.

Bella caught him round the neck and kissed him, and ran out for ever.

She ran up-stairs, and sat down on the floor in her own room, and cried abundantly. But the day was declining and she had no time to lose. She opened all the places where she kept her dresses; selected only those she had brought with her, leaving all the rest; and made a great misshapen bundle of them, to be sent for afterwards.

'I won't take one of the others,' said Bella, tying the knots of the bundle very tight, in the severity of her resolution. 'I'll leave all the presents behind, and begin again entirely on my own account.' That the resolution might be thoroughly carried into practice, she even changed the dress she wore, for that in which she had come to the grand mansion. Even the bonnet she put on, was the bonnet that had mounted into the Boffin chariot at Holloway.

'Now, I am complete,' said Bella. 'It's a little trying, but I have steeped my eyes in cold water, and I won't cry any more. You have been a pleasant room to me, dear room. Adieu! We shall never see each other again.'

With a parting kiss of her fingers to it, she softly closed the door and went with a light foot down the great staircase, pausing and listening as she went, that she might meet none of the household. No one chanced to be about, and she got down to the hall in quiet. The door of the late Secretary's room stood open. She peeped in as she passed, and divined from the emptiness of his table, and the general appearance of things, that he was already gone. Softly opening the great hall door, and softly closing it upon herself, she turned and kissed it on the outside—insensible old combination of wood and iron that it was!—before she ran away from the house at a swift pace.

'That was well done!' panted Bella, slackening in the next street, and subsiding into a walk. ''If I had left myself any breath to cry with, I should have cried again. Now poor dear darling little Pa, you are going to see your lovely woman unexpectedly.'

Chapter 16

The Feast of the Three Hobgoblins

THE City looked unpromising enough, as Bella made her way along its gritty streets. Most of its money-mills were slackening sail, or had left off grinding for the day. The master-millers had already departed, and the journeymen were departing. There was a jaded aspect on the business lanes and courts, and the very pavements had a weary appearance, confused by the tread of a million of feet. There must be hours of night to temper down the day's distraction of so feverish a place. As yet the worry of the newly-stopped whirling and grinding on the part of the money-mills seemed to linger in the air, and the quiet was more like the prostration of a spent giant than the repose of one who was renewing his strength.

If Bella thought, as she glanced at the mighty Bank, how agreeable it would be to have an hour's gardening there, with a bright copper shovel, among the money, still she was not in an avaricious vein. Much improved in that respect, and with certain half-formed images which had little gold in their composition, dancing before her bright eyes, she arrived in the drug-flavoured region of Mincing Lane, with the sensation of having just opened a drawer in a chemist's shop.

The counting-house of Chicksey, Veneering, and Stobbles was pointed out by an elderly female accustomed to the care of offices, who dropped upon Bella out of a public-house, wiping her mouth, and accounted for its humidity on natural principles well known to the physical sciences, by explaining that she had looked in at the door to see what o'clock it was. The counting-house was a wall-eyed ground floor by a dark gateway, and Bella was considering, as she approached it, could there be any precedent in the City for her going in and asking for R. Wilfer, when whom should she see, sitting at one of the windows with the plate-glass sash raised, but R. Wilfer himself, preparing to take a slight refection!

On approaching nearer, Bella discerned that the refection had the appearance of a small cottage-loaf and a pennyworth of milk. Simultaneously with this discovery on her part, her father discovered her, and invoked the echoes of Mincing Lane to exclaim 'My gracious me!'

He then came cherubically flying out without a hat, and embraced her, and handed her in. 'For it's after hours and I am all alone, my dear,' he explained, 'and am having—as I sometimes do when they are all gone—a quiet tea.'

Looking round the office, as if her father were a captive and this his cell, Bella hugged him and choked him to her heart's content.

'I never was so surprised, my dear!' said her father. 'I couldn't believe my eyes. Upon my life, I thought they had taken to lying! The idea of your coming down the Lane yourself! Why didn't you send the footman down the Lane, my dear?'

'I have brought no footman with me, Pa.'

'Oh indeed! But you have brought the elegant turn-out, my love?'

'No, Pa.'

'You never can have walked, my dear?'

'Yes, I have Pa.'

He looked so very much astonished, that Bella could not make up her mind to break it to him just yet.

'The consequence is, Pa, that your lovely woman feels a little faint, and would very much like to share your tea.'

The cottage loaf and the pennyworth of milk had been set forth on a sheet of paper on the window-seat. The cherubic pocket-knife, with the first bit of the loaf still on its point, lay beside them where it had been hastily thrown down. Bella took the bit off, and put it in her mouth. 'My dear child,' said her father, 'the idea of your partaking of such lowly fare! But at least you must have your own loaf and your own penn'orth. One moment, my dear. The Dairy is just over the way and round the corner.'

Regardless of Bella's dissuasions he ran out, and quickly returned with the new supply. 'My dear child,' he said, as he spread it on another piece of paper before her, 'the idea of a splendid—!' and then looked at her figure, and stopped short.

'What's the matter, Pa?'

'—of a splendid female,' he resumed more slowly, 'putting up with such accommodation as the present!—Is that a new dress you have on, my dear?'

'No, Pa, an old one. Don't you remember it?'

'Why, I *thought* I remembered it, my dear!'

'You should, for you bought it, Pa.'

'Yes, I *thought* I bought it my dear!' said the cherub, giving himself a little shake, as if to rouse his faculties.

'And have you grown so fickle that you don't like your own taste, Pa dear?'

'Well, my love,' he returned, swallowing a bit of the cottage loaf with considerable effort, for it seemed to stick by the way: 'I should have thought it was hardly sufficiently splendid for existing circumstances.'

'And so, Pa,' said Bella, moving coaxingly to his side instead of remaining opposite, 'you sometimes have a quiet tea here all alone? I am not in the tea's way, if I draw my arm over your shoulder like this, Pa?'

'Yes, my dear, and no, my dear. Yes to the first question, and Certainly Not to the second. Respecting the quiet tea, my dear, why you see the occupations of the day are sometimes a little wearing; and if there's nothing interposed between the day and your mother, why *she* is sometimes a little wearing, too.'

'I know, Pa.'

'Yes, my dear. So sometimes I put a quiet tea at the window here, with a little quiet contemplation of the Lane (which comes soothing), between the day, and domestic—'

'Bliss,' suggested Bella, sorrowfully.

'And domestic Bliss,' said her father, quite contented to accept the phrase.

Bella kissed him. 'And it is in this dark dingy place of captivity, poor dear, that you pass all the hours of your life when you are not at home?'

'Not at home, or not on the road there, or on the road here, my love. Yes. You see that little desk in the corner?'

'In the dark corner, furthest both from the light and from the fireplace? The shabbiest desk of all the desks?'

'Now, does it really strike you in that point of view, my dear?' said her father, surveying it artistically with his head on one side: 'that's mine. That's called Rumty's Perch.'

'Whose Perch?' asked Bella with great indignation.

'Rumty's. You see, being rather high and up two steps they call it a Perch. And they call *me* Rumty.'

'How dare they!' exclaimed Bella.

'They're playful, Bella my dear; they're playful. They're more or less younger than I am, and they're playful. What does it matter? It might be Surly, or Sulky, or fifty disagreeable things that I really shouldn't like to be considered. But Rumty! Lor, why not Rumty?'

To inflict a heavy disappointment on this sweet nature, which had been, through all her caprices, the object of her recognition, love, and admiration from infancy, Bella felt to be the hardest task of her hard day. 'I should have done better,' she thought, 'to tell him at first; I should have done better to tell him just now, when he had some slight misgiving; he is quite happy again, and I shall make him wretched.'

He was falling back on his loaf and milk, with the pleasantest composure, and Bella stealing her arm a little closer about him, and at the same time sticking up his hair with an irresistible propensity to play with him founded on the habit of her whole life, had prepared herself to say: 'Pa dear, don't be cast down, but I must tell you something disagreeable!' when he interrupted her in an unlooked-for manner.

'My gracious me!' he exclaimed, invoking the Mincing Lane echoes as before. 'This is very extraordinary!'

'What is, Pa?'

'Why here's Mr Rokesmith now!'

'No, no, Pa, no,' cried Bella, greatly flurried. 'Surely not.'

'Yes there is! Look here!'

Sooth to say, Mr Rokesmith not only passed the window, but came into the counting-house. And not only came into the counting-house, but, finding himself alone there with Bella and her father, rushed at Bella and caught her in his arms, with the rapturous words 'My dear, dear girl; my gallant, generous, disinterested, courageous, noble girl!' And not only that even, (which one might have thought astonishment enough for one dose), but Bella, after hanging her head for a moment, lifted it up and laid it on his breast, as if that were her head's chosen and lasting resting-place!

'I knew you would come to him, and I followed you,' said Rokesmith. 'My love, my life! You ARE mine?'

To which Bella responded, 'Yes, I AM yours if you think me worth taking!' And after that, seemed to shrink to next to nothing in the clasp of his arms, partly because it was such a strong one on his part, and partly because there was such a yielding to it on hers.

The cherub, whose hair would have done for itself, under the influence of this amazing spectacle, what Bella had just now done for it, staggered back into the window-seat from which he had risen, and surveyed the pair with his eyes dilated to their utmost.

'But we must think of dear Pa,' said Bella; 'I haven't told dear Pa; let us speak to Pa.' Upon which they turned to do so.

'I wish first, my dear,' remarked the cherub faintly, 'that you'd have the kindness to sprinkle me with a little milk, for I feel as if I was—Going.'

In fact, the good little fellow had become alarmingly limp, and his senses seemed to be rapidly escaping, from the knees upward. Bella sprinkled him with kisses instead of milk, but gave him a little of that article to drink; and he gradually revived under her caressing care.

'We'll break it to you gently, dearest Pa,' said Bella.

'My dear,' returned the cherub, looking at them both, 'you broke so much in the first—Gush, if I may so express myself— that I think I am equal to a good large breakage now.'

'Mr Wilfer,' said John Rokesmith, excitedly and joyfully, 'Bella takes me, though I have no fortune, even no present occupation; nothing but what I can get in the life before us. Bella takes me!'

'Yes, I should rather have inferred, my dear sir,' returned the cherub feebly, 'that Bella took you, from what I have within these few minutes remarked.'

'You don't know, Pa,' said Bella, 'how ill I have used him!'

'You don't know, sir,' said Rokesmith, 'what a heart she has!'

'You don't know, Pa,' said Bella, 'what a shocking creature I was growing, when he saved me from myself!'

'You don't know, sir,' said Rokesmith, 'what a sacrifice she has made for me!'

'My dear Bella,' replied the cherub, still pathetically scared, 'and my dear John Rokesmith, if you will allow me so to call you—'

'Yes do, Pa, do!' urged Bella. '*I* allow you, and my will is his law. Isn't it—dear John Rokesmith?'

There was an engaging shyness in Bella, coupled with an engaging tenderness of love and confidence and pride, in thus first calling him by name, which made it quite excusable in John Rokesmith to do what he did. What he did was, once more to give her the appearance of vanishing as aforesaid.

'I think, my dears,' observed the cherub, 'that if you could make it convenient to sit one on one side of me, and the other on the other, we should get on rather more consecutively, and make things rather plainer. John Rokesmith mentioned, a while ago, that he had no present occupation.'

'None,' said Rokesmith.

'No, Pa, none,' said Bella.

'From which I argue,' proceeded the cherub, 'that he has left Mr Boffin?'

'Yes, Pa. And so—'

'Stop a bit, my dear. I wish to lead up to it by degrees. And that Mr Boffin has not treated him well?'

'Has treated him most shamefully, dear Pa!' cried Bella with a flashing face.

'Of which,' pursued the cherub, enjoining patience with his hand, 'a certain mercenary young person distantly related to myself, could not approve? Am I leading up to it right?'

'Could not approve, sweet Pa,' said Bella, with a tearful laugh and a joyful kiss.

'Upon which,' pursued the cherub, 'the certain mercenary young person distantly related to myself, having previously observed and mentioned to myself that prosperity was spoiling Mr Boffin, felt that she must not sell her sense of what was right and what was wrong, and what was true and what was false, and what was just and what was unjust, for any price that could be paid to her by any one alive? Am I leading up to it right?'

With another tearful laugh Bella joyfully kissed him again.

'And therefore—and therefore,' the cherub went on in a glowing voice, as Bella's hand stole gradually up his waistcoat to his neck, 'this mercenary young person distantly related to myself, refused the price, took off the splendid fashions that were part of it, put on the comparatively poor dress that I had last given her, and trusting to my supporting her in what was right, came straight to me. Have I led up to it?'

Bella's hand was round his neck by this time, and her face was on it.

'The mercenary young person distantly related to myself,' said her good father, 'did well! The mercenary young person distantly related to myself, did not trust to me in vain! I admire this mercenary young person distantly related to myself, more in this dress than if she had come to me in China silks, Cashmere shawls, and Golconda diamonds. I love this young person dearly. I say to the man of this young person's heart, out of my heart and with all of it, ''My blessing on this engagement betwixt you, and she brings you a good fortune when she brings you the poverty she has accepted for your sake and the honest truth's!'' '

The stanch little man's voice failed him as he gave John Rokesmith his hand, and he was silent, bending his face low over his daughter. But, not for long. He soon looked up, saying in a sprightly tone:

'And now, my dear child, if you think you can entertain John Rokesmith for a minute and a half, I'll run over to the Dairy, and fetch *him* a cottage loaf and a drink of milk, that we may all have tea together.'

It was, as Bella gaily said, like the supper provided for the three nursery hobgoblins at their house in the forest, without their thunderous low growlings of the alarming discovery, 'Somebody's been drinking *my* milk!' It was a delicious repast; by far the most delicious that Bella, or John Rokesmith, or even R. Wilfer had ever made. The uncongenial oddity of its surroundings, with the two brass knobs of the iron safe of Chicksey, Veneering, and Stobbles staring from a corner, like the eyes of some dull dragon, only made it the more delightful.

'To think,' said the cherub, looking round the office with unspeakable enjoyment, 'that anything of a tender nature should come off here, is what tickles me. To think that ever I should have seen my Bella folded in the arms of her future husband, *here,* you know!'

It was not until the cottage loaves and the milk had for some time disappeared, and the foreshadowings of night were creeping over Mincing Lane, that the cherub by degrees became a little nervous, and said to Bella, as he cleared his throat:

'Hem!—Have you thought at all about your mother, my dear?'

'Yes, Pa.'

'And your sister Lavvy, for instance, my dear?'

'Yes, Pa. I think we had better not enter into particulars at home. I think it will be quite enough to say that I had a difference with Mr Boffin, and have left for good.'

'John Rokesmith being acquainted with your Ma, my love,' said her father, after some slight hesitation, 'I need have no delicacy in hinting before him that you may perhaps find your Ma a little wearing.'

'A little, patient Pa?' said Bella with a tuneful laugh: the tunefuller for being so loving in its tone.

'Well! We'll say, strictly in confidence among ourselves, wearing; we won't qualify it,' the cherub stoutly admitted. 'And your sister's temper is wearing.'

'I don't mind, Pa.'

'And you must prepare yourself, you know, my precious,' said her father, with much gentleness, 'for our looking very poor and meagre at home, and being at the best but very uncomfortable, after Mr Boffin's house.'

'I don't mind, Pa. I could bear much harder trials—for John.'

The closing words were not so softly and blushingly said but that John heard them, and showed that he heard them by again assisting Bella to another of those mysterious disappearances.

'Well!' said the cherub gaily, and not expressing disapproval, 'when you—when you come back from retirement, my love, and reappear on the surface, I think it will be time to lock up and go.'

If the counting-house of Chicksey, Veneering, and Stobbles had ever been shut up by three happier people, glad as most people were to shut it up, they must have been superlatively happy indeed. But first Bella mounted upon Rumty's Perch, and said, 'Show me what you do here all day long, dear Pa. Do you write like this?' laying her round cheek upon her plump left arm, and losing sight of her pen in waves of hair, in a highly unbusinesslike manner. Though John Rokesmith seemed to like it.

So, the three hobgoblins, having effaced all traces of their feast, and swept up the crumbs, came out of Mincing Lane to walk to Holloway; and if two of the hobgoblins didn't wish the distance twice as long as it was, the third hobgoblin was much mistaken. Indeed, that modest spirit deemed himself so much in the way of their deep enjoyment of the journey, that he apologetically remarked: 'I think, my dears, I'll take the lead on the other side of the road, and seem not to belong to you.' Which he did, cherubically strewing the path with smiles, in the absence of flowers.

It was almost ten o'clock when they stopped within view of Wilfer Castle; and then, the spot being quiet and deserted, Bella began a series of disappearances which threatened to last all night.

'I think, John,' the cherub hinted at last, 'that if you can spare me the young person distantly related to myself, I'll take her in.'

'I can't spare her,' answered John, 'but I must lend her to you.—My Darling!' A word of magic which caused Bella instantly to disappear again.

'Now, dearest Pa,' said Bella, when she became visible,

'put your hand in mine, and we'll run home as fast as ever we can run, and get it over. Now, Pa. Once!—'

'My dear,' the cherub faltered, with something of a craven air, 'I was going to observe that if your mother—'

'You mustn't hang back, sir, to gain time,' cried Bella, putting out her right foot; 'do you see that, sir? That's the mark; come up to the mark, sir. Once! Twice! Three times and away, Pa!' Off she skimmed, bearing the cherub along, nor ever stopped, nor suffered him to stop, until she had pulled at the bell. 'Now, dear Pa,' said Bella, taking him by both ears as if he were a pitcher, and conveying his face to her rosy lips, 'we are in for it!'

Miss Lavvy came out to open the gate, waited on by that attentive cavalier and friend of the family, Mr George Sampson. 'Why, it's never Bella!' exclaimed Miss Lavvy starting back at the sight. And then bawled, 'Ma! Here's Bella!'

This produced, before they could get into the house, Mrs Wilfer. Who, standing in the portal, received them with ghostly gloom, and all her other appliances of ceremony.

'My child is welcome, though unlooked for,' said she, at the time presenting her cheek as if it were a cool slate for visitors to enrol themselves upon. 'You too, R. W., are welcome, though late. Does the male domestic of Mrs Boffin hear me there?' This deep-toned inquiry was cast forth into the night, for response from the menial in question.

'There is no one waiting, Ma, dear,' said Bella.

'There is no one waiting?' repeated Mrs Wilfer in majestic accents.

'No, Ma, dear.'

A dignified shiver pervaded Mrs Wilfer's shoulders and gloves, as who should say, 'An Enigma!' and then she marched at the head of the procession to the family keeping-room, where she observed:

'Unless, R. W.': who started on being solemnly turned upon: 'you have taken the precaution of making some addition to our frugal supper on your way home, it will prove but a distasteful one to Bella. Cold neck of mutton and a lettuce can ill compete with the luxuries of Mr Boffin's board.'

'Pray don't talk like that, Ma dear,' said Bella; 'Mr Boffin's board is nothing to me.'

But, here Miss Lavinia, who had been intently eyeing Bella's bonnet, struck in with 'Why, Bella!'

'Yes, Lavvy, I know.'

The Irrepressible lowered her eyes to Bella's dress, and stooped to look at it, exclaiming again: 'Why, Bella!'

'Yes, Lavvy, I know what I have got on. I was going to tell Ma when you interrupted. I have left Mr Boffin's house for good, Ma, and I have come home again.'

Mrs Wilfer spake no word, but, having glared at her offspring for a minute or two in an awful silence, retired into her corner of state backward, and sat down: like a frozen article on sale in a Russian market.

'In short, dear Ma,' said Bella, taking off the depreciated bonnet and shaking out her hair, 'I have had a very serious difference with Mr Boffin on the subject of his treatment of a member of his household, and it's a final difference, and there's an end of all.'

'And I am bound to tell you, my dear,' added R. W., submissively, 'that Bella has acted in a truly brave spirit, and with a truly right feeling. And therefore I hope, my dear, you'll not allow yourself to be greatly disappointed.'

'George!' said Miss Lavvy, in a sepulchral, warning voice, founded on her mother's; 'George Sampson, speak! What did I tell you about those Boffins?'

Mr Sampson perceiving his frail bark to be labouring among shoals and breakers, thought it safest not to refer back to any particular thing that he had been told, lest he should refer back to the wrong thing. With admirable seamanship he got his bark into deep water by murmuring 'Yes indeed.'

'Yes! I told George Sampson, as George Sampson tells you,' said Miss Lavvy, 'that those hateful Boffins would pick a quarrel with Bella, as soon as her novelty had worn off. Have they done it, or have they not? Was I right, or was I wrong? And what do you say to us, Bella, of your Boffins now?'

'Lavvy and Ma,' said Bella, 'I say of Mr and Mrs Boffin what I always have said; and I always shall say of them what I always have said. But nothing will induce me to quarrel with any one to-night. I hope you are not sorry to see me, Ma dear,' kissing her; 'and I hope you are not sorry to see me, Lavvy,' kissing her too; 'and as I notice the lettuce Ma mentioned, on the table, I'll make the salad.'

Bella playfully setting herself about the task, Mrs Wilfer's impressive countenance followed her with glaring eyes, presenting a combination of the once popular sign of the Saracen's Head, with a piece of Dutch clock-work, and suggesting to an imaginative mind that from the composition of the salad, her daughter might prudently omit the vinegar. But no word issued from the majestic matron's lips. And this was more terrific to her husband (as perhaps she knew) than any flow of eloquence with which she could have edified the company.

'Now, Ma dear,' said Bella in due course, 'the salad's ready, and it's past supper-time.'

Mrs Wilfer rose, but remained speechless. 'George!' said Miss Lavinia in her voice of warning, 'Ma's chair!' Mr Sampson flew to the excellent lady's back, and followed her up close, chair in hand, as she stalked to the banquet. Arrived at the table, she took her rigid seat, after favouring Mr Sampson with a glare for himself, which caused the young gentleman to retire to his place in much confusion.

The cherub not presuming to address so tremendous an object, transacted her supper through the agency of a third person, as 'Mutton to your Ma, Bella, my dear'; and 'Lavvy, I dare say your Ma would take some lettuce if you were to put it on her plate.' Mrs Wilfer's manner of receiving those viands was marked by petrified absence of mind; in which state, likewise, she partook of them, occasionally laying down her knife and fork, as saying within her own spirit, 'What is this I am doing?' and glaring at one or other of the party, as if in indignant search of information. A magnetic result of such glaring was, that the person glared at could not by any means successfully pretend to be ignorant of the fact: so that a bystander, without beholding Mrs Wilfer at all, must have known at whom she was glaring, by seeing her refracted from the countenance of the beglared one.

Miss Lavinia was extremely affable to Mr Sampson on this special occasion, and took the opportunity of informing her sister why.

'It was not worth troubling you about, Bella, when you were in a sphere so far removed from your family as to make it a matter in which you could be expected to take very little interest,' said Lavinia with a toss of her chin; 'but George Sampson is paying his addresses to me.'

Bella was glad to hear it. Mr Sampson became thoughtfully red, and felt called upon to encircle Miss Lavinia's waist with his arm; but, encountering a large pin in the young lady's belt, scarified a finger, uttered a sharp exclamation, and attracted the lightning of Mrs Wilfer's glare.

'George is getting on very well,' said Miss Lavinia—which might not have been supposed at the moment—'and I dare say we shall be married, one of these days. I didn't care to mention it when you were with your Bof—' here Miss Lavinia checked herself in a bounce, and added more placidly, 'when you were with Mr and Mrs Boffin; but now I think it sisterly to name the circumstance.'

'Thank you, Lavvy dear. I congratulate you.'

'Thank you, Bella. The truth is, George and I did discuss whether I should tell you; but I said to George that you wouldn't be much interested in so paltry an affair, and that it was far more likely you would rather detach yourself from us altogether, than have him added to the rest of us.'

'That was a mistake, dear Lavvy,' said Bella.

'It turns out to be,' replied Miss Lavinia; 'but circumstances have changed, you know, my dear. George is in a new situation, and his prospects are very good indeed. I shouldn't have had the courage to tell you so yesterday, when you would have thought his prospects poor, and not worth notice; but I feel quite bold to-night.'

'When did you begin to feel timid, Lavvy?' inquired Bella, with a smile.

'I didn't say that I ever felt timid, Bella,' replied the Irrepressible. 'But perhaps I might have said, if I had not been restrained by delicacy towards a sister's feelings, that I have for some time felt independent; too independent, my dear, to subject myself to have my intended match (you'll prick yourself again, George) looked down upon. It is not that I could have blamed you for looking down upon it, when you were looking up to a rich and great match, Bella; it is only that I was independent.'

Whether the Irrepressible felt slighted by Bella's declaration that she would not quarrel, or whether her spitefulness was evoked by Bella's return to the sphere of Mr George Sampson's courtship, or whether it was a necessary fillip to her spirits that she should come into collision with somebody on the present occasion,—anyhow she made a dash at her stately parent now, with the greatest impetuosity.

'Ma, pray don't sit staring at me in that intensely aggravating manner! If you see a black on my nose, tell me so; if you don't, leave me alone.'

'Do you address Me in those words?' said Mrs Wilfer. 'Do you presume?'

'Don't talk about presuming, Ma, for goodness' sake. A girl who is old enough to be engaged, is quite old enough to object to be stared at as if she was a Clock.'

'Audacious one!' said Mrs Wilfer. 'Your grandmamma, if

so addressed by one of her daughters, at any age, would have insisted on her retiring to a dark apartment.'

'My grandmamma,' returned Lavvy, folding her arms and leaning back in her chair, 'wouldn't have sat staring people out of countenance, I think.'

'She would!' said Mrs Wilfer.

'Then it's a pity she didn't know better,' said Lavvy. 'And if my grandmamma wasn't in her dotage when she took to insisting on people's retiring to dark apartments, she ought to have been. A pretty exhibition my grandmamma must have made of herself! I wonder whether she ever insisted on people's retiring into the ball of St Paul's; and if she did, how she got them there!'

'Silence!' proclaimed Mrs Wilfer. 'I command silence!'

'I have not the slightest intention of being silent, Ma,' returned Lavinia coolly, 'but quite the contrary. I am not going to be eyed as if *I* had come from the Boffins, and sit silent under it. I am not going to have George Sampson eyed as if *he* had come from the Boffins, and sit silent under it. If Pa thinks proper to be eyed as if *he* had come from the Boffins also, well and good. I don't chose to. And I won't!'

Lavinia's engineering having made this crooked opening at Bella, Mrs Wilfer strode into it.

'You rebellious spirit! You mutinous child! Tell me this, Lavinia. If, in violation of your mother's sentiments, you had condescended to allow yourself to be patronized by the Boffins, and if you had come from those halls of slavery—'

'That's mere nonsense, Ma,' said Lavinia.

'How!' exclaimed Mrs Wilfer, with sublime severity.

'Halls of slavery, Ma, is mere stuff and nonsense,' returned the unmoved Irrepressible.

'I say, presumptuous child, if you had come from the neighbourhood of Portland Place, bending under the yoke of patronage and attended by its domestics in glittering garb to visit me, do you think my deep-seated feelings could have been expressed in looks?'

'All I think about it, is,' returned Lavinia, 'that I should wish them expressed to the right person.'

'And if,' pursued her mother, 'if, making light of my warnings that the face of Mrs Boffin alone was a face teeming with evil, you had clung to Mrs Boffin instead of to me, and had after all come home rejected by Mrs Boffin, trampled under foot by Mrs Boffin, and cast out by Mrs Boffin, do you think my feelings could have been expressed in looks?'

Lavinia was about replying to her honoured parent that she might as well have dispensed with her looks altogether then, when Bella rose and said, 'Good night, dear Ma. I have had a tiring day, and I'll go to bed.' This broke up the agreeable party. Mr George Sampson shortly afterwards took his leave, accompanied by Miss Lavinia with a candle as far as the hall, and without a candle as far as the garden gate; Mrs Wilfer, washing her hands of the Boffins, went to bed after the manner of Lady Macbeth; and R. W. was left alone among the dilapidations of the supper table, in a melancholy attitude.

But, a light footstep roused him from his meditations, and it was Bella's. Her pretty hair was hanging all about her, and she had tripped down softly, brush in hand, and barefoot, to say good-night to him.

'My dear, you most unquestionably *are* a lovely woman,' said the cherub, taking up a tress in his hand.

'Look here, sir,' said Bella; 'when your lovely woman marries, you shall have that piece if you like, and she'll make you a chain of it. Would you prize that remembrance of the dear creature?'

'Yes, my precious.'

'Then you shall have it if you're good, sir. I am very, very sorry, dearest Pa, to have brought home all this trouble.'

'My pet,' returned her father, in the simplest good faith, 'don't make yourself uneasy about that. It really is not worth mentioning, because things at home would have taken pretty much the same turn any way. If your mother and sister don't find one subject to get at times a little wearing on, they find another. We're never out of a wearing subject, my dear, I assure you. I am afraid you find your old room with Lavvy, dreadfully inconvenient, Bella?'

'No I don't, Pa; I don't mind. Why don't I mind, do you think, Pa?'

'Well, my child, you used to complain of it when it wasn't such a contrast as it must be now. Upon my word, I can only answer, because you are so much improved.'

'No, Pa. Because I am so thankful and so happy!'

Here she choked him until her long hair made him sneeze, and then she laughed until she made him laugh, and then she choked him again that they might not be overheard.

'Listen, sir,' said Bella. 'Your lovely woman was told her fortune to-night on her way home. It won't be a large fortune, because if the lovely woman's Intended gets a certain appointment that he hopes to get soon, she will marry on a hundred and fifty pounds a year. But that's at first, and even if it should never be more, the lovely woman will make it quite enough. But that's not all, sir. In the fortune there's a certain fair man—a little man, the fortune-teller said—who, it seems, will always find himself near the lovely woman, and will always have kept, expressly for him, such a peaceful corner in the lovely woman's little house as never was. Tell me the name of that man, sir.'

"Is he a Knave in the pack of cards?' inquired the cherub, with a twinkle in his eyes.

'Yes!' cried Bella, in high glee, choking him again. 'He's the Knave of Wilfers! Dear Pa, the lovely woman means to look forward to this fortune that has been told for her, so delightfully, and to cause it to make her a much better lovely woman than she ever has been yet. What the little fair man is expected to do, sir, is to look forward to it also, by saying to himself when he is in danger of being over-worried, "I see land at last!" '

'I see land at last!' repeated her father.

'There's a dear Knave of Wilfers!' exclaimed Bella; then putting out her small white bare foot, 'That's the mark, sir. Come to the mark. Put your boot against it. We keep to it together, mind! Now, sir, you may kiss the lovely woman before she runs away, so thankful and so happy. O yes, fair little man, so thankful and so happy!'

Chapter 17
A Social Chorus

AMAZEMENT sits enthroned upon the countenances of Mr and Mrs Alfred Lammle's circle of acquaintance, when the disposal of their first-class furniture and effects (including a Billiard Table in capital letters), 'by auction, under a bill of sale,' is publicly announced on a waving hearthrug in Sackville Street. But, no-body is half so much amazed as Hamilton Veneering, Esquire, M.P. for Pocket-Breaches, who instantly begins to find out that

the Lammles are the only people ever entered on his soul's
register, who are *not* the oldest and dearest friends he has in the
world. Mrs Veneering, W.M.P. for Pocket-Breaches, like a
faithful wife shares her husband's discovery and inexpressible
astonishment. Perhaps the Veneerings twain may deem the last
unutterable feeling particularly due to their reputation, by reason
that once upon a time some of the longer heads in the City are
whispered to have shaken themselves, when Veneering's extensive dealings and great wealth were mentioned. But, it is certain
that neither Mr nor Mrs Veneering can find words to wonder in,
and it becomes necessary that they give to the oldest and dearest
friends they have in the world, a wondering dinner.

For, it is by this time noticeable that, whatever befals, the
Veneerings must give a dinner upon it. Lady Tippins lives in a
chronic state of invitation to dine with the Veneerings, and in a
chronic state of inflammation arising from the dinners. Boots and
Brewer go about in cabs, with no other intelligible business on
earth than to beat up people to come and dine with the Veneerings. Veneering pervades the legislative lobbies, intent upon
entrapping his fellow-legislators to dinner. Mrs Veneering dined
with five-and-twenty bran-new faces over night; calls upon them
all to-day; sends them every one a dinner-card to-morrow, for the
week after next; before that dinner is digested, calls upon their
brothers and sisters, their sons and daughters, their nephews and
nieces, their aunts and uncles and cousins, and invites them all to
dinner. And still, as at first, howsoever, the dining circle wid-
ens, it is to be observed that all the diners are consistent in
appearing to go to the Veneerings, not to dine with Mr and Mrs
Veneering (which would seem to be the last thing in their
minds), but to dine with one another.

Perhaps, after all,—who knows?—Veneering may find this
dining, though expensive, remunerative, in the sense that it
makes champions. Mr Podsnap, as a representative man, is not
alone in caring very particularly for his own dignity, if not for
that of his acquaintances, and therefore in angrily supporting the
acquaintances who have taken out his Permit, lest, in their being
lessened, he should be. The gold and silver camels, and the
ice-pails, and the rest of the Veneering table decorations, make a
brilliant show, and when I, Podsnap, casually remark elsewhere
that I dined last Monday with a gorgeous caravan of camels, I
find it personally offensive to have it hinted to me that they are
broken-kneed camels, or camels labouring under suspicion of
any sort. 'I don't display camels myself, I am above them: I am

a more solid man; but these camels have basked in the light of my countenance, and how dare you, sir, insinuate to me that I have irradiated any but unimpeachable camels?'

The camels are polishing up in the Analytical's pantry for the dinner of wonderment on the occasion of the Lammles going to pieces, and Mr Twemlow feels a little queer on the sofa at his lodgings over the stable yard in Duke Street, Saint James's, in consequence of having taken two advertised pills at about midday, on the faith of the printed representation accompanying the box (price one and a penny halfpenny, government stamp included), that the same 'will be found highly salutary as a precautionary measure in connection with the pleasures of the table.' To whom, while sickly with the fancy of an insoluble pill sticking in his gullet, and also with the sensation of a deposit of warm gum languidly wandering within him a little lower down, a servant enters with the announcement that a lady wishes to speak with him.

'A lady!' says Twemlow, pluming his ruffled feathers. 'Ask the favour of the lady's name.'

The lady's name is Lammle. The lady will not detain Mr Twemlow longer than a very few minutes. The lady is sure that Mr Twemlow will do her the kindness to see her, on being told that she particularly desires a short interview. The lady has no doubt whatever of Mr Twemlow's compliance when he hears her name. Has begged the servant to be particular not to mistake her name. Would have sent in a card, but has none.

'Show the lady in.' Lady shown in, comes in.

Mr Twemlow's little rooms are modestly furnished, in an old-fashioned manner (rather like the housekeeper's room at Snigsworthy Park), and would be bare of mere ornament, were it not for a full-length engraving of the sublime Snigsworth over the chimneypiece, snorting at a Corinthian column, with an enormous roll of paper at his feet, and a heavy curtain going to tumble down on his head; those accessories being understood to represent the noble lord as somehow in the act of saving his country.

'Pray take a seat, Mrs Lammle.' Mrs Lammle takes a seat and opens the conversation.

'I have no doubt, Mr Twemlow, that you have heard of a reverse of fortune having befallen us. Of course you have heard of it, for no kind of news travels so fast—among one's friends especially.'

Mindful of the wondering dinner, Twemlow, with a little twinge, admits the imputation.

'Probably it will not,' says Mrs Lammle, with a certain hardened manner upon her, that makes Twemlow shrink, 'have surprised you so much as some others, after what passed between us at the house which is now turned out at windows. I have taken the liberty of calling upon you, Mr Twemlow, to add a sort of postscript to what I said that day.'

Mr Twemlow's dry and hollow cheeks become more dry and hollow at the prospect of some new complication.

'Really,' says the uneasy little gentleman, 'really, Mrs Lammle, I should take it as a favour if you could excuse me from any further confidence. It has never been one of the objects of my life—which, unfortunately, has not had many objects—to be inoffensive, and to keep out of cabals and interferences.'

Mrs Lammle, by far the more observant of the two, scarcely finds it necessary to look at Twemlow while he speaks, so easily does she read him.

'My postscript—to retain the term I have used'—says Mrs Lammle, fixing her eyes on his face, to enforce what she says herself—'coincides exactly with what you say, Mr Twemlow. So far from troubling you with any new confidence, I merely wish to remind you what the old one was. So far from asking you for interference, I merely wish to claim your strict neutrality.'

Twemlow going on to reply, she rests her eyes again, knowing her ears to be quite enough for the contents of so weak a vessel.

'I can, I suppose,' says Twemlow, nervously, 'offer no reasonable objection to hearing anything that you do me the honour to wish to say to me under those heads. But if I may, with all possible delicacy and politeness, entreat you not to range beyond them, I—I beg to do so.'

'Sir,' says Mrs Lammle, raising her eyes to his face again, and quite daunting him with her hardened manner, 'I imparted to you a certain piece of knowledge, to be imparted again, as you thought best, to a certain person.'

'Which I did,' says Twemlow.

'And for doing which, I thank you; though, indeed, I scarcely know why I turned traitress to my husband in the matter, for the girl is a poor little fool. I was a poor little fool once myself; I can find no better reason.' Seeing the effect she produces on him by her indifferent laugh and cold look, she keeps her eyes upon him as she proceeds. 'Mr Twemlow, if you should chance to see my husband, or to see me, or to see both of us, in the favour or confidence of any one else—whether of our common acquaintance or not, is of no consequence—you have no right to use against us the knowledge I intrusted you with, for one special purpose which has been accomplished. This is what I came to say. It is not a stipulation; to a gentleman it is simply a reminder.'

Twemlow sits murmuring to himself with his hand to his forehead.

'It is so plain a case,' Mrs Lammle goes on, 'as between me (from the first relying on your honour) and you, that I will not waste another word upon it.' She looks steadily at Mr Twemlow, until, with a shrug, he makes her a little one-sided bow, as though saying 'Yes, I think you have a right to rely upon me,' and then she moistens her lips, and shows a sense of relief.

'I trust I have kept the promise I made through your servant, that I would detain you a very few minutes. I need trouble you no longer, Mr Twemlow.'

'Stay!' says Twemlow, rising as she rises. 'Pardon me a moment. I should never have sought you out, madam, to say what I am going to say, but since you have sought me out and are here, I will throw it off my mind. Was it quite consistent, in candour, with our taking that resolution against Mr Fledgeby, that you should afterwards address Mr Fledgeby as your dear and confidential friend, and entreat a favour of Mr Fledgeby? Always supposing that you did; I assert no knowledge of my own on the subject; it has been represented to me that you did.'

'Then he told you?' retorts Mrs Lammle, who again has saved her eyes while listening, and uses them with strong effect while speaking.

'Yes.'

'It is strange that he should have told you the truth,' says Mrs Lammle, seriously pondering. 'Pray where did a circumstance so very extraordinary happen?'

Twemlow hesitates. He is shorter than the lady as well as weaker, and, as she stands above him with her hardened manner and her well-used eyes, he finds himself at such a disadvantage that he would like to be of the opposite sex.

'May I ask where it happened, Mr Twemlow? In strict confidence?'

'I must confess,' says the mild little gentleman, coming to his answer by degrees, 'that I felt some compunctions when Mr Fledgeby mentioned it. I must admit that I could not regard myself in an agreeable light. More particularly, as Mr Fledgeby did, with great civility, which I could not feel that I deserved from him, render me the same service that you had entreated him to render you.'

It is a part of the true nobility of the poor gentleman's soul to say this last sentence. 'Otherwise,' he has reflected, 'I shall assume the superior position of having no difficulties of my own, while I know of hers. Which would be mean, very mean.'

'Was Mr Fledgeby's advocacy as effectual in your case as in ours?' Mrs Lammle demands.

'As *in*effectual.'

'Can you make up your mind to tell me where you saw Mr Fledgeby, Mr Twemlow?'

'I beg your pardon. I fully intended to have done so. The reservation was not intentional. I encountered Mr Fledgeby, quite by accident, on the spot.—By the expression, on the spot, I mean at Mr Riah's in Saint Mary Axe.'

'Have you the misfortune to be in Mr Riah's hands then?'

'Unfortunately, madam,' returns Twemlow, 'the one money-obligation to which I stand committed, the one debt of my life (but it is a just debt; pray observe that I don't dispute it), has fallen into Mr Riah's hands.'

'Mr Twemlow,' says Mrs Lammle, fixing his eyes with hers: which he would prevent her doing if he could, but he can't; 'it has fallen into Mr Fledgeby's hands. Mr Riah is his mask. It has fallen in Mr Fledgeby's hands. Let me tell you that, for your guidance. The information may be of use to you, if only to prevent your credulity, in judging another man's truthfulness by your own, from being imposed upon.'

'Impossible!' cries Twemlow, standing aghast. 'How do you know it?'

'I scarcely know how I know it. The whole train of circumstances seemed to take fire at once, and show it to me.'

'Oh! Then you have no proof.'

'It is very strange,' says Mrs Lammle, coldly and boldly, and with some disdain, 'how like men are to one another in some things, though their characters are as different as can be! No two men can have less affinity between them, one would say, than Mr Twemlow and my husband. Yet my husband replies to me "You have no proof," and Mr Twemlow replies to me with the very same words!'

'But why, madam?' Twemlow ventures gently to argue.

'Consider why the very same words? Because they state the fact. Because you *have* no proof.'

'Men are very wise in their way,' quoth Mrs Lammle, glancing haughtily at the Snigsworth portrait, and shaking out her dress before departing; 'but they have wisdom to learn. My husband, who is not over-confiding, ingenuous, or inexperienced, sees this plain thing no more than Mr Twemlow does— because there is no proof! Yet I believe five women out of six, in my place, would see it as clearly as I do. However, I will never rest (if only in remembrance of Mr Fledgeby's having kissed my hand) until my husband does see it. And you will do well for yourself to see it from this time forth, Mr Twemlow, though I *can* give you no proof.'

As she moves towards the door, Mr Twemlow, attending on her, expresses his soothing hope that the condition of Mr Lammle's affairs is not irretrievable.

'I don't know,' Mrs Lammle answers, stopping, and sketching out the pattern of the paper on the wall with the point of her parasol; 'it depends. There may be an opening for him dawning now, or there may be none. We shall soon find out. If none, we are bankrupt here, and must go abroad, I suppose.'

Mr Twemlow, in his good-natured desire to make the best of it, remarks that there are pleasant lives abroad.

'Yes,' returns Mrs Lammle, still sketching on the wall; 'but I doubt whether billiard-playing, card-playing, and so forth, for the means to live under suspicion at a dirty table-d'hôte, is one of them.'

It is much for Mr Lammle, Twemlow politely intimates (though greatly shocked), to have one always beside him who is attached to him in all his fortunes, and whose restraining influence will prevent him from courses that would be discreditable and ruinous. As he says it, Mrs Lammle leaves off sketching, and looks at him.

'Restraining influence, Mr Twemlow? We must eat and drink, and dress, and have a roof over our heads. Always beside him and attached in all his fortunes? Not much to boast of in that; what can a woman at my age do? My husband and I deceived one another when we married; we must bear the consequences of the deception—that is to say, bear one another, and bear the burden of scheming together for to-day's dinner and to-morrow's breakfast—till death divorces us.'

With those words, she walks out into Duke Street, Saint James's. Mr Twemlow returning to his sofa, lays down his

aching head on its slippery little horsehair bolster, with a strong
internal conviction that a painful interview is not the kind of
thing to be taken after the dinner pills which are so highly
salutary in connexion with the pleasures of the table.

But, six o'clock in the evening finds the worthy little gentleman getting better, and also getting himself into his obsolete
little silk stockings and pumps, for the wondering dinner at the
Veneerings. And seven o'clock in the evening finds him trotting
out into Duke Street, to trot to the corner and save a sixpence in
coach-hire.

Tippins the divine has dined herself into such a condition by
this time, that a morbid mind might desire her, for a blessed
change, to sup at last, and turn into bed. Such a mind has Mr
Eugene Wrayburn, whom Twemlow finds contemplating Tippins
with the moodiest of visages, while that playful creature rallies
him on being so long overdue at the woolsack. Skittish is
Tippins with Mortimer Lightwood too, and has raps to give him
with her fan for having been best man at the nuptials of these
deceiving what's-their-names who have gone to pieces. Though,
indeed, the fan is generally lively, and taps away at the men in
all directions, with something of a grisly sound suggestive of the
clattering of Lady Tippins's bones.

A new race of intimate friends has sprung up at Veneering's
since he went into Parliament for the public good, to whom Mrs
Veneering is very attentive. These friends, like astronomical
distances, are only to be spoken of in the very largest figures.
Boots says that one of them is a Contractor who (it has been
calculated) gives employment, directly and indirectly, to five
hundred thousand men. Brewer says that another of them is a
Chairman, in such request at so many Boards, so far apart, that
he never travels less by railway than three thousand miles a
week. Buffer says that another of them hadn't a sixpence eighteen months ago, and, through the brilliancy of his genius in
getting those shares issued at eighty-five, and buying them all up
with no money and selling them at par for cash, has now three
hundred and seventy-five thousand pounds—Buffer particularly
insisting on the odd seventy-five, and declining to take a
farthing less. With Buffer, Boots, and Brewer, Lady Tippins is
eminently facetious on the subject of these Fathers of the Scrip-
Church: surveying them through her eyeglass, and inquiring
whether Boots and Brewer and Buffer think they will make her
fortune if she makes love to them? with other pleasantries of that
nature. Veneering, in his different way, is much occupied with

the Fathers too, piously retiring with them into the conservatory, from which retreat the word 'Committee' is occasionally heard, and where the Fathers instruct Veneering how he must leave the valley of the piano on his left, take the level of the mantelpiece, cross by an open cutting at the candelabra, seize the carrying-traffic at the console, and cut up the opposition root and branch at the window curtains.

Mr and Mrs Podsnap are of the company, and the Fathers descry in Mrs Podsnap a fine woman. She is consigned to a Father—Boots's Father, who employs five hundred thousand men—and is brought to anchor on Veneering's left; thus affording opportunity to the sportive Tippins on his right (he, as usual, being mere vacant space), to entreat to be told something about those loves of Navvies, and whether they really do live on raw beefsteaks, and drink porter out of their barrows. But, in spite of such little skirmishes it is felt that this was to be a wondering dinner, and that the wondering must not be neglected. Accordingly, Brewer, as the man who has the greatest reputation to sustain, becomes the interpreter of the general instinct.

'I took,' says Brewer in a favourable pause, 'a cab this morning, and I rattled off to that Sale.'

Boots (devoured by envy) says, 'So did I.'

Buffer says, 'So did I'; but can find nobody to care whether he did or not.

'And what was it like?' inquires Veneering.

'I assure you,' replies Brewer, looking about for anybody else to address his answer to, and giving the preference to Lightwood; 'I assure you, the things were going for a song. Handsome things enough, but fetching nothing.'

'So I heard this afternoon,' says Lightwood.

Brewer begs to know now, would it be fair to ask a professional man how—on—earth—these—people—ever—did—come—*to*—such—*a*—total smash? (Brewer's divisions being for emphasis.)

Lightwood replies that he was consulted certainly, but could give no opinion which would pay off the Bill of Sale, and therefore violates no confidence in supposing that it came of their living beyond their means.

'But how,' says Veneering, 'CAN people do that!'

Hah! That is felt on all hands to be a shot in the bull's eye. How CAN people do that! The Analytical Chemist going round with champagne, looks very much as if *he* could give them a pretty good idea how people did that, if he had a mind.

'How,' says Mrs Veneering, laying down her fork to press her aquiline hands together at the tips of the fingers, and addressing the Father who travels the three thousand miles per week: 'how a mother can look at her baby, and know that she lives beyond her husband's means, I cannot imagine.'

Eugene suggests that Mrs Lammle, not being a mother, had no baby to look at.

'True,' says Mrs Veneering, 'but the principle is the same.'

Boots is clear that the principle is the same. So is Buffer. It is the unfortunate destiny of Buffer to damage a cause by espousing it. The rest of the company have meekly yielded to the proposition that the principle is the same, until Buffer says it is; when instantly a general murmur arises that the principle is not the same.

'But I don't understand,' says the Father of the three hundred and seventy-five thousand pounds, '—if these people spoken of, occupied the position of being in society—they were in society?'

Veneering is bound to confess that they dined here, and were even married from here.

'Then I don't understand,' pursues the Father, 'how even their living beyond their means could bring them to what has been termed a total smash. Because, there is always such a thing as an adjustment of affairs, in the case of people of any standing at all.'

Eugene (who would seem to be in a gloomy state of suggestiveness), suggests, 'Suppose you have no means and live beyond them?'

This is too insolvent a state of things for the Father to entertain. It is too insolvent a state of things for any one with any self-respect to entertain, and is universally scouted. But, it is so amazing how any people can have come to a total smash, that everybody feels bound to account for it specially. One of the Fathers says, 'Gaming table.' Another of the Fathers says, 'Speculated without knowing that speculation is a science.' Boots says 'Horses.' Lady Tippins says to her fan, 'Two establishments.' Mr Podsnap, saying nothing, is referred to for his opinion; which he delivers as follows; much flushed and extremely angry:

'Don't ask me. I desire to take no part in the discussion of these people's affairs. I abhor the subject. It is an odious subject, an offensive subject, a subject that makes me sick, and I—' And with his favourite right-arm flourish which sweeps away everything and settles it for ever, Mr Podsnap sweeps these inconveniently unexplainable wretches who have lived beyond their means and gone to total smash, off the face of the universe.

Eugene, leaning back in his chair, is observing Mr Podsnap with an irreverent face, and may be about to offer a new suggestion, when the Analytical is beheld in collision with the Coachman; the Coachman manifesting a purpose of coming at the company with a silver salver, as though intent upon making a collection for his wife and family; the Analytical cutting him off at the sideboard. The superior stateliness, if not the superior generalship, of the Analytical prevails over a man who is as nothing off the box; and the Coachman, yielding up his salver, retires defeated.

Then, the Analytical, perusing a scrap of paper lying on the salver, with the air of a literary Censor, adjusts it, takes his time about going to the table with it, and presents it to Mr Eugene Wrayburn. Whereupon the pleasant Tippins says aloud, 'The Lord Chancellor has resigned!'

With distracting coolness and slowness—for he knows the curiosity of the Charmer to be always devouring—Eugene makes a pretence of getting out an eyeglass, polishing it, and reading the paper with difficulty, long after he has seen what is written on it. What is written on it in wet ink, is:

'Young Blight.'

'Waiting?' says Eugene over his shoulder, in confidence, with the Analytical.

'Waiting,' returns the Analytical in responsive confidence.

Eugene looks 'Excuse me,' towards Mrs Veneering, goes out, and finds Young Blight, Mortimer's clerk, at the hall-door.

'You told me to bring him, sir, to wherever you was, if he come while you was out and I was in,' says that discreet young gentleman, standing on tiptoe to whisper; 'and I've brought him.'

'Sharp boy. Where is he?' asks Eugene.

'He's in a cab, sir, at the door. I thought it best not to show him, you see, if it could be helped; for he's a-shaking all over, like—' Blight's simile is perhaps inspired by the surrounding dishes of sweets—'like Glue Monge.'

'Sharp boy again,' returns Eugene. 'I'll go to him.'

Goes out straightway, and, leisurely leaning his arms on the open window of a cab in waiting, looks in at Mr Dolls: who has brought his own atmosphere with him, and would seem from its odour to have brought it, for convenience of carriage, in a rum-cask.

'Now Dolls, wake up!'

'Mist Wrayburn? Drection! Fifteen shillings!'

After carefully reading the dingy scrap of paper handed to him, and as carefully tucking it into his waistcoat pocket, Eugene tells out the money; beginning incautiously by telling the first shilling into Mr Dolls's hand, which instantly jerks it out of window; and ending by telling the fifteen shillings on the seat.

'Give him a ride back to Charing Cross, sharp boy, and there get rid of him.'

Returning to the dining-room, and pausing for an instant behind the screen at the door, Eugene overhears, above the hum and clatter, the fair Tippins saying: 'I am dying to ask him what he was called out for!'

'Are you?' mutters Eugene, 'then perhaps if you can't ask him, you'll die. So I'll be a benefactor to society, and go. A stroll and a cigar, and I can think this over. Think this over.' Thus, with a thoughtful face, he finds his hat and cloak, unseen of the Analytical, and goes his way.

BOOK THE FOURTH
A TURNING

Chapter 1
Setting Traps

PLASHWATER WEIR MILL LOCK looked tranquil and pretty on an evening in the summer time. A soft air stirred the leaves of the fresh green trees, and passed like a smooth shadow over the river, and like a smoother shadow over the yielding grass. The voice of the falling water, like the voices of the sea and the wind, were as an outer memory to a contemplative listener; but not particularly so to Mr Riderhood, who sat on one of the blunt wooden levers of his lock-gates, dozing. Wine must be got into a butt by some agency before it can be drawn out; and the wine of sentiment never having been got into Mr Riderhood by any agency, nothing in nature tapped him.

As the Rogue sat, ever and again nodding himself off his balance, his recovery was always attended by an angry stare and growl, as if, in the absence of any one else, he had aggressive inclinations towards himself. In one of these starts the cry of 'Lock, ho! Lock!' prevented his relapse into a doze. Shaking himself as he got up like the surly brute he was, he gave his growl a responsive twist at the end, and turned his face downstream to see who hailed.

It was an amateur-sculler, well up to his work though taking it easily, in so light a boat that the Rogue remarked: 'A little less on you, and you'd a'most ha' been a Wagerbut'; then went to work at his windlass handles and sluices, to let the sculler in. As the latter stood in his boat, holding on by the boat-hook to the woodwork at the lock side, waiting for the gates to open, Rogue Riderhood recognized his 'T'other governor,' Mr Eugene Wrayburn; who was, however, too indifferent or too much engaged to recognize him.

The creaking lock-gates opened slowly, and the light boat passed in as soon as there was room enough, and the creaking lock-gates closed upon it, and it floated low down in the dock between the two sets of gates, until the water should rise and the second gates should open and let it out. When Riderhood had run to his second windlass and turned it, and while he leaned against the lever of that gate to help it to swing open presently, he noticed, lying to rest under the green hedge by the towing-path astern of the Lock, a Bargeman.

The water rose and rose as the sluice poured in, dispersing the scum which had formed behind the lumbering gates, and sending the boat up, so that the sculler gradually rose like an apparition against the light from the bargeman's point of view. Riderhood observed that the bargeman rose too, leaning on his arm, and seemed to have his eyes fastened on the rising figure.

But, there was the toll to be taken, as the gates were now complaining and opening. The T'other governor tossed it ashore, twisted in a piece of paper, and as he did so, knew his man.

'Ay, ay? It's you, is it, honest friend?' said Eugene, seating himself preparatory to resuming his sculls. 'You got the place, then?'

'I got the place, and no thanks to you for it, nor yet none to Lawyer Lightwood,' gruffly answered Riderhood.

'We saved our recommendation, honest fellow,' said Eugene, 'for the next candidate—the one who will offer himself when you are transported or hanged. Don't be long about it; will you be so good?'

So imperturbable was the air with which he gravely bent to his work that Riderhood remained staring at him, without having found a retort, until he had rowed past a line of wooden objects by the weir, which showed like huge teetotums standing at rest in the water, and was almost hidden by the drooping boughs on the left bank, as he rowed away, keeping out of the opposing current. It being then too late to retort with any effect—if that could ever have been done—the honest man confined himself to cursing and growling in a grim under-tone. Having then got his gates shut, he crossed back by his plank lock-bridge to the towing-path side of the river.

If, in so doing, he took another glance at the bargeman, he did it by stealth. He cast himself on the grass by the Lock side, in an indolent way, with his back in that direction, and, having gathered a few blades, fell to chewing them. The dip of Eugene Wrayburn's sculls had become hardly audible in his ears when the bargeman passed him, putting the utmost width that he could between them, and keeping under the hedge. Then, Riderhood sat up and took a long look at his figure, and then cried: 'Hi–i–i! Lock, ho! Lock! Plashwater Weir Mill Lock!'

The bargeman stopped, and looked back.

'Plashwater Weir Mill Lock, T'otherest gov–er–nor–or–or–or!' cried Mr. Riderhood, with his hands to his mouth.

The bargeman turned back. Approaching nearer and nearer, the bargeman became Bradley Headstone, in rough water-side second-hand clothing.

'Wish I may die,' said Riderhood, smiting his right leg, and laughing, as he sat on the grass, 'if you ain't ha' been a imitating me, T'otherest governor! Never thought myself so good-looking afore!'

Truly, Bradley Headstone had taken careful note of the honest man's dress in the course of that night-walk they had had together. He must have committed it to memory, and slowly got it by heart. It was exactly reproduced in the dress he now wore. And whereas, in his own schoolmaster clothes, he usually looked as if they were the clothes of some other man, he now looked, in the clothes of some other man or men, as if they were his own.

'*This* your Lock?' said Bradley, whose surprise had a genuine air; 'they told me, where I last inquired, it was the third I should come to. This is only the second.'

'It's my belief, governor,' returned Riderhood, with a wink and shake of his head, 'that you've dropped one in your counting. It ain't Locks as *you*'ve been giving your mind to. No, no!'

As he expressively jerked his pointing finger in the direction the boat had taken, a flush of impatience mounted into Bradley's face, and he looked anxiously up the river.

'It ain't Locks as *you*'ve been a reckoning up,' said Riderhood, when the schoolmaster's eyes came back again. 'No, no!'

'What other calculations do you suppose I have been occupied with? Mathematics?'

'I never heerd it called that. It's a long word for it. Hows'ever, p'raps you call it so,' said Riderhood, stubbornly chewing his grass.

'It. What?'

'I'll say them, instead of it, if you like,' was the coolly growled reply. 'It's safer talk too.'

'What do you mean that I should understand by them?'

'Spites, affronts, offences giv' and took, deadly aggrawations, such like,' answered Riderhood.

Do what Bradley Headstone would, he could not keep that

former flush of impatience out of his face, or so master his eyes
as to prevent their again looking anxiously up the river.

'Ha ha! Don't be afeerd, T'otherest,' said Riderhood. 'The
T'other's got to make way agin the stream, and he takes it easy.
You can soon come up with him. But wot's the good of saying
that to you! *You* know how fur you could have outwalked him
betwixt anywheres about where he lost the tide—say Richmond—
and this, if you had a mind to it.'

'You think I have been following him?' said Bradley.

'I KNOW you have,' said Riderhood.

'Well! I have, I have,' Bradley admitted. 'But,' with another anxious look up the river, 'he may land.'

'Easy you! He won't be lost if he does land,' said Riderhood.
'He must leave his boat behind him. He can't make a bundle or a
parcel on it, and carry it ashore with him under his arm.'

'He was speaking to you just now,' said Bradley, kneeling
on one knee on the grass beside the Lock-keeper. 'What did he
say?'

'Cheek,' said Riderhood.

'What?'

'Cheek,' repeated Riderhood, with an angry oath; 'cheek is
what he said. He can't say nothing but cheek. I'd ha' liked to
plump down aboard of him, neck and crop, with a heavy jump,
and sunk him.'

Bradley turned away his haggard face for a few moments,
and then said, tearing up a tuft of grass:

'Damn him!'

'Hooroar!' cried Riderhood. 'Does you credit! Hooroar! I
cry chorus to the T'otherest.'

'What turn,' said Bradley, with an effort at self-repression
that forced him to wipe his face, 'did his insolence take to-day?'

'It took the turn,' answered Riderhood, with sullen ferocity,
'of hoping as I was getting ready to be hanged.'

'Let him look to that,' cried Bradley. 'Let him look to that!
It will be bad for him when men he has injured, and at whom he
has jeered, are thinking of getting hanged. Let *him* get ready for
his fate, when that comes about. There was more meaning in
what he said than he knew of, or he wouldn't have had brains
enough to say it. Let him look to it; let him look to it! When men
he has wronged, and on whom he has bestowed his insolence,
are getting ready to be hanged, there is a death-bell ringing. And
not for them.'

Riderhood, looking fixedly at him, gradually arose from his

recumbent posture while the schoolmaster said these words with the utmost concentration of rage and hatred. So, when the words were all spoken, he too kneeled on one knee on the grass, and the two men looked at one another.

'Oh!' said Riderhood, very deliberately spitting out the grass he had been chewing. 'Then, I make out, T'otherest, as he is a-going to her?'

'He left London,' answered Bradley, 'yesterday. I have hardly a doubt, this time, that at last he is going to her.'

'You ain't sure, then?'

'I am as sure here,' said Bradley, with a clutch at the breast of his coarse shirt, 'as if it was written there;' with a blow or a stab at the sky.

'Ah! But judging from the looks on you,' retorted Riderhood, completely ridding himself of his grass, and drawing his sleeve across his mouth, 'you've made ekally sure afore, and have got disapinted. It has told upon you.'

'Listen,' said Bradley, in a low voice, bending forward to lay his hand upon the Lock-keeper's shoulder. 'These are my holidays.'

'Are they, by George!' muttered Riderhood, with his eyes on the passion-wasted face. 'Your working days must be stiff 'uns, if these is your holidays.'

'And I have never left him,' pursued Bradley, waving the interruption aside with an impatient hand, 'since they began. And I never will leave him now, till I have seen him with her.'

'And when you have seen him with her?' said Riderhood.

'—I'll come back to you.'

Riderhood stiffened the knee on which he had been resting, got up, and looked gloomily at his new friend. After a few moments they walked side by side in the direction the boat had taken, as if by tacit consent; Bradley pressing forward, and Riderhood holding back; Bradley getting out his neat prim purse into his hand (a present made him by penny subscription among his pupils); and Riderhood, unfolding his arms to smear his coat-cuff across his mouth with a thoughtful air.

'I have a pound for you,' said Bradley.

'You've two,' said Riderhood.

Bradley held a sovereign between his fingers. Slouching at his side with his eyes upon the towing-path, Riderhood held his left hand open, with a certain slight drawing action towards himself. Bradley dipped in his purse for another sovereign, and two chinked in Riderhood's hand, the drawing action of which, promptly strengthening, drew them home to his pocket.

'Now, I must follow him,' said Bradley Headstone. 'He takes this river-road—the fool!—to confuse observation, or divert attention, if not solely to baffle me. But he must have the power of making himself invisible before he can shake Me off.'

Riderhood stopped. 'If you don't get disapinted agin, T'otherest, maybe you'll put up at the Lock-house when you come back?'

'I will.'

Riderhood nodded, and the figure of the bargeman went its way along the soft turf by the side of the towing-path, keeping near the hedge and moving quickly. They had turned a point from which a long stretch of river was visible. A stranger to the scene might have been certain that here and there along the line of hedge a figure stood, watching the bargeman, and waiting for him to come up. So he himself had often believed at first, until his eyes became used to the posts, bearing the dagger that slew Wat Tyler, in the City of London shield.

Within Mr Riderhood's knowledge all daggers were as one. Even to Bradley Headstone, who could have told to the letter without book all about Wat Tyler, Lord Mayor Walworth, and the King, that it is dutiful for youth to know, there was but one subject living in the world for every sharp destructive instrument that summer evening. So, Riderhood looking after him as he went, and he with his furtive hand laid upon the dagger as he passed it, and his eyes upon the boat, were much upon a par.

The boat went on, under the arching trees, and over their tranquil shadows in the water. The bargeman skulking on the opposite bank of the stream, went on after it. Sparkles of light showed Riderhood when and where the rower dipped his blades, until, even as he stood idly watching, the sun went down and the landscape was dyed red. And then the red had the appearance of fading out of it and mounting up to Heaven, as we say that blood, guiltily shed, does.

Turning back towards his Lock (he had not gone out of view of it), the Rogue pondered as deeply as it was within the contracted power of such a fellow to do. 'Why did he copy my clothes? He could have looked like what he wanted to look like, without that.' This was the subject-matter in his thoughts; in which, too, there came lumbering up, by times, like any half floating and half sinking rubbish in the river, the question, Was it done by accident? The setting of a trap for finding out whether it was accidentally done, soon superseded, as a practical piece of cunning, the abstruser inquiry why otherwise it was done. And he devised a means.

Rogue Riderhood went into his Lock-house, and brought forth, into the now sober grey light, his chest of clothes. Sitting on the grass beside it, he turned out, one by one, the articles it contained, until he came to a conspicuous bright red neckerchief stained black here and there by wear. It arrested his attention, and he sat pausing over it, until he took off the rusty colourless wisp that he wore round his throat, and substituted the red neckerchief, leaving the long ends flowing. 'Now,' said the Rogue, 'if arter he sees me in this neckhankecher, I see him in a sim'lar neckhankecher, it won't be accident!' Elated by his device, he carried his chest in again and went to supper.

'Lock ho! Lock!' It was a light night, and a barge coming down summoned him out of a long doze. In due course he had let the barge through and was alone again, looking to the closing of his gates, when Bradley Headstone appeared before him, standing on the brink of the Lock.

'Halloa!' said Riderhood. 'Back a'ready, T'otherest?'

'He has put up for the night, at an Angler's Inn,' was the fatigued and hoarse reply. 'He goes on, up the river, at six in the morning. I have come back for a couple of hours' rest.'

'You want 'em,' said Riderhood, making towards the school-master by his plank bridge.

'I don't want them,' returned Bradley, irritably, 'because I would rather not have them, but would much prefer to follow him all night. However, if he won't lead, I can't follow. I have been waiting about, until I could discover, for a certainty, at what time he starts; if I couldn't have made sure of it, I should have stayed there.—This would be a bad pit for a man to be flung into with his hands tied. These slippery smooth walls would give him no chance. And I suppose those gates would suck him down?'

'Suck him down, or swaller him up, he wouldn't get out,' said Riderhood. 'Not even, if his hands warn't tied, he wouldn't. Shut him in at both ends, and I'd give him a pint o' old ale ever to come up to me standing here.'

Bradley looked down with a ghastly relish. 'You run about the brink, and run across it, in this uncertain light, on a few inches width of rotten wood,' said he. 'I wonder you have no thought of being drowned.'

'I can't be!' said Riderhood.

'You can't be drowned?'

'No!' said Riderhood, shaking his head with an air of thorough conviction, 'it's well known. I've been brought out o' drowning, and I can't be drowned. I wouldn't have that there busted B'low-bridger aware on it, or her people might make it tell agin' the damages I mean to get. But it's well known to water-side characters like myself, that him as has been brought out o' drowning, can never be drowned.'

Bradley smiled sourly at the ignorance he would have corrected in one of his pupils, and continued to look down into the water, as if the place had a gloomy fascination for him.

'You seem to like it,' said Riderhood.

He took no notice, but stood looking down, as if he had not heard the words. There was a very dark expression on his face; an expression that the Rogue found it hard to understand. It was fierce, and full of purpose; but the purpose might have been as much against himself as against another. If he had stepped back for a spring, taken a leap, and thrown himself in, it would have been no surprising sequel to the look. Perhaps his troubled soul, set upon some violence, did hover for the moment between that violence and another.

'Didn't you say,' asked Riderhood, after watching him for a while with a sidelong glance, 'as you had come back for a couple o' hours' rest?' But, even then he had to jog him with his elbow before he answered.

'Eh? Yes.'

'Hadn't you better come in and take your couple o' hours' rest?'

'Thank you. Yes.'

With the look of one just awakened, he followed Riderhood into the Lock-house, where the latter produced from a cupboard some cold salt beef and half a loaf, some gin in a bottle, and some water in a jug. The last he brought in, cool and dripping, from the river.

'There, T'otherest,' said Riderhood, stooping over him to put it on the table. 'You'd better take a bite and a sup, afore you takes your snooze.' The draggling ends of the red neckerchief caught the schoolmaster's eyes. Riderhood saw him look at it.

'Oh!' thought that worthy. 'You're a-taking notice, are you? Come! You shall have a good squint at it then.' With which reflection he sat down on the other side of the table, threw open his vest, and made a pretence of re-tying the neckerchief with much deliberation.

Bradley ate and drank. As he sat at his platter and mug, Riderhood saw him, again and yet again, steal a look at the neckerchief, as if he were correcting his slow observation and prompting his sluggish memory. 'When you're ready for your snooze,' said that honest creature, 'chuck yourself on my bed in the corner, T'otherest. It'll be broad day afore three. I'll call you early.'

'I shall require no calling,' answered Bradley. And soon afterwards, divesting himself only of his shoes and coat, laid himself down.

Riderhood, leaning back in his wooden arm-chair with his arms folded on his breast, looked at him lying with his right hand clenched in his sleep and his teeth set, until a film came over his own sight, and he slept too. He awoke to find that it was daylight, and that his visitor was already astir, and going out to the riverside to cool his head:—'Though I'm blest,' muttered Riderhood at the Lock-house door, looking after him, 'if I think there's water enough in all the Thames to do *that* for you!' Within five minutes he had taken his departure, and was passing on into the calm distance as he had passed yesterday. Riderhood knew when a fish leaped, by his starting and glancing round.

'Lock ho! Lock!' at intervals all day, and 'Lock ho! Lock!' thrice in the ensuing night, but no return of Bradley. The second day was sultry and oppressive. In the afternoon, a thunderstorm came up, and had but newly broken into a furious sweep of rain when he rushed in at the door, like the storm itself.

'You've seen him with her!' exclaimed Riderhood, starting up.

'I have.'

'Where?'

'At his journey's end. His boat's hauled up for three days. I heard him give the order. Then, I saw him wait for her and meet her. I saw them'—he stopped as though he were suffocating, and began again—'I saw them walking side by side, last night.'

'What did you do?'

'Nothing.'

'What are you going to do?'

He dropped into a chair, and laughed. Immediately afterward, a great spirt of blood burst from his nose.

'How does that happen?' asked Riderhood.

'I don't know. I can't keep it back. It has happened twice— three times—four times—I don't know how many times—since last night. I taste it, smell it, see it, it chokes me, and then it breaks out like this.'

He went into the pelting rain again with his head bare, and, bending low over the river, and scooping up the water with his two hands, washed the blood away. All beyond his figure, as Riderhood looked from the door, was a vast dark curtain in solemn movement towards one quarter of the heavens. He raised his head and came back, wet from head to foot, but with the lower parts of his sleeves, where he had dipped into the river, streaming water.

'Your face is like a ghost's,' said Riderhood.

'Did you ever see a ghost?' was the sullen retort.

'I mean to say, you're quite wore out.'

'That may well be. I have had no rest since I left here. I don't remember that I have so much as sat down since I left here.'

'Lie down now, then,' said Riderhood.

'I will, if you'll give me something to quench my thirst first.'

The bottle and jug were again produced, and he mixed a weak draught, and another, and drank both in quick succession. 'You asked me something,' he said then.

'No, I didn't,' replied Riderhood.

'I tell you,' retorted Bradley, turning upon him in a wild and desperate manner, 'you asked me something, before I went out to wash my face in the river.'

'Oh! Then?' said Riderhood, backing a little. 'I asked you wot you wos a-going to do.'

'How can a man in this state know?' he answered, protesting with both his tremulous hands, with an action so vigorously angry that he shook the water from his sleeves upon the floor, as if he had wrung them. 'How can I plan anything, if I haven't sleep?'

'Why, that's what I as good as said,' returned the other. 'Didn't I say lie down?'

'Well, perhaps you did.'

'Well! Anyways I says it again. Sleep where you slept last; the sounder and longer you can sleep, the better you'll know afterwards what you're up to.'

His pointing to the truckle bed in the corner, seemed gradually to bring that poor couch to Bradley's wandering remembrance. He slipped off his worn down-trodden shoes, and cast himself heavily, all wet as he was, upon the bed.

Riderhood sat down in his wooden arm-chair, and looked through the window at the lightning, and listened to the thunder.

But, his thoughts were far from being absorbed by the thunder and the lightning, for again and again and again he looked very curiously at the exhausted man upon the bed. The man had turned up the collar of the rough coat he wore, to shelter himself from the storm, and had buttoned it about his neck. Unconscious of that, and of most things, he had left the coat so, both when he had laved his face in the river, and when he had cast himself upon the bed; though it would have been much easier to him if he had unloosened it.

The thunder rolled heavily, and the forked lightning seemed to make jagged rents in every part of the vast curtain without, as Riderhood sat by the window, glancing at the bed. Sometimes, he saw the man upon the bed, by a red light; sometimes, by a blue; sometimes, he scarcely saw him in the darkness of the storm; sometimes he saw nothing of him in the blinding glare of palpitating white fire. Anon, the rain would come again with a tremendous rush, and the river would seem to rise to meet it, and a blast of wind, bursting upon the door, would flutter the hair and dress of the man, as if invisible messengers were come around the bed to carry him away. From all these phases of the storm, Riderhood would turn, as if they were interruptions— rather striking interruptions possibly, but interruptions still—of his scrutiny of the sleeper.

'He sleeps sound,' he said within himself; 'yet he's that up to me and that noticing of me that my getting out of my chair may wake him, when a rattling peal won't; let alone my touching of him.'

He very cautiously rose to his feet. 'T'otherest,' he said, in a low, calm voice, 'are you a lying easy? There's a chill in the air, governor. Shall I put a coat over you?'

No answer.

'That's about what it is a'ready, you see,' muttered Riderhood in a lower and a different voice; 'a coat over you, a coat over you!'

The sleeper moving an arm, he sat down again in his chair, and feigned to watch the storm from the window. It was a grand spectacle, but not so grand as to keep his eyes, for half a minute together, from stealing a look at the man upon the bed.

It was at the concealed throat of the sleeper that Riderhood so often looked so curiously, until the sleep seemed to deepen into the stupor of the dead-tired in mind and body. Then, Riderhood came from the window cautiously, and stood by the bed.

'Poor man!' he murmured in a low tone, with a crafty face,

and a very watchful eye and ready foot, lest he should start up; 'this here coat of his must make him uneasy in his sleep. Shall I loosen it for him, and make him more comfortable? Ah! I think I ought to do it, poor man. I think I will.'

He touched the first button with a very cautious hand, and a step backward. But, the sleeper remaining in profound unconsciousness, he touched the other buttons with a more assured hand, and perhaps the more lightly on that account. Softly and slowly, he opened the coat and drew it back.

The draggling ends of a bright-red neckerchief were then disclosed, and he had even been at the pains of dipping parts of it in some liquid, to give it the appearance of having become stained by wear. With a much-perplexed face, Riderhood looked from it to the sleeper, and from the sleeper to it, and finally crept back to his chair, and there, with his hand to his chin, sat long in a brown study, looking at both.

Chapter 2
The Golden Dustman Rises a Little

MR and Mrs Lammle had come to breakfast with Mr and Mrs Boffin. They were not absolutely uninvited, but had pressed themselves with so much urgency on the golden couple, that evasion of the honour and pleasure of their company would have been difficult, if desired. They were in a charming state of mind, were Mr and Mrs Lammle, and almost as fond of Mr and Mrs Boffin as of one another.

'My dear Mrs Boffin,' said Mrs Lammle, 'it imparts new life to me, to see my Alfred in confidential communication with Mr Boffin. The two were formed to become intimate. So much simplicity combined with so much force of character, such natural sagacity united to such amiability and gentleness—these are the distinguishing characteristics of both.'

This being said aloud, gave Mr Lammle an opportunity, as he came with Mr Boffin from the window to the breakfast table, of taking up his dear and honoured wife.

'My Sophronia,' said that gentleman, 'your too partial estimate of your husband's character—'

'No! Not too partial, Alfred,' urged the lady, tenderly moved; 'never say that.'

'My child, your favourable opinion, then, of your husband—you don't object to that phrase, darling?'

'How can I, Alfred?'

'Your favourable opinion then, my Precious, does less than justice to Mr Boffin, and more than justice to me.'

'To the first charge, Alfred, I plead guilty. But to the second, oh no, no!'

'Less than justice to Mr Boffin, Sophronia,' said Mr Lammle, soaring into a tone of moral grandeur, 'because it represents Mr Boffin as on my lower level; more than justice to me, Sophronia, because it represents me as on Mr Boffin's higher level. Mr Boffin bears and forbears far more than I could.'

'Far more than you could for yourself, Alfred?'

'My love, that is not the question.'

'Not the question, Lawyer?' said Mrs Lammle, archly.

'No, dear Sophronia. From my lower level, I regard Mr Boffin as too generous, as possessed of too much clemency, as being too good to persons who are unworthy of him and ungrateful to him. To those noble qualities I can lay no claim. On the contrary, they rouse my indignation when I see them in action.'

'Alfred!'

'They rouse my indignation, my dear, against the unworthy persons, and give me a combative desire to stand between Mr Boffin and all such persons. Why? Because, in my lower nature I am more worldly and less delicate. Not being so magnanimous as Mr Boffin, I feel his injuries more than he does himself, and feel more capable of opposing his injurers.'

It struck Mrs Lammle that it appeared rather difficult this morning to bring Mr and Mrs Boffin into agreeable conversation. Here had been several lures thrown out, and neither of them had uttered a word. Here were she, Mrs Lammle, and her husband discoursing at once affectingly and effectively, but discoursing alone. Assuming that the dear old creatures were impressed by what they heard, still one would like to be sure of it, the more so, as at least one of the dear old creatures was somewhat pointedly referred to. If the dear old creatures were too bashful or too dull to assume their required places in the discussion, why then it would seem desirable that the dear old creatures should be taken by their heads and shoulders and brought into it.

'But is not my husband saying in effect,' asked Mrs Lammle, therefore, with an innocent air, of Mr and Mrs Boffin, 'that he becomes unmindful of his own temporary misfortunes in his admiration of another whom he is burning to serve? And is not that making an admission that his nature is a generous one? I am wretched in argument, but surely this is so, dear Mr and Mrs Boffin?'

Still, neither Mr and Mrs Boffin said a word. He sat with his eyes on his plate, eating his muffins and ham, and she sat shyly looking at the teapot. Mrs Lammle's innocent appeal was merely thrown into the air, to mingle with the steam of the urn. Glancing towards Mr and Mrs Boffin, she very slightly raised her eyebrows, as though inquiring of her husband: 'Do I notice anything wrong here?'

Mr Lammle, who had found his chest effective on a variety of occasions, manœuvred his capacious shirt front into the largest demonstration possible, and then smiling retorted on his wife, thus:

'Sophronia, darling, Mr and Mrs Boffin will remind you of the old adage, that self-praise is no recommendation.'

'Self-praise, Alfred? Do you mean because we are one and the same?'

'No, my dear child. I mean that you cannot fail to remember, if you reflect for a single moment, that what you are pleased to compliment me upon feeling in the case of Mr Boffin, you have yourself confided to me as your own feeling in the case of Mrs Boffin.'

('I shall be beaten by this Lawyer,' Mrs Lammle gaily whispered to Mrs Boffin. 'I am afraid I must admit it, if he presses me, for it's damagingly true.')

Several white dints began to come and go about Mr Lammle's nose, as he observed that Mrs Boffin merely looked up from the teapot for a moment with an embarrassed smile, which was no smile, and then looked down again.

'Do you admit the charge, Sophronia?' inquired Alfred, in a rallying tone.

'Really, I think,' said Mrs Lammle, still gaily, 'I must throw myself on the protection of the Court. Am I bound to answer that question, my Lord?' To Mr Boffin.

'You needn't, if you don't like, ma'am,' was his answer. 'It's not of the least consequence.'

Both husband and wife glanced at him, very doubtfully. His

manner was grave, but not coarse, and derived some dignity from a certain repressed dislike of the tone of the conversation.

Again Mrs Lammle raised her eyebrows for instruction from her husband. He replied in a slight nod, 'Try 'em again.'

'To protect myself against the suspicion of covert self-laudation, my dear Mrs Boffin,' said the airy Mrs Lammle therefore, 'I must tell you how it was.'

'No. Pray don't,' Mr Boffin interposed.

Mrs Lammle turned to him laughingly. 'The Court objects?'

'Ma'am,' said Mr Boffin, 'the Court (if I am the Court) does object. The Court objects for two reasons. First, because the Court don't think it fair. Secondly, because the dear old lady, Mrs Court (if I am Mr) gets distressed by it.'

A very remarkable wavering between two bearings—between her propitiatory bearing there, and her defiant bearing at Mr Twemlow's—was observable on the part of Mrs Lammle as she said: 'What does the Court not consider fair?'

'Letting you go on,' replied Mr Boffin, nodding his head soothingly, as who should say, We won't be harder on you than we can help; we'll make the best of it. 'It's not above-board and it's not fair. When the old lady is uncomfortable, there's sure to be good reason for it. I see she is uncomfortable, and I plainly see this is the good reason wherefore. *Have* you breakfasted, ma'am.'

Mrs Lammle, settling into her defiant manner, pushed her plate away, looked at her husband, and laughed; but by no means gaily.

'Have *you* breakfasted, sir?' inquired Mr Boffin.

'Thank you,' replied Alfred, showing all his teeth. 'If Mrs Boffin will oblige me, I'll take another cup of tea.'

He spilled a little of it over the chest which ought to have been so effective, and which had done so little; but on the whole drank it with something of an air, though the coming and going dints got almost as large, the while, as if they had been made by pressure of the teaspoon. 'A thousand thanks,' he then observed. 'I have breakfasted.'

'Now, which,' said Mr Boffin softly, taking out a pocket-book, 'which of you two is Cashier?'

'Sophronia, my dear,' remarked her husband, as he leaned back in his chair, waving his right hand towards her, while he hung his left hand by the thumb in the arm-hole of his waistcoat: 'it shall be your department.'

'I would rather,' said Mr Boffin, 'that it was your hus-

band's, ma'am, because—but never mind, because. I would
rather have to do with him. However, what I have to say, I will
say with as little offence as possible; if I can say it without any, I
shall be heartily glad. You two have done me a service, a very
great service, in doing what you did (my old lady knows what it
was), and I have put into this envelope a bank note for a hundred
pound. I consider the service well worth a hundred pound, and I
am well pleased to pay the money. Would you do me the favour
to take it, and likewise to accept my thanks?'

With a haughty action, and without looking towards him,
Mrs Lammle held out her left hand, and into it Mr Boffin put
the little packet. When she had conveyed it to her bosom, Mr
Lammle had the appearance of feeling relieved, and breathing
more freely, as not having been quite certain that the hundred
pounds were his, until the note had been safely transferred out of
Mr Boffin's keeping into his own Sophronia's.

'It is not impossible,' said Mr Boffin, addressing Alfred,
'that you have had some general idea, sir, of replacing Rokesmith,
in course of time?'

'It is not,' assented Alfred, with a glittering smile and a
great deal of nose, 'not impossible.'

'And perhaps, ma'am,' pursued Mr Boffin, addressing
Sophronia, 'you have been so kind as to take up my old lady in
your own mind, and to do her the honour of turning the question
over whether you mightn't one of these days have her in charge,
like? Whether you mightn't be a sort of Miss Bella Wilfer to her,
and something more?'

'I should hope,' returned Mrs Lammle, with a scornful look
and in a loud voice, 'that if I were anything to your wife, sir, I
could hardly fail to be something more than Miss Bella Wilfer,
as you call her.'

'What do *you* call her, ma'am?' asked Mr Boffin.

Mrs Lammle disdained to reply, and sat defiantly beating
one foot on the ground.

'Again I think I may say, that's not impossible. Is it, sir?'
asked Mr Boffin, turning to Alfred.

'It is not,' said Alfred, smiling assent as before, 'not
impossible.'

'Now,' said Mr Boffin, gently, 'it won't do. I don't wish
to say a single word that might be afterwards remembered as
unpleasant; but it won't do.'

'Sophronia, my love,' her husband repeated in a bantering
manner, 'you hear? It won't do.'

'No,' said Mr Boffin, with his voice still dropped, 'it really won't. You positively must excuse us. If you'll go your way, we'll go ours, and so I hope this affair ends to the satisfaction of all parties.'

Mrs Lammle gave him the look of a decidedly dissatisfied party demanding exemption from the category; but said nothing.

'The best thing we can make of the affair,' said Mr Boffin, 'is a matter of business, and as a matter of business it's brought to a conclusion. You have done me a great service, a very great service, and I have paid for it. Is there any objection to the price?'

Mr and Mrs Lammle looked at one another across the table, but neither could say that there was. Mr Lammle shrugged his shoulders, and Mrs Lammle sat rigid.

'Very good,' said Mr Boffin. 'We hope (my old lady and me) that you'll give us credit for taking the plainest and honestest short-cut that could be taken under the circumstances. We have talked it over with a deal of care (my old lady and me), and we have felt that at all to lead you on, or even at all to let you go on of your own selves, wouldn't be the right thing. So, I have openly given you to understand that—' Mr Boffin sought for a new turn of speech, but could find none so expressive as his former one, repeated in a confidential tone, '—that it won't do. If I could have put the case more pleasantly I would; but I hope I haven't put it very unpleasantly; at all events I haven't meant to. So,' said Mr Boffin, by way of peroration, 'wishing you well in the way you go, we now conclude with the observation that perhaps you'll go it.'

Mr Lammle rose with an impudent laugh on his side of the table, and Mrs Lammle rose with a disdainful frown on hers. At this moment a hasty foot was heard on the staircase, and Georgiana Podsnap broke into the room, unannounced and in tears.

'Oh, my dear Sophronia,' cried Georgiana, wringing her hands as she ran up to embrace her, 'to think that you and Alfred should be ruined! Oh, my poor dear Sophronia, to think that you should have had a Sale at your house after all your kindness to me! Oh, Mr and Mrs Boffin, pray forgive me for this intrusion, but you don't know how fond I was of Sophronia when Pa wouldn't let me go there any more, or what I have felt for Sophronia since I heard from Ma of her having been brought low in the world. You don't, you can't, you never can, think, how I have lain awake at night and cried for my good Sophronia, my first and only friend!'

Mrs Lammle's manner changed under the poor silly girl's embraces, and she turned extremely pale: directing one appealing look, first to Mrs Boffin, and then to Mr Boffin. Both understood her instantly, with a more delicate subtlety than much better educated people, whose perception came less directly from the heart, could have brought to bear upon the case.

'I haven't a minute,' said poor little Georgiana, 'to stay. I am out shopping early with Ma, and I said I had a headache and got Ma to leave me outside in the phaeton, in Piccadilly, and ran round to Sackille Street, and heard that Sophronia was here, and then Ma came to see, oh such a dreadful old stony woman from the country in a turban in Portland Place, and I said I wouldn't go up with Ma but would drive round and leave cards for the Boffins, which is taking a liberty with the name; but oh my goodness I am distracted, and the phaeton's at the door, and what would Pa say if he knew it!'

'Don't ye be timid, my dear,' said Mrs Boffin. 'You came in to see us.'

'Oh, no, I didn't,' cried Georgiana. 'It's very impolite, I know, but I came to see my poor Sophronia, my only friend. Oh! how I felt the separation, my dear Sophronia, before I knew you were brought low in the world, and how much more I feel it now!'

There were actually tears in the bold woman's eyes, as the soft-headed and soft-hearted girl twined her arms about her neck.

'But I've come on business,' said Georgiana, sobbing and drying her face, and then searching in a little reticule, 'and if I don't despatch it I shall have come for nothing, and oh good gracious! what would Pa say if he knew of Sackville Street, and what would Ma say if she was kept waiting on the doorsteps of that dreadful turban, and there never were such pawing horses as ours unsettling my mind every moment more and more when I want more mind than I have got, by pawing up Mr Boffin's street where they have no business to be. Oh! where is, where is it? Oh! I can't find it!' All this time sobbing, and searching in the little reticule.

'What do you miss, my dear?' asked Mr Boffin, stepping forward.

'Oh! it's little enough,' replied Georgiana, 'because Ma always treats me as if I was in the nursery (I am sure I wish I was!), but I hardly ever spend it and it has mounted up to fifteen pounds, Sophronia, and I hope three five-pound notes are better than nothing, though so little, so little! And now I have found that—oh, my goodness! there's the other gone next! Oh no, it isn't, here it is!'

With that, always sobbing and searching in the reticule, Georgiana produced a necklace.

'Ma says chits and jewels have no business together,' pursued Georgiana, 'and that's the reason why I have no trinkets except this, but I suppose my aunt Hawkinson was of a different opinion, because she left me this, though I used to think she might just as well have buried it, for it's always kept in jewellers' cotton. However, here it is, I am thankful to say, and of use at last, and you'll sell it, dear Sophronia, and buy things with it.'

'Give it to me,' said Mr Boffin, gently taking it. 'I'll see that it's properly disposed of.'

'Oh! are you such a friend of Sophronia's, Mr Boffin?' cried Georgiana. 'Oh, how good of you! Oh, my gracious! there was something else, and it's gone out of my head! Oh no, it isn't, I remember what it was. My grandmamma's property, that'll come to me when I am of age, Mr Boffin, will be all my own, and neither Pa nor Ma nor anybody else will have any control over it, and what I wish to do is to make some of it over somehow to Sophronia and Alfred, by signing something somewhere that'll prevail on somebody to advance them something. I want them to have something handsome to bring them up in the world again. Oh, my goodness me! Being such a friend of my dear Sophronia's, you won't refuse me, will you?'

'No, no,' said Mr Boffin, 'it shall be seen to.'

'Oh, thank you, thank you!' cried Georgiana. 'If my maid had a little note and half a crown, I could run round to the pastry-cook's to sign something, or I could sign something in the Square if somebody would come and cough for me to let 'em in with the key, and would bring a pen and ink with 'em and a bit of blotting-paper. Oh, my gracious! I must tear myself away, or Pa and Ma will both find out! Dear, dear Sophronia, good, good-bye!'

The credulous little creature again embraced Mrs Lammle most affectionately, and then held out her hand to Mr Lammle.

'Good-bye, dear Mr Lammle—I mean Alfred. You won't think after to-day that I have deserted you and Sophronia because you have been brought low in the world, will you? Oh me! oh me! I have been crying my eyes out of my head, and Ma will be sure to ask me what's the matter. Oh, take me down, somebody, please, please, please!'

Mr Boffin took her down, and saw her driven away, with

her poor little red eyes and weak chin peering over the great apron of the custard-coloured phaeton, as if she had been ordered to expiate some childish misdemeanour by going to bed in the daylight, and were peeping over the counterpane in a miserable flutter of repentance and low spirits. Returning to the breakfast-room, he found Mrs Lammle still standing on her side of the table, and Mr Lammle on his.

'I'll take care,' said Mr Boffin, showing the money and the necklace, 'that these are soon given back.'

Mrs Lammle had taken up her parasol from a side table, and stood sketching with it on the pattern of the damask cloth, as she had sketched on the pattern of Mr Twemlow's papered wall.

'You will not undeceive her I hope, Mr Boffin?' she said, turning her head towards him, but not her eyes.

'No,' said Mr Boffin.

'I mean, as to the worth and value of her friend,' Mrs Lammle explained, in a measured voice, and with an emphasis on her last word.

'No,' he returned. 'I may try to give a hint at her home that she is in want of kind and careful protection, but I shall say no more than that to her parents, and I shall say nothing to the young lady herself.'

'Mr and Mrs Boffin,' said Mrs Lammle, still sketching, and seeming to bestow great pains upon it, 'there are not many people, I think, who, under the circumstances, would have been so considerate and sparing as you have been to me just now. Do you care to be thanked?'

'Thanks are always worth having,' said Mrs Boffin, in her ready good nature.

'Then thank you both.'

'Sophronia,' asked her husband, mockingly, 'are you sentimental?'

'Well, well, my good sir,' Mr Boffin interposed, 'it's a very good thing to think well of another person, and it's a very good thing to be thought well of *by* another person. Mrs Lammle will be none the worse for it, if she is.'

'Much obliged. But I asked Mrs Lammle if she was.'

She stood sketching on the table-cloth, with her face clouded and set, and was silent.

'Because,' said Alfred, 'I am disposed to be sentimental myself, on your appropriation of the jewels and the money, Mr Boffin. As our little Georgiana said, three five-pound notes are better than nothing, and if you sell a necklace you can buy things with the produce.'

'*If* you sell it,' was Mr Boffin's comment, as he put it in his pocket.

Alfred followed it with his looks, and also greedily pursued the notes until they vanished into Mr Boffin's waistcoat pocket. Then he directed a look, half exasperated and half jeering, at his wife. She still stood sketching; but, as she sketched, there was a struggle within her, which found expression in the depth of the few last lines the parasol point indented into the table-cloth, and then some tears fell from her eyes.

'Why, confound the woman,' exclaimed Lammle, 'she *is* sentimental!'

She walked to the window, flinching under his angry stare, looked out for a moment, and turned round quite coldly.

'You have had no former cause of complaint on the senti-mental score, Alfred, and you will have none in future. It is not worth your noticing. We go abroad soon, with the money we have earned here?'

'You know we do; you know we must.'

'There is no fear of my taking any sentiment with me. I should soon be eased of it, if I did. But it will be all left behind. It *is* all left behind. Are you ready, Alfred?'

'What the deuce have I been waiting for but you, Sophronia?'

'Let us go then. I am sorry I have delayed our dignified departure.'

She passed out and he followed her. Mr and Mrs Boffin had the curiosity softly to raise a window and look after them as they went down the long street. They walked arm-in-arm, showily enough, but without appearing to interchange a syllable. It might have been fanciful to suppose that under their outer bearing there was something of the shamed air of two cheats who were linked together by concealed handcuffs; but, not so, to suppose that they were haggardly weary of one another, of themselves, and of all this world. In turning the street corner they might have turned out of this world, for anything Mr and Mrs Boffin ever saw of them to the contrary; for, they set eyes on the Lammles never more.

Chapter 3
The Golden Dustman Sinks Again

THE evening of that day being one of the reading evenings at the Bower, Mr Boffin kissed Mrs Boffin after a five o'clock dinner, and trotted out, nursing his big stick in both arms, so that, as of old, it seemed to be whispering in his ear. He carried so very attentive an expression on his countenance that it appeared as if the confidential discourse of the big stick required to be followed closely. Mr Boffin's face was like the face of a thoughtful listener to an intricate communication, and, in trotting along, he occasionally glanced at that companion with the look of a man who was interposing the remark: 'You don't mean it!'

Mr Boffin and his stick went on alone together, until they arrived at certain cross-ways where they would be likely to fall in with any one coming, at about the same time, from Clerkenwell to the Bower. Here they stopped, and Mr Boffin consulted his watch.

'It wants five minutes, good, to Venus's appointment,' said he. 'I'm rather early.'

But Venus was a punctual man, and, even as Mr Boffin replaced his watch in its pocket, was to be descried coming towards him. He quickened his pace on seeing Mr Boffin already at the place of meeting, and was soon at his side.

'Thank'ee, Venus,' said Mr Boffin. 'Thank'ee, thank'ee, thank'ee!'

It would not have been very evident why he thanked the anatomist, but for his furnishing the explanation in what he went on to say.

'All right, Venus, all right. Now, that you've been to see me, and have consented to keep up the appearance before Wegg of remaining in it for a time, I have got a sort of a backer. All right, Venus. Thank'ee, Venus. Thank'ee, thank'ee, thank'ee!'

Mr Venus shook the proffered hand with a modest air, and they pursued the direction of the Bower.

'Do you think Wegg is likely to drop down upon me to-night, Venus?' inquired Mr Boffin, wistfully, as they went along.

'I think he is, sir.'

'Have you any particular reason for thinking so, Venus?'

'Well, sir,' returned that personage, 'the fact is, he has given me another look-in, to make sure of what he calls our stock-in-trade being correct, and he has mentioned his intention that he was not to be put off beginning with you the very next time you should come. And this,' hinted Mr Venus, delicately, 'being the very next time, you know, sir—'

—'Why, therefore you suppose he'll turn to at the grind-stone, eh, Wegg?' said Mr Boffin.

'Just so, sir.'

Mr Boffin took his nose in his hand, as if it were already excoriated, and the sparks were beginning to fly out of that feature. 'He's a terrible fellow, Venus; he's an awful fellow. I don't know how ever I shall go through with it. You must stand by me, Venus, like a good man and true. You'll do all you can to stand by me, Venus; won't you?'

Mr Venus replied with the assurance that he would; and Mr Boffin, looking anxious and dispirited, pursued the way in silence until they rang at the Bower gate. The stumping approach of Wegg was soon heard behind it, and as it turned upon its hinges he became visible with his hand on the lock.

'Mr Boffin, sir?' he remarked. 'You're quite a stranger!'

'Yes. I've been otherwise occupied, Wegg.'

'Have you indeed, sir?' returned the literary gentleman, with a threatening sneer. 'Hah! I've been looking for you, sir, rather what I may call specially.'

'You don't say so, Wegg?'

'Yes, I do say so, sir. And if you hadn't come round to me to-night, dash my wig if I wouldn't have come round to you to-morrow. Now! I tell you!'

'Nothing wrong, I hope, Wegg?'

'Oh no, Mr Boffin,' was the ironical answer. 'Nothing wrong! What should be wrong in Boffinses Bower! Step in, sir.

' "If you'll come to the Bower I've shaded for you,
    Your bed shan't be roses all spangled with doo:
  Will you, will you, will you, will you, come to
    the Bower?

> Oh, won't you, won't you, won't you, won't you,
>   come to the Bower?'' '

An unholy glare of contradiction and offence shone in the eyes
of Mr Wegg, as he turned the key on his patron, after ushering
him into the yard with this vocal quotation. Mr Boffin's air was
crest-fallen and submissive. Whispered Wegg to Venus, as they
crossed the yard behind him: 'Look at the worm and minion;
he's down in the mouth already.' Whispered Venus to Wegg:
'That's because I've told him. I've prepared the way for you.'

Mr Boffin, entering the usual chamber, laid his stick upon
the settle usually reserved for him, thrust his hands into his
pockets, and, with his shoulders raised and his hat drooping back
upon them, looking disconsolately at Wegg. 'My friend and
partner, Mr Venus, gives me to understand,' remarked that man
of might, addressing him, 'that you are aware of our power over
you. Now, when you have took your hat off, we'll go into that
pint.'

Mr Boffin shook it off with one shake, so that it dropped on
the floor behind him, and remained in his former attitude with
his former rueful look upon him.

'First of all, I'm a-going to call you Boffin, for short,' said
Wegg. 'If you don't like it, it's open to you to lump it.'

'I don't mind it, Wegg,' Mr Boffin replied.

'That's lucky for you, Boffin. Now, do you want to be read
to?'

'I don't particularly care about it to-night, Wegg.'

'Because if you did want to,' pursued Mr Wegg, the brilliancy of whose point was dimmed by his having been unexpectedly answered: 'you wouldn't be. I've been your slave long
enough. I'm not to be trampled under-foot by a dustman any
more. With the single exception of the salary, I renounce the
whole and total sitiwation.'

'Since you say it is to be so, Wegg,' returned Mr Boffin,
with folded hands, 'I suppose it must be.'

'*I* suppose it must be,' Wegg retorted. 'Next (to clear the
ground before coming to business), you've placed in this yard a
skulking, a sneaking, and a sniffing, menial.'

'He hadn't a cold in his head when I sent him here,' said
Mr Boffin.

'Boffin!' retorted Wegg, 'I warn you not to attempt a joke
with me!'

Here Mr Venus interposed, and remarked that he conceived

Mr Boffin to have taken the description literally; the rather, for-asmuch as he, Mr Venus, had himself supposed the menial to have contracted an affliction or a habit of the nose, involving a serious drawback on the pleasures of social intercourse, until he had discovered that Mr Wegg's description of him was to be accepted as merely figurative.

'Any how, and every how,' said Wegg, 'he has been planted here, and he is here. Now, I won't have him here. So I call upon Boffin, before I say another word, to fetch him in and send him packing to the right-about.'

The unsuspecting Sloppy was at that moment airing his many buttons within view of the window. Mr Boffin, after a short interval of impassive discomfiture, opened the window and beckoned him to come in.

'I call upon Boffin,' said Wegg, with one arm a-kimbo and his head on one side, like a bullying counsel pausing for an answer from a witness, 'to inform that menial that I am Master here!'

In humble obedience, when the button-gleaming Sloppy entered Mr Boffin said to him: 'Sloppy, my fine fellow, Mr Wegg is Master here. He doesn't want you, and you are to go from here.'

'For good!' Mr Wegg severely stipulated.

'For good,' said Mr Boffin.

Sloppy stared, with both his eyes and all his buttons, and his mouth wide open; but was without loss of time escorted forth by Silas Wegg, pushed out at the yard gate by the shoulders, and locked out.

'The atmospear,' said Wegg, stumping back into the room again, a little reddened by his late exertion, 'is now freer for the purposes of respiration. Mr Venus, sir, take a chair. Boffin, you may sit down.'

Mr Boffin, still with his hands ruefully stuck in his pockets, sat on the edge of the settle, shrunk into a small compass, and eyed the potent Silas with conciliatory looks.

'This gentleman,' said Silas Wegg, pointing out Venus, 'this gentleman, Boffin, is more milk and watery with you than I'll be. But he hasn't borne the Roman yoke as I have, nor yet he hasn't been required to pander to your depraved appetite for miserly characters.'

'I never meant, my dear Wegg—' Mr Boffin was begin-ning, when Silas stopped him.

'Hold your tongue, Boffin! Answer when you're called

upon to answer. You'll find you've got quite enough to do. Now, you're aware—are you—that you're in possession of property to which you've no right at all? Are you aware of that?'

'Venus tells me so,' said Mr Boffin, glancing towards him for any support he could give.

'*I* tell you so,' returned Silas. 'Now, here's my hat, Boffin, and here's my walking-stick. Trifle with me, and instead of making a bargain with you, I'll put on my hat and take up my walking-stick, and go out, and make a bargain with the rightful owner. Now, what do you say?'

'I say,' returned Mr Boffin, leaning forward in alarmed appeal, with his hands on his knees, 'that I am sure I don't want to trifle, Wegg. I have said so to Venus.'

'You certainly have, sir,' said Venus.

'You're too milk and watery with our friend, you are indeed,' remonstrated Silas, with a disapproving shake of his wooden head. 'Then at once you confess yourself desirous to come to terms, do you, Boffin? Before you answer, keep this hat well in your mind, and also this walking-stick.'

'I am willing, Wegg, to come to terms.'

'Willing won't do, Boffin. I won't take willing. Are you desirous to come to terms? Do you ask to be allowed as a favour to come to terms?' Mr Wegg again planted his arm, and put his head on one side.

'Yes.'

'Yes what?' said the inexorable Wegg: 'I won't take yes. I'll have it out of you in full, Boffin.'

'Dear me!' cried that unfortunate gentleman. 'I am so worrited! I ask to be allowed to come to terms, supposing your document is all correct.'

'Don't you be afraid of that,' said Silas, poking his head at him. 'You shall be satisfied by seeing it. Mr Venus will show it you, and I'll hold you the while. Then you want to know what the terms are. Is that about the sum and substance of it? Will you or won't you answer, Boffin?' For he had paused a moment.

'Dear me!' cried that unfortunate gentleman again, 'I am worrited to that degree that I'm almost off my head. You hurry me so. Be so good as name the terms, Wegg.'

'Now, mark, Boffin,' returned Silas: 'Mark 'em well, because they're the lowest terms and the only terms. You'll throw your Mound (the little Mound as comes to you any way) into the general estate, and then you'll divide the whole property into three parts, and you'll keep one and hand over the others.'

Mr Venus's mouth screwed itself up, as Mr Boffin's face lengthened itself; Mr Venus not having been prepared for such a rapacious demand.

'Now, wait a bit, Boffin,' Wegg proceeded, 'there's something more. You've been a squandering this property—laying some of it out on yourself. *That* won't do. You've bought a house. You'll be charged for it.'

'I shall be ruined, Wegg!' Mr Boffin faintly protested.

'Now, wait a bit, Boffin; there's something more. You'll leave me in sole custody of these Mounds till they're all laid low. If any waluables should be found in 'em, I'll take care of such waluables. You'll produce your contract for the sale of the Mounds, that we may know to a penny what they're worth, and you'll make out likewise an exact list of all the other property. When the Mounds is cleared away to the last shovel-full, the final diwision will come off.'

'Dreadful, dreadful, dreadful! I shall die in a workhouse!' cried the Golden Dustman, with his hands to his head.

'Now, wait a bit, Boffin; there's something more. You've been unlawfully ferreting about this yard. You've been seen in the act of ferreting about this yard. Two pair of eyes at the present moment brought to bear upon you, have seen you dig up a Dutch bottle.'

'It was mine, Wegg,' protested Mr Boffin. 'I put it there myself.'

'What was in it, Boffin?' inquired Silas.

'Not gold, not silver, not bank notes, not jewels, nothing that you could turn into money, Wegg; upon my soul!'

'Prepared, Mr Venus,' said Wegg, turning to his partner with a knowing and superior air, 'for an ewasive answer on the part of our dusty friend here, I have hit out a little idea which I think will meet your views. We charge that bottle against our dusty friend at a thousand pound.'

Mr Boffin drew a deep groan.

'Now, wait a bit, Boffin; there's something more. In your employment is an under-handed sneak, named Rokesmith. It won't answer to have *him* about, while this business of ours is about. He must be discharged.'

'Rokesmith is already discharged,' said Mr Boffin, speaking in a muffled voice, with his hands before his face, as he rocked himself on the settle.

'Already discharged, is he?' returned Wegg, surprised. 'Oh! Then, Boffin, I believe there's nothing more at present.'

The unlucky gentleman continuing to rock himself to and fro, and to utter an occasional moan, Mr Venus besought him to bear up against his reverses, and to take time to accustom himself to the thought of his new position. But, his taking time was exactly the thing of all others that Silas Wegg could not be induced to hear of. 'Yes or no, and no half measures!' was the motto which that obdurate person many times repeated; shaking his fist at Mr Boffin, and pegging his motto into the floor with his wooden leg, in a threatening and alarming manner.

At length, Mr Boffin entreated to be allowed a quarter of an hour's grace, and a cooling walk of that duration in the yard. With some difficulty Mr Wegg granted this great favour, but only on condition that he accompanied Mr Boffin in his walk, as not knowing what he might fraudulently unearth if he were left to himself. A more absurd sight than Mr Boffin in his mental irritation trotting very nimbly, and Mr Wegg hopping after him with great exertion, eager to watch the slightest turn of an eyelash, lest it should indicate a spot rich with some secret, assuredly had never been seen in the shadow of the Mounds. Mr Wegg was much distressed when the quarter of an hour expired, and came hopping in, a very bad second.

'I can't help myself!' cried Mr Boffin, flouncing on the settle in a forlorn manner, with his hands deep in his pockets, as if his pockets had sunk. 'What's the good of my pretending to stand out, when I can't help myself? I must give in to the terms. But I should like to see the document.'

Wegg, who was all for clinching the nail he had so strongly driven home, announced that Boffin should see it without an hour's delay. Taking him into custody for that purpose, or overshadowing him as if he really were his Evil Genius in visible form, Mr Wegg clapped Mr Boffin's hat upon the back of his head, and walked him out by the arm, asserting a proprietorship over his soul and body that was at once more grim and more ridiculous than anything in Mr Venus's rare collection. That light-haired gentleman followed close upon their heels, at least backing up Mr Boffin in a literal sense, if he had not had recent opportunities of doing so spiritually; while Mr Boffin, trotting on as hard as he could trot, involved Silas Wegg in frequent collisions with the public, much as a pre-occupied blind man's dog may be seen to involve his master.

Thus they reached Mr Venus's establishment, somewhat heated by the nature of their progress thither. Mr Wegg, especially, was in a flaming glow, and stood in the little shop, panting and mopping his head with his pocket-handkerchief, speechless for several minutes.

Meanwhile, Mr Venus, who had left the duelling frogs to fight it out in his absence by candlelight for the public delectation, put the shutters up. When all was snug, and the shop-door fastened, he said to the perspiring Silas: 'I suppose, Mr Wegg, we may now produce the paper?'

'Hold on a minute, sir,' replied that discreet character; 'hold on a minute. Will you obligingly shove that box—which you mentioned on a former occasion as containing miscellanies— towards me in the midst of the shop here?'

Mr Venus did as he was asked.

'Very good,' said Silas, looking about: 've–ry good. Will you hand me that chair, sir, to put a-top of it?'

Venus handed him the chair.

'Now, Boffin,' said Wegg, 'mount up here and take your seat, will you?'

Mr Boffin, as if he were about to have his portrait painted, or to be electrified, or to be made a Freemason, or to be placed at any other solitary disadvantage, ascended the rostrum prepared for him.

'Now, Mr Venus,' said Silas, taking off his coat, 'when I catches our friend here round the arms and body, and pins him tight to the back of the chair, you may show him what he wants to see. If you'll open it and hold it well up in one hand, sir, and a candle in the other, he can read it charming.'

Mr Boffin seemed rather inclined to object to these precautionary arrangements, but, being immediately embraced by Wegg, resigned himself. Venus then produced the document, and Mr Boffin slowly spelt it out aloud: so very slowly, that Wegg, who was holding him in the chair with the grip of a wrestler, became again exceedingly the worse for his exertions. 'Say when you've put it safe back, Mr Venus,' he uttered with difficulty, 'for the strain of this is terrimenjious.'

At length the document was restored to its place; and Wegg, whose uncomfortable attitude had been that of a very persevering man unsuccessfully attempting to stand upon his head, took a seat to recover himself. Mr Boffin, for his part, made no attempt to come down, but remained aloft disconsolate.

'Well, Boffin!' said Wegg, as soon as he was in a condition to speak. 'Now, you know.'

'Yes, Wegg,' said Mr Boffin, meekly. 'Now, I know.'

'You have no doubts about it, Boffin.'

'No, Wegg. No, Wegg. None,' was the slow and sad reply.

'Then, take care, you,' said Wegg, 'that you stick to your conditions. Mr Venus, if on this auspicious occasion, you should happen to have a drop of anything not quite so mild as tea in the 'ouse, I think I'd take the friendly liberty of asking you for a specimen of it.'

Mr Venus, reminded of the duties of hospitality, produced some rum. In answer to the inquiry, 'Will you mix it, Mr Wegg?' that gentleman pleasantly rejoined, 'I think not, sir. On so auspicious an occasion, I prefer to take it in the form of a Gum-Tickler.'

Mr Boffin, declining rum, being still elevated on his pedestal, was in a convenient position to be addressed. Wegg having eyed him with an impudent air at leisure, addressed him, therefore, while refreshing himself with his dram.

'Bof–fin!'

'Yes, Wegg,' he answered, coming out of a fit of abstraction, with a sigh.

'I haven't mentioned one thing, because it's a detail that comes of course. You must be followed up, you know. You must be kept under inspection.'

'I don't quite understand,' said Mr Boffin.

'Don't you?' sneered Wegg. 'Where's your wits, Boffin? Till the Mounds is down and this business completed, you're accountable for all the property, recollect. Consider yourself accountable to me. Mr Venus here being too milk and watery with you, I am the boy for you.'

'I've been a-thinking,' said Mr Boffin, in a tone of despondency, 'that I must keep the knowledge from my old lady.'

'The knowledge of the diwision, d'ye mean?' inquired Wegg, helping himself to a third Gum-Tickler—for he had already taken a second.

'Yes. If she was to die first of us two she might then think all her life, poor thing, that I had got the rest of the fortune still, and was saving it.'

'I suspect, Boffin,' returned Wegg, shaking his head sagaciously, and bestowing a wooden wink upon him, 'that you've found out some account of some old chap, supposed to be a Miser, who got himself the credit of having much more money than he had. However, *I* don't mind.'

'Don't you see, Wegg?' Mr Boffin feelingly represented to him: 'don't you see? My old lady has got so used to the property. It would be such a hard surprise.'

'I don't see it at all,' blustered Wegg. 'You'll have as much as I shall. And who are you?'

'But then, again,' Mr Boffin gently represented; 'my old lady has very upright principles.'

'Who's your old lady,' returned Wegg, 'to set herself up for having uprighter principles than mine?'

Mr Boffin seemed a little less patient at this point than at any other of the negotiations. But he commanded himself, and said tamely enough: 'I think it must be kept from my old lady, Wegg.'

'Well,' said Wegg, contemptuously, though, perhaps, perceiving some hint of danger otherwise, 'keep it from your old lady. I ain't going to tell her. I can have you under close inspection without that. I'm as good a man as you, and better. Ask me to dinner. Give me the run of your 'ouse. I was good enough for you and your old lady once, when I helped you out with your weal and hammers. Was there no Miss Elizabeth, Master George, Aunt Jane, and Uncle Parker, before *you* two?'

'Gently, Mr Wegg, gently,' Venus urged.

'Milk and water-erily you mean, sir,' he returned, with some little thickness of speech, in consequence of the Gum-Ticklers having tickled it. 'I've got him under inspection, and I'll inspect him.

> ' "Along the line the signal ran
> England expects as this present man
> Will keep Boffin to his duty."

—Boffin, I'll see you home.'

Mr Boffin descended with an air of resignation, and gave himself up, after taking friendly leave of Mr Venus. Once more, Inspector and Inspected went through the streets together, and so arrived at Mr Boffin's door.

But even there, when Mr Boffin had given his keeper good-night, and had let himself in with his key, and had softly closed the door, even there and then, the all-powerful Silas must needs claim another assertion of his newly-asserted power.

'Bof–fin!' he called through the keyhole.

'Yes, Wegg,' was the reply through the same channel.

'Come out. Show yourself again. Let's have another look at you!'

Mr Boffin—ah, how fallen from the high estate of his honest simplicity!—opened the door and obeyed.

'Go in. You may get to bed now,' said Wegg, with a grin.

The door was hardly closed, when he again called through the keyhole:

'Bof—fin!'

'Yes, Wegg.'

This time Silas made no reply, but laboured with a will at turning an imaginary grindstone outside the keyhole, while Mr Boffin stooped at it within; he then laughed silently, and stumped home.

Chapter 4

A Runaway Match

CHERUBIC Pa arose with as little noise as possible from beside majestic Ma, one morning early, having a holiday before him. Pa and the lovely woman had a rather particular appointment to keep.

Yet Pa and the lovely woman were not going out together. Bella was up before four, but had no bonnet on. She was waiting at the foot of the stairs—was sitting on the bottom stair, in fact—to receive Pa when he came down, but her only object seemed to be to get Pa well out of the house.

'Your breakfast is ready, sir,' whispered Bella, after greeting him with a hug, 'and all you have to do, is, to eat it up and drink it up, and escape. How do you feel, Pa?'

'To the best of my judgement, like a housebreaker new to the business, my dear, who can't make himself quite comfortable till he is off the premises.'

Bella tucked her arm in his with a merry noiseless laugh, and they went down to the kitchen on tiptoe; she stopping on every separate stair to put the tip of her forefinger on her rosy lips, and then lay it on his lips, according to her favourite petting way of kissing Pa.

'How do you feel, my love?' asked R. W., as she gave him his breakfast.

'I feel as if the Fortune-teller was coming true, dear Pa, and the fair little man was turning out as was predicted.'

'Ho! Only the fair little man?' said her father.

Bella put another of those finger-seals upon his lips, and then said, kneeling down by him as he sat at table: 'Now, look here, sir. If you keep well up to the mark this day, what do you think you deserve? What did I promise you should have, if you were good, upon a certain occasion?'

'Upon my word I don't remember, Precious. Yes, I do, though. Wasn't it one of these beau–tiful tresses?' with his caressing hand upon her hair.

'Wasn't it, too!' returned Bella, pretending to pout. 'Upon my word! Do you know, sir, that the Fortune-teller would give five thousand guineas (if it was quite convenient to him, which it isn't) for the lovely piece I have cut off for you? You can form no idea, sir, of the number of times he kissed quite a scrubby little piece—in comparison—that I cut off for *him*. And he wears it, too, round his neck, I can tell you! Near his heart!' said Bella, nodding. 'Ah! very near his heart! However, you have been a good, good boy, and you are the best of all the dearest boys that ever were, this morning, and here's the chain I have made of it, Pa, and you must let me put it round your neck with my own loving hands.'

As Pa bent his head, she cried over him a little, and then said (after having stopped to dry her eyes on his white waistcoat, the discovery of which incongruous circumstance made her laugh): 'Now, darling Pa, give me your hands that I may fold them together, and do you say after me:—My little Bella.'

'My little Bella,' repeated Pa.

'I am very fond of you.'

'I am very fond of you, my darling,' said Pa.

'You mustn't say anything not dictated to you, sir. You daren't do it in your responses at Church, and you mustn't do it in your responses out of Church.'

'I withdraw the darling,' said Pa.

'That's a pious boy! Now again:—You were always—'

'You were always,' repeated Pa.

'A vexatious—'

'No you weren't,' said Pa.

'A vexatious (do you hear, sir?), a vexatious, capricious, thankless, troublesome, Animal; but I hope you'll do better in the time to come, and I bless you and forgive you!' Here, she quite forgot that it was Pa's turn to make the responses, and clung to his neck. 'Dear Pa, if you knew how much I think this morning of what you told me once, about the first time of our seeing old Mr Harmon, when I stamped and screamed and beat you with my detestable little bonnet! I feel as if I had been stamping and screaming and beating you with my hateful little bonnet, ever since I was born, darling!'

'Nonsense, my love. And as to your bonnets, they have always been nice bonnets, for they have always become you—or you have become them; perhaps it was that—at every age.'

'Did I hurt you much, poor little Pa?' asked Bella, laughing (notwithstanding her repentance), with fantastic pleasure in the picture, 'when I beat you with my bonnet?'

'No, my child. Wouldn't have hurt a fly!'

'Ay, but I am afraid I shouldn't have beat you at all, unless I had meant to hurt you,' said Bella. 'Did I pinch your legs, Pa?'

'Not much, my dear; but I think it's almost time I—'

'Oh, yes!' cried Bella. 'If I go on chattering, you'll be taken alive. Fly, Pa, fly!'

So, they went softly up the kitchen stairs on tiptoe, and Bella with her light hand softly removed the fastenings of the house door, and Pa, having received a parting hug, made off. When he had gone a little way, he looked back. Upon which, Bella set another of those finger seals upon the air, and thrust out her little foot expressive of the mark. Pa, in appropriate action, expressed fidelity to the mark, and made off as fast as he could go.

Bella walked thoughtfully in the garden for an hour and more, and then, returning to the bedroom where Lavvy the Irrepressible still slumbered, put on a little bonnet of quiet, but on the whole of sly appearance, which she had yesterday made. 'I am going for a walk, Lavvy,' she said, as she stooped down and kissed her. The Irrepressible, with a bounce in the bed, and a remark that it wasn't time to get up yet, relapsed into unconsciousness, if she had come out of it.

Behold Bella tripping along the streets, the dearest girl afoot under the summer sun! Behold Pa waiting for Bella behind a pump, at least three miles from the parental roof-tree. Behold Bella and Pa aboard an early steamboat for Greenwich.

Were they expected at Greenwich? Probably. At least, Mr John Rokesmith was on the pier looking out, about a couple of hours before the coaly (but to him gold-dusty) little steamboat got her steam up in London. Probably. At least, Mr John Rokesmith seemed perfectly satisfied when he descried them on board. Probably. At least, Bella no sooner stepped ashore than she took Mr John Rokesmith's arm, without evincing surprise, and the two walked away together with an ethereal air of happiness which, as it were, wafted up from the earth and drew after them a gruff and glum old pensioner to see it out. Two wooden legs had this gruff and glum old pensioner, and, a minute before Bella stepped out of the boat, and drew that confiding little arm of hers through Rokesmith's, he had had no object in life but tobacco, and not enough of that. Stranded was Gruff and Glum in a harbour of everlasting mud, when all in an instant Bella floated him, and away he went.

Say, cherubic parent taking the lead, in what direction do we steer first? With some such inquiry in his thoughts, Gruff and Glum, stricken by so sudden an interest that he perked his neck and looked over the intervening people, as if he were trying to stand on tiptoe with his two wooden legs, took an observation of R. W. There was no 'first' in the case, Gruff and Glum made out; the cherubic parent was bearing down and crowding on direct for Greenwich church, to see his relations.

For, Gruff and Glum, though most events acted on him simply as tobacco-stoppers, pressing down and condensing the quids within him, might be imagined to trace a family resemblance between the cherubs in the church architecture, and the cherub in the white waistcoat. Some remembrance of old Valentines, wherein a cherub, less appropriately attired for a proverbially uncertain climate, had been seen conducting lovers to the altar, might have been fancied to inflame the ardour of his timber toes. Be it as it might, he gave his moorings the slip, and followed in chase.

The cherub went before, all beaming smiles; Bella and John Rokesmith followed; Gruff and Glum stuck to them like wax. For years, the wings of his mind had gone to look after the legs of his body; but Bella had brought them back for him per steamer, and they were spread again.

He was a slow sailer on a wind of happiness, but he took a cross cut for the rendezvous, and pegged away as if he were scoring furiously at cribbage. When the shadow of the church-porch swallowed them up, victorious Gruff and Glum likewise presented himself to be swallowed up. And by this time the cherubic parent was so fearful of surprise, that, but for the two wooden legs on which Gruff and Glum was reassuringly mounted, his conscience might have introduced, in the person of that pensioner, his own stately lady disguised, arrived at Greenwich in a car and griffins, like the spiteful Fairy at the christenings of the Princesses, to do something dreadful to the marriage service.

And truly he had a momentary reason to be pale of face, and to whisper to Bella, 'You don't think that can be your Ma; do you, my dear?' on account of a mysterious rustling and a stealthy movement somewhere in the remote neighbourhood of the organ, though it was gone directly and was heard no more. Albeit it was heard of afterwards, as will afterwards be read in this veracious register of marriage.

Who taketh? I, John, and so do I, Bella. Who giveth? I., R. W. Forasmuch, Gruff and Glum, as John and Bella have consented together in holy wedlock, you may (in short) consider it done, and withdraw your two wooden legs from this temple. To the foregoing purport, the Minister speaking, as directed by the Rubric, to the People, selectly represented in the present instance by G. and G. above mentioned.

And now, the church-porch having swallowed up Bella Wilfer for ever and ever, had it not in its power to relinquish that young woman, but slid into the happy sunlight, Mrs John Rokesmith instead. And long on the bright steps stood Gruff and Glum, looking after the pretty bride, with a narcotic consciousness of having dreamed a dream.

After which, Bella took out from her pocket a little letter, and read it aloud to Pa and John; this being a true copy of the same.

'DEAREST MA,

I hope you won't be angry, but I am most happily married to Mr John Rokesmith, who loves me better than I can ever deserve, except by loving him with all my heart. I thought it best not to mention it beforehand, in case it should cause any little difference at home. Please tell darling Pa. With love to Lavvy,

Ever dearest Ma,
Your affectionate daughter,
BELLA
(P.S.—Rokesmith).'

Then, John Rokesmith put the queen's countenance on the letter—when had Her Gracious Majesty looked so benign as on that blessed morning!—and then Bella popped it into the post-office, and said merrily, 'Now, dearest Pa, you are safe, and will never be taken alive!'

Pa was, at first, in the stirred depths of his conscience, so far from sure of being safe yet, that he made out majestic matrons lurking in ambush among the harmless trees of Greenwich Park, and seemed to see a stately countenance tied up in a well-known pocket-handkerchief glooming down at him from a window of the Observatory, where the Familiars of the Astronomer Royal nightly outwatch the winking stars. But, the minutes passing on and no Mrs Wilfer in the flesh appearing, he became more confident, and so repaired with good heart and appetite to Mr and Mrs John Rokesmith's cottage on Blackheath, where breakfast was ready.

A modest little cottage but a bright and a fresh, and on the snowy tablecloth the prettiest of little breakfasts. In waiting, too, like an attendant summer breeze, a fluttering young damsel, all pink and ribbons, blushing as if she had been married instead of Bella, and yet asserting the triumph of her sex over both John and Pa, in an exulting and exalted flurry: as who should say, 'This is what you must all come to, gentlemen, when we choose to bring you to book.' This same young damsel was Bella's serving-maid, and unto her did deliver a bunch of keys, commanding treasures in the way of dry-saltery, groceries, jams and pickles, the investigation of which made pastime after breakfast, when Bella declared that 'Pa must taste everything, John dear, or it will never be lucky,' and when Pa had all sorts of things poked into his mouth, and didn't quite know what to do with them when they were put there.

Then they, all three, out for a charming ride, and for a charming stroll among heath in bloom, and there behold the identical Gruff and Glum with his wooden legs horizontally disposed before him, apparently sitting meditating on the vicissitudes of life! To whom said Bella, in her light-hearted surprise: 'Oh! How do you do again? What a dear old pensioner you are!' To which Gruff and Glum responded that he see her married this morning, my Beauty, and that if it warn't a liberty he wished her ji and the fairest of fair wind and weather; further, in a general way requesting to know what cheer? and scrambling up on his two wooden legs to salute, hat in hand, ship-shape, with the gallantry of a man-of-warsman and a heart of oak.

It was a pleasant sight, in the midst of the golden bloom, to see this salt old Gruff and Glum, waving his shovel hat at Bella, while his thin white hair flowed free, as if she had once more launched him into blue water again. 'You are a charming old pensioner,' said Bella, 'and I am so happy that I wish I could make you happy, too.' Answered Gruff and Glum, 'Give me leave to kiss your hand, my Lovely, and it's done!' So it was

done to the general contentment; and if Gruff and Glum didn't in
the course of the afternoon splice the main brace, it was not for
want of the means of inflicting that outrage on the feelings of the
Infant Bands of Hope.

But, the marriage dinner was the crowning success, for
what had bride and bridegroom plotted to do, but to have and to
hold that dinner in the very room of the very hotel where Pa and
the lovely woman had once dined together! Bella sat between Pa
and John, and divided her attentions pretty equally, but felt it
necessary (in the waiter's absence before dinner) to remind Pa
that she was *his* lovely woman no longer.

'I am well aware of it, my dear,' returned the cherub, 'and I
resign you willingly.'

'Willingly, sir? You ought to be brokenhearted.'

'So I should be, my dear, if I thought that I was going to
lose you.'

'But you know you are not; don't you, poor dear Pa? You
know that you have only made a new relation who will be as
fond of you and as thankful to you—for my sake and your own
sake both—as I am; don't you, dear little Pa? Look here, Pa!'
Bella put her finger on her own lip, and then on Pa's, and then
on her own lip again, and then on her husband's. 'Now, we are a
partnership of three, dear Pa.'

The appearance of dinner here cut Bella short in one of her
disappearances: the more effectually, because it was put on
under the auspices of a solemn gentleman in black clothes and a
white cravat, who looked much more like a clergyman than *the*
clergyman, and seemed to have mounted a great deal higher in
the church: not to say, scaled the steeple. This dignitary, conferring in secrecy with John Rokesmith on the subject of punch and
wines, bent his head as though stooping to the Papistical practice of receiving auricular confession. Likewise, on John's offering a suggestion which didn't meet his views, his face became
overcast and reproachful, as enjoining penance.

What a dinner! Specimens of all the fishes that swim in the
sea, surely had swum their way to it, and if samples of the fishes
of divers colours that made a speech in the Arabian Nights (quite
a ministerial explanation in respect of cloudiness), and then
jumped out of the frying-pan, were not to be recognized, it was
only because they had all become of one hue by being cooked in
batter among the whitebait. And the dishes being seasoned with
Bliss—an article which they are sometimes out of, at Greenwich—

were of perfect flavour, and the golden drinks had been bottled in the golden age and hoarding up their sparkles ever since.

The best of it was, that Bella and John and the cherub had made a covenant that they would not reveal to mortal eyes any appearance whatever of being a wedding party. Now, the supervising dignitary, the Archbishop of Greenwich, knew this as well as if he had performed the nuptial ceremony. And the loftiness with which his Grace entered into their confidence without being invited, and insisted on a show of keeping the waiters out of it, was the crowning glory of the entertainment.

There was an innocent young waiter of a slender form and with weakish legs, as yet unversed in the wiles of waiterhood, and but too evidently of a romantic temperament, and deeply (it were not too much to add hopelessly) in love with some young female not aware of his merit. This guileless youth, descrying the position of affairs, which even his innocence could not mistake, limited his waiting to languishing admiringly against the sideboard when Bella didn't want anything, and swooping at her when she did. Him, his Grace the Archbishop perpetually obstructed, cutting him out with his elbow in the moment of success, despatching him in degrading quest of melted butter, and, when by any chance he got hold of any dish worth having, bereaving him of it, and ordering him to stand back.

'Pray excuse him, madam,' said the Archbishop in a low stately voice; 'he is a very young man on liking, and we *don't* like him.'

This induced John Rokesmith to observe—by way of making the thing more natural—'Bella, my love, this is so much more successful than any of our past anniversaries, that I think we must keep our future anniversaries here.'

Whereunto Bella replied, with probably the least successful attempt at looking matronly that ever was seen: 'Indeed, I think so, John, dear.'

Here the Archbishop of Greenwich coughed a stately cough to attract the attention of three of his ministers present, and staring at them, seemed to say: 'I call upon you by your fealty to believe this!'

With his own hands he afterwards put on the dessert, as remarking to the three guests, 'The period has now arrived at which we can dispense with the assistance of those fellows who are not in our confidence,' and would have retired with complete dignity but for a daring action issuing from the misguided brain of the young man on liking. He finding, by ill-fortune, a piece of

orange flower somewhere in the lobbies now approached unde-
tected with the same in a finger-glass, and placed it on Bella's
right hand. The Archbishop instantly ejected and excommuni-
cated him; but the thing was done.

'I trust, madam,' said his Grace, returning alone, 'that you
will have the kindness to overlook it, in consideration of its
being the act of a very young man who is merely here on liking,
and who will never answer.'

With that, he solemnly bowed and retired, and they all burst
into laughter, long and merry. 'Disguise is of no use,' said Bella;
'they all find me out; I think it must be, Pa and John dear,
because I look so happy!'

Her husband feeling it necessary at this point to demand one
of those mysterious disappearances on Bella's part, she dutifully
obeyed; saying in a softened voice from her place of concealment:

'You remember how we talked about the ships that day, Pa?'

'Yes, my dear.'

'Isn't it strange, now, to think that there was no John in all
the ships, Pa?'

'Not at all, my dear.'

'Oh, Pa! Not at all?'

'No, my dear. How can we tell what coming people are aboard
the ships that may be sailing to us now from the unknown seas!'

Bella remaining invisible and silent, her father remained at
his dessert and wine, until he remembered it was time for him to
get home to Holloway. 'Though I positively cannot tear myself
away,' he cherubically added, '—it would be a sin—without
drinking to many, many happy returns of this most happy day.'

'Here! ten thousand times!' cried John. 'I fill my glass and
my precious wife's.'

'Gentlemen,' said the cherub, inaudibly addressing, in his
Anglo-Saxon tendency to throw his feelings into the form of a
speech, the boys down below, who were bidding against each
other to put their heads in the mud for sixpence: 'Gentlemen—
and Bella and John—you will readily suppose that it is not my
intention to trouble you with many observations on the present
occasion. You will also at once infer the nature and even the
terms of the toast I am about to propose on the present occasion.
Gentlemen—and Bella and John—the present occasion is an
occasion fraught with feelings that I cannot trust myself to
express. But gentlemen—and Bella and John—for the part I have
had in it, for the confidence you have placed in me, and for the
affectionate good-nature and kindness with which you have de-

termined not to find me in the way, when I am well aware that I cannot be otherwise than in it more or less, I do most heartily thank you. Gentlemen—and Bella and John—my love to you, and may we meet, as on the present occasion, on many future occasions; that is to say, gentlemen—and Bella and John—on many happy returns of the present happy occasion.'

Having thus concluded his address, the amiable cherub embraced his daughter, and took his flight to the steamboat which was to convey him to London, and was then lying at the floating pier, doing its best to bump the same to bits. But, the happy couple were not going to part with him in that way, and before he had been on board two minutes, there they were, looking down at him from the wharf above.

'Pa, dear!' cried Bella, beckoning him with her parasol to approach the side, and bending gracefully to whisper.

'Yes, my darling.'

'Did I beat you much with that horrid little bonnet, Pa?'

'Nothing to speak of, my dear.'

'Did I pinch your legs, Pa?'

'Only nicely, my pet.'

'You are sure you quite forgive me, Pa? Please, Pa, please, forgive me quite!' Half laughing at him and half crying to him, Bella besought him in the prettiest manner; in a manner so engaging and so playful and so natural, that her cherubic parent made a coaxing face as if she had never grown up, and said, 'What a silly little Mouse it is!'

'But you do forgive me that, and everything else; don't you, Pa?'

'Yes, my dearest.'

'And you don't feel solitary or neglected, going away by yourself; do you, Pa?'

'Lord bless you! No, my Life!'

'Good-bye, dearest Pa. Good-bye!'

'Good-bye, my darling! Take her away, my dear John. Take her home!'

So, she leaning on her husband's arm, they turned homeward by a rosy path which the gracious sun struck out for them in its setting. And O there are days in this life, worth life and worth death. And O what a bright old song it is, that O 'tis love, 'tis love, 'tis love, that makes the world go round!

Chapter 5
Concerning the Mendicant's Bride

THE impressive gloom with which Mrs Wilfer received her husband on his return from the wedding, knocked so hard at the door of the cherubic conscience, and likewise so impaired the firmness of the cherubic legs, that the culprit's tottering condition of mind and body might have roused suspicion in less occupied persons than the grimly heroic lady, Miss Lavinia, and that esteemed friend of the family, Mr George Sampson. But, the attention of all three being fully possessed by the main fact of the marriage, they had happily none to bestow on the guilty conspirator; to which fortunate circumstance he owed the escape for which he was in nowise indebted to himself.

'You do not, R. W.' said Mrs Wilfer from her stately corner, 'inquire for your daughter Bella.'

'To be sure, my dear,' he returned, with a most flagrant assumption of unconsciousnes, 'I did omit it. How—or perhaps I should rather say where—*is* Bella?'

'Not here,' Mrs Wilfer proclaimed, with folded arms.

The cherub faintly muttered something to the abortive effect of 'Oh, indeed, my dear!'

'Not here,' repeated Mrs Wilfer, in a stern sonorous voice. 'In a word, R.W., you have no daughter Bella.'

'No daughter Bella, my dear?'

'No. Your daughter Bella,' said Mrs Wilfer, with a lofty air of never having had the least copartnership in that young lady: of whom she now made reproachful mention as an article of luxury which her husband had set up entirely on his own account, and in direct opposition to her advice: '—your daughter Bella has bestowed herself upon a Mendicant.'

'Good gracious, my dear!'

'Show your father his daughter Bella's letter, Lavinia,' said Mrs Wilfer, in her monotonous Act of Parliament tone, and waving her hand. 'I think your father will admit it to be documentary proof of what I tell him. I believe your father is acquainted with his daughter Bella's writing. But I do not know. He may tell you he is not. Nothing will surprise me.'

'Posted at Greenwich, and dated this morning,' said the Irrepressible, flouncing at her father in handing him the evidence. 'Hopes Ma won't be angry, but is happily married to Mr John Rokesmith, and didn't mention it beforehand to avoid words, and please tell darling you, and love to me, and I should like to know what you'd have said if any other unmarried member of the family had done it!'

He read the letter, and faintly exclaimed 'Dear me!'

'You may well say Dear me!' rejoined Mrs Wilfer, in a deep tone. Upon which encouragement he said it again, though scarcely with the success he had expected; for the scornful lady then remarked, with extreme bitterness: 'You said that before.'

'It's very surprising. But I suppose, my dear,' hinted the cherub, as he folded the letter after a disconcerting silence, 'that we must make the best of it? Would you object to my pointing out, my dear, that Mr John Rokesmith is not (so far as I am acquainted with him), strictly speaking, a Mendicant.'

'Indeed?' returned Mrs Wilfer, with an awful air of politeness. 'Truly so? I was not aware that Mr John Rokesmith was a gentleman of landed property. But I am much relieved to hear it.'

'I doubt if you *have* heard it, my dear,' the cherub submitted with hesitation.

'Thank you,' said Mrs Wilfer. 'I make false statements, it appears? So be it. If my daughter flies in my face, surely my husband may. The one thing is not more unnatural than the other. There seems a fitness in the arrangement. By all means!' Assuming, with a shiver of resignation, a deadly cheerfulness.

But, here the Irrepressible skirmished into the conflict, dragging the reluctant form of Mr Sampson after her.

'Ma,' interposed the young lady, 'I must say I think it would be much better if you would keep to the point, and not hold forth about people's flying into people's faces, which is nothing more nor less than impossible nonsense.'

'How!' exclaimed Mrs Wilfer, knitting her dark brows.

'Just im-possible nonsense, Ma,' returned Lavvy, 'and George Sampson knows it is, as well as I do.'

Mrs Wilfer suddenly becoming petrified, fixed her indignant eyes upon the wretched George: who, divided between the support due from him to his love, and the support due from him to his love's mamma, supported nobody, not even himself.

'The true point is,' pursued Lavinia, 'that Bella has behaved in a most unsisterly way to me, and might have severely compromised me with George and with George's family, by making off and getting married in this very low and disreputable manner—with some pew-opener or other, I suppose, for a bridesmaid—when she ought to have confided in me, and ought to have said, "If, Lavvy, you consider it due to your engagement with George, that you should countenance the occasion by being present, then Lavvy, I beg you to *be* present, keeping my secret from Ma and Pa." As of course I should have done.'

'As of course you would have done? Ingrate!' exclaimed Mrs Wilfer. 'Viper!'

'I say! You know ma'am. Upon my honour you mustn't,' Mr Sampson remonstrated, shaking his head seriously, 'With the highest respect for you, ma'am, upon my life you mustn't. No really, you know. When a man with the feelings of a gentleman finds himself engaged to a young lady, and it comes (even on the part of a member of the family) to vipers, you know!—I would merely put it to your own good feeling, you know,' said Mr Sampson, in rather lame conclusion.

Mrs Wilfer's baleful stare at the young gentleman in acknowledgment of his obliging interference was of such a nature that Miss Lavinia burst into tears, and caught him round the neck for his protection.

'My own unnatural mother,' screamed the young lady, 'wants to annihilate George! But you shan't be annihilated, George. I'll die first!'

Mr Sampson, in the arms of his mistress, still struggled to shake his head at Mrs Wilfer, and to remark: 'With every sentiment of respect for you, you know, ma'am—vipers really doesn't do you credit.'

'You shall not be annihilated, George!' cried Miss Lavinia. 'Ma shall destroy me first, and then she'll be contented. Oh, oh, oh! Have I lured George from his happy home to expose him to this! George, dear, be free! Leave me, ever dearest George, to Ma and to my fate. Give my love to your aunt, George dear, and implore her not to curse the viper that has crossed your path and blighted your existence. Oh, oh, oh!' The young lady who, hysterically speaking, was only just come of age, and had never gone off yet, here fell into a highly creditable crisis, which, regarded as a first performance, was very successful; Mr Sampson, bending over the body meanwhile, in a state of distraction, which induced him to address Mrs Wilfer in the inconsistent expressions: 'Demon—with the highest respect for you—behold your work!'

The cherub stood helplessly rubbing his chin and looking on, but on the whole was inclined to welcome this diversion as one in which, by reason of the absorbent properties of hysterics, the previous question would become absorbed. And so, indeed, it proved, for the Irrepressible gradually coming to herself, and asking with wild emotion, 'George dear, are you safe?' and further, 'George love, what has happened? Where is Ma?' Mr Sampson, with words of comfort, raised her prostrate form, and handed her to Mrs Wilfer as if the young lady were something in the nature of refreshments. Mrs Wilfer with dignity partaking of the refreshments, by kissing her once on the brow (as if accepting an oyster), Miss Lavvy, tottering, returned to the protection of Mr Sampson; to whom she said, 'George dear, I am afraid I have been foolish; but I am still a little weak and giddy; don't let go my hand, George!' And whom she afterwards greatly agitated at intervals, by giving utterance, when least expected, to a sound between a sob and a bottle of soda water, that seemed to rend the bosom of her frock.

Among the most remarkable effects of this crisis may be mentioned its having, when peace was restored, an inexplicable moral influence, of an elevating kind, on Miss Lavinia, Mrs Wilfer, and Mr George Sampson, from which R. W. was altogether excluded, as an outsider and non-sympathizer. Miss Lavinia assumed a modest air of having distinguished herself; Mrs Wilfer, a serene air of forgiveness and resignation; Mr Sampson, an air of having been improved and chastened. The influence pervaded the spirit in which they returned to the previous question.

'George dear,' said Lavvy, with a melancholy smile, 'after what has passed, I am sure Ma will tell Pa that he may tell Bella we shall all be glad to see her and her husband.'

Mr Sampson said he was sure of it too; murmuring how eminently he respected Mrs Wilfer, and ever must, and ever would. Never more eminently, he added, than after what had passed.

'Far be it from me,' said Mrs Wilfer, making deep proclamation from her corner, 'to run counter to the feelings of a child of mine, and of a Youth,' Mr Sampson hardly seemed to like that word, 'who is the object of her maiden preference. I may feel—nay, know—that I have been deluded and deceived. I may feel—nay, know—that I have been set aside and passed over. I may feel—nay, know—that after having so far overcome my repugnance towards Mr and Mrs Boffin as to receive them under this roof, and to consent to your daughter Bella's,' here turning to her husband, 'residing under theirs, it were well if your daughter Bella,' again turning to her husband, 'had profited in a worldly point of view by a connection so distasteful, so disreputable, I may feel—nay, know—that in uniting herself to Mr Rokesmith she has united herself to one who is, in spite of shallow sophistry, a Mendicant. And I may feel well assured that your daughter Bella,' again turning to her husband, 'does not exalt her family by becoming a Mendicant's bride. But I suppress what I feel, and say nothing of it.'

Mr Sampson murmured that this was the sort of thing you might expect from one who had ever in her own family been an example and never an outrage. And ever more so (Mr Sampson added, with some degree of obscurity,) and never more so, than in and through what had passed. He must take the liberty of adding, that what was true of the mother was true of the youngest daughter, and that he could never forget the touching feelings that the conduct of both had awakened within him. In conclusion, he did hope that there wasn't a man with a beating heart who was capable of something that remained undescribed, in consequence of Miss Lavinia's stopping him as he reeled in his speech.

'Therefore, R. W.,' said Mrs Wilfer, resuming her discourse and turning to her lord again, 'let your daughter Bella come when she will, and she will be received. So,' after a short pause, and an air of having taken medicine in it, 'so will her husband.'

'And I beg, Pa,' said Lavinia, 'that you will not tell Bella what I have undergone. It can do no good, and it might cause her to reproach herself.'

'My dearest girl,' urged Mr Sampson, 'she ought to know it.'

'No, George,' said Lavinia, in a tone of resolute self-denial. 'No, dearest George, let it be buried in oblivion.'

Mr Sampson considered that, 'too noble.'

'Nothing is too noble, dearest George,' returned Lavinia. 'And Pa, I hope you will be careful not to refer before Bella, if you can help it, to my engagement to George. It might seem like reminding her of her having cast herself away. And I hope, Pa, that you will think it equally right to avoid mentioning George's rising prospects, when Bella is present. It might seem like taunting her with her own poor fortunes. Let me ever remember that I am her younger sister, and ever spare her painful contrasts, which could not but wound her sharply.'

Mr Sampson expressed his belief that such was the demeanour of Angels. Miss Lavvy replied with solemnity, 'No, dearest George. I am but too well aware that I am merely human.'

Mrs Wilfer, for her part, still further improved the occasion by sitting with her eyes fastened on her husband, like two great black notes of interrogation, severely inquiring, Are you looking into your breast? Do you deserve your blessings? Can you lay your hand upon your heart and say that you are worthy of so hysterical a daughter? I do not ask you if you are worthy of such a wife—put Me out of the question—but are you sufficiently conscious of, and thankful for, the pervading moral grandeur of the family spectacle on which you are gazing? These inquiries proved very harassing to R. W. who, besides being a little disturbed by wine, was in perpetual terror of committing himself by the utterance of stray words that would betray his guilty foreknowledge. However, the scene being over, and—all things considered—well over, he sought refuge in a doze; which gave his lady immense offence.

'Can you think of your daughter Bella, and sleep?' she disdainfully inquired.

To which he mildly answered, 'Yes, I think I can, my dear.'

'Then,' said Mrs Wilfer, with solemn indignation, 'I would recommend you, if you have a human feeling, to retire to bed.'

'Thank you, my dear,' he replied; 'I think it *is* the best place for me.' And with these unsympathetic words very gladly withdrew.

Within a few weeks afterwards, the Mendicant's bride (arm-in-arm with the Mendicant) came to tea, in fulfilment of an engagement made through her father. And the way in which the Mendicant's bride dashed at the unassailable position so considerately to be held by Miss Lavvy, and scattered the whole of the works in all directions in a moment, was triumphant.

'Dearest Ma,' cried Bella, running into the room with a radiant face, 'how do you do, dearest Ma?' And then embraced her, joyously. 'And Lavvy darling, how do *you* do, and how's George Sampson, and how is he getting on, and when are you going to be married, and how rich are you going to grow? You must tell me all about it, Lavvy dear, immediately. John, love, kiss Ma and Lavvy, and then we shall all be at home and comfortable.'

Mrs Wilfer stared, but was helpless. Miss Lavinia stared, but was helpless. Apparently with no compunction, and assuredly with no ceremony, Bella tossed her bonnet away, and sat down to make the tea.

'Dearest Ma and Lavvy, you both take sugar, I know. And Pa (you good little Pa), you don't take milk. John does. I didn't before I was married; but I do now, because John does. John dear, did you kiss Ma and Lavvy? Oh, you did! Quite correct, John dear; but I didn't see you do it, so I asked. Cut some bread and butter, John; that's a love. Ma likes it doubled. And now you must tell me, dearest Ma and Lavvy, upon your words and honours! Didn't you for a moment—just a moment—think I was a dreadful little wretch when I wrote to say I had run away?'

Before Mrs Wilfer could wave her gloves, the Mendicant's bride in her merriest affectionate manner went on again.

'I think it must have made you rather cross, dear Ma and Lavvy, and I know I deserved that you should be very cross. But you see I had been such a heedless, heartless creature, and had led you so to expect that I should marry for money, and so to make sure that I was incapable of marrying for love, that I thought you couldn't believe me. Because, you see, you didn't know how much of Good, Good, Good, I had learnt from John. Well! So I was sly about it, and ashamed of what you supposed me to be, and fearful that we couldn't understand one another and might come to words, which we should all be sorry for afterwards, and so I said to John that if he liked to take me without any fuss, he might. And as he did like, I let him. And we were married at Greenwich church in the presence of nobody—except an unknown individual who dropped in,' here her eyes sparkled more brightly, 'and half a pensioner. And now, isn't it nice, dearest Ma and Lavvy, to know that no words have been said which any of us can be sorry for, and that we are all the best of friends at the pleasantest of teas!'

Having got up and kissed them again, she slipped back to her chair (after a loop on the road to squeeze her husband round the neck) and again went on.

'And now you will naturally want to know, dearest Ma and Lavvy, how we live, and what we have got to live upon. Well! And so we live on Blackheath, in the charm—ingest of dolls' houses, de–lightfully furnished, and we have a clever little servant who is de–cidedly pretty, and we are economical and orderly, and do everything by clockwork, and we have a hundred and fifty pounds a year, and we have all we want, and more. And lastly, if you would like to know in confidence, as perhaps you may, what is my opinion of my husband, my opinion is—that I almost love him!'

'And if you would like to know in confidence, as perhaps you may,' said her husband, smiling, as he stood by her side, without her having detected his approach, 'my opinion of my wife, my opinion is—' But Bella started up, and put her hand upon his lips.

'Stop, sir! No, John, dear! Seriously! Please not yet a while! I want to be something so much worthier than the doll in the doll's house.'

'My darling, are you not?'

'Not half, not a quarter, so much worthier as I hope you may some day find me! Try me through some reverse, John—try me through some trial—and tell them after *that,* what you think of me.'

'I will, my Life,' said John. 'I promise it.'

'That's my dear John. And you won't speak a word now; will you?'

'And I won't,' said John, with a very expressive look of admiration around him, 'speak a word now!'

She laid her laughing cheek upon his breast to thank him, and said, looking at the rest of them sideways out of her bright eyes: 'I'll go further, Pa and Ma and Lavvy. John don't suspect it—he has no idea of it—but I quite love him!'

Even Mrs Wilfer relaxed under the influence of her married daughter, and seemed in a majestic manner to imply remotely that if R. W. had been a more deserving object, she too might have condescended to come down from her pedestal for his beguilement. Miss Lavinia, on the other hand, had strong doubts of the policy of the course of treatment, and whether it might not spoil Mr Sampson, if experimented on in the case of that young gentleman. R. W. himself was for his part convinced that he was father of one of the most charming of girls, and that Rokesmith was the most favoured of men; which opinion, if propounded to him, Rokesmith would probably not have contested.

The newly-married pair left early, so that they might walk at leisure to their starting-place from London, for Greenwich. At first they were very cheerful and talked much; but after a while, Bella fancied that her husband was turning somewhat thoughtful. So she asked him:

'John dear, what's the matter?'

'Matter, my love?'

'Won't you tell me,' said Bella, looking up into his face, 'what you are thinking of?'

'There's not much in the thought, my soul. I was thinking whether you wouldn't like me to be rich?'

'You rich, John?' repeated Bella, shrinking a little.

'I mean, really rich. Say, as rich as Mr Boffin. You would like that?'

'I should be almost afraid to try, John dear. Was he much the better for his wealth? Was I much the better for the little part I once had in it?'

'But all people are not the worse for riches, my own.'

'Most people?' Bella musingly suggested with raised eyebrows.

'Nor even most people, it may be hoped. If you were rich, for instance, you would have a great power of doing good to others.'

'Yes, sir, for instance,' Bella playfully rejoined; 'but should I exercise the power, for instance? And again, sir, for instance; should I, at the same time, have a great power of doing harm to myself?'

Laughing and pressing her arm, he retorted: 'But still, again for instance; would you exercise that power?'

'I don't know,' said Bella, thoughtfully shaking her head. 'I hope not. I think not. But it's so easy to hope not and think not, without the riches.'

'Why don't you say, my darling—instead of that phrase—being poor?' he asked, looking earnestly at her.

'Why don't I say, being poor! Because I am not poor. Dear John, it's not possible that you suppose I think we are poor?'

'I do, my love.'

'Oh John!'

'Understand me, sweetheart. I know that I am rich beyond all wealth in having you; but I think *of* you, and think *for* you. In such a dress as you are wearing now, you first charmed me, and in no dress could you ever look, to my thinking, more graceful or more beautiful. But you have admired many finer dresses this very day; and is it not natural that I wish I could give them to you?'

'It's very nice that you should wish it, John. It brings these tears of grateful pleasure into my eyes, to hear you say so with such tenderness. But I don't want them.'

'Again,' he pursued, 'we are now walking through the muddy streets. I love those pretty feet so dearly, that I feel as if I could not bear the dirt to soil the sole of your shoe. Is it not natural that I wish you could ride in a carriage?'

'It's very nice,' said Bella, glancing downward at the feet in question, 'to know that you admire them so much, John dear, and since you do, I am sorry that these shoes are a full size too large. But I don't want a carriage, believe me.'

'You would like one if you could have one, Bella?'

'I shouldn't like it for its own sake, half so well as such a wish for it. Dear John, your wishes are as real to me as the wishes in the Fairy story, that were all fulfilled as soon as spoken. Wish me everything that you can wish for the woman you dearly love, and I have as good as got it, John. I have better than got it, John!'

They were not the less happy for such talk, and home was not the less home for coming after it. Bella was fast developing a perfect genius for home. All the loves and graces seemed (her husband thought) to have taken domestic service with her, and to help her to make home engaging.

Her married life glided happily on. She was alone all day, for, after an early breakfast her husband repaired every morning to the City, and did not return until their late dinner hour. He was 'in a China house,' he explained to Bella: which she found quite satisfactory, without pursuing the China house into minuter details than a wholesale vision of tea, rice, odd-smelling silks, carved boxes, and tight-eyed people in more than double-soled shoes, with their pigtails pulling their heads of hair off, painted on transparent procelain. She always walked with her husband to the railroad, and was always there again to meet him; her old coquettish ways a little sobered down (but not much), and her dress as daintily managed as if she managed nothing else. But, John gone to business and Bella returned home, the dress would be laid aside, trim little wrappers and aprons would be substituted, and Bella, putting back her hair with both hands, as if she were making the most business-like arrangements for going dramatically distracted, would enter on the household affairs of the day. Such weighing and mixing and chopping and grating, such dusting and washing and polishing, such snipping and weeding and trowelling and other small gardening, such making and mending and folding and airing, such diverse arrangements, and above all such severe study! For Mrs J. R., who had never been wont to do too much at home as Miss B. W., was under the constant necessity of referring for advice and support to a sage volume entitled The Complete British Family Housewife, which she would sit consulting, with her elbows on the table and her temples on her hands, like some perplexed enchantress poring over the Black Art. This, principally because the Complete British Housewife, however sound a Briton at heart, was by no means an expert Briton at expressing herself with clearness in the British tongue, and sometimes might have issued her directions to equal purpose in the Kamskatchan language. In any crisis of this nature, Bella would suddenly exclaim aloud, 'Oh you ridiculous old thing, what do you mean by that? You must have been drinking!' And having made this marginal note, would try the Housewife again, with all her dimples screwed into an expression of profound research.

There was likewise a coolness on the part of the British Housewife, which Mrs John Rokesmith found highly exasperating. She would say, 'Take a salamander,' as if a general should command a private to catch a Tartar. Or, she would casually issue the order, 'Throw in a handful—' of something entirely unattainable. In these, the Housewife's most glaring moments of unreason, Bella would shut her up and knock her on the table, apostrophising her with the compliment, 'O you ARE a stupid old Donkey! Where am I to get it, do you think?'

Another branch of study claimed the attention of Mrs John Rokesmith for a regular period every day. This was the mastering of the newspaper, so that she might be close up with John on general topics when John came home. In her desire to be in all things his companion, she would have set herself with equal zeal to master Algebra, or Euclid, if he had divided his soul between her and either. Wonderful was the way in which she would store up the City Intelligence, and beamingly shed it upon John in the course of the evening; incidentally mentioning the commodities that were looking up in the markets, and how much gold had been taken to the Bank, and trying to look wise and serious over it until she would laugh at herself most charmingly and would say, kissing him: 'It all comes of my love, John dear.'

For a City man, John certainly did appear to care as little as might be for the looking up or looking down of things, as well as for the gold that got taken to the Bank. But he cared, beyond all expression, for his wife, as a most precious and sweet commodity that was always looking up, and that never was worth less than all the gold in the world. And she, being inspired by her affection, and having a quick wit and a fine ready instinct, made amazing progress in her domestic efficiency, though, as an endearing creature, she made no progress at all. This was her husband's verdict, and he justified it by telling her that she had begun her married life as the most endearing creature that could possibly be.

'And you have such a cheerful spirit!' he said, fondly. 'You are like a bright light in the house.'

'Am I truly, John?'

'Are you truly? Yes, indeed. Only much more, and much better.'

'Do you know, John dear,' said Bella, taking him by a button of his coat, 'that I sometimes, at odd moments—don't laugh, John, please.'

Nothing should induce John to do it, when she asked him not to do it.

'—That I sometimes think, John, I feel a little serious.'

'Are you too much alone, my darling?'

'O dear, no, John! The time is so short that I have not a moment too much in the week.'

'Why serious, my life, then? When serious?'

'When I laugh, I think,' said Bella, laughing as she laid her head upon his shoulder. 'You wouldn't believe, sir, that I feel serious now? But I do.' And she laughed again, and something glistened in her eyes.

'Would you like to be rich, pet?' he asked her coaxingly.

'Rich, John! How *can* you ask such goose's questions?'

'Do you regret anything, my love?'

'Regret anything? No!' Bella confidently answered. But then, suddenly changing, she said, between laughing and glistening: 'Oh yes, I do though. I regret Mrs Boffin.'

'I, too, regret that separation very much. But perhaps it is only temporary. Perhaps things may so fall out, as that you may sometimes see her again—as that we may sometimes see her again.' Bella might be very anxious on the subject, but she scarcely seemed so at the moment. With an absent air, she was investigating that button on her husband's coat, when Pa came in to spend the evening.

Pa had his special chair and his special corner reserved for him on all occasions, and—without disparagement of his domestic joys—was far happier there, than anywhere. It was always pleasantly droll to see Pa and Bella together; but on this present evening her husband thought her more than usually fantastic with him.

'You are a very good little boy,' said Bella, 'to come unexpectedly, as soon as you could get out of school. And how have they used you at school to-day, you dear?'

'Well, my pet,' replied the cherub, smiling and rubbing his hands as she sat him down in his chair, 'I attend two schools. There's the Mincing Lane establishment, and there's your mother's Academy. Which might you mean, my dear?'

'Both,' said Bella.

'Both, eh? Why, to say the truth, both have taken a little out of me to-day, my dear, but that was to be expected. There's no royal road to learning; and what is life but learning!'

'And what do you do with yourself when you have got your learning by heart, you silly child?'

'Why then, my dear,' said the cherub, after a little consideration, 'I suppose I die.'

'You are a very bad boy,' retorted Bella, 'to talk about dismal things and be out of spirits.'

'My Bella,' rejoined her father, 'I am not out of spirits. I am as gay as a lark.' Which his face confirmed.

'Then if you are sure and certain it's not you, I suppose it must be I,' said Bella; 'so I won't do so any more. John dear, we must give this little fellow his supper, you know.'

'Of course we must, my darling.'

'He has been grubbing and grubbing at school,' said Bella, looking at her father's hand and lightly slapping it, 'till he's not fit to be seen. O what a grubby child!'

'Indeed, my dear,' said her father, 'I was going to ask to be allowed to wash my hands, only you find me out so soon.'

'Come here, sir!' cried Bella, taking him by the front of his coat, 'come here and be washed directly. You are not to be trusted to do it for yourself. Come here, sir!'

The cherub, to his genial amusement, was accordingly conducted to a little washing-room, where Bella soaped his face and rubbed his face, and soaped his hands and rubbed his hands, and splashed him and rinsed him and toweled him, until he was as red as beet-root, even to his very ears: 'Now you must be brushed and combed, sir,' said Bella, busily. 'Hold the light, John. Shut your eyes, sir, and let me take hold of your chin. Be good directly, and do as you are told!'

Her father being more than willing to obey, she dressed his hair in her most elaborate manner, brushing it out straight, parting it, winding it over her fingers, sticking it up on end, and constantly falling back on John to get a good look at the effect of it. Who always received her on his disengaged arm, and detained her, while the patient cherub stood waiting to be finished.

'There!' said Bella, when she had at last completed the final touches. 'Now, you are something like a genteel boy! Put your jacket on, and come and have your supper.'

The cherub investing himself with his coat was led back to his corner—where, but for having no egotism in his pleasant nature, he would have answered well enough for that radiant though self-sufficient boy, Jack Horner—Bella with her own hands laid a cloth for him, and brought him his supper on a tray. 'Stop a moment,' said she, 'we must keep his little clothes clean;' and tied a napkin under his chin, in a very methodical manner.

While he took his supper, Bella sat by him, sometimes admonishing him to hold his fork by the handle, like a polite child, and at other times carving for him, or pouring out his drink. Fantastic as it all was, and accustomed as she ever had been to make a plaything of her good father, ever delighted that she should put him to that account, still there was an occasional something on Bella's part that was new. It could not be said that she was less playful, whimsical, or natural, than she always had been; but it seemed, her husband thought, as if there were some rather graver reason than he had supposed for what she had so lately said, and as if, throughout all this, there were glimpses of an underlying seriousness.

It was a circumstance in support of this view of the case, that when she had lighted her father's pipe, and mixed him his glass of grog, she sat down on a stool between her father and her husband, leaning her arm upon the latter, and was very quiet. So quiet, that when her father rose to take his leave, she looked round with a start, as if she had forgotten his being there.

'You go a little way with Pa, John?'

'Yes, my dear. Do you?'

'I have not written to Lizzie Hexam since I wrote and told her that I really had a lover—a whole one. I have often thought I would like to tell her how right she was when she pretended to read in the live coals that I would go through fire and water for him. I am in the humour to tell her so to-night, John, and I'll stay at home and do it.'

'You are tired.'

'Not at all tired, John dear, but in the humour to write to Lizzie. Good night, dear Pa. Good night, you dear, good, gentle Pa!'

Left to herself, she sat down to write, and wrote Lizzie a long letter. She had but completed it and read it over, when her husband came back. 'You are just in time, sir,' said Bella; 'I am going to give you your first curtain lecture. It shall be a parlour-curtain lecture. You shall take this chair of mine when I have folded my letter, and I will take the stool (though you ought to take it, I can tell you, sir, if it's the stool of repentance), and you'll soon find yourself taken to task soundly.'

Her letter folded, sealed, and directed, and her pen wiped, and her middle finger wiped, and her desk locked up and put away, and these transactions performed with an air of severe business sedateness, which the Complete British Housewife might have assumed, and certainly would not have rounded off and broken down in with a musical laugh, as Bella did: she placed her husband in his chair, and placed herself upon her stool.

'Now, sir! To begin at the beginning. What is your name?'

A question more decidedly rushing at the secret he was keeping from her, could not have astounded him. But he kept his countenance and his secret, and answered, 'John Rokesmith, my dear.'

'Good boy! Who gave you that name?'

With a returning suspicion that something might have betrayed him to her, he answered, interrogatively, 'My godfathers and my godmothers, dear love?'

'Pretty good!' said Bella. 'Not goodest good, because you hesitate about it. However, as you know your Catechism fairly, so far, I'll let you off the rest. Now, I am going to examine you out of my own head. John dear, why did you go back, this evening, to the question you once asked me before—would I like to be rich?'

Again, his secret! He looked down at her as she looked up at him, with her hands folded on his knee, and it was as nearly told as ever secret was.

Having no reply ready, he could do no better than embrace her.

'In short, dear John,' said Bella, 'this is the topic of my lecture: I want nothing on earth, and I want you to believe it.'

'If that's all, the lecture may be considered over, for I do.'

'It's not all, John dear,' Bella hesitated. 'It's only Firstly. There's a dreadful Secondly, and a dreadful Thirdly to come—as I used to say to myself in sermon-time when I was a very small-sized sinner at church.'

'Let them come, my dearest.'

'Are you sure, John dear; are you absolutely certain in your innermost heart of hearts—?'

'Which is not in my keeping,' he rejoined.

'No, John, but the key is.—Are you absolutely certain that down at the bottom of that heart of hearts, which you have given to me as I have given mine to you, there is no remembrance that I was once very mercenary?'

'Why, if there were no remembrance in me of the time you speak of,' he softly asked her with his lips to hers, 'could I love you quite as well as I do; could I have in the Calendar of my life the brightest of its days; could I whenever I look at your dear face, or hear your dear voice, see and hear my noble champion? It can never have been that which made you serious, darling?'

'No John, it wasn't that, and still less was it Mrs Boffin, though I love her. Wait a moment, and I'll go on with the lecture. Give me a moment, because I like to cry for joy. It's so delicious, John dear, to cry for joy.'

She did so on his neck, and, still clinging there, laughed a little when she said, 'I think I am ready now for Thirdly, John.'

'*I* am ready for Thirdly,' said John, 'whatever it is.'

'I believe, John,' pursued Bella, 'that you believe that I believe—'

'My dear child,' cried her husband gaily, 'what a quantity of believing!'

'Isn't there?' said Bella, with another laugh. 'I never knew such a quantity! It's like verbs in an exercise. But I can't get on with less believing. I'll try again. I believe, dear John, that you believe that I believe that we have as much money as we require, and that we want for nothing.'

'It is strictly true, Bella.'

'But if our money should by any means be rendered not so much—if we had to stint ourselves a little in purchases that we can afford to make now—would you still have the same confidence in my being quite contented, John?'

'Precisely the same confidence, my soul.'

'Thank you, John dear, thousands upon thousands of times. And I may take it for granted, no doubt,' with a little faltering, 'that you would be quite as contented yourself, John? But, yes, I know I may. For, knowing that I should be so, how surely I may know that you would be so; you who are so much stronger, and firmer, and more reasonable and more generous, than I am.'

'Hush!' said her husband, 'I must not hear that. You are all wrong there, though otherwise as right as can be. And now I am brought to a little piece of news, my dearest, that I might have told you earlier in the evening. I have strong reason for confidently believing that we shall never be in the receipt of a smaller income than our present income.'

She might have shown herself more interested in the intelligence; but she had returned to the investigation of the coat-button that had engaged her attention a few hours before, and scarcely seemed to heed what he said.

'And now we have got to the bottom of it at last,' cried her husband, rallying her, 'and this is the thing that made you serious?'

'No dear,' said Bella, twisting the button and shaking her head, 'it wasn't this.'

'Why then, Lord bless this little wife of mine, there's a Fourthly!' exclaimed John.

'This worried me a little, and so did Secondly,' said Bella, occupied with the button, 'but it was quite another sort of seriousness—a much deeper and quieter sort of seriousness—that I spoke of, John dear.'

As he bent his face to hers, she raised hers to meet it, and laid her little right hand on his eyes, and kept it there.

'Do you remember, John, on the day we were married, Pa's speaking of the ships that might be sailing towards us from the unknown seas?'

'Perfectly, my darling!'

'I think . . . among them . . . there is a ship upon the ocean . . . bringing . . to you and me . . . a little baby, John.'

Chapter 6
A Cry for Help

THE Paper Mill had stopped work for the night, and the paths and roads in its neighbourhood were sprinkled with clusters of people going home from their day's labour in it. There were men, women, and children in the groups, and there was no want of lively colour to flutter in the gentle evening wind. The mingling of various voices and the sound of laughter made a cheerful impression upon the ear, analogous to that of the fluttering colours upon the eye. Into the sheet of water reflecting the flushed sky in the foreground of the living picture, a knot of urchins were casting stones, and watching the expansion of the rippling circles. So, in the rosy evening, one might watch the ever-widening beauty of the landscape—beyond the newly-released workers wending home—beyond the silver river—beyond the deep green fields of corn, so prospering, that the loiterers in their narrow threads of pathway seemed to float immersed breast-high—beyond the hedgerows and the clumps of trees—beyond the windmills on the ridge—away to where the sky appeared to meet the earth, as if there were no immensity of space between mankind and Heaven.

It was a Saturday evening, and at such a time the village dogs, always much more interested in the doings of humanity than in the affairs of their own species, were particularly active. At the general shop, at the butcher's and at the public-house, they evinced an inquiring spirit never to be satiated. Their especial interest in the public-house would seem to imply some latent rakishness in the canine character; for little was eaten there, and they, having no taste for beer or tobacco (Mrs Hubbard's dog is said to have smoked, but proof is wanting), could only have been attracted by sympathy with loose convivial habits. Moreover, a most wretched fiddle played within; a fiddle so unutterably vile, that one lean long-bodied cur, with a better ear than the rest, found himself under compulsion at intervals to go round the corner and howl. Yet, even he returned to the public-house on each occasion with the tenacity of a confirmed drunkard.

Fearful to relate, there was even a sort of little Fair in the village. Some despairing gingerbread that had been vainly trying to dispose of itself all over the country, and had cast a quantity of dust upon its head in its mortification, again appealed to the public from an infirm booth. So did a heap of nuts, long, long exiled from Barcelona, and yet speaking English so indifferently as to call fourteen of themselves a pint. A Peep-show which had originally started with the Battle of Waterloo, and had since made it every other battle of later date by altering the Duke of Wellington's nose, tempted the student of illustrated history. A Fat Lady, perhaps in part sustained upon postponed pork, her professional associate being a Learned Pig, displayed her life-size picture in a low dress as she appeared when presented at Court, several yards round. All this was a vicious spectacle as

any poor idea of amusement on the part of the rougher hewers of
wood and drawers of water in this land of England ever is and
shall be. They *must not* vary the rheumatism with amusement.
They may vary it with fever and ague, or with as many rheu-
matic variations as they have joints; but positively not with
entertainment after their own manner.

The various sounds arising from this scene of depravity, and
floating away into the still evening air, made the evening, at any
point which they just reached fitfully, mellowed by the distance, more still by contrast. Such was the stillness of the
evening to Eugene Wrayburn, as he walked by the river with his
hands behind him.

He walked slowly, and with the measured step and preoccupied air of one who was waiting. He walked between the two
points, an osier-bed at this end and some floating lilies at that,
and at each point stopped and looked expectantly in one direction.

'It is very quiet,' said he.

It was very quiet. Some sheep were grazing on the grass by
the river-side, and it seemed to him that he had never before
heard the crisp tearing sound with which they cropped it. He
stopped idly, and looked at them.

'You are stupid enough, I suppose. But if you are clever
enough to get through life tolerably to your satisfaction, you
have got the better of me, Man as I am, and Mutton as you are!'

A rustle in a field beyond the hedge attracted his attention.
'What's here to do?' he asked himself, leisurely going towards
the gate and looking over. 'No jealous paper-miller? No pleasures of the chase in this part of the country? Mostly fishing
hereabouts!'

The field had been newly mown, and there were yet the
marks of the scythe on the yellow-green ground, and the track of
wheels where the hay had been carried. Following the tracks
with his eyes, the view closed with the new hayrick in a corner.

Now, if he had gone on to the hayrick, and gone round it?
But, say that the event was to be, as the event fell out, and how
idle are such suppositions! Besides, if he had gone; what is there
of warning in a Bargeman lying on his face?

'A bird flying to the hedge,' was all he thought about it; and
came back, and resumed his walk.

'If I had not a reliance on her being truthful,' said Eugene,
after taking some half-dozen turns, 'I should begin to think she
had given me the slip for the second time. But she promised, and
she is a girl of her word.'

Turning again at the water-lilies, he saw her coming, and advanced to meet her.

'I was saying to myself, Lizzie, that you were sure to come, though you were late.'

'I had to linger through the village as if I had no object before me, and I had to speak to several people in passing along, Mr Wrayburn.'

'Are the lads of the village—and the ladies—such scandal-mongers?' he asked, as he took her hand and drew it through his arm.

She submitted to walk slowly on, with downcast eyes. He put her hand to his lips, and she quietly drew it away.

'Will you walk beside me, Mr Wrayburn, and not touch me?' For, his arm was already stealing round her waist.

She stopped again, and gave him an earnest supplicating look. 'Well, Lizzie, well!' said he, in an easy way though ill at ease with himself, 'don't be unhappy, don't be reproachful.'

'I cannot help being unhappy, but I do not mean to be reproachful. Mr Wrayburn, I implore you to go away from this neighbourhood, to-morrow morning.'

'Lizzie, Lizzie, Lizzie!' he remonstrated. 'As well be reproachful as wholly unreasonable. I can't go away.'

'Why not?'

'Faith!' said Eugene in his airily candid manner. 'Because you won't let me. Mind! I don't mean to be reproachful either. I don't complain that you design to keep me here. But you do it, you do it.'

'Will you walk beside me, and not touch me;' for, his arm was coming about her again; 'while I speak to you very seriously, Mr Wrayburn?'

'I will do anything within the limits of possibility, for you, Lizzie,' he answered with pleasant gaiety as he folded his arms. 'See here! Napoleon Buonaparte at St Helena.'

'When you spoke to me as I came from the Mill the night before last,' said Lizzie, fixing her eyes upon him with the look of supplication which troubled his better nature, 'you told me that you were much surprised to see me, and that you were on a solitary fishing excursion. Was it true?'

'It was not,' replied Eugene composedly, 'in the least true. I came here, because I had information that I should find you here.'

'Can you imagine why I left London, Mr Wrayburn?'

'I am afraid, Lizzie,' he openly answered, 'that you left

London to get rid of me. It is not flattering to my self-love, but I am afraid you did.'

'I did.'

'How could you be so cruel?'

'O Mr Wrayburn,' she answered, suddenly breaking into tears, 'is the cruelty on my side! O Mr Wrayburn, Mr Wrayburn, is there no cruelty in your being here to-night!'

'In the name of all that's good—and that is not conjuring you in my own name, for Heaven knows I am not good'—said Eugene, 'don't be distressed!'

'What else can I be, when I know the distance and the difference between us? What else can I be, when to tell me why you came here, is to put me to shame!' said Lizzie, covering her face.

He looked at her with a real sentiment of remorseful tenderness and pity. It was not strong enough to impell him to sacrifice himself and spare her, but it was a strong emotion.

'Lizzie! I never thought before, that there was a woman in the world who could affect me so much by saying so little. But don't be hard in your construction of me. You don't know what my state of mind towards you is. You don't know how you haunt me and bewilder me. You don't know how the cursed carelessness that is over-officious in helping me at every other turning of my life, WON'T help me here. You have struck it dead, I think, and I sometimes almost wish you had struck me dead along with it.'

She had not been prepared for such passionate expressions, and they awakened some natural sparks of feminine pride and joy in her breast. To consider, wrong as he was, that he could care so much for her, and that she had the power to move him so!

'It grieves you to see me distressed, Mr Wrayburn; it grieves me to see you distressed. I don't reproach you. Indeed I don't reproach you. You have not felt this as I feel it, being so different from me, and beginning from another point of view. You have not thought. But I entreat you to think now, think now!'

'What am I to think of?' asked Eugene, bitterly.

'Think of me.'

'Tell me how *not* to think of you, Lizzie, and you'll change me altogether.'

'I don't mean in that way. Think of me, as belonging to another station, and quite cut off from you in honour. Remember that I have no protector near me, unless I have one in your noble heart. Respect my good name. If you feel towards me, in one particular, as you might if I was a lady, give me the full claims of a lady upon your generous behaviour. I am removed from you and your family by being a working girl. How true a gentleman to be as considerate of me as if I was removed by being a Queen!'

He would have been base indeed to have stood untouched by her appeal. His face expressed contrition and indecision as he asked:

'Have I injured you so much, Lizzie?'

'No, no. You may set me quite right. I don't speak of the past, Mr Wrayburn, but of the present and the future. Are we not here now, because through two days you have followed me so closely where there are so many eyes to see you, that I consented to this appointment as an escape?'

'Again, not very flattering to my self-love,' said Eugene, moodily; 'but yes. Yes. Yes.'

'Then I beseech you, Mr Wrayburn, I beg and pray you, leave this neighbourhood. If you do not, consider to what you will drive me.'

He did consider within himself for a moment or two, and then retorted, 'Drive you? To what shall I drive you, Lizzie?'

'You will drive me away. I live here peacefully and re-spected, and I am well employed here. You will force me to quit this place as I quitted London, and—by following me again—will force me to quit the next place in which I may find refuge, as I quitted this.'

'Are you so determined, Lizzie—forgive the word I am going to use, for its literal truth—to fly from a lover?'

'I am so determined,' she answered resolutely, though trembling, 'to fly from such a lover. There was a poor woman died here but a little while ago, scores of years older than I am, whom I found by chance, lying on the wet earth. You may have heard some account of her?'

'I think I have,' he answered, 'if her name was Higden.'

'Her name was Higden. Though she was so weak and old, she kept true to one purpose to the very last. Even at the very last, she made me promise that her purpose should be kept to, after she was dead, so settled was her determination. What she did, I can do. Mr Wrayburn, if I believed—but I do not believe—that you could be so cruel to me as to drive me from place to place to wear me out, you should drive me to death and not do it.'

He looked full at her handsome face, and in his own handsome face there was a light of blended admiration, anger, and reproach, which she—who loved him so in secret—whose heart had long been so full, and he the cause of its overflowing—drooped before. She tried hard to retain her firmness, but he saw it melting away under his eyes. In the moment of its dissolution, and of his first full knowledge of his influence upon her, she dropped, and he caught her on his arm.

'Lizzie! Rest so a moment. Answer what I ask you. If I had not been what you call removed from you and cut off from you, would you have made this appeal to me to leave you?'

'I don't know, I don't know. Don't ask me, Mr Wrayburn. Let me go back.'

'I swear to you, Lizzie, you shall go directly. I swear to you, you shall go alone. I'll not accompany you, I'll not follow you, if you will reply.'

'How can I, Mr Wrayburn? How can I tell you what I should have done, if you had not been what you are?'

'If I had not been what you make me out to be,' he struck in, skilfully changing the form of words, 'would you still have hated me?'

'O Mr Wrayburn,' she replied appealingly, and weeping, 'you know me better than to think I do!'

'If I had not been what you make me out to be, Lizzie, would you still have been indifferent to me?'

'O Mr Wrayburn,' she answered as before, 'you know me better than that too!'

There was something in the attitude of her whole figure as he supported it, and she hung her head, which besought him to be merciful and not force her to disclose her heart. He was not merciful with her, and he made her do it.

'If I know you better than quite to believe (unfortunate dog though I am!) that you hate me, or even that you are wholly indifferent to me, Lizzie, let me know so much more from yourself before we separate. Let me know how you would have dealt with me if you had regarded me as being what you would have considered on equal terms with you.'

'It is impossible, Mr Wrayburn. How can I think of you as being on equal terms with me? If my mind could put you on equal terms with me, you could not be yourself. How could I remember, then, the night when I first saw you, and when I went out of the room because you looked at me so attentively? Or, the night that passed into the morning when you broke to me that my father was dead? Or, the nights when you used to come to see me at my next home? Or, your having known how uninstructed I was, and having caused me to be taught better? Or, my having so looked up to you and wondered at you, and at first thought you so good to be at all mindful of me?'

'Only "at first" thought me so good, Lizzie? What did you think me after "at first"? So bad?'

'I don't say that. I don't mean that. But after the first wonder and pleasure of being noticed by one so different from any one who had ever spoken to me, I began to feel that it might have been better if I had never seen you.'

'Why?'

'Because you *were* so different,' she answered in a lower voice. 'Because it was so endless, so hopeless. Spare me!'

'Did you think for me at all, Lizzie?' he asked, as if he were a little stung.

'Not much, Mr Wrayburn. Not much until to-night.'

'Will you tell me why?'

'I never supposed until to-night that you needed to be thought for. But if you do need to be; if you do truly feel at heart that you have indeed been towards me what you have called yourself to-night, and that there is nothing for us in this life but separation; then Heaven help you, and Heaven bless you!'

The purity with which in these words she expressed something of her own love and her own suffering, made a deep impression on him for the passing time. He held her, almost as if she were sanctified to him by death, and kissed her, once, almost as he might have kissed the dead.

'I promised that I would not accompany you, nor follow you. Shall I keep you in view? You have been agitated, and it's growing dark.'

'I am used to be out alone at this hour, and I entreat you not to do so.'

'I promise. I can bring myself to promise nothing more to-night, Lizzie, except that I will try what I can do.'

'There is but one means, Mr Wrayburn, of sparing yourself and of sparing me, every way. Leave this neighbourhood to-morrow morning.'

'I will try.'

As he spoke the words in a grave voice, she put her hand in his, removed it, and went away by the river-side.

'Now, could Mortimer believe this?' murmured Eugene, still remaining, after a while, where she had left him. 'Can I even believe it myself?'

He referred to the circumstance that there were tears upon his hand, as he stood covering his eyes. 'A most ridiculous position this, to be found out in!' was his next thought. And his next struck its root in a little rising resentment against the cause of the tears.

'Yet I have gained a wonderful power over her, too, let her be as much in earnest as she will!'

The reflection brought back the yielding of her face and form as she had drooped under his gaze. Contemplating the reproduction, he seemed to see, for the second time, in the appeal and in the confession of weakness, a little fear.

'And she loves me. And so earnest a character must be very earnest in that passion. She cannot choose for herself to be strong in this fancy, wavering in that, and weak in the other. She must go through with her nature, as I must go through with mine. If mine exacts its pains and penalties all round, so must hers, I suppose.'

Pursuing the inquiry into his own nature, he thought, 'Now, if I married her. If, outfacing the absurdity of the situation in correspondence with M. R. F., I astonished M. R. F. to the utmost extent of his respected powers, by informing him that I had married her, how would M. R. F. reason with the legal mind? ''You wouldn't marry for some money and some station, because you were frightfully likely to become bored. Are you less frightfully likely to become bored, marrying for no money and no station? Are you sure of yourself?'' Legal mind, in spite of forensic protestations, must secretly admit, ''Good reasoning on the part of M. R. F. *Not* sure of myself.'' '

In the very act of calling this tone of levity to his aid, he felt it to be profligate and worthless, and asserted her against it.

'And yet,' said Eugene, 'I should like to see the fellow (Mortimer excepted) who would undertake to tell me that this was not a real sentiment on my part, won out of me by her beauty and her worth, in spite of myself, and that I would not be true to her. I should particularly like to see the fellow to-night who would tell me so, or who would tell me anything that could be construed to her disadvantage; for I am wearily out of sorts with one Wrayburn who cuts a sorry figure, and I would far rather be out of sorts with somebody else. ''Eugene, Eugene,

Eugene, this is a bad business.'' Ah! So go the Mortimer Lightwood bells, and they sound melancholy to-night.'

Strolling on, he thought of something else to take himself to
task for. 'Where is the analogy, Brute Beast,' he said impatiently, 'between a woman whom your father coolly finds out for
you and a woman whom you have found out for yourself, and
have ever drifted after with more and more of constancy since
you first set eyes upon her? Ass! Can you reason no better than
that?'

But, again he subsided into a reminiscence of his first full
knowledge of his power just now, and of her disclosure of her
heart. To try no more to go away, and to try her again, was the
reckless conclusion it turned uppermost. And yet again, 'Eugene, Eugene, Eugene, this is a bad business!' And, 'I wish I
could stop the Lightwood peal, for it sounds like a knell.'

Looking above, he found that the young moon was up, and
that the stars were beginning to shine in the sky from which the
tones of red and yellow were flickering out, in favour of the
calm blue of a summer night. He was still by the river-side.
Turning suddenly, he met a man, so close upon him that Eugene,
surprised, stepped back, to avoid a collision. The man carried
something over his shoulder which might have been a broken
oar, or spar, or bar, and took no notice of him, but passed on.

'Halloa, friend!' said Eugene, calling after him, 'are you
blind?'

The man made no reply, but went his way.

Eugene Wrayburn went the opposite way, with his hands
behind him and his purpose in his thoughts. He passed the
sheep, and passed the gate, and came within hearing of the
village sounds, and came to the bridge. The inn where he stayed,
like the village and the mill, was not across the river, but on that
side of the stream on which he walked. However, knowing the
rushy bank and the back-water on the other side to be a retired
place, and feeling out of humour for noise or company, he
crossed the bridge, and sauntered on: looking up at the stars as
they seemed one by one to be kindled in the sky, and looking
down at the river as the same stars seemed to be kindled deep in
the water. A landing-place overshadowed by a willow, and a
pleasure-boat lying moored there among some stakes, caught his
eye as he passed along. The spot was in such dark shadow, that
he paused to make out what was there, and then passed on again.

The rippling of the river seemed to cause a correspondent
stir in his uneasy reflections. He would have laid them asleep if

he could, but they were in movement, like the stream, and all tending one way with a strong current. As the ripple under the moon broke unexpectedly now and then, and palely flashed in a new shape and with a new sound, so parts of his thoughts started, unbidden, from the rest, and revealed their wickedness. 'Out of the question to marry her,' said Eugene, 'and out of the question to leave her. The crisis!'

He had sauntered far enough. Before turning to retrace his steps, he stopped upon the margin, to look down at the reflected night. In an instant, with a dreadful crash, the reflected night turned crooked, flames shot jaggedly across the air, and the moon and stars came bursting from the sky.

Was he struck by lightning? With some incoherent half-formed thought to that effect, he turned under the blows that were blinding him and mashing his life, and closed with a murderer, whom he caught by a red neckerchief—unless the raining down of his own blood gave it that hue.

Eugene was light, active, and expert; but his arms were broken, or he was paralysed, and could do no more than hang on to the man, with his head swung back, so that he could see nothing but the heaving sky. After dragging at the assailant, he fell on the bank with him, and then there was another great crash, and then a splash, and all was done.

Lizzie Hexam, too, had avoided the noise, and the Saturday movement of people in the straggling street, and chose to walk alone by the water until her tears should be dry, and she could so compose herself as to escape remark upon her looking ill or unhappy on going home. The peaceful serenity of the hour and place, having no reproaches or evil intentions within her breast to contend against, sank healingly into its depths. She had meditated and taken comfort. She, too, was turning homeward, when she heard a strange sound.

It startled her, for it was like a sound of blows. She stood still, and listened. It sickened her, for blows fell heavily and cruelly on the quiet of the night. As she listened, undecided, all was silent. As she yet listened, she heard a faint groan, and a fall into the river.

Her old bold life and habit instantly inspired her. Without vain waste of breath in crying for help where there were none to hear, she ran towards the spot from which the sounds had come. It lay between her and the bridge, but it was more removed from her than she had thought; the night being so very quiet, and sound travelling far with the help of water.

At length, she reached a part of the green bank, much and newly trodden, where there lay some broken splintered pieces of wood and some torn fragments of clothes. Stooping, she saw that the grass was bloody. Following the drops and smears, she saw that the watery margin of the bank was bloody. Following the current with her eyes, she saw a bloody face turned up towards the moon, and drifting away.

Now, merciful Heaven be thanked for that old time, and grant, O Blessed Lord, that through thy wonderful workings it may turn to good at last! To whomsoever the drifting face belongs, be it man's or woman's, help my humble hands, Lord God, to raise it from death and restore it to some one to whom it must be dear!

It was thought, fervantly thought, but not for a moment did the prayer check her. She was away before it welled up in her mind, away, swift and true, yet steady above all—for without steadiness it could never be done—to the landing-place under the willow-tree, where she also had seen the boat lying moored among the stakes.

A sure touch of her old practised hand, a sure step of her old practised foot, a sure light balance of her body, and she was in the boat. A quick glance of her practised eye showed her, even through the deep dark shadow, the sculls in a rack against the red-brick garden-wall. Another moment, and she had cast off (taking the line with her), and the boat had shot out into the moonlight, and she was rowing down the stream as never other woman rowed on English water.

Intently over her shoulder, without slackening speed, she looked ahead for the driving face. She passed the scene of the struggle—yonder it was, on her left, well over the boat's stern—she passed on her right, the end of the village street, a hilly street that almost dipped into the river; its sounds were growing faint again, and she slackened; looking as the boat drove, everywhere, everywhere, for the floating face.

She merely kept the boat before the stream now, and rested on her oars, knowing well that if the face were not soon visible, it had gone down, and she would overshoot it. An untrained sight would never have seen by the moonlight what she saw at the length of a few strokes astern. She saw the drowning figure rise to the surface, slightly struggle, and as if by instinct turn over on its back to float. Just so had she first dimly seen the face which she now dimly saw again.

Firm of look and firm of purpose, she intently watched its

coming on, until it was very near; then, with a touch unshipped her sculls, and crept aft in the boat, between kneeling and crouching. Once, she let the body evade her, not being sure of her grasp. Twice, and she had seized it by its bloody hair.

It was insensible, if not virtually dead; it was mutilated, and streaked the water all about it with dark red streaks. As it could not help itself, it was impossible for her to get it on board. She bent over the stern to secure it with the line, and then the river and its shores rang to the terrible cry she uttered.

But, as if possessed by supernatural spirit and strength, she lashed it safe, resumed her seat, and rowed in, desperately, for the nearest shallow water where she might run the boat aground. Desperately, but not wildly, for she knew that if she lost distinctness of intention, all was lost and gone.

She ran the boat ashore, went into the water, released him from the line, and by main strength lifted him in her arms and laid him in the bottom of the boat. He had fearful wounds upon him, and she bound them up with her dress torn into strips. Else, supposing him to be still alive, she foresaw that he must bleed to death before he could be landed at his inn, which was the nearest place for succour.

This done very rapidly, she kissed his disfigured forehead, looked up in anguish to the stars, and blessed him and forgave him, 'if she had anything to forgive.' It was only in that instant that she thought of herself, and then she thought of herself only for him.

Now, merciful Heaven be thanked for that old time, enabling me, without a wasted moment, to have got the boat afloat again, and to row back against the stream! And grant, O Blessed Lord God, that through poor me he may be raised from death, and preserved to some one else to whom he may be dear one day, though never dearer than to me!

She rowed hard—rowed desperately, but never wildly—and seldom removed her eyes from him in the bottom of the boat. She had so laid him there, as that she might see his disfigured face; it was so much disfigured that his mother might have covered it, but it was above and beyond disfigurement in her eyes.

The boat touched the edge of the patch of inn lawn, sloping gently to the water. There were lights in the windows, but there chanced to be no one out of doors. She made the boat fast, and again by main strength took him up, and never laid him down until she laid him down in the house.

Surgeons were sent for, and she sat supporting his head. She had oftentimes heard in days that were gone, how doctors would lift the hand of an insensible wounded person, and would drop it if the person were dead. She waited for the awful moment when the doctors might lift this hand, all broken and bruised, and let it fall.

The first of the surgeons came, and asked, before proceeding to his examination, 'Who brought him in?'

'I brought him in, sir,' answered Lizzie, at whom all present looked.

'You, my dear? You could not lift, far less carry, this weight.'

'I think I could not, at another time, sir; but I am sure I did.'

The surgeon looked at her with great attention, and with some compassion. Having with a grave face touched the wounds upon the head, and the broken arms, he took the hand.

O! would he let it drop?

He appeared irresolute. He did not retain it, but laid it gently down, took a candle, looked more closely at the injuries on the head, and at the pupils of the eyes. That done, he replaced the candle and took the hand again. Another surgeon then coming in, the two exchanged a whisper, and the second took the hand. Neither did he let it fall at once, but kept it for a while and laid it gently down.

'Attend to the poor girl,' said the first surgeon then. 'She is quite unconscious. She sees nothing and hears nothing. All the better for her! Don't rouse her, if you can help it; only move her. Poor girl, poor girl! She must be amazingly strong of heart, but it is much to be feared that she has set her heart upon the dead. Be gentle with her.'

Chapter 7
Better to Be Abel Than Cain

DAY was breaking at Plashwater Weir Mill Lock. Stars were yet visible, but there was dull light in the east that was not the light of night. The moon had gone down, and a mist crept along the banks of the river, seen through which the trees were the ghosts of trees, and the water was the ghost of water. This earth looked spectral, and so did the pale stars: while the cold eastern glare, expressionless as to heat or colour, with the eye of the firmament quenched, might have been likened to the stare of the dead.

Perhaps it was so likened by the lonely Bargeman, standing on the brink of the lock. For certain, Bradley Headstone looked that way, when a chill air came up, and when it passed on murmuring, as if it whispered something that made the phantom trees and water tremble—or threaten—for fancy might have made it either.

He turned away, and tried the Lock-house door. It was fastened on the inside.

'Is he afraid of me?' he muttered, knocking.

Rogue Riderhood was soon roused, and soon undrew the bolt and let him in.

'Why, T'otherest, I thought you had been and got lost! Two nights away! I a'most believed as you'd giv' me the slip, and I had as good as half a mind for to advertise you in the newspapers to come for'ard.'

Bradley's face turned so dark on this hint, that Riderhood deemed it expedient to soften it into a compliment.

'But not you, governor, not you,' he went on, stolidly shaking his head. 'For what did I say to myself arter having amused myself with that there stretch of a comic idea, as a sort of a playful game? Why, I says to myself, "He's a man o' honour." That's what *I* says to myself. "He's a man o' double honour."'

Very remarkably, Riderhood put no question to him. He

had looked at him on opening the door, and he now looked at him again (stealthily this time), and the result of his looking was, that he asked him no question.

'You'll be for another forty on 'em, governor, as I judges, afore you turns your mind to breakfast,' said Riderhood, when his visitor sat down, resting his chin on his hand, with his eyes on the ground. And very remarkably again: Riderhood feigned to set the scanty furniture in order, while he spoke, to have a show of reason for not looking at him.

'Yes. I had better sleep, I think,' said Bradley, without changing his position.

'I myself should recommend it, governor,' assented Riderhood. 'Might you be anyways dry?'

'Yes. I should like a drink,' said Bradley; but without appearing to attend much.

Mr Riderhood got out his bottle, and fetched his jug-full of water, and administered a potation. Then, he shook the coverlet of his bed and spread it smooth, and Bradley stretched himself upon it in the clothes he wore. Mr Riderhood poetically remarking that he would pick the bones of his night's rest, in his wooden chair, sat in the window as before; but, as before, watched the sleeper narrowly until he was very sound asleep. Then, he rose and looked at him close, in the bright daylight, on every side, with great minuteness. He went out to his Lock to sum up what he had seen.

'One of his sleeves is tore right away below the elber, and the t'other's had a good rip at the shoulder. He's been hung on to, pretty tight, for his shirt's all tore out of the neck-gathers. He's been in the grass and he's been in the water. And he's spotted, and I know with what, and with whose. Hooroar!'

Bradley slept long. Early in the afternoon a barge came down. Other barges had passed through, both ways, before it; but the Lock-keeper hailed only this particular barge, for news, as if he had made a time calculation with some nicety. The men on board told him a piece of news, and there was a lingering on their part to enlarge upon it.

Twelve hours had intervened since Bradley's lying down, when he got up. 'Not that I swaller it,' said Riderhood, squinting at his Lock, when he saw Bradley coming out of the house, 'as you've been a sleeping all the time, old boy!'

Bradley came to him, sitting on his wooden lever, and asked what o'clock it was? Riderhood told him it was between two and three.

'When are you relieved?' asked Bradley.

'Day arter to-morrow, governor.'

'Not sooner?'

'Not a inch sooner, governor.'

On both sides, importance seemed attached to this question of relief. Riderhood quite petted his reply; saying a second time, and prolonging a negative roll of his head, 'n–n–not a inch sooner, governor.'

'Did I tell you I was going on to-night?' asked Bradley.

'No, governor,' returned Riderhood, in a cheerful, affable, and conversational manner, 'you did not tell me so. But most like you meant to it and forgot to it. How, otherways, could a doubt have come into your head about it, governor?'

'As the sun goes down, I intend to go on,' said Bradley.

'So much the more necessairy is a Peck,' returned Riderhood. 'Come in and have it, T'otherest.'

The formality of spreading a tablecloth not being observed in Mr Riderhood's establishment, the serving of the 'peck' was the affair of a moment; it merely consisting in the handing down of a capacious baking dish with three-fourths of an immense meat pie in it, and the production of two pocket-knives, an earthenware mug, and a large brown bottle of beer.

Both ate and drank, but Riderhood much the more abundantly. In lieu of plates, that honest man cut two triangular pieces from the thick crust of the pie, and laid them, inside uppermost, upon the table: the one before himself, and the other before his guest. Upon these platters he placed two goodly portions of the contents of the pie, thus imparting the unusual interest to the entertainment that each partaker scooped out the inside of his plate, and consumed it with his other fare, besides having the sport of pursuing the clots of congealed gravy over the plain of the table, and successfully taking them into his mouth at last from the blade of his knife, in case of their not first sliding off it.

Bradley Headstone was so remarkably awkward at these exercises, that the Rogue observed it.

'Look out, T'otherest!' he cried, 'you'll cut your hand!'

But, the caution came too late, for Bradley gashed it at the instant. And, what was more unlucky, in asking Riderhood to tie it up, and in standing close to him for the purpose, he shook his hand under the smart of the wound, and shook blood over Riderhood's dress.

When dinner was done, and when what remained of the

platters and what remained of the congealed gravy had been put back into what remained of the pie, which served as an economical investment for all miscellaneous savings, Riderhood filled the mug with beer and took a long drink. And now he did look at Bradley, and with an evil eye.

'T'otherest!' he said, hoarsely, as he bent across the table to touch his arm. 'The news has gone down the river afore you.'

'What news?'

'Who do you think,' said Riderhood, with a hitch of his head, as if he disdainfully jerked the feint away, 'picked up the body? Guess.'

'I am not good at guessing anything.'

'She did. Hooroar! You had him there agin. She did.'

The convulsive twitching of Bradley Headstone's face, and the sudden hot humour that broke out upon it, showed how grimly the intelligence touched him. But he said not a single word, good or bad. He only smiled in a lowering manner, and got up and stood leaning at the window, looking through it. Riderhood followed him with his eyes. Riderhood cast down his eyes on his own besprinkled clothes. Riderhood began to have an air of being better at a guess than Bradley owned to being.

'I have been so long in want of rest,' said the schoolmaster, 'that with your leave I'll lie down again.'

'And welcome, T'otherest!' was the hospitable answer of his host. He had laid himself down without waiting for it, and he remained upon the bed until the sun was low. When he arose and came out to resume his journey, he found his host waiting for him on the grass by the towing-path outside the door.

'Whenever it may be necessary that you and I should have any further communication together,' said Bradley, 'I will come back. Good-night!'

'Well, since no better can be,' said Riderhood, turning on his heel, 'Good-night!' But he turned again as the other set forth, and added under his breath, looking after him with a leer: 'You wouldn't be let to go like that, if my Relief warn't as good as come. I'll catch you up in a mile.'

In a word, his real time of relief being that evening at sunset, his mate came lounging in, within a quarter of an hour. Not staying to fill up the utmost margin of his time, but borrowing an hour or so, to be repaid again when he should relieve his reliever, Riderhood straightway followed on the track of Bradley Headstone.

He was a better follower than Bradley. It had been the

calling of his life to slink and skulk and dog and waylay, and he
knew his calling well. He effected such a forced march on
leaving the Lock House that he was close up with him—that is to
say, as close up with him as he deemed it convenient to be—
before another Lock was passed. His man looked back pretty
often as he went, but got no hint of him. *He* knew how to take
advantage of the ground, and where to put the hedge between
them, and where the wall, and when to duck, and when to drop,
and had a thousand arts beyond the doomed Bradley's slow
conception.

But, all his arts were brought to a standstill, like himself,
when Bradley, turning into a green lane or riding by the river-
side—a solitary spot run wild in nettles, briars, and brambles,
and encumbered with the scathed trunks of a whole hedgerow of
felled trees, on the outskirts of a little wood—began stepping on
these trunks and dropping down among them and stepping on
them again, apparently as a schoolboy might have done, but
assuredly with no schoolboy purpose, or want of purpose.

'What are you up to?' muttered Riderhood, down in the
ditch, and holding the hedge a little open with both hands. And
soon his actions made a most extraordinary reply. 'By George
and the Draggin!' cried Riderhood, 'if he ain't a going to bathe!'

He had passed back, on and among the trunks of trees
again, and has passed on to the water-side and had begun un-
dressing on the grass. For a moment it had a suspicious look of
suicide, arranged to counterfeit accident. 'But you wouldn't have
fetched a bundle under your arm, from among that timber, if
such was your game!' said Riderhood. Nevertheless it was a
relief to him when the bather after a plunge and a few strokes
came out. 'For I shouldn't,' he said in a feeling manner, 'have
liked to lose you till I had made more money out of you
neither.'

Prone in another ditch (he had changed his ditch as his man
had changed his position), and holding apart so small a patch of
the hedge that the sharpest eyes could not have detected him,
Rogue Riderhood watched the bather dressing. And now gradually came the wonder that he stood up, completely clothed,
another man, and not the Bargeman.

'Aha!' said Riderhood. 'Much as you was dressed that
night. I see. You're a taking me with you, now. You're deep.
But I knows a deeper.'

When the bather had finished dressing, he kneeled on the
grass, doing something with his hands, and again stood up with

his bundle under his arm. Looking all around him with great attention, he then went to the river's edge, and flung it in as far, and yet as lightly as he could. It was not until he was so decidedly upon his way again as to be beyond a bend of the river and for the time out of view, that Riderhood scrambled from the ditch.

'Now,' was his debate with himself, 'shall I foller you on, or shall I let you loose for this once, and go a fishing?' The debate continuing, he followed, as a precautionary measure in any case, and got him again in sight. 'If I was to let you loose this once,' said Riderhood then, still following, 'I could make you come to me agin, or I could find you out in one way or another. If I wasn't to go a fishing, others might.—I'll let you loose this once, and go a fishing!' With that, he suddenly dropped the pursuit and turned.

The miserable man whom he had released for the time, but not for long, went on towards London. Bradley was suspicious of every sound he heard, and of every face he saw, but was under a spell which very commonly falls upon the shedder of blood, and had no suspicion of the real danger that lurked in his life, and would have it yet. Riderhood was much in his thoughts—had never been out of his thoughts since the night-adventure of their first meeting; but Riderhood occupied a very different place there, from the place of pursuer; and Bradley had been at the pains of devising so many means of fitting that place to him, and of wedging him into it, that his mind could not compass the possibility of his occupying any other. And this is another spell against which the shedder of blood for ever strives in vain. There are fifty doors by which discovery may enter. With infinite pains and cunning, he double locks and bars forty-nine of them, and cannot see the fiftieth standing wide open.

Now, too, was he cursed with a state of mind more wearing and more wearisome than remorse. He had no remorse; but the evil-doer who can hold that avenger at bay, cannot escape the slower torture of incessantly doing the evil deed again and doing it more efficiently. In the defensive declarations and pretended confessions of murderers, the pursuing shadow of this torture may be traced through every lie they tell. If I had done it as alleged, is it conceivable that I would have made this and this mistake? If I had done it as alleged, should I have left that unguarded place which that false and wicked witness against me so infamously deposed to? The state of that wretch who continually finds the weak spots in his own crime, and strives to strengthen them when it is unchangeable, is a state that aggravates the offence by doing the deed a thousand times instead of once; but it is a state, too, that tauntingly visits the offence upon a sullen unrepentant nature with its heaviest punishment every time.

Bradley toiled on, chained heavily to the idea of his hatred and his vengeance, and thinking how he might have satiated both in many better ways than the way he had taken. The instrument might have been better, the spot and the hour might have been better chosen. To batter a man down from behind in the dark, on the brink of a river, was well enough, but he ought to have been instantly disabled, whereas he had turned and seized his assailant; and so, to end it before chance-help came, and to be rid of him, he had been hurriedly thrown backward into the river before the life was fully beaten out of him. Now if it could be done again, it must not be so done. Supposing his head had been held down under water for a while. Supposing the first blow had been truer. Supposing he had been shot. Supposing he had been strangled. Suppose this way, that way, the other way. Suppose anything but getting unchained from the one idea, for that was inexorably impossible.

The school reopened next day. The scholars saw little or no change in their master's face, for it always wore its slowly labouring expression. But, as he heard his classes, he was always doing the deed and doing it better. As he paused with his piece of chalk at the black board before writing on it, he was thinking of the spot, and whether the water was not deeper and the fall straighter, a little higher up, or a little lower down. He had half a mind to draw a line or two upon the board, and show himself what he meant. He was doing it again and improving on the manner, at prayers, in his mental arithmetic, all through his questioning, all through the day.

Charley Hexam was a master now, in another school, under another head. It was evening, and Bradley was walking in his garden observed from behind a blind by gentle little Miss Peecher, who contemplated offering him a loan of her smelling salts for headache, when Mary Anne, in faithful attendance, held up her arm.

'Yes, Mary Anne?'

'Young Mr Hexam, if you please, ma'am, coming to see Mr Headstone.'

'Very good, Mary Anne.'

Again Mary Anne held up her arm.

'You may speak, Mary Anne?'

'Mr Headstone has beckoned young Mr Hexam into his house, ma'am, and he has gone in himself without waiting for young Mr Hexam to come up, and now *he* has gone in too, ma'am, and has shut the door.'

'With all my heart, Mary Anne.'

Again Mary Anne's telegraphic arm worked.

'What more, Mary Anne?'

'They must find it rather dull and dark, Miss Peecher, for the parlour blind's down, and neither of them pulls it up.'

'There is no accounting,' said good Miss Peecher with a little sad sigh which she repressed by laying her hand on her neat methodical boddice, 'there is no accounting for tastes, Mary Anne.'

Charley, entering the dark room, stopped short when he saw his old friend in its yellow shade.

'Come in, Hexam, come in.'

Charley advanced to take the hand that was held out to him; but stopped again, short of it. The heavy, bloodshot eyes of the schoolmaster, rising to his face with an effort, met his look of scrutiny.

'Mr Headstone, what's the matter?'

'Matter? Where?'

'Mr Headstone, have you heard the news? This news about the fellow, Mr Eugene Wrayburn? That he is killed?'

'He is dead, then!' exclaimed Bradley.

Young Hexam standing looking at him, he moistened his lips with his tongue, looked about the room, glanced at his former pupil, and looked down. 'I heard of the outrage,' said Bradley, trying to constrain his working mouth, 'but I had not heard the end of it.'

'Where were you,' said the boy, advancing a step as he lowered his voice, 'when it was done? Stop! I don't ask that. Don't tell me. If you force your confidence upon me, Mr Headstone, I'll give up every word of it. Mind! Take notice. I'll give up it, and I'll give up you. I will!'

The wretched creature seemed to suffer acutely under this renunciation. A desolate air of utter and complete loneliness fell upon him, like a visible shade.

'It's for me to speak, not you,' said the boy. 'If you do, you'll do it at your peril. I am going to put your selfishness before you, Mr Headstone—your passionate, violent, and ungovernable selfishness—to show you why I can, and why I will, have nothing more to do with you.'

He looked at young Hexam as if he were waiting for a scholar to go on with a lesson that he knew by heart and was deadly tired of. But he had said his last word to him.

'If you had any part—I don't say what—in this attack,' pursued the boy; 'or if you know anything about it—I don't say how much—or if you know who did it—I go no closer—you did an injury to me that's never to be forgiven. You know that I took you with me to his chambers in the Temple when I told him my opinion of him, and made myself responsible for my opinion of you. You know that I took you with me when I was watching him with a view to recovering my sister and bringing her to her senses; you know that I have allowed myself to be mixed up with you, all through this business, in favouring your desire to marry my sister. And how do you know that, pursuing the ends of your own violent temper, you have not laid me open to suspicion? Is that your gratitude to me, Mr Headstone?'

Bradley sat looking steadily before him at the vacant air. As often as young Hexam stopped, he turned his eyes towards him, as if he were waiting for him to go on with the lesson, and get it done. As often as the boy resumed, Bradley resumed his fixed face.

'I am going to be plain with you, Mr Headstone,' said young Hexam, shaking his head in a half-threatening manner, 'because this is no time for affecting not to know things that I do know—except certain things at which it might not be very safe for you, to hint again. What I mean is this: if you were a good master, I was a good pupil. I have done you plenty of credit, and in improving my own reputation I have improved yours quite as much. Very well then. Starting on equal terms, I want to put before you how you have shown your gratitude to me, for doing all I could to further your wishes with reference to my sister. You have compromised me by being seen about with me, endeavouring to counteract this Mr Eugene Wrayburn. That's the first thing you have done. If my character, and my now dropping you, help me out of that, Mr Headstone, the deliverance is to be attributed to me, and not to you. No thanks to you for it!'

The boy stopping again, he moved his eyes again.

'I am going on, Mr Headstone, don't you be afraid. I am going on to the end, and I have told you beforehand what the end is. Now, you know my story. You are as well aware as I am, that I have had many disadvantages to leave behind me in life. You have heard me mention my father, and you are sufficiently acquainted with the fact that the home from which I, as I

may say, escaped, might have been a more creditable one than it
was. My father died, and then it might have been supposed that
my way to respectability was pretty clear. No. For then my sister
begins.'

He spoke as confidently, and with as entire an absence of
any tell-tale colour in his cheek, as if there were no softening old
time behind him. Not wonderful, for there *was* none in his
hollow empty heart. What is there but self, for selfishness to see
behind it?

'When I speak of my sister, I devoutly wish that you had
never seen her, Mr Headstone. However, you did see her, and
that's useless now. I confided in you about her. I explained her
character to you, and how she interposed some ridiculous fanciful notions in the way of our being as respectable as I tried for.
You fell in love with her, and I favoured you with all my might.
She could not be induced to favour you, and so we came into
collision with this Mr Eugene Wrayburn. Now, what have you
done? Why, you have justified my sister in being firmly set
against you from first to last, and you have put me in the wrong
again! And why have you done it? Because, Mr Headstone, you
are in all your passions so selfish, and so concentrated upon
yourself, that you have not bestowed one proper thought on me.'

The cool conviction with which the boy took up and held
his position, could have been derived from no other vice in
human nature.

'It is,' he went on, actually with tears, 'an extraordinary
circumstance attendant on my life, that every effort I make
towards perfect respectability, is impeded by somebody else
through no fault of mine! Not content with doing what I have put
before you, you will drag my name into notoriety through dragging my sister's—which you are pretty sure to do, if my suspicions have any foundation at all—and the worse you prove to be,
the harder it will be for me to detach myself from being associated with you in people's minds.'

When he had dried his eyes and heaved a sob over his
injuries, he began moving towards the door.

'However, I have made up my mind that I will become
respectable in the scale of society, and that I will not be dragged
down by others. I have done with my sister as well as with you.
Since she cares so little for me as to care nothing for undermin-
ing my respectability, she shall go her way and I will go mine.
My prospects are very good, and I mean to follow them alone.
Mr Headstone, I don't say what you have got upon your con-

science, for I don't know. Whatever lies upon it, I hope you will see the justice of keeping wide and clear of me, and will find a consolation in completely exonerating all but yourself. I hope, before many years are out, to succeed the master in my present school, and the mistress being a single woman, though some years older than I am, I might even marry her. If it is any comfort to you to know what plans I may work out by keeping myself strictly respectable in the scale of society, these are the plans at present occurring to me. In conclusion, if you feel a sense of having injured me, and a desire to make some small reparation, I hope you will think how respectable you might have been yourself, and will contemplate your blighted existence.'

Was it strange that the wretched man should take this heavily to heart? Perhaps he had taken the boy to heart, first, through some long laborious years; perhaps through the same years he had found his drudgery lightened by communication with a brighter and more apprehensive spirit than his own; perhaps a family resemblance of face and voice between the boy and his sister, smote him hard in the gloom of his fallen state. For whichsoever reason, or for all, he drooped his devoted head when the boy was gone, and shrank together on the floor, and grovelled there, with the palms of his hands tight-clasping his hot temples, in unutterable misery, and unrelieved by a single tear.

Rogue Riderhood had been busy with the river that day. He had fished with assiduity on the previous evening, but the light was short, and he had fished unsuccessfully. He had fished again that day with better luck, and had carried his fish home to Plashwater Weir Mill Lock-house, in a bundle.

Chapter 8
A Few Grains of Pepper

THE dolls' dressmaker went no more to the business-premises of
Pubsey and Co. in St Mary Axe, after chance had disclosed to
her (as she supposed) the flinty and hypocritical character of Mr
Riah. She often moralized over her work on the tricks and the
manners of that venerable cheat, but made her little purchases
elsewhere, and lived a secluded life. After much consultation
with herself, she decided not to put Lizzie Hexam on her guard
against the old man, arguing that the disappointment of finding
him out would come upon her quite soon enough. Therefore, in
her communication with her friend by letter, she was silent on
this theme, and principally dilated on the backslidings of her bad
child, who every day grew worse and worse.

'You wicked old boy,' Miss Wren would say to him, with a
menacing forefinger, 'you'll force me to run away from you,
after all, you will; and then you'll shake to bits, and there'll be
nobody to pick up the pieces!'

At this foreshadowing of a desolate decease, the wicked old
boy would whine and whimper, and would sit shaking himself
into the lowest of low spirits, until such time as he could shake
himself out of the house and shake another threepennyworth into
himself. But dead drunk or dead sober (he had come to such a
pass that he was least alive in the latter state), it was always on
the conscience of the paralytic scarecrow that he had betrayed his
sharp parent for sixty threepennyworths of rum, which were all
gone, and that her sharpness would infallibly detect his having
done it, sooner or later. All things considered therefore, and
addition made of the state of his body to the state of his mind,
the bed on which Mr Dolls reposed was a bed of roses from
which the flowers and leaves had entirely faded, leaving him to
lie upon the thorns and stalks.

On a certain day, Miss Wren was alone at her work, with

the house-door set open for coolness, and was trolling in a small sweet voice a mournful little song which might have been the song of the doll she was dressing, bemoaning the brittleness and meltability of wax, when whom should she descry standing on the pavement, looking in at her, but Mr Fledgeby.

'I thought it was you?' said Fledgeby, coming up the two steps.

'Did you?' Miss Wren retorted. 'And I thought it was you, young man. Quite a coincidence. You're not mistaken, and I'm not mistaken. How clever we are!'

'Well, and how are you?' said Fledgeby.

'I am pretty much as usual, sir,' replied Miss Wren. 'A very unfortunate parent, worried out of my life and senses by a very bad child.'

Fledgeby's small eyes opened so wide that they might have passed for ordinary-sized eyes, as he stared about him for the very young person whom he supposed to be in question.

'But you're not a parent,' said Miss Wren, 'and consequently it's of no use talking to you upon a family subject.—To what am I to attribute the honour and favour?'

'To a wish to improve your acquaintance,' Mr Fledgeby replied.

Miss Wren, stopping to bite her thread, looked at him very knowingly.

'We never meet now,' said Fledgeby; 'do we?'

'No,' said Miss Wren, chopping off the word.

'So I had a mind,' pursued Fledgeby, 'to come and have a talk with you about our dodging friend, the child of Israel.'

'So *he* gave you my address; did he?' asked Miss Wren.

'I got it out of him,' said Fledgeby, with a stammer.

'You seem to see a good deal of him,' remarked Miss Wren, with shrewd distrust. 'A good deal of him you seem to see, considering.'

'Yes, I do,' said Fledgeby. 'Considering.'

'Haven't you,' inquired the dressmaker, bending over the doll on which her art was being exercised, 'done interceding with him yet?'

'No,' said Fledgeby, shaking his head.

'La! Been interceding with him all this time, and sticking to him still?' said Miss Wren, busy with her work.

'Sticking to him is the word,' said Fledgeby.

Miss Wren pursued her occupation with a concentrated air, and asked, after an interval of silent industry:

'Are you in the army?'

'Not exactly,' said Fledgeby, rather flattered by the question.

'Navy?' asked Miss Wren.

'N–no,' said Fledgeby. He qualified these two negatives, as if he were not absolutely in either service, but was almost in both.

'What are you then?' demanded Miss Wren.

'I am a gentleman, I am,' said Fledgeby.

'Oh!' assented Jenny, screwing up her mouth with an appearance of conviction. 'Yes, to be sure! That accounts for your having so much time to give to interceding. But only to think how kind and friendly a gentleman you must be!'

Mr Fledgeby found that he was skating round a board marked Dangerous, and had better cut out a fresh track. 'Let's get back to the dodgerest of the dodgers,' said he. 'What's he up to in the case of your friend the handsome gal? He must have some object. What's his object?'

'Cannot undertake to say, sir, I am sure!' returned Miss Wren, composedly.

'He won't acknowledge where she's gone,' said Fledgeby; 'and I have a fancy that I should like to have another look at her. Now I know he knows where she is gone.'

'Cannot undertake to say, sir, I am sure!' Miss Wren again rejoined.

'And you know where she is gone,' hazarded Fledgeby.

'Cannot undertake to say, sir, really,' replied Miss Wren.

The quaint little chin met Mr Fledgeby's gaze with such a baffling hitch, that that agreeable gentleman was for some time at a loss how to resume his fascinating part in the dialogue. At length he said:

'Miss Jenny!—That's your name, if I don't mistake?'

'Probably you don't mistake, sir,' was Miss Wren's cool answer; 'because you had it on the best authority. Mine, you know.'

'Miss Jenny! Instead of coming up and being dead, let's come out and look alive. It'll pay better, I assure you,' said Fledgeby, bestowing an inveigling twinkle or two upon the dressmaker. 'You'll find it pay better.'

'Perhaps,' said Miss Jenny, holding out her doll at arm's length, and critically contemplating the effect of her art with her scissors on her lips and her head thrown back, as if her interest lay there, and not in the conversation; 'perhaps you'll explain your meaning, young man, which is Greek to me.—You must have another touch of blue in your trimming, my dear.' Having addressed the last remark to her fair client, Miss Wren proceeded to snip at some blue fragments that lay before her, among fragments of all colours, and to thread a needle from a skein of blue silk.

'Look here,' said Fledgeby.—'Are you attending?'

'I am attending, sir,' replied Miss Wren, without the slightest appearance of so doing. 'Another touch of blue in your trimming, my dear.'

'Well, look here,' said Fledgeby, rather discouraged by the circumstances under which he found himself pursuing the conversation. 'If you're attending—'

('Light blue, my sweet young lady,' remarked Miss Wren, in a sprightly tone, 'being best suited to your fair complexion and your flaxen curls.')

'I say, if you're attending,' proceeded Fledgeby, 'it'll pay better in this way. It'll lead in a roundabout manner to your buying damage and waste of Pubsey and Co. at a nominal price, or even getting it for nothing.'

'Aha!' thought the dressmaker. 'But you are not so roundabout, Little Eyes, that I don't notice your answering for Pubsey and Co. after all! Little Eyes, Little Eyes, you're too cunning by half.'

'And I take it for granted,' pursued Fledgeby, 'that to get the most of your materials for nothing would be well worth your while, Miss Jenny?'

'You may take it for granted,' returned the dressmaker with many knowing nods, 'that it's always well worth my while to make money.'

'Now,' said Fledgeby approvingly, 'you're answering to a sensible purpose. Now, you're coming out and looking alive! So I make so free, Miss Jenny, as to offer the remark, that you and Judah were too thick together to last. You can't come to be intimate with such a deep file as Judah without beginning to see a little way into him, you know,' said Fledgeby with a wink.

'I must own,' returned the dressmaker, with her eyes upon her work, 'that we are not good friends at present.'

'I know you're not good friends at present,' said Fledgeby. 'I know all about it. I should like to pay off Judah, by not letting him have his own deep way in everything. In most things he'll get it by hook or by crook, but—hang it all!—don't let him have his own deep way in everything. That's too much.' Mr Fledgeby said this with some display of indignant warmth, as if he was counsel in the cause for Virtue.

'How can I prevent his having his own way?' began the dressmaker.

'Deep way, I called it,' said Fledgeby.

'—His own deep way, in anything?'

'I'll tell you,' said Fledgeby. 'I like to hear you ask it, because it's looking alive. It's what I should expect to find in one of your sagacious understanding. Now, candidly.'

'Eh?' cried Miss Jenny.

'I said, now candidly,' Mr Fledgeby explained, a little put out.

'Oh-h!'

'I should be glad to countermine him, respecting the handsome gal, your friend. He means something there. You may depend upon it, Judah means something there. He has a motive, and of course his motive is a dark motive. Now, whatever his motive is, it's necessary to his motive'—Mr Fledgeby's constructive powers were not equal to the avoidance of some tautology here—'that it should be kept from me, what he has done with her. So I put it to you, who know: What *has* he done with her? I ask no more. And is that asking much, when you understand that it will pay?'

Miss Jenny Wren, who had cast her eyes upon the bench again after her last interruption, sat looking at it, needle in hand but not working, for some moments. She then briskly resumed her work, and said with a sidelong glance of her eyes and chin at Mr Fledgeby;

'Where d'ye live?'

'Albany, Piccadilly,' replied Fledgeby.

'When are you at home?'

'When you like.'

'Breakfast-time?' said Jenny, in her abruptest and shortest manner.

'No better time in the day,' said Fledgeby.

'I'll look in upon you to-morrow, young man. Those two ladies,' pointing to dolls, 'have an appointment in Bond Street at ten precisely. When I've dropped 'em there, I'll drive round to you.' With a weird little laugh, Miss Jenny pointed to her crutch-stick as her equipage.

'This is looking alive indeed!' cried Fledgeby, rising.

'Mark you! I promise you nothing,' said the dolls' dressmaker, dabbing two dabs at him with her needle, as if she put out both his eyes.

'No no. *I* understand,' returned Fledgeby. 'The damage and waste question shall be settled first. It shall be made to pay; don't you be afraid. Good-day, Miss Jenny.'

'Good-day, young man.'

Mr Fledgeby's prepossessing form withdrew itself; and the little dressmaker, clipping and snipping and stitching, and stitching and snipping and clipping, fell to work at a great rate; musing and muttering all the time.

'Misty, misty, misty. Can't make it out. Little Eyes and the wolf in a conspiracy? Or Little Eyes and the wolf against one another? Can't make it out. My poor Lizzie, have they both designs against you, either way? Can't make it out. Is Little Eyes Pubsey, and the wolf Co? Can't make it out. Pubsey true to Co, and Co to Pubsey? Pubsey false to Co, and Co to Pubsey? Can't make it out. What said Little Eyes? "Now, candidly?" Ah! However the cat jumps, *he's* a liar. That's all I can make out at present; but you may go to bed in the Albany, Piccadilly, with *that* for your pillow, young man!' Thereupon, the little dressmaker again dabbed out his eyes separately, and making a loop in the air of her thread and deftly catching it into a knot with her needle, seemed to bowstring him into the bargain.

For the terrors undergone by Mr Dolls that evening when his little parent sat profoundly meditating over her work, and when he imagined himself found out, as often as she changed her attitude, or turned her eyes towards him, there is no adequate name. Moreover it was her habit to shake her head at that wretched old boy whenever she caught his eye as he shivered and shook. What are popularly called 'the trembles' being in full force upon him that evening, and likewise what are popularly called 'the horrors,' he had a very bad time of it; which was not made better by his being so remorseful as frequently to moan 'Sixty threepennorths.' This imperfect sentence not being at all intelligible as a confession, but sounding like a Gargantuan order for a dram, brought him into new difficulties by occasioning his parent to pounce at him in a more than usually snappish manner, and to overwhelm him with bitter reproaches.

What was a bad time for Mr Dolls, could not fail to be a bad time for the dolls' dressmaker. However, she was on the alert next morning, and drove to Bond Street, and set down the two ladies punctually, and then directed her equipage to conduct her to the Albany. Arrived at the doorway of the house in which

Mr Fledgeby's chambers were, she found a lady standing there in a travelling dress, holding in her hand—of all things in the world—a gentleman's hat.

'You want some one?' said the lady in a stern manner.

'I am going up stairs to Mr Fledgeby's.'

'You cannot do that at this moment. There is a gentleman with him. I am waiting for the gentleman. His business with Mr Fledgeby will very soon be transacted, and then you can go up. Until the gentleman comes down, you must wait here.'

While speaking, and afterwards, the lady kept watchfully between her and the staircase, as if prepared to oppose her going up, by force. The lady being of a stature to stop her with a hand, and looking mightily determined, the dressmaker stood still.

'Well? Why do you listen?' asked the lady.

'I am not listening,' said the dressmaker.

'What do you hear?' asked the lady, altering her phrase.

'Is it a kind of a spluttering somewhere?' said the dressmaker, with an inquiring look.

'Mr Fledgeby in his shower-bath, perhaps,' remarked the lady, smiling.

'And somebody's beating a carpet, I think?'

'Mr Fledgeby's carpet, I dare say,' replied the smiling lady.

Miss Wren had a reasonably good eye for smiles, being well accustomed to them on the part of her young friends, though their smiles mostly ran smaller than in nature. But she had never seen so singular a smile as that upon this lady's face. It twitched her nostrils open in a remarkable manner, and contracted her lips and eyebrows. It was a smile of enjoyment too, though of such a fierce kind that Miss Wren thought she would rather not enjoy herself than do it in that way.

'Well!' said the lady, watching her. 'What now?'

'I hope there's nothing the matter!' said the dressmaker.

'Where?' inquired the lady.

'I don't know where,' said Miss Wren, staring about her. 'But I never heard such odd noises. Don't you think I had better call somebody?'

'I think you had better not,' returned the lady with a significant frown, and drawing closer.

On this hint, the dressmaker relinquished the idea, and stood looking at the lady as hard as the lady looked at her. Meanwhile the dressmaker listened with amazement to the odd noises which still continued, and the lady listened too, but with a coolness in which there was no trace of amazement.

Soon afterwards, came a slamming and banging of doors; and then came running down stairs, a gentleman with whiskers, and out of breath, who seemed to be red-hot.

'Is your business done, Alfred?' inquired the lady.

'Very thoroughly done,' replied the gentleman, as he took his hat from her.

'You can go up to Mr Fledgeby as soon as you like,' said the lady, moving haughtily away.

'Oh! And you can take these three pieces of stick with you,' added the gentleman politely, 'and say, if you please, that they come from Mr Alfred Lammle, with his compliments on leaving England. Mr Alfred Lammle. Be so good as not to forget the name.'

The three pieces of stick were three broken and frayed fragments of a stout lithe cane. Miss Jenny taking them wonderingly, and the gentleman repeating with a grin, 'Mr Alfred Lammle, if you'll be so good. Compliments, on leaving England,' the lady and gentleman walked away quite deliberately, and Miss Jenny and her crutch-stick went up stairs. 'Lammle, Lammle, Lammle?' Miss Jenny repeated as she panted from stair to stair, 'where have I heard that name? Lammle, Lammle? I know! Saint Mary Axe!'

With a gleam of new intelligence in her sharp face, the dolls' dressmaker pulled at Fledgeby's bell. No one answered; but, from within the chambers, there proceeded a continuous spluttering sound of a highly singular and unintelligible nature.

'Good gracious! Is Little Eyes choking?' cried Miss Jenny.

Pulling at the bell again and getting no reply, she pushed the outer door, and found it standing ajar. No one being visible on her opening it wider, and the spluttering continuing, she took the liberty of opening an inner door, and then beheld the extraordinary spectacle of Mr Fledgeby in a shirt, a pair of Turkish trousers, and a Turkish cap, rolling over and over on his own carpet, and spluttering wonderfully.

'Oh Lord!' gasped Mr Fledgeby. 'Oh my eye! Stop thief! I am strangling. Fire! Oh my eye! A glass of water. Give me a glass of water. Shut the door. Murder! Oh Lord!' And then rolled and spluttered more than ever.

Hurrying into another room, Miss Jenny got a glass of water, and brought it for Fledgeby's relief: who, gasping, spluttering, and rattling in his throat betweenwhiles, drank some water, and laid his head faintly on her arm.

'Oh my eye!' cried Fledgeby, struggling anew. 'It's salt and snuff. It's up my nose, and down my throat, and in my wind-pipe. Ugh! Ow! Ow! Ow! Ah–h–h–h!' And here, crowing fearfully, with his eyes starting out of his head, appeared to be contending with every mortal disease incidental to poultry.

'And Oh my Eye, I'm so sore!' cried Fledgeby, starting, over on his back, in a spasmodic way that caused the dressmaker to retreat to the wall. 'Oh I smart so! Do put something to my back and arms, and legs and shoulders. Ugh! It's down my throat again and can't come up. Ow! Ow! Ow! Ah–h–h–h! Oh I smart so!' Here Mr Fledgeby bounded up, and bounded down, and went rolling over and over again.

The dolls' dressmaker looked on until he rolled himself into a corner with his Turkish slippers uppermost, and then, resolving in the first place to address her ministration to the salt and snuff, gave him more water and slapped his back. But, the latter application was by no means a success, causing Mr Fledgeby to scream, and to cry out, 'Oh my eye! don't slap me! I'm covered with weales and I smart so!'

However, he gradually ceased to choke and crow, saving at intervals, and Miss Jenny got him into an easy-chair: where, with his eyes red and watery, with his features swollen, and with some half-dozen livid bars across his face, he presented a most rueful sight.

'What ever possessed you to take salt and snuff, young man?' inquired Miss Jenny.

'I didn't take it,' the dismal youth replied. 'It was crammed into my mouth.'

'Who crammed it?' asked Miss Jenny.

'He did,' answered Fledgeby. 'The assassin. Lammle. He rubbed it into my mouth and up my nose and down my throat—Ow! Ow! Ow! Ah–h–h–h! Ugh—to prevent my crying out, and then cruelly assaulted me.'

'With this?' asked Miss Jenny, showing the pieces of cane.

'That's the weapon,' said Fledgeby, eyeing it with the air of an acquaintance. 'He broke it over me. Oh I smart so! How did you come by it?'

'When he ran down stairs and joined the lady he had left in the hall with his hat'—Miss Jenny began.

'Oh!' groaned Mr Fledgeby, writhing, 'she was holding his hat, was she? I might have known she was in it.'

'When he came down stairs and joined the lady who wouldn't let me come up, he gave me the pieces for you, and I was to say,

"With Mr Alfred Lammle's compliments on his leaving England." ' Miss Jenny said it with such spiteful satisfaction, and such a hitch of her chin and eyes as might have added to Mr Fledgeby's miseries, if he could have noticed either, in his bodily pain with his hand to his head.

'Shall I go for the police?' inquired Miss Jenny, with a nimble start towards the door.

'Stop! No, don't!' cried Fledgeby. 'Don't, please. We had better keep it quiet. Will you be so good as shut the door? Oh I do smart so!'

In testimony of the extent to which he smarted, Mr Fledgeby came wallowing out of the easy-chair, and took another roll on the carpet.

'Now the door's shut,' said Mr Fledgeby, sitting up in anguish, with his Turkish cap half on and half off, and the bars on his face getting bluer, 'do me the kindness to look at my back and shoulders. They must be in an awful state, for I hadn't got my dressing-gown on, when the brute came rushing in. Cut my shirt away from the collar; there's a pair of scissors on that table. Oh!' groaned Mr Fledgeby, with his hand to his head again. 'How I do smart, to be sure!'

'There?' inquired Miss Jenny, alluding to the back and shoulders.

'Oh Lord, yes!' moaned Fledgeby, rocking himself. 'And all over! Everywhere!'

The busy little dressmaker quickly snipped the shirt away, and laid bare the results of as furious and sound a thrashing as even Mr Fledgeby merited. 'You may well smart, young man!' exclaimed Miss Jenny. And stealthily rubbed her little hands behind him, and poked a few exultant pokes with her two forefingers over the crown of his head.

'What do you think of vinegar and brown paper?' inquired the suffering Fledgeby, still rocking and moaning. 'Does it look as if vinegar and brown paper was the sort of application?'

'Yes,' said Miss Jenny, with a silent chuckle. 'It looks as if it ought to be Pickled.'

Mr Fledgeby collapsed under the word 'Pickled,' and groaned again. 'My kitchen is on this floor,' he said; 'you'll find brown paper in a dresser-drawer there, and a bottle of vinegar on a shelf. Would you have the kindness to make a few plasters and put 'em on? It can't be kept too quiet.'

'One, two—hum—five, six. You'll want six,' said the dressmaker.

'There's smart enough,' whimpered Mr Fledgeby, groaning and writhing again, 'for sixty.'

Miss Jenny repaired to the kitchen, scissors in hand, found the brown paper and found the vinegar, and skilfully cut out and steeped six large plasters. When they were all lying ready on the dresser, an idea occurred to her as she was about to gather them up.

'I think,' said Miss Jenny with a silent laugh, 'he ought to have a little pepper? Just a few grains? I think the young man's tricks and manners make a claim upon his friends for a little pepper?'

Mr Fledgeby's evil star showing her the pepper-box on the chimneypiece, she climbed upon a chair, and got it down, and sprinkled all the plasters with a judicious hand. She then went back to Mr Fledgeby, and stuck them all on him: Mr Fledgeby uttering a sharp howl as each was put in its place.

'There, young man!' said the dolls' dressmaker. 'Now I hope you feel pretty comfortable?'

Apparently, Mr Fledgeby did not, for he cried by way of answer, 'Oh–h how I do smart!'

Miss Jenny got his Persian gown upon him, extinguished his eyes crookedly with his Persian cap, and helped him to his bed: upon which he climbed groaning. 'Business between you and me being out of the question to-day, young man, and my time being precious,' said Miss Jenny then, 'I'll make myself scarce. Are you comfortable now?'

'Oh my eye!' cried Mr Fledgeby. 'No, I ain't. Oh–h–h! how I do smart!'

The last thing Miss Jenny saw, as she looked back before closing the room door, was Mr Fledgeby in the act of plunging and gambolling all over his bed, like a porpoise or dolphin in its native element. She then shut the bedroom door, and all the other doors, and going down stairs and emerging from the Albany into the busy streets, took omnibus for Saint Mary Axe: pressing on the road all the gaily-dressed ladies whom she could see from the window, and making them unconscious lay-figures for dolls, while she mentally cut them out and basted them.

Chapter 9
Two Places Vacated

SET down by the omnibus at the corner of Saint Mary Axe, and trusting to her feet and her crutch-stick within its precincts, the dolls' dressmaker proceeded to the place of business of Pubsey and Co. All there was sunny and quiet externally, and shady and quiet internally. Hiding herself in the entry outside the glass door, she could see from that post of observation the old man in his spectacles sitting writing at his desk.

'Boh!' cried the dressmaker, popping in her head at the glass-door. 'Mr Wolf at home?'

The old man took his glasses off, and mildly laid them down beside him. 'Ah Jenny, is it you? I thought you had given me up.'

'And so I had given up the treacherous wolf of the forest,' she replied; 'but, godmother, it strikes me you have come back. I am not quite sure, because the wolf and you change forms. I want to ask you a question or two, to find out whether you are really godmother or really wolf. May I?'

'Yes, Jenny, yes.' But Riah glanced towards the door, as if he thought his principal might appear there, unseasonably.

'If you're afraid of the fox,' said Miss Jenny, 'you may dismiss all present expectations of seeing that animal. *He* won't show himself abroad, for many a day.'

'What do you mean, my child?'

'I mean, godmother,' replied Miss Wren, sitting down beside the Jew, 'that the fox has caught a famous flogging, and that if his skin and bones are not tingling, aching, and smarting at this present instant, no fox did ever tingle, ache, and smart.' Therewith Miss Jenny related what had come to pass in the Albany, omitting the few grains of pepper.

'Now, godmother,' she went on, 'I particularly wish to ask you what has taken place here, since I left the wolf here?

Because I have an idea about the size of a marble, rolling about in my little noddle. First and foremost, are you Pubsey and Co., or are you either? Upon your solemn word and honour.'

The old man shook his head.

'Secondly, isn't Fledgeby both Pubsey and Co.?'

The old man answered with a reluctant nod.

'My idea,' exclaimed Miss Wren, 'is now about the size of an orange. But before it gets any bigger, welcome back, dear godmother!'

The little creature folded her arms about the old man's neck with great earnestness, and kissed him. 'I humbly beg your forgiveness, godmother. I am truly sorry. I ought to have had more faith in you. But what could I suppose when you said nothing for yourself, you know? I don't mean to offer that as a justification, but what could I suppose, when you were a silent party to all he said? It did look bad; now didn't it?'

'It looked so bad, Jenny,' responded the old man, with gravity, 'that I will straightway tell you what an impression it wrought upon me. I was hateful in mine own eyes. I was hateful to myself, in being so hateful to the debtor and to you. But more than that, and worse than that, and to pass out far and broad beyond myself—I reflected that evening, sitting alone in my garden on the housetop, that I was doing dishonour to my ancient faith and race. I reflected—clearly reflected for the first time—that in bending my neck to the yoke I was willing to wear, I bent the unwilling necks of the whole Jewish people. For it is not, in Christian countries, with the Jews as with other peoples. Men say, "This is a bad Greek, but there are good Greeks. This is a bad Turk, but there are good Turks." Not so with the Jews. Men find the bad among us easily enough—among what peoples are the bad not easily found?—but they take the worst of us as samples of the best; they take the lowest of us as presentations of the highest; and they say "All Jews are alike." If, doing what I was content to do here, because I was grateful for the past and have small need of money now, I had been a Christian, I could have done it, compromising no one but my individual self. But doing it as a Jew, I could not choose but compromise the Jews of all conditions and all countries. It is a little hard upon us, but it is the truth. I would that all our people remembered it! Though I have little right to say so, seeing that it came home so late to me.'

The dolls' dressmaker sat holding the old man by the hand, and looking thoughtfully in his face.

'Thus I reflected, I say, sitting that evening in my garden on the housetop. And passing the painful scene of that day in review before me many times, I always saw that the poor gentleman believed the story readily, because I was one of the Jews—that you believed the story readily, my child, because I was one of the Jews—that the story itself first came into the invention of the originator thereof, because I was one of the Jews. This was the result of my having had you three before me, face to face, and seeing the thing visibly presented as upon a theatre. Wherefore I perceived that the obligation was upon me to leave this service. But Jenny, my dear,' said Riah, breaking off, 'I promised that you should pursue your questions, and I obstruct them.'

'On the contrary, godmother; my idea is as large now as a pumpkin—and *you* know what a pumpkin is, don't you? So you gave notice that you were going? Does that come next?' asked Miss Jenny with a look of close attention.

'I indited a letter to my master. Yes. To that effect.'

'And what said Tingling-Tossing-Aching-Screaming-Scratching-Smarter?' asked Miss Wren with an unspeakable enjoyment in the utterance of those honourable titles and in the recollection of the pepper.

'He held me to certain months of servitude, which were his lawful term of notice. They expire to-morrow. Upon their expiration—not before—I had meant to set myself right with my Cinderella.'

'My idea is getting so immense now,' cried Miss Wren, clasping her temples, 'that my head won't hold it! Listen, godmother; I am going to expound. Little Eyes (that's Screaming-Scratching-Smarter) owes you a heavy grudge for going. Little Eyes casts about how best to pay you off. Little Eyes thinks of Lizzie. Little Eyes says to himself, "I'll find out where he has placed that girl, and I'll betray his secret because it's dear to him." Perhaps Little Eyes thinks, "I'll make love to her myself too;" but that I can't swear—all the rest I can. So, Little Eyes comes to me, and I go to Little Eyes. That's the way of it. And now the murder's all out, I'm sorry,' added the dolls' dressmaker, rigid from head to foot with energy as she shook her little fist before her eyes, 'that I didn't give him Cayenne pepper and chopped pickled Capsicum!'

This expression of regret being but partially intelligible to Mr Riah, the old man reverted to the injuries Fledgeby had received, and hinted at the necessity of his at once going to tend that beaten cur.

'Godmother, godmother, godmother!' cried Miss Wren irritably, 'I really lose all patience with you. One would think you believed in the Good Samaritan. How can you be so inconsistent?'

'Jenny dear,' began the old man gently, 'it is the custom of our people to help—'

'Oh! Bother your people!' interposed Miss Wren, with a toss of her head. 'If your people don't know better than to go and help Little Eyes, it's a pity they ever got out of Egypt. Over and above that,' she added, 'he wouldn't take your help if you offered it. Too much ashamed. Wants to keep it close and quiet, and to keep you out of the way.'

They were still debating this point when a shadow darkened the entry, and the glass door was opened by a messenger who brought a letter unceremoniously addressed, 'Riah.' To which he said there was an answer wanted.

The letter, which was scrawled in pencil uphill and downhill and round crooked corners, ran thus:

'OLD RIAH,

Your accounts being all squared, go. Shut up the place, turn out directly, and send me the key by bearer. Go. You are an unthankful dog of a Jew. Get out.

F.'

The dolls' dressmaker found it delicious to trace the screaming and smarting of Little Eyes in the distorted writing of this epistle. She laughed over it and jeered at it in a convenient corner (to the great astonishment of the messenger) while the old man got his few goods together in a black bag. That done, the shutters of the upper windows closed, and the office blind pulled down, they issued forth upon the steps with the attendant messenger. There, while Miss Jenny held the bag, the old man locked the house door, and handed over the key to him; who at once retired with the same.

'Well, godmother,' said Miss Wren, as they remained upon the steps together, looking at one another. 'And so you're thrown upon the world!'

'It would appear so, Jenny, and somewhat suddenly.'

'Where are you going to seek your fortune?' asked Miss Wren.

The old man smiled, but looked about him with a look of having lost his way in life, which did not escape the dolls' dressmaker.

'Verily, Jenny,' said he, 'the question is to the purpose, and
more easily asked than answered. But as I have experience of the
ready goodwill and good help of those who have given occupation to Lizzie, I think I will seek them out for myself.'

'On foot?' asked Miss Wren, with a chop.

'Ay!' said the old man. 'Have I not my staff?'

It was exactly because he had his staff, and presented so
quaint an aspect, that she mistrusted his making the journey.

'The best thing you can do,' said Jenny, 'for the time being,
at all events, is to come home with me, godmother. Nobody's
there but my bad child, and Lizzie's lodging stands empty.' The
old man when satisfied that no inconvenience could be entailed
on any one by his compliance, readily complied; and the singularly-
assorted couple once more went through the streets together.

Now, the bad child having been strictly charged by his
parent to remain at home in her absence, of course went out;
and, being in the very last stage of mental decrepitude, went out
with two objects; firstly, to establish a claim he conceived
himself to have upon any licensed victualler living, to be supplied with threepennyworth of rum for nothing; and secondly,
to bestow some maudlin remorse on Mr Eugene Wrayburn, and
see what profit came of it. Stumblingly pursuing these two
designs—they both meant rum, the only meaning of which he
was capable—the degraded creature staggered into Covent Garden Market and there bivouacked, to have an attack of the
trembles succeeded by an attack of the horrors, in a doorway.

This market of Covent Garden was quite out of the creature's line of road, but it had the attraction for him which it has
for the worst of the solitary members of the drunken tribe. It may
be the companionship of the nightly stir, or it may be the
companionship of the gin and beer that slop about among carters
and hucksters, or it may be the companionship of the trodden
vegetable refuse which is so like their own dress that perhaps
they take the Market for a great wardrobe; but be it what it may,
you shall see no such individual drunkards on doorsteps anywhere, as there. Of dozing women-drunkards especially, you
shall come upon such specimens there, in the morning sunlight,
as you might seek out of doors in vain through London. Such
stale vapid rejected cabbage-leaf and cabbage-stalk dress, such
damaged-orange countenance, such squashed pulp of humanity,
are open to the day nowhere else. So, the attraction of the
Market drew Mr Dolls to it, and he had out his two fits of

trembles and horrors in a doorway on which a woman had had out her sodden nap a few hours before.

There is a swarm of young savages always flitting about this same place, creeping off with fragments of orange-chests, and mouldy litter—Heaven knows into what holes they can convey them, having no home!—whose bare feet fall with a blunt dull softness on the pavement as the policeman hunts them, and who are (perhaps for that reason) little heard by the Powers that be, whereas in top-boots they would make a deafening clatter. These, delighting in the trembles and the horrors of Mr Dolls, as in a gratuitous drama, flocked about him in his doorway, butted at him, leaped at him, and pelted him. Hence, when he came out of his invalid retirement and shook off that ragged train, he was much bespattered, and in worse case than ever. But, not yet at his worst; for, going into a public-house, and being supplied in stress of business with his rum, and seeking to vanish without payment, he was collared, searched, found penniless, and admonished not to try that again, by having a pail of dirty water cast over him. This application superinduced another fit of the trembles; after which Mr Dolls, as finding himself in good cue for making a call on a professional friend, addressed himself to the Temple.

There was nobody at the chambers but Young Blight. That discreet youth, sensible of a certain incongruity in the association of such a client with the business that might be coming some day, with the best intentions temporized with Dolls, and offered a shilling for coach-hire home. Mr Dolls, accepting the shilling, promptly laid it out in two threepennyworths of conspiracy against his life, and two threepennyworths of raging repentance. Returning to the Chambers with which burden, he was descried coming round into the court, by the wary young Blight watching from the window: who instantly closed the outer door, and left the miserable object to expend his fury on the panels.

The more the door resisted him, the more dangerous and imminent became that bloody conspiracy against his life. Force of police arriving, he recognized in them the conspirators, and laid about him hoarsely, fiercely, staringly, convulsively, foamingly. A humble machine, familiar to the conspirators and called by the expressive name of Stretcher, being unavoidably sent for, he was rendered a harmless bundle of torn rags by being strapped down upon it, with voice and consciousness gone out of him, and life fast going. As this machine was borne out at the

Temple gate by four men, the poor little dolls' dressmaker and her Jewish friend were coming up the street.

'Let us see what it is,' cried the dressmaker. 'Let us make haste and look, godmother.'

The brisk little crutch-stick was but too brisk. 'O gentlemen, gentlemen, he belongs to me!'

'Belongs to you?' said the head of the party, stopping it.

'O yes, dear gentlemen, he's my child, out without leave. My poor bad, bad boy! and he don't know me, he don't know me! O what shall I do,' cried the little creature, wildly beating her hands together, 'when my own child don't know me!'

The head of the party looked (as well he might) to the old man for explanation. He whispered, as the dolls' dressmaker bent over the exhausted form and vainly tried to extract some sign of recognition from it: 'It's her drunken father.'

As the load was put down in the street, Riah drew the head of the party aside, and whispered that he thought the man was dying. 'No, surely not?' returned the other. But he became less confident, on looking, and directed the bearers to 'bring him to the nearest doctor's shop.'

Thither he was brought; the window becoming from within, a wall of faces, deformed into all kinds of shapes through the agency of globular red bottles, green bottles, blue bottles, and other coloured bottles. A ghastly light shining upon him that he didn't need, the beast so furious but a few minutes gone, was quiet enough now, with a strange mysterious writing on his face, reflected from one of the great bottles, as if Death had marked him: 'Mine.'

The medical testimony was more precise and more to the purpose than it sometimes is in a Court of Justice. 'You had better send for something to cover it. All's over.'

Therefore, the police sent for something to cover it, and it was covered and borne through the streets, the people falling away. After it, went the dolls' dressmaker, hiding her face in the Jewish skirts, and clinging to them with one hand, while with the other she plied her stick. It was carried home, and, by reason that the staircase was very narrow, it was put down in the parlour—the little working-bench being set aside to make room for it—and there, in the midst of the dolls with no speculation in their eyes, lay Mr Dolls with no speculation in his.

Many flaunting dolls had to be gaily dressed, before the money was in the dressmaker's pocket to get mourning for Mr Dolls. As the old man, Riah, sat by, helping her in such small ways as he could, he found it difficult to make out whether she really did realize that the deceased had been her father.

'If my poor boy,' she would say, 'had been brought up better, he might have done better. Not that I reproach myself. I hope I have no cause for that.'

'None indeed, Jenny, I am very certain.'

'Thank you, godmother. It cheers me to hear you say so. But you see it is so hard to bring up a child well, when you work, work, work, all day. When he was out of employment, I couldn't always keep him near me. He got fractious and nervous, and I was obliged to let him go into the streets. And he never did well in the streets, he never did well out of sight. How often it happens with children!'

'Too often, even in this sad sense!' thought the old man.

'How can I say what I might have turned out myself, but for my back having been so bad and my legs so queer, when I was young!' the dressmaker would go on. 'I had nothing to do but work, and so I worked. I couldn't play. But my poor unfortunate child could play, and it turned out the worse for him.'

'And not for him alone, Jenny.'

'Well! I don't know, godmother. He suffered heavily, did my unfortunate boy. He was very, very ill sometimes. And I called him a quantity of names;' shaking her head over her work, and dropping tears. 'I don't know that his going wrong was much the worse for me. If it ever was, let us forget it.'

'You are a good girl, you are a patient girl.'

'As for patience,' she would reply with a shrug, 'not much of that, godmother. If I had been patient, I should never have called him names. But I hope I did it for his good. And besides, I felt my responsibility as a mother, so much. I tried reasoning, and reasoning failed. I tried coaxing, and coaxing failed. I tried scolding and scolding failed. But I was bound to try everything, you know, with such a charge upon my hands. Where would have been my duty to my poor lost boy, if I had not tried everything!'

With such talk, mostly in a cheerful tone on the part of the industrious little creature, the day-work and the night-work were beguiled until enough of smart dolls had gone forth to bring into the kitchen, where the working-bench now stood, the sombre stuff that the occasion required, and to bring into the house the other sombre preparations. 'And now,' said Miss Jenny, 'having knocked off my rosy-cheeked young friends, I'll knock off my white-cheeked self.' This referred to her making her own dress,

which at last was done. 'The disadvantage of making for yourself,' said Miss Jenny, as she stood upon a chair to look at the
result in the glass, 'is, that you can't charge anybody else for the
job, and the advantage is, that you haven't to go out to try on.
Humph! Very fair indeed! If He could see me now (whoever he
is) I hope he wouldn't repent of his bargain!'

The simple arrangements were of her own making, and
were stated to Riah thus:

'I mean to go alone, godmother, in my usual carriage, and
you'll be so kind as keep house while I am gone. It's not far off.
And when I return, we'll have a cup of tea, and a chat over
future arrangements. It's a very plain last house that I have been
able to give my poor unfortunate boy; but he'll accept the will
for the deed if he knows anything about it; and if he doesn't
know anything about it,' with a sob, and wiping her eyes, 'why,
it won't matter to him. I see the service in the Prayer-book says,
that we brought nothing into this world and it is certain we can
take nothing out. It comforts me for not being able to hire a lot
of stupid undertaker's things for my poor child, and seeming as
if I was trying to smuggle 'em out of this world with him, when
of course I must break down in the attempt, and bring 'em all
back again. As it is, there'll be nothing to bring back but me,
and that's quite consistent, for *I* shan't be brought back, some
day!'

After that previous carrying of him in the streets, the wretched
old fellow seemed to be twice buried. He was taken on the
shoulders of half a dozen blossom-faced men, who shuffled with
him to the churchyard, and who were preceded by another
blossom-faced man, affecting a stately stalk, as if he were a
Policeman of the D(eath) Division, and ceremoniously pretending not to know his intimate acquaintances, as he led the pag-
eant. Yet, the spectacle of only one little mourner hobbling after,
caused many people to turn their heads with a look of interest.

At last the troublesome deceased was got into the ground, to
be buried no more, and the stately stalker stalked back before the
solitary dressmaker, as if she were bound in honour to have no
notion of the way home. Those Furies, the conventionalities,
being thus appeased, he left her.

'I must have a very short cry, godmother, before I cheer up
for good,' said the little creature, coming in. 'Because after all a
child is a child, you know.'

It was a longer cry than might have been expected. Howbeit, it wore itself out in a shadowy corner, and then the dress-

maker came forth, and washed her face, and made the tea. 'You wouldn't mind my cutting out something while we are at tea, would you?' she asked her Jewish friend, with a coaxing air.

'Cinderella, dear child,' the old man expostulated, 'will you never rest?'

'Oh! It's not work, cutting out a pattern isn't,' said Miss Jenny, with her busy little scissors already snipping at some paper. 'The truth is, godmother, I want to fix it while I have it correct in my mind.'

'Have you seen it to-day then?' asked Riah.

'Yes, godmother. Saw it just now. It's a surplice, that's what it is. Thing our clergymen wear, you know,' explained Miss Jenny, in consideration of his professing another faith.

'And what have you to do with that, Jenny?'

'Why, godmother,' replied the dressmaker, 'you must know that we Professors who live upon our taste and invention, are obliged to keep our eyes always open. And you know already that I have many extra expenses to meet just now. So, it came into my head while I was weeping at my poor boy's grave, that something in my way might be done with a clergyman.'

'What can be done?' asked the old man.

'Not a funeral, never fear!' returned Miss Jenny, anticipating his objection with a nod. 'The public don't like to be made melancholy, I know very well. I am seldom called upon to put my young friends into mourning; not into real mourning, that is; Court mourning they are rather proud of. But a doll clergyman, my dear,—glossy black curls and whiskers—uniting two of my young friends in matrimony,' said Miss Jenny, shaking her forefinger, 'is quite another affair. If you don't see those three at the altar in Bond Street, in a jiffy, my name's Jack Robinson!'

With her expert little ways in sharp action, she had got a doll into whitey-brown paper orders, before the meal was over, and was displaying it for the edification of the Jewish mind, when a knock was heard at the street-door. Riah went to open it, and presently came back, ushering in, with the grave and courteous air that sat so well upon him, a gentleman.

The gentleman was a stranger to the dressmaker; but even in the moment of his casting his eyes upon her, there was something in his manner which brought to her remembrance Mr Eugene Wrayburn.

'Pardon me,' said the gentleman. 'You are the dolls' dressmaker?'

'I am the dolls' dressmaker, sir.'

'Lizzie Hexam's friend?'

'Yes, sir,' replied Miss Jenny, instantly on the defensive. 'And Lizzie Hexam's friend.'

'Here is a note from her, entreating you to accede to the request of Mr Mortimer Lightwood, the bearer. Mr Riah chances to know that I am Mr Mortimer Lightwood, and will tell you so.'

Riah bent his head in corroboration.

'Will you read the note?'

'It's very short,' said Jenny, with a look of wonder, when she had read it.

'There was no time to make it longer. Time was so very precious. My dear friend Mr Eugene Wrayburn is dying.'

The dressmaker clasped her hands, and uttered a little piteous cry.

'Is dying,' repeated Lightwood, with emotion, 'at some distance from here. He is sinking under injuries received at the hands of a villain who attacked him in the dark. I come straight from his bedside. He is almost always insensible. In a short restless interval of sensibility, or partial sensibility, I made out that he asked for you to be brought to sit by him. Hardly relying on my own interpretation of the indistinct sounds he made, I caused Lizzie to hear them. We were both sure that he asked for you.'

The dressmaker, with her hands still clasped, looked affrightedly from the one to the other of her two companions.

'If you delay, he may die with his request ungratified, with his last wish—intrusted to me—we have long been much more than brothers—unfulfilled. I shall break down, if I try to say more.'

In a few moments the black bonnet and the crutch-stick were on duty, the good Jew was left in possession of the house, and the dolls' dressmaker, side by side in a chaise with Mortimer Lightwood, was posting out of town.

Chapter 10

The Doll's Dressmaker
Discovers a Word

A DARKENED and hushed room; the river outside the windows flowing on to the vast ocean; a figure on the bed, swathed and bandaged and bound, lying helpless on its back, with its two useless arms in splints at its sides. Only two days of usage so familiarized the little dressmaker with this scene, that it held the place occupied two days ago by the recollections of years.

He had scarcely moved since her arrival. Sometimes his eyes were open, sometimes closed. When they were open, there was no meaning in their unwinking stare at one spot straight before them, unless for a moment the brow knitted into a faint expression of anger, or a surprise. Then, Mortimer Lightwood would speak to him, and on occasions he would be so far roused as to make an attempt to pronounce his friend's name. But, in an instant consciousness was gone again, and no spirit of Eugene was in Eugene's crushed outer form.

They provided Jenny with materials for plying her work, and she had a little table placed at the foot of his bed. Sitting there, with her rich shower of hair falling over the chair-back, they hoped she might attract his notice. With the same object, she would sing, just above her breath, when he opened his eyes, or she saw his brow knit into that faint expression, so evanescent that it was like a shape made in water. But as yet he had not heeded. The 'they' here mentioned were the medical attendant; Lizzie, who was there in all her intervals of rest; and Lightwood, who never left him.

The two days became three, and the three days became four. At length, quite unexpectedly, he said something in a whisper.

'What was it, my dear Eugene?'

'Will you, Mortimer—'

'Will I—?'

—'Send for her?'

'My dear fellow, she is here.'

Quite unconscious of the long blank, he supposed that they were still speaking together.

The little dressmaker stood up at the foot of the bed, humming her song, and nodded to him brightly. 'I can't shake hands, Jenny,' said Eugene, with something of his old look; 'but I am very glad to see you.'

Mortimer repeated this to her, for it could only be made out by bending over him and closely watching his attempts to say it. In a little while, he added:

'Ask her if she has seen the children.'

Mortimer could not understand this, neither could Jenny herself, until he added:

'Ask her if she has smelt the flowers.'

'Oh! I know!' cried Jenny. 'I understand him now!' Then, Lightwood yielded his place to her quick approach, and she said, bending over the bed, with that better look: 'You mean my long bright slanting rows of children, who used to bring me ease and rest? You mean the children who used to take me up, and make me light?'

Eugene smiled, 'Yes.'

'I have not seen them since I saw you. I never see them now, but I am hardly ever in pain now.'

'It was a pretty fancy,' said Eugene.

'But I have heard my birds sing,' cried the little creature, 'and I have smelt my flowers. Yes, indeed I have! And both were most beautiful and most Divine!'

'Stay and help to nurse me,' said Eugene, quietly. 'I should like you to have the fancy here, before I die.'

She touched his lips with her hand, and shaded her eyes with that same hand as she went back to her work and her little low song. He heard the song with evident pleasure, until she allowed it gradually to sink away into silence.

'Mortimer.'

'My dear Eugene.'

'If you can give me anything to keep me here for only a few minutes—'

'To keep you here, Eugene?'

'To prevent my wandering away I don't know where—for I begin to be sensible that I have just come back, and that I shall lose myself again—do so, dear boy!'

Mortimer gave him such stimulants as could be given him

with safety (they were always at hand, ready), and bending over him once more, was about to caution him, when he said:

'Don't tell me not to speak, for I must speak. If you knew the harassing anxiety that gnaws and wears me when I am wandering in those places—where are those endless places, Mortimer? They must be at an immense distance!'

He saw in his friend's face that he was losing himself; for he added after a moment: 'Don't be afraid—I am not gone yet. What was it?'

'You wanted to tell me something, Eugene. My poor dear fellow, you wanted to say something to your old friend—to the friend who has always loved you, admired you, imitated you, founded himself upon you, been nothing without you, and who, God knows, would be here in your place if he could!'

'Tut, tut!' said Eugene with a tender glance as the other put his hand before his face. 'I am not worth it. I acknowledge that I like it, dear boy, but I am not worth it. This attack, my dear Mortimer; this murder—'

His friend leaned over him with renewed attention, saying: 'You and I suspect some one.'

'More than suspect. But, Mortimer, while I lie here, and when I lie here no longer, I trust to you that the perpetrator is never brought to justice.'

'Eugene?'

'Her innocent reputation would be ruined, my friend. She would be punished, not he. I have wronged her enough in fact; I have wronged her still more in intention. You recollect what pavement is said to be made of good intentions. It is made of bad intentions too. Mortimer, I am lying on it, and I know!'

'Be comforted, my dear Eugene.'

'I will, when you have promised me. Dear Mortimer, the man must never be pursued. If he should be accused, you must keep him silent and save him. Don't think of avenging me; think only of hushing the story and protecting her. You can confuse the case, and turn aside the circumstances. Listen to what I say to you. It was not the schoolmaster, Bradley Headstone. Do you hear me? Twice; it was not the schoolmaster, Bradley Headstone. Do you hear me? Three times; it was not the schoolmaster, Bradley Headstone.'

He stopped, exhausted. His speech had been whispered, broken, and indistinct; but by a great effort he had made it plain enough to be unmistakable.

'Dear fellow, I am wandering away. Stay me for another moment, if you can.'

Lightwood lifted his head at the neck, and put a wine-glass to his lips. He rallied.

'I don't know how long ago it was done, whether weeks, days, or hours. No matter. There is inquiry on foot, and pursuit. Say! Is there not?'

'Yes.'

'Check it; divert it! Don't let her be brought in question. Shield her. The guilty man, brought to justice, would poison her name. Let the guilty man go unpunished. Lizzie and my reparation before all! Promise me!'

'Eugene, I do. I promise you!'

In the act of turning his eyes gratefully towards his friend, he wandered away. His eyes stood still, and settled into that former intent unmeaning stare.

Hours and hours, days and nights, he remained in this same condition. There were times when he would calmly speak to his friend after a long period of unconsciousness, and would say he was better, and would ask for something. Before it could be given him, he would be gone again.

The dolls' dressmaker, all softened compassion now, watched him with an earnestness that never relaxed. She would regularly change the ice, or the cooling spirit, on his head, and would keep her ear at the pillow betweenwhiles, listening for any faint words that fell from him in his wanderings. It was amazing through how many hours at a time she would remain beside him, in a crouching attitude, attentive to his slightest moan. As he could not move a hand, he could make no sign of distress; but, through this close watching (if through no secret sympathy or power) the little creature attained an understanding of him that Lightwood did not possess. Mortimer would often turn to her, as if she were an interpreter between this sentient world and the insensible man; and she would change the dressing of a wound, or ease a ligature, or turn his face, or alter the pressure of the bedclothes on him, with an absolute certainty of doing right. The natural lightness and delicacy of touch which had become very refined by practice in her miniature work, no doubt was involved in this; but her perception was at least as fine.

The one word, Lizzie, he muttered millions of times. In a certain phase of his distressful state, which was the worst to those who tended him, he would roll his head upon the pillow, incessantly repeating the name in a hurried and impatient manner, with the misery of a disturbed mind, and the monotony of a machine. Equally, when he lay still and staring, he would repeat it for hours without cessation, but then, always in a tone of subdued warning and horror. Her presence and her touch upon his breast or face would often stop this, and then they learned to expect that he would for some time remain still, with his eyes closed, and that he would be conscious on opening them. But, the heavy disappointment of their hope—revived by the welcome silence of the room—was, that his spirit would glide away again and be lost, in the moment of their joy that it was there.

This frequent rising of a drowning man from the deep, to sink again, was dreadful to the beholders. But, gradually the change stole upon him that it became dreadful to himself. His desire to impart something that was on his mind, his unspeakable yearning to have speech with his friend and make a communication to him, so troubled him when he recovered consciousness, that its term was thereby shortened. As the man rising from the deep would disappear the sooner for fighting with the water, so he in his desperate struggle went down again.

One afternoon when he had been lying still, and Lizzie, unrecognized, had just stolen out of the room to pursue her occupation, he uttered Lightwood's name.

'My dear Eugene, I am here.'

'How long is this to last, Mortimer?'

Lightwood shook his head. 'Still, Eugene, you are no worse than you were.'

'But I know there's no hope. Yet I pray it may last long enough for you to do to me one last service, and for me to do one last action. Keep me here a few moments, Mortimer. Try, try!'

His friend gave him what aid he could, and encouraged him to believe that he was more composed, though even then his eyes were losing the expression they so rarely recovered.

'Hold me here, dear fellow, if you can. Stop my wandering away. I am going!'

'Not yet, not yet. Tell me, dear Eugene, what is it I shall do?'

'Keep me here for only a single minute. I am going away again. Don't let me go. Hear me speak first. Stop me—stop me!'

'My poor Eugene, try to be calm.'

'I do try. I try so hard. If you only knew how hard! Don't let me wander till I have spoken. Give me a little more wine.'

Lightwood complied. Eugene, with a most pathetic struggle against the unconsciousness that was coming over him, and with a look of appeal that affected his friend profoundly, said:

'You can leave me with Jenny, while you speak to her and
tell her what I beseech of her. You can leave me with Jenny,
while you are gone. There's not much for you to do. You won't
be long away.'

'No, no, no. But tell me what it is that I shall do, Eugene!'

'I am going! You can't hold me.'

'Tell me in a word, Eugene!'

His eyes were fixed again, and the only word that came
from his lips was the word millions of times repeated. Lizzie,
Lizzie, Lizzie.

But, the watchful little dressmaker had been vigilant as ever
in her watch, and she now came up and touched Lightwood's
arm as he looked down at his friend, despairingly.

'Hush!' she said, with her finger on her lips. 'His eyes are
closing. He'll be conscious when he next opens them. Shall I
give you a leading word to say to him?'

'O Jenny, if you could only give me the right word!'

'I can. Stoop down.'

He stooped, and she whispered in his ear. She whispered in
his ear one short word of a single syllable. Lightwood started,
and looked at her.

'Try it,' said the little creature, with an excited and exultant
face. She then bent over the unconscious man, and, for the first
time, kissed him on the cheek, and kissed the poor maimed hand
that was nearest to her. Then, she withdrew to the foot of the
bed.

Some two hours afterwards, Mortimer Lightwood saw his
consciousness come back, and instantly, but very tranquilly, bent
over him.

'Don't speak, Eugene. Do no more than look at me, and
listen to me. You follow what I say.'

He moved his head in assent.

'I am going on from the point where we broke off. Is the
word we should soon have come to—is it—Wife?'

'O God bless you, Mortimer!'

'Hush! Don't be agitated. Don't speak. Hear me, dear
Eugene. Your mind will be more at peace, lying here, if you
make Lizzie your wife. You wish me to speak to her, and tell her
so, and entreat her to be your wife. You ask her to kneel at this
bedside and be married to you, that your reparation may be
complete. Is that so?'

'Yes. God bless you! Yes.'

'It shall be done, Eugene. Trust it to me. I shall have to go away for some few hours, to give effect to your wishes. You see this is unavoidable?'

'Dear friend, I said so.'

'True. But I had not the clue then. How do you think I got it?'

Glancing wistfully around, Eugene saw Miss Jenny at the foot of the bed, looking at him with her elbows on the bed, and her head upon her hands. There was a trace of his whimsical air upon him, as he tried to smile at her.

'Yes indeed,' said Lightwood, 'the discovery was hers. Observe, my dear Eugene; while I am away you will know that I have discharged my trust with Lizzie, by finding her here, in my present place at your bedside, to leave you no more. A final word before I go. This is the right course of a true man, Eugene. And I solemnly believe, with all my soul, that if Providence should mercifully restore you to us, you will be blessed with a noble wife in the preserver of your life, whom you will dearly love.'

'Amen. I am sure of that. But I shall not come through it, Mortimer.'

'You will not be the less hopeful or less strong, for this, Eugene.'

'No. Touch my face with yours, in case I should not hold out till you come back. I love you, Mortimer. Don't be uneasy for me while you are gone. If my dear brave girl will take me, I feel persuaded that I shall live long enough to be married, dear fellow.'

Miss Jenny gave up altogether on this parting taking place between the friends, and sitting with her back towards the bed in the bower made by her bright hair, wept heartily, though noiselessly. Mortimer Lightwood was soon gone. As the evening light lengthened the heavy reflections of the trees in the river, another figure came with a soft step into the sick room.

'Is he conscious?' asked the little dressmaker, as the figure took its station by the pillow. For, Jenny had given place to it immediately, and could not see the sufferer's face, in the dark room, from her new and removed position.

'He is conscious, Jenny,' murmured Eugene for himself. 'He knows his wife.'

Chapter 11

Effect is Given
to the Dolls' Dressmaker's Discovery

MRS JOHN ROKESMITH sat at needlework in her neat little room, beside a basket of neat little articles of clothing, which presented so much of the appearance of being in the dolls' dressmaker's way of business, that one might have supposed she was going to set up in opposition to Miss Wren. Whether the Complete British Family Housewife had imparted sage counsel anent them, did not appear, but probably not, as that cloudy oracle was nowhere visible. For certain, however, Mrs John Rokesmith stitched at them with so dexterous a hand, that she must have taken lessons of somebody. Love is in all things a most wonderful teacher, and perhaps love (from a pictorial point of view, with nothing on but a thimble), had been teaching this branch of needlework to Mrs John Rokesmith.

It was near John's time for coming home, but as Mrs John was desirous to finish a special triumph of her skill before dinner, she did not go out to meet him. Placidly, though rather consequentially smiling, she sat stitching away with a regular sound, like a sort of dimpled little charming Dresden-china clock by the very best maker.

A knock at the door, and a ring at the bell. Not John; or Bella would have flown out to meet him. Then who, if not John? Bella was asking herself the question, when that fluttering little fool of a servant fluttered in, saying, 'Mr Lightwood!'

Oh good gracious!

Bella had but time to throw a handkerchief over the basket, when Mr Lightwood made his bow. There was something amiss with Mr Lightwood, for he was strangely grave and looked ill.

With a brief reference to the happy time when it had been his privilege to know Mrs Rokesmith as Miss Wilfer, Mr Lightwood explained what was amiss with him and why he came. He came bearing Lizzie Hexam's earnest hope that Mrs John Rokesmith would see her married.

Bella was so fluttered by the request, and by the short narrative he had feelingly given her, that there never was a more timely smelling-bottle than John's knock. 'My husband,' said Bella; 'I'll bring him in.'

But, that turned out to be more easily said than done; for, the instant she mentioned Mr Lightwood's name, John stopped, with his hand upon the lock of the room door.

'Come up stairs, my darling.'

Bella was amazed by the flush in his face, and by his sudden turning away. 'What can it mean?' she thought, as she accompanied him up stairs.

'Now, my life,' said John, taking her on his knee, 'tell me all about it.'

All very well to say, 'Tell me all about it;' but John was very much confused. His attention evidently trailed off, now and then, even while Bella told him all about it. Yet she knew that he took a great interest in Lizzie and her fortunes. What could it mean?

'You will come to this marriage with me, John dear?'

'N–no, my love; I can't do that.'

'You can't do that, John?'

'No, my dear, it's quite out of the question. Not to be thought of.'

'Am I to go alone, John?'

'No, my dear, you will go with Mr Lightwood.'

'Don't you think it's time we went down to Mr Lightwood, John dear?' Bella insinuated.

'My darling, it's almost time you went, but I must ask you to excuse me to him altogether.'

'You never mean, John dear, that you are not going to see him? Why, he knows you have come home. I told him so.'

'That's a little unfortunate, but it can't be helped. Unfortunate or fortunate, I positively cannot see him, my love.'

Bella cast about in her mind what could be his reason for this unaccountable behaviour; as she sat on his knee looking at him in astonishment and pouting a little. A weak reason presented itself.

'John dear, you never can be jealous of Mr Lightwood?'

'Why, my precious child,' returned her husband, laughing outright: 'how could I be jealous of him? Why should I be jealous of him?'

'Because, you know, John,' pursued Bella, pouting a little more, 'though he did rather admire me once, it was not my fault.'

'It was your fault that I admired you,' returned her husband, with a look of pride in her, 'and why not your fault that he admired you? But, I jealous on that account? Why, I must go distracted for life, if I turned jealous of every one who used to find my wife beautiful and winning!'

'I am half angry with you, John dear,' said Bella, laughing a little, 'and half pleased with you; because you are such a stupid old fellow, and yet you say nice things, as if you meant them. Don't be mysterious, sir. What harm do you know of Mr Lightwood?'

'None, my love.'

'What has he ever done to you, John?'

'He has never done anything to me, my dear. I know no more against him than I know against Mr Wrayburn; he has never done anything to me; neither has Mr Wrayburn. And yet I have exactly the same objection to both of them.'

'Oh, John!' retorted Bella, as if she were giving him up for a bad job, as she used to give up herself. 'You are nothing better than a sphinx! And a married sphinx isn't a—isn't a nice confidential husband,' said Bella, in a tone of injury.

'Bella, my life,' said John Rokesmith, touching her cheek, with a grave smile, as she cast down her eyes and pouted again; 'look at me. I want to speak to you.'

'In earnest, Blue Beard of the secret chamber?' asked Bella, clearing her pretty face.

'In earnest. And I confess to the secret chamber. Don't you remember that you asked me not to declare what I thought of your higher qualities until you had been tried?'

'Yes, John dear. And I fully meant it, and I fully mean it.'

'The time will come, my darling—I am no prophet, but I say so,—when you *will* be tried. The time will come, I think, when you will undergo a trial through which you will never pass quite triumphantly for me, unless you can put perfect faith in me.'

'Then you may be sure of me, John dear, for I can put perfect faith in you, and I do, and I always, always will. Don't judge me by a little thing like this, John. In little things, I am a little thing myself—I always was. But in great things, I hope not; I don't mean to boast, John dear, but I hope not!'

He was even better convinced of the truth of what she said

than she was, as he felt her loving arms about him. If the Golden Dustman's riches had been his to stake, he would have staked them to the last farthing on the fidelity through good and evil of her affectionate and trusting heart.

'Now, I'll go down to, and go away with, Mr Lightwood,' said Bella, springing up. 'You are the most creasing and tumbling Clumsy-Boots of a packer, John, that ever was; but if you're quite good, and will promise never to do so any more (though I don't know what you have done!) you may pack me a little bag for a night, while I get my bonnet on.'

He gaily complied, and she tied her dimpled chin up, and shook her head into her bonnet, and pulled out the bows of her bonnet-strings, and got her gloves on, finger by finger, and finally got them on her little plump hands, and bade him good-bye and went down. Mr Lightwood's impatience was much relieved when he found her dressed for departure.

'Mr Rokesmith goes with us?' he said, hesitating, with a look towards the door.

'Oh, I forgot!' replied Bella. 'His best compliments. His face is swollen to the size of two faces, and he is to go to bed directly, poor fellow, to wait for the doctor, who is coming to lance him.'

'It is curious,' observed Lightwood, 'that I have never yet seen Mr Rokesmith, though we have been engaged in the same affairs.'

'Really?' said the unblushing Bella.

'I begin to think,' observed Lightwood, 'that I never shall see him.'

'These things happen so oddly sometimes,' said Bella with a steady countenance, 'that there seems a kind of fatality in them. But I am quite ready, Mr Lightwood.'

They started directly, in a little carriage that Lightwood had brought with him from never-to-be-forgotten Greenwich; and from Greenwich they started directly for London; and in London they waited at a railway station until such time as the Reverend Frank Milvey, and Margaretta his wife, with whom Mortimer Lightwood had been already in conference, should come and join them.

That worthy couple were delayed by a portentous old parishioner of the female gender, who was one of the plagues of their lives, and with whom they bore with most exemplary sweetness and good-humour, notwithstanding her having an infection of absurdity about her, that communicated itself to everything with which, and everybody with whom, she came in contact. She was a member of the Reverend Frank's congregation, and made a point of distinguishing herself in that body, by conspicuously weeping at everything, however cheering, said by the Reverend Frank in his public ministration; also by applying to herself the various lamentations of David, and complaining in a personally injured manner (much in arrear of the clerk and the rest of the respondents) that her enemies were digging pit-falls about her, and breaking her with rods of iron. Indeed, this old widow discharged herself of that portion of the Morning and Evening Service as if she were lodging a complaint on oath and applying for a warrant before a magistrate. But this was not her most inconvenient characteristic, for that took the form of an impression, usually recurring in inclement weather and at about daybreak, that she had something on her mind and stood in immediate need of the Reverend Frank to come and take it off. Many a time had that kind creature got up, and gone out to Mrs Sprodgkin (such was the disciple's name), suppressing a strong sense of her comicality by his strong sense of duty, and perfectly knowing that nothing but a cold would come of it. However, beyond themselves, the Reverend Frank Milvey and Mrs Milvey seldom hinted that Mrs Sprodgkin was hardly worth the trouble she gave; but both made the best of her, as they did of all their troubles.

This very exacting member of the fold appeared to be endowed with a sixth sense, in regard of knowing when the Reverend Frank Milvey least desired her company, and with promptitude appearing in his little hall. Consequently, when the Reverend Frank had willingly engaged that he and his wife would accompany Lightwood back, he said, as a matter of course: 'We must make haste to get out, Margaretta, my dear, or we shall be descended on by Mrs Sprodgkin.' To which Mrs Milvey replied, in her pleasantly emphatic way, 'Oh *yes,* for she *is* such a marplot, Frank, and *does* worry so!' Words that were scarcely uttered when their theme was announced as in faithful attendance below, desiring counsel on a spiritual matter. The points on which Mrs Sprodgkin sought elucidation being seldom of a pressing nature (as Who begat Whom, or some information concerning the Amorites), Mrs Milvey on this special occasion resorted to the device of buying her off with a present of tea and sugar, and a loaf and butter. These gifts Mrs Sprodgkin accepted, but still insisted on dutifully remaining in the hall, to curtsey to the Reverend Frank as he came forth. Who, incautiously saying in his genial manner, 'Well, Sally, there you are!' involved himself in a discursive address from Mrs Sprodgkin, revolving around the result that she regarded tea and sugar in the light of myrrh and frankincense, and considered bread and butter identical with locusts and wild honey. Having communicated this edifying piece of information, Mrs Sprodgkin was left still unadjourned in the hall, and Mr and Mrs Milvey hurried in a heated condition to the railway station. All of which is here recorded to the honour of that good Christian pair, representatives of hundreds of other good Christian pairs as conscientious and as useful, who merge the smallness of their work in its greatness, and feel in no danger of losing dignity when they adapt themselves to incomprehensible humbugs.

'Detained at the last moment by one who had a claim upon me,' was the Reverend Frank's apology to Lightwood, taking no thought of himself. To which Mrs Milvey added, taking thought for him, like the championing little wife she was; 'Oh yes, detained at the last moment. But *as* to the claim, Frank, I *must* say that I *do* think you are *over*-considerate sometimes, and allow *that* to be a *little* abused.'

Bella felt conscious, in spite of her late pledge for herself, that her husband's absence would give disagreeable occasion for surprise to the Milveys. Nor could she appear quite at her ease when Mrs Milvey asked:

'*How* is Mr Rokesmith, and *is* he gone before us, or *does* he follow us?'

It becoming necessary, upon this, to send him to bed again and hold him in waiting to be lanced again, Bella did it. But not half as well on the second occasion as on the first; for, a twice-told white one seems almost to become a black one, when you are not used to it.

'Oh *dear*!' said Mrs Milvey, 'I am *so* sorry! Mr Rokesmith took *such* an interest in Lizzie Hexam, when we were there before. And if we had *only* known of his face, we *could* have given him something that would have kept it down long enough for so *short* a purpose.'

By way of making the white one whiter, Bella hastened to stipulate that he was not in pain. Mrs Milvey was *so* glad of it.

'I don't know *how* it is,' said Mrs Milvey, 'and I am *sure* you don't, Frank, but the clergy and their wives seem to *cause* swelled faces. Whenever I take notice of a child in the school, it seems to me as if its face swelled *instantly*. Frank *never* makes acquaintance with a new old woman, but she gets the face-ache.

And another thing is, we *do* make the poor children sniff so. I don't know *how* we do it, and I should be so glad not to; but the *more* we take notice of them, the *more* they sniff. Just as they do when the text is given out.—Frank, that's a schoolmaster. I have seen him somewhere.'

The reference was to a young man of reserved appearance, in a coat and waistcoat of black, and pantaloons of pepper and salt. He had come into the office of the station, from its interior, in an unsettled way, immediately after Lightwood had gone out to the train; and he had been hurriedly reading the printed bills and notices on the wall. He had had a wandering interest in what was said among the people waiting there and passing to and fro. He had drawn nearer, at about the time when Mrs Milvey mentioned Lizzie Hexam, and had remained near, since: though always glancing towards the door by which Lightwood had gone out. He stood with his back towards them, and his gloved hands clasped behind him. There was now so evident a faltering upon him, expressive of indecision whether or no he should express his having heard himself referred to, that Mr Milvey spoke to him.

'I cannot recall your name,' he said, 'but I remember to have seen you in your school.'

'My name is Bradley Headstone, sir,' he replied, backing into a more retired place.

'I ought to have remembered it,' said Mr Milvey, giving him his hand. 'I hope you are well? A little overworked, I am afraid?'

'Yes, I am overworked just at present, sir.'

'Had no play in your last holiday time?'

'No, sir.'

'All work and no play, Mr Headstone, will not make dulness, in your case, I dare say; but it will make dyspepsia, if you don't take care.'

'I will endeavour to take care, sir. Might I beg leave to speak to you, outside, a moment?'

'By all means.'

It was evening, and the office was well lighted. The schoolmaster, who had never remitted his watch on Lightwood's door, now moved by another door to a corner without, where there was more shadow than light; and said, plucking at his gloves:

'One of your ladies, sir, mentioned within my hearing a name that I am acquainted with; I may say, well acquainted with. The name of the sister of an old pupil of mine. He was my pupil for a long time, and has got on and gone upward rapidly. The name of Hexam. The name of Lizzie Hexam.' He seemed to be a shy man, struggling against nervousness, and spoke in a very constrained way. The break he set between his last two sentences was quite embarrassing to his hearer.

'Yes,' replied Mr Milvey. 'We are going down to see her.'

'I gathered as much, sir. I hope there is nothing amiss with the sister of my old pupil? I hope no bereavement has befallen her. I hope she is in no affliction? Has lost no—relation?'

Mr Milvey thought this a man with a very odd manner, and a dark downward look; but he answered in his usual open way.

'I am glad to tell you, Mr Headstone, that the sister of your old pupil has not sustained any such loss. You thought I might be going down to bury some one?'

'That may have been the connexion of ideas, sir, with your clerical character, but I was not conscious of it.—Then you are not, sir?'

A man with a very odd manner indeed, and with a lurking look that was quite oppressive.

'No. In fact,' said Mr Milvey, 'since you are so interested in the sister of your old pupil, I may as well tell you that I am going down to marry her.'

The schoolmaster started back.

'Not to marry her, myself,' said Mr Milvey, with a smile, 'because I have a wife already. To perform the marriage service at her wedding.'

Bradley Headstone caught hold of a pillar behind him. If Mr Milvey knew an ashy face when he saw it, he saw it then.

'You are quite ill, Mr Headstone!'

'It is not much, sir. It will pass over very soon. I am accustomed to be seized with giddiness. Don't let me detain you, sir; I stand in need of no assistance, I thank you. Much obliged by your sparing me these minutes of your time.'

As Mr Milvey, who had no more minutes to spare, made a suitable reply and turned back into the office, he observed the schoolmaster to lean against the pillar with his hat in his hand, and to pull at his neckcloth as if he were trying to tear it off. The Reverend Frank accordingly directed the notice of one of the attendants to him, by saying: 'There is a person outside who seems to be really ill, and to require some help, though he says he does not.'

Lightwood had by this time secured their places, and the departure-bell was about to be rung. They took their seats, and were beginning to move out of the station, when the same attendant came running along the platform, looking into all the carriages.

'Oh! You are here, sir!' he said, springing on the step, and holding the window-frame by his elbow, as the carriage moved. 'That person you pointed out to me is in a fit.'

'I infer from what he told me that he is subject to such attacks. He will come to, in the air, in a little while.'

He was took very bad to be sure, and was biting and knocking about him (the man said) furiously. Would the gentleman give him his card, as he had seen him first? The gentleman did so, with the explanation that he knew no more of the man attacked than that he was a man of a very respectable occupation, who had said he was out of health, as his appearance would of itself have indicated. The attendant received the card, watched his opportunity for sliding down, slid down, and so it ended.

Then, the train rattled among the house-tops, and among the ragged sides of houses torn down to make way for it, and over the swarming streets, and under the fruitful earth, until it shot across the river: bursting over the quiet surface like a bombshell, and gone again as if it had exploded in the rush of smoke and steam and glare. A little more, and again it roared across the river, a great rocket: spurning the watery turnings and doublings with ineffable contempt, and going straight to its end, as Father Time goes to his. To whom it is no matter what living waters run high or low, reflect the heavenly lights and darknesses, produce their little growth of weeds and flowers, turn here, turn there, are noisy or still, are troubled or at rest, for their course has one sure termination, though their sources and devices are many.

Then, a carriage ride succeeded, near the solemn river, stealing away by night, as all things steal away, by night and by day, so quietly yielding to the attraction of the loadstone rock of Eternity; and the nearer they drew to the chamber where Eugene lay, the more they feared that they might find his wanderings done. At last they saw its dim light shining out, and it gave them hope: though Lightwood faltered as he thought: 'If he were gone, she would still be sitting by him.'

But he lay quiet, half in stupor, half in sleep. Bella, entering with a raised admonitory finger, kissed Lizzie softly, but said not a word. Neither did any of them speak, but all sat down at the foot of the bed, silently waiting. And now, in this nightwatch, mingling with the flow of the river and with the rush of the train, came the questions into Bella's mind again: What could be in the depths of that mystery of John's? Why was it that he had never been seen by Mr Lightwood, whom he still avoided? When would that trial come, through which her faith in, and her duty to, her dear husband, was to carry her, rendering him triumphant? For, that had been his term. Her passing through the trial was to make the man she loved with all her heart, triumphant. Term not to sink out of sight in Bella's breast.

Far on in the night, Eugene opened his eyes. He was sensible, and said at once: 'How does the time go? Has our Mortimer come back?'

Lightwood was there immediately, to answer for himself. 'Yes, Eugene, and all is ready.'

'Dear boy!' returned Eugene with a smile, 'we both thank you heartily. Lizzie, tell them how welcome they are, and that I would be eloquent if I could.'

'There is no need,' said Mr Milvey. 'We know it. Are you better, Mr Wrayburn?'

'I am much happier,' said Eugene.

'Much better too, I hope?'

Eugene turned his eyes towards Lizzie, as if to spare her, and answered nothing.

Then, they all stood around the bed, and Mr Milvey, opening his book, began the service; so rarely associated with the shadow of death; so inseparable in the mind from a flush of life and gaiety and hope and health and joy. Bella thought how different from her own sunny little wedding, and wept. Mrs Milvey overflowed with pity, and wept too. The dolls' dressmaker, with her hands before her face, wept in her golden bower. Reading in a low clear voice, and bending over Eugene, who kept his eyes upon him, Mr Milvey did his office with suitable simplicity. As the bridegroom could not move his hand, they touched his fingers with the ring, and so put it on the bride. When the two plighted their troth, she laid her hand on his and kept it there. When the ceremony was done, and all the rest departed from the room, she drew her arm under his head, and laid her own head down upon the pillow by his side.

'Undraw the curtains, my dear girl,' said Eugene, after a while, 'and let us see our wedding-day.'

The sun was rising, and his first rays struck into the room, as she came back, and put her lips to his. 'I bless the day!' said Eugene. 'I bless the day!' said Lizzie.

'You have made a poor marriage of it, my sweet wife,' said

Eugene. 'A shattered graceless fellow, stretched at his length here, and next to nothing for you when you are a young widow.'

'I have made the marriage that I would have given all the world to dare to hope for,' she replied.

'You have thrown yourself away,' said Eugene, shaking his head. 'But you have followed the treasure of your heart. My justification is, that you had thrown that away first, dear girl!'

'No. I had given it to you.'

'The same thing, my poor Lizzie!'

'Hush! hush! A very different thing.'

There were tears in his eyes, and she besought him to close them. 'No,' said Eugene, again shaking his head; 'let me look at you, Lizzie, while I can. You brave devoted girl! You heroine!'

Her own eyes filled under his praises. And when he mustered strength to move his wounded head a very little way, and lay it on her bosom, the tears of both fell.

'Lizzie,' said Eugene, after a silence: 'when you see me wandering away from this refuge that I have so ill deserved, speak to me by my name, and I think I shall come back.'

'Yes, dear Eugene.'

'There!' he exclaimed, smiling. 'I should have gone then, but for that!'

A little while afterwards, when he appeared to be sinking into insensibility, she said, in a calm loving voice: 'Eugene, my dear husband!' He immediately answered: 'There again! You see how you can recall me!' And afterwards, when he could not speak, he still answered by a slight movement of his head upon her bosom.

The sun was high in the sky, when she gently disengaged herself to give him the stimulants and nourishment he required. The utter helplessness of the wreck of him that lay cast ashore there, now alarmed her, but he himself appeared a little more hopeful

'Ah, my beloved Lizzie!' he said, faintly. 'How shall I ever pay all I owe you, if I recover!'

'Don't be ashamed of me,' she replied, 'and you will have more than paid all.'

'It would require a life, Lizzie, to pay all; more than a life.'

'Live for that, then; live for me, Eugene; live to see how hard I will try to improve myself, and never to discredit you.'

'My darling girl,' he replied, rallying more of his old manner than he had ever yet got together. 'On the contrary, I have been thinking whether it is not the best thing I can do, to die.'

'The best thing you can do, to leave me with a broken heart?'

'I don't mean that, my dear girl. I was not thinking of that. What I was thinking of was this. Out of your compassion for me, in this maimed and broken state, you make so much of me—you think so well of me—you love me so dearly.'

'Heaven knows I love you dearly!'

'And Heaven knows I prize it! Well. If I live, you'll find me out.'

'I shall find out that my husband has a mine of purpose and energy, and will turn it to the best account?'

'I hope so, dearest Lizzie,' said Eugene, wistfully, and yet somewhat whimsically. 'I hope so. But I can't summon the vanity to think so. How can I think so, looking back on such a trifling wasted youth as mine! I humbly hope it; but I daren't believe it. There is a sharp misgiving in my conscience that if I were to live, I should disappoint your good opinion and my own—and that I ought to die, my dear!'

Chapter 12
The Passing Shadow

THE winds and tides rose and fell a certain number of times, the earth moved round the sun a certain number of times, the ship upon the ocean made her voyage safely, and brought a baby-Bella home. Then who so blest and happy as Mrs John Rokesmith, saving and excepting Mr John Rokesmith!

'Would you not like to be rich *now*, my darling?'

'How can you ask me such a question, John dear? Am I not rich?'

These were among the first words spoken near the baby Bella as she lay asleep. She soon proved to be a baby of wonderful intelligence, evincing the strongest objection to her grandmother's society, and being invariably seized with a painful acidity of the stomach when that dignified lady honoured her with any attention.

It was charming to see Bella contemplating this baby, and
finding out her own dimples in that tiny reflection, as if she were
looking in the glass without personal vanity. Her cherubic father
justly remarked to her husband that the baby seemed to make her
younger than before, reminding him of the days when she had a
pet doll and used to talk to it as she carried it about. The world
might have been challenged to produce another baby who had
such a store of pleasant nonsense said and sung to it, as Bella
said and sung to this baby; or who was dressed and undressed as
often in four-and-twenty hours as Bella dressed and undressed
this baby; or who was held behind doors and poked out to stop
its father's way when he came home, as this baby was; or, in a
word, who did half the number of baby things, through the lively
invention of a gay and proud young mother, that this inexhaustible baby did.

The inexhaustible baby was two or three months old, when
Bella began to notice a cloud upon her husband's brow. Watching it, she saw a gathering and deepening anxiety there, which
caused her great disquiet. More than once, she awoke him
muttering in his sleep; and, though he muttered nothing worse
than her own name, it was plain to her that his restlessness
originated in some load of care. Therefore, Bella at length put in
her claim to divide this load, and bear her half of it.

'You know, John dear,' she said, cheerily reverting to their
former conversation, 'that I hope I may safely be trusted in great
things. And it surely cannot be a little thing that causes you so
much uneasiness. It's very considerate of you to try to hide from
me that you are uncomfortable about something, but it's quite
impossible to be done, John love.'

'I admit that I am rather uneasy, my own.'

'Then please to tell me what about, sir.'

But no, he evaded that. 'Never mind!' thought Bella, resolutely. 'John requires me to put perfect faith in him, and he shall
not be disappointed.'

She went up to London one day, to meet him, in order that
they might make some purchases. She found him waiting for her
at her journey's end, and they walked away together through the
streets. He was in gay spirits, though still harping on that notion
of their being rich; and he said, now let them make believe that
yonder fine carriage was theirs, and that it was waiting to take
them home to a fine house they had; what would Bella, in that
case, best like to find in the house? Well! Bella didn't know:
already having everything she wanted, she couldn't say. But, by

degrees she was led on to confess that she would like to have for the inexhaustible baby such a nursery as never was seen. It was to be 'a very rainbow for colours', as she was quite sure baby noticed colours; and the staircase was to be adorned with the most exquisite flowers, as she was absolutely certain baby noticed flowers; and there was to be an aviary somewhere, of the loveliest little birds, as there was not the smallest doubt in the world that baby noticed birds. Was there nothing else? No, John dear. The predilections of the inexhaustible baby being provided for, Bella could think of nothing else.

They were chatting on in this way, and John had suggested, 'No jewels for your own wear, for instance?' and Bella had replied laughing. O! if he came to that, yes, there might be a beautiful ivory case of jewels on her dressing-table; when these pictures were in a moment darkened and blotted out.

They turned a corner, and met Mr Lightwood.

He stopped as if he were petrified by the sight of Bella's husband, who in the same moment had changed colour.

'Mr Lightwood and I have met before,' he said.

'Met before, John?' Bella repeated in a tone of wonder. 'Mr Lightwood told me he had never seen you.'

'I did not then know that I had,' said Lightwood, discomposed on her account. 'I believed that I had only heard of—Mr Rokesmith.' With an emphasis on the name.

'When Mr Lightwood saw me, my love,' observed her husband, not avoiding his eye, but looking at him, 'my name was Julius Handford.'

Julius Handford! The name that Bella had so often seen in old newspapers, when she was an inmate of Mr Boffin's house! Julius Handford, who had been publicly entreated to appear, and for intelligence of whom a reward had been publicly offered!

'I would have avoided mentioning it in your presence,' said Lightwood to Bella, delicately; 'but since your husband mentions it himself, I must confirm his strange admission. I saw him as Mr Julius Handford, and I afterwards (unquestionably to his knowledge) took great pains to trace him out.'

'Quite true. But it was not my object or my interest,' said Rokesmith, quietly, 'to be traced out.'

Bella looked from the one to the other, in amazement.

'Mr Lightwood,' pursued her husband, 'as chance has brought us face to face at last—which is not to be wondered at, for the wonder is, that, in spite of all my pains to the contrary, chance has not confronted us together sooner—I have only to remind

you that you have been at my house, and to add that I have not
changed my residence.'

'Sir,' returned Lightwood, with a meaning glance towards
Bella, 'my position is a truly painful one. I hope that no com-
plicity in a very dark transaction may attach to you, but you
cannot fail to know that your own extraordinary conduct has laid
you under suspicion.'

'I know it has,' was all the reply.

'My professional duty,' said Lightwood hesitating, with
another glance towards Bella, 'is greatly at variance with my
personal inclination; but I doubt, Mr Handford, or Mr Rokesmith,
whether I am justified in taking leave of you here, with your
whole course unexplained.'

Bella caught her husband by the hand.

'Don't be alarmed, my darling. Mr Lightwood will find that
he is quite justified in taking leave of me here. At all events,'
added Rokesmith, 'he will find that I mean to take leave of him
here.'

'I think, sir,' said Lightwood, 'you can scarcely deny that
when I came to your house on the occasion to which you have
referred, you avoided me of a set purpose.'

'Mr Lightwood, I assure you I have no disposition to deny
it, or intention to deny it. I should have continued to avoid you,
in pursuance of the same set purpose, for a short time longer, if
we had not met now. I am going straight home, and shall remain
at home to-morrow until noon. Hereafter, I hope we may be
better acquainted. Good-day.'

Lightwood stood irresolute, but Bella's husband passed him
in the steadiest manner, with Bella on his arm; and they went
home without encountering any further remonstrance or molesta-
tion from any one.

When they had dined and were alone, John Rokesmith said
to his wife, who had preserved her cheerfulness: 'And you don't
ask me, my dear, why I bore that name?'

'No, John love. I should dearly like to know, of course;'
(which her anxious face confirmed;) 'but I wait until you can tell
me of your own free will. You asked me if I could have perfect
faith in you, and I said yes, and I meant it.'

It did not escape Bella's notice that he began to look
triumphant. She wanted no strengthening in her firmness; but if
she had had need of any, she would have derived it from his
kindling face.

'You cannot have been prepared, my dearest, for such a

discovery as that this mysterious Mr Handford was identical with your husband?'

'No, John dear, of course not. But you told me to prepare to be tried, and I prepared myself.'

He drew her to nestle closer to him, and told her it would soon be over, and the truth would soon appear. 'And now,' he went on, 'lay stress, my dear, on these words that I am going to add. I stand in no kind of peril, and I can by possibility be hurt at no one's hand.'

'You are quite, quite sure of that, John dear?'

'Not a hair of my head! Moreover, I have done no wrong, and have injured no man. Shall I swear it?'

'No, John!' cried Bella, laying her hand upon his lips, with a proud look. 'Never to me!'

'But circumstances,' he went on '—I can, and I will, disperse them in a moment—have surrounded me with one of the strangest suspicions ever known. You heard Mr Lightwood speak of a dark transaction?'

'Yes, John.'

'You are prepared to hear explicitly what he meant?'

'Yes, John.'

'My life, he meant the murder of John Harmon, your allotted husband.'

With a fast palpitating heart, Bella grasped him by the arm. 'You cannot be suspected, John?'

'Dear love, I can be—for I am!'

There was silence between them, as she sat looking in his face, with the colour quite gone from her own face and lips. 'How dare they!' she cried at length, in a burst of generous indignation. 'My beloved husband, how dare they!'

He caught her in his arms as she opened hers, and held her to his heart. 'Even knowing this, you can trust me, Bella?'

'I can trust you, John dear, with all my soul. If I could not trust you, I should fall dead at your feet.'

The kindling triumph in his face was bright indeed, as he looked up and rapturously exclaimed, what had he done to deserve the blessing of this dear confiding creature's heart! Again she put her hand upon his lips, saying, 'Hush!' and then told him, in her own little natural pathetic way, that if all the world were against him, she would be for him; that if all the world repudiated him, she would believe him; that if he were infamous in other eyes, he would be honoured in hers; and that, under the worst unmerited suspicion, she could devote her life to consoling him, and imparting her own faith in him to their little child.

A twilight calm of happiness then succeeding to their radiant noon, they remained at peace, until a strange voice in the room startled them both. The room being by that time dark, the voice said, 'Don't let the lady be alarmed by my striking a light,' and immediately a match rattled, and glimmered in a hand. The hand and the match and the voice were then seen by John Rokesmith to belong to Mr Inspector, once meditatively active in this chronicle.

'I take the liberty,' said Mr Inspector, in a business-like manner, 'to bring myself to the recollection of Mr Julius Handford, who gave me his name and address down at our place a considerable time ago. Would the lady object to my lighting the pair of candles on the chimneypiece, to throw a further light upon the subject? No? Thank you, ma'am. Now, we look cheerful.'

Mr Inspector, in a dark-blue buttoned-up frock coat and pantaloons, presented a serviceable, half-pay, Royal Arms kind of appearance, as he applied his pocket handkerchief to his nose and bowed to the lady.

'You favoured me, Mr Handford,' said Mr Inspector, 'by writing down your name and address, and I produce the piece of paper on which you wrote it. Comparing the same with the writing on the fly-leaf of this book on the table—and a sweet pretty volume it is—I find the writing of the entry, "Mrs John Rokesmith. From her husband on her birthday"—and very gratifying to the feelings such memorials are—to correspond exactly. Can I have a word with you?'

'Certainly. Here, if you please,' was the reply.

'Why,' retorted Mr Inspector, again using his pocket handkerchief, 'though there's nothing for the lady to be at all alarmed at, still, ladies are apt to take alarm at matters of business—being of that fragile sex that they're not accustomed to them when not of a strictly domestic character—and I do generally make it a rule to propose retirement from the presence of ladies, before entering upon business topics. Or perhaps,' Mr Inspector hinted, 'if the lady was to step up-stairs, and take a look at baby now!'

'Mrs Rokesmith,'—her husband was beginning; when Mr Inspector, regarding the words as an introduction, said, 'Happy I am sure, to have the honour.' And bowed, with gallantry.

'Mrs Rokesmith,' resumed her husband, 'is satisfied that she can have no reason for being alarmed, whatever the business is.'

'Really? Is that so?' said Mr Inspector. 'But it's a sex to live and learn from, and there's nothing a lady can't accomplish when she once fully gives her mind to it. It's the case with my own wife. Well, ma'am, this good gentleman of yours has given rise to a rather large amount of trouble which might have been avoided if he had come forward and explained himself. Well you see! He *didn't* come forward and explain himself. Consequently, now that we meet, him and me, you'll say—and say right—that there's nothing to be alarmed at, in my proposing to him *to* come forward—or, putting the same meaning in another form, to come along with me—*and* explain himself.'

When Mr Inspector put it in that other form, 'to come along with me,' there was a relishing roll in his voice, and his eye beamed with an official lustre.

'Do you propose to take me into custody?' inquired John Rokesmith, very coolly.

'Why argue?' returned Mr Inspector in a comfortable sort of remonstrance; 'ain't it enough that I propose that you shall come along with me?'

'For what reason?'

'Lord bless my soul and body!' returned Mr Inspector, 'I wonder at it in a man of your education. Why argue?'

'What do you charge against me?'

'I wonder at you before a lady,' said Mr Inspector, shaking his head reproachfully: 'I wonder, brought up as you have been, you haven't a more delicate mind! I charge you, then, with being some way concerned in the Harmon Murder. I don't say whether before, or in, or after, the fact. I don't say whether with having some knowledge of it that hasn't come out.'

'You don't surprise me. I foresaw your visit this afternoon.'

'Don't!' said Mr Inspector. 'Why, why argue? It's my duty to inform you that whatever you say, will be used against you.'

'I don't think it will.'

'But I tell you it will,' said Mr Inspector. 'Now, having received the caution, do you still say that you foresaw my visit this afternoon?'

'Yes. And I will say something more, if you will step with me into the next room.'

With a reassuring kiss on the lips of the frightened Bella, her husband (to whom Mr Inspector obligingly offered his arm), took up a candle, and withdrew with that gentleman. They were a full half-hour in conference. When they returned, Mr Inspector looked considerably astonished.

'I have invited this worthy officer, my dear,' said John, 'to make a short excursion with me in which you shall be a sharer. He will take something to eat and drink, I dare say, on your invitation, while you are getting your bonnet on.'

Mr Inspector declined eating, but assented to the proposal of a glass of brandy and water. Mixing this cold, and pensively consuming it, he broke at intervals into such soliloquies as that he never did know such a move, that he never had been so gravelled, and that what a game was this to try the sort of stuff a man's opinion of himself was made of! Concurrently with these comments, he more than once burst out a laughing, with the half-enjoying and half-piqued air of a man, who had given up a good conundrum, after much guessing, and been told the answer. Bella was so timid of him, that she noted these things in a half-shrinking, half-perceptive way, and similarly noted that there was a great change in his manner towards John. That coming-along-with-him deportment was now lost in long musing looks at John and at herself, and sometimes in slow heavy rubs of his hand across his forehead, as if he were ironing out the creases which his deep pondering made there. He had had some coughing and whistling satellites secretly gravitating towards him about the premises, but they were now dismissed, and he eyed John as if he had meant to do him a public service, but had unfortunately been anticipated. Whether Bella might have noted anything more, if she had been less afraid of him, she could not determine; but it was all inexplicable to her, and not the faintest flash of the real state of the case broke in upon her mind. Mr Inspector's increased notice of herself, and knowing way of raising his eyebrows when their eyes by any chance met, as if he put the question 'Don't you see?' augmented her timidity, and, consequently, her perplexity. For all these reasons, when he and she and John, at towards nine o'clock of a winter evening went to London, and began driving from London Bridge, among low-lying water-side wharves and docks and strange places, Bella was in the state of a dreamer; perfectly unable to account for her being there, perfectly unable to forecast what would happen next, or whither she was going, or why; certain of nothing in the immediate present, but that she confided in John, and that John seemed somehow to be getting more triumphant. But what a certainty was that!

They alighted at last at the corner of a court, where there was a building with a bright lamp and wicket gate. Its orderly appearance was very unlike that of the surrounding neighbourhood, and was explained by the inscription POLICE STATION.

'We are not going in here, John?' said Bella, clinging to him.

'Yes, my dear; but of our own accord. We shall come out again as easily, never fear.'

The whitewashed room was pure white as of old, the methodical book-keeping was in peaceful progress as of old, and some distant howler was banging against a cell door as of old. The sanctuary was not a permanent abiding-place, but a kind of criminal Pickford's. The lower passions and vices were regularly ticked off in the books, warehoused in the cells, carted away as per accompanying invoice, and left little mark upon it.

Mr Inspector placed two chairs for his visitors, before the fire, and communed in a low voice with a brother of his order (also of a half-pay, and Royal Arms aspect), who, judged only by his occupation at the moment, might have been a writing-master, setting copies. Their conference done, Mr Inspector returned to the fireplace, and, having observed that he would step round to the Fellowships and see how matters stood, went out. He soon came back again, saying, 'Nothing could be better, for they're at supper with Miss Abbey in the bar;' and then they all three went out together.

Still, as in a dream, Bella found herself entering a snug old-fashioned public-house, and found herself smuggled into a little three-cornered room nearly opposite the bar of that establishment. Mr Inspector achieved the smuggling of herself and John into this queer room, called Cosy in an inscription on the door, by entering in the narrow passage first in order, and suddenly turning round upon them with extended arms, as if they had been two sheep. The room was lighted for their reception.

'Now,' said Mr Inspector to John, turning the gas lower; 'I'll mix with 'em in a casual way, and when I say Identification, perhaps you'll show yourself.'

John nodded, and Mr Inspector went alone to the half-door of the bar. From the dim doorway of Cosy, within which Bella and her husband stood, they could see a comfortable little party of three persons sitting at supper in the bar, and could hear everything that was said.

The three persons were Miss Abbey and two male guests. To whom collectively, Mr Inspector remarked that the weather was getting sharp for the time of year.

'It need be sharp to suit your wits, sir,' said Miss Abbey. 'What have you got in hand now?'

'Thanking you for your compliment: not much, Miss Abbey,' was Mr Inspector's rejoinder.

'Who have you got in Cosy?' asked Miss Abbey.

'Only a gentleman and his wife, Miss.'

'And who are they? If one may ask it without detriment to your deep plans in the interests of the honest public?' said Miss Abbey, proud of Mr Inspector as an administrative genius.

'They are strangers in this part of the town, Miss Abbey. They are waiting till I shall want the gentleman to show himself somewhere, for half a moment.'

'While they're waiting,' said Miss Abbey, 'couldn't you join us?'

Mr Inspector immediately slipped into the bar, and sat down at the side of the half-door, with his back towards the passage, and directly facing the two guests. 'I don't take my supper till later in the night,' said he, 'and therefore I won't disturb the compactness of the table. But I'll take a glass of flip, if that's flip in the jug in the fender.'

'That's flip,' replied Miss Abbey, 'and it's my making, and if even you can find out better, I shall be glad to know where.' Filling him, with hospitable hands, a steaming tumbler, Miss Abbey replaced the jug by the fire; the company not having yet arrived at the flip-stage of their supper, but being as yet skirmishing with strong ale.

'Ah–h!' cried Mr Inspector. 'That's the smack! There's not a Detective in the Force, Miss Abbey, that could find out better stuff than that.'

'Glad to hear you say so,' rejoined Miss Abbey. 'You ought to know, if anybody does.'

'Mr Job Potterson,' Mr Inspector continued, 'I drink your health. Mr Jacob Kibble, I drink yours. Hope you have made a prosperous voyage home, gentlemen both.'

Mr Kibble, an unctuous broad man of few words and many mouthfuls, said, more briefly than pointedly, raising his ale to his lips: 'Same to you.' Mr Job Potterson, a semi-seafaring man of obliging demeanour, said, 'Thank you, sir.'

'Lord bless my soul and body!' cried Mr Inspector. 'Talk of trades, Miss Abbey, and the way they set their marks on men' (a subject which nobody had approached); 'who wouldn't know your brother to be a Steward! There's a bright and ready twinkle in his eye, there's a neatness in his action, there's a smartness in his figure, there's an air of reliability about him in case you wanted a basin, which points out the steward! And Mr Kibble; ain't he Passenger, all over? While there's that mercantile cut upon him which would make you happy to give him credit for five hundred pound, don't you see the salt sea shining on him too?'

'*You* do, I dare say,' returned Miss Abbey, 'but *I* don't. And as for stewarding, I think it's time my brother gave that up, and took his House in hand on his sister's retiring. The House will go to pieces if he don't. I wouldn't sell it for any money that could be told out, to a person that I couldn't depend upon to be a Law to the Porters, as I have been.'

'There you're right, Miss,' said Mr Inspector. 'A better kept house is not known to our men. What do I say? Half so well a kept house is not known to our men. Show the Force the Six Jolly Fellowship Porters, and the Force—to a constable—will show you a piece of perfection, Mr Kibble.'

That gentleman, with a very serious shake of his head, subscribed the article.

'And talk of Time slipping by you, as if it was an animal at rustic sports with its tail soaped,' said Mr Inspector (again, a subject which nobody had approached); 'why, well you may. Well you may. How has it slipped by us, since the time when Mr Job Potterson here present, Mr Jacob Kibble here present, and an Officer of the Force here present, first came together on a matter of Identification!'

Bella's husband stepped softly to the half-door of the bar, and stood there.

'How has Time slipped by us,' Mr Inspector went on slowly, with his eyes narrowly observant of the two guests, 'since we three very men, at an Inquest in this very house—Mr Kibble? Taken ill, sir?'

Mr Kibble had staggered up, with his lower jaw dropped, catching Potterson by the shoulder, and pointing to the half-door. He now cried out: 'Potterson! Look! Look there!' Potterson started up, started back, and exclaimed: 'Heaven defend us, what's that!' Bella's husband stepped back to Bella, took her in his arms (for she was terrified by the unintelligible terror of the two men), and shut the door of the little room. A hurry of voices succeeded, in which Mr Inspector's voice was busiest; it gradually slackened and sank; and Mr Inspector reappeared. 'Sharp's the word, sir!' he said, looking in with a knowing wink. 'We'll get your lady out at once.' Immediately, Bella and her husband were under the stars, making their way back, alone, to the vehicle they had kept in waiting.

All this was most extraordinary, and Bella could make nothing of it but that John was in the right. How in the right, and how suspected of being in the wrong, she could not divine. Some vague idea that he had never really assumed the name of Handford, and that there was a remarkable likeness between him and that mysterious person, was her nearest approach to any definite explanation. But John was triumphant; that much was made apparent; and she could wait for the rest.

When John came home to dinner next day, he said, sitting down on the sofa by Bella and baby-Bella: 'My dear, I have a piece of news to tell you. I have left the China House.'

As he seemed to like having left it, Bella took it for granted that there was no misfortune in the case.

'In a word, my love,' said John, 'the China House is broken and abolished. There is no such thing any more.'

'Then, are you already in another House, John?'

'Yes, my darling. I am in another way of business. And I am rather better off.'

The inexhaustible baby was instantly made to congratulate him, and to say, with appropriate action on the part of a very limp arm and a speckled fist: 'Three cheers, ladies and gemplemorums. Hoo—ray!'

'I am afraid, my life,' said John, 'that you have become very much attached to this cottage?'

'Afraid I have, John? Of course I have.'

'The reason why I said afraid,' returned John, 'is, because we must move.'

'O John!'

'Yes, my dear, we must move. We must have our head-quarters in London now. In short, there's a dwelling-house rent-free, attached to my new position, and we must occupy it.'

'That's a gain, John.'

'Yes, my dear, it is undoubtedly a gain.'

He gave her a very blithe look, and a very sly look. Which occasioned the inexhaustible baby to square at him with the speckled fists, and demand in a threatening manner what he meant?

'My love, you said it was a gain, and *I* said it was a gain. A very innocent remark, surely.'

'I won't,' said the inexhaustible baby, '—allow—you—to—make—game—of—my—venerable—Ma.' At each division administering a soft facer with one of the speckled fists.

John having stooped down to receive these punishing visitations, Bella asked him, would it be necessary to move soon? Why yes, indeed (said John), he did propose that they should move very soon. Taking the furniture with them, of course? (said Bella). Why, no (said John), the fact was, that the house was—in a sort of a kind of a way—furnished already.

The inexhaustible baby, hearing this, resumed the offensive, and said: 'But there's no nursery for me, sir. What do you mean, marble-hearted parent?' To which the marble-hearted parent rejoined that there was a—sort of a kind of a—nursery, and it might be 'made to do'. 'Made to do?' returned the Inexhaustible, administering more punishment, 'what do you take me for?' And was then turned over on its back in Bella's lap, and smothered with kisses.

'But really, John dear,' said Bella, flushed in quite a lovely manner by these exercises, 'will the new house, just as it stands, do for baby? That's the question.'

'I felt that to be the question,' he returned, 'and therefore I arranged that you should come with me and look at it, to-morrow morning.' Appointment made, accordingly, for Bella to go up with him to-morrow morning; John kissed; and Bella delighted.

When they reached London in pursuance of their little plan, they took coach and drove westward. Not only drove westward, but drove into that particular westward division, which Bella had seen last when she turned her face from Mr Boffin's door. Not only drove into that particular division, but drove at last into that very street. Not only drove into that very street, but stopped at last at that very house.

'John dear!' cried Bella, looking out of window in a flutter. 'Do you see where we are?'

'Yes, my love. The coachman's quite right.'

The house-door was opened without any knocking or ringing, and John promptly helped her out. The servant who stood holding the door, asked no question of John, neither did he go before them or follow them as they went straight up-stairs. It was only her husband's encircling arm, urging her on, that prevented Bella from stopping at the foot of the staircase. As they ascended, it was seen to be tastefully ornamented with most beautiful flowers.

'O John!' said Bella, faintly. 'What does this mean?'

'Nothing, my darling, nothing. Let us go on.'

Going on a little higher, they came to a charming aviary, in which a number of tropical birds, more gorgeous in colour than the flowers, were flying about; and among those birds were gold and silver fish, and mosses, and water-lilies, and a fountain, and all manner of wonders.

'O my dear John!' said Bella. 'What does this mean?'

'Nothing, my darling, nothing. Let us go on.'

They went on, until they came to a door. As John put out his hand to open it, Bella caught his hand.

'I don't know what it means, but it's too much for me. Hold me, John, love.'

John caught her up in his arm, and lightly dashed into the room with her.

Behold Mr and Mrs Boffin, beaming! Behold Mrs Boffin clapping her hands in an ecstacy, running to Bella with tears of joy pouring down her comely face, and folding her to her breast, with the words: 'My deary deary, deary girl, that Noddy and me saw married and couldn't wish joy to, or so much as speak to! My deary, deary, deary, wife of John and mother of his little child! My loving loving, bright bright, Pretty Pretty! Welcome to your house and home, my deary!'

Chapter 13

Showing How the Golden Dustman Helped to Scatter Dust

IN all the first bewilderment of her wonder, the most bewilderingly wonderful thing to Bella was the shining countenance of Mr Boffin. That his wife should be joyous, open-hearted, and genial, or that her face should express every quality that was large and trusting, and no quality that was little or mean, was accordant with Bella's experience. But, that he, with a perfectly beneficent air and a plump rosy face, should be standing there, looking at her and John, like some jovial good spirit, was marvellous. For, how had he looked when she last saw him in that very room (it was the room in which she had given him that piece of her mind at parting), and what had become of all those crooked lines of suspicion, avarice, and distrust, that twisted his visage then?

Mrs Boffin seated Bella on the large ottoman, and seated herself beside her, and John her husband seated himself on the other side of her, and Mr Boffin stood beaming at every one and everything he could see, with surpassing jollity and enjoyment. Mrs Boffin was then taken with a laughing fit of clapping her hands, and clapping her knees, and rocking herself to and fro, and then with another laughing fit of embracing Bella, and rocking her to and fro—both fits, of considerable duration.

'Old lady, old lady,' said Mr Boffin, at length; 'if you don't begin somebody else must.'

'I'm a going to begin, Noddy, my dear,' returned Mrs Boffin. 'Only it isn't easy for a person to know where to begin, when a person is in this state of delight and happiness. Bella, my dear. Tell me, who's this?'

'Who is this?' repeated Bella. 'My husband.'

'Ah! But tell me his name, deary!' cried Mrs Boffin.

'Rokesmith.'

'No, it ain't!' cried Mrs Boffin, clapping her hands, and shaking her head. 'Not a bit of it.'

'Handford then,' suggested Bella.

'No, it ain't!' cried Mrs Boffin, again clapping her hands and shaking her head. 'Not a bit of it.'

'At least, his name is John, I suppose?' said Bella.

'Ah! I should think so, deary!' cried Mrs Boffin. 'I should hope so! Many and many is the time I have called him by his name of John. But what's his other name, his true other name? Give a guess, my pretty!'

'I can't guess,' said Bella, turning her pale face from one to another.

'*I* could,' cried Mrs Boffin, 'and what's more, I did! I found him out, all in a flash as I may say, one night. Didn't I, Noddy?'

'Ay! That the old lady did!' said Mr Boffin, with stout pride in the circumstance.

'Harkee to me, deary,' pursued Mrs Boffin, taking Bella's hands between her own, and gently beating on them from time to time. 'It was after a particular night when John had been disappointed—as he thought—in his affections. It was after a night when John had made an offer to a certain young lady, and the certain young lady had refused it. It was after a particular night, when he felt himself cast-away-like, and had made up his mind to go seek his fortune. It was the very next night. My Noddy wanted a paper out of his Secretary's room, and I says to

Noddy, "I am going by the door, and I'll ask him for it." I tapped at his door, and he didn't hear me. I looked in, and saw him a sitting lonely by his fire, brooding over it. He chanced to look up with a pleased kind of smile in my company when he saw me, and then in a single moment every grain of the gunpowder that had been lying sprinkled thick about him ever since I first set eyes upon him as a man at the Bower, took fire! Too many a time had I seen him sitting lonely, when he was a poor child, to be pitied, heart and hand! Too many a time had I seen him in need of being brightened up with a comforting word! Too many and too many a time to be mistaken, when that glimpse of him come at last! No, no! I just makes out to cry, "I know you now! You're John!" And he catches me as I drops.—So what,' says Mrs Boffin, breaking off in the rush of her speech to smile most radiantly, 'might you think by this time that your husband's name was, dear?'

'Not,' returned Bella, with quivering lips; 'not Harmon? That's not possible?'

'Don't tremble. Why not possible, deary, when so many things are possible?' demanded Mrs Boffin, in a soothing tone.

'He was killed,' gasped Bella.

'Thought to be,' said Mrs Boffin. 'But if ever John Harmon drew the breath of life on earth, that is certainly John Harmon's arm round your waist now, my pretty. If ever John Harmon had a wife on earth, that wife is certainly you. If ever John Harmon and his wife had a child on earth, that child is certainly this.'

By a master-stroke of secret arrangement, the inexhaustible baby here appeared at the door, suspended in mid-air by invisible agency. Mrs Boffin, plunging at it, brought it to Bella's lap, where both Mrs and Mr Boffin (as the saying is) 'took it out of' the Inexhaustible in a shower of caresses. It was only this timely appearance that kept Bella from swooning. This, and her husband's earnestness in explaining further to her how it had come to pass that he had been supposed to be slain, and had even been suspected of his own murder; also, how he had put a pious fraud upon her which had preyed upon his mind, as the time for its disclosure approached, lest she might not make full allowance for the object with which it had originated, and in which it had fully developed.

'But bless ye, my beauty!' cried Mrs Boffin, taking him up short at this point, with another hearty clap of her hands. 'It wasn't John only that was in it. We was all of us in it.'

'I don't,' said Bella, looking vacantly from one to another, 'yet understand—'

'Of course you don't, my deary,' exclaimed Mrs Boffin. 'How can you till you're told! So now I am a going to tell you. So you put your two hands between my two hands again,' cried the comfortable creature, embracing her, 'with that blessed little picter lying on your lap, and you shall be told all the story. Now, I'm a going to tell the story. Once, twice, three times, and the horses is off. Here they go! When I cries out that night, "I know you now, you're John!"—which was my exact words; wasn't they, John?'

'Your exact words,' said John, laying his hand on hers.

'That's a very good arrangement,' cried Mrs Boffin. 'Keep it there, John. And as we was all of us in it, Noddy you come and lay yours a top of his, and we won't break the pile till the story's done.'

Mr Boffin hitched up a chair, and added his broad brown right hand to the heap.

'That's capital!' said Mrs Boffin, giving it a kiss. 'Seems quite a family building; don't it? But the horses is off. Well! When I cries out that night, "I know you now! you're John!" John catches of me, it is true; but I ain't a light weight, bless ye, and he's forced to let me down. Noddy, he hears a noise, and in he trots, and as soon as I anyways comes to myself I calls to him, "Noddy, well I might say as I did say, that night at the Bower, for the Lord be thankful this is John!" On which he gives a heave, and down he goes likewise, with his head under the writing-table. This brings me round comfortable, and that brings him round comfortable, and then John and him and me we all fall a crying for joy.'

'Yes! They cry for joy, my darling,' her husband struck in. 'You understand? These two, whom I come to life to disappoint and dispossess, cry for joy!'

Bella looked at him confusedly, and looked again at Mrs Boffin's radiant face.

'That's right, my dear, don't you mind him,' said Mrs Boffin, 'stick to me. Well! Then we sits down, gradually gets cool, and holds a confabulation. John, he tells us how he is despairing in his mind on accounts of a certain fair young person, and how, if I hadn't found him out, he was going away to seek his fortune far and wide, and had fully meant never to come to life, but to leave the property as our wrongful inheritance for ever and a day. At which you never see a man so

frightened as my Noddy was. For to think that he should have
come into the property wrongful, however innocent, and—more
than that—might have gone on keeping it to his dying day,
turned him whiter than chalk.'

'And you too,' said Mr Boffin.

'Don't you mind him, neither, my deary,' resumed Mrs
Boffin; 'stick to me. This brings up a confabulation regarding the
certain fair young person; when Noddy he gives it as his opinion
that she is a deary creetur. ''She may be a leetle spoilt, and
nat'rally spoilt,'' he says, ''by circumstances, but that's only the
surface, and I lay my life,'' he says, ''that she's the true golden
gold at heart.'' '

'So did you,' said Mr Boffin.

'Don't you mind him a single morsel, my dear,' proceeded
Mrs Boffin, 'but stick to me. Then says John, O, if he could but
prove so! Then we both of us ups and says, that minute, ''Prove
so!'' '

With a start, Bella directed a hurried glance towards Mr
Boffin. But, he was sitting thoughtfully smiling at that broad
brown hand of his, and either didn't see it, or would take no
notice of it.

' ''Prove it, John!'' we says,' repeated Mrs Boffin. ' ''Prove
it and overcome your doubts with triumph, and be happy for the
first time in your life, and for the rest of your life.'' This puts
John in a state, to be sure. Then we says, ''What will content
you? If she was to stand up for you when you was slighted, if
she was to show herself of a generous mind when you was
oppressed, if she was to be truest to you when you was poorest
and friendliest, and all this against her own seeming interest,
how would that do?'' ''Do?'' says John, ''it would raise me to
the skies.'' ''Then,'' says my Noddy, ''make your preparations
for the ascent, John, it being my firm belief that up you go!'' '

Bella caught Mr Boffin's twinkling eye for half an instant;
but he got it away from her, and restored it to his broad brown
hand.

'From the first, you was always a special favourite of
Noddy's,' said Mrs Boffin, shaking her head. 'O you were! And
if I had been inclined to be jealous, I don't know what I mightn't
have done to you. But as I wasn't—why, my beauty,' with a
hearty laugh and an embrace, 'I made you a special favourite of
my own too. But the horses is coming round the corner. Well!
Then says my Noddy, shaking his sides till he was fit to make
'em ache again: ''Look out for being slighted and oppressed,

John, for if ever a man had a hard master, you shall find me from this present time to be such to you." And then he began!' cried Mrs Boffin, in an ecstacy of admiration. 'Lord bless you, then he began! And how he *did* begin; didn't he!'

Bella looked half frightened, and yet half laughed.

'But, bless you,' pursued Mrs Boffin, 'if you could have seen him of a night, at that time of it! The way he'd sit and chuckle over himself! The way he'd say "I've been a regular brown bear to-day," and take himself in his arms and hug himself at the thoughts of the brute he had pretended. But every night he says to me: "Better and better, old lady. What did we say of her? She'll come through it, the true golden gold. This'll be the happiest piece of work we ever done." And then he'd say, "I'll be a grislier old growler to-morrow!" and laugh, he would, till John and me was often forced to slap his back, and bring it out of his windpipes with a little water.'

Mr Boffin, with his face bent over his heavy hand, made no sound, but rolled his shoulders when thus referred to, as if he were vastly enjoying himself.

'And so, my good and pretty,' pursued Mrs Boffin, 'you was married, and there was we hid up in the church-organ by this husband of yours; for he wouldn't let us out with it then, as was first meant. "No," he says, "she's so unselfish and contented, that I can't afford to be rich yet. I must wait a little longer." Then, when baby was expected, he says, "She is such a cheerful, glorious housewife that I can't afford to be rich yet. I must wait a little longer." Then when baby was born, he says, "She is so much better than she ever was, that I can't afford to be rich yet. I must wait a little longer." And so he goes on and on, till I says outright, "Now, John, if you don't fix a time for setting her up in her own house and home, and letting us walk out of it, I'll turn Informer." Then he says he'll only wait to triumph beyond what we ever thought possible, and to show her to us better than even we ever supposed; and he says, "She shall see me under suspicion of having murdered myself, and *you* shall see how trusting and how true she'll be." Well! Noddy and me agreed to that, and he was right, and here you are, and the horses is in, and the story is done, and God bless you my Beauty, and God bless us all!'

The pile of hands dispersed, and Bella and Mrs Boffin took a good long hug of one another: to the apparent peril of the inexhaustible baby, lying staring in Bella's lap.

'But *is* the story done?' said Bella, pondering. 'Is there no more of it?'

'What more of it should there be, deary?' returned Mrs Boffin, full of glee.

'Are you sure you have left nothing out of it?' asked Bella.

'I don't think I have,' said Mrs Boffin, archly.

'John dear,' said Bella, 'you're a good nurse; will you please hold baby?' Having deposited the Inexhaustible in his arms with those words, Bella looked hard at Mr Boffin, who had moved to a table where he was leaning his head upon his hand with his face turned away, and, quietly settling herself on her knees at his side, and drawing one arm over his shoulder, said: 'Please I beg your pardon, and I made a small mistake of a word when I took leave of you last. Please I think you are better (not worse) than Hopkins, better (not worse) than Dancer, better (not worse) than Blackberry Jones, better (not worse) than any of them! Please something more!' cried Bella, with an exultant ringing laugh as she struggled with him and forced him to turn his delighted face to hers. 'Please I have found out something not yet mentioned. Please I don't believe you are a hard-hearted miser at all, and please I don't believe you ever for one single minute were!'

At this, Mrs Boffin fairly screamed with rapture, and sat beating her feet upon the floor, clapping her hands, and bobbing herself backwards and forwards, like a demented member of some Mandarin's family.

'O, I understand you now, sir!' cried Bella. 'I want neither you nor any one else to tell me the rest of the story. I can tell it to *you*, now, if you would like to hear it.'

'Can you, my dear?' said Mr Boffin. 'Tell it then.'

'What?' cried Bella, holding him prisoner by the coat with both hands. 'When you saw what a greedy little wretch you were the patron of, you determined to show her how much misused and misprized riches could do, and often had done, to spoil people; did you? Not caring what she thought of you (and Goodness knows *that* was of no consequence!) you showed her, in yourself, the most detestable sides of wealth, saying in your own mind, "This shallow creature would never work the truth out of her own weak soul, if she had a hundred years to do it in; but a glaring instance kept before her may open even her eyes and set her thinking." That was what you said to yourself; was it, sir?'

'I never said anything of the sort,' Mr Boffin declared in a state of the highest enjoyment.

'Then you ought to have said it, sir,' returned Bella, giving him two pulls and one kiss, 'for you must have thought and meant it. You saw that good fortune was turning my stupid head and hardening my silly heart—was making me grasping, calculating, insolent, insufferable—and you took the pains to be the dearest and kindest fingerpost that ever was set up anywhere, pointing out the road that I was taking and the end it led to. Confess instantly!'

'John,' said Mr Boffin, one broad piece of sunshine from head to foot, 'I wish you'd help me out of this.'

'You can't be heard by counsel, sir,' returned Bella. 'You must speak for yourself. Confess instantly!'

'Well, my dear,' said Mr Boffin, 'the truth is, that when we did go in for the little scheme that my old lady has pinted out, I did put it to John, what did he think of going in for some such general scheme as *you* have pinted out? But I didn't in any way so word it, because I didn't in any way so mean it. I only said to John, wouldn't it be more consistent, me going in for being a reg'lar brown bear respecting him, to go in as a reg'lar brown bear all round?'

'Confess this minute, sir,' said Bella, 'that you did it to correct and amend me!'

'Certainly, my dear child,' said Mr Boffin, 'I didn't do it to harm you; you may be sure of that. And I did hope it might just hint a caution. Still, it ought to be mentioned that no sooner had my old lady found out John, than John made known to her and me that he had had his eye upon a thankless person by the name of Silas Wegg. Partly for the punishment of which Wegg, by leading him on in a very unhandsome and underhanded game that he was playing, them books that you and me bought so many of together (and, by-the-by, my dear, he wasn't Blackberry Jones, but Blewberry) was read aloud to me by that person of the name of Silas Wegg aforesaid.'

Bella, who was still on her knees at Mr Boffin's feet, gradually sank down into a sitting posture on the ground, as she meditated more and more thoughtfully, with her eyes upon his beaming face.

'Still,' said Bella, after this meditative pause, 'there remain two things that I cannot understand. Mrs Boffin never supposed any part of the change in Mr Boffin to be real; did she?—You never did; did you?' asked Bella, turning to her.

'No!' returned Mrs Boffin, with a most rotund and glowing negative.

'And yet you took it very much to heart,' said Bella. 'I remember its making you very uneasy, indeed.'

'Ecod, you see Mrs John has a sharp eye, John!' cried Mr Boffin, shaking his head with an admiring air. 'You're right, my dear. The old lady nearly blowed us into shivers and smithers, many times.'

'Why?' asked Bella. 'How did that happen, when she was in your secret?'

'Why, it was a weakness in the old lady,' said Mr Boffin; 'and yet, to tell you the whole truth and nothing but the truth, I'm rather proud of it. My dear, the old lady thinks so high of me that she couldn't abear to see and hear me coming out as a reg'lar brown one. Couldn't abear to make-believe as I meant it! In consequence of which, we was everlastingly in danger with her.'

Mrs Boffin laughed heartily at herself; but a certain glistening in her honest eyes revealed that she was by no means cured of that dangerous propensity.

'I assure you, my dear,' said Mr Boffin, 'that on the celebrated day when I made what has since been agreed upon to be my grandest demonstration—I allude to Mew says the cat, Quack quack says the duck, and Bow-wow-wow says the dog—I assure you, my dear, that on that celebrated day, them flinty and unbeliving words hit my old lady so hard on my account, that I had to hold her, to prevent her running out after you, and defending me by saying I was playing a part.'

Mrs Boffin laughed heartily again, and her eyes glistened again, and it then appeared, not only that in that burst of sarcastic eloquence Mr Boffin was considered by his two fellow-conspirators to have outdone himself, but that in his own opinion it was a remarkable achievement. 'Never thought of it afore the moment, my dear!' he observed to Bella. 'When John said, if he had been so happy as to win your affections and possess your heart, it come into my head to turn round upon him with "Win her affections and possess her heart! Mew says the cat, Quack quack says the duck, and Bow-wow-wow says the dog." I couldn't tell you how it come into my head or where from, but it had so much the sound of a rasper that I own to you it astonished myself. I was awful nigh bursting out a laughing though, when it made John stare!'

'You said, my pretty,' Mrs Boffin reminded Bella, 'that there was one other thing you couldn't understand.'

'O yes!' cried Bella, covering her face with her hands; 'but that I never shall be able to understand as long as I live. It is, how John could love me so when I so little deserved it, and how you, Mr and Mrs Boffin, could be so forgetful of yourselves, and take such pains and trouble, to make me a little better, and after all to help him to so unworthy a wife. But I am very very grateful.'

It was John Harmon's turn then—John Harmon now for good, and John Rokesmith for nevermore—to plead with her (quite unnecessarily) in behalf of his deception, and to tell her, over and over again, that it had been prolonged by her own winning graces in her supposed station of life. This led on to many interchanges of endearment and enjoyment on all sides, in the midst of which the Inexhaustible being observed staring, in a most imbecile manner, on Mrs Boffin's breast, was pronounced to be supernaturally intelligent as to the whole transaction, and was made to declare to the ladies and gemplemorums, with a wave of the speckled fist (with difficulty detached from an exceedingly short waist), 'I have already informed my venerable Ma that I know all about it!'

Then, said John Harmon, would Mrs John Harmon come and see her house? And a dainty house it was, and a tastefully beautiful; and they went through it in procession; the Inexhaustible on Mrs Boffin's bosom (still staring) occupying the middle station, and Mr Boffin bringing up the rear. And on Bella's exquisite toilette table was an ivory casket, and in the casket were jewels the like of which she had never dreamed of, and aloft on an upper floor was a nursery garnished as with rainbows; 'though we were hard put to it,' said John Harmon, 'to get it done in so short a time.'

The house inspected, emissaries removed the Inexhaustible, who was shortly afterwards heard screaming among the rainbows; whereupon Bella withdrew herself from the presence and knowledge of gemplemorums, and the screaming ceased, and smiling Peace associated herself with that young olive branch.

'Come and look in, Noddy!' said Mrs Boffin to Mr Boffin.

Mr Boffin, submitting to be led on tiptoe to the nursery door, looked in with immense satisfaction, although there was nothing to see but Bella in a musing state of happiness, seated in a little low chair upon the hearth, with her child in her fair young arms, and her soft eyelashes shading her eyes from the fire.

'It looks as if the old man's spirit had found rest at last; don't it?' said Mrs Boffin.

'Yes, old lady.'

'And as if his money had turned bright again, after a long long rust in the dark, and was at last a beginning to sparkle in the sunlight?'

'Yes, old lady.'

'And it makes a pretty and a promising picter; don't it?'

'Yes, old lady.'

But, aware at the instant of a fine opening for a point, Mr Boffin quenched that observation in this—delivered in the grisliest growling of the regular brown bear. 'A pretty and a hopeful picter? Mew, Quack quack, Bow-wow!' And then trotted silently downstairs, with his shoulders in a state of the liveliest commotion.

Chapter 14

Checkmate to the Friendly Move

MR AND MRS JOHN HARMON had so timed their taking possession of their rightful name and their London house, that the event befel on the very day when the last wagon-load of the last Mound was driven out at the gates of Boffin's Bower. As it jolted away, Mr Wegg felt that the last load was correspondingly removed from his mind, and hailed the auspicious season when that black sheep, Boffin, was to be closely sheared.

Over the whole slow process of levelling the Mounds, Silas had kept watch with rapacious eyes. But, eyes no less rapacious had watched the growth of the Mounds in years bygone, and had vigilantly sifted the dust of which they were composed. No valuables turned up. How should there be any, seeing that the old hard jailer of Harmony Jail had coined every waif and stray into money, long before?

Though disappointed by this bare result, Mr Wegg felt too sensibly relieved by the close of the labour, to grumble to any great extent. A foreman-representative of the dust contractors, purchasers of the Mounds, had worn Mr Wegg down to skin and bone. This supervisor of the proceedings, asserting his employers' rights to cart off by daylight, nightlight, torchlight, when they would, must have been the death of Silas if the work had lasted much longer. Seeming never to need sleep himself, he would reappear, with a tied-up broken head, in fantail hat and velveteen smalls, like an accursed goblin, at the most unholy and untimely hours. Tired out by keeping close ward over a long day's work in fog and rain, Silas would have just crawled to bed and be dozing, when a horrid shake and rumble under his pillow would announce an approaching train of carts, escorted by this Demon of Unrest, to fall to work again. At another time, he would be rumbled up out of his soundest sleep, in the dead of the night; at another, would be kept at his post eight-and-forty hours on end. The more his persecutor besought him not to trouble himself to turn out, the more suspicious was the crafty Wegg that indications had been observed of something hidden somewhere, and that attempts were on foot to circumvent him. So continually broken was his rest through these means, that he led the life of having wagered to keep ten thousand dog-watches in ten thousand hours, and looked piteously upon himself as always getting up and yet never going to bed. So gaunt and haggard had he grown at last, that his wooden leg showed disproportionate, and presented a thriving appearance in contrast with the rest of his plagued body, which might almost have been termed chubby.

However, Wegg's comfort was, that all his disagreeables were now over, and that he was immediately coming into his property. Of late, the grindstone did undoubtedly appear to have been whirling at his own nose rather than Boffin's, but Boffin's nose was now to be sharpened fine. Thus far, Mr Wegg had let his dusty friend off lightly, having been baulked in that amiable design of frequently dining with him, by the machinations of the sleepless dustman. He had been constrained to depute Mr Venus to keep their dusty friend, Boffin, under inspection, while he himself turned lank and lean at the Bower.

To Mr Venus's museum Mr Wegg repaired when at length the Mounds were down and gone. It being evening, he found that gentleman, as he expected, seated over his fire; but did not find him, as he expected, floating his powerful mind in tea.

'Why, you smell rather comfortable here!' said Wegg, seeming to take it ill, and stopping and sniffing as he entered.

'I *am* rather comfortable, sir,' said Venus.

'You don't use lemon in your business, do you?' asked Wegg, sniffing again.

'No, Mr Wegg,' said Venus. 'When I use it at all, I mostly use it in cobblers' punch.'

'What do you call cobblers' punch?' demanded Wegg, in a worse humour than before.

'It's difficult to impart the receipt for it, sir,' returned Venus, 'because, however particular you may be in allotting your materials, so much will still depend upon the individual gifts, and there being a feeling thrown into it. But the groundwork is gin.'

'In a Dutch bottle?' said Wegg gloomily, as he sat himself down.

'Very good, sir, very good!' cried Venus. 'Will you partake, sir?'

'Will I partake?' returned Wegg very surlily. 'Why, of course I will! *Will* a man partake, as has been tormented out of his five senses by an everlasting dustman with his head tied up! *Will* he, too! As if he wouldn't!'

'Don't let it put you out, Mr Wegg. You don't seem in your usual spirits.'

'If you come to that, you don't seem in your usual spirits,' growled Wegg. 'You seem to be setting up for lively.'

This circumstance appeared, in his then state of mind, to give Mr Wegg uncommon offence.

'And you've been having your hair cut!' said Wegg, missing the usual dusty shock.

'Yes, Mr Wegg. But don't let that put you out, either.'

'And I am blest if you ain't getting fat!' said Wegg, with culminating discontent. 'What are you going to do next?'

'Well, Mr Wegg,' said Venus, smiling in a sprightly manner, 'I suspect you could hardly guess what I am going to do next.'

'I don't want to guess,' retorted Wegg. 'All I've got to say is, that it's well for you that the diwision of labour has been what it has been. It's well for you to have had so light a part in this business, when mine has been so heavy. You haven't had *your* rest broke, I'll be bound.'

'Not at all, sir,' said Venus. 'Never rested so well in all my life, I thank you.'

'Ah!' grumbled Wegg, 'you should have been me. If you had been me, and had been fretted out of your bed, and your sleep, and your meals, and your mind, for a stretch of months together, *you*'d have been out of condition and out of sorts.'

'Certainly, it has trained you down, Mr Wegg,' said Venus, contemplating his figure with an artist's eye. 'Trained you down very low, it has! So weazen and yellow is the kivering upon your bones, that one might almost fancy you had come to give a look-in upon the French gentleman in the corner, instead of me.'

Mr Wegg, glancing in great dudgeon towards the French gentleman's corner, seemed to notice something new there, which induced him to glance at the opposite corner, and then to put on his glasses and stare at all the nooks and corners of the dim shop in succession.

'Why, you've been having the place cleaned up!' he exclaimed.

'Yes, Mr Wegg. By the hand of adorable woman.'

'Then what you're going to do next, I suppose, is to get married?'

'That's it, sir.'

Silas took off his glasses again—finding himself too intensely disgusted by the sprightly appearance of his friend and partner to bear a magnified view of him—and made the inquiry:

'To the old party?'

'Mr Wegg!' said Venus, with a sudden flush of wrath. 'The lady in question is not a old party.'

'I meant,' exclaimed Wegg, testily, 'to the party as formerly objected?'

'Mr Wegg,' said Venus, 'in a case of so much delicacy, I must trouble you to say what you mean. There are strings that must not be played upon. No sir! Not sounded, unless in the most respectful and tuneful manner. Of such melodious strings is Miss Pleasant Riderhood formed.'

'Then it *is* the lady as formerly objected?' said Wegg.

'Sir,' returned Venus with dignity, 'I accept the altered phrase. It is the lady as formerly objected.'

'When is it to come off?' asked Silas.

'Mr Wegg,' said Venus, with another flush. 'I cannot permit it to be put in the form of a Fight. I must temperately but firmly call upon you, sir, to amend that question.'

'When is the lady,' Wegg reluctantly demanded, constraining his ill temper in remembrance of the partnership and its stock in trade, 'a going to give her 'and where she has already given her 'art?'

'Sir,' returned Venus, 'I again accept the altered phrase, and with pleasure. The lady is a going to give her 'and where she has already given her 'art, next Monday.'

'Then the lady's objection has been met?' said Silas.

'Mr Wegg,' said Venus, 'as I did name to you, I think, on a former occasion, if not on former occasions—'

'On former occasions,' interrupted Wegg.

'—What,' pursued Venus, 'what the nature of the lady's objection was, I may impart, without violating any of the tender confidences since sprung up between the lady and myself, how it has been met, through the kind interference of two good friends of mine: one, previously acquainted with the lady: and one, not. The pint was thrown out, sir, by those two friends when they did me the great service of waiting on the lady to try if a union betwixt the lady and me could not be brought to bear—the pint, I say, was thrown out by them, sir, whether if, after marriage, I confined myself to the articulation of men, children, and the lower animals, it might not relieve the lady's mind of her feeling respecting being—as a lady—regarded in a bony light. It was a happy thought, sir, and it took root.'

'It would seem, Mr Venus,' observed Wegg, with a touch of distrust, 'that you are flush of friends?'

'Pretty well, sir,' that gentleman answered, in a tone of placid mystery. 'So-so, sir. Pretty well.'

'However,' said Wegg, after eyeing him with another touch of distrust, 'I wish you joy. One man spends his fortune in one way, and another in another. You are going to try matrimony. I mean to try travelling.'

'Indeed, Mr Wegg?'

'Change of air, sea-scenery, and my natural rest, I hope may bring me round after the persecutions I have undergone from the dustman with his head tied up, which I just now mentioned. The tough job being ended and the Mounds laid low, the hour is come for Boffin to stump up. Would ten to-morrow morning suit you, partner, for finally bringing Boffin's nose to the grindstone?'

Ten to-morrow morning would quite suit Mr Venus for that excellent purpose.

'You have had him well under inspection, I hope?' said Silas.

Mr Venus had had him under inspection pretty well every day.

'Suppose you was just to step round to-night then, and give him orders from me—I say from me, because he knows *I* won't be played with—to be ready with his papers, his accounts, and his cash, at that time in the morning?' said Wegg. 'And as a matter of form, which will be agreeable to your own feelings, before we go out (for I'll walk with you part of the way, though my leg gives under me with weariness), let's have a look at the stock in trade.'

Mr Venus produced it, and it was perfectly correct; Mr Venus undertook to produce it again in the morning, and to keep tryst with Mr Wegg on Boffin's doorstep as the clock struck ten. At a certain point of the road between Clerkenwell and Boffin's house (Mr Wegg expressly insisted that there should be no prefix to the Golden Dustman's name) the partners separated for the night.

It was a very bad night; to which succeeded a very bad morning. The streets were so unusually slushy, muddy, and miserable, in the morning, that Wegg rode to the scene of action; arguing that a man who was, as it were, going to the Bank to draw out a handsome property, could well afford that trifling expense.

Venus was punctual, and Wegg undertook to knock at the door, and conduct the conference. Door knocked at. Door opened.

'Boffin at home?'

The servant replied that *Mr* Boffin was at home.

'He'll do,' said Wegg, 'though it ain't what I call him.'

The servant inquired if they had any appointment?

'Now, I tell you what, young fellow,' said Wegg, 'I won't have it. This won't do for me. I don't want menials. I want Boffin.'

They were shown into a waiting-room, where the all-powerful Wegg wore his hat, and whistled, and with his forefinger stirred up a clock that stood upon the chimneypiece, until he made it strike. In a few minutes they were shown upstairs into what used to be Boffin's room; which, besides the door of entrance, had folding-doors in it, to make it one of a suite of rooms when occasion required. Here, Boffin was seated at a library-table, and here Mr Wegg, having imperiously motioned the servant to withdraw, drew up a chair and seated himself, in his hat, close beside him. Here, also, Mr Wegg instantly underwent the remarkable experience of having his hat twitched off his head and thrown out of a window, which was opened and shut for the purpose.

'Be careful what insolent liberties you take in that gentleman's presence,' said the owner of the hand which had done this, 'or I will throw you after it.'

Wegg involuntarily clapped his hand to his bare head, and stared at the Secretary. For, it was he addressed him with a severe countenance, and who had come in quietly by the folding-doors.

'Oh!' said Wegg, as soon as he recovered his suspended power of speech. 'Very good! I gave directions for *you* to be dismissed. And you ain't gone, ain't you? Oh! We'll look into this presently. Very good!'

'No, nor *I* ain't gone,' said another voice.

Somebody else had come in quietly by the folding-doors. Turning his head, Wegg beheld his persecutor, the ever-wakeful dustman, accoutred with fantail hat and velveteen smalls complete. Who, untying his tied-up broken head, revealed a head that was whole, and a face that was Sloppy's.

'Ha, ha, ha, gentlemen!' roared Sloppy in a peal of laughter, and with immeasurable relish. 'He never thought as I could sleep standing, and often done it when I turned for Mrs Higden! He never thought as I used to give Mrs Higden the Police-news in different voices! But I did lead him a life all through it, gentlemen, I hope I really and truly DID!' Here, Mr Sloppy opening his mouth to a quite alarming extent, and throwing back his head to peal again, revealed incalculable buttons.

'Oh!' said Wegg, slightly discomfited, but not much as yet: 'one and one is two not dismissed, is it? Bof–fin! Just let me ask a question. Who set this chap on, in this dress, when the carting began? Who employed this fellow?'

'I say!' remonstrated Sloppy, jerking his head forward. 'No fellows, or *I*'ll throw you out of winder!'

Mr Boffin appeased him with a wave of his hand, and said: 'I employed him, Wegg.'

'Oh! You employed him, Boffin? Very good. Mr Venus, we raise our terms, and we can't do better than proceed to business. Bof–fin! I want the room cleared of these two scum.'

'That's not going to be done, Wegg,' replied Mr Boffin, sitting composedly on the library-table, at one end, while the Secretary sat composedly on it at the other.

'Bof–fin! Not going to be done?' repeated Wegg. 'Not at your peril?'

'No, Wegg,' said Mr Boffin, shaking his head good-humouredly. 'Not at my peril, and not on any other terms.'

Wegg reflected a moment, and then said: 'Mr Venus, will you be so good as hand me over that same dockyment?'

'Certainly, sir,' replied Venus, handing it to him with much politeness. 'There it is. Having now, sir, parted with it, I wish to make a small observation: not so much because it is anyways necessary, or expresses any new doctrine or discovery, as because it is a comfort to my mind. Silas Wegg, you are a precious old rascal.'

Mr Wegg, who, as if anticipating a compliment, had been beating time with the paper to the other's politeness until this unexpected conclusion came upon him, stopped rather abruptly.

'Silas Wegg,' said Venus, 'know that I took the liberty of taking Mr Boffin into our concern as a sleeping partner, at a very early period of our firm's existence.'

'Quite true,' added Mr Boffin; 'and I tested Venus by making him a pretended proposal or two; and I found him on the whole a very honest man, Wegg.'

'So Mr Boffin, in his indulgence, is pleased to say,' Venus remarked: 'though in the beginning of this dirt, my hands were not, for a few hours, quite as clean as I could wish. But I hope I made early and full amends.'

'Venus, you did,' said Mr Boffin. 'Certainly, certainly, certainly.'

Venus inclined his head with respect and gratitude. 'Thank you, sir. I am much obliged to you, sir, for all. For your good opinion now, for your way of receiving and encouraging me when I first put myself in communication with you, and for the influence since so kindly brought to bear upon a certain lady, both by yourself and by Mr John Harmon.' To whom, when thus making mention of him, he also bowed.

Wegg followed the name with sharp ears, and the action with sharp eyes, and a certain cringing air was infusing itself into his bullying air, when his attention was re-claimed by Venus.

'Everything else between you and me, Mr Wegg,' said Venus, 'now explains itself, and you can now make out, sir, without further words from me. But totally to prevent any unpleasantness or mistake that might arise on what I consider an important point, to be made quite clear at the close of our acquaintance, I beg the leave of Mr Boffin and Mr John Harmon to repeat an observation which I have already had the pleasure of bringing under your notice. You are a precious old rascal!'

'You are a fool,' said Wegg, with a snap of his fingers, 'and I'd have got rid of you before now, if I could have struck out any way of doing it. I have thought it over, I can tell you. You may go, and welcome. You leave the more for me. Because, you know,' said Wegg, dividing his next observation between Mr Boffin and Mr Harmon, 'I am worth my price, and I mean to have it. This getting off is all very well in its way, and it tells with such an anatomical Pump as this one,' pointing out Mr

Venus, 'but it won't do with a Man. I am here to be bought off, and I have named my figure. Now, buy me, or leave me.'

'I'll leave you, Wegg,' said Mr Boffin, laughing, 'as far as I am concerned.'

'Bof–fin!' replied Wegg, turning upon him with a severe air, 'I understand *your* new-born boldness. I see the brass underneath *your* silver plating. *You* have got *your* nose out of joint. Knowing that you've nothing at stake, you can afford to come the independent game. Why, you're just so much smeary glass to see through, you know! But Mr Harmon is in another sitiwation. What Mr Harmon risks, is quite another pair of shoes. Now, I've heerd something lately about this being Mr Harmon—I make out now, some hints that I've met on that subject in the newspaper—and I drop you, Bof–fin, as beneath my notice. I ask Mr Harmon whether he has any idea of the contents of this present paper?'

'It is a will of my late father's, of more recent date than the will proved by Mr Boffin (address whom again, as you have addressed him already, and I'll knock you down), leaving the whole of his property to the Crown,' said John Harmon, with as much indifference as was compatible with extreme sternness.

'Right you are!' cried Wegg. 'Then,' screwing the weight of his body upon his wooden leg, and screwing his wooden head very much on one side, and screwing up one eye: 'then, I put the question to you, what's this paper worth?'

'Nothing,' said John Harmon.

Wegg had repeated the word with a sneer, and was entering on some sarcastic retort, when, to his boundless amazement, he found himself gripped by the cravat; shaken until his teeth chattered; shoved back, staggering, into a corner of the room; and pinned there.

'You scoundrel!' said John Harmon, whose seafaring hold was like that of a vice.

'You're knocking my head against the wall,' urged Silas faintly.

'I mean to knock your head against the wall,' returned John Harmon, suiting his action to his words, with the heartiest good will; 'and I'd give a thousand pounds for leave to knock your brains out. Listen, you scoundrel, and look at that Dutch bottle.'

Sloppy held it up, for his edification.

'That Dutch bottle, scoundrel, contained the latest will of the many wills made by my unhappy self-tormenting father. That will gives everything absolutely to my noble benefactor and yours, Mr Boffin, excluding and reviling me, and my sister (then already dead of a broken heart), by name. That Dutch bottle was found by my noble benefactor and yours, after he entered on possession of the estate. That Dutch bottle distressed him beyond measure, because, though I and my sister were both no more, it cast a slur upon our memory which he knew we had done nothing in our miserable youth, to deserve. That Dutch bottle, therefore, he buried in the Mound belonging to him, and there it lay while you, you thankless wretch, were prodding and poking—often very near it, I dare say. His intention was, that it should never see the light; but he was afraid to destroy it, lest to destroy such a document, even with his great generous motive, might be an offence at law. After the discovery was made here who I was, Mr Boffin, still restless on the subject, told me, upon certain conditions impossible for such a hound as you to appreciate, the secret of that Dutch bottle. I urged upon him the necessity of its being dug up, and the paper being legally produced and established. The first thing you saw him do, and the second thing has been done without your knowledge. Consequently, the paper now rattling in your hand as I shake you—and I should like to shake the life out of you—is worth less than the rotten cork of the Dutch bottle, do you understand?'

Judging from the fallen countenance of Silas as his head wagged backwards and forwards in a most uncomfortable manner, he did understand.

'Now, scoundrel,' said John Harmon, taking another sailor-like turn on his cravat and holding him in his corner at arms' length, 'I shall make two more short speeches to you, because I hope they will torment you. Your discovery was a genuine discovery (such as it was), for nobody had thought of looking into that place. Neither did we know you had made it, until Venus spoke to Mr Boffin, though I kept you under good observation from my first appearance here, and though Sloppy has long made it the chief occupation and delight of his life, to attend you like your shadow. I tell you this, that you may know we knew enough of you to persuade Mr Boffin to let us lead you on, deluded, to the last possible moment, in order that your disappointment might be the heaviest possible disappointment. That's the first short speech, do you understand?'

Here, John Harmon assisted his comprehension with another shake.

'Now, scoundrel,' he pursued, 'I am going to finish. You supposed me just now, to be the possessor of my father's property.—So I am. But through any act of my father's, or by any right I have? No. Through the munificence of Mr Boffin. The conditions that he made with me, before parting with the secret of the Dutch bottle, were, that I should take the fortune, and that he should take his Mound and no more. I owe everything I possess, solely to the disinterestedness, uprightness, tenderness, goodness (there are no words to satisfy me) of Mr and Mrs Boffin. And when, knowing what I knew, I saw such a mud-worm as you presume to rise in this house against this noble soul, the wonder is,' added John Harmon through his clenched teeth, and with a very ugly turn indeed on Wegg's cravat, 'that I didn't try to twist your head off, and fling *that* out of window! So. That's the last short speech, do you understand?'

Silas, released, put his hand to his throat, cleared it, and looked as if he had a rather large fishbone in that region. Simultaneously with this action on his part in his corner, a singular, and on the surface an incomprehensible, movement was made by Mr Sloppy: who began backing towards Mr Wegg along the wall, in the manner of a porter or heaver who is about to lift a sack of flour or coals.

'I am sorry, Wegg,' said Mr Boffin, in his clemency, 'that my old lady and I can't have a better opinion of you than the bad one we are forced to entertain. But I shouldn't like to leave you, after all said and done, worse off in life than I found you. Therefore say in a word, before we part, what it'll cost to set you up in another stall.'

'And in another place,' John Harmon struck in. 'You don't come outside these windows.'

'Mr Boffin,' returned Wegg in avaricious humiliation: 'when I first had the honour of making your acquaintance, I had got together a collection of ballads which was, I may say, above price.'

'Then they can't be paid for,' said John Harmon, 'and you had better not try, my dear sir.'

'Pardon me, Mr Boffin,' resumed Wegg, with a malignant glance in the last speaker's direction, 'I was putting the case to you, who, if my senses did not deceive me, put the case to me. I had a very choice collection of ballads, and there was a new stock of gingerbread in the tin box. I say no more, but would rather leave it to you.'

'But it's difficult to name what's right,' said Mr Boffin uneasily, with his hand in his pocket, 'and I don't want to go beyond what's right, because you really have turned out such a very bad fellow. So artful, and so ungrateful you have been, Wegg; for when did I ever injure you?'

'There was also,' Mr Wegg went on, in a meditative manner, 'a errand connection, in which I was much respected. But I would not wish to be deemed covetous, and I would rather leave it to you, Mr Boffin.'

'Upon my word, I don't know what to put it at,' the Golden Dustman muttered.

'There was likewise,' resumed Wegg, 'a pair of trestles, for which alone a Irish person, who was deemed a judge of trestles, offered five and six—a sum I would not hear of, for I should have lost by it—and there was a stool, a umbrella, a clothes-horse, and a tray. But I leave it to you, Mr Boffin.'

The Golden Dustman seeming to be engaged in some abstruse calculation, Mr Wegg assisted him with the following additional items.

'There was, further, Miss Elizabeth, Master George, Aunt Jane, and Uncle Parker. Ah! When a man thinks of the loss of such patronage as that; when a man finds so fair a garden rooted up by pigs; he finds it hard indeed, without going high, to work it into money. But I leave it wholly to you, sir.'

Mr Sloppy still continued his singular, and on the surface his incomprehensible, movement.

'Leading on has been mentioned,' said Wegg with a melancholy air, 'and it's not easy to say how far the tone of my mind may have been lowered by unwholesome reading on the subject of Misers, when you was leading me and others on to think you one yourself, sir. All I can say is, that I felt my tone of mind a lowering at the time. And how can a man put a price upon his mind! There was likewise a hat just now. But I leave the ole to you, Mr Boffin.'

'Come!' said Mr Boffin. 'Here's a couple of pound.'

'In justice to myself, I couldn't take it, sir.'

The words were but out of his mouth when John Harmon lifted his finger, and Sloppy, who was now close to Wegg, backed to Wegg's back, stooped, grasped his coat collar behind with both hands, and deftly swung him up like the sack of flour or coals before mentioned. A countenance of special discontent and amazement Mr Wegg exhibited in this position, with his buttons almost as prominently on view as Sloppy's own, and with his wooden leg in a highly unaccommodating state. But, not for many seconds was his countenance visible in the room; for, Sloppy lightly trotted out with him and trotted down the staircase,

Mr Venus attending to open the street door. Mr Sloppy's instructions had been to deposit his burden in the road; but, a scavenger's cart happening to stand unattended at the corner, with its little ladder planted against the wheel, Mr S. found it impossible to resist the temptation of shooting Mr Silas Wegg into the cart's contents. A somewhat difficult feat, achieved with great dexterity, and with a prodigious splash.

Chapter 15

What Was Caught
in the Traps That Were Set

How Bradley Headstone had been racked and riven in his mind since the quiet evening when by the river-side he had risen, as it were, out of the ashes of the Bargeman, none but he could have told. Not even he could have told, for such misery can only be felt.

First, he had to bear the combined weight of the knowledge of what he had done, of that haunting reproach that he might have done it so much better, and of the dread of discovery. This was load enough to crush him, and he laboured under it day and night. It was as heavy on him in his scanty sleep, as in his red-eyed waking hours. It bore him down with a dread unchanging monotony, in which there was not a moment's variety. The overweighted beast of burden, or the overweighted slave, can for certain instants shift the physical load, and find some slight respite even in enforcing additional pain upon such a set of muscles or such a limb. Not even that poor mockery of relief could the wretched man obtain, under the steady pressure of the infernal atmosphere into which he had entered.

Time went by, and no visible suspicion dogged him; time went by, and in such public accounts of the attack as were renewed at intervals, he began to see Mr Lightwood (who acted as lawyer for the injured man) straying further from the fact, going wider of the issue, and evidently slackening in his zeal. By degrees, a glimmering of the cause of this began to break on Bradley's sight. Then came the chance meeting with Mr Milvey at the railway station (where he often lingered in his leisure hours, as a place where any fresh news of his deed would be circulated, or any placard referring to it would be posted), and then he saw in the light what he had brought about.

For, then he saw that through his desperate attempt to separate those two for ever, he had been made the means of uniting them. That he had dipped his hands in blood, to mark himself a miserable fool and tool. That Eugene Wrayburn, for his wife's sake, set him aside and left him to crawl along his blasted course. He thought of Fate, or Providence, or be the directing Power what it might, as having put a fraud upon him—overreached him—and in his impotent mad rage bit, and tore, and had his fit.

New assurance of the truth came upon him in the next few following days, when it was put forth how the wounded man had been married on his bed, and to whom, and how, though always in a dangerous condition, he was a shade better. Bradley would far rather have been seized for his murder, than he would have read that passage, knowing himself spared, and knowing why.

But, not to be still further defrauded and overreached— which he would be, if implicated by Riderhood, and punished by the law for his abject failure, as though it had been a success—he kept close in his school during the day, ventured out warily at night, and went no more to the railway station. He examined the advertisements in the news for any sign that Riderhood acted on his hinted threat of so summoning him to renew their acquaintance, but found none. Having paid him handsomely for the support and accommodation he had had at the Lock House, and knowing him to be a very ignorant man who could not write, he began to doubt whether he was to be feared at all, or whether they need ever meet again.

All this time, his mind was never off the rack, and his raging sense of having been made to fling himself across the chasm which divided those two, and bridge it over for their coming together, never cooled down. This horrible condition brought on other fits. He could not have said how many, or when; but he saw in the faces of his pupils that they had seen him in that state, and that they were possessed by a dread of his relapsing.

One winter day when a slight fall of snow was feathering the sills and frames of the schoolroom windows, he stood at his black board, crayon in hand, about to commence with a class; when, reading in the countenances of those boys that there was something wrong, and that they seemed in alarm for him, he turned his eyes to the door towards which they faced. He then saw a slouching man of forbidding appearance standing in the midst of the school, with a bundle under his arm; and saw that it was Riderhood.

He sat down on a stool which one of his boys put for him, and he had a passing knowledge that he was in danger of falling, and that his face was becoming distorted. But, the fit went off for that time, and he wiped his mouth, and stood up again.

'Beg your pardon, governor! By your leave!' said Riderhood, knuckling his forehead, with a chuckle and a leer. 'What place may this be?'

'This is a school.'

'Where young folks learns wot's right?' said Riderhood, gravely nodding. 'Beg your pardon, governor! By your leave! But who teaches this school?'

'I do.'

'You're the master, are you, learned governor?'

'Yes. I am the master.'

'And a lovely thing it must be,' said Riderhood, 'fur to learn young folks wot's right, and fur to know wot *they* know wot you do it. Beg your pardon, learned governor! By your leave!—That there black board; wot's it for?'

'It is for drawing on, or writing on.'

'Is it though!' said Riderhood. 'Who'd have thought it, from the looks on it! *Would* you be so kind as write your name upon it, learned governor?' (In a wheedling tone.)

Bradley hesitated for a moment; but placed his usual signature, enlarged, upon the board.

'I ain't a learned character myself,' said Riderhood, surveying the class, 'but I do admire learning in others. I should dearly like to hear these here young folks read that there name off, from the writing.'

The arms of the class went up. At the miserable master's nod, the shrill chorus arose: 'Bradley Headstone!'

'No?' cried Riderhood. 'You don't mean it? Headstone! Why, that's in a churchyard. Hooroar for another turn!'

Another tossing of arms, another nod, and another shrill chorus: 'Bradley Headstone!'

'I've got it now!' said Riderhood, after attentively listening, and internally repeating: 'Bradley. I see. Chris'en name, Bradley sim'lar to Roger which is my own. Eh? Fam'ly name, Headstone, sim'lar to Riderhood which is my own. Eh?'

Shrill chorus. 'Yes!'

'Might you be acquainted, learned governor,' said Riderhood, 'with a person of about your own heighth and breadth, and wot 'ud pull down in a scale about your own weight, answering to a name sounding summat like Totherest?'

With a desperation in him that made him perfectly quiet, though his jaw was heavily squared; with his eyes upon Riderhood; and with traces of quickened breathing in his nostrils; the schoolmaster replied, in a suppressed voice, after a pause: 'I think I know the man you mean.'

'I thought you knowed the man I mean, learned governor. I want the man.'

With a half glance around him at his pupils, Bradley returned: 'Do you suppose he is here?'

'Begging your pardon, learned governor, and by your leave,' said Riderhood, with a laugh, 'how could I suppose he's here, when there's nobody here but you, and me, and these young lambs wot you're a learning on? But he is most excellent company, that man, and I want him to come and see me at my Lock, up the river.'

'I'll tell him so.'

'D'ye think he'll come?' asked Riderhood.

'I am sure he will.'

'Having got your word for him,' said Riderhood, 'I shall count upon him. P'raps you'd so fur obleege me, learned governor, as tell him that if he don't come precious soon, I'll look him up.'

'He shall know it.'

'Thankee. As I says a while ago,' pursued Riderhood, changing his hoarse tone and leering round upon the class again, 'though not a learned character my own self, I do admire learning in others, to be sure! Being here and having met with your kind attention, Master, might I, afore I go, ask a question of these here young lambs of yourn?'

'If it is in the way of school,' said Bradley, always sustaining his dark look at the other, and speaking in his suppressed voice, 'you may.'

'Oh! It's in the way of school!' cried Riderhood. 'I'll pound it, Master, to be in the way of school. Wot's the diwisions of water, my lambs? Wot sorts of water is there on the land?'

Shrill chorus: 'Seas, rivers, lakes, and ponds.'

'Seas, rivers, lakes, and ponds,' said Riderhood. 'They've got all the lot, Master! Blowed if I shouldn't have left out lakes, never having clapped eyes upon one, to my knowledge. Seas, rivers, lakes, and ponds. Wot is it, lambs, as they ketches in seas, rivers, lakes, and ponds?'

Shrill chorus (with some contempt for the ease of the question): 'Fish!'

'Good a-gin!' said Riderhood. 'But wot else is it, my lambs, as they sometimes ketches in rivers?'

Chorus at a loss. One shrill voice: 'Weed!'

'Good agin!' cried Riderhood. 'But it ain't weed neither. You'll never guess, my dears. Wot is it, besides fish, as they sometimes ketches in rivers? Well! I'll tell you. It's suits o' clothes.'

Bradley's face changed.

'Leastways, lambs,' said Riderhood, observing him out of the corners of his eyes, 'that's wot I my own self sometimes ketches in rivers. For strike me blind, my lambs, if I didn't ketch in a river the wery bundle under my arm!'

The class looked at the master, as if appealing from the irregular entrapment of this mode of examination. The master looked at the examiner, as if he would have torn him to pieces.

'I ask your pardon, learned governor,' said Riderhood, smearing his sleeve across his mouth as he laughed with a relish, 'tain't fair to the lambs, I know. It wos a bit of fun of mine. But upon my soul I drawed this here bundle out of a river! It's a Bargeman's suit of clothes. You see, it had been sunk there by the man as wore it, and I got it up.'

'How do you know it was sunk by the man who wore it?' asked Bradley.

' 'Cause I see him do it,' said Riderhood.

They looked at each other. Bradley, slowly withdrawing his eyes, turned his face to the black board and slowly wiped his name out.

'A heap of thanks, Master,' said Riderhood, 'for bestowing so much of your time, and of the lambses' time, upon a man as hasn't got no other recommendation to you than being a honest man. Wishing to see at my Lock up the river, the person as we've spoke of, and as you've answered for, I takes my leave of the lambs and of their learned governor both.'

With those words, he slouched out of the school, leaving the master to get through his weary work as he might, and leaving the whispering pupils to observe the master's face until he fell into the fit which had been long impending.

The next day but one was Saturday, and a holiday. Bradley rose early, and set out on foot for Plashwater Weir Mill Lock.

He rose so early that it was not yet light when he began his journey. Before extinguishing the candle by which he had dressed himself, he made a little parcel of his decent silver watch and its decent guard, and wrote inside the paper: 'Kindly take care of these for me.' He then addressed the parcel to Miss Peecher, and left it on the most protected corner of the little seat in her little porch.

It was a cold hard easterly morning when he latched the garden gate and turned away. The light snowfall which had feathered his schoolroom windows on the Thursday, still lingered in the air, and was falling white, while the wind blew black. The tardy day did not appear until he had been on foot two hours, and had traversed a greater part of London from east to west. Such breakfast as he had, he took at the comfortless public-house where he had parted from Riderhood on the occasion of their night-walk. He took it, standing at the littered bar, and looked loweringly at a man who stood where Riderhood had stood that early morning.

He outwalked the short day, and was on the towing-path by the river, somewhat footsore, when the night closed in. Still two or three miles short of the Lock, he slackened his pace then, but went steadily on. The ground was now covered with snow, though thinly, and there were floating lumps of ice in the more exposed parts of the river, and broken sheets of ice under the shelter of the banks. He took heed of nothing but the ice, the snow, and the distance, until he saw a light ahead, which he knew gleamed from the Lock House window. It arrested his steps, and he looked all around. The ice, and the snow, and he, and the one light, had absolute possession of the dreary scene. In the distance before him, lay the place where he had struck the worse than useless blows that mocked him with Lizzie's presence there as Eugene's wife. In the distance behind him, lay the place where the children with pointing arms had seemed to devote him to the demons in crying out his name. Within there, where the light was, was the man who as to both distances could give him up to ruin. To these limits had his world shrunk.

He mended his pace, keeping his eyes upon the light with a strange intensity, as if he were taking aim at it. When he approached it so nearly as that it parted into rays, they seemed to fasten themselves to him and draw him on. When he struck the door with his hand, his foot followed so quickly on his hand, that he was in the room before he was bidden to enter.

The light was the joint product of a fire and a candle.

Between the two, with his feet on the iron fender, sat Riderhood, pipe in mouth.

He looked up with a surly nod when his visitor came in. His visitor looked down with a surly nod. His outer clothing removed, the visitor then took a seat on the opposite side of the fire.

'Not a smoker, I think?' said Riderhood, pushing a bottle to him across the table.

'No.'

They both lapsed into silence, with their eyes upon the fire.

'You don't need to be told I am here,' said Bradley at length. 'Who is to begin?'

'I'll begin,' said Riderhood, 'when I've smoked this here pipe out.'

He finished it with great deliberation, knocked out the ashes on the hob, and put it by.

'I'll begin,' he then repeated, 'Bradley Headstone, Master, if you wish it.'

'Wish it? I wish to know what you want with me.'

'And so you shall.' Riderhood had looked hard at his hands and his pockets, apparently as a precautionary measure lest he should have any weapon about him. But, he now leaned forward, turning the collar of his waistcoat with an inquisitive finger, and asked, 'Why, where's your watch?'

'I have left it behind.'

'I want it. But it can be fetched. I've took a fancy to it.'

Bradley answered with a contemptuous laugh.

'I want it,' repeated Riderhood, in a louder voice, 'and I mean to have it.'

'That is what you want of me, is it?'

'No,' said Riderhood, still louder; 'it's on'y part of what I want of you. I want money of you.'

'Anything else?'

'Everythink else!' roared Riderhood, in a very loud and furious way. 'Answer me like that, and I won't talk to you at all.'

Bradley looked at him.

'Don't so much as look at me like that, or I won't talk to you at all,' vociferated Riderhood. 'But, instead of talking, I'll bring my hand down upon you with all its weight,' heavily smiting the table with great force, 'and smash you!'

'Go on,' said Bradley, after moistening his lips.

'O! I'm a going on. Don't you fear but I'll go on full-fast enough for you, and fur enough for you, without your telling.

Look here, Bradley Headstone, Master. You might have split the T'other governor to chips and wedges, without my caring, except that I might have come upon you for a glass or so now and then. Else why have to do with you at all? But when you copied my clothes, and when you copied my neckhankercher, and when you shook blood upon me after you had done the trick, you did wot I'll be paid for and paid heavily for. If it come to be throw'd upon you, you was to be ready to throw it upon me, was you? Where else but in Plashwater Weir Mill Lock was there a man dressed according as described? Where else but in Plashwater Weir Mill Lock was there a man as had had words with him coming through in his boat? Look at the Lock-keeper in Plashwater Weir Mill Lock, in them same answering clothes and with that same answering red neckhankercher, and see whether his clothes happens to be bloody or not. Yes, they do happen to be bloody. Ah, you sly devil!'

Bradley, very white, sat looking at him in silence.

'But two could play at your game,' said Riderhood, snapping his fingers at him half a dozen times, 'and I played it long ago; long afore you tried your clumsy hand at it; in days when you hadn't begun croaking your lecters or what not in your school. I know to a figure how you done it. Where you stole away, I could steal away arter you, and do it knowinger than you. I know how you come away from London in your own clothes, and where you changed your clothes, and hid your clothes. I see you with my own eyes take your own clothes from their hiding-place among them felled trees, and take a dip in the river to account for your dressing yourself, to any one as might come by. I see you rise up Bradley Headstone, Master, where you sat down Bargeman. I see you pitch your Bargeman's bundle into the river. I hooked your Bargeman's bundle out of the river. I've got your Bargeman's clothes, tore this way and that way with the scuffle, stained green with the grass, and spattered all over with what bust from the blows. I've got them, and I've got you. I don't care a curse for the T'other governor, alive or dead, but I care a many curses for my own self. And as you laid your plots agin me and was a sly devil agin me, I'll be paid for it—I'll be paid for it—I'll be paid for it—till I've drained you dry!'

Bradley looked at the fire, with a working face, and was silent for a while. At last he said, with what seemed an inconsistent composure of voice and feature:

'You can't get blood out of a stone, Riderhood.'

'I can get money out of a schoolmaster though.'

'You can't get out of me what is not in me. You can't wrest from me what I have not got. Mine is but a poor calling. You have had more than two guineas from me, already. Do you know how long it has taken me (allowing for a long and arduous training) to earn such a sum?'

'I don't know, nor I don't care. Yours is a 'spectable calling. To save your 'spectability, it's worth your while to pawn every article of clothes you've got, sell every stick in your house, and beg and borrow every penny you can get trusted with. When you've done that and handed over, I'll leave you. Not afore.'

'How do you mean, you'll leave me?'

'I mean as I'll keep you company, wherever you go, when you go away from here. Let the Lock take care of itself. I'll take care of you, once I've got you.'

Bradley again looked at the fire. Eyeing him aside, Riderhood took up his pipe, refilled it, lighted it, and sat smoking. Bradley leaned his elbows on his knees, and his head upon his hands, and looked at the fire with a most intent abstraction.

'Riderhood,' he said, raising himself in his chair, after a long silence, and drawing out his purse and putting it on the table. 'Say I part with this, which is all the money I have; say I let you have my watch; say that every quarter, when I draw my salary, I pay you a certain portion of it.'

'Say nothink of the sort,' retorted Riderhood, shaking his head as he smoked. 'You've got away once, and I won't run the chance agin. I've had trouble enough to find you, and shouldn't have found you, if I hadn't seen you slipping along the street overnight, and watched you till you was safe housed. I'll have one settlement with you for good and all.'

'Riderhood, I am a man who has lived a retired life. I have no resources beyond myself. I have absolutely no friends.'

'That's a lie,' said Riderhood. 'You've got one friend as I knows of; one as is good for a Savings-Bank book, or I'm a blue monkey!'

Bradley's face darkened, and his hand slowly closed on the purse and drew it back, as he sat listening for what the other should go on to say.

'I went into the wrong shop, fust, last Thursday,' said Riderhood. 'Found myself among the young ladies, by George! Over the young ladies, I see a Missis. That Missis is sweet enough upon you, Master, to sell herself up, slap, to get you out of trouble. Make her do it then.'

Bradley stared at him so very suddenly that Riderhood, not quite knowing how to take it, affected to be occupied with the encircling smoke from his pipe; fanning it away with his hand, and blowing it off.

'You spoke to the mistress, did you?' inquired Bradley, with that former composure of voice and feature that seemed inconsistent, and with averted eyes.

'Poof! Yes,' said Riderhood, withdrawing his attention from the smoke. 'I spoke to her. I didn't say much to her. She was put in a fluster by my dropping in among the young ladies (I never did set up for a lady's man), and she took me into her parlour to hope as there was nothink wrong. I tells her, "O no, nothink wrong. The master's my wery good friend." But I see how the land laid, and that she was comfortable off.'

Bradley put the purse in his pocket, grasped his left wrist with his right hand, and sat rigidly contemplating the fire.

'She couldn't live more handy to you than she does,' said Riderhood, 'and when I goes home with you (as of course I am a going), I recommend you to clean her out without loss of time. You can marry her, arter you and me have come to a settlement. She's nice-looking, and I know you can't be keeping company with no one else, having been so lately disapinted in another quarter.'

Not one other word did Bradley utter all that night. Not once did he change his attitude, or loosen his hold upon his wrist. Rigid before the fire, as if it were a charmed flame that was turning him old, he sat, with the dark lines deepening in his face, its stare becoming more and more haggard, its surface turning whiter and whiter as if it were being overspread with ashes, and the very texture and colour of his hair degenerating.

Not until the late daylight made the window transparent, did this decaying statue move. Then it slowly arose, and sat in the window looking out.

Riderhood had kept his chair all night. In the earlier part of the night he had muttered twice or thrice that it was bitter cold; or that the fire burnt fast, when he got up to mend it; but, as he could elicit from his companion neither sound nor movement, he had afterwards held his peace. He was making some disorderly preparations for coffee, when Bradley came from the window and put on his outer coat and hat.

'Hadn't us better have a bit o' breakfast afore we start?' said Riderhood. 'It ain't good to freeze a empty stomach, Master.'

Without a sign to show that he heard, Bradley walked out of

the Lock House. Catching up from the table a piece of bread, and taking his Bargeman's bundle under his arm, Riderhood immediately followed him. Bradley turned towards London. Riderhood caught him up, and walked at his side.

The two men trudged on, side by side, in silence, full three miles. Suddenly, Bradley turned to retrace his course. Instantly, Riderhood turned likewise, and they went back side by side.

Bradley re-entered the Lock House. So did Riderhood. Bradley sat down in the window. Riderhood warmed himself at the fire. After an hour or more, Bradley abruptly got up again, and again went out, but this time turned the other way. Riderhood was close after him, caught him up in a few paces, and walked at his side.

This time, as before, when he found his attendant not to be shaken off, Bradley suddenly turned back. This time, as before, Riderhood turned back along with him. But, not this time, as before, did they go into the Lock House, for Bradley came to a stand on the snow-covered turf by the Lock, looking up the river and down the river. Navigation was impeded by the frost, and the scene was a mere white and yellow desert.

'Come, come, Master,' urged Riderhood, at his side. 'This is a dry game. And where's the good of it? You can't get rid of me, except by coming to a settlement. I am a going along with you wherever you go.'

Without a word of reply, Bradley passed quickly from him over the wooden bridge on the lock gates. 'Why, there's even less sense in this move than t'other,' said Riderhood, following. 'The Weir's there, and you'll have to come back, you know.'

Without taking the least notice, Bradley leaned his body against a post, in a resting attitude, and there rested with his eyes cast down. 'Being brought here,' said Riderhood, gruffly, 'I'll turn it to some use by changing my gates.' With a rattle and a rush of water, he then swung-to the lock gates that were standing open, before opening the others. So, both sets of gates were, for the moment, closed.

'You'd better by far be reasonable, Bradley Headstone, Master,' said Riderhood, passing him, 'or I'll drain you all the dryer for it, when we do settle.—Ah! Would you!'

Bradley had caught him round the body. He seemed to be girdled with an iron ring. They were on the brink of the Lock, about midway between the two sets of gates.

'Let go!' said Riderhood, 'or I'll get my knife out and slash you wherever I can cut you. Let go!'

Bradley was drawing to the Lock-edge. Riderhood was drawing away from it. It was a strong grapple, and a fierce struggle, arm and leg. Bradley got him round, with his back to the Lock, and still worked him backward.

'Let go!' said Riderhood. 'Stop! What are you trying at? You can't drown Me. Ain't I told you that the man as has come through drowning can never be drowned? I can't be drowned.'

'I can be!' returned Bradley, in a desperate, clenched voice. 'I am resolved to be. I'll hold you living, and I'll hold you dead. Come down!'

Riderhood went over into the smooth pit, backward, and Bradley Headstone upon him. When the two were found, lying under the ooze and scum behind one of the rotting gates, Riderhood's hold had relaxed, probably in falling, and his eyes were staring upward. But, he was girdled still with Bradley's iron ring, and the rivets of the iron ring held tight.

Chapter 16
Persons and Things in General

MR AND MRS JOHN HARMON'S first delightful occupation was, to set all matters right that had strayed in any way wrong, or that might, could, would, or should, have strayed in any way wrong, while their name was in abeyance. In tracing out affairs for which John's fictitious death was to be considered in any way responsible, they used a very broad and free construction; regarding, for instance, the dolls' dressmaker as having a claim on their protection, because of her association with Mrs Eugene Wrayburn, and because of Mrs Eugene's old association, in her turn, with the dark side of the story. It followed that the old man, Riah, as a good and serviceable friend to both, was not to be disclaimed. Nor even Mr Inspector, as having been trepanned into an industrious hunt on a false scent. It may be remarked, in connexion with that worthy officer, that a rumor shortly afterwards pervaded the Force, to the effect that he had confided to Miss Abbey Potterson, over a jug of mellow flip in the bar of the Six

Jolly Fellowship Porters, that he 'didn't stand to lose a farthing' through Mr Harmon's coming to life, but was quite as well satisfied as if that gentleman had been barbarously murdered, and he (Mr Inspector) had pocketed the government reward.

In all their arrangements of such nature, Mr and Mrs John Harmon derived much assistance from their eminent solicitor, Mr Mortimer Lightwood; who laid about him professionally with such unwonted despatch and intention, that a piece of work was vigorously pursued as soon as cut out; whereby Young Blight was acted on as by that transatlantic dram which is poetically named An Eye-Opener, and found himself staring at real clients instead of out of window. The accessibility of Riah proving very useful as to a few hints towards the disentanglement of Eugene's affairs, Lightwood applied himself with infinite zest to attacking and harassing Mr Fledgeby: who, discovering himself in danger of being blown into the air by certain explosive transactions in which he had been engaged, and having been sufficiently flayed under his beating, came to a parley and asked for quarter. The harmless Twemlow profited by the conditions entered into, though he little thought it. Mr Riah unaccountably melted; waited in person on him over the stable yard in Duke Street, St James's, no longer ravening but mild, to inform him that payment of interest as heretofore, but henceforth at Mr Lightwood's offices, would appease his Jewish rancour; and departed with the secret that Mr John Harmon had advanced the money and become the creditor. Thus, was the sublime Snigsworth's wrath averted, and thus did he snort no larger amount of moral grandeur at the Corinthian column in the print over the fireplace, than was normally in his (and the British) constitution.

Mrs Wilfer's first visit to the Mendicant's bride at the new abode of Mendicancy, was a grand event. Pa had been sent for into the City, on the very day of taking possession, and had been stunned with astonishment, and brought-to, and led about the house by one ear, to behold its various treasures, and had been enraptured and enchanted. Pa had also been appointed Secretary, and had been enjoined to give instant notice of resignation to Chicksey, Veneering, and Stobbles, for ever and ever. But Ma came later, and came, as was her due, in state.

The carriage was sent for Ma, who entered it with a bearing worthy of the occasion, accompanied, rather than supported, by Miss Lavinia, who altogether declined to recognize the maternal majesty. Mr. George Sampson meekly followed. He was received in the vehicle, by Mrs Wilfer, as if admitted to the honour of assisting at a funeral in the family, and she then issued the order, 'Onward!' to the Mendicant's menial.

'I wish to goodness, Ma,' said Lavvy, throwing herself back among the cushions, with her arms crossed, 'that you'd loll a little.'

'How!' repeated Mrs Wilfer. 'Loll!'

'Yes, Ma.'

'I hope,' said the impressive lady, 'I am incapable of it.'

'I am sure you look so, Ma. But why one should go out to dine with one's own daughter or sister, as if one's under-petticoat was a blackboard, I do *not* understand.'

'Neither do I understand,' retorted Mrs Wilfer, with deep scorn, 'how a young lady can mention the garment in the name of which you have indulged. I blush for you.'

'Thank you, Ma,' said Lavvy, yawning, 'but I can do it for myself, I am obliged to you, when there's any occasion.'

Here, Mr Sampson, with the view of establishing harmony, which he never under any circumstances succeeded in doing, said with an agreeable smile: 'After all, you know, ma'am, we know it's there.' And immediately felt that he had committed himself.

'We know it's there!' said Mrs Wilfer, glaring.

'Really, George,' remonstrated Miss Livinia, 'I must say that I don't understand your allusions, and that I think you might be more delicate and less personal.'

'Go it!' cried Mr Sampson, becoming, on the shortest notice, a prey to despair. 'Oh yes! Go it, Miss Lavinia Wilfer!'

'What you may mean, George Sampson, by your omnibus-driving expressions, I cannot pretend to imagine. Neither,' said Miss Lavinia, 'Mr George Sampson, do I wish to imagine. It is enough for me to know in my own heart that I am not going to—' having imprudently got into a sentence without providing a way out of it, Miss Lavinia was constrained to close with 'going to it'. A weak conclusion which, however, derived some appearance of strength from disdain.

'Oh yes!' cried Mr Sampson, with bitterness. 'Thus it ever is. I never—'

'If you mean to say,' Miss Lavvy cut him short, 'that you never brought up a young gazelle, you may save yourself the trouble, because nobody in this carriage supposes that you ever did. We know you better.' (As if this were a home-thrust.)

'Lavinia,' returned Mr Sampson, in a dismal vein, 'I did not mean to say so. What I did mean to say, was, that I never expected to retain my favoured place in this family, after Fortune shed her beams upon it. Why do you take me,' said Mr Sampson, 'to the glittering halls with which I can never compete, and then taunt me with my moderate salary? Is it generous? Is it kind?'

The stately lady, Mrs Wilfer, perceiving her opportunity of delivering a few remarks from the throne, here took up the altercation.

'Mr Sampson,' she began, 'I cannot permit you to misrepresent the intentions of a child of mine.'

'Let him alone, Ma,' Miss Lavvy interposed with haughtiness. 'It is indifferent to me what he says or does.'

'Nay, Lavinia,' quoth Mrs Wilfer, 'this touches the blood of the family. If Mr George Sampson attributes, even to my youngest daughter—'

('I don't see why you should use the word "even", Ma,' Miss Lavvy interposed, 'because I am quite as important as any of the others.')

'Peace!' said Mrs Wilfer, solemnly. 'I repeat, if Mr George Sampson attributes, to my youngest daughter, grovelling motives, he attributes them equally to the mother of my youngest daughter. That mother repudiates them, and demands of Mr George Sampson, as a youth of honour, what he *would* have? I may be mistaken—nothing is more likely—but Mr George Sampson,' proceeded Mrs Wilfer, majestically waving her gloves, 'appears to me to be seated in a first-class equipage. Mr George Sampson appears to me to be on his way, by his own admission, to a residence that may be termed Palatial. Mr George Sampson appears to me to be invited to participate in the—shall I say the—Elevation which has descended on the family with which he is ambitious, shall I say to Mingle? Whence, then, this tone on Mr Sampson's part?'

'It is only, ma'am,' Mr Sampson explained, in exceedingly low spirits, 'because, in a pecuniary sense, I am painfully conscious of my unworthiness. Lavinia is now highly connected. Can I hope that she will still remain the same Lavinia as of old? And is it not pardonable if I feel sensitive, when I see a disposition on her part to take me up short?'

'If you are not satisfied with your position, sir,' observed Miss Lavinia, with much politeness, 'we can set you down at any turning you may please to indicate to my sister's coachman.'

'Dearest Lavinia,' urged Mr Sampson, pathetically, 'I adore you.'

'Then if you can't do it in a more agreeable manner,' returned the young lady, 'I wish you wouldn't.'

'I also,' pursued Mr Sampson, 'respect you, ma'am, to an extent which must ever be below your merits, I am well aware, but still up to an uncommon mark. Bear with a wretch, Lavinia, bear with a wretch, ma'am, who feels the noble sacrifices you make for him, but is goaded almost to madness,' Mr Sampson slapped his forehead, 'when he thinks of competing with the rich and influential.'

'When you have to compete with the rich and influential, it will probably be mentioned to you,' said Miss Lavvy, 'in good time. At least, it will if the case is *my* case.'

Mr Sampson immediately expressed his fervent opinion that this was 'more than human', and was brought upon his knees at Miss Lavinia's feet.

It was the crowning addition indispensable to the full enjoyment of both mother and daughter, to bear Mr Sampson, a grateful captive, into the glittering halls he had mentioned, and to parade him through the same, at once a living witness of their glory, and a bright instance of their condescension. Ascending the staircase, Miss Lavinia permitted him to walk at her side, with the air of saying: 'Notwithstanding all these surroundings, I am yours as yet, George. How long it may last is another question, but I am yours as yet.' She also benignantly intimated to him, aloud, the nature of the objects upon which he looked, and to which he was unaccustomed: as, 'Exotics, George,' 'An aviary, George,' 'An ormolu clock, George,' and the like. While, through the whole of the decorations, Mrs Wilfer led the way with the bearing of a Savage Chief, who would feel himself compromised by manifesting the slightest token of surprise or admiration.

Indeed, the bearing of this impressive woman, throughout the day, was a pattern to all impressive women under similar circumstances. She renewed the acquaintance of Mr and Mrs Boffin, as if Mr and Mrs Boffin had said of her what she had said of them, and as if Time alone could quite wear her injury out. She regarded every servant who approached her, as her sworn enemy, expressly intending to offer her affronts with the dishes, and to pour forth outrages on her moral feelings from the decanters. She sat erect at table, on the right hand of her son-in-law, as half suspecting poison in the viands, and as bearing up with native force of character against other deadly ambushes. Her carriage towards Bella was as a carriage towards a young lady of good position, whom she had met in society a few years ago. Even when, slightly thawing under the influence of sparkling champagne, she related to her son-in-law some passages of domestic interest concerning her papa, she infused into the narrative such Arctic suggestions of her having been an unappreciated blessing to mankind, since her papa's days, and also of that gentleman's having been a frosty impersonation of a frosty race, as struck cold to the very soles of the feet of the hearers. The Inexhaustible being produced, staring, and evidently intending a weak and washy smile shortly, no sooner beheld her, than it was striken spasmodic and inconsolable. When she took her leave at last, it would have been hard to say whether it was with the air of going to the scaffold herself, or of leaving the inmates of the house for immediate execution. Yet, John Harmon enjoyed it all merrily, and told his wife, when he and she were alone, that her natural ways had never seemed so dearly natural as beside this foil, and that although he did not dispute her being her father's daughter, he should ever remain stedfast in the faith that she could not be her mother's.

This visit was, as has been said, a grand event. Another event, not grand but deemed in the house a special one, occurred at about the same period; and this was, the first interview between Mr Sloppy and Miss Wren.

The dolls' dressmaker, being at work for the Inexhaustible upon a full-dressed doll some two sizes larger than that young person, Mr Sloppy undertook to call for it, and did so.

'Come in, sir,' said Miss Wren, who was working at her bench. 'And who may you be?'

Mr Sloppy introduced himself by name and buttons.

'Oh indeed!' cried Jenny. 'Ah! I have been looking forward to knowing you. I heard of your distinguishing yourself.'

'Did you, Miss?' grinned Sloppy. 'I am sure I am glad to hear it, but I don't know how.'

'Pitching somebody into a mud-cart,' said Miss Wren.

'Oh! That way!' cried Sloppy. 'Yes, Miss.' And threw back his head and laughed.

'Bless us!' exclaimed Miss Wren, with a start. 'Don't open your mouth as wide as that, young man, or it'll catch so, and not shut again some day.'

Mr Sloppy opened it, if possible, wider, and kept it open until his laugh was out.

'Why, you're like the giant,' said Miss Wren, 'when he

came home in the land of Beanstalk, and wanted Jack for supper.'

'Was he good-looking, Miss?' asked Sloppy.

'No,' said Miss Wren. 'Ugly.'

Her visitor glanced round the room—which had many comforts in it now, that had not been in it before—and said: 'This is a pretty place, Miss.'

'Glad you think so, sir,' returned Miss Wren. 'And what do you think of Me?'

The honesty of Mr Sloppy being severely taxed by the question, he twisted a button, grinned, and faltered.

'Out with it!' said Miss Wren, with an arch look. 'Don't you think me a queer little comicality?' In shaking her head at him after asking the question, she shook her hair down.

'Oh!' cried Sloppy, in a burst of admiration. 'What a lot, and what a colour!'

Miss Wren, with her usual expressive hitch, went on with her work. But, left her hair as it was; not displeased by the effect it had made.

'You don't live here alone; do you, Miss?' asked Sloppy.

'No,' said Miss Wren, with a chop. 'Live here with my fairy godmother.'

'With;' Mr Sloppy couldn't make it out; 'with who did you say, Miss?'

'Well!' replied Miss Wren, more seriously. 'With my second father. Or with my first, for that matter.' And she shook her head, and drew a sigh. 'If you had known a poor child I used to have here,' she added, 'you'd have understood me. But you didn't, and you can't. All the better!'

'You must have been taught a long time,' said Sloppy, glancing at the array of dolls in hand, 'before you came to work so neatly, Miss, and with such a pretty taste.'

'Never was taught a stitch, young man!' returned the dressmaker, tossing her head. 'Just gobbled and gobbled, till I found out how to do it. Badly enough at first, but better now.'

'And here have I,' said Sloppy, in something of a self-reproachful tone, 'been a learning and a learning, and here has Mr Boffin been a paying and a paying, ever so long!'

'I have heard what your trade is,' observed Miss Wren; 'it's cabinet-making.'

Mr Sloppy nodded. 'Now that the Mounds is done with, it is. I'll tell you what, Miss. I should like to make you something.'

'Much obliged. But what?'

'I could make you,' said Sloppy, surveying the room, 'I could make you a handy set of nests to lay the dolls in. Or I could make you a handy little set of drawers, to keep your silks and threads and scraps in. Or I could turn you a rare handle for that crutch-stick, if it belongs to him you call your father.'

'It belongs to me,' returned the little creature, with a quick flush of her face and neck. 'I am lame.'

Poor Sloppy flushed too, for there was an instinctive delicacy behind his buttons, and his own hand had struck it. He said, perhaps, the best thing in the way of amends that could be said. 'I am very glad it's yours, because I'd rather ornament it for you than for any one else. Please may I look at it?'

Miss Wren was in the act of handing it to him over her bench, when she paused. 'But you had better see me use it,' she said, sharply. 'This is the way. Hoppetty, Kicketty, Pep-peg-peg. Not pretty; is it?'

'It seems to me that you hardly want it at all,' said Sloppy.

The little dressmaker sat down again, and gave it into his hand, saying, with that better look upon her, and with a smile: 'Thank you!'

'And as concerning the nests and the drawers,' said Sloppy, after measuring the handle on his sleeve, and softly standing the stick aside against the wall, 'why, it would be a real pleasure to me. I've heerd tell that you can sing most beautiful; and I should be better paid with a song than with any money, for I always loved the likes of that, and often giv' Mrs Higden and Johnny a comic song myself, with "Spoken" in it. Though that's not your sort, I'll wager.'

'You are a very kind young man,' returned the dressmaker; 'a really kind young man. I accept your offer.—I suppose He won't mind,' she added as an afterthought, shrugging her shoulders; 'and if he does, he may!'

'Meaning him that you call your father, Miss,' asked Sloppy.

'No, no,' replied Miss Wren. 'Him, Him, Him!'

'Him, him, him?' repeated Sloppy; staring about, as if for Him.

'Him who is coming to court and marry me,' returned Miss Wren. 'Dear me, how slow you are!'

'Oh! *Him*!' said Sloppy. And seemed to turn thoughtful and a little troubled. 'I never thought of him. When is he coming, Miss?'

'What a question!' cried Miss Wren. 'How should *I* know!'

'Where is he coming from, Miss?'

'Why, good gracious, how can *I* tell! He is coming from somewhere or other, I suppose, and he is coming some day or other, I suppose. *I* don't know any more about him, at present.'

This tickled Mr Sloppy as an extraordinarily good joke, and he threw back his head and laughed with measureless enjoyment. At the sight of him laughing in that absurd way, the dolls' dressmaker laughed very heartily indeed. So they both laughed, till they were tired.

'There, there, there!' said Miss Wren. 'For goodness' sake, stop, Giant, or I shall be swallowed up alive, before I know it. And to this minute you haven't said what you've come for.'

'I have come for little Miss Harmonses doll,' said Sloppy.

'I thought as much,' remarked Miss Wren, 'and here is little Miss Harmonses doll waiting for you. She's folded up in silver paper, you see, as if she was wrapped from head to foot in new Bank notes. Take care of her, and there's my hand, and thank you again.'

'I'll take more care of her than if she was a gold image,' said Sloppy, 'and there's both *my* hands, Miss, and I'll soon come back again.'

But, the greatest event of all, in the new life of Mr and Mrs John Harmon, was a visit from Mr and Mrs Eugene Wrayburn. Sadly wan and worn was the once gallant Eugene, and walked resting on his wife's arm, and leaning heavily upon a stick. But, he was daily growing stronger and better, and it was declared by the medical attendants that he might not be much disfigured by-and-by. It was a grand event, indeed, when Mr and Mrs Eugene Wraybrun came to stay at Mr and Mrs John Harmon's house: where, by the way, Mr and Mrs Boffin (exquisitely happy, and daily cruising about, to look at shops,) were likewise staying indefinitely.

To Mr Eugene Wrayburn, in confidence, did Mrs John Harmon impart what she had known of the state of his wife's affections, in his reckless time. And to Mrs John Harmon, in confidence, did Mr Eugene Wrayburn impart that, please God, she should see how his wife had changed him!

'I make no protestations,' said Eugene; '—who does, who means them!—I have made a resolution.'

'But would you believe, Bella,' interposed his wife, coming to resume her nurse's place at his side, for he never got on well without her: 'that on our wedding day he told me he almost thought the best thing he could do, was to die?'

'As I didn't do it, Lizzie,' said Eugene, 'I'll do that better thing you suggested—for your sake.'

That same afternoon, Eugene lying on his couch in his own room upstairs, Lightwood came to chat with him, while Bella took his wife out for a ride. 'Nothing short of force will make her go,' Eugene had said; so, Bella had playfully forced her.

'Dear old fellow,' Eugene began with Lightwood, reaching up his hand, 'you couldn't have come at a better time, for my mind is full, and I want to empty it. First, of my present, before I touch upon my future. M. R. F., who is a much younger cavalier than I, and a professed admirer of beauty, was so affable as to remark the other day (he paid us a visit of two days up the river there, and much objected to the accommodation of the hotel), that Lizzie ought to have her portrait painted. Which, coming from M. R. F., may be considered equivalent to a melodramatic blessing.'

'You are getting well,' said Mortimer, with a smile.

'Really,' said Eugene, 'I mean it. When M. R. F. said that, and followed it up by rolling the claret (for which he called, and I paid), in his mouth, and saying, "My dear son, why do you drink this trash?" it was tantamount—in him—to a paternal benediction on our union, accompanied with a gush of tears. The coolness of M. R. F. is not to be measured by ordinary standards.'

'True enough,' said Lightwood.

'That's all,' pursued Eugene, 'that I shall ever hear from M. R. F. on the subject, and he will continue to saunter through the world with his hat on one side. My marriage being thus solemnly recognized at the family altar, I have no further trouble on that score. Next, you really have done wonders for me, Mortimer, in easing my money-perplexities, and with such a guardian and steward beside me, as the preserver of my life (I am hardly strong yet, you see, for I am not man enough to refer to her without a trembling voice—she is so inexpressibly dear to me, Mortimer!), the little that I can call my own will be more than it ever has been. It need be more, for you know what it always has been in my hands. Nothing.'

'Worse than nothing, I fancy, Eugene. My own small income (I devoutly wish that my grandfather had left it to the Ocean rather than to me!) has been an effective Something, in the way of preventing me from turning to at Anything. And I think yours has been much the same.'

'There spake the voice of wisdom,' said Eugene. 'We are shepherds both. In turning to at last, we turn to in earnest. Let us

say no more of that, for a few years to come. Now, I have had
an idea, Mortimer, of taking myself and my wife to one of the
colonies, and working at my vocation there.'

'I should be lost without you, Eugene; but you may be
right.'

'No,' said Eugene, emphatically. 'Not right. Wrong!'

He said it with such a lively—almost angry—flash, that
Mortimer showed himself greatly surprised.

'You think this thumped head of mine is excited?' Eugene
went on, with a high look; 'not so, believe me. I can say to you
of the healthful music of my pulse what Hamlet said of his. My
blood is up, but wholesomely up, when I think of it. Tell me!
Shall I turn coward to Lizzie, and sneak away with her, as if I
were ashamed of her! Where would your friend's part in this
world be, Mortimer, if she had turned coward to him, and on
immeasurably better occasion?'

'Honourable and stanch,' said Lightwood. 'And yet,
Eugene—'

'And yet what, Mortimer?'

'And yet, are you sure that you might not feel (for her sake,
I say for her sake) any slight coldness towards her on the part
of—Society?'

'O! You and I may well stumble at the word,' returned
Eugene, laughing. 'Do we mean our Tippins?'

'Perhaps we do,' said Mortimer, laughing also.

'Faith, we DO!' returned Eugene, with great animation.
'We may hide behind the bush and beat about it, but we DO!
Now, my wife is something nearer to my heart, Mortimer, than
Tippins is, and I owe her a little more than I owe to Tippins, and
I am rather prouder of her than I ever was of Tippins. Therefore,
I will fight it out to the last gasp, with her and for her, here, in
the open field. When I hide her, or strike for her, faint-heartedly,
in a hole or a corner, do you whom I love next best upon earth,
tell me what I shall most righteously deserve to be told:—that she
would have done well to turn me over with her foot that night
when I lay bleeding to death, and spat in my dastard face.'

The glow that shone upon him as he spoke the words, so
irradiated his features that he looked, for the time, as though he
had never been mutilated. His friend responded as Eugene would
have had him respond, and they discoursed of the future until
Lizzie came back. After resuming her place at his side, and
tenderly touching his hands and his head, she said:

'Eugene, dear, you made me go out, but I ought to have

stayed with you. You are more flushed than you have been for many days. What have you been doing?'

'Nothing,' replied Eugene, 'but looking forward to your coming back.'

'And talking to Mr Lightwood,' said Lizzie, turning to him with a smile. 'But it cannot have been Society that disturbed you.'

'Faith, my dear love!' retorted Eugene, in his old airy manner, as he laughed and kissed her, 'I rather think it *was* Society though!'

The word ran so much in Mortimer Lightwood's thoughts as he went home to the Temple that night, that he resolved to take a look at Society, which he had not seen for a considerable period.

Chapter 17
The Voice of Society

BEHOVES Mortimer Lightwood, therefore, to answer a dinner card from Mr and Mrs Veneering requesting the honour, and to signify that Mr Mortimer Lightwood will be happy to have the other honour. The Veneerings have been, as usual, indefatigably dealing dinner cards to Society, and whoever desires to take a hand had best be quick about it, for it is written in the Books of the Insolvent Fates that Veneering shall make a resounding smash next week. Yes. Having found out the clue to that great mystery how people can contrive to live beyond their means, and having over-jobbed his jobberies as legislator deputed to the Universe by the pure electors of Pocket-Breaches, it shall come to pass next week that Veneering will accept the Chiltern Hundreds, that the legal gentleman in Britannia's confidence will again accept the Pocket-Breaches Thousands, and that the Veneerings will retire to Calais, there to live on Mrs Veneering's diamonds (in which Mr Veneering, as a good husband, has from time to time invested considerable sums), and to relate to Neptune and others, how that, before Veneering retired from Parliament, the House of Commons was composed of himself and the six hundred and fifty-seven dearest and oldest friends he had in the world. It shall likewise come to pass, at as nearly as possible the same period, that Society will discover that it always did despise Veneering, and distrust Veneering, and that when it went to Veneering's to dinner it always had misgivings—though very secretly at the time, it would seem, and in a perfectly private and confidential manner.

The next week's books of the Insolvent Fates, however, being not yet opened, there is the usual rush to the Veneerings, of the people who go to their house to dine with one another and not with them. There is Lady Tippins. There are Podsnap the Great, and Mrs Podsnap. There is Twemlow. There are Buffer, Boots, and Brewer. There is the Contractor, who is Providence to five hundred thousand men. There is the Chairman, travelling three thousand miles per week. There is the brilliant genius who turned the shares into that remarkably exact sum of three hundred and seventy five thousand pounds, no shillings, and nopence.

To whom, added Mortimer Lightwood, coming in among them with a reassumption of his old languid air, founded on Eugene, and belonging to the days when he told the story of the man from Somewhere.

That fresh fairy, Tippins, all but screams at sight of her false swain. She summons the deserter to her with her fan; but the deserter, predetermined not to come, talks Britain with Podsnap. Podsnap always talks Britain, and talks as if he were a sort of Private Watchman employed, in the British interests, against the rest of the world. 'We know what Russia means, sir,' says Podsnap; 'we know what France wants; we see what America is up to; but we know what England is. That's enough for us.'

However, when dinner is served, and Lightwood drops into his old place over against Lady Tippins, she can be fended off no longer. 'Long banished Robinson Crusoe,' says the charmer, exchanging salutations, 'how did you leave the Island?'

'Thank you,' says Lightwood. 'It made no complaint of being in pain anywhere.'

'Say, how did you leave the savages?' asks Lady Tippins.

'They were becoming civilized when I left Juan Fernandez,' says Lightwood. 'At least they were eating one another, which looked like it.'

'Tormentor!' returns the dear young creature. 'You know what I mean, and you trifle with my impatience. Tell me something, immediately, about the married pair. You were at the wedding.'

'Was I, by-the-by?' Mortimer pretends, at great leisure, to consider. 'So I was!'

'How was the bride dressed? In rowing costume?'

Mortimer looks gloomy, and declines to answer.

'I hope she steered herself, skiffed herself, paddled herself, larboarded and starboarded herself, or whatever the technical term may be, to the ceremony?' proceeds the playful Tippins.

'However she got to it, she graced it,' says Mortimer.

Lady Tippins with a skittish little scream, attracts the general attention. 'Graced it! Take care of me if I faint, Veneering. He means to tell us, that a horrid female waterman is graceful!'

'Pardon me. I mean to tell you nothing, Lady Tippins,' replies Lightwood. And keeps his word by eating his dinner with a show of the utmost indifference.

'You shall not escape me in this way, you morose backwoodsman,' retorts Lady Tippins. 'You shall not evade the question, to screen your friend Eugene, who has made this exhibition of himself. The knowledge shall be brought home to you that such a ridiculous affair is condemned by the voice of Society. My dear Mrs Veneering, do let us resolve ourselves into a Committee of the whole House on the subject.'

Mrs Veneering, always charmed by this rattling sylph, cries: 'Oh yes! Do let us resolve ourselves into a Committee of the whole House! So delicious!' Veneering says, 'As many as are of that opinion, say Aye,—contrary, No—the Ayes have it.' But nobody takes the slightest notice of his joke.

'Now, I am Chairwoman of Committees!' cries Lady Tippins.

('What spirits she has!' exclaims Mrs Veneering; to whom likewise nobody attends.)

'And this,' pursues the sprightly one, 'is a Committee of the whole House to what-you-may-call-it—elicit, I suppose—the voice of Society. The question before the Committee is, whether a young man of very fair family, good appearance, and some talent, makes a fool or a wise man of himself in marrying a female waterman, turned factory girl.'

'Hardly so, I think,' the stubborn Mortimer strikes in. 'I take the question to be, whether such a man as you describe, Lady Tippins, does right or wrong in marrying a brave woman (I say nothing of her beauty), who has saved his life, with a wonderful energy and address; whom he knows to be virtuous, and possessed of remarkable qualities; whom he has long admired, and who is deeply attached to him.'

'But, excuse me,' says Podsnap, with his temper and

shirt-collar about equally rumpled; 'was this young woman ever a female waterman?'

'Never. But she sometimes rowed in a boat with her father, I believe.'

General sensation against the young woman. Brewer shakes his head. Boots shakes his head. Buffer shakes his head.

'And now, Mr Lightwood, was she ever,' pursues Podsnap, with his indignation rising high into those hair-brushes of his, 'a factory girl?'

'Never. But she had some employment in a paper mill, I believe.'

General sensation repeated. Brewer says, 'Oh dear!' Boots says, 'Oh dear!' Buffer says, 'Oh dear!' All, in a rumbling tone of protest.

'Then all *I* have to say is,' returns Podsnap, putting the thing away with his right arm, 'that my gorge rises against such a marriage—that it offends and disgusts me—that it makes me sick—and that I desire to know no more about it.'

('Now I wonder,' thinks Mortimer, amused, 'whether *you* are the Voice of Society!')

'Hear, hear, hear!' cries Lady Tippins. 'Your opinion of this *mésalliance,* honourable colleagues of the honourable member who has just sat down?'

Mrs Podsnap is of opinion that in these matters there should be an equality of station and fortune, and that a man accustomed to Society should look out for a woman accustomed to Society and capable of bearing her part in it with—an ease and elegance of carriage—that. Mrs Podsnap stops there, delicately intimating that every such man should look out for a fine woman as nearly resembling herself as he may hope to discover.

('Now I wonder,' thinks Mortimer, 'whether *you* are the Voice!')

Lady Tippins next canvasses the Contractor, of five hundred thousand power. It appears to this potentate, that what the man in question should have done, would have been, to buy the young woman a boat and a small annuity, and set her up for herself. These things are a question of beefsteaks and porter. You buy the young woman a boat. Very good. You buy her, at the same time, a small annuity. You speak of that annuity in pounds sterling, but it is in reality so many pounds of beefsteaks and so many pints of porter. On the one hand, the young woman has the boat. On the other hand, she consumes so many pounds of beefsteaks and so many pints of porter. Those beefsteaks and that porter are the fuel to that young woman's engine. She derives therefrom a certain amount of power to row the boat; that power will produce so much money; you add that to the small annuity; and thus you get at the young woman's income. That (it seems to the Contractor) is the way of looking at it.

The fair enslaver having fallen into one of her gentle sleeps during the last exposition, nobody likes to wake her. Fortunately, she comes awake of herself, and puts the question to the Wandering Chairman. The Wanderer can only speak of the case as if it were his own. If such a young woman as the young woman described, had saved his own life, he would have been very much obliged to her, wouldn't have married her, and would have got her a berth in an Electric Telegraph Office, where young women answer very well.

What does the Genius of the three hundred and seventy-five thousand pounds, no shillings, and nopence, think? He can't say what he thinks, without asking: Had the young woman any money?

'No,' says Lightwood, in an uncompromising voice; 'no money.'

'Madness and moonshine,' is then the compressed verdict of the Genius. 'A man may do anything lawful, for money. But for no money!—Bosh!'

What does Boots say?

Boots says he wouldn't have done it under twenty thousand pound.

What does Brewer say?

Brewer says what Boots says.

What does Buffer say?

Buffer says he knows a man who married a bathing-woman, and bolted.

Lady Tippins fancies she has collected the suffrages of the whole Committee (nobody dreaming of asking the Veneerings for their opinion), when, looking round the table through her eyeglass, she perceives Mr Twemlow with his hand to his forehead.

Good gracious! My Twemlow forgotten! My dearest! My own! What is his vote?

Twemlow has the air of being ill at ease, as he takes his hand from his forehead and replies.

'I am disposed to think,' says he, 'that this is a question of the feelings of a gentleman.'

'A gentleman can have no feelings who contracts such a marriage,' flushes Podsnap.

'Pardon me, sir,' says Twemlow, rather less mildly than usual, 'I don't agree with you. If this gentleman's feelings of gratitude, of respect, of admiration, and affection, induced him (as I presume they did) to marry this lady—'

'This lady!' echoes Podsnap.

'Sir,' returns Twemlow, with his wristbands bristling a little, '*you* repeat the word; *I* repeat the word. This lady. What else would you call her, if the gentleman were present?'

This being something in the nature of a poser for Podsnap, he merely waves it away with a speechless wave.

'I say,' resumes Twemlow, 'if such feelings on the part of this gentleman, induced this gentleman to marry this lady, I think he is the greater gentleman for the action, and makes her the greater lady. I beg to say, that when I use the word, gentleman, I use it in the sense in which the degree may be attained by any man. The feelings of a gentleman I hold sacred, and I confess I am not comfortable when they are made the subject of sport or general discussion.'

'I should like to know,' sneers Podsnap, 'whether your noble relation would be of your opinion.'

'Mr Podsnap,' retorts Twemlow, 'permit me. He might be, or he might not be. I cannot say. But, I could not allow even him to dictate to me on a point of great delicacy, on which I feel very strongly.'

Somehow, a canopy of wet blanket seems to descend upon the company, and Lady Tippins was never known to turn so very greedy or so very cross. Mortimer Lightwood alone brightens. He has been asking himself, as to every other member of the Committee in turn, 'I wonder whether you are the Voice!' But he does not ask himself the question after Twemlow has spoken, and he glances in Twemlow's direction as if he were grateful. When the company disperse—by which time Mr and Mrs Veneering have had quite as much as they want of the honour, and the guests have had quite as much as *they* want of the other honour—Mortimer sees Twemlow home, shakes hands with him cordially at parting, and fares to the Temple, gaily.

POSTSCRIPT

IN LIEU OF PREFACE

WHEN I devised this story, I foresaw the likelihood that a class of readers and commentators would suppose that I was at great pains to conceal exactly what I was at great pains to suggest: namely, that Mr John Harmon was not slain, and that Mr John Rokesmith was he. Pleasing myself with the idea that the supposition might in part arise out of some ingenuity in the story, and thinking it worth while, in the interests of art, to hint to an audience that an artist (of whatever denomination) may perhaps be trusted to know what he is about in his vocation, if they will concede him a little patience, I was not alarmed by the anticipation.

To keep for a long time unsuspected, yet always working itself out, another purpose originating in that leading incident, and turning it to a pleasant and useful account at last, was at once the most interesting and the most difficult part of my design. Its difficulty was much enhanced by the mode of publication; for, it would be very unreasonable to expect that many readers, pursuing a story in portions from month to month through nineteen months, will, until they have it before them complete, perceive the relations of its finer threads to the whole pattern which is always before the eyes of the story-weaver at his loom. Yet, that I hold the advantages of the mode of publication to outweigh its disadvantages, may be easily believed of one who revived it in the Pickwick Papers after long disuse, and has pursued it ever since.

There is sometimes an odd disposition in this country to dispute as improbable in fiction, what are the commonest experiences in fact. Therefore, I note here, though it may not be at all necessary, that there are hundreds of Will Cases (as they are called), far more remarkable than that fancied in this book; and that the stores of the Prerogative Office teem with instances of testators who have made, changed, contradicted, hidden, forgotten, left cancelled, and left uncancelled, each many more wills than were ever made by the elder Mr Harmon of Harmony Jail.

In my social experiences since Mrs Betty Higden came upon the scene and left it, I have found Circumlocutional champions disposed to be warm with me on the subject of my view of the Poor Law. My friend Mr Bounderby could never see any difference between leaving the Coketown 'hands' exactly as they were, and requiring them to be fed with turtle soup and venison out of gold spoons. Idiotic propositions of a parallel nature have been freely offered for my acceptance, and I have been called upon to admit that I would give Poor Law relief to anybody, anywhere, anyhow. Putting this nonsense aside, I have observed a suspicious tendency in the champions to divide into two parties; the one, contending that there are no deserving Poor who prefer death by slow starvation and bitter weather, to the mercies of some Relieving Officers and some Union Houses; the other, admitting that there are such Poor, but denying that they have any cause or reason for what they do. The records in our newspapers, the late exposure by THE LANCET, and the common sense and senses of common people, furnish too abundant evidence against both defences. But, that my view of the Poor Law may not be mistaken or misrepresented, I will state it. I believe there has been in England, since the days of the STUARTS, no law so often infamously administered, no law so often openly violated, no law habitually so ill-supervised. In the majority of the shameful cases of disease and death from destitution, that shock the Public and disgrace the country, the illegality is quite equal to the inhumanity—and known language could say no more of their lawlessness.

On Friday the Ninth of June in the present year, Mr and Mrs Boffin (in their manuscript dress of receiving Mr and Mrs Lammle at breakfast) were on the South Eastern Railway with me, in a terribly destructive accident. When I had done what I could to help others, I climbed back into my carriage—nearly turned over a viaduct, and caught aslant upon the turn—to extricate the worthy couple. They were much soiled, but otherwise unhurt. The same happy result attended Miss Bella Wilfer on her wedding day, and Mr Riderhood inspecting Bradley

Headstone's red neckerchief as he lay asleep. I remember with devout thankfulness that I can never be much nearer parting company with my readers for ever, than I was then, until there shall be written against my life, the two words with which I have this day closed this book:—THE END.

September 2nd, 1865.

Bantam Classics bring you the world's greatest literature— books that have stood the test of time. These beautifully designed books will be proud additions to your bookshelf. You'll want all these time-tested classics for your own reading pleasure.

Titles by the Brontës:

☐ 21140	JANE EYRE Charlotte Brontë	$1.95
☐ 21258	WUTHERING HEIGHTS Emily Brontë	$2.50

Titles by Charles Dickens:

☐ 21123	THE PICKWICK PAPERS	$4.95
☐ 21223	BLEAK HOUSE	$4.95
☐ 21265	NICHOLAS NICKLEBY	$4.95
☐ 21342	GREAT EXPECTATIONS	$2.95
☐ 21176	A TALE OF TWO CITIES	$2.50
☐ 21016	HARD TIMES	$2.25
☐ 21102	OLIVER TWIST	$2.50
☐ 21244	A CHRISTMAS CAROL & OTHER VICTORIAN TALES	$1.95

Titles by Henry James:

☐ 21127	PORTRAIT OF A LADY	$3.50
☐ 21059	THE TURN OF THE SCREW	$1.95

Look for them at your bookstore or use this page to order:

Bantam Books, Dept. CL3, 414 East Golf Road, Des Plaines, IL 60016

Please send me the items I have checked above. I am enclosing $_____ (please add $2.00 to cover postage and handling). Send check or money order, no cash or C.O.D.s please.

Mr/Ms _____

Address _____

City/State _____ Zip_____

CL3–12/89

Please allow four to six weeks for delivery.
Prices and availability subject to change without notice.

Bantam Classics bring you the world's greatest literature—books that have stood the test of time—at specially low prices. These beautifully designed books will be proud additions to your bookshelf. You'll want all these time-tested classics for your own reading pleasure.

Titles by Mark Twain:

☐	21079	**ADVENTURES OF HUCKLEBERRY FINN**	$1.95
☐	21128	**ADVENTURES OF TOM SAWYER**	$1.95
☐	21195	**COMPLETE SHORT STORIES**	$4.95
☐	21143	**A CONNECTICUT YANKEE IN KING ARTHUR'S COURT**	$2.95
☐	21349	**LIFE ON THE MISSISSIPPI**	$2.50
☐	21256	**THE PRINCE AND THE PAUPER**	$2.25
☐	21158	**PUDD'NHEAD WILSON**	$2.25

Other Great Classics:

☐	21274	**BILLY BUDD** Herman Melville	$2.95
☐	21311	**MOBY DICK** Herman Melville	$2.25
☐	21233	**THE CALL OF THE WILD & WHITE FANG** Jack London	$2.50
☐	21011	**THE RED BADGE OF COURAGE** Stephen Crane	$1.75
☐	21350	**THE COUNT OF MONTE CRISTO** Alexander Dumas	$4.95